The
Future
Burns Bright

Book Three : *Against Time*

(First Edition)

by

Marcus B. Shields

For additional information about *The Future Burns Bright,* surf to :

http://abfbook.telostic.com

For Vîrya

Table of Contents

Prologue..7

Against Time...11

THE JOKE'S ON *THEM*..11
BEAT YOU TO FAYETTEVILLE...17
SMOKE FROM A NOT-SO-DISTANT FIRE...28
BAD NEWS AT THE KEROSENE PUMP..45
FANCY MEETING YOU HERE... BROTHER...50
TURN THAT RADIO ON...59
BRIDGE TO NOWHERE..62
DOWN FLOATS THE BOAT, WITHOUT A PADDLE..............................69
TROUBLE JUST ROUND THE BEND...80
MAY I HAVE THIS DANCE?...89
DON'T LOOK UNDER THAT TARP..109
LET'S MAKE A DEAL...117
FARMER JONES, YOU'VE JUST MET ONE.......................................123
EVERY PLACE HAS A BACK-DOOR..127
TEXAS SHOOTIN'-GALLERY...134
EVERY ONE'S GOT TO COUNT FOR TWO...147
THE SHATTERING SHIELD...150
SCALPS AT ARROW AND SIERRA MADRE...164
HOT RED, HOT-HEAD BUBBLE...169
THEIR MASTERS' VOICE...171
PLEASE... NO MORE FUNERALS...174
A SON FOR DESPERATE TIMES..184
RAMÒN'S *MORDEDURA*..206
BREAKING IN... AND BREAKING THE NEWS......................................214
A WHIFF OF DEATH..219
DOUBLE-BOGEY..222
INTERCEPTED..224
OUT OF GAS... OUT OF LUCK...227
PIT-STOP, WITH INCOMING...233
AN ADDRESS FROM YOUR LAST AND NEXT PRESIDENT.....................243
STOP THE CONVOY, GRAB A TABLE..249
UP AND OVER..261
WAKE UP, YVONNE..268
OVERTAKEN BY EVENTS... SO TAKING OVER....................................276
FLIGHT-PLAN AND BAD OUTCOME, CONFIRMED................................280

THE HENDRICKS FINGER..288
A FRIENDLY CHAT ABOUT ARMAGEDDON..................................294
A WHITEMAN IS DISARMED...306
UNFRIENDLY *FIRE*...308
ALL ABOARD FOR PARTS EAST...314
TO JOIN OUR FUEHRER IN HELL..329
NOT WHO YOU HAD COUNTED ON..331
FEAR HER... BUT MORE, FEAR HER FAMILY................................334
DEATH, EN ROUTE TO D.C..355
SACRIFICES AND THE SECOND TEST..361
KNAVES AND PLANS FOR A MASSACRE..366
CASS MOUNTAIN DROP-OFF...378
BIRD IN FLIGHT..386
THE CAPTAIN AND HIS SHIP...390
TWO NOW FOR YOU, MS. CHU...394
AWAKE AND ON HER WAY..396
TO THE DEADLY HEAVENS ABOVE..406
FIRE IN ANY DIRECTION BUT "DOWN"..410
FIND THE KEY OF SOLOMON..415
TURN THE KEY OF SOLOMON...419

Prologue

Since this book is the third volume of the sequel to a predecessor series, it is strongly suggested that you should enjoy…

Angel of Mailànkh (Book One)
Doubt Me Not (Book Two)
Angel and The Empire (Book Three)
Children of The Fire (Book Four)

Of *The Angel Brings Fire* series, and then…

Storm In The North (Book One)
The Race (Book Two)

Of *The Future Burns Bright* series…

Before starting to read *Against Time*.

With that said, it is recognized that for various reasons, some readers will have happened upon *Against Time,* without having convenient access to the preceding books of the series.

We have therefore provided the following brief synopsis of the events of *The Race,* so that the reader can make sense of some of the characters and themes involved.

Marcus Shields

Author

The Future Burns Bright (Book Two) – The Race, begins with the competing "Mars Gang" (led by Sam Jacobson) and "FBI" (led by Minnie Chu) teams, being deposited by the Storied Watcher in the Pacific Northwest, and in Florida, respectively.

Both parties set out on their quests, but immediately run into various challenges.

Chu's group is initially paid almost no attention by the government, but is then abruptly sequestered into confinement in a building in downtown Pittsburgh. Chu has a tense meeting with a sinister man who is actually the malevolent CIA director, with ambitious plans to murder the Storied Watcher and to re-impose totalitarian repression on the United States. While this is going on, the former JPL scientist, Sylvia Abruzzio, is forced to kill a CIA agent, and she – along with the ex-President's Chief of Staff (Jerry Kaysten) and Abruzzio's alien-powered dog Rainbow, must flee and to go into hiding, eventually taking shelter with Abruzzio's childhood friend, Moira Sullivan.

For their part, as they begin their journey, Jacobson's group is riven with internal disagreements as to how to proceed, and they are faced with logistical difficulties.

Other dangers are building in the background.

The cynical, cruel former Vice-President – who has taken over the government, and who is on an obsessive quest to kill Karéin-Mayréij – has put a price on the heads of the Mars Gang's members. However, unknown to both him and almost everyone else, a group of terrorists named "The Muslim Salvation League" has tracked the missing Pakistani H-bomb to the Los Angeles area, and is planning to find, capture and detonate it as soon as possible.

They have competition for ownership of this lethal weapon, specifically from both a group of racist skinheads named the "Aryan Brotherhood" and from the sinister Prince of Venom – Sebastiàn – whose alien-powers, derived from his early friendship with the Storied Watcher – are growing in like measure to the size of his gangster army. Sebastiàn has evolved an "insect-plague" attack that literally eats its victims down to the bone, and he uses it to horrendous effect against the Aryan Brotherhood's equally-brutal-and-cruel warriors. But the Brotherhood – which has physical control of the bomb – fights back savagely, and is planning to set off the nuke in Hollywood, so as to kill as many Jews and minorities as possible. But the necessary preparations are not yet complete, and Sebastiàn's army hopes to capture it before this can happen.

Karéin-Mayréij herself has left for the reaches of the South Atlantic, using her burgeoning powers to hollow out a cavernous redoubt underneath desolate, isolated Bouvet Island, wherein she hopes to deposit (and keep safe) the majority of the Compton refugees and her other hangers-on. She is thus effectively out of the picture while Jacobson and his Mars Gang slowly work their way across the central United States.

While traveling on a highway through the central United States, in the aftermath of a tornado (which Jacobson's "more-than-human" followers manage to extinguish by the clever use of their alien-powers), the Mars Gang meets up with the Storied Watcher's former lover, Donny Wade. The ex-astronauts (and others) are unaware that they are being followed by a group of underground hackers calling themselves the "Digital NRA", who manage to affix a tracking device to "Wolf", the fire-using bounty-hunter; and Jacobson's team – frustrated at being "stonewalled" and persecuted by the increasingly-repressive, authoritarian American government – engages in an escalating series of provocations, culminating in a spectacular attack against the gold repository at Fort Knox.

This success is quickly overshadowed when the hackers manage to communicate with the Mars Gang, warning Jacobson and Boyd that the U.S. government is targeting their families for kidnap, torture and eventual murder. In an atmosphere of near-panic, the Mars Gang is forced to abruptly revise their plans, with Jacobson and the rest of the group taking a stolen U.S. Army aircraft to Texas to rescue the former Mars mission commander's wife and children, while Boyd – who is now able to fly on his own – heads to a location in West Virginia to *rendez-vous* with his own family.

Meanwhile, Chu's FBI group has problems of their own. At the behest of the scheming, fanatical "Brother Harold" Crowford – the leader of the "Klan of Jesus Christ" group of religious terrorists – Chu and her two compatriots, Otis Boatman and Will Hendricks, are forcibly ushered on board the U.S. government's Airborne Command Post, which aircraft is the temporary headquarters of the *faux*-President, as he tries to evade a possible attack by the Mars Gang or even the Storied Watcher herself.

Unknown to anyone other than himself – and a hapless junior Christian terrorist who unwittingly stumbles aboard – Brother Harold has smuggled a nuclear weapon, stolen earlier from the U.S. Air Force, on board the Airborne Command Post. He plans to use the bomb in a trap set for Karéin-Mayréij, with Minnie Chu as the bait.

Chu is put under great pressure by the imposter-President to betray Jacobson and the Mars Gang, but she resists, albeit at the price of being stripped of her rank and then placed into solitary confinement on the plane.

The two other ex-FBI-agents are not so lucky; they are thrown out of the aircraft while it is flying high in the air, but they manage to cheat death by invoking their nascent alien-powers, as the plunge earthward. They land in the Appalachian mountains and encounter some suspicious hillbillies, but are eventually able to convince them to provide shelter.

The other half of the Chu team – Jerry Kaysten and Sylvia Abruzzio – have been working, in parallel, on a plan to rescue the former President, who was deposed in a *coup*. Along with Moira Sullivan and the Storied Watcher's animate arm-shield, *Vîrya* I'ëà'b' – who has gone adventuring on her own, to the dismay of her alien mother – Abruzzio tracks the ex-President to a private gated community in Arnold Air Force Base in Tennessee, where – along with the rest of his family – he is being held under house-arrest.

After some initial confusion, Abruzzio, Kaysten and the living-shield are welcomed by the former U.S. leader, but he balks at being recruited into their plans to stage a counter-*coup*. The Abruzzio scheme is about to fall apart when news of the Mars Gang's devastating attack on Fort Knox becomes available, prompting the former (legitimate) President to call the current (false) President (the former Vice-President), pleading with the latter to cease the hostilities with the Mars Gang and with the alien, and to cut a deal with both hostile parties.

The request is curtly rejected, as the foolhardy imposter-President incorrectly believes that the U.S. military has enough firepower to simply slay the Storied Watcher and the members of the Mars Gang outright. He also threatens the safety of the original (legitimate) President's family; so the latter – now out of palatable options – reluctantly agrees to sign on to Abruzzio and Kaysten's plan.

The Race closes with the brutal, hulking skinhead warriors of the Aryan Brotherhood, pledging to seek out and destroy Sebastiàn and his sinister, deadly insect-attack – thereby clearing the way to fomenting a nuclear atrocity in downtown Los Angeles. And Harold Crowford of The Klan of Jesus Christ, has hidden a *second* hydrogen bomb, on board an aircraft flying over the most heavily-populated areas of the United States.

The Storied Watcher is thousands of miles away. Her followers are all preoccupied with fighting for their own lives, and those of their families.

Who will save America?

Against Time

The Joke's On *Them*

"I don't hear *anything*," argued the former President, "But I'll take your word for it, Ms. Abruzzio. Kathy – can you pack for the both of us, please? Matt, Clairie – one suitcase-worth each –"

"But *Daddy*," interjected the teenage girl, "I can't *possibly* get all my clothes, my cosmetics, my video-games and my shoes into just one –"

He quickly stepped forward and took hold of his daughter by the shoulders.

"Sweetheart," he cajoled and instructed, "This is serious business, and you've got a lot of growing-up to do, right now. I tried to hide these dangers from you, Mom and Matt... but they've caught up with us. You don't have a choice, and I don't have time to argue –"

"But –" she repeated.

"Nobility comes this day to you, Clairie... your brother, father and mother, too," inscrutably interjected Abruzzio. "I pray that you will be worthy of it. You should do what your Dad requests."

"Pack at least one full change, and make it comfortable stuff, like you're going on a hike or something," commanded the former President. "*Go!*"

The teenager had rarely heard this tone of voice, but its import was unmistakable. She mutely nodded, wheeled in place and ran down the hall toward her room, accompanied in so doing by her brother. The wife had already disappeared in the other direction, after motioning for the female guard-cum-waiter to go with her.

"They're nice kids, you know, sir," offered the JPL scientist. "But you're right... things are going to start happening *very* fast from now on – and there won't be much leeway for mistakes. I've been, uhh, noticing the volume increasing on some of the military radio frequencies over the past few minutes... Jerry – you hearing it too?"

"Yeah," confirmed the former Chief of Staff. "Engines, sirens, coming from the direction we took to get here... I figure we got two to three minutes before they show."

"Ms. Abruzzio," interrupted the ex-President, "You said you had 'noticed' the government's radio traffic? But I don't see you carrying a receiver... is your friend 'Veer-ya' providing that capability?"

"Nope," replied the scientist. "All in my head. Too much chatter, in fact. Have to filter it out, if I want to stay sane."

The former American leader was about to pursue the line of questioning, but he was pre-empted in turn by Kaysten.

"Sylvia," he asked, "What's the plan? If LEA blocks the front exit to the street, there's no *way* we're going to get the Boss and his family to where

Moira's waiting. We could get Miss Flying Razor-Blade to do a number on 'em, so we could break out of here, but –"

"You will *not* attack law enforcement, or the military, if you want cooperation out of me," demanded the former President. "They're patriotic policemen and soldiers who are simply doing their duty. Is that clear?"

"That's what *I* was going to say, sir," unctuously echoed Kaysten.

"Yes," stated Abruzzio, "And it's been our practice not to take the first shot, but be aware, Mr. President, that if our lives or safety, or those of innocent bystanders – including yourself and your family – are put in peril, I *will* use force to defend us. It makes me sick to think of hurting or killing anyone, and I'll avoid it if I possibly can, but over the past few days I've learned that sometimes it *can't* be helped. I don't have to explain what the alternative is likely to be, if your former Vice-President's planning what I *think* he's planning. Is *that* clear?"

"Yes, and let's hope it doesn't come to that," acknowledged the former U.S. leader. "Goddamn George, anyway... I *never* should have let him take over."

"Yeah, well, sir, there are a *lot* of things that some of us might have done differently, with the benefit of hindsight," allowed the JPL scientist.

"They're getting nearer," warned Kaysten. "Listen, Sylvia – I got an angle on tying 'em up for a while out front, but it won't last forever, and that's assuming that they aren't planning some kind of BS like dropping paratroopers on the roof or behind the house, as well. We gotta figure out how we all get *out* of here, preferably in one piece."

"Mr. President... the yacht that's tied up at the dock, behind and below us – you know how to operate it?" asked Abruzzio, as, invisibly to all except Kaysten and the living-shield, she pressed her quick-intellect-skill to its limits.

"Of *course* I do," he replied. "I take it out fishing and so on, twice a week. But if you're planning on us all sailing to freedom, I don't think that'll work, Ms. Abruzzio – the Retention Reservoir's a small place; they'd notice us the minute we cast off. There's nowhere to dock or beach the yacht on its far shore, and on top of that, it's miles to nowhere in every direction except east, and the base – which is to the east – will be heavily-patrolled, *especially* under these circumstances. They picked a good place to imprison us, is what I'm saying."

"Sir, does the yacht have a secondary-boat... a skiff, an inflatable safety-raft, that kind of thing?" pressed the JPL scientist.

"Yeah," he confirmed. "If the light were better, you could see it tied on to the transom, down there – just undo two clasps and she falls down. Aluminum-composite hull, big enough to seat six – but what's the point? What are you proposing to do... just row away in it?"

There was a faint kaleidoscope in Abruzzio's eyes, as, with a far-off look, she replied, "*Something* like that. It has places where someone can, uhh, hold on tight, if there's a storm or something... right?"

"*Sure* it does," he said. "And poly-plastic covers over the stem and stern, to keep out rough seas... not much use here on the Reservoir, of course. Look, Ms. Abruzzio, I really think –"

She stepped backward, toward the picture-window – which opened completely without any apparent human intervention – while traces of the *Fire* illuminated her body, from underneath her clothes.

Abruzzio stepped out on to the home's open-air balcony overlooking the AEDC Retention Reservoir, the yacht and much of the mostly-dark expanse of Arnold Air Force Base. Effortlessly, she hopped backward and upward, coming to rest with her feet on the upper guard-rail.

"Ms. Abruzzio!" cried the alarmed former President. "It's fifty feet or more, down from there! Get back here, or you'll be *killed!*"

"Jerry," instructed the more-than-a-woman, with her eyes now glowing bright, while her war-song began to pick up the beat, "Keep 'em talking, as long as you can, then hop a ride on Little One, down to the wharf! Mr. President – get your family dockside, thirty seconds from now!"

"I'm on it!" purposefully vowed Kaysten, striding toward the door and the sounds of oncoming police-cars.

"But – but –"stammered the flustered, frightened, ex-U.S. leader.

"*Do it!*" commanded Abruzzio, as she stepped backward into the void, and disappeared from view, below the balcony.

Jerry Kaysten, former Chief of Staff to the President of the United States and now he knew-not-what, stood tall and straight on the front step of his boss's mansion, with an open door behind him.

He had about twenty seconds in which to slick back his hair, straighten his tie and otherwise spiff himself up, before the first set of three police-cars, accompanied by two third-generation, Kevlar-II-armored, JMVV-3 military utility vehicles, arrived at the front gate.

As could have been predicted, black-garbed, combat-geared soldiers poured out of the Army trucks, followed in close order by a group of at least six police officers. The soldiers, brandishing auto-rifles as they went, dashed rapidly to either side of the building, while the cops crouched behind relatively hidden firing-positions and called out a brusque demand, using some kind of bullhorn.

"You, there, in front of the house!" shouted the voice. "Stand still, and get your hands up, unless you want to get shot!"

Kaysten, trying not to let his nerves get the better of him, complied, slowly raising his arms. He was, however, reassured by the knowledge – a presence, made evident by no mundane sense, but rather an esoteric one – that somewhere close by, *Vìrya I'ëà'b'* stood guard.

Okay, he mused, *Here goes.*

Calling on the power, the Fire, *the whatever... Karéin, let's hope that tongue of yours wasn't as forked, as your teeth (oww!) were sharp.*

Gotta remember that one... Jerry, you're a card – should be dealt with...

He called back to his assailants.

"Hey there, guys... no problemo! I'm on your side... and that's a *fact*, Jack!"

There were the babbling sounds of what appeared to be confusion, on the other side of the loudspeaker.

"What the hell you talkin' about?" responded whoever had the bullhorn. "Who are you? What are you doing here, mister? Please, uhh, state your name..."

An impressed and increasingly-confident Kaysten realized that – somehow, perhaps with this 'warm-sight' thingamajig – he could see where all his interlocutors were hiding; and, no longer caring if his eyes, ears or other body-parts were externally-glowing, he reached deep-down and asked for the *Fire* to come to his tongue.

In the best imitation of a late-night TV comic he could muster, while his pleasant, lilting (though exciting), war-song started to issue from all points of the night, the former Chief of Staff went on, "Name's Jerry Kaysten – or, as that ba-donk-a-donk lil' space-cadet-girl used to say, 'Jerrrr-eeee Kayyy-steen, The Magnificent'. Okay, so I *did* make the 'Magnificent' thing up... so sue me! Great to be with you folks, tonight – hope you checked your wives – 'scuse me, your *guns* – back at the gate! Sorry, I *always* get that wrong... I'd say it was Freudian, if I knew who that 'Freud' guy actually is, but, well, I failed both Psych and Sex Education, you know?"

He noticed a few quickly-stifled chuckles from the hidden soldiers and policemen, and – bizarrely – some amused "chirps" issuing from his unseen, demi-human companion.

"Shut your ears, honey," whispered Kaysten. "If you have any, that is."

"Hey... ever hear *this* one," continued the former Chief of Staff. "A priest, a rabbi and a naïve alien angel from Mars who just ended up on Earth, walk into a bar, and –"

"What the fuck..." he heard one of the entrenched cops saying, over burgeoning, though suppressed, giggles. "Come *on*, Tom... act *professional*, for Christ's sake... we're on a *mission*, here."

An adrenaline rush of excitement surged through Kaysten's bloodstream as he perceived what was happening; though he wasn't deliberately shouting, his voice seemed to be borne aloft on the night-breezes, and his eyes could see faint wisps of the *Fire* carrying his charged words right at the intended victims.

"So," he crowed, adding a feigned, supernaturally-infectious chuckle of his own, "The barkeeper says, 'is this a joke?' The priest says, 'it's not a joke'; the rabbi says, 'it's not a joke'; and, know what the alien-girl says? Give up? Well, *she* goes, 'could you explain... what is this hoo-man thing called a joke?'"

He couldn't tell if it was natural, or if it was part of the *Amaiish*-ability, but momentarily, the former Chief of Staff found himself laughing at his own jest; it was all he could do to keep his hands in the air.

But, in fact, he needn't have had to have done so. As Kaysten regained his composure, signs of unnatural risibility began to echo from every human being within earshot, and, within seconds, he heard the sounds of weapons being dropped, of bodies falling to the ground, and of desperate gasps for air, as his now-helpless victims were so uncontrollably shrieking in convulsive paroxysms of laughter that they hadn't time to properly breathe.

Shit, the abashed super-human realized.

She warned me that it could kill... didn't she?

But she didn't tell me how to turn it off! If it can *be turned off, that is.*

Okay. Let's hope it wears off by itself, before they literally laugh themselves to death.

Only one thing for me to do... I'm outta here!

As he called upon his other power and rocketed backward into the house, his ears got a fleeting impression of yet another victim – the President's guard-woman – who was herself doubled up on the floor, teary-eyed with hilarity, howling and shaking with irresistible mirth.

Ha ha, mused a smugly self-satisfied Kaysten, while dashing for the interior stairs leading town to the boat-dock.

Joke's on you!

"Uh-oh... hearing cars... they'll be here any *second,*" warned Abruzzio, as she made rapid "come-on" hand-gestures, ushering the President's family down to the dock. "Everybody, congregate right here!"

Each one of the former First Family was lugging at least one suitcase, with the teenagers carrying more. As they hurried down the concrete steps leading from underneath the mansion to the dock, the President's wife exclaimed, "Clark, what on Earth are we going to do – if the police are here, we can't possibly outrun them in the yacht, and –"

"She can't possibly have survived jumping off that railing, either," grunted the ex-President, as he dropped a duffel-bag at Abruzzio's feet, and asked the JPL scientist, "How'd you do that, anyway?"

"Easy," replied Abruzzio. "I flew... *that's* how."

While the newly-arrived gaped in disbelief, she wheeled in place, directed her telekinesis at the two catch-clasps that attached the rescue-skiff to the much larger yacht, and pulled the locking-catches open. The little boat fell backward toward the dock, and might have been damaged in landing on the latter, except that its velocity was degraded by another of the JPL scientist's mental "pushes", just before impact.

"Quickly now – everybody into the boat!" demanded Abruzzio. "Stow the loose gear forward and rearward, so it can't easily be thrown out, in a tight turn!"

"This is, if you don't mind my saying, Madam," protested the ex-President, "*Crazy*. Look at the stern of the yacht – you've forgotten the oars... they're still stuck on there, and if you think we're going to evade the military by *rowing* away, well –"

The JPL scientist heard Kaysten's war-song, coming from the front of the mansion. It sounded different, somehow, as if her fellow more-than-human had crossed a metaphysical bridge.

"We aren't 'rowing', anywhere," retorted Abruzzio, with her eyes aglow, the *Fire* showing within her breast, and her war-song beginning to rise. "We're going to *soar*, above the clouds – under *my* power. Now get in, unless you want to miss the boat and answer to that arsehole Vice-President of yours. *Sir*. Rainbow – you too, honey."

"*Neaaat!*" enthusiastically exclaimed the teenage girl. She and her brother, followed by a very reluctant, shaken former President, his wife, and finally the little dog, rapidly clambered or hopped into the skiff.

There were now curt, warlike voices in the dark, on either side of the house.

"First Family located!" shouted one of these. "Along with one intruder!"

Just loud enough for even the humans to hear, a metallic, radio-communications voice – apparently coming from a helmeted earphone or on-board speaker – barked, "Permission to engage – eliminate the terrorist – secure the hostages!"

An alarmed – though, grimly-determined – Abruzzio brought her power to full-bore, and the display, plus its accompanying, thrilling war-song, simultaneously terrified and awed the ex-President and his family.

The JPL scientist stood on the dock with her feet firmly planted, her arms raised and her fingers set in a claw-like arrangement. She was surrounded by a whirling, rainbow-hued 'bubble', whose subdued, elfin light illuminated the area for several dozens of feet in all directions, and whose translucent substance made her figure shimmering, indistinct and difficult to clearly identify – *except* for her brightly-glowing, multi-colored eyes, which were easily-visible through the rainbow-barrier and which imparted a sinister, demonic appearance.

"Take one shot at *me*, or any of the people who I'm protecting," she defiantly yelled back, "And I'll radiate the eyeballs out of your head, the flesh off your bones! If you're lucky, you'll die fast... more than I can say for everybody in the half-mile behind you! Get the hell *out* of here! Three – *two* –"

The buzzing, humming sound of the Storied Watcher's arm-shield, came to Abruzzio's ears, and she whispered, "*Virya I'ëa'b*' – hold thou here, and protect me from their bang-sticks, if thou please."

"Ms. *Abruzzio!*" angrily shouted the ex-President, from his crouching vantage-point within the skiff. "I will *not* permit this – if for no reason other than, you'll hit Marnie – she's still in there!"

What do I care about that pathetic, weak little hum... whoa, Sylvia, silently reflected the scientist.

It's going to your head... control, control... okay. Beneath me... beneath us... but they still got a right to life.

Yeah. Got it down.

Oh... shit! Damn lucky he stopped me – I could have hit Jerry!

Her self-questioning was apropos, because, at that precise moment, Abruzzio felt a blast of air, like a gale from nowhere had buffeted her body. Out of the corner of her eye, she perceived the flickering image of a humanoid figure, but this flashed past so quickly that even with all the alien-second-sight powers at full-tilt, the scientist could not properly focus.

At the limit of her empowered hearing, she could make out words of panic among the arriving, military and police reinforcements; there were comments like, "first team incapacitated by a nerve agent, request NBC cleanup!"

Not willing to take her eyes off the SWAT-geared soldiers who had accosted her, Abruzzio said out loud, "That *you*, Jerry?"

"Already in the boat," came back the proud response. "Didn't you see me go by? Wicked stuff, Sylvia – like everybody else is moving in slow-motion, or maybe it's that I'm sped-up, or, whatever... you know, 'andale, arriba, meep meep' kinda thing – like the cartoons, but it's *real!* I'm *lovin'* it... although I'm a bit tired... burns me out fast, *that's* for sure."

"For God's sake, Jerry, your *eyes* –" she heard the ex-President say.

"Congratulations, my brother," solemnly offered Abruzzio. "That is one impressive power she's granted you."

She paused for a second, and then added, "Now... see... *mine.*"

The melodic, exciting beat of Abruzzio's personal war-song surged yet more, as – to the amazement of those in the boat, save the puppy and Kaysten – she levitated herself to a spot about five feet directly above the mid-point of the skiff.

With a dignified, downward glance and the look of might in her kaleidoscope eyes, the former JPL scientist locked her telekinesis on to the rescue-boat, which rocked a little bit, then stabilized and lifted about three inches clear of the dock.

Then Abruzzio turned her eyes to the heavens.

"Now... we *fly!*" her godly voice declared.

Beat You To Fayetteville

Bad enough having to cruise at God-knows-how-fast through the night, at low altitude through a mountain-range, after only a day or two of being able to fly in the first place, ruefully mused Brent Boyd, as he streaked through an Appalachian valley, dangerously close to the tree-line.

But having to do so while flying on my back, five minutes out of every ten, eyes upward to the sky, looking for "hostiles"... a whole new quantum of "nerve-wracking", that's for sure – but at least I've got Karéin's infra-sight to pierce the darkness and sort of see where I'm going; without that, this trip would be damn terrifying.

Wish I had a nice TFR, right about now, but that's a minor thing, compared to not having been tracked by the Air Force since leaving Radcliff...

Well, that is... I think I escaped their notice...

He had used I-64 as a guideline, accepting the fact that a crow's-flight-path would have saved him a few minutes on the trip. Though he had stayed at least a mile away from the highway, and had done his best to keep the cloak-of-shadows raised in every direction except above and directly ahead of his head (a very necessary step, considering that his entire body glowed like a 1,000-Watt light-bulb, whenever he used more than a thimble's-worth of *Amaiish*), the former Mars mission pilot worried about the fast-paced, weirdo melodic-rock "music" that seemed to stick to him like a stray puppy.

No matter how hard he tried (sometimes, successfully) to dial back the volume, *it*, was always there, no doubt echoing across the surroundings in a way guaranteed to attract attention – though he never got tired of hearing the tune.

Got the junction with Route 612 a few miles back, he realized.

Should be coming up on – yeah, there *it is, the Whipple Store, where Laura talked me into buying all those antiques, just before I left for Mars... I wasn't in much of a mind to argue, considering what had happened to the expedition before my own...*

Those were the days, when everything was as uncomplicated as it can get, when you're a rookie astronaut. You might just not be coming back, so you do a lot of compromising...

He streaked right over the building, trying to concentrate on the business of low-level flight while ignoring the incongruity of the situation and the startled glances of those below, who had heard Boyd's thrill-inducing psycho-music.

Hey, folks – here's the guy who bargained you down from $250 to $125 on that nice Colonial rocking-chair... where am I? Just look up... but don't blink!

Even if he hadn't been glowing from the tips of his toes to the top of his head, you wouldn't have missed the brilliance of Boyd's broad, proud grin.

Okay – there's the curve of Route 19, north – let's stay a click or so to the left, and follow her up to Fayetteville... right, there's Oak Hill... let's detour straight north over the country club, fewer human ears to wake up...

Making good time... there's Newtown... Midway... Lochgelly... the airport – let's go across 19 and hope nobody sees us, not much traffic on the road anyway, this time of night – hooray, there's South Court Street!

Cut north again, gotta find somewhere "discreet" to put down... how about near the back of the left side of the Soldiers and Sailors Museum?

Kind of appropriate, wouldn't you say?

Doing his level best to suppress his musical accompaniment, Boyd completely enshrouded himself in his ebon shroud (a move that made precise judgments about the distance-to-ground well-nigh impossible, as he found out the hard way when he relaxed his flight-power, about two feet too far off the surface of the museum parking-lot).

After a few muffled curses and dusting himself off, the former Mars mission pilot peeked out from behind the two panel-vans that had hidden his sudden "downfall" from street-view. The surroundings were very dark and there was a chill in the air.

No traffic on West Maple... okay, here I go. God, I can't wait to hold Laura again!

He raced across the street and stopped momentarily to look at the Morris Harvey House, which hadn't changed very much since the halcyon days in which Boyd had proposed to his then-girlfriend, at this three-story, impeccably-restored, gray-and-white Victorian bed-and-breakfast place. It was early in the growing-season and the mini-maze of manicured shrubs surrounding the house was lacking in foliage, but everything else, including the open porch which encircled most of the building, was just as he had remembered it.

He looked around in every direction but could not see any trace of his wife's '35, dark-green Patriotic family-van, parked on the Fayetteville streets.

Parking-lot's out back, Boyd realized. *Well, either they're here, or they aren't. Okay, then.*

He strode up to the front door and gave it a loud knock. After a short delay, it opened, revealing the face of an elderly Caucasian woman.

"Can I help you, young man?" she pleasantly asked. "It's after hours... I was getting ready for bed. We usually don't get inquiries this late in the evening, you know."

"I'm looking for Mrs., uhh, Wayne, Ma'am," he replied. "My wife. She and our kids were due in here, as of several hours ago. Could you page her, please?"

A puzzled look appeared on the old woman's brow.

"Mrs... 'Wayne'?" she said. "No, I'm sorry, we've got two rooms out of six booked, but there's nobody by *that* name, here. Did she have a reservation?"

Oh God, he worried, with a churning gut.

If she got intercepted on the way up here – and Karéin didn't zero in on her, in time –

A crestfallen Boyd answered, "No... I don't think she would have. Have you had a phone call, or NeoNet message, lately, by anyone inquiring about room rates, availability... that kind of thing?"

With a gentle laugh, the hostess observed, "Well, son, we get inquiries of that kind, several times per day, you know, but as I said, I don't remember anyone identifying themselves as a 'Mrs. Wayne', or, in fact, any name remotely *like* that. If she has a mobile communicator, why don't you just give her a call, and see where she's at?"

"I, uhh, don't *have* one on me," stammered Boyd. "Left it at home... darnedest thing. Sorry."

"Well, come on in here, then," offered the old lady, "You can call her from our land-line. We don't have all this fancy-dancy video-stuff on it, mind you... but you can still do a voice call."

Damn, he considered.

Risky to do that... they're almost certainly tracing every call made to Laura's mobile number. I could just wait here for her and the kids... but if she's been caught, I might be waiting forever. Lesser of two evils, I suppose...

"Yeah... thank you... that'd be *super*," he said, trying to sound grateful.

The hostess smiled and ushered him into the familiar confines of this period-piece of a house, its polished-brass, plush-stuffed-furniture and hardwood interiors providing a welcome refuge from the techno-junk that seemingly intruded everywhere else, these days. But one such device *did* exist, here : a '20s-vintage, digital voice-phone, which had been hidden behind the reception-desk, and which was duly made available to the former astronaut.

Nervously, he entered his wife's mobile-communicator number into the keypad, reflexively scanning the area and noting that other than for the hostess, nobody else was around.

Beep... beep... beep... beep... beep... beep...

He listened through another six more of the ring-tones and then pressed the "disconnect" button.

He tried again, through seven ring-tones.

There was no answer.

"Seems her phone's off the hook," observed the hostess. "Would you like to have a seat and wait here, for a while?"

"No... thanks, but I don't think that's a good idea," he responded.

Boyd took a couple of steps toward the door, but thought better of it.

"Mind if I try just one more time?" he requested.

"Oh, of *course* – *anything* for such a nicely-dressed young man," smiled the old woman.

If you only knew where this dress-suit has been, and what's underneath it, he mused, while again entering his wife's communicator-number into the keypad.

Beep... beep... beep...

All of a sudden, the line went to "active mode" and a confused cacophony beset Boyd's enhanced hearing; he could make out road-noise and the sounds of several voices – barely recognizable as his younger children – shouting in the background.

"Hello?" exclaimed the stressed voice of a young girl. "Who's *this?*"

"Wendy? *Wendy?* That *you?*" was all he could think of to say.

"Yes, it's me," came back the reply. "Mom... *Mom!* I think it's *Daddy!*"

"Can't talk now!" he heard Laura shouting. "I got to keep my eyes on the road – think we lost them at that last turn, but they'll try to cut us off, up ahead – honey, get out the map, we've got to –"

"Laura... *Laura!*" shrieked Boyd. "It's *Brent,* here! Where *are* you?"

"It's Wendy here, Daddy," interrupted his daughter's voice. "Daddy, I'm *scared* – we've been driving all *day*, there's these men following us in these big, black cars, and they had these guns, they were *shooting* at us –"

"Wendy, sweetheart – I want you to listen *very* carefully to what I'm about to say... are you listening, dear?" quickly replied the former Mars mission pilot.

"Y-yes, Daddy," she answered.

"You have to tell me *exactly* where you are, honey," cajoled Boyd. "Do you know where you are, now?"

He momentarily muted the phone with one hand and furiously motioned to the hostess.

"I need a map – *right now!*" he barked, as if he meant it. With a look of concern on her face, the elderly woman began to rummage behind her desk.

"I think we're on... Mommy, what road are we on, again?" Boyd heard his daughter ask, evidently to her mother.

There was a short pause, and then Wendy again came on the line.

"Mommy says we're on, uhh, Interstate 81, going south... she says we're getting close to the turn-off for Route 64... but the bad men might be waiting for us, up there. What're we gonna *do*, Daddy! What's going *on?*"

"Everything's going to be okay, sweetheart," he reassured. "Here's what I want you and Mommy to do – hold on just a sec –"

A panicking Boyd fumbled with the map. His eyes rapidly scanned the layout of the local West Virginia roads and terrain, and after no more than a couple more seconds, he again addressed his daughter.

"Wendy," he ordered, "I want you to tell Mommy to pull the car over, beneath the underpass where the Lee Highway – that's Route 11 – goes over Interstate 64. Can you tell her that, right now?"

There was a confused exchange of babbling at the remote end of the conversation, and then Wendy spoke up.

"Mommy says, 'what's the point of doing that', and she wants to know 'where you are now'," conveyed the daughter.

"I'm near Fayetteville," stated the former astronaut, "And tell her there's no time to explain more, but I'll be there in less than ten minutes. You'll know I'm coming because you'll hear some real neat music, coming from all around – and if any of the bad guys show up before I do, tell them to leave you alone... or *else*. Can you tell that to your mother, sweetheart?"

"Yeah, Daddy," replied the girl. She proceeded to make good on the promise, to the obvious sounds of incredulity on the part of Boyd's wife.

"Mommy says that's more than 60 *miles* from here," voiced Wendy, "And there's no *way* you could –"

"Tell Mommy that I love you and her and Brent and Nicky very much, and that Daddy's on his way," countered Boyd. "Remember – under the overpass!"

Though he very much wanted not to, he cut the connection and, with map-in-hand, turned to address the hostess.

"Ma'am," he announced, "Thank you *so* much – I swear that in time, you won't regret having helped me; but for the immediate future, if anyone asks... forget that you ever *met* me, and tell them, that if they threaten or hurt you... I'll *kill* them. Got that?"

"Well... yes," stammered the old lady, "But why would anyone be after a nice young man like *you*, son?"

"Want to know why?" he answered, as his *Fire* began to blaze inside, as his eyes displayed their sinister glow and his enervating, exciting war-music began to roar.

"*This* is why," exclaimed Brent Boyd, one second before he dashed out the front door of the Morris Harvey House and rocketed skyward, executing a brutal high-G reverse-turn, heading to the south-east.

"When's Daddy going to be here?" whined the off-blond-haired, skinny ten-year-old girl, as she fidgeted in the passenger-seat of the family-van.

"Soon, honey," evaded Laura Boyd, while scanning back and forth, up and down the highway and trying to hide her fear from the kids. She did some compulsive puttering too, removing her schoolteacher-glasses, cleaning them and putting them back on, while ruffling her auburn, close-cropped coiffure.

She had carefully backed the van into the rather narrow space between the two concrete supports that raised the Lee Highway over the Interstate, going upward almost to the trees on the upper level. In the unlit darkness, you'd have had to have been looking carefully, to have seen the vehicle. Not that there was much traffic, anyway; there had only been three cars in the last twelve minutes.

"Why can't I use the game-tablet or turn on a light, Mommy?" came the voice of a dark-haired boy, a few years younger than the girl, from one of the back seats.

"I've already *told* you twice, Brent," replied the mother. "We have to keep things *absolutely* dark and quiet in here, so the bad men don't find us –"

"Roofer's whining," interrupted the boy. "I think he's got to go out and do his business."

"Well, Roofer will have to wait," ordered Laura Boyd. "Nobody's getting out of the car, until Daddy –"

She did a double-take at something far away, south-east on I-64, then shouted, "Everybody – *get down!*"

The children, knowing that it wasn't a joke, instantly complied, diving to the floor, as the woman bent over in the driver-seat.

An automobile raced by, going north-west; then another, then a third. They waited for several seconds, and then the mother cautiously raised her head.

She anxiously looked to the left and to her relief saw no other vehicles approaching. But when she turned her attention to the right, to her dismay, Laura Boyd saw that one of the three just-passed cars – evidently a SUV of some sort, though it was far enough away to be hard to precisely identify – had slowed down. It pulled over to the side of the road, and, a couple of seconds later, so did the two other black vehicles. Her worst fears were realized in the next moment, when the rear-guard SUV reversed course and began to slowly drive toward them, going the wrong way down the northbound side of Interstate 64.

"Everybody keep quiet!" whispered the woman.

But despite this entreaty, something was playing... *music*. At first – though even at initial, muted volume, it was clearly recognizable as some kind of fast-paced rock with pop overtones, with a pulsing, foot-tapping beat – the tune was barely perceptible; but its gain-level was increasing with each passing second, and though Laura Boyd subconsciously knew that this song, whatever it was, deserved a place of honor in her personal collection... now, was anything but the time to be enjoying it.

"*Brent! Wendy! Nicky!*" desperately hissed the mother. "Whoever's playing that, turn it off, *right now!*"

"I *can't*," complained the boy, from his hiding-place, under the back-seat. "My player's in the suitcase, and its battery's drained!"

"I can hear it too," added the ten-year-old, from underneath the passenger-side glove-compartment. "It's coming from, like, all around... not just the radio. How's that possible, Mommy?"

"I don't know, Wendy dear, but hush up, now –" demanded an inwardly-petrified Laura Boyd.

Maybe I should tell them how much Mommy loves them, she mused.

She heard a vehicle's tires come to a stop, some distance away, and then discerned a sound like its car-doors opening. Then someone spoke into the static of a radio-device.

"Located a vehicle under the Lee Highway overpass, possibly abandoned," reported a husky, male voice.

There was a pause, and then she heard, "Control... you gettin' this? Somebody's playin' *music* over the link – tell 'em to cut it out, we're on a Class Two fugitive-chase here, you're screwin' up our comms!"

There were footsteps approaching, as the terrified woman cowered on the floor of her van.

"Draw weapons and engage anyone making a break from it," cracked a remote voice.

There was a shouted command.

"*You in the van!* You're under arrest on charges of being accessories to terrorist activities! Show yourselves, with hands in the air! You got ten seconds, and we shoot, whether you're in there or not!"

The music was now... everywhere, and its exciting, got-to-get-up-and-dance beat was almost irresistible.

Shot to death to the tune of the latest Indie band, thought a frustrated, tearful Laura Boyd.

Brent, my love – where are you!

God, to see you, one last time!

And – as if in answer to a prayer – now, she heard a new voice outside the family-van; it was one that seemingly for eons had been available, only over phone- and computer-channels... never, in-person.

"You so much as *raise* those fucking guns – and I'll cut you down where you stand!" defiantly exclaimed her husband.

"What the *fuck?*" came back the confused reply, accompanied with expletives of similar nature from at least three other outside voices. "Vinnie, Mel... *you* say that?"

There was more confusion, as the familiar, tough-yet-gentle voice of Brent Boyd again was heard. It sounded like he was standing between the on-coming Men-In-Black and the van, although the wife was still too frightened to dare raise her head to car-window-level.

"Listen up, you Agency pricks," he challenged, "You're now being targeted by someone who can kill you with just a *thought* – but I'll play nice, just this once... turn around, get your asses out of here, and tell those who sent you, that *next* time, there won't be any survivors. You've got five seconds. *Move!*"

"I can't see him," shouted one of the other government agents. "Team, go to vision-enhance-mode!"

"Laura – kids – *stay down, with your eyes closed!*" shouted Brent Boyd, one second before a surpassingly-brilliant light-burst, akin to being inside a mirror-filled room with an old-fashioned photo-flash-bulb going off in its middle, bathed even the interior of the van – not to mention, its surroundings – with a hatefully-powerful surge of photo-voltaic energy.

There were screams of pain and distress, now coming from outside.

"Can't see... can't *see!*" shrieked a guy who seemed to have fallen to the ground.

"Me neither!" moaned another voice. "God, God, *motherfucker*, it *hurts*, my eyes, my *eyes!*"

"Where *is* he – in the van, the *van!*" yelled another voice. "Shoot the *fuck* out of it! Use the launcher –"

The music was now veritably roaring, and in the next second, Laura Boyd heard her husband yell, "*Shine!*"

There was a strange, other-worldly noise, utterly new to her ears; it had a sweet-singing, chiming, sizzling "*ba-zappp!*" sound. This was immediately followed by more screams and then the shock-wave of a powerful explosion.

Slowly, the outside scene – and the strange rock music – began to quiet down, although the sinister sounds of disintegrating metal and flames consuming a motor-vehicle evidently several dozens of feet away, were also audible.

Footsteps rapidly approached the front passenger-door. It opened, but all that was on the outside was a coal-black, amorphous shape, one that completely obscured the feeble background light and concrete-overpass-supports that should have been visible, behind it.

The music quickly ebbed away.

"*Wendy... Laura!*" called a blessedly-familiar voice. "Oh... sorry... forgot..."

In a split-second, the figure of Brent Boyd – a bit of five o'clock shadow on his cheeks and chin, wearing black lace-up dress-shoes and evidently dressed in a business-suit, albeit without a tie – appeared in the car-doorway. The scenery further out was, however, still completely blocked out by the strange, black shroud behind the ex-astronaut. There was an elfin glow in his eyes, but this quickly vanished and those onlooking told themselves that the effect must have been a light-reflection or something akin.

"Oh God – *Brent!*" cried the wife, as she almost crushed her daughter, while diving across the middle of the van to embrace her husband. "I never thought I'd *see* you –"

For many seconds, they just hugged, while murmuring private lovers' greetings and consolations. Then Boyd turned his attentions to each of his children in turn, offering "have I got a story to tell all of you". He even kissed the top of the dog's head.

After a too-brief re-acquaintance session, the former Mars mission pilot ushered his daughter out of the passenger seat (she took a place next to the boy in the back row) and instructed, "Laura, honey – get us out of here; those guys aren't in any shape to threaten us, but there'll be reinforcements on the way... *drive. Boot it!*"

As she reconnected her seat-belts and shoulder-restraints and restarted the engine, the over-wrought, stressed-out wife managed, "S...sh...sure, Brent... but which way? Where to? And... I'm a nervous wreck, right about now... isn't there any way that you could..."

"Northwest on I-64," he directed. "I got a map with me, I'll figure out where we're going on the way. Kids... try to keep your heads down, don't look out the windows – Daddy's orders."

The van bumped up the shoulder, gaining speed rapidly on the north-bound lanes of the Interstate.

The wife didn't have much time to observe the aftermath of the recent confrontation, as she pulled out from under the overpass; but she *did* see several, apparently-dead, black-suited bodies lying hither and yon, as well as three black SUVs in various states of disrepair, with odd-looking scorch-marks on their nearest-facing sides.

It was as if someone had taken a huge, intensely-hot blow-torch to the unlucky automobiles; one of them had almost been sliced in half, by whatever sinister weapon had been deployed, here.

"By the way, Laura, sweetheart... I'd love to take over at the wheel, but the reason why I'm not driving is that I may need to, uhh, *defend* us, at any minute," said Boyd. "Don't be surprised if I open the door and fly out of here – I'll never leave you or the kids again, but I may need some tactical mobility... attacking from above, kind of thing. You got all the on-board tracking-gear, like the trip-computer and the satellite-map, turned off?"

"Yes – I disconnected them back at home, before we set out, but you're not making any *sense*," protested the wife. "And how'd you *get* here, anyway? I didn't see you drive up –"

"Laura," he calmly replied, "I... *flew* here, that's how. Remember what I said over the phone, a couple of days ago?"

"What do you mean – you 'flew' here?" persisted Laura Boyd. "Like, in a helicopter, or –"

"I meant, 'all by myself', honey," related the ex-astronaut. "I don't need a helicopter, or an airplane, or a balloon, or... *anything*. Not sure exactly *how* I do it, but Karéin mentioned something about 'the skills latent within you, by which you will bend the mighty waves of that force called gravity'... I'm guessing that my average airspeed was into the high hundreds of miles per hour, going from Fayetteville to here."

"And I'll spare you your next question," he continued. "Yes, it *was* me who taught those Agency creeps out there a harsh lesson, and no, I *didn't* need a gun to do it. Laura... I'm a *demi-god*, now; I'm powerful beyond anything you can imagine. I've already had a hydrogen bomb dropped on my head – okay, just a little ways off my head – and lived to tell about it. As long as all of you are with me, you're completely safe... our enemies don't have a *chance*. The 'music' that you heard back there is what the Storied Watcher calls a 'war-song'... not so great for the surprise-element but I'm learning to live with it."

"You're *Superman* now, Daddy? *Neaattt!*" piped up the excited voice of the boy, from the back seat.

Boyd tried not to literally beam a smile, and succeeded in doing so only figuratively, as he reached behind him and grinned at his son.

"*Something* like that, Brent," proudly offered the ex-astronaut. "But let me tell you, it's not all it's cracked up to be... I got most of the government on my tail. Same goes for Commander Jacobson, Cherie Tanaka, Devon White and a few others who you haven't yet met. It looks like that S.O.B.-of-a-President is hunting down the families of all of us, except for Devon's, because Saquina and her kids are already safe – and they, along with the three who went with me to Mars, have also gained a big ol' whack of these 'alien-powers'... long story there."

He looked down at the map and, without thinking too much of it, held up an instantly-glowing finger to illuminate this document, a move that won him a chorus of amazed and awed "oohs" and "aahs" from the back seat.

"Oh, sorry," he sheepishly commented, "I guess I've gotten a bit too used to having parts of my body act like a lantern."

"Brent... what's going *on*?" stammered the perplexed wife. "How on Earth are you... *doing* that?"

"The Storied Watcher granted me powers over light and darkness," he explained, in matter-of-fact manner. "On top of a lot of other little alien-tricks... I'll fill you in on the whole thing when there's time, but suffice it to say, dear, that if I decide to use enough of Karéin's '*Fire*' – it's called '*Amaiish*' in her language – in powering-up my little personal flashlight, well... you saw what happened to those Agency vehicles, back there?"

"My God," she grimly repeated. "That was... *you?*"

"It was a small fraction of what I'm capable of, Laura," he mentioned. "You have no *idea*... and neither do they."

Silence fell over the conversation for a few seconds, and then again, the wife spoke up.

"Are you still... *human?*" she carefully ventured.

"Laura – kids – I promised never to lie to you," answered Boyd. "And I won't start doing so, now."

He paused and then said, "Am I 'human'? No... I guess I'd have to honestly say, that I'm not, and I haven't been since I met Karéin on Mars, though I hadn't the foggiest idea of what I was getting myself into, on that day. I don't know *what* you'd call me, but I'm *still* the man – okay, the 'more-than-a-man' – who loves all of you more than he loves life itself. Whether or not you believe me... I'm telling you the truth, dear... and whether or not you'll have me as a husband and father, and whether or not I can be with you, I'll never stop loving you, or caring for you, or defending you. That's about it, I guess."

"*I* believe you, Daddy... and I want you to *stay* being our Daddy," came the voice of Wendy, from directly behind the ex-astronaut, and with watering eyes, he reached back and exulted in the feeling of her hand grasping his own.

"Well, human or otherwise," offered Laura Boyd, "You're all I've got, Brent... and of *course* I still love you. We saw the news-broadcasts from that thing with the tornado down South, but I couldn't *believe* that... anyway. Where are we going?"

"Thinking... *thinking*," temporized the former Mars mission pilot, as he intensely studied the map. "Okay... remember that little private campground we stayed at in the old trailer, a couple years after we got married, where is it again... yeah, up 629, about fourteen miles up the road from here... ought to be far enough for us to pull over, do our best to hide the van and then catch up, make some short-term plans. It's so late that in these parts, they'll all be in bed by now... nobody should notice us. Just keep going and take the turn-off when you see Douthat Road turn-off, with the shopping-center coming up on the right."

"Got it," she replied, while boosting the speed as much as she dared, without being certain to draw the attention of the State Troopers. "I'll get us there, but... what do we do afterwards, Brent? Where do we *go?*"

"Oh... *that's* easy," he said, with an insouciantly-arched eyebrow. "We wait until Sam Jacobson and the rest of the crew come to pick us up. Back at the Fort Knox Army base, Cherie Tanaka and I, uhh, 'appropriated' an Air Force transport-plane – vertical-takeoff-and-landing, so you don't need a runway – for all of us to ride in. The Commander's off to Texas to rescue *his* family... then he's going to double back to the Morris Harvey House in Fayetteville, where we'll have to wait until he arrives. With me so far?"

"Yeah, but... what if those, uhh, 'government' people, figure this all out, and show up at the Harvey House, before us?" she argued. "And even if that doesn't happen... when and if we get on Commander Jacobson's airplane... where do we go, then?"

"Well," he confidently offered, "First, I'll fly ahead and scout out Fayetteville, and it's really simple... I'll give anybody who's planning an ambush, five minutes to scram, or I'll vaporize them. For the record, I made quite a spectacular exit from the Harvey House when I was up there a few minutes ago, but it was late and I don't think a lot of people – one old lady excepted – saw me. And as to your second question, honey... want to know what we're going to do, after everybody's accounted for, and on the transport?"

"Not sure I do," said the wife, trying to keep her eyes on the road ahead, while scanning every so often for signs of pursuit. "But you might as well tell me, Brent."

"It's really quite straight-forward," stated the ex-astronaut. "Then, we're going to find Air Force One, and overthrow the President of the United States."

Smoke From A Not-So-Distant Fire

The depressing routine of doing the proverbial "S.F.A." had, by now, stretched over days – *weeks*, in fact – and Karlie Tillman had almost come to welcome her intermittent anxiety-attacks, as relief from the boredom.

Those, and the dreams : fleeting, nocturnal glances of she knew-not-what, of exotic battle-scenes, of faces that somehow seemed familiar (but that she couldn't quite place), of... *impossible* things, like "being thrown from somewhere way high up, falling through the clouds... yet landing like a feather".

The dream-images had been especially vivid at one point; but lately, they had diminished.

That *worried* her.

So did the strange, deep-red and deep-purple colors that seemed to appear in random places, when the terror of the falling-dream forced her involuntarily-awake.

Now, the ex-waitress looked over the drab, gray-upon-steel confines of the holding-cell, which contained nothing that she could possibly have used to have killed herself with (she *had* considered it, actually; but the bedsheets were made of some paper-like substance, which would never have held her full weight, even if twisted into a makeshift rope).

Going nuts, she morosely reflected, trying – and again failing – to stretch high enough to see out the single, tiny window to the outside world.

It had steel bars and a thick pane of glass to close off even the theoretical chance of escape, and although it couldn't be opened to let in a whiff of fresh air, Karlie could have sworn she'd heard the sweet calls of crickets and songbirds, far-off, somewhere behind, out in the free, uncomplicated, mostly-sane world that – until all the Crazy Things started happening – she had inhabited.

She slumped back onto the bed, staring vacantly at the opposite concrete wall.

I've read that damn Bible, front to back, six times or more.

Why can't I have some other book in here?

How many days has it been? How many weeks?

Lost count...

Why are they keeping me here?

I didn't do anything!

The cell-block had at least ten individual cells – Karlie's was the middle one, on the south side of a central-corridor – but as far as she could tell, she was alone here. There was at least one additional block to the east and the west, separated from hers by a concrete wall and a locked steel door, on either end.

Occasionally, she had heard faint sounds of street-criminals and other unfortunates being temporarily accommodated (and, apparently, being beaten within an inch of their lives) in the block to the east, and she wondered how she could do so at all, considering the distance from "here" to "there"; but repeated calls to someone – *anyone* – for camaraderie, or just conversation of any type, went un-answered.

Meals – uniformly made of some freeze-dried substance that looked like cardboard, and tasted the same – were delivered only once a day, by a team of no less than four big, heavily-armed, black-SWAT-geared guards, whose faces were invariably concealed by riot-gear-helmets and mirror-sunglass visors.

Each time, Karlie marveled at the spectacle, as any one of these guys could have easily overpowered her – *who the H are they worried about?* – she mused; and although after they marched off, she wolfed every last bit of the unappealing stuff as if she was famished... really, she wasn't.

She wondered about *that*, too.

Not even as much as an appetizer back at the Santa Esmerelda, she had noted. *I know I should feel hungry... but I don't.*

They got me on drugs – that's gotta *be it. Some kind of fuckin' experiment.*

But I'm just a waitress, *for Cripe's sakes!*

What do they want with me?

That family – yeah, they told me – something "bad" happened to 'em.

But I had nothin' to do with that!

Okay... so I served them breakfast – is that a crime, these days?

They asked me 'bout it, over and over again, for two days, *when they first brought Ossie, his old lady, and me, in – and I never* saw *that hippie-girl before, or afterwards.*

Is just servin' her, a 'Fed'ral offense', or something?

What's she got to do with that shit that went down in D.C.? They sure clammed up when I asked 'em for details on that...

Guess everything's a crime, if they want you bad enough.

But why they want me, *in the first place?*

Realizing – for the umpteenth time – that none of it made sense, Karlie sighed and slumped with her back against the concrete wall, her long legs hanging a considerable distance past the edge of the cell-cot.

She closed her eyes and tried to doze off, over the space of a few minutes.

The effort was to no avail, but not for the usual reasons. This time, something entirely new – a very loud, deep-pitched "boom" that shook the whole cell-block, popping-sounds and shouting way off in the distance, apparently coming from top-side – assailed her senses.

She sniffed the air a few times.

Smells like... uhh... smoke? the ex-waitress asked herself.

Hah – serves the fuckers right... somebody set his mattress on fire.

She looked down at her own furnishings.

Okay... no mattress here. Maybe somebody else got one, though.

And these bed-sheets – they're paper – they'd burn... right?

Now, Karlie could clearly hear alarmed screams coming from the east and above. There were more of the "pop-pop-pop" noises, which – worryingly – reminded her of what gunshots were supposed to sound like.

Then came fire-alarm-bells. The scent of burning-things was unmistakable.

A trickle of water came down the corridor, heading from east to west. It covered most of the outside floor and started to infiltrate her own cell. She laid out a towel underneath the bottom of the iron-barred gate between the cell and the corridor; it retarded, but did not stop, the burgeoning flow.

"Hey – *hey!*" called the alarmed ex-waitress. "What's goin' *on?* Hey – anybody!"

There was no reply – except, at the limit of her hearing, she could just make out ominous words and phrases like "evacuate", "out of control" and "at large".

The smell of smoke was becoming unpleasantly-oppressive as it started to form a perceptible layer over the floor-water, although – strangely – Karlie's lungs didn't protest, however much contaminated air she was breathing in.

Then the overhead-lights and the one small lamp on her folding-cell-table went out, being replaced after a delay of perhaps a second or two with emergency-illumination from a battery-powered set, high on the eastern far wall, above and to the right of the security-door.

Hmm... didn't know the damn things put out that funny kind of light, mused Karlie.

Why the hell'd they shine so everything's got that really dark red edge to it?

Must be some kinda high-tech 'emergency' thing, 'cause I can see stuff perfectly well in that red-light... maybe it cuts through smoke better...

She looked down again. The towel was now totally-soaked, and the water was gushing through and past it, covering most of the cell-floor. The ex-waitress' slippers were also becoming waterlogged.

"Help! *Hellllppp!*" shouted an increasingly-frightened Karlie. "Hey, uhh, jailer! You guard-guys! *Anybody!* I'm gettin' *flooded* in here!"

There was no answer.

Some of the water sloshed into a low-lying A/C-socket, and for a second or two, the ex-waitress was terrified of being electrocuted; but it was immediately apparent that the power had been cut here, too, and there was neither a hiss, nor a spark, nor a shock.

Fortunately, at this point the flow seemed to abate, leaving the floor mostly covered with a half-inch thick layer of water with a few dry-spots here and there. However, the smoke continued to waft down from somewhere above, producing an almost impenetrably dense cloud – at least to mundane human eyes. This continued for several more minutes, with the stench of smoke and airborne chemicals within it, becoming steadily more distasteful. There was faint yelling from the east, but it died down to a whimper and then... nothing.

Even though she intuitively knew that she should be gasping for air and risking unconsciousness, somehow, Karlie was coping remarkably well with the increasing lack of oxygen. She knew this because she had no trouble in repeating her cries for assistance, even louder than before.

And *this* time, there was an answer – but not the one that she had expected. At the limit of her ability to hear, came a faint response.

"Karlie? *Karlie?* That *you?*"

"Yeah, it's me!" she eagerly called out. "Who's – wait a minute – uhh – Ossie? *Ossie?*"

Initially, there wasn't any more talking back, and the ex-waitress felt the pangs of frustration returning.

"Ossie! *Ossie!* Where *is* ya?" she frantically shouted.

"Hold on," came back a distant answer.

She heard a rattling-noise, off to the left, somewhere past the western end of the corridor. This was followed, in short order, by some low-level swearing in what sounded like Spanish, and then, by a clanging impact-noise, a "plop" and "splash", each after the other. Finally, there was the sound of a steel-door swinging on its hinges, along with low ripples of displaced water coming from the west.

In another six or seven seconds, much to Karlie's elation, the rotund, gold-toothed, tan-faced and wonderfully-familiar figure of Osvaldo Jiminez – his orange-colored prison-gear pant-legs rolled up to well over his knees, carrying slippers in one hand and what looked like an iron bar in the other.

"Ossie – *Ossie!*" gushed the ex-waitress. "Never thought I'd *see* ya again!"

"*Igualmente,*" he replied. "Had me in a cell all by myself since we got here... way back there, that way."

He motioned to the west.

"So what the fuck's goin' *on?*" she queried. "And... how'd ya get out?"

She didn't see a key (either conventional or electronic) anywhere on his person. He was squinting in his usual manner, but didn't seem to be bothered by the clouds of smoke wafting about.

"No idea, *chica,*" answered Jiminez, "On both questions. 'Cept I think there's somethin' heavy goin' down upstairs, 'cause I hear this big 'boom', gunshots, people yellin' 'fire' and so on... I banged my eatin'-plate on the cell-bars, nobody listens of course – then the smoke 'n water starts comin' and I figure, 'Ossie you're *screwed*, time to pray to La Santa Maria'. So I do that... sit around for a minute or two, and I realize that God ain't comin' my way today, so... so..."

"So... *what?*" pressed Karlie. "Ya still ain't told me how ya sprung yourself."

"Well... maybe it was a miracle... or I don' know what you'd call it," he explained. "See, I got pissed off – much as I ever been – I mean, drownin' or dyin' from smoke-inhalation, that ain't right, is it? I start punchin' and kickin' at the bars on the cell, all I do is hurt my hands and feet... finally, I'm 'bout to give up and in disgust... I spit at the damn thing. Hit it right on the lock, not that I was aimin', and... well..."

"What?" demanded the man's ex-employee.

"You not gonna *believe* this, *chica,*" offered Jiminez, "But... 'bout a second after I hork on it... fuckin' bars just... uhh... *melt* – like ice-cream in July, you know? Nothin' left at all, where I hit it. Couldn't *believe* it, so I spit on my fingers to be sure, and it smelled a bit different, but didn't hurt me none – tried it again on the bars and *seguro*, there they go. Pushed it open, just walked out. Then I heard you callin', and I got up to the door between this corridor and the one I was in, it was locked, so I spit on that one as well... melted same way, catch fell off on the other side... then I walked in here."

"What's all this talk about horkin' on things and them meltin'?" countered the ex-waitress. "Come *on*, Ossie... what *really* happened back there? Look – it don't matter to me if ya had to crack a few knuckles to get out of this shithole... or even if ya had to do more than that... know what I mean?"

"Think I'm shittin' you?" argued Jiminez.

"Yeah... of *course* ya is," answered Karlie. "But why don't ya just –"

"Stand back," interrupted the former restaurant-owner.

The ex-waitress shuffled backwards by perhaps a foot or two, and then by another few inches as she saw her former boss pucker up and let fly with a large gob of saliva. He missed the target – apparently he had been aiming at the lock sealing Karlie in the cell, but instead struck an area slightly above it – and a second or two afterwards, the steel bar-structure hit by Jiminez' spit began to... *deliquesce*.

A slurry of melted metal – looking very much like liquid solder – flowed down from the impact-spot, creating in turn a shallow impression on everything that it touched. It missed the lock, however, causing the restaurant-owner to let fly a second shot, and this time Jiminez' aim was true; he hit the lock square-on, resulting in a steaming, pulpy mess where solid brass (or bronze), had been a few seconds beforehand.

Some of what was left of this sinister concoction made it as far as the floor, where it hissed and sputtered upon contacting the water and concrete, leaving another slight depression.

A wide-eyed Karlie stared in disbelief.

"Jaysus, Ossie... what the... *what* the..." she gasped.

"I don' *know*," he pleaded.

After a second or two of shock, the ex-waitress managed,

"Ossie... that's fuckin' *weird* – what they *do* to you, man? I mean... doesn't that spit, like, burn you up inside, or..."

"Nothin' – *nothin'!*" he protested. "They knocked me around quite a bit, interrogated me for hours – days – 'specially about that hippie-girl that we served up, don' know shit about her anyways... but no 'speriments, no *drogas* that I'm aware of – *¡lo juro!* And like I told you – I feel *fine*, 'cept for missin' the home cookin' back at the *Esmerelda*. I got no idea of what's goin' on, *chica*... none at all."

"I... I... don't know what to *say*," stammered Karlie.

"Here," he offered, giving the cell-door a firm yank.

The lock – its mechanism melted to nothingness – immediately snapped in two, leaving Karlie with a clear path through the puddles of dirty water and floating *bric-a-brac*, out to freedom... or some facsimile thereof.

"I... gotta get some things," muttered Karlie, as – though preoccupied and bewildered by what she had just witnessed – she gathered the very few personal items that had been allowed her (a duplicate set of prison-clothes, a toothbrush and plastic hairbrush, a writing-pad and crayon, some non-toxic makeup and lipstick and a few other small things) into the paper-like fabric of one of her pillow-cases.

She quickly folded a bed-sheet and a hand-towel into the other pillow-case, remembering at the last minute to also grab the half-roll of toilet-paper that remained on its hook.

"That's it, I guess," she added, while moving with trepidation past the melted cell-locking-assembly, out into the hallway. "Take anything with ya from yours, Ossie?"

"No *señorita*," he stated. "All happened kind of fast, I suppose."

"Still can't *believe* it," observed the ex-waitress. "Time for that later. Listen... where we goin'?"

The Mexican returned a classic "deer-in-the-headlights" stare.

"No idea, *chica*," he replied, after a second or two of consideration. "'Cept out of here would be a good start... you know?"

As she set a path toward the eastern cells and – hopefully – freedom, Karlie asked, "Listen, Ossie... you see any of them guards, or policemen? Back there, I mean."

"Nothin'," he replied, while stepping from side to side to avoid the most-part of the water. "Guess they run away or somethin' – not sure why."

They had reached the eastern cell-block, and both of them heard – at the edge of their ability, though they could not precisely interpret the nature of the crisis – far-off shouts of panic and mayhem.

A visual review of this gray-painted, concrete-and-steel prison-area revealed plentiful signs of recent occupation (including, ominously, blood-stains in a few spots). All the cells were shut tight; most were unoccupied, but two near the end furthest from where Karlie had been held, accommodated apparently-lifeless male bodies, staring glassy-eyed up at the ceiling.

"Smoke must've got to 'em," observed Jiminez.

"Why not us?" countered Karlie.

"You tell *me*, *chica*," muttered the restaurant-owner. "I smell buckets of *la mierda* in every breath I take, feel like pukin' every second, but I'm still goin' – for how long, I don' know. *¡Que vamos!*"

Turning her stare from the scene, the waitress grimly nodded and went forward.

They came to a set of stairs that ascended about ten feet to a small platform, then another ten up to a very robust-looking, reinforced steel-door. Though the bottom-part of this thing was flush with the floor and it looked like its locking-mechanism was engaged, water was spraying out from it at each edge, as far as about a quarter of the way from its bottom extremity; and smoke was leaking through further up. Its particulate haze enveloped the entire ceiling of the room.

As the two ascended the stairs, Jiminez commented, "That ain't good, *señorita* – maybe a flood behind it. We better be ready."

"Yeah," agreed the ex-waitress.

She extended a hand to the lever on the door, touched it, flinched momentarily and then withdrew her hand.

"Feels a bit warm," observed Karlie. "Damn... fire out there?"

"Maybe," evenly answered the former restaurant-owner. "Watch out– here I go."

He spat at what appeared to be the door's locking-apparatus, and this melted immediately; but even after a good swift kick on Jiminez' part, it refused to budge.

"Must be somethin' anchoring it in place," he theorized. "Okay, then– I'll get the hinges."

Three more shots of expectorate, aimed with increasing expertise at equidistant points on the right-hand side of the portal, seemed to do the trick, as the door began to shimmy and shake, with increasing amounts of both smoke and water issuing from its bottom and top halves.

"Uh-oh– gonna *go*–" warned Jiminez, about a half-second before the door's right side gave way, releasing a flood of dirty, debris-filled water that swept both of the refugees off their feet, sending both the ex-waitress and her former boss careening down the second half-staircase to the intermediate landing. In between panicked yelps, Karlie thought she caught glimpses of charred and burned flotsam and jetsam – mostly burnt wood, with shards of paper, melted plastic and rubber – passing by her in the deluge; she took hold of a guard-rail, interrupting her descent, while Jiminez grabbed one of her legs and thus also came to a stop on the platform.

The dirty, charcoal-laden water was still gushing by and a pall of smoke – significantly denser, darker and more replete with chemical-smells than what had previously been bothering them – started to descend from the half-open top-half of the doorway.

"Ossie – *Ossie* – y'*okay*?" shouted a sputtering, gasping Karlie, as she tried to right herself against the onrushing deluge.

"Yeah," Jiminez called back, "But we gotta get *out* of here – I can barely *breathe!*"

"Me either!" yelled the ex-waitress. "Thought I could handle the smoke, but it's *gettin'* to me!"

"Stay low... crouch... *crawl!*" he advised. "Hard to move with this water shootin' at us, but I'll back you up – push you from behind. Got it?"

"Yeah," she agreed, with a quick nod.

Barely keeping their heads above the flood – which showed no signs of abating – the two shuffled awkwardly forward, stumbling once or twice as they mounted the higher half-staircase, but eventually succeeding in reaching the breached door. The opening on its right side was barely large enough to allow one person to traverse it, and Jiminez – being still somewhat rotund despite weeks of inadequate prison-food – was able to squeeze past only with considerable difficulty.

The floor in the area that they emerged into had once been covered by a carpet; but its waterlogged fibers were now under about a foot of filthy water with a thin film of creosote-like black-stuff on top, and the stifling, chemical-contaminated smoke was everywhere; it seemed to be pouring down from a stairway-entrance, far in front of them, to the left. Karlie and Jiminez, already short of breath, had to keep their mouths and nostrils just above water-level to avail themselves of any oxygen whatsoever.

This place might, at one time, have been a holding- or receiving-area, judging from the rows of half-melted plastic-and-metal chairs strewn haphazardly, hither and yon, and from the shattered, glass dividing-windows. Black scorch-marks were visible on the walls and on almost every other horizontal and vertical surface; some of the drywall and wood-finishings had been charred almost all the way through, and in places above the waterline, fires were still burning, albeit at low intensity. Through the haze the two could barely make out what appeared to be impact-craters of various sizes, in some of the wall-sections.

Then Karlie screamed.

"What – what?" demanded Jiminez.

"L-look – *there* –" she stuttered, pointing to a mangled, bloodied, half-charred human male torso – missing both legs, one eye and much of its nose – that floated by. It was carried to the doorway that they had just exited and then jammed in the open-space leading to the lower levels.

A quick visual scan of the water-surface revealed at least three or four other corpses (or remnants of them), evidently two male policemen or guards and what must have been a female office-worker, floating or at rest in different places. All of these had suffered variations of the same grisly injuries.

"Ossie... what ya think... *happened* here?" inquired the ex-waitress, in a tremulous voice.

"*No sé,*" he replied. "Bomb, maybe?"

"But who'd – anyway," said Karlie. "What we gonna *do*?"

"Head out," he suggested. "You hear them sounds from above?"

"Yeah," she confirmed, "Something breaking, cracking..."

"Structure could be givin' way, *señorita*," warned Jiminez. "You don' want to be here, if it does."

She vigorously nodded in the affirmative.

Then, after looking around yet again, she asked, "Which way?"

"Don' know," replied Jiminez.

The situation seemed impossible; the way in front of them to the left and right was jammed with charred, shattered debris. Something collapsed up ahead, causing more groaning-sounds coming from the walls and sending a billowing cloud of dust and ashes coming straight at them.

A desperate Karlie glanced behind her right shoulder.

"There, Ossie!" she shouted. "Door open back there – almost out of the water – behind us –"

There was indeed such a portal; its glass inside-window was cracked and holed in several places, but it seemed mostly intact, and was still on its hinges.

"What if it's a dead-end?" he protested. "We get trapped, and –"

"What if it isn't?" she argued. "I'm *goin'!*"

Coming up to as much as a full crouch, the ex-waitress moved with unusual speed through the murky water – Jiminez could have sworn that the stuff was parting in front of her – to the remains of what looked like a carpeted-area going off to the right and behind.

She dashed through, followed about a second-and-a-half by the restaurateur, who slammed the door shut just as the dust-cloud arrived. Some of it got through the perforations in the portal, but the latter provided reasonably effective protection against the worst of the gas-and-ashes that were starting to accumulate on the other side.

A faint moan was heard from some far-off place.

Karlie and Ossie straightened up, as they found that the air in here was more breathable (albeit, with a strongly-unpleasant smoke-odor). They looked in the opposite direction from the door and quickly discovered why; this was a carpeted corridor leading to another building at ground-level, and it originally had large glass windows running all the way down on the left – although all of these were now badly-damaged, with two or three of them shattered altogether.

"There's our break," exulted Jiminez. "Come on – we can jump through one of them windows, make it out onto the grass –"

"Broken glass all over... wait... what's that – oh, *shit* –" stammered the ex-waitress.

They cast their vision down to the end of the corridor. Its originally-red, tastefully-designed shag was now shot ragged, with small pieces of once-airborne debris extending a long way down it. Near the end of the corridor were three casualties that must have been hit by the whatever-it-was, just as they entered the area through a door at its opposite end.

Two of these unfortunates were likely dead, judging from the severity of their injuries and various other obvious factors, but one other – a fit-looking, tanned, Caucasian, rusty-haired man who couldn't have been more than about twenty or so, dressed in a bloodstained dark blue business-jacket, white shirt and navy-blue slacks, plus shiny, lace-up dress-shoes – was trying to come to his feet by propping himself up on the wall.

"Hey – hey you!" called Karlie. "Ya need some *help?*"

The man sent back a glassy-eyed nod in the affirmative.

"*Santa Maria*, Karlie," protested Jiminez, "We got enough problems – he one of *them*, you know – we gotta get *out* of here!"

"Then *you* go," countered the ex-waitress, "Gonna check him out – only be a sec or two, anyways."

She raced over to the man, to the background-noise of more structural-rumbling and a new burst of smoke-infused dust coming from the area they had just exited.

Karlie did a shocked double-take, upon getting close enough to see the details. The poor guy had been hit by shrapnel – apparently nothing with enough mass to penetrate his body-cavity – but his jacket on the left side and back bore numerous small gashes, some of which were bleeding profusely, despite the man's half-dazed attempts to staunch the outflow.

"Holy *shit!*" exclaimed the former waitress, as she fumbled around for something to use as an absorbent, eventually settling on serviettes lying around what might have been an overturned food-cart. "Ya sure took one, or two, for the team there, mister... what the hell *happened* here?"

"Don't... don't know," he slowly replied in some kind of hard-to-place Commonwealth accent. "Had just walked through the doors with... with... those two poor buggers... guess they're goners now, by the look of 'em... and then it's like the whole *world* blew up in front of my face. Must've been out for a while... just managed to get to my feet... oww, my side hurts, feels like I got hit with buckshot..."

"Can ya move?" asked Karlie.

"Barely," he replied. "Why?"

"We – that's Ossie over there, he's my bud – we gotta *go*," she said. "Building might come down any minute."

"Mind if I tag along?" requested the man. "'Safety in numbers' and all that. There's a side-exit to the lawn back through these doors behind us, just 'round to the left... get us outside..."

"*No problemo*," cooperatively agreed Karlie, positioning herself under the guy's bad side – which, thanks to her impromptu bandage-job, had been reduced to an ugly as opposed to alarming state – and then helping him limp forward (though, her personal belongings in the bed-sheet made this effort, cumbersome and awkward). "What'd ya say your name was again?"

"Trevor... Trevor Marshall," he weakly forced out. "Senior Inspector, Australian Federal Police Counter-Terrorism Force Signals Group... on O.S.-duty up here in America, tryin' to track down blighters from the Salvation League – well, looks like maybe they found *me* first, wouldn't you say, ha ha... hey, wait a minute – your *clothes* –"

"What *about* 'em?" challenged Karlie.

"Marks you as a prisoner, hun," warily observed the wounded-guy.

Jiminez – who, though exasperated – had, by now, reluctantly followed his former employee down to the vicinity, interjected, "Listen, *señor*... we was framed, or somethin' – all I ever done was run a little *cantina* up in Idaho, with Karlie here waitin' on tables – and then the next thing we know, we gettin' slapped in handcuffs and sent down here, after hours and hours of them yellin' at us about an 'alien' or whatever *mierda* that was... you want us to just leave you here, that's *bueno para mi*... you know?"

"Yeah – Ossie's right about that," echoed the ex-waitress. "We only just got out of where they was keepin' us down below, by the skin of our teeth, before the whole damn place flooded out. We ain't done *nothing*, man! I *swear* it!"

The wounded-man tried to raise his hands in resignation, but only managed to get them half-way before the pain made the gesture too difficult to complete.

"Peace, mates," he wearily muttered, "Certainly wouldn't be the *first* time I've heard of bull-dust like that going on, up here – three-quarters of the blighters your American police-friends dragged in front of me, half-cactus from a few hours of tender love in the old divvy-van, they didn't have a scrap of useful information – waste of time, if you ask – anyway. Shall we go?"

"You got any idea what he's *talkin'* about, Ossie?" inquired a bewildered Karlie, as she tried to support Marshall in the direction of the exit-doorway.

"*No señorita,*" said Jiminez, with a bemused grin. "Barely learned how they talk *Inglès* up here in the States... no chance with that."

With the Australian wheezing, grimacing and still somehow managing to show a rueful grin, the three advanced to the doorway, which, unfortunately, was jammed shut by debris; a few quick kicks by Jiminez and Karlie together dealt with this, and in ten or twelve seconds they had exited the building altogether, out the side-entrance that Marshall had mentioned a short while beforehand.

They were now in an outside patio, with a stone floor, pre-formed concrete chairs and tables and a couple of decorative trees to break up the sterility of the area's decor. Just past this was a well-manicured lawn leading to a paved driveway extending far to the south but curving off to the east, just north of them. Another, narrower stretch of grass and a 6-foot-fall chain-link fence separated the driveway from a public double-lane road, running north and south.

"Fucking terrorists – come out with your hands *up!*" barked a hostile-sounding voice coming from a loudspeaker somewhere.

Karlie caught a glimpse of a couple of unmarked police cruisers and a number of police officers, to the north, on their left.

"*¡La mierda!*" cursed a frustrated Jiminez. "They fixin' to arrest us all over again!"

"What got you nicked in here for, mates?" suspiciously inquired Marshall, through a cough.

"I *told* ya – *nothing!*" complained the ex-waitress. "Mistaken identity, I guess... listen, Ossie, ya think we should – oh, *shit! **Run!***"

Her warning came none too soon – with a low, earthquake-like rumble, the part of the building to the northwest that they had just vacated began to disintegrate.

Dodging razor-sharp shards of broken glass, large chunks of concrete and jagged pieces of torn metal as they dashed outward across the patio, the panicked refugees glanced upward over their shoulders.

The north-western building – all seven to ten stories of it – was coming down. The entire side furthest from the door that they had exited, collapsed in on itself, producing a gray, billowing cloud of dust, chemical-haze and airborne detritus, coming at them with alarming speed.

The stuff was so opaque – even to the strangely-heightened senses of the waitress and her former boss – that they couldn't tell if within it, were potentially fatally-large remnants of the building. There was no time to test the theory, as they sprinted desperately toward the lawn-edge, away from the disaster-site.

They had just stepped on to the grass leading to the side-driveway, when – in suitably eerie, inexplicable fashion – time (or, at least, a second or two of it), seemed to slow to a crawl, at least from the perspective of Karlie and Jiminez.

The Mexican's heart skipped several beats as he saw the police-forces to his left suddenly open fire and aiming to kill, without any additional verbal warning; many of the pistol- and rifle-rounds thus launched weren't well-aimed, but enough of them were to make short work of the escapees.

That's how it happens, fatalistically mused Jiminez.

God gives you enough time to own up to your sins, before –

¡Mi señor bendecido... confieso todos mis pecados! Santa Maria –

But the invocation was a moot point, for reasons that his mind couldn't process. Marshall and Jiminez were on the right, and Karlie was slightly further to the north, so she was first-in-line to be struck by the LEA fusillade... or, *would* have been – *except* for –

Given that he somehow knew how each clock-tick of perceptible time must have been, in reality, about eight or more of actual time, the *thing* must have taken no more than a split-second or two, to have manifested itself.

The three of them were astonished to see brief, mirror-reflection-like flashes of light appearing an inch or so distant from Karlie's head, neck, shoulders, hands, waist, knees and feet; from each of these blazed a pencil-thin, subdued-red-glowing line of some laser-beam-like projection, connecting with the originating-points of the adjoining beams, until collectively they formed something looking rather like a diamond-shaped computer wire-frame diagram, interposed between the waitress and the incoming shots.

A hail of erstwhile-lethal gunshots struck this delicate-looking virtual-reality construct, and... ricocheted off harmlessly in all directions, each leaving a faint smoke-trail, as if the bullet had either been set afire or melted, upon coming into contact.

And that wasn't all; from one or two of the many impact-points, streaked some kind of retaliatory discharge, loosely-following the flight-path of the bullet that had triggered the counter-attack. Whatever this was, it traveled much too fast to be dodged or effectively reacted to, and a shocked Karlie watched it hit two of the crouching policemen, resulting in a shower of sparks, what looked like flames from something having been set alight, screams of consternation and words sounding like "heavily-armed gang, requesting reinforcements".

She winced in momentary discomfort; each bullet-strike felt like a pin-prick, but the sensation was followed close-on by a weird, luxurious rush of warmth and alertness, almost like downing a can of high-test cola in one slurp. She didn't notice the fact that something inside her body seemed to be... *glowing.*

And there was something *else* – a subdued, almost-imperceptible but still-audible echo of some kind of weird, fast-paced electro-rock music that started playing from everywhere and nowhere.

The rapid-thinking environment now went away as abruptly as it had manifested itself, and the strange wire-frame began to flicker as Karlie pushed Marshall and Jiminez to the south, away from their tormentors. They almost tripped over each other in so doing, because the waitress insisted on still facing the police-encampment and the other two had to trot backwards and sideways to avoid turning their backs.

This decision on Karlie's part proved a wise one, as a second – then, a third – barrage of gunshots was launched at the hapless refugees; but each of these was met by the same, ethereal force-shield, and each resulted in a fusillade of energy-discharges and more casualties – some of them undoubtedly serious or worse – among the angry, frustrated police-force.

The three, though sprinting to the south along the side of an adjoining building in unnaturally-rapid style (considering Marshall's near-deadweight non-contribution), would likely have become bogged down in a fire-fight with the authorities.

However, at this point, the north-western building from which they had exited, collapsed altogether. As they backed away as quickly as they could, Karlie, Marshall and Jiminez saw about half of the east-facing side of the building shear off and come crashing down into the police-encampment.

There couldn't have been many, or – perhaps – any, survivors; the area was covered smashed glass and in shattered concrete. Mercifully, the sight was visible only for a second or two, as a cloud of dust and debris, billowing out to the east, shielded it from view. And as this happened, the waitress' strange protective-*whatever*, flickered and disappeared, along with the unrequited music-track.

"Oh my... my *God*," gasped Karlie. "Did ya see *that...*"

Jiminez crossed himself, and then ruefully grunted, "Don' know why I do that, though – *putos* was tryin' to kill us!"

"That's what they *do* when they see somebody who they think's a 'terrorist', you know," observed Marshall. "Listen, mates – something really barmy's going on here – what the hell *was* that? Anyway, if I know your Bureau and Chicago Police half as well as I know me auntie in Melbourne, I'd wager they've got us tagged as 'terrorists', 'gangsters', what have-you; and that means we'd better rack off out of here while we've got some cover via that outback-cloud between us and whosoever left of them poor buggers. Come *on!*"

The other two didn't need much convincing, and they continued moving away from the battle-scene as quickly as possible, around the corner of the southern building; and around this time, the Australian – though obviously in considerable pain – began to regain the ability to walk on his own, albeit at no more than the speed of a hobbling, slow walk.

As they turned the corner, Karlie, Jiminez and Marshall instantly found themselves in the midst of a burgeoning crowd – probably encompassing a couple hundred or more – including not only some individuals who were likely from the prison-complex that they had just exited, but also a much larger number of ordinary civilians and morbidly-fascinated passers-by.

"What in God's name's going *on* up there?" asked a matronly Caucasian woman.

"Whole *building* came down," answered the waitress. "We just about got *killed* gettin' out of there. Hey, lady – call 9-1-1 – okay? There's people *hurt* up there!"

And more than a few of 'em might be dead because of me, she silently considered.

But what the hell did I do, anyway?

The civilian-woman nodded and pulled out a mobile-communicator, while the three refugees moved discreetly onward.

"Thank God," whispered Marshall, as they reached a point about halfway across the south-facing wall of the building. They could see another gate, now crowded with emergency-vehicles and people – mostly civilians – everywhere.

"Safety in numbers, I reckon," he added. "Stick with me, and if anybody asks about those funny trakkies you're wearing, I'll tell 'em that I'm just 'evacuating' you to another facility... we'll get somewhere safe, figure it out and settle up later. As you might guess, I've got a few things to get straight, between us. That work for you?"

"*Claro que sì,*" agreed Jiminez.

"Yeah – considerin' that we got no other options that won't get us arrested or shot, a block away from here," unhappily echoed Karlie.

So they moved at a deliberate but brisk pace, with the Australian reverting to being supported at the shoulders by the other two, toward the entrance-gate at the south-west corner of the building-compound, dodging gawkers, voggers, the first contingents of TV news-crews as they arrived on-scene, as well as the occasional police-officer (from whom Karlie and Jiminez demurely hid their eyes, *en passant*).

The two former prisoners had to muffle their alarm when they were challenged by rifle-toting guards just as they were about to transit the gate; but a quick disclaimer from Marshall to the effect of "that's alright, mate, these wankers are in my custody – they're taking me to a walk-in clinic", plus a check of his 3D smart-card identity-badge – the thing had been made ragged by shrapnel, but its circuitry was somehow still functioning – got them waved through with a perfunctory shrug.

The Australian motioned them across a two-lane side-street labeled "S. Leavitt", and then on a north-west course across a small, nondescript city park, until, after a trip of about a half-block, they were midway down a street marked "Washburne Avenue".

Marshall pointed to a mid-size Patriotic – a high-end, metallic-gold-painted sedan with lots of chrome, leather seats and "all the toys" – on the other side of the avenue.

"There's my Yank Tank – had to park her here because they're out of space in the Bureau lot," he offered, fumbling inside his many-holed jacket for a miniature key-fob. Relief was plainly visible on his face when he eventually located it.

"They wanted to put me in a kombi... but I pulled some strings to get something a little more, uhh, 'respectable'," he explained. "Would one of you mind driving? After what went down back there, I'm still a bit zonked... you know?"

"No shit, and the faster we get out of here, the better," agreed the waitress. "Ossie?"

"Fine," volunteered Jiminez, as he received the key-toss from Marshall. "I was on the road a lot, gettin' supplies for the *cantina*. 'Cept this rig's a lot better than my old *coche*, back in Idaho."

Rapidly, they all got into the automobile, with the Australian in the back, Karlie in the front passenger-seat and Ossie in the driver's-seat.

"Which way?" asked the former restaurant-owner.

"Right on South Oakley, broad left on Roosevelt Road – that's a big one, traffic's barmy and the lights are crazy, watch out when you get to the intersection – then a bit to the west, take a right on South Western, get us up to I-290, that's the 'Eisenhower Expressway' by the way... I'll direct you from there. Unfortunately, my hotel-flat's quite a ways out of town, in some place called 'Oak Brook'... fair Australia's anything but flush – they picked the cheapest place they could get away with. Okay?"

"Yeah... okay," echoed Jiminez, as he marveled at the panoply of high-tech devices that the luxury-car had at his disposal, while trying to get the feel of driving this particular vehicle. Somehow, the holographic 3D display that popped up, seemingly from nowhere, had correctly interpreted the driving-directions as Marshall had dictated them, and the path was perfectly laid-out on a mini-map in front of him.

Karlie looked backward, to the east. She gasped at the scene of destruction.

"Sweet Baby *Jaysus*," she gasped. "Whole front of that place... it's... *gone!*"

And she was right.

Now, they could clearly see the cause of the conflagration that had almost killed them, but that had latterly freed them : the north side of the building nearest to Roosevelt Road, had been replaced by a huge crater, from which flames were issuing and grayish-black smoke was billowing. Glass windows on either side of the street were either cracked or completely blown out, for at least a city block on either side of the crater, and there were people lying injured all over the immediate area.

"Yeah... surprised I'm still here talking to you," contemplatively acknowledged the Australian. "Luck of the draw, I s'pose... I was carrying a report for some blokes in the North Building, and if I'd been even twenty seconds earlier leaving my desk... poor bastards... not a buckley's chance..."

His voice subsided.

The Mexican-American had to drive cautiously, because the side-roads were already becoming clogged with other vehicles – including, ominously, a number of heavily-armored, military personnel-carriers – drawn by the commotion that they were trying to leave behind. But eventually, the Patriotic and its crew managed to clear the local traffic-jams and head out northward toward the highway.

For about a mile after they departed the disaster-scene, Marshall maintained a silent demeanor that might have been intentional, but was probably just as much due to exhaustion and the debilitating effects of the wounds he bore. However, as they were almost ready to turn onto the Interstate, he again raised his voice.

"So, mates," he asked, "I think I've more than kept my side of the bargain here – we all know that I could've turned you two in to what's left of the FBI back there, and probably I should have, but 'curiosity killed the cat'... you know?"

"FBI?" responded Jiminez, never taking his eyes off the road, except to periodically check behind them for signs of pursuit (fortunately, none seemed to be forthcoming). "'That who's been raggin' on us?"

"That Chinese woman who arrested us was FBI... or so she told us," mentioned Karlie.

"Well, they're the blokes who owned that headquarters back there," noted the Australian. "Though they weren't the only ones using it – your Yank government seems to have more spy agencies than we got sharks off Bondi, and a lot of 'em are so secret they didn't even let me know their names. But let's stay on the subject... shall we? You can start by telling me *exactly* why and how you got in there, luv; and when you're done with *that,* you can explain what the hell happened when we were getting shot at, and should have carked it right there."

The waitress sighed, shook her head and replied,

"I've said it a million times to a thousand people, Mister –"

"Just 'Trevor' will do," he reassured.

"Yeah, fine... 'Trevor', whatever," she confirmed. "I'm Karlie Tillman, by the way... Ossie's last name is 'Jiminez', he was my boss at the Santa Esmerelda Restaurant back up in Idaho, and as to how the hell we got put in a prison down here in, uhh – where *are* we, anyways?"

"Chicago," disclosed the Australian.

"*Chicago?* What the H –" complained Karlie. "But okay... see, up there at the restaurant, nothin' really happens very much, we just get a few truckers through there, and then, of course, the Big Thing with the comet goes down... you remember that?"

"*I'd* say," remarked Marshall. "Bloody close call for everybody..."

"Yeah... no shit," agreed the waitress. "So a couple of days after we was all breathin' a sigh of relief that we didn't get, like, blasted by that 'Lucifer' thing, I'm gettin' back to waiting tables at the Santa Esmerelda, 'back to life, back to reality' kinda thing, and in wanders this cute little hippie-chick, about seventeen or eighteen years old or so and a bit shorter than me, not bad-lookin' but dirty and ragged as all get-out, couldn't talk worth shit, looked stoned out of her mind or disoriented all the time, real space-cadet –"

"Just a minute," interrupted the Australian. "What'd you say she looked like? Did she say what her name was? Was there anything... uhh... *unusual*, about her?"

"Like I *told* ya," diffidently answered the waitress, "She looked like she'd just been in a car-crash or somethin' – had some kind of an army-uniform on, 'cept it was all torn-up, burn-marks here and there, but she wasn't bleedin' or anything like that, so we didn't have to do any first-aid on her. And 'weird'? Yeah, I guess you'd say that about her – this chickie was one of a kind, *that's* for sure. For example, she didn't know how to use cutlery, and she slurped up almost all the sugar we had, until I caught her and made her lay off. What was the other question?"

"Her *name* – did she tell you her name?" repeated Marshall.

His voice was rising, as if with intense expectation.

"Did she... hmm... what was it again... funny, you know, she was so unusual, you'd think that it'd come right to me... oh wait, *I* remember! 'Sar-ee', or something like that – yeah, *that's* what she called herself."

"'Sar-ee' – that it? You *sure?*" pressed the Australian.

"Listen, Trevor... what's it to ya, anyway? Why ya so interested in this girl?" asked Karlie.

"Yeah," chimed in Jiminez. "We never see her again, after she goes out with some family from... where was it – oh yeah – from Michigan. What's the big deal here?"

A weary, bemused look appeared on the face of the Australian.

"Well, mates," he said, "Let's just say that I've seen some intel-briefings... and now, I know why you were in that jail."

Bad News At The Kerosene Pump

"Hate to stop like this, while Yvonne and the kids *need* me," grumbled Jacobson, as he returned from the pump at the darkened, closed-down municipal airport, just south-east of Magnolia, Arkansas, with the fuel-line draped over his shoulder, leaving the cage that normally locked the hose in place "after hours", looking rather worse for the wear.

"Yeah, well, Cap'n," offered White, while connecting the fuel-line to a receptacle underneath the V-37's slate-gray fuselage, "Understand how y'all feel – but we're gonna look pretty damn stupid if we show up like the cavalry, and then we run out of gas. Assumin' the tank underground here's full, we should be good to get to the *rendez-vous* point back east, with just a bit left over... *if* I'm calculatin' it all right – of course... that 'calculatin' stuff always *was* more Brent's thing than mine."

"Let's just get gassed up and get out of here, ASAP," requested the Mars mission commander.

White nodded and initiated the flow.

For perhaps two minutes, the situation remained quiet, with the two former Mars astronauts continuing to pump Jet-A fuel into the V-37, while observing that Donny and Sammie had exited the aircraft so they could share a cigarette (there had been lively arguments about this *en route;* but neither Jacobson nor Tanaka would relent). Wolf, meanwhile, had taken his two mutts – including the previously-wounded one, which – though still limping – did look a bit more healthy – off to a nearby grass-field, to "do their business", and the elder Wades had accompanied Tanaka into the airfield's rudimentary main-office-and-lounge, in hopes of scrounging up provisions and necessities for the trip.

Misha had elected to remain on-board the plane.

As the aircraft's local gauges were showing almost "full", the face of the Science Officer, with something halfway between alarm and anger showing prominently upon it, appeared just outside the doorway to the lounge.

"Sam!" she shouted. "Come quick!"

"What is it?" he replied, covering the fifty or more feet to her proximity in scarcely more than a single bound.

"Rigged up the communicator to use the Neo connection here as an access-point," explained Tanaka. "Got through to the hackers... this guy, name of 'Any Nobody', says he's got an important update for us. You can talk through the computer-mike. Go ahead."

While Callum and Marie Wade, their arms full of chocolate bars, bags of potato chips and soda-pop, watched passively on from the shadows of this almost-completely-unlit place, Jacobson spoke up.

"If you know my voice, you know who I am," he said. "My co-worker tells me there's new information. What is it?"

"Hi, man," responded whoever was at the other end. "And yeah, we got a voice-print-confirm... hate to tell you this, Mister Jacobson, but looks like something *bad's* already gone down at that address you gave us – what was it again, oh, yeah, '17104 Saint Therese Road, Manor, Texas' –"

"What's happened?" interrupted an instantly-desperate Jacobson.

"So," said 'Any Nobody', "We sorta hacked in to the home security and enviro-control systems – good thing we did, because not an hour after we got root, the Man tried to do so as well, but we had it properly locked-down at that point, of course – and we got a video-feed from the outside cameras. 'Bout ten minutes ago, there were images of a bunch of dudes in black combat-gear – you know, the whole SWAT-thing – sneakin' around outside the house. We set off the inside alarms before the Man cut the outside Neo-link and we lost the signal – maybe that would've given your folks a little heads'-up, can't say for sure – but beyond that there wasn't much more we could do, 'cept –"

"*Shit!*" bellowed Jacobson, as he pounded his fist on a nearby desk, loudly enough that the windows rattled. "Why didn't you tell us *immediately*, when –"

Several of those outside abandoned whatever they were doing and raced toward the lounge.

"Hey – hey – hold *on*, man!" stammered the hacker. "I know how you're feelin' – *believe* me I do – had people close to me, grabbed the same way – and we *did* ping you... but you were off the Net at the time, we couldn't even see a MAC address for your box."

"We were in the air, running in EMCON-mode," mentioned the former Mars mission commander. "We've turned off everything other than what's absolutely necessary to fly the plane... I shouldn't have to explain why that's necessary."

"No doubt *'bout* it, dude," continued 'Any Nobody'. "Anyway... minute we realized what was goin' down, we tapped all of our Lone Star sleepers and those within 50 miles of the Texas border, any direction... we've also got root on most of the road-surveillance cameras in the Austin area, and we're pretty sure we got an ID on the black-SUV convoy that's got your folks. They're headin' north on State Route 195, and we got some radio-traffic intercepts – only bits 'n bytes, you understand, crypto they're usin's pretty decent – but we're bettin' they're headin' for Fort Hood... Army Air Base over there, specifically –"

"God fucking *damn!*" spat Jacobson. "Yvonne and the kids get put on a plane, and we'll *never* catch up with them!"

"If it's of any use, man," interjected the hacker, "They seem to be drivin' fairly slow up 195... prolly less than speed-limit, judgin' from what our feet-on-the-street've been sayin' at each way-point. We've got some shit put on the highway to slow 'em down – fake 'Construction-Zone' LED-sign-messages, oil-spills dumped here 'n there by our local-boys, tied 'em up in Hutto as soon as we found out – but that assumes that they don't detour."

White – who had finished refueling the V-37 a few seconds before and who had raced in with the others – ruefully commented, "Well – at least they can't take 'em back to Amchitka... *that's* for sure. We just gotta do the next ten of them shit-holes the Agency got hidden away... right?"

"Yeah," absent-mindedly acknowledged Jacobson. "Anybody got a map? Yes – over there, the ATC zone thing, on the wall – flashlight, please!"

With the hacker still listening in, the former Mars mission leader furiously pondered his options. "Okay... look," he announced, "We're... here. They, are going... there, and they've already got a ten-minute head-start on us... damn it to *hell!* There's no *way* we can intercept them – the plane's just too *slow!*"

Now, Tanaka's solemn face and wide, moist eyes appeared over Jacobson's shoulder.

She softly proposed, "Sam... you're right, the plane's too slow – but *I'm*, not. I can make it to there – what's the distance, again? Looks to be a little over 350 miles, right? I'm *sure* I can get there ahead of them –"

He matched her glance with barely-suppressed tears of his own, which the shaken more-than-human man awkwardly tried to wipe.

"Cherie... you'd do that... for *me?*" he asked.

"Sam," she answered, holding her face very close to his, "Of *course* I would. I kind of *owe* you one, you know?"

More like I owe your wife one, silently sent Tanaka, to a rueful nod by Jacobson.

He added, "But you'd be going *alone* – through the dark – and even if you freed them, and for God's sake be careful in doing so – we'd still be at least an *hour* behind you, maybe two; how would you protect Yvonne, Jen, Jeannie and Riley, until we arrive? To say nothing of the fact that the military will redirect all their air assets to the area, the minute they get the first distress signal from wherever you intercept the convoy?"

"Don't know, Sam," evaded Tanaka. "I guess you'll just have to trust me."

Yeah... like Yvonne trusted me, he mused.

Don't do this to yourself, she sent back.

I'll settle with her... for both of us.

The bounty-hunter, who had been leaning on the wall just inside the doorway, offered, "Want some company, hun? I dealt with the Army... wouldn't mind tryin' my hand against the Air Force."

Tanaka countered, "Keep up that 'honey' stuff and you're bound to get stung, by either a bee, me or a fighter-plane, Wolf – but anyway... how fast can you fly?"

He shrugged and said, "Don't rightly know... sure *seemed* like I was bootin' it good, back at the Fort. Few hundred miles per hour, maybe? Your guess is as good as mine... *Ms.* Cherie."

"That's *better*," she coolly responded. "The 'Ms.' part, I mean. As for the airspeed factor – if you're right, that's impressive, but I don't think that'll cut it. I've estimated my own top speed at over five hundred miles per hour, and that's in maneuvering flight; I can probably do even better, on a straight-line trip like this, even though it's low-altitude."

He shrugged again.

"Your loss," mentioned Wolf. "Guess I'm all dressed up to be a shootin' star, and nowhere to go."

"*Wait* a minute," suggested Jacobson. "That's actually *perfect* – Cherie, why don't you go straight there, and Wolf, you follow on behind her at your best cruising-speed. You can deal with any second-echelon forces that the government sends to re-capture my family. All I ask is, 'try to keep loss of life to a minimum'... okay?"

They saw a third instance of the bounty-hunter's patented dismissive shrugs.

"Do my best, Mister Space Man," offered Wolf, with an evil-looking smirk, "Although... sometimes my 'best' just ain't good enough, I reckon."

"You *know* what I mean," countered the former Mars mission pilot. "Cherie... you got any objection to that?"

"Under the circumstances, we all have to take some chances, so... no," answered the Science Officer, "Except, Wolf... don't push your speed – you can't keep up with me, so you might as well just cruise along and preserve your strength for combat, if that becomes necessary. You and I will no doubt be aware of each other's presence just by the war-songs, but be very careful to stay out of the line-of-fire, if I have to let loose against the government's forces. I'm not sure how far my lightening-attack travels, but it might still be dangerous at a much greater distance compared to how far I can accurately aim it."

He phlegmatically nodded assent.

"If you're approaching a battlefield," instructed Tanaka, "Make sure you have your fire-shield at full power for protection. Just be aware that you'll stand out like a sore thumb to the Air Force's infra-red tracking-gear, even if you dial back the flame-stuff to the minimum needed to keep you airborne – which you'll probably have to do to fly safely at low altitude, so you can use *Um'nàhr'é* to see and avoid ground obstacles. If you get jumped by too many fighters, or gunships, or whatever, I'll come to your aid and try to take off some of the pressure. Understood?"

"I'll make a note of that – though I got no clue what this 'oomna' thing is – and much obliged," he offered. "And don't you get too close neither, when I let 'er rip... I can *feel* this *Fire* shit – the 'alien' kind, as well as the barbecue kind – it's, uhh *growin'* in me... dogs, too. Though, sad to say, I think I'm gonna have to leave 'em back in the plane... hard flyin' upside down, with one under each arm, you know?"

"Yeah," she acknowledged. "Now... in case we get separated, we should have a place to meet... let's see..."

The more-than-a-woman intensely studied the air-traffic-control map, estimating distances and travel-times with a plastic ruler which flew from a table, several feet away, into her hand.

"I'm estimating that I should be able to intercept them when their trip is about 70 to 80 per cent complete, which would place them near where State Road 2484 intersects with the highway," she announced. "Look – there's a 'White Airport' a half-mile south of there, probably just a grass strip in somebody's back yard, but it'll do. Wolf, come here – have a careful look at this... think you can navigate to it? Weather reports show clear all the way there, but there's a front coming in from the west, so that might not hold."

"*Sure* I do," he grunted, after striding over to stand by her side, then reaching up and roughly ripping the map from the wall. "Read the fucker by fire-light... I'll be okay."

"I'd box your ears for grabbing that all for yourself, but *Vîrya Sài'ymë* got a good look at it," muttered Tanaka.

"Then it's decided," proclaimed Jacobson. "We all head for this 'White Airport' place, after Cherie, God willing, frees my family, and we wait there until everyone arrives. Ordinarily I'd want much better battle-plans, but time's of the essence, and we've wasted too much of it already."

He went over to the computer-mike and again addressed the hacker.

"Listen, Mister 'Nobody'... again, I can't thank you guys enough," he congratulated. "Can you do us a real favor and keep tracking the Agency convoy, as much as you're able? I'll check up with you as soon as I find a safe place to set her down and find a connection to the network."

"Gotcha, man," came back the response. "Oh, and there's one *other* thing... there's a lot of chatter on the Fed channels about some kind of 'terrorist' thing goin' down up Chicago-way – you folks got a hand in that? Anything we can do for you, if so?"

Jacobson, Tanaka, White and the bounty-hunter looked back and forth at each other; then Jacobson said,

"Not that we know of... it *could* have been Minnie's group..."

"Who's *that?*" demanded an obviously-interested hacker.

"Uhh... nobody you need to worry about, for the time being," deflected Jacobson. "Listen – we have to get going, ASAP."

'Any Nobody' replied, "10-4, dude... 'we own the logical'... now, it's time for you guys to show us *how you*, own the physical. Give 'em a fuckin' piece of my *mind*, man. Good idea to hang 'er up now – key's gettin' stale. Good huntin', space cowboys."

The connection went dead.

Jacobson turned to Tanaka, but she beat him to the hug.

"I won't let you, or them, down, Sam... I *swear* it," she vowed, in a voice both steely and compassionate.

As he released her, all he said was, "Please, God..."

The former Mars mission Science Officer, with charges of *Amaiish* glowing and darting throughout her body as her eyes lit up from behind, called to the bounty-hunter; and the others were already feeling an alarming surge of heat, because Wolf's own, formidable powers, quickly became manifest.

"Brother," she sang, as her body was – in the blink of an eye – encased in a translucent simile of the Storied Watcher's own scale-mail, complete with arm-buckler and skull-cap, "It's time for us to fly."

They dashed out of the airstrip-lounge, and a second later – to the ethereal sounds of very different, yet somehow complimentary, other-worldly war-songs – two super-beings rocketed into the dark, Arkansas skies.

Fancy Meeting You Here... Brother

Despite the excitement of what had been going on, Harold Crowford, chief Christian minister to a profoundly disinterested-in-matters-metaphysical

President of the United States, had actually gotten some sleep, over what remained of the previous night.

Now, with the dawning sun peeking over the horizon to the east, he strode down the starboard-side corridor on Air Force One, heading toward the aircraft's tail. Just aft of the plane's huge, silver wings, he stepped from the tan- to the blue-carpeted floor, then stopped at a doorway.

He knocked.

"Open up," he requested. "President's Spiritual Adviser here."

There were the sounds of minor confusion on the other side of the door, which opened up after a few seconds.

A young, male, Caucasian Presidential staffer, without necktie, appeared in the doorway.

"What can we do for you, sir?" he asked.

"Well, it's pretty borin' stuff," prevaricated Crowford, silently excusing himself for the sin, "As maybe you boys might have guessed, other than for helpin' the President ask for divine guidance within the present crises, and other than for sayin' benedictions over his meals, there isn't much for me to do while cooped up on this-here airplane; so he's asked me to – uhh – run some errands for him... keep these hands away from the Devil, by keepin' 'em busy, kind of thing. Latest one is, I'm s'posed to be checkin' out the status of some gallery repair-parts. Any of you know anythin' about that?"

There were blank looks all around, between the man in the doorway and the two others – both similar, nondescript, male Executive Wing staffers – inside the room. But, eventually, one of them mentioned, "Sir, that's not our department... but I bet the Logistics Chief would know about it. Want me to page him?"

"Would you mind doin' that for me?" unctuously replied Crowford. "I'd be much obliged. But I'd like to chat with this gentleman in person, if you all don't mind."

"No problem," responded the staffer.

He picked up one of the white-handled phone hand-sets (the tan one was locked in place) and entered a number on the keypad.

There were three "beeps" and then the line activated.

"Hey, Chief... Charlie Banks here... how's it goin'?" spoke the bureaucrat. "Know what you mean... been quite a challenge for us, too, what with all these unplanned ups and downs, and there's never a chance to change planes... no *kidding*. Anyway – I've got the President's Spiritual Adviser – what's your name again, sir?"

"Crowford," interjected the Christian leader. "Harold Crowford."

"Yeah, so I got a 'Mr. Crowford' here, and he wants to talk to you about some shipment or something. You got a minute?" said the staffer. "We're in the Second Executive Assistants Room, main level. Okay. Thanks a lot."

The man looked up at the Spiritual Adviser and said, "He'll be up here in a minute, sir. Want to wait in here with us?"

"Oh, no, that's okay," demurred Crowford. "I'll just wait for him out here in the hallway. You all can get on with your business."

The staffer smiled, nodded and closed the door.

The wait was a short one; it was somewhat less than 60 seconds before a short, past-middle-age, pug-ugly Caucasian guy with thinning black hair and a prominent gap between two of his front teeth, wearing a single-piece Air Force working-uniform, showed up. The man was accompanied by two rather taller, younger under-studies, both in similar garb.

"Darren Aliotti here," he announced, offering a hand-shake, with a broad, friendly-looking grin. "Along with my two partners-in-crime, Airmen First Class Stanton and Michelberg. I'm Logistics Chief of this big rig – very nice to meet you, Mr. Crowford, sir."

"Likewise, I'm sure," politely responded the Spiritual Adviser. "I'll get right to the point, here – I believe you're in possession of somethin' that I need to check up on. 'Case you're wondering why it's *me* doin' this, well, that's just the Old Man tryin' to get me to work for my pay, I 'spose... not too much to do around here, for a man of the cloth."

"Know what you mean, sir," pleasantly offered Aliotti. "If you want to 'check up' on things aboard this 'plane, you've come to the right man. *My* job's to keep track of everything that goes on or off here... 'course, the Secret Service's got a hand in that, as well. What in particular you lookin' for?"

"There's a long list of things, but the most important one's some 'cookin'-stove' type thing," dissembled Crowford, as he retrieved a printed manifest-page from his shirt-pocket. "Let's see, what'd they call it again... yeah, *here* it is... 'Replacement Secondary Galley APU, New Model W-91 LEP'. President wants me to verify that it's here and will get set up, next time we're on the ground for a full repair-cycle – somethin' about 'his steaks aren't gettin' cooked right' or some-such thing... personally, I think they're just fine, but then again I like 'em rare, and I'm not about to argue with the Old Man... you know?"

"Sure know about *that*," agreed the Logistics Chief. "Gotta keep the Old Man happy... right? But I think you're in luck today, Mr. Crowford – I *personally* saw that shipment get lifted on-board, and a damn heavy – oh, sorry, forgot about your position there, sir –"

"That's quite alright," convivially stated the Spiritual Adviser. "Not the *worst* I've heard up in the bow of this-here vessel, if you know what I mean."

"Thanks, sir," said Aliotti. "Well, anyway, what I *meant* to say is, that 'Galley' thing was a bit heavier than we'd anticipated it to be, but we got it on-board, alright. It's down in one of the cargo-holds, and I'll take you to have a look at it in a minute, but there *was* one, uhh, 'problem' that we encountered while on the tarmac, where we got the shipment, that you should know about."

Crowford tried his best to maintain a poker-face, as he asked, "What would *that* be?"

"Well, sir," explained the Logistics Chief, "Policy's that *everything* – and I *do* mean, 'everything' – that happens on this 'plane, has to match the paperwork that authorizes that activity – no exceptions! In this case, we had a mismatch between the weight of what was delivered, as opposed to what was listed on the manifest, and it was a big enough one to get the attention of an auditor. Normally, that'd mean the goods would've been left back on the runway, but because it was a direct order from the Executive Office, we sort of over-rode the protocol and took this 'Gallery Replacement' gear aboard, anyway."

"What's the problem, then?" inquired the Christian leader.

"Thing is, sir," continued Aliotti, "My personal, uhh, butt, is on the line, if we fail an audit of the real weight versus the listed weight of the item, they'll dock me six weeks worth of pay – unless, somebody else signed off on the paperwork discrepancy. The only person who was in a position to do that, was the MP at the airfield, who escorted the shipment up to this rig... some guy by name of 'Grassleigh', as I recall –"

"Oh, *now* I get it," sighed a relieved Crowford. "Makes sense, I s'pose... better he gets *his* pay docked, than you get *yours*. Ha... teach that boy to fill out his forms right! Well, I was in the military, in a previous life... a lesson we all have to learn, sooner or later."

"You got *that* right, sir," echoed the Logistics Chief, "*My* first time only cost me three days' pay... so I guess I got off easy. But anyway, what I was gonna say was, if you want this 'W-91 Galley' thing to actually get *installed*, I'll need you – or somebody else from up front – to take over possession of it, from the MP. You'll have to give me your sign-off, in other words."

"Fine, *fine*," quickly replied the Spiritual Adviser. "Where do I sign?"

"At the bottom of the manifest, sir," noted Aliotti. "Oh, but don't worry about doin' that right now – you can only do it in the physical presence of the last person to have formal possession of the item, but that's no 'biggie', since to comply with the rules, we had to take *him* aboard, too. He's cooling his heels back in the Security Area –"

An immediately alarmed and confused Crowford cut in,

"What'd you say, there?"

"Oh, just that this 'Grassleigh' guy's on-board, so there won't be any problem in you meetin' up with him and doing the sign-over, sir," casually remarked the Logistics Chief. "I'm sure he'll be only too happy to do it... frankly, I think he's worried about gettin' in deep doo-doo with his base C.O., once word gets back to Camp Douglas Field. Last time I saw him, which was a few hours ago, he seemed real nervous – not unusual for a young fella takin' his first steps aboard this 'very important aircraft', of course. Listen... you wanna inspect the goods first, before we visit SFC Simon Grassleigh back where all those Secret Service folks hang out, to do the sign-off? We really *should* do it in that order, you know... 'protocol'. Drives me crazy, but we gotta follow the rules... right?"

Why in Tarnation would a MP willingly do somethin' like that? pondered Crowford.

What went on down there?

The Spiritual Adviser hoped that Aliotti didn't notice the worried, 'staring-off-into-space' look on his face, as he quietly replied,

"Yeah, for sure... let's... follow the rules... get this over with."

All that Brother Harold had said, upon being ushered down to the aft cargo hold underneath the aircraft's main deck and upon seeing the *thing*, was, "Well... there it is."

He hadn't gotten too close – although he did use a handy flashlight to carefully study what was before him as much as was possible, considering that *it*, was only slightly visible between the slats of the cargo-crate, in which *it* was encased. The Christian leader thought that he caught a glimpse of a small slot or recess, near the front and top of what was inside the crate.

As Aliotti preceded him up the rear access stairs, Crowford commented, "Sure *is* cluttered down here... I'm not the tallest man in the world, but I really had to do some contortions to get past all the luggage 'n such. Considerin' that this thing's supposed to go into the galley... how you gonna get it up there?"

The Logistics Chief cheerfully volunteered, "Oh, that's no problem... tell you a little secret : some of the main-level areas – 'specially the ones that might have to have gear swapped out every so often, like the communications deck and the galley, for example – they got access-doors in the floor underneath 'em, open up right into the cargo-deck. Just pull back the carpet, unscrew a couple of bolts and bingo! You can lift up or drop down, just about *anything*. Though, *this* sucker's so heavy, you'll probably need Specialist Stanton's power-lift to hoist it up there. Don't worry – next repair-stop, we'll get it done before you even know anything's happened."

"Well... that's good to know," was all that Brother Harold had replied.

The two men ascended the top-most of the rear access stairs and, now joined by Aliotti's two junior logistics-crew-members, they reversed direction and walked a few feet to their right, until they were in front of a door marked "Security Detail – PRIVATE".

Aliotti knocked, announcing as he did this, "Yo, Bradley! You in there?"

"He's up front, doing planning for our next stop," came a voice from inside the room. "Just a sec."

A couple of footsteps were heard, and then the door opened, revealing a brush-cut, well-muscled, olive-skinned man dressed in trademark Secret Service fashion : white shirt, gray-and-mauve tie, dark gray dress-pants, black leather belt and black, lace-up dress-shoes.

"Oh, hi, Robbie," greeted the Logistics Chief. "You subbin' for Brad?"

"Yep," responded the Secret Service man.

Through the doorway, Crowford could see at least two other agents – both similarly-garbed – plus one empty chair. There were two individuals (as far apart from each other, as could have been arranged in this relatively tightly-constrained space), whose presence seemed out-of-place.

One of these – who had removed her shoes and pulled her shapely legs up on to the seat, within which she was restrained by a robust-looking set of straps and buckles – he recognized as the loud-mouthed, rebellious, Chinese-American FBI agent, upon whom he had staked far too much of his own credibility.

Then, the Spiritual Adviser's gaze came to rest on the second passenger, a tall, thin, fair-haired Caucasian sort dressed in an ill-fitting military police uniform, who had been hiding his face. The man was looking down at the floor, in a peculiar way.

"Hey, Grassleigh!" called Aliotti. "You're in luck... nice fella here standing here with me's willing to take that damn – 'scuse me, *darn* – thing off your hands! Get your butt over here so we can sign off on the paperwork, will you?"

The MP dawdled, as if he didn't want to look up, or move at all, and out of the corner of his eye, Crowford noticed that the Asian-American FBI agent had awoken from her half-sleep. She seemed to be mildly interested in what was going on.

"*Grassleigh!*" repeated the annoyed Logistics Chief. "Come *on*, man, we ain't got all *day!*"

Finally, the military policeman looked up, straight into the eyes of Spiritual Adviser Harold Crowford... who tried desperately to avoid showing emotion.

Sweet baby Jaysus! silently inveighed the Christian leader.

How's this possible?

I told that boy to get it on-board and then get out of Dodge! I didn't tell him to get on-board, himself! What on Earth's he doin' here, posin' as a soldier?

How could he do this to me?

And... what to do now?

I'm amazed that these Secret Service boys ain't got to the bottom of it, already... but that's got to be only a matter of time.

When they do figure it out, I'll be off to meet the Lord soon after that, for sure... and I don't fancy a noose, them stickin' poison-needles in my arm or the firin'-squad... at least, not before the mission's complete.

And anyway... meetin' my Savior's the plan, one way or another. I just need it to be in the same ball of fire that sends the Devil-Girl back where she belongs.

Think fast, Harold, think fast... and call on His divine guidance!

He saw – though, considering the urgency of what else was going on, it did not seem very significant – that the FBI agent was now staring at him in an oddly determined manner.

Crowford managed, "Pleased to meet you, son."

"Oh yeah... same here, sir," weakly responded the disguised man who – there was no reasonable doubt – could be recognized as none other than Brother Martin.

"Well, we'd better get this 'sign-off' thing dealt with –" started the Spiritual Adviser; but he was interrupted by the monumentally-annoying former FBI team-leader.

"Sir," she said, addressing her comments to the Secret Service man who had answered the door, "Something's *wrong* here – you had better do a –"

What in Tarnation? thought a shocked Brother Harold.

How could she possibly know – no, she couldn't... could she?

She's been cooped up in that chair since – and she's got no evidence!

Unless... wait a minute... wait, just a minute... you ain't foolin' me, harlot!

I was right about you, all the time!

And... there's my ticket to reel in the Devil-Girl... I just gotta get it set up!

Father God – surely dost Thou show me the way!

"What *you* ought to do, young lady," quickly countered the Christian leader, with an accusatory finger pointed in the Chinese-American woman's direction, "Is keep that big mouth of yours shut! You're already in a big heap o' trouble, on account of havin' refused a direct order from your Commander-In-Chief. Mister, uhh, 'Robert' – that's your name, right? I wouldn't believe a thing she says... she's a traitor – and a lyin' one to boot."

"Yeah... I got briefed on that situation," grunted the Secret Service man.

Turning to the former FBI agent, he dismissively mentioned, "You *know* you have no standing here, Ms. Chu... nobody takes you seriously. Do all of us a *big* favor and refrain from interfering in any more of our business, will you? We're all *very* busy here, you know!"

The woman glared, shook her head in frustration and muttered some intemperate remarks, but then clammed up.

"Listen, sir," spoke up Brother Harold, "We're probably not gonna get a word in edgewise, what with *her* in this room... and I got a couple of things I need to ask this 'Grassleigh' fella about what I'm signin' off on. Would you all mind very much if I head off to the visitor's-lounge with that young man, get the facts straight, and then come back here and sign off in your presence?"

The Secret Service man shrugged.

"Makes no difference to me, he replied. "Chief... that okay by you?"

"Sure – as long as he keeps his entire signature in the right box at the bottom of the form," said Aliotti. "Don't forget... they can reject it if it isn't filled out to spec. Gotta think like an auditor... they pick on any damn little thing."

"Oh... I'll make sure everythin's one hundred per cent neat 'n clean," reassured the Christian leader.

"Fine – you got ten minutes," said the Logistics Chief. "I got some boxes of toilet-paper to count. See you back here then."

Brother Harold beckoned to the so-called "SFC Grassleigh" with his index finger, and as the younger man got up and went out, eyes straight ahead so as to avoid looking anyone in the face, the door to the security detail room closed behind him. From its other, hidden side, the Spiritual Adviser could hear a strenuous argument breaking out, with the woman's voice haranguing the Secret Service agent about something-or-other.

Fortunately, there were only two other people – a young, male Air Force orderly and somebody who might have been a member of the flight-crew – in the Air Force One visitor's lounge, which was not far from the security room; and both of these appeared to be catching up on their sleep. Even better, both of these men were at the other end of the lounge, so Brother Harold was able to usher his under-study to one of the two seats nearest the windows.

He lowered his head and leaned forward, a gesture which was reciprocated by his disguised under-study.

Now almost whispering, the Christian leader said, "Boy – what in the Lord's name are you *doin'* here?"

There was a tear in Brother Martin's eye as, with a trembling voice, he replied, "It's... it's a long story, sir... things went badly wrong, down on the runway, where we were supposed to make the, uhh, *delivery*. I had to take matters into my own hands... or the entire project would have failed, right then and there. I'm *sorry*, sir!"

"If you're tellin' the truth, I suppose I can't rightly blame you for doin' what you had to do," allowed Brother Harold. "But how in Tarnation are you dressed up as some kind of a *soldier*? Where'd you get the uniform... it hardly fits, you know... and they're bound to catch on to that kind of clumsy disguise!"

"Uniform belongs to the MP who was supposed to escort us to the plane, sir," explained the younger man, his voice so quiet as to almost be inaudible. "He found out... I had to *deal* with him, if you know what I mean. Oh, sir... I've *sinned*... I have *blood* on my hands..."

It sounded as if he was about to cry.

"Keep it together," demanded the Spiritual Adviser. "That's an *order*, son! We are too close – too close by *far* – to have you give us away, with all your blubberin'. We both got to think, and act, fast and clear... God's *countin'* on us to do no less."

Brother Martin nodded.

"Good," continued Brother Harold, "And let me tell you somethin' that neither one of us knew, right up to one minute ago. Remember that Chinese woman back there in the room with them Secret Service boys?"

Again, the under-study mutely nodded in acknowledgment.

"I'm about ninety-nine per cent sure that she's one of the Devil-Girl's accursed slaves," stated the Christian Man, with unsuppressed relish, "Don't ask me *how* I know – but I do. She put up a pretty good act of feignin' that she's a child of God – don't mind sayin', I almost fell for it myself – but *she's* gonna be the one whose cries for help, are gonna lead that spawn of Satan, right here. And I guess I don't have to explain to you, son, what *that* means, for me... and you."

"I'm so... *scared*, sir," protested the nerve-wracked younger man. "I know you prepared me for this kind of thing happening... but I never thought –"

"Son," came back the fatherly answer, "You know that more than anythin' on this-here Earth, I want to take your hand and give you the peace of knowin' that soon, we'll both be in Paradise, lookin' up in joy at our Blessed Lord and Savior, Jesus Christ; but doin' that here and now, is a chance that neither one of us can take. I promise you, when the time comes, we'll be together, sayin' our final 'goodbyes' to this tainted life. You understand?"

"Yes... yes... I do," unenthusiastically replied Brother Martin.

"Now," resumed Brother Harold, "We both got some very quick thinkin' to do, and whatever's decided, we got to execute *perfectly* – even one itty-bitty little slip-up, and I'll assure you, them Secret Service guys *will* catch us... don't under-estimate 'em, boy... they're very, *very* good at what they do."

"You can be *sure* of that, sir," said the younger man, with a half-head-nod.

"You still got your key?" inquired the Christian leader.

"Yep," confirmed Brother Martin. "Right in here –"

He fumbled for something in a side-pocket on the pant-legs of his uniform, and the object of his attentions almost fell out on the floor, when, at the last second, Brother Harold desperately and silently gestured for the key not to be removed.

"That's good," remarked the Spiritual Adviser. "Whatever you do, don't lose that, or let 'em take it off you... I've still got mine, of course."

"I'll guard it with my *life*, sir," vowed the disguised Christian underling.

"Okay, so here's the plan," said Brother Harold. "I'm sort of makin' this up as I go... but fortunately, it's not too far off what I had originally been thinkin' of, and why here the Lord comes and reveals this 'Chu' harlot right to me – if *that* ain't a sign, I don't know what one would be! First, you stick by this 'Grassleigh' thing... if they get wise or say that somethin' don't match up, tell 'em that them computer-things have screwed up again. I'll cover for you as best I can, keepin' in mind that I can't get 'em riled up about me, as well. It won't keep 'em off your tail forever; but it'll take 'em time to prove their suspicions, and, obviously... we don't need, or have, that much time, anyway."

"Yeah," agreed Brother Martin, with a nervous, *sotto voce* giggle.

"Second," directed the Christian leader, "My problem's gonna be 'how to get this 'Chu' whore, set up so she'll call out to the Devil, to come save her... leave *that* one to me. When I get the whole thing goin', it may take a while for the Evil One to actually get here, and both of us may have to delay things, in the meantime. You'll have to be creative – throw a switch you ain't supposed to be touchin', set off an alarm... anythin' that will cause a diversion for a few minutes. The, uhh, 'package', by the way, is in the aft cargo-bay, almost directly below where we're now sittin', as it turns out; that area is accessible by them stairs that I came up, just around the corner from this-here lounge."

"Saw the stairs on my way here," offered the younger man. "Is there a lock on the door to the cargo-hold?"

"I'll make sure it isn't workin'," noted Brother Harold. "And I want you to position yourself so that you can get down there on one minute's notice, when you hear the word "key" mentioned out of my lips, twice within the same sentence – whether or not you hear it on the intercom or if I'm sittin' right next to you, or the President, or whoever, at the time. You got that?"

"Yeah," quietly promised the disguised Christian acolyte.

"Now listen *very* carefully," demanded the Spiritual Adviser. "When you hear the word "turn" from me, twice in one sentence... you put that key in, and God's will be done. Don't worry about bein' alone, because I'll be on my way down there – I'll do my best to stop anyone who chases either of us or tries to, uhh, stop the operation... if for whatever reason you're unable to execute your orders, I'll do it with my key, as soon as I get there. And if it's of any interest, son... apart from my word of honor as a Christian bathed and born again in the holy, cleansin' blood of Jesus, that I won't let you down in those final moments, don't forget... even if I bailed out of the aircraft, I'd still be much too close to... well, *you* know... right?"

"I... I just wish we could pray, sir," stammered Brother Martin.

"We will, son... we will... I *swear* it," reassured Brother Harold. "As those last seconds count down, we'll both be on our knees, chantin' the sacred words that our Savior Himself taught us... and triumphant we'll rise, to take our place among the saints and martyrs who've gone before us. Don't doubt it for so much as a *second*, son; and if you see any sign of waverin' on my part – I'm just a weak and filthy sinner myself, after all – you slap me hard on the face, and remind me of my vows... you *understand?*"

"It will be very hard to do anything like that, sir," earnestly replied the disguised man, "But with God's help... I have faith that we'll succeed."

"Amen!" contentedly agreed the Christian leader.

"Now," he added, producing a pen, "I guess we'd better sign off on that little ol' 'manifest'... don't you think?"

Turn That Radio On

Hendricks and Boatman had each taken turns in standing guard while the other one "caught 40 winks", and it was after 9:30 p.m. before they felt well-rested and well-fed enough to contemplate heading off the mountain. Newly-dressed in West Virginia backwoods garb, with their dress-clothes stored in a couple of backpacks, they boarded the hillbillies' long-bed pickup-truck (the third agent had to clamber into the confined spaces of the rear-cabin, as it was much too small for Boatman's bulk; the black agent rode in the passenger-seat) and began the bumpy ride downward.

They had gone perhaps two or three miles, when Hendricks, bending forward and trying his best to ignore how perilously-close they were to going off the road with each hairpin-turn, noticed the presence of a techno-contraption, complete with a complex array of LCD-displays, knobs and buttons, located discreetly underneath the passenger-side glove-compartment.

"Hey man... mind telling me what that thing is?" he asked.

"What y'all *think* it is?" dismissively remarked Billy-Ray. "Guess you FBI boys don't do a lot of work with th' local po-lice... it's a radio-scanner, of course. Got 'er rigged with one of them special Brazilian computer-chips that lets us tap in to th' 'crypted channels that ATF uses – don' always get all of 'em, but enough to give us a head start, most of th' time... don' mind sayin', it's saved our bacon more than once, while we's runnin' th' product 'cross county lines 'n so on. I remembers th' days when a man didn' need all this fancy-ass shit just to make a livin'... but them days is long gone, I 'spose."

"Mind if we use it to see what the local cops are up to, right now?" asked the third agent.

"Why y'all want to do *that*, boy?" countered the mountain-man driver.

"They might be looking for us," offered Hendricks. "It'd be helpful to know if they are, before we get arrested."

The other hillbilly, who was to the left of Boatman in the back-cabin, let out a belching laugh and said, "Boy's got a point, Billy-Ray... if'n he an' Mister Blackie here really *did* get kicked out of some damn plane, well, they's probably important enough to get picked up if'n they's showin' their faces down in Lewisburg town."

"Well, fine, then," grunted the driver.

He reached out his right hand, hit a button on the radio-scanner and then entered an access-code; the front-panel display on the device lit up, and immediately the quad-speaker audio-system within the pickup-truck began to broadcast typical LEA chatter, with intermittent announcements of traffic accidents, bar-fights, arrests for "drunk and disorderly conduct" and for street prostitution, and other run-of-the-mill, local-cop-type night-time happenings. There was also – curiously – talk of some kind of "serious terrorist attack" on a police headquarters in Chicago; evidently hundreds of officers and civilian staff had been killed in a bombing, with "fugitives on the loose" in the Illinois and Indiana regions.

Hendricks and Boatman listened carefully for a few minutes and continued to do so, only casually, for about another ten.

Eventually, the black ex-FBI agent reduced the volume and commented, "Well, not much of a surprise there, young man; after all, them folks up in Air Force One – or maybe it's 'Air Force Whatever', don't rightly know, considerin' it ain't properly marked up as such – they think we're pushin' up the daisies, right about now. Even if they *were* lookin' for us, which I doubt... they probably wouldn't let the police from these parts, in on the hunt. So I think we're okay –"

"Just a sec," suddenly demanded the third agent, "Turn it up, will you?"

"Sure, but what... *wait* a minute," said Boatman. "Hey you two – keep it down – this sounds *interestin'* –"

"What's so –" countered Billy-Ray; but the third agent growled, "Shut *up*, man!"

So the driver, not terribly happy about being ordered about but wise to the situation, held his tongue.

A ghostly voice came over the speakers.

"Two-twelve Clifton, over," stated someone who sounded like a State Trooper in a patrol-car, "Please say again... didn't get your last message. Over."

"Six-nineteen Tri-State dispatch," came the reply, "No code for either of these events – nothing in the book like what seems to be goin' on – but priority on both is high as it gets. You are authorized to cross the Virginia state line. Please acknowledge. Over."

"Two-twelve Clifton, acknowledged," came the first voice. "Got no problem with the one down on I-64... but why y'all callin' us out on somethin' from Tennessee? Over."

"Both suspected Priority One terrorist incidents," stated the dispatchers. "Federal resources are on the way but your orders are to head immediately to the last known location of the one that's closest to you. Please state which you can get to first. Over."

"Two-twelve Clifton," sounded the State Trooper. "Wow... okay. That'd be the one on the Interstate. Can you describe the situation? What're we getting ourselves into? Over."

"Six-nineteen dispatch," said the second voice, "Don't know a lot right now, but we've been advised, 'terrorists using exotic weapons', and 'Federal agents down'. Adversaries may traveling with a female Caucasian, name of 'Laura Boyd', plus three school-age children, in a dark green or blue '30s-model Patriotic van... we're running the license check now. Be advised, adversaries are presumed armed and *extremely* dangerous. Observe and report the moment you have contact. Over."

"Holy *shit*," breathed Hendricks, looking intently at his friend, as he spoke. "That's gotta be Brent's old lady – but what the hell's *she* doing –"

"Listen up," countermanded Boatman, straining to make out every word that was coming from the speakers.

"Two-twelve Clifton, heard and understood," spoke the State Trooper. "Heading to Lee Highway and I-64, will check out the road west and east of that junction. Just out of interest, though... what's the other one? Over."

"Six-nineteen dispatch," came the second voice, "You're not gonna *believe* this, Earl... but we're being told that it's a, uhh... 'UFO', that's apparently kidnapped a senior official of the Federal government. Was heading north from Arnold Air Force Base... that's near Manchester, Tennessee, by the way. Over."

"Two-twelve Clifton," sounded the obviously-astonished trooper, "Say again, please – did you say, a *'UFO'*? Over."

"Six-nineteen dispatch," repeated the other voice, "Yeah, that's *exactly* what I said. But don't worry about the Arnold situation... Air National Guard's scrambling to deal with it, problem is, it's apparently 'low and slow', hard to track. Can you give me your ETA to the one near Lexington? Over."

"Two-twelve Clifton," came the reply, "ETA about ten minutes. Listen... is any of this related to the terrorist activity down at Fort Knox? Over."

"You're damn right it is," muttered Boatman, with a rueful grin.

"Who the H is *that*?" wondered Hendricks, out loud. "Tanaka? No, *can't* be... she was outrunning *missiles* up there on the island... right? But she was the only one who could –"

"Your guess is as good as mine, young man," offered the African-American ex-agent. "

"Six-nineteen dispatch," responded the dispatcher, "Unknown at this time, but be on your guard. Got to go now – six other calls to make. Over."

"Two-twelve Clifton... on our way," said the State Trooper. "Over and out."

Boatman turned to address the driver.

"Step on it," he ordered.

"I'm already doin' *eighty*," protested Billy-Ray. "Any more'n that, they get us on that ra-dar –"

"And one other thing," continued the big, black ex-agent.

"Yeah?" asked the driver.

"We're takin' a left, at White Sulfur Springs," said Boatman.

Bridge To Nowhere

The black-suited ones – to a man (there were no females, and no non-Caucasians, among them) dressed in white business-shirts (each with a different-colored plain-pattern tie), black leather belts and well-polished, black lace-up leather shoes – had hardly said a word to each other, since picking up their "passengers", just outside Austin, Texas. But at least the trademark sunglasses had been doffed in consideration of the somber, inky-blackness outside.

The conversation, such as it was, had been limited to periodic progress-checks on the dark, tinted-window SUV's encrypted-radio system, as the convoy of three nearly-identical, armored vehicles, rolled up the highway.

Man-In-Black Number One – whose attention was normally completely fixed on the road, inasmuch as he was the driver and had to keep track of the identical SUV, which was traveling about fifty feet ahead – allowed himself a momentary glance out the window to his left.

"Front coming in," he mumbled.

"Rain tonight," added the big, tough-looking guy in the passenger-seat.

"Not a problem," offered the driver. "We'll make it to Fort Hood *long* before any falls 'round here."

"Umm-hmm," agreed Man-In-Black Number Two.

Man-In-Black Number One asked, "How are they doing?"

The other guy looked behind him, into the rear of the vehicle, which had been stripped of its normal, luxurious appointments; the area, which was separated from the driver's-compartment by a metal partition, looked pretty much like a paddy-wagon. Five unconscious, Caucasian figures – one just-past-middle-age, heavy-set, blond-going-on-white-haired woman, two shapely teenage girls (one blond, one dark-haired), one younger teen girl and a good-looking 12ish brown-haired boy – lay unconscious, gagged and tightly trussed-up in straight-jacket-like restraints.

"How you *think* they're doing?" snorted Man-In-Black Number Two. "They're breathing... that's about it."

"Yeah... stupid question," admitted the driver.

There was relative quiet, except for road-noise, for a few minutes. Then the guy in the passenger-seat looked side-wise at the instrument-panel.

"You turn the radio on?" he asked.

"No," came the answer.

"Why am I hearing music?" demanded Man-In-Black Number Two.

"What are you talking ab... *oh*," said the driver. "Yeah, heard it too... but it's gone now... right?"

The other man nodded.

"Right," he confirmed.

"Well, there were a couple of trucks going south, on the other side," mentioned Man-In-Black Number One. "Good ol' boys just playing their stereos pretty loud, I guess."

"Yeah," said a relieved Man-In-Black Number Two.

He stopped talking for a second or two, then commented, "But don't those farmers only like country?"

The driver shrugged.

"Bound to be one or two rockers, in a state *this* big," he observed.

"Yeah," said the guy in the passenger-seat.

Northward they continued, on Texas State Route 195.

The convoy had proceeded in the pre-determined direction, for less than two minutes. They had just passed a sprawling set of farm-fields and were on a bridge over the almost-dry Lampasas Riverbed, when – to the consternation and alarm of Man-In-Black Number One – the lead SUV's brake-lights flashed and that vehicle skidded to an abrupt stop.

"What the *fuck* –" angrily inveighed the driver, while he frantically jammed on the brakes; he only missed the rear-bumper of the convoy-lead vehicle by about six inches.

"Find out what the hell's going on!" he ordered.

"On it," spoke Man-In-Black, a second before he unholstered his service pistol, opened the passenger-side door, dropped down to the highway-pavement and disappeared into the darkness.

There were the sounds of agitated discussion, and then a somewhat familiar face – that of the driver of the leading SUV – appeared below the driver-side window.

"We got a *problem*," announced the gruff voice of this tallish, muscular Caucasian man.

"What?" asked the driver.

"Some kind of roadblock, up ahead, just before the bridge ends," claimed the other man. "Bunch of piled-up tree-trunks, complete with leaves on 'em, and a few big rocks in the pile, too."

"*Shit*," complained Man-In-Black Number One. "You think it might be –"

But he checked his speech in mid-sentence, upon hearing the faint sounds of the same kind of far-off rock-music that had momentarily appeared earlier. There was a flash, and a loud "bang" sound off to the left behind the tree-stand that lined the river-bank, then another, then several more, from a point two or three hundred feet behind the convoy's hindmost vehicle.

"*Ambush!*" yelled the Man-In-Black down below the driver.

"Secure the detainees!" he added. "Defensive formation!"

"I'll get H.Q. on the line," shouted Man-In-Black Number One, as the guy from the lead SUV high-tailed it back to his own car.

Counter-intuitively, nothing happened for the next minute or so, and, indeed, the surroundings were unnervingly quiet, with naught but cricket-chirps and the occasional call of a night-bird, to disturb the silence.

The driver heard an order on the part of the convoy-leader to the vehicle bringing up the rear, to volt-face and reconnoiter the highway behind them; so the hindmost SUV turned around and slowly drove southward down Route 195. It had gone no more than about a hundred feet, when it, too, stopped suddenly.

A call came in over the radio.

Man-In-Black Number One picked up the mike.

"ToughLove Two here, over," he stated.

"ToughLove One here, over," chimed in a voice from the leading SUV.

"ToughLove Three multi-cast, over," came the voice of the driver of the rear-most SUV. "Think we're seeing same fuckin' kind of thing down here, at the other end of the bridge," he advised. "Tree-trunks and rocks. Zack got out and checked out these trees with the flashlight – weird, look like they were, uhh, I don't know, like, burned-off or something – like, what I mean is, not sliced with a saw, or anything like that. A few of 'em are still smoldering where they got cut. Over."

What the fuck's that? mused the confused and frustrated Man-In-Black, at the steering-wheel of the middle SUV.

Same fuckin' music – but there's no cars going south on the other side of the highway –

"Rodge," sounded the convoy-leader, from the first SUV. "You see any IEDs, or other hazards, in or around the pile? Over."

"That's a 'negative', far as we can tell," indicated the driver of the rear-most SUV. "What about the frontal barrier, Pete? Over."

"Same here," said the convoy-leader. "Okay, well, I don't like this, guys, but we can't just *sit* here... H.Q.'s saying it's at least a half-hour, maybe more, before they can even get a 'copter here to assist. I'm gonna get Karl to scout the pile at the north end of the bridge for IEDs or booby-traps, then we'll use the chains to pull this shit out of the way. There aren't too many of these trees, shouldn't take too long, and we can just dodge around the rocks... I hope. Come back here, and form up. Over."

"Roger that... over," sounded the voice of the rear-most SUV driver.

Man-In-Black Number One heard the third-SUV driver calling, "Yo, Zack! Back here, on the double!"

And then he heard something else; something, to put it mildly, that was completely unexpected. It was a pleasant-but-firm female voice, coming from a spot behind the driver's-compartment of his vehicle, apparently between the side of the SUV and the waist-high safety-rail on the west side of the bridge, overlooking the Lampasas River.

"Stick your head out of that car-window," it warned, "And I'll blow it off your shoulders. Where are the Jacobson family members? Which car?"

Man-In-Black Number One, following Agency protocol, clammed up.

"*Listen*, asshole," hissed the woman-voice from behind the driver's seat, "I know they're in one of these three vehicles... and I'm betting it's yours. If I have to kill every one of you, to get at them... that's what I'll do. *Talk!*"

The voice of the convoy-leader came over the radio.

"ToughLove Two," he inquired, "Form up. We need you to help pull this shit out of the way. Over."

"ToughLove One," slowly half-whispered the driver, "That's a 'negative'. I say again, that's a 'negative'. I have a *situation* here."

At this point, the passenger-side door opened, and Man-In-Black Number Two only narrowly escaped being shot by the driver's at-the-ready pistol. The other man was about to say something, but was dissuaded by a head-shake and hand-gesture pointing behind and over the driver's left shoulder.

Also following protocol, Man-In-Black Number Two mutely nodded, again readied his gun and exited the SUV, turning southward and closing the side-door as he went.

About three seconds later, while the increasingly-agitated voice of the convoy-leader began to press for more information over the radio, the vehicle briefly rocked back and forth as if it had just passed a large tractor-trailer at high speed; then, the accursed, exciting-beat rock-music began to play loudly enough to echo clearly across the Texas plain.

There was a muffled scream, one gun-shot, the sound of something splashing into the shallow remnants of the river, some thirty or forty feet below, and then silence.

As every available Agency agent ahead of and behind the middle SUV came running with guns drawn, to his astonishment, Man-In-Black Number One saw the driver's-side door open, all by itself. In the next half-second, to his dismay, he felt himself being simultaneously being crushed and pulled out of the seat, by some hateful, unseen, pincer-force.

The driver caught the briefest of glances at a youngish, dark-haired, Eurasian woman, her otherwise-attractive visage spoiled by a pair of demoniacally-glowing eyes, as he tumbled ass-over-teakettle out of the SUV, on a trajectory heading clear off the bridge and towards a likely-fatal plunge into the riverbed.

Mercifully, at the last moment, he managed to grab hold of the guard-rail.

With his legs kicking helplessly into the void below and most of his body hanging precariously over the side of the bridge, the panicked man yelled for assistance as he marveled at what happened next.

His SUV – with, as far as he could tell from his limited vantage-point, no-one in the driver's-seat – gunned its engine and roared toward the tree-trunk barrier at the north end of the bridge, narrowly missing two Agency agents, as it went. These men, along with everyone else around, opened a rapid-fire hail of gunshots at the fleeing vehicle, but their efforts were to no avail, as the pistol-rounds bounced ineffectively off the SUV's armored side-panels.

As it approached the northern barrier, a translucently-glowing left arm reached out of the driver's-side window; there was a brilliant, multi-colored flash and a thundering-, booming-sound that momentarily overwhelmed the still-background-throbbing rock-beat.

The barricade exploded, with its constituent tree-trunks, some of them now enveloped in fire, being flung in every direction like so much stove-kindling. The purloined SUV charged forward, driving at high speed northward on Route 195, as the strange music started to fade into the distance.

"*Shit!*" screamed the convoy-leader. "Get in the cars! Pursue!"

"*Help!*" shrieked Man-In-Black Number One. "Hands are slippin'! *Help me*, for God's sake!"

"Who's that – oh, shit, it's –" called one of the other agents.

"Hey, Todd, we got a chance," shouted another. "Damn thing's stopped, up the road there!"

"Well don't just *stand* there," loudly demanded the convoy-leader. "Go *get* 'em!"

All of a sudden, the unwelcome, fast-paced, weirdo rock-music-track returned in full form, and it was coming from a point about a hundred feet off the highway, just above what was left of the north-most barricade.

The Agency men turned their eyes upward, and saw the same glowing-eyed, godly-looking woman whose appearance had lately caused Man-In-Black Number One such consternation. She was surrounded by a dim 'bubble' of some sort, vaguely reminiscent of what would be made by the familiar child's toy.

"You're very lucky that the Jacobson family is – as far as I can tell – still alive and well," called this fearsome being, her voice reverberating over the surroundings in a thoroughly unnatural way. "Because if any one of them weren't... you'd already be dead."

"Who *are* you?" shouted the convoy-leader.

"No concern of yours," she haughtily replied. "But I *do* have two things to tell you."

"What?" he asked.

"One – raise or fire any of those guns, and I'll blow your asses to Kingdom Come!" she growled. "My attack flies at the speed of light, in case you think you can out-draw me. Two – you need to turn tail, get out of here, southbound, specifically – and tell the sonofabitch posing as 'President', that he'd better stop trying to kidnap our relatives and release the ones that he's already got his filthy mitts on... *especially* my mother. Touch one hair on her head and I'll flatten this whole fucking *country*, regardless of what my fellow super-beings do or don't want to do. Oh, and advise our impostor 'President' to give himself up, before we track him down and have to vaporize him. Understand?"

"Our orders are to pursue and recover the detainees," bravely stated the most senior Man-In-Black.

"Slow *learners*, I see," sniffed the glowing, super-human being, as she floated, apparently without any independent means of propulsion, high over Route 195. "Here... I'll make it easy for you to decide which way you're going."

The angry – but, by now, thoroughly shocked – Agency men were confronted by a fusillade of hellish, blue-yellow-red-green-and-white lightening-bolts issuing downward.

They were sure that this was going to be the last thing that they would ever see, in *this* life, at least; but, in fact, she had been aiming at the section of the Lampasas River Bridge just north of where her self-created barricade had been. The luckless concrete struck by this lethal barrage immediately exploded, disintegrating into variable-size chunks that rocketed with alarming speed, hither and yon.

A gap at least seven feet long was thus instantly opened between the landward parts of Route 195 and the bridge on which the two remaining CIA SUVs, were now positioned. The Men-In-Black dove behind these two cars, which were the only obstacles that afforded any cover whatsoever.

"If I were you, I'd start driving backward, before this whole thing crumbles into the drink," taunted the glowing, floating enemy. "Oops... you *can't* go back... can you? Here – I'll fix *that* one for you, too."

At unbelievable speed, the flying-woman darted over their heads, coming to hover at a spot just behind the southern tree-trunk-barrier. Her music surged even more, and the nonplussed agents saw the pile of debris being somehow parted from the middle, as if it was being pushed to the east and west sides of the bridge by an invisible bulldozer. A second later their tormentor reversed course, flew north again and stopped just above the chasm preventing access to Route 195 north of the Lampasas River.

"I could – and should – disintegrate all of you... *vermin*," she ominously threatened. "If for no reason other than what I've seen the likes of you do to helpless civilians, including children. But unlike the government of this country, murder's not my 'thing'. How's the song go, again? 'Hit the road, Jack, and don't you come back no more, no more no *more* no more'..."

For a second, the stunned Agency Men-In-Black just stood there, unable to comprehend what they were dealing with. Then the convoy-leader mumbled, "Uhh... contact H.Q... contact the base... we need military assets here..."

"Remember I said that I'm not into slaughtering people who can't fight back?" accosted the flying-woman. "I *could* change my mind, you know."

As if to reinforce the point, she loosed a couple of lower-powered, albeit still very lethal, lightening-bolts over their heads.

"I am the One Of Thunder," her majestic voice pronounced. "The One Of Fire, is on his way, due to arrive here, any minute now; and *trust* me, you don't want to be standing around, when *he* shows up – ever heard of 'shoot first and ask questions later'? *Scram!*"

Coming finally to his senses, the convoy-leader gave a hand-signal; the other Men-In-Black rapidly dashed into their cars, reversed direction and drove at a fast pace, southward on the north-bound lanes of Route 195.

"Help... *help!*" screeched the guy who was trying to hang on to the guard-rail (and who was slowly losing the fight, as the thing's sharp edges cut into his fingers). In dismay, he watched the two remaining SUVs drive past, paying no attention to his predicament.

A second later, something with powerful kinetic energy – like coming down fast on a trampoline whose springs had been tightened too much – struck the soles of his shoes, propelling the hapless Man-In-Black Number One, over the guard-rail. He fell roughly on to the highway-pavement, suffering various cuts and bruises in the process; but, he was alive.

"Much more mercy from me, than you got from your fellow-spooks," came the receding voice of the mysterious, flying super-being. "I'd *think* about that, if I were you."

After the shaken man picked himself up and watched the tail-lights of the two Agency-controlled SUVs disappearing to the south – there was a near-collision with a northbound-driving vehicle of some sort, almost at the limits of his vision – he turned to look in the other direction. His own vehicle was driving away, and the flying-woman had also vanished from sight.

The Director probably thinks I'm dead by now, he reflected.

And considering the penalty for failure on a Class 1 mission like this... I might as well be.

Man-In-Black Number One pondered his options, and came to a conclusion :

I'll need a change of clothes.

He turned and began a fast walk to the south.

Down Floats The Boat, Without A Paddle

Only one person – a guy in a warehouse-type, brown uniform – had come to bother Moira Sullivan, in the nerve-wracked hours that she had spent waiting parked in her Ford General on the grass beside the dumpsters, behind the Oak Plaza shopping center in Manchester, Tennessee.

The spot had been well-chosen; her vehicle was mostly surrounded by trees and other obstacles and was invisible from McArthur Street, but nonetheless had easy access to that route.

He had knocked on her car-door and asked, "What y'all *doin'* here, lady?"; to which she had truthfully replied, "I'm just waiting for somebody."

"Well, don't try nothin'," the warehouse-worker had advised, "'Cause we got security in there. But don't worry if you're dealin' or buyin' th' shit, 'cause *lots* of folks do that, 'round these parts. Y'all got a good price for it, let me know... maybe I'll take some off your hands, honey."

Sullivan had nodded and smiled in a vapid manner. The gesture must have worked, because the man walked away without further comment. She then put the seat back and tried fitfully to doze off. Attempts to bury her attentions in any of the three Calico Cat women's romance novels that she had resourcefully brought along for the ride, proved no more successful.

This is insane, she thought.

I'm waiting from my dearest childhood friend – who's a half- uhh- alien, now... is that right, Moira? – to show up with... who?

Is this really going on?

Gotta be a hallucination... come on, Moira, it must have been the booze, the pills, or...

No. I saw it, I heard it, I... felt it.

How's that song go – "Too late, to turn back now..."

A few large delivery-trucks showed up from time to time, backed up to the shopping-mall's rear loading-bays, gave up their cargo and then drove away.

At length, the traffic dwindled to almost nothing, and, to deal with the boredom and tension, Sullivan turned on her car-radio (though not her engine or headlights). She switched from channel to channel and tried to listen to the honky-tonk stuff that dominated the airwaves around here, but found that she couldn't tolerate it for more than a short while.

Again, she tried channel-hopping; there was a soft-rock station that sounded promising, but its signal wavered and faded into static.

Okay, then, resolved the woman.

I guess the news is at least a human voice that I can listen to.

Thunder 107.9 it is...

For about fifteen minutes, a bored Sullivan paid little attention to the summary of local and national sports news and gossip, with extensive coverage of NCAA championships and baseball training-camps; sports – except for tennis, at which she made a noble effort, though she was far from good at it – had never been her thing.

At length, she reached for the power-button, but instead quickly muted the radio's broadcast, upon hearing a kind of crashing- or banging-sound, possibly a few miles off to the south-east. She listened carefully for more such noise but none was forthcoming, so she gradually increased the volume.

Sullivan was about to give up on the radio entirely, when finally she heard, "And now, turning to national news..."

Quickly, she reached forward and turned the gain up to speaking-level.

"Tonight, we have reports of numerous road closures and local investigations being implemented by federal and state law enforcement authorities, in and around the Tri-State area," spoke a male announcer, "Due to, quote, 'apprehended and on-going terrorist activity', unquote. Federal authorities have, as of yet, declined to comment as to whether this activity is related to the bombing of the FBI headquarters in Chicago, and they have refused to elaborate about threats to Tennessee residents, although they have asked those without a need to travel, to stay off the Interstates and state highways."

As Sullivan concentrated to commit all this to memory, the news-reader continued, "Thunder News *has* been able to determine that there has been one incident south of Manchester and north of Tullahoma in this state, and, apparently, another somewhere near Lexington in western Virginia."

Where's that? she wondered, while fumbling for a map and cursing the strict orders to leave all the fancy-dancy geo-location computer-map-stuff, disabled.

"These are, of course," mentioned the radio-voice, "On top of the still-evolving hostage stand-off at Fort Knox, although, according to authorities, the latter situation is, quote, 'well under-hand and in its wrap-up phases, with complete victory on the part of our brave soldiers and law enforcement officers, now in sight', unquote. According to a recent government press release, the terrorist group known as the 'Mars Gang', which had previously been under siege within the Fort Knox compound, has now succumbed to vastly superior government firepower, although Administration spokesmen have warned us that recovering what's left of the bodies of the terrorists may require days to weeks."

Oh my God, thought the woman.

Sylvia's friends... the poor buggers...

But the news-reader wasn't finished.

"In order to maintain order and to track down and eradicate the several terrorist cells that may still be active, effective as of midnight tonight, the Administration has decided to re-impose martial law, applicable to all parts of the United States east of the Mississippi River," he said. "The government warns that, quote, 'while this tough measure is an essential tool in the fight against terrorism and will be maintained for as long as necessary, we will not hesitate to use lethal force, without warning, against anyone who stands in the way of American democracy, wherever he or she may happen to be', unquote. A curfew from dusk to dawn will exist in those parts of the country covered by the announcement, although leniency will be extended to travelers on a case-by-case basis tonight, to accommodate those who may not yet be aware of the change in the law."

Sullivan had had enough of this depressing news; but, mercifully, the topic changed to the usual recounting of local drug busts, prostitution arrests and car-crashes, and instead of turning the damn thing off completely, she just reduced the volume. A second or so later, she did a double-take at the station-setting.

That's funny, she mused.

Some kind of screw-up with the tuner, or something?

It's supposed to be a talk-station, but there's music coming from it –

Uh-oh – that ain't any run-of-the-mill pop-rock tune – it's gotta be –

Trying to contain the giddy excitement rushing through her bloodstream, the woman opened the car-door and tumbled outside. She looked in all directions and even grabbed the cheap night-vision-enhancement binoculars that Abruzzio had fished out of Sullivan's basement; but, despite a careful search around the Ford General, there was no visual sign of her former classmate, even though the latter's rhythmic, hypnotic-beat war-song was now loud enough to be heard clearly.

Then Sullivan thought to look upward, and while gaping in astonishment, she reflexively stepped backward until her back was against the car.

What in God's name? she thought.

Fifty feet in the air, descending rapidly... white or gray, oblong shape...

But it looks like the bottom of a... boat? What the H?

She remained transfixed against the side of the Ford General, as the unidentified flying object revealed itself; it was, indeed, a boat of decent size, almost as long as her own vehicle, with weather-proof coverings at its stem and stern, and an open area amidships, in which the now-familiar figure of Jerry Kaysten was seated, his arms holding on to both sides of the vessel for self-stabilization.

And a few feet above the thing, surrounded by a shimmering, translucent 'bubble' of some sort – its colors subtly and continuously changing from place to place on its surface – was someone who Sullivan barely could recognize as her girlhood friend : Sylvia Abruzzio, floating in mid-air, feet pointing down with no obvious means of support, with her arms stretched out as if waiting to be crucified.

As the flying-skiff came to a gliding, gentle landing about ten feet from the car, Abruzzio – whose eyes were glowing in eerie, kaleidoscopic fashion – turned her head toward Sullivan and remarked, "*Miss* us, Moira?"

Sullivan just gulped.

This can't be the Sylvia who I knew, she silently reflected.

What's happened *to the shy, introverted book-worm who I had to teach how to put on eye-liner?*

"I'm still her... though, new and improved," responded Abruzzio, as she gradually lowered her arms – in so doing, gliding to an upright landing close to Sullivan – even though no words had yet passed her friend's lips.

The weirdo-music quickly ebbed away, as did the bubble and the ocular glow, thereby restoring Abruzzio to some semblance of a normal human being. She looked up at an apparently empty part of the sky and called out, "*Vìrya I'ëà'b'* ... maintain thou thy guard above, if thee please."

There was an odd-sounding "chirp", a slight breeze and a flickering in the starlight.

"Jerry... they okay?" asked Abruzzio, directing the question to Kaysten.

The man momentarily ducked his head under the bow and stern covered-places, then re-emerged and offered, "They look a bit shook up, but... yeah, they're fine... I think."

He again stooped down and mentioned to persons unknown, "Sir – we're here. You can get out now."

"Sylvia..." started Sullivan.

"Yeah?" replied the former JPL scientist.

"That was, uhh, quite an entrance," uneasily noted Sullivan.

"You know what?" said Abruzzio.

"No... what," replied the human woman.

"When I started out on this thing, there isn't a *chance* that I could have done, what I just did, Moira," remarked the scientist. "And Jerry's been growing apace, as well."

"How so?" asked Sullivan.

"All I can say is, 'don't listen to any of his jokes'," quipped Abruzzio.

Sullivan was about to inquire further, but her attentions turned to the lifeboat, which, evidently, had accommodated passengers other than the two more-than-humans. The ambient light wasn't very good and the woman had to strain to make out features, but after little "Rainbow" bounded outward, the first ones to step out of the vessel were a handsome, dark-haired young Caucasian college-boy and his slightly-younger and -shorter sister; then, along with a late-middle-aged, well-dressed and reasonably fit woman, there appeared a gray-haired, good-looking, late-fiftyish man who looked like the proverbial Chairman-Of-The-Board stereotype.

"Sylvia," whispered the woman, "Is that –"

A contented smile showed on Abruzzio's face as she nodded affirmatively and interrupted, saying out loud, "Mr. President – and First Family – I'd like you to meet my dearest of friends, Moira Sullivan."

Nervously, Sullivan stepped forward and offered her hand, which was taken in the President's firm, vigorous grasp.

"Very nice to meet you, Ms. Sullivan," he said. "Oh, and I'd like to introduce my wife Kathy and my two children, Matt and Clairie."

There was a perfunctory murmur of similar greetings from the three other newcomers.

"It's... uhh... an honor, sir..." stammered the woman, completely unprepared for being in such august company.

The President turned to address Abruzzio.

"Listen, Madam," he said in a determined, almost-upset tone of voice, "I thought I *told* you, 'no attacks on members of the Armed Forces'. What *happened* up there? While we were hunkered down below, I mean."

"What 'happened', sir?" defensively answered the former JPL scientist. "Oh, that's easy to explain... you see, I guess I'm not much of a 'fast-flier' – after all, the boat, with all of you in it, weighs quite a bit and my telekinesis is rather rusty, these days. I tried to stay as low as possible and keep out of the line of sight, but just as we got to the edge of the lake, one of the Army's helicopters started chasing us; I tried using some, uhh, 'visual' and radio-jamming tricks to throw them off, but they were too close, I couldn't make it convincing enough I guess... the first sounds that you heard – you know, the ones that sounded like popcorn popping – were the soldiers in there, shooting at us. *Vîrya I'ëà'b'* cut the rotor off the top of one 'copter and then sliced its tail off, as well. It went down in the Reservoir."

"My God," muttered the President. "Were there any... survivors?"

"Yeah," defiantly riposted Abruzzio. "Five in the boat, one carrying it aloft, and that dear little one who deflected the bullets that they fired at us, while trying to kill us... kill, *you*. Sir – what do you want me to *say*? The helicopter went down at low altitude, and I'd assume that if its inhabitants can swim, at least *some* of them would have made it. But I wasn't about to go back and fish them out, since my main goal – and that of 'Daughter Tornado Diamond-Curtain' – is the safety of you and your family. *Vîrya I'ëà'b'* probably saved your life back there... you could at least say 'thanks'."

The frustrated ex-President cast a glance to a random part of the sky and mumbled, "Thanks, I guess... to whoever you are, wherever you are."

One of the flying-buckler's trademark, happy-sounding "chirps", came back as a response. This was answered by an inappropriately-loud bark on the part of Abruzzio's mutt.

Sullivan spoke up. "Who? Oh... the... *shield*. Yeah. Right," she observed.

"You *know* about that thing?" asked the ex-President.

"Yeah... we've, uhh... *met*, sir," mentioned the woman.

"There, there, *Vîrya I'ëà'b'*," interjected Abruzzio. "He intends not to demean thee. Just give him *time*, if thou please."

Another "chirp" came from somewhere up above.

"Well," sighed the former U.S. leader, "I suppose that's one of the things that we can talk about at more length, later. In the meantime, Ms. Abruzzio... what's the plan?"

"Get your things into Moira's car – you'll have to pack them in carefully, as there won't be a lot of space for your personal belongings, plus the seven of us, in there – and no, I *haven't* forgotten thee, Little One, but thou need to fly outside, to defend. Then we get out of here," explained the JPL scientist.

"And then we do what?" inquired the President's son.

"We discuss that while we're getting out of here," deflected Abruzzio. "My proposal would be for all of us to chant the name of the Storied Watcher until she graces us with her presence, then we take our chances –"

"Easy for *you* to say," interrupted the former First Lady. "It's not *your* life that would be at risk, by doing that."

"Ma'am," countered the scientist, "*My* life's been in continuous jeopardy since at least the fiasco back at the Tucson Hotel, so I don't think I have anything to apologize about, on *that* front."

"For what it's worth, Ma'am," said Sullivan to the First Lady, "If you're feeling 'in over your head' about all this... join the club. I feel awfully inadequate, just being a plain old American girl with a day-job, in the company of half-aliens like Sylvia and Jerry."

"Aww, come *on*, Moira," smirked Kaysten, "All *I* can do is tell a joke or two, and then belt it out of there, when the crowd thinks I've bombed out."

"Don't believe him," said Abruzzio. "He *always* leaves 'em in stitches... as in, 'need lots of, to put their guts back in, after they've been laughed right out'. Now, if you don't want all of us to get nicely 'bombed', I'd suggest you get your stuff into the car, so we can beetle on out of here. The Arnold Air Force Base guys are probably trying to calculate our exit-path, as we speak, and I'd prefer to avoid another show-down with the authorities – I don't think I have to explain why, Mr. President... right?"

"You certainly *don't*, Ms. Abruzzio," ruefully agreed the ex-President. "Kathy, Matt, Clairie – come on, let's get the baggage off the boat and into the car."

Abruzzio silently nodded assent as, along with Kaysten and Sullivan, she joined the former First Family in man-handling the baggage into the back of the Ford General. The task was made considerably easier by the sudden re-appearance (an event that nearly caused the ex-First-Lady a heart-attack) of *Vîrya I'ëà'b'*, whose load-carrying capacity came in very handy.

After no more than a minute of such efforts, the car had various pieces of personal belongings squirreled away into almost every available nook and cranny. Sullivan was about to start the Ford General, but she was motioned to stop by Abruzzio, who seemed to be standing still and concentrating on something.

"Just a second, Moira – I think I hear –" remarked the former JPL scientist. In the next second, the sound of military jet engines roared overhead, and several of the party thought that Abruzzio's warning was about to come true; but, mercifully, the aircraft just streaked by in a blur, without either a bombing-run or even a second pass.

"What was *that?*" demanded the ex-First Lady, from her vantage-point beside her husband, in the middle of the vehicle's back-seats.

"Fighter-planes," explained Abruzzio.

"Shit," cursed Kaysten, "What if they come back and drop –"

"Chance we'll have to take, Jerry," stated the scientist. "Let's not make it any easier for them – come *on*, everybody, hop aboard."

As those of the group who weren't already in the car headed toward it, they saw the flying-boat being dragged to a dumpster, evidently by Abruzzio's telekinetic powers. The refuse-container's hinged top-cover – which must have weighed several hundred pounds – self-opened. The skiff floated up and into the container, which was again shut.

"That's, *that*, I suppose," commented the former JPL scientist, as she got into the SUV. "Hopefully it'll be a while until they catch on to where it got left. Moira, you drive; I'll have to stay in the passenger-seat, and if it looks like we're about to encounter trouble – from any direction – I'll try to cloak the whole car, but I can only do that reliably when we're stopped, so pull over, if that happens. It'll be almost impossible to see where you're going, in that case, anyway. Rainbow, honey, you look out the back window and warn Mommy if any bad people start following us. Understood?"

The puppy gave a happy "yip" and wormed itself through the pile of suitcases and duffel-bags in the back of the car, coming to a stop with its little face so close to the back window that the glass was immediately obscured by nostril-condensation.

The rest of them also clambered in, though it was a tight fit, with the ex-President's son sitting on top of his unhappy sister's lap while Kaysten did the same, on the knees of an obviously-uncomfortable former First Lady.

"Seat-belts, everybody," requested Sullivan, although only Abruzzio and the ex-President could really comply. "Here we go."

The SUV rounded the side of the Oak Plaza Shopping Center, driving only within the marked lanes of the mall's front parking-lot. It came to the junction with McArthur Street and turned right, with Sullivan carefully holding her top speed to slightly below the marked limit.

Abruzzio rolled down her window and said, apparently to no-one, "*Vîrya I'ëà'b*', please soar in hidden-guise, warn us of foes on the wing, and defend us, if thou can."

"Damn... I think I heard the kid reply to you," offered Kaysten, though no sound from the Storied Watcher's lost war-child, had come through to the interior of the vehicle. "That is, I think I *thought* the kid reply to you, or... oh, *forget* it," he muttered. "You know, Mr. President... this 'alien' stuff, isn't all it's cracked up to be."

"I'll have to take your word for that, Jerry," patiently sighed the former U.S. leader.

As Sullivan's overcrowded car drove slowly northward up McArthur Street, Abruzzio – while warily scanning back and forth with a dim, kaleidoscopic glow just visible in her eyes – remarked, "About the planes... did you notice their direction? I think they were going to the west, and judging from their speed, they couldn't have been from Arnold. Peculiar – I don't think that they were hunting *us*."

"Well then where *would* they be going, Ms. Abruzzio?" asked the ex-President's daughter. "Wherever it is, I want to go in the other way."

"Fort Knox, maybe?" offered the son. "No, wait a minute – that's north of here, isn't it?"

"Sylvia," cautiously mentioned Sullivan, "I think I should tell you... I had the radio on, for a while when you were away. The government's saying that they've, uhh, bombed Fort Knox into ratshit... oops, sorry, Mr. President."

"No problem," he politely replied.

"Anyway," related the woman, "They're claiming that the, uhh, 'terrorists', are all dead, and that the Bullion Repository has now been recaptured. I'm terribly sorry, Sylvia. About your friends, I mean."

Abruzzio let out a contemptuous laugh.

"Don't be," she counseled. "If that's Sam Jacobson and Company that they're talking about – which is who I *assume* they're talking about – there isn't a *chance* of that being true. But there *is* something very peculiar about that report... namely, 'given that Sam and his people are likely still alive and royally pissed off, why would they abandon the Fort Knox project, and where are they now'?"

"Maybe they went off to, like, take over Wall Street, or something," proposed the ex-President's son.

"I doubt it, Matt," countered the JPL scientist. "Sam's highly resourceful – he wouldn't do something predictable, like that. I honestly don't know... I sure wish I had some way to communicate with him."

"There's more," offered Sullivan.

"What?" asked Abruzzio.

"The news guy was saying that there have been some more terrorist attacks, one south of Manchester and another to the north of Tullahoma here in Tennessee," explained Sullivan. "And there's been yet another, around Lexington – the 'Lexington' in Virginia, that is. You think those might have been done by this 'Jacobson' guy?"

"Hmm," mused the JPL scientist. "Now that, *is* awfully strange. It's not like Sam to break up his team... did they say what exactly was going on? Like, important land-marks, military bases, government buildings, *et cetera*, being attacked?"

"Didn't say," answered the driver. "Listen, Sylvia... more immediate thing... I'm going north right now, and I think we're fine if we stay on the side-streets, but that radio guy also said that there's martial law being imposed everywhere east of the Mississippi, so we can't take any of the state highways or the Interstates. There's supposed to be a curfew after dark, too. So we could get pulled over just for driving anywhere. Thought you should know."

"Where exactly are we driving to, Ms. Abruzzio?" asked the ex-President.

"We're going, uhh, away from Arnold Air Force Base," temporized Abruzzio.

"That wasn't what I wanted to know," he persisted. "What's our destination?"

"I don't, uhh... *have* one," mumbled the former JPL scientist. "Not in the short-term, that is."

"Oh for God's sake," complained the ex-First Lady. "Clark, I *told* you this was an insane idea –"

"Compared to *what?*" he retorted. "Kathy, I *know* she's making this up as she goes, but I also know George well enough to guess at what he had in store for us, if we had waited around back at the house. For better or worse, I'm afraid we're stuck with these two, for the time being."

"Gee – thanks for the ringing endorsement, Mr. President," muttered Abruzzio.

"Get me on the Presidential Airborne Command Post, and you'll *have* it, and then some, Ms. Abruzzio," he pledged. "I've still got some people in high-up places who'll support me, when I cut George down to size and put an end to this entire fiasco with you, Jacobson and the alien."

"*That's* the spirit, sir!" unctuously added Kaysten.

The former U.S. leader paused for a second or two and then commented, "You know, Madam... I *do* have to admit, that *was* an amazing feat that you accomplished back there... lifting us all up in the boat, I mean. How do you *do* it, anyway? If, say, we saw Air Force One flying overhead... would you be able to catch up to her?"

Abruzzio leaned back in her seat, momentarily closed her eyes as if concentrating, and her now-familiar, exciting-and-rhythmic war-song beat began to sound, although it quickly ebbed away.

She turned her head to look directly at the former Chief Executive.

"I've kind of been wondering about that subject, myself, lately," she confessed. "As to how my telekinesis works, it's hard to explain... it's like I concentrate on something in a determined way, and it just... *comes*, that's the best I can describe it. It's kind of like reaching out with your arms and hands – you can grasp, pull forward, push away, punch, and so on – and to fly, you just 'push' against the ground; there's a range limit to it, which means the effect is weaker, the higher I get. I've noticed that it's much easier to do against an inanimate object than a living one, particularly a human being who's deliberately trying to, uhh, 'elude my grasp'. And when I activate it – when I use anything of the *Fire*, in fact – there's a thrill, a rush, like adrenaline, I guess... I feel mighty, noble... *superior*. It's an amazing feeling, of that I'll attest."

"That's *so* cool!" gushed the fascinated, awed teenage girl.

"You're right," acknowledged Abruzzio, with a far-off, but proud, look on her face. "It's *incredibly* cool. As a scientist, I can't *wait* to do some tests on it, and I can't believe that I was almost stupid enough to refuse this blessing, when Karéin offered it to me. A whole new world... a new *universe*..."

After falling quiet for some time, she continued, "I honestly don't know about the airplane, sir... I haven't had a lot of time or opportunity to experiment, obviously, but right now, I'd doubt that I could match the speed and altitude at which Air Force One cruises. My guess is, it would have to be flying low and slow, for me to get you near it... and that leaves unaddressed, the question of how we'd get them to open the door and let you on board."

"Yeah... you're probably right... ahh, just an idea, after all," sighed the ex-President.

"Well, speaking of ideas," interjected Sullivan, "Anybody got any, about where I should be driving to?"

"It's-your-turn-for-a-bright-idea" glances were exchanged, but none spoke up until the former President broke the silence.

"Alright," he observed, "We had better think this whole thing through, if we're to have a chance of success, and we can start by comparing the assets and tools that we have at our disposal, compared to those that George has, at his –"

"Yeah, sir," sourly mentioned Kaysten, "Like, specifically... we've got one real super-human, one under-performing super-human-wannabe – yours truly – and a cute little free-flying buzz-saw, with nowhere to run or stay, while *he's* got the whole Army, Navy, Air Force, Agency and God knows what else, to come after us with –"

"Now, *now*, Jerry," tut-tutted the ex-President, "You've been in the Executive Branch... you know how the game's played. The government's a slow-moving beast, and furthermore, George has to divide his attentions between a number of fronts, not only the laundry-list of 'normal' crises like for example what's going on around L.A., but also the tom-foolery that this 'Jacobson' guy's been doing at Fort Knox, and maybe the two or three other ones that Ms. Sullivan's so kindly informed us of."

"Call me 'Moira', sir," pleasantly interjected Sullivan.

"I don't mind if you use 'Sylvia', for me sir," added Abruzzio. "But you'd better stick with the formalities for 'Daughter Tornado Diamond-Curtain'."

"Yeah... *that's* for sure," spoke Kaysten. "And the V-P's not very good at multi-tasking... especially if he's counting on Bezomorton to run interference for him. John always forgets which way to put the toilet paper roll back on, never mind what 'crisis' is the most important, today."

The ex-Chief Executive smiled as he went on, saying, "Secondly, don't forget, even if George *has* sent out some kind of warning that 'the former President's been kidnapped by aliens and has likely been brainwashed by them', it'll be hours or days before that message sinks down to the junior ranks and the local military and LEA commanders. The fact that about sixty per cent of the military's job has been outsourced to GrayWar, will also make it harder for George to get his orders consistently enforced. We can use those factors, and whatever authority that I have left personally, to our advantage."

"What are you thinking of, here, sir?" asked the former Chief of Staff.

"Well," elaborated the ex-President, "If I'm going to pull off this half-baked *putsch*, I've got to find a dramatic way of relieving George of power, then take my chances with the Joint Chiefs and Secret Service, maybe the Bureau too... the Agency's obviously a write-off, so we'll need to think of how we can neutralize their sleeper-agents as quickly as possible. Do you have any, uhh, super-human way to recognize them?"

"Hate to disappoint you there, sir," piped up Kaysten, "No such luck, on this side of the aisle. But *Minnie* can... and as you heard back there, she's already on the plane."

"Okay," said the former U.S. leader. "Now, I figure what we need most, right now, is some way for me to make it clear to the public, that I'm 'back in the saddle again', as it were; don't forget, when it comes to politics, perception *is* reality. Secondly, we need *information*... specifically, where George is hanging out, and also, what the hell's going on with this 'Jacobson' guy. From what you said, Moira, there's almost certainly much more happening than we know about, right now... and as long as George knows the details, and we don't, that's a big ace he's got in the hole, against us. Finally, we've got to find some way of communicating not only with Jacobson – if for no reason other than to tell him to lay off – but with other elements of the government, who might support me."

"Sounds interesting, so far," commented Abruzzio. "What were you planning on doing, precisely? Maybe show up to an Air Force base, flash your ID-badge, and go from there?"

"Something like that," offered the ex-President. "But I had somewhere a bit more, ahh, *familiar*, in mind."

"Where?" quickly replied Kaysten; and in the next second, a wide grin came over his face.

"Sir – of course – that's *perfect!*" he exclaimed. "I can't *wait!*"

Perhaps it was a guess, or maybe it was some nascent supernatural ability, that brought the revelation to Abruzzio's mind.

"Sir," she protested, "You can't be *serious!* That's probably the most carefully-guarded place in the *country*, especially after Karéin showed up and trashed it... not to mention, the government would have to assume that the Mars Gang might also try to attack it. The Vice-President's undoubtedly got it under careful watch, just in case you try something like this. Your chances will be marginal, at best!"

"Sylvia," he patiently replied, "If I'm not seen there... who'd believe that I'm the 'real' President?"

She just stared in frustration for a few seconds, until Kaysten unhelpfully remarked, "He's *got* you there, you know, Sylvia."

The more-than-a-woman moved so she was again staring forward through the windshield, shook her head and rolled her eyes.

"Well... it was an insane idea to drop in to Arnold and shanghai you from there... this one's not that much worse, I suppose," she muttered.

"Would all of you mind telling me what you're talking about?" protested Sullivan.

"Moira," directed Abruzzio, "Have we got enough gas to make it as far as the White House?"

Trouble Just Round The Bend

"Keep it on that channel," demanded Boatman, as the pickup-truck sped eastward on I-64, with the pitch-dark woods of rural Virginia looming oppressively to the right and left.

"Ain't so easy t'do," complained the driver. "Fed'rals got some kinda thang where it jumps back 'n forth. Y'all hear it fadin', y'all gotta tell it to seek agin."

"Yeah," acknowledged Hendricks, fidgeting anxiously as he spoke. "Keep your speed up – we got to boot it, what with that broadcast back there about martial law and curfews all over the place. Wish there was some way other than the Interstate to get where we're going."

"Well, sorry to disappoint y'all, city-boy," snorted Billy-Ray, "But 'less y'all done figured out how to jump right over a mountain or two, this's the only route that's gonna get y'all there."

"Jump over a mountain," absent-mindedly reflected the third agent. "Good idea, man. Give me a little time... I'll figure it out."

"Boy's been into th' product back there in th' cabin, when we's not lookin' at him," offered the driver.

"Yeah," nervously agreed Dorsie.

"He ain't," countered Boatman, with a knowing chuckle.

"Ain't, *what?*" asked the hillbilly in the back-seat.

"Ain't done any stuff, ain't affected by it if he did, and ain't kiddin' about takin' a little hop over a mountain," patiently stated the big, former FBI-agent.

Neither of the hillbillies cared to carry this line of conversation any further, so for a few minutes, all that was heard within the cab of the pickup-truck was road-noise and various inscrutable, jargon-laden, fading-in-and-fading-out police-band call-signs and incident-codes. Fortunately, they hadn't seen or been accosted by any military or police-vehicles, although both Boatman and

Hendricks did pick up the far-off sounds of what must have been helicopter-turbines.

They had just sped by a town down in a valley, while continuing on the highway, which was elevated on a series of road-bridges. Far ahead, I-64 looked to be turning to the right.

"Anybody know what place that was? Back there... turn-off from the rest-stop exit-ramp, I mean," idly inquired the third agent.

"Covington, Virginny," mumbled Dorsie. "Few hookers 'n honky-tonk bars, if'n y'all into that... not much else."

"Well, I'm more of a rock – *whoa!*" replied Hendricks, the tone of his voice morphing rapidly from small-talk to frantic warning. "Trouble ahead – we'd better –"

The driver tried to slow down in preparation for a full stop, but it was too late. They were almost at the bend in the road, and clearly-visible beyond it was a law enforcement checkpoint, complete with at least three squad-cars, six uniformed LEA officers, and a camouflaged, wheeled military APC of some sort. There was no real highway-median in these parts; the westbound and eastbound lanes of I-64 were separated by a concrete divider (although seven or eight lengths of this had been moved to block traffic on both lanes, thereby also facilitating movement for officials behind the barrier). On either side were wooden barricades, portable light-posts and orange traffic-management cones. The highway was completely closed off in both directions, with the forested walls of the surrounding mountains rising on the left and the right. For whatever reason, there did not appear to be any civilian vehicles, except for their own, waiting for clearance.

"*Shit!*" cursed Billy-Ray, as he brought his truck to a very slow forward speed. "Fed-ral boys up yonder done seen us for *sure!* Y'all want me to turn an' try a run for it?"

"Peace, brother," countermanded Boatman. "That'd be failure in our mission to find out, err, whatever's goin' on, past this-here junction... and failure *ain't* an option, today. Besides... with all of us packed in here, you ain't gonna outrun any squad-car in this truck and besides *that*, where you gonna run *to*? There's only this highway and that side-road runnin' beside it. Just pull up and let me do the talkin'."

"Y'all full of *shit*," protested Billy-Ray. "They don't close th' highway for no ord'nary thang... don't even do it if'n there's an' 'scaped convict or sim'lar. Y'all gonna get us *killed*, boy!"

"Just keep drivin', and keep that mouth of yours shut," ordered the big black agent. "Oh, but there's one other thing."

"What?" asked a exasperated Dorsie.

"You hear some nice, fast, crazy-soundin' music... you get your heads down and keep 'em there... and make sure you know where your guns are," calmly instructed Boatman.

"I *knowed* it was a fuckin' stupid thang, givin' you boys so much as the time of day," ruefully commented a clearly-worried Billy-Ray.

"We're gonna be *fine*... just, *fine*," unconvincingly reassured Hendricks, as the truck came to a gentle stop, upon being gestured to do so by an average-sized, dark-haired, Caucasian Virginia State Trooper.

With his side-arm prominently at the ready and with two of his fellow-officers – a big one brandishing a shotgun and the other with a long-barreled revolver – covering him from positions about ten feet behind, the Trooper approached until he was about six feet from the driver's-side door and called out, "Road's closed, and this entire highway's now under martial law; we've got orders to impound vehicles and imprison drivers who venture out on it, unless they've got a very good reason why they're here. You all got such a reason, sir?"

"We... we was..." started Billy-Ray; but he was interrupted by Boatman.

"'Scuse me, officer," spoke the big black ex-agent, while leaning over the driver's lap, "But what my friend's meanin' to say is, 'we got important business – specifically, his wife's havin' a baby – up the road, past Clifton Forge'... that's why he's a bit nervous, tonight. I'm Doctor Bateauhomme, and this young man in the back seat, he's my intern, Bill Hendriques... he's comin' along to learn the procedure. My friend Billy-Ray here's the proud father, and his friend Dorsie there... he's the uncle. But you better let us through quick, 'less, of course, you all want to do the deliverin' yourselves."

Hendricks tried desperately not to laugh out loud, hoping all the while that the cops couldn't see the smirk on his face.

"Yeah... *sure* you are, sir," replied the State Trooper. "Never heard that Clifton's short of doctors, especially with that MacKay fella bein' there and doin' that for the past seventeen years. Well... one way or another, we got to inspect the truck and check your ID. Could you all step out on to the road, please?"

There were anxious stares back and forth.

Boatman quietly advised, "Come on, boys, let's make the man happy – let's do what he says... don't want to be playin' him no *music*, right?"

"Sure don't," whispered Hendricks, as he unbuckled. "Because upon hearing anything like *that*, well... I'd be diving for cover, as if my life *depended* on it, you know?"

The mountain-men – though certainly not strangers to the rough-stuff – were acutely aware of the latent peril of the situation, and they sullenly complied with the State Trooper's demands, slowly clambering out of the truck and joining Hendricks and Boatman on the surface of I-64.

The second State Trooper – a big, pot-bellied, brush-cut, Gary-Busey-like Caucasian guy, almost the black ex-agent's size – pointed a microphone-like thing at the four travelers and said to his leader, "Well, anyway, they don't show no concealed guns... 'less they's them newfangled see-ramic things."

He grunted in Boatman's direction, "You know, sir, you and your, uhh, 'intern' buddy there don't look very much like a doctor... don't they usually wear, like, a suit, or somethin'?"

"Shore *do*," quickly countered Boatman, "Mine's back in the ho-tel room... this was an emergency call, 'come-as-you-are' kind of thing."

"Where's your doctor-bag?" snorted the third State Trooper, who was white, greasy-haired, hook-nosed and almost as tall as Hendricks.

"I *told* you," complained the black ex-agent, "We had to rush out here... if everything goes according to nature's plan, I won't need what's in my case, but we're wastin' *time* here –"

"Yeah. Sure," grunted the shortest of the LEA officials. "Can I see your ID, please, sir?"

"Left *that* back at home, too," argued Boatman.

"Okay... so we got 'travellin' without authorization on a closed thoroughfare', 'lyin' to a police officer', and 'unable to show proof of citizenship when so demanded'," maliciously offered the first of the State Troopers.

With a dismissive hand-wave, he added, "You boys all line up so we can put the cuffs on – real slow-like, and no lip or funny-business... we got standin' orders to shoot anyone tryin' to run out on us."

A desperate Boatman replied, "Okay, okay... so you don't believe me... that's fine, officer, but before you all do anythin' rash... mind if I speak with you *privately?* I promise that my friends ain't gonna do nothin', in the meantime. Right, boys?"

The frustrated mountain-men sourly muttered agreement, while Hendricks, with a telling tone-of-voice, mentioned, "Love to listen in, man... bet I *can*."

The black ex-agent nodded and began walking slowly to one side, proceeding until he was about ten feet away from his three co-travelers.

"You stop right there, boy," demanded the shorter and darker-haired of the State Troopers.

"Oh, certainly, sir," said the big, former FBI-agent. He motioned for the man to come over.

"Jesse, Tom – any of them, includin' this one – makes a move, you know what to do," spoke the State Trooper leader, as he briskly walked over to be within earshot of Boatman.

"Shore do," ominously pronounced the other two Troopers. Their guns were prominently drawn.

"Okay, boy," curtly requested the leading State Trooper, "What you got to say? Maybe if you start tellin' me the truth, 'stead of a bunch of horse-shit like bein' some kind of 'doctor', I'll just give you over-night in the jail, hundred-dollar bail-bond and then get your ass out of town, kind of thing."

"Listen, sir," cajoled Boatman in a half-whisper, "I'm only doin' this because Will – he's the taller, red-haired fella over there, he's with me, the other two guys is just some folks we picked up on the way, they offered us a ride –

and I, we're former Federal agents – FBI, ourselves... we are, or were, on your side, Trooper, and we don't want this to turn out badly, for either you or us."

"'Zat *right?*" chuckled the State Trooper. "First you're a 'doctor', now you're a 'Bureau Agent', and no ID for neither one of you. Tell me *another* one, boy."

"Look," persisted the big black guy, "You all want the truth – I'll *give* it to you, and you better listen up good, because I don't want anyone to get hurt. Truth is, Will 'n me, we *were* with the Bureau, but we aren't any more – and that's because we've been hangin' around with Her Alien Angel-ness, name of 'Karéin-Mayréij'... you know, the one who smashed that comet?"

"Oh, for fuck's *sake* –" guffawed the policeman.

"There's more," continued Boatman. "If you followed any of Karéin's recent doin's, you'd know that she's so damn powerful that she makes Superman look like, I don't know, Superbaby, or somethin'. I'm warnin' you now, sir, that Will and me, we've inherited a small part of her powers... we don't want any trouble, but if you don't just back off and let us go past here, you and your friends is gonna end up crippled or dead –"

"I've heard *enough* of this, boy," snapped the State Trooper. "I got six guys behind me ready to fire, two with ARs, and these parts's *crawlin'* with law enforcement back-up, not to mention the military bein' on the way, too... and I don't see no guns on any of you. You're wastin' my *time*, boy – for what reason I don't know, but I reckon I might find out if I give you, say, three weeks in the lock-up. Now start *movin'!*"

He turned his head, and shouted, "Rest of you boys get your hands up, where I can see 'em!"

All three of the others did so, but Hendricks' unenthusiastic gesture resulted in his palms being lifted no higher than an inch below his shoulders.

"Listen, officer," pleaded Billy-Ray, "We ain't with them two city-boys... we's from mountains, back West Virginny way. They done car-jacked us – we wanted to turn 'em in, but –"

"Oh yeah," taunted the biggest of the State Troopers. "Two fuckin' unarmed city-slickers 'car-jacked' 'couple of local-boys like you, but y'all just drove 'em here, 'cross state lines, out of the goodness of your heart. Don't know if I should laugh or cry. *Jaysus*, Tom – that must be damn good moonshine they got up there... 'mind me to try some, 'soon as we get it out of that truck."

Boatman slowly stepped back by about two steps, and though he had also raised his hands, without taking his eyes off the three State Troopers (while noting the positions of the three others who were encamped at the barricades, approximately fifty or so feet distant), he called out, "Will?"

"With you all the way, 'bro," came the answer.

Hendricks addressed the two State Troopers standing in front of himself and the mountain-men.

"You better fuckin' pay *attention* to what Otis said, man," warned the third agent. "Billy-Ray, Dorsie – remember what I said about playin' some tunes?"

"Yeah," nervously offered the truck-driver.

"Enough foot-draggin'," commanded the leading State Trooper. "Jesse – cuff 'em!"

The biggest of the State Troopers had only taken one foot-step forward, when – to the astonishment of the Troopers, though not the mountain-men – two war-songs (one deep, bass-inflected and rhythmic, the other rapid-fire-staccato) began to echo from everywhere and nowhere. In the next instant, Boatman and Hendricks both took on demonic-guise, with the third agent's eyes shinning blue-white, while those of the black ex-agent took on a subdued, brownish-orange glow.

Instantly, the hulking, brush-cut State Trooper lowered his shotgun and fired it straight at Hendricks – or, rather, at where the third agent *had* been, a split-second before. From a standing start, the former FBI agent executed a spinning leap at least ten feet into the air, and as he reached the zenith of the jump, a newly-impressed Boatman noticed that the third agent's palms were... *on fire*, with the momentum and direction of his movement enveloping his body in a cork-screw-pattern shroud of flame-trails.

The big, black former agent had no time to pause in admiration of this feat, however, because he was himself confronted by two angrily-armed opponents. While Dorsie and Billy-Ray scrambled for cover behind the truck and shouts of alarm – along with the sounds of guns being grabbed – came from the three LEA officers back at the barricade, the State Trooper commander opened fire with his semi-auto pistol, spraying rounds wildly. Worse still, from a different direction, the taller of the Troopers raised his revolver and also let fly.

Despite dodging faster than any human being of his size and girth could do, given the range and the crossfire, Boatman could hardly avoid being hit, and – for a moment or two – he felt such searing pain at several impact-points upon his torso and pelvis, that the big black more-than-a-human was sure that he was about to die. The kinetic-energy of the two or three best-aimed incoming pistol-rounds had knocked him back by at least two feet; but – to the former agent's own amazement – he was still on his feet.

And, despite wincing from the bullet-bruises, he was quite... alive.

"Fucker's got a *jacket!*" yelled the leading State Trooper. "Aim for the head!"

Oh, no, you don't, grimly resolved Boatman. *Thick skull or not – don't fancy takin' one in the eyes.*

Fire, *I'm callin' you now!*

With the iridescent tendrils of *Amaiish*-energy lighting up his body from inside, Boatman brought his big hands together in a vigorous clapping-motion, while stomping one foot ahead of him, propelling an invisible – but impressively-powerful – shock-wave, tearing up the highway-pavement while rocketing at the two hapless State Troopers, whose bloodied, instantly-unconscious, rag-doll figures were literally sent flying, as if body-slammed by an unseen wrecking-ball. The more-than-human's assailants careened helplessly backward in a parabolic trajectory, crashing down upon the remnants of the barricade, whose sand-bags and wooden-planks had also – despite being over fifty feet away – been scattered by Boatman's brutal assault.

Hendricks, meanwhile, had come down on top of the State Trooper calling himself "Jesse"; the third agent's massively-energetic flying drop-kick was delivered with a boot enveloped in flame, so that the stunned policeman's short hair started to smolder, as, bleeding profusely from a massive gash in his scalp, he collapsed down to the highway-surface.

"Shit," gasped Billy-Ray, from his hidden, crouching vantage-point, behind the pickup-truck, "Think his neck's broke –"

But the fracas wasn't over. The mountain-men saw two camouflaged figures rapidly disembark from the parked military-vehicle behind what was left of the barricade, while two more State Troopers from the further-off reserve-group (the third of whom, might have been struck by Boatman's shock-wave, and was evidently hors du combat) dashed for cover and readied weapons.

The third agent landed in a classic martial-arts pose that would have looked like a self-conscious fake, under any other circumstances. He turned and shouted to Boatman, "ARs, up ahead – I'll *get* 'em – careful where you aim!"

"How'd you learn – never mind," exclaimed the big, black ex-agent. "Go right, I'll go left!"

It was hard to know if Hendricks had gotten the message, because before Boatman was able to finish talking, the third agent had already launched into another impossibly-high, flame-bedecked, super-kangaroo-like leaps. To the black ex-agent's dismay, he saw that one of the State Troopers at the barricade-area had raised an auto-rifle and was spraying rounds at the airborne third-agent.

His aim's off, realized the forward-charging Boatman, *but if he empties a full clip, he's bound to –*

Suddenly, two brilliant-red-orange flame-bolts, each leaving a prominent smoke-trail, issued from Hendricks' hands, streaking downward at the State Trooper with the auto-rifle. One of these missiles missed but the other struck the unfortunate LEA official, igniting his clothing and taking him immediately out of the battle, one second before the third agent landed and proceeded to beat him senseless with a series of lightening-fast martial-arts kicks.

The one remaining State Trooper was raising his own auto-rifle when he was hit by Boatman's second shock-wave. Fortunately for the Trooper, the black ex-agent had decided to unleash his attack at relatively long range, and the policeman did not suffer the kind of bone-shattering impact that had been inflicted on his two fallen colleagues; he was knocked back, arse-over-teakettle, striking his head on the side of a squad-car and thereafter collapsing prone.

Coming to a stop just in front of the splintered remains of the barricades, Boatman did a wary, alien-sense-enabled scan of the surroundings, looking out for other hidden opponents, but all he saw were the figures of the guys who had been in the military-vehicle; they had fled the scene, and were scrambling up the steep slope on the south side of the highway.

The flames on and around Hendricks flickered out, as he did a shorter jump, landing next to his more-than-human co-adventurer.

"Don't see any more of 'em," breathlessly offered the third agent. "What about you?"

"That'd be a 'no'," confirmed Boatman. "You okay, young man?"

"Yeah," said Hendricks. "Few scratches, but the flames, or the *Fire*, or the... oh, hell, I got no *idea* what – must have kept the bullets away from me. But I saw *you* take some, man! Might be a med-pack in that APC over there, I'll –"

"Relax," answered the big black ex-agent, with a wan smile. "Just some bruises... nothin' worse."

He looked around and grimaced upon seeing the clearly-lifeless bodies of the two State Troopers who had confronted him. The sides of the corpses that had been directly exposed to his shock-wave were pulped, as if they had run into a brick wall at hundreds of miles per hour. It looked like every bone in their bodies had been crushed; the surfaces that had been struck were shredded and abraded, as if they had come into contact with a huge belt-sander or wood-rasp.

"May God forgive me," quietly spoke an obviously-horrified Boatman, as he wiped a tear from his cheek. "It's so damn hard to *control*... wouldn't have hit 'em with the whole thing, if..."

Hendricks put a sympathetic hand on the black ex-agent's shoulder.

"Don't sweat it, bro'," he consoled. "Pretty sure I caved in that big Trooper's skull back there, when I came down on him. We all got a lot of soul-searching to do... just, not now."

"Yeah," ruefully agreed Boatman.

The heightened hearing of both of the more-than-humans revealed the sounds of the doors to the pickup-truck, in the process of being opened.

"Want me to stop 'em?" asked the third agent.

"No," requested Boatman. "But you might want to go and talk to 'em, while I see if I can get this military vehicle goin'."

With that, he broke into a fast trot toward the APC.

"Gotcha," responded Hendricks, as he zoomed upward and westward, landing – after a jump of at least fifty feet – right in front of the pickup-truck, within which both Billy-Ray and Dorsie had just positioned themselves. The mountain-men already had the key in the ignition.

Billy-Ray cringed upon seeing the third agent's glowing-eyed, lethally-empowered figure appear just outside the pickup-truck's driver-side door; the mountain-man's case of nerves wasn't helped by Hendricks' war-song, which, though more muted, was still playing in the background.

"Hey, man," announced the third agent, "How's it goin'?"

"F-fine... jus' fine, city-boy," stammered the driver. "We's fixin' to get out of here, if'n y'all don't mind too much."

"Well," smugly offered the third agent, "Here's how *I* see it –"

"How y'all see *anythin'*, with your eyes shinin' like that?" asked Dorsie. "Y'all look jus' like a devil –"

"Oh, I see perfectly well," countered Hendricks. "As a matter of fact, I see and hear a shitload more than *you* do, and whatever I look like, I'm no devil... 'matter of fact, I'm kind of a groupie for an *angel*, you know? Listen, man... I think we both know, Otis and I could bust your ass if we wanted to stop you from doing the jet out of here, but that's not our style... *capiche*?"

"'Zat mean... we kin go?" nervously asked Dorsie.

"After I'm finished saying what I want to say, yeah," affirmed the third agent.

"We's listenin'," carefully replied Billy-Ray.

"Okay," continued Hendricks, "So, here's the deal : we'll take you two with us, protect you as best we can... maybe introduce your sorry asses to Her Alien Highness herself, if you're up to it, and she is... no promises there. All you gotta do is use your brains, if you got any that is, keep your heads down when the heavy stuff hits, and so on. With me so far?"

"Yeah," grunted Dorsie. "But what's in it for *us*? 'Part from leavin' our brewin'-business wide-open, for the next fucker who show up wantin' a lil' free moonshine 'n synth?"

"Well, let's start by asking ourselves, 'what you suppose is gonna happen to you guys, when the LEA catches up with you, after what just went down here?'", remarked the third agent. "At least three dead State Troopers – Otis and I didn't *mean* to, you understand, but like I told you, our powers are, uhh, kind of a blunt instrument – and from being in the Bureau, I can attest, the punishment for that is summary execution... or, worse –"

"What's worse than bein' killed?" nervously snorted Billy-Ray.

"There is... and I've seen it," countered Hendricks. "Close-up. *Trust* me on this one, man. Anyway... with good luck, I figure you might make it a ways off the main road, before the Feds pick you up, with bad luck you'll get nabbed a half-mile from here, and don't forget that going back means you're driving on the wrong side of the road. With *crazy*-good luck, you might make it back to that mountain of yours, before the Feds tear it – and that still you got up there – apart, when they come looking for you with blood in their eyes. However you cut it... you're *fucked*, now, man. You're only slightly less fucked if you come along with Otis and me, but 'slightly's better than nothing... am I right?"

The mountain-men fell silent for a few seconds, and then Dorsie spoke up.

"Boy's got a point," he offered.

"Y'all talkin' *shit*," protested Billy-Ray. "It's *them* who smoked them Troopers... not us!"

"Y'all think th' Fed-rals gonna care?" countered Dorsie. "City-boys got no ID – we do – an' if what they's sayin's true, 'bout droppin' out of a plane I means – 'far as th' Fed-rals thinkin', they's *daid*... so we got a bunch of daid Troopers, two livin' billies on th' scene, an' no other livin' man to pin it on – come *on*, Billy-Ray, y'all *knows* what gonna happen!"

"Well y'all want to take your chances with them, you go to it," defiantly replied the driver. "I'm done with this weirdo shit... I'm *out* of here!"

With a frustrated and sad grimace, but without another response, Dorsie debarked from the truck. He walked around to stand beside Hendricks and mutely stared at the driver.

"Y'all bein' fuckin' *stupid*, Dorsie," pleaded Billy-Ray, through a rolled-down driver-side window. "Turnin' your back on your own kind... your own blood."

"Listen, man," offered Hendricks, his voice soft and introspective, "I'm not really up on all this 'blood' stuff... but if it *means* anything, Otis and me, we're now in on the world's most exclusive 'family' – specifically the one belonging to a cute little alien chick called the 'Storied Watcher' – and your friend here might have a shot at it, too. Don't throw your chance away, man. Be the stupidest mistake you ever made."

"'Zat right, city-boy?" retorted Billy-Ray. "Well, I already got one fam'ly, an' it suits me jus' fine. You 'n Dorsie want another, that's your business."

"Hey," wistfully spoke the other mountain-man, "Y'all take care of yourself."

There was a long stare by the driver, while he revved the pickup-truck's engine. Then he said,

"You too, Dorsie."

Solemnly, Dorsie nodded, while Billy-Ray – his eyes trained straight forward – began to drive westward, down the east-bound lanes of Interstate 64.

"Okay," proposed Will Hendricks, as his eyes returned to normal guise and the war-music ebbed to nothingness, "Let's go find Otis."

May I Have This Dance?

As he reclined in one of the re-purposed bus-seats within the dimly-lit, *faux*-executive-jet-like interior of the *Mailànkh Express*, Billings just as unnerved as he had always been, about how easily Tommy had taken to playing with the... *thing.*

Indeed, the kid endlessly talked to it as if it was really alive (*was* it? despite one or two cringe-inducing attempts, back in the woods, at "joining" with it – no, okay, with *him*, gotta remember the weird little bugger's pompous sense of self – the salesman still had his doubts). Tommy went around with the damn dagger strapped to his right leg, without the slightest concern... despite the fact that it was almost as long as his tibia, and despite the fact that anywhere within a couple of inches of it, the thing's hellish cold made Billings feel like he had been ice-fishing, with his fingers as bait.

The kid had begged his adoptive mother for the flaming-yellow one, too; but she had demurred, saying something about, "easier to thaw those things which you all purchased back from stalwart Grayson's home-town, than to reconstitute them, if they be calcined by bright-burning young *Væran Ksé'l'ch'*" (whatever *that* meant – it annoyed Billings no end, when she used that highfalutin' medieval-times lingo; but a guy had to pick his battles, after all).

Now, his girlfriend's animate-battle-knife-type-thingie was vibrating and making some kind of extra-bizarre humming-sound, while Tommy held it in his hand, quite unperturbed by its killing-cold aura, staring intently and mumbling something in an "off-somewhere" conversation.

They were now only about twenty-five minutes out of Grand Cayman, and the salesman still felt damp, despite Saquina White's game attempts to drive the last droplets of salt water out of his garments.

He sure as hell *had* learned some important stuff, back there; especially the part about how hard ordinary water can feel, when you hit it after having fallen, say, about a hundred feet.

The first two times, he had just suffered through it, but on the third – after savagely vowing to "head back to Tucson, drink it dry and just *pretend* that I'm getting smashed" – she had partly relented, and had held his hand, cramming his mind with crazy-ass feelings of swimming through air, sort of like doing the same in water but without the dog-paddle, as he plummeted downward.

Amazingly, as he neared the wave-tops, he slowed, and then... *floated*.
Upward.

He was still too scared shitless to look down – even when it was so dark that Mars eyes or not, he couldn't really tell how far up he was. But the realization that he had learned how to – after a fashion – *fly*, was, well... a bit too much to get his head around.

"Ah, but Bob," she had teased, "Now, my love, if you want to *have* me... perhaps no more shall you chase me on foot – rather, through the very clouds and skies!"

There's always a catch, he realized.

"Know I shouldn't feel cold," complained Billings. "Still do."

"Well, Bob," smilingly offered the astronaut's wife, "Y'all can dry 'em off yourself, you know. 'Member what she said y'all could do? Just turn it on for a few seconds – no more than that, or them pants of yours are gonna end up even more 'air-conditioned'."

Shaking his head, the salesman replied, "Oh, *no*, you don't. Every time I use that shit – cover your ears, kids – it makes my flesh crawl... it just reminds me of the last time I had to... for *real*. Like... down *there*, you know?"

"Yeah," she quietly acknowledged. "Bad memories... Devon told me all 'bout that. Well, it's your choice, after all."

Suddenly, his sense of balance – newly-refined, like all the others – told of a downward-sloping trajectory.

"*Væran Ss'éth'ch*' wants me to let you know, on behalf of Mom," announced Tommy, "That we're coming in to land."

"Well, nice of her to tell us," grumbled Billings. "Since I can't see sh... nothing, I mean – outside. At least with *my* little hidey-cloak, I can rig it to let the purple stuff in. With *hers*, I'm as blind as a bat."

"Yeah," mentioned Ramirez. "I've sorta been at odds myself... I mean, with the trip to Amchitka, I at least had something to do, tiring though it was. Guess we're all just back to being passengers, along for the ride."

"Mom's saying – through *Væran Ss'éth'ch*' – that from what my sisters tell her – we're just outside, uhh... where's 'Paska-goula'?" related the boy. "She says we're gonna put down at a, uhh, place with a bunch of boats, right near the edge of the water –"

"Well ask your mother, why... oh, *forget* it," muttered the salesman. "I wish she had traveled in here with us... wouldn't have to use young Ice Prince *Ss'éth'ch*' as an intercom."

"You forgot his title, Mister Billings," whispered the boy.

"No, I didn't," answered the salesman. "I *overlooked* it. There's a difference."

The dagger vibrated and gave off a noise that could never have been heard by human ears; in this company, however, it sounded like a petulant whine.

"Yeah... right... but come *on*, Mister Billings," pleasantly replied Tommy. "Remember, Mom *told* you – it's a lot easier for her to drag us through the air, as well as to protect us, if she's on the outside. I sure know what she means, after being in that big battle with the fighter-planes that we had over the ocean. You should've *seen* –"

Billings was about to say something smart, but the boy paused for a second, stared at the dagger and then called out, "Mom says, 'fasten your seat-belts, and return your seats to their upright positions'."

Well, alien goddess or not... she's still got a sense of humor, admitted Billings, to himself.

After a further delay of no more than perhaps another thirty or forty seconds, the *Mailànkh Express* came to a gentle, complete stop, and shortly thereafter, the vessel's main hatchway-entrance opened up. The Storied Watcher's teenager-pretty visage peered inward. Her weirding-armor had already been hidden in places unseen, and she was wearing a stylish combination of chic clothes purloined from Brazil's finer shops, along with sandals and a pair of tight-fitting track-pants.

"Hurry, everyone," demanded Karéin-Mayréij, "I tamped down my war-song as much as I could, and have parked our flying-refuge as best I could to provide it some cover... but as long as this portal remains open, passers-by cannot help but wax curious."

I never could understand all that Shakespeare-era-talk, mentally grumbled Billings, as he scrambled out the hatch and down its recessed, auto-appearing staircase. Immediately, he noticed the sticky, clammy heat and humidity of... wherever they were.

"But it is good and proper, my love," she commented, with a cheery kiss planted on his cheek. "For if one's cant is never formal, then a change to the familiar is no sign of friendship or affection."

"Whatever, honey," pleasantly replied the salesman.

He looked around, and was immediately worried. The *Express* had been deposited, facing southward toward the sea, on a gravel mustering-area which also accommodated between fifteen and twenty pleasure-boats and yachts of various sizes and types. Unfortunately, the new arrival was significantly larger and obviously of different shape; had it not been well after sundown, the alien-ship would have stood out like the proverbial sore thumb. Perhaps another twelve to twenty boats were docked on piers located on a bayou inlet, on the left, while ahead and to the right were four (thankfully, unoccupied) tennis-courts, and just before the seashore, was a moderately-large club-building.

"What the Dickens are we *doing* here, Sari?" asked Billings. "And where is, 'here'?"

The Storied Watcher turned, did a head-gesture at the air-ship. Its entrance-portal closed, and its outline became fuzzy and indistinct; this close, even a human being could undoubtedly notice its presence, but from further away, you'd really have had to be looking for it.

"Well, first of all, my love," she offered, "I had hoped that, upon again making land-fall in this 'America' empire, my war-children would pick up a trace of their lost sister; lamentably, as you say, Bob... 'no such luck'. But that means of communication is fickle at the best of times, and dear *Vîrya I'ëà'b' may* just be out of range. As to the 'where' of it, we are on the southern coast, near a city named 'Pas-ka-goul-ah'... I thought it not prudent to go too far inland, until we had a chance to hear of recent goings-on in your 'America'. And on the way in, I observed that over yonder, is a meeting-hall wherein many people seem to be congregating... do you not hear the music coming from in there?"

Indeed, she was right; the faint sounds of something like Tommy Dorsey or Les Brown, were coming from the club-house near the sea-shore.

"Hmm," observed Billings, "Sounds like old-time stuff... big band, I think. Bit dated but nice, none the less... good for the nerves, and God knows *that* would be a 'plus'. Now if I could just have a *real* drink."

"I am not familiar with that style of song, but if you say that it is good... that is enough for me, dear Bob," she flattered. "Thus, let us go there and see if they might have a tee-vee which we can use, to assess the current situation."

"'Zat a good idea, Karéin?" asked Saquina White. "I mean... there's prolly a price on our heads, 'round here. Somebody might *recognize* us."

"Yeah, but," argued Ramirez, "What are we supposed to do... go around with masks on, all the time?"

"He gots a point, Miz White," offered Melissa. "An' 'sides... anyone rag on us, we jus' fly 'way... right?"

"I've hardly got the hang of doing that, you know," replied the Tex-Mex scientist. "And if we wanted to draw attention to ourselves, well..."

"I counsel you all to keep your greatness in check, until the time – which surely will come – when it need be revealed and used," requested Karéin-Mayréij. "Now let us hurry to this meeting-place, for it is late and they may close down, at any time."

The travelers heeded her advice, and proceeded up to the lodge's front-entrance, which was wide-open, as was another door on the opposite wall, which looked out over the Gulf of Mexico. Inside was a wooden-floored dance-hall, with subdued lighting and 1940s-era band-music issuing from overhead speakers (at the front end of the dance-floor was a band-stand, but no live musicians seemed to be present). Out on the floor were seven or eight middle-aged-to-elderly, semi-formally-dressed couples slowly executing a two-step. There was a bar-and-restaurant section, which was more well-illuminated, at the far back end of the building.

"Ahh," happily remarked the alien-girl, "The dignified art of couple-dancing! Bob... do you know how to do this?"

"I'm all left feet," he evaded.

"Then I shall instruct one of them to act as if it were the right," she persisted. "Come on!"

And with that, the helpless – but, truth be told, weakly-resisting – salesman, was dragged out on to the dance-floor.

While the other four watched enviously from wall-side, the Storied Watcher proved true to her word : Billings' feet seemed to take on a life of their own, and he and his alien girlfriend moved effortlessly to the pleasant chords of *Corcovado*, then *Tuxedo Junction*, then *Desafinado*, and, finally, *Coffee Time*.

He had never been much for dancing, but the envious stares that he received from some of the locals (after all, she could have been his daughter), went a long way to stiffen his resolve.

"Ahh, Sari," he contentedly murmured, while holding her close to his chest, "It's a fool's paradise doing this, I know; but... count me as a happy fool."

"No, my love," she gently argued, "I will count both of us, as just... happy."

With the elfin head of the most powerful being ever to walk the face of the Earth, snugly nestled by his chin, Bob Billings of Tucson, Arizona – in a world of his own – swayed to the music.

Meanwhile, while the two more-than-human love-birds made the best use of their personal private-time, Ramirez led Saquina White, Melissa Claremont and Tommy George, down the right-hand side of the dance-floor, toward the back of the lodge.

With considerable interest, the more-than-human troupe noted that there was a flat-screen television situated just below the ceiling, at the junction of the rear-wall and the one on the south side of the building; it could be seen from in front of the serving-counter, behind which was an opening that provided access to the kitchen, but was almost invisible from the dance-floor. Unfortunately, the TV was turned off.

Ramirez approached the serving-counter and accosted the short-order cook – an elderly, white-haired, portly, stubble-cheeked Caucasian guy with a stained smock and a white, '50s-replica soda-jerk hat – who was polishing up beer-steins.

"Whoa," the man exclaimed, "A Mexican, and a bunch of bl... uhh, excuse me... forgot my manners, there. How'd you all get past the front gate, son?"

"Oh, we kind of just, uhh, 'dropped in', you might say," disingenuously responded the former scientist.

"Hah... likely story," grunted the cook. "Well, we don't got much security... folks sneak in here all the time, but it ain't usually for dancin', more like tryin' to steal things. For what it's worth, we're supposed to have a dress-code, but it's pretty near closin'-time anyway... no point in throwin' you all out, I guess. Want anythin' to eat? Got some tuna-fish sandwiches left."

"Oh, thanks, but, no," demurred Ramirez. "We kind of, uhh, ate on the plane, you know? Actually, what we were hoping was –"

As the Amerindian boy's voice cut in, Ramirez noticed that somehow, Tommy had managed to hop up and deposit himself on a nearby bar-stool, even though the seat of the thing was almost level with the top of his head.

"I'd like a Double-Jolt Cola, please, mister," demanded Tommy.

"Yo, me too!" added Melissa, her face already in a coltish half-pout.

"Y'all *know* y'all ain't gonna get no buzz out of it," whispered Saquina White, to the two youngsters. "What with this-here 'immunity' thing –."

"I still want one," persisted the boy.

"He yours?" asked the cook of Ramirez, pointing at Tommy.

"Oh... no," hastily responded the former JPL scientist. "Tommy's actually the son of Bob and Sari, over there – see, out on the floor? Yeah, those two."

"Hmmph," nonchalantly offered the cook. "Well, *he's* a lucky man, I'd say... whew! What a *catch*, eh?"

"Uhh... yeah, y'all could say that," said an obviously-bemused Saquina White, while Tommy and Melissa giggled profusely.

"Anyway," convivially mentioned the guy at the counter, "We'd just be throwin' some of it out, and we're not far from closin' time anyway, so anythin' you want – anythin' *dry*, that is – it's on the house."

"Yeah!" called out both of the children, as the man began to pour some cola into a pair of tall, chilled tumblers.

"So what I was wondering," continued Ramirez, "Is, 'is there any way that you could get that TV up there going'?"

"Well, we don't usually run it when there's a dance goin' on," replied the cook. "Few folks find it distractin'... but since we're almost done for the night anyway, and 'long as you all are okay with the sound bein' off... sure."

"Could you just turn the sound way down low?" asked the scientist, while the cook reached for a remote-control, touched a button on it and brought the television to life.

"Can't be loud enough to hear outside of back here," warned the man behind the counter, with a shrug. "'They always pump the volume way up on them damn commercials, so I don't know what you all are gonna get out of it, but... oh well."

He pushed the "volume up" control until it hit about the "2" position (on a scale of 1 to 20). The first thing that showed up was an old Hollywood animated movie about pirates accompanied by animated vegetables wearing various corporate trademarks, and a corpulent pink-and-purple dragon; Tommy complained vociferously when Ramirez directed the cook to keep flicking through the available stations, until, after trying over thirty-five of them, they finally hit a channel affiliated with the Disney News Network.

"What's the matter," jovially asked the cook, "You folks miss the evenin' news, today?"

"*Somethin'* like that," offered Saquina White. "We've sort of been out of town for a while."

"Oh?" he replied, with mild interest. "Where 'bouts?"

"South," she evaded.

"Well, there's not much... oh, *I* get it... Florida, right?" he commented.

"Island south of there, actually," stepped in Ramirez. "Went around in a private, uhh, *vessel*... pleasure-cruise, you know? Gotta tell you, though, was a bad deal... water was too cold for swimming, all the time we were down there."

Tommy and Melissa broke out in malicious giggles.

"Yeah, well, it *happens*," pleasantly agreed the cook. "Times bein' what they are, good luck at gettin' a refund on your trip."

"No kiddin'," deadpanned the scientist. "Look, man... we've been out a while, and we're trying to catch up on goings-on back home, you know? And as you're getting close to closing-time, while they're playing through all the Blaine Maine celebrity gossip up there on Disney... mind giving us an update on what's been happening? Had some problems with all that video and radio stuff, on the cruise I mean, so we've kind of been in the dark."

"Heh, heh, well," chuckled the cook, "If you don't mind me dronin' on, as I'm prone to do... sure. How 'long you folks been out?"

"Few weeks," semi-prevaricated Saquina White.

"Okay, well," offered the guy behind the counter, "Most important thing to mention is that damn curfew-and-martial-law thing they're imposin', as of tonight... as we seem to find ourselves east of the big river, I guess we're caught up in all that. By the way, a bunch of them out on the dance-floor will be organizin' a convoy to head out of here, when they finally go home... might ease things with the State Troopers a bit, so if you want to tag along –"

"'Curfew'? 'Martial law'?" worriedly interrupted Ramirez. "What's all that about?"

"Man, you folks sure *have* been out of the loop," harrumphed the cook. "It's all that 'terrorist' business that's been goin' down, last few days," he explained. "Government's sayin' that they got the Kentucky thing under control – terrorists are dead, supposedly –"

Anxious, wide-eyed stares circulated back and forth within the *incognito* group of more-than-humans.

"Oh my sweet Lord *Jaysus*," gasped a blanching Saquina White. "Hector – y'all think that they really – what about *Devon* –"

Her face wore a look of sheer horror.

"Don't know," gravely answered Ramirez. "But we better tell those two."

He vigorously motioned out to the floor with a "come hither" gesture, but as it turned out, the alien-girl and her escort had cut short their their dancing and were already on the way. In about three seconds they were within human earshot.

"You heard?" quietly remarked the former JPL scientist.

"Yes," answered the Storied Watcher.

"How could *she* have –" started the cook; but he was pre-empted by Billings.

"You think it's possible?" inquired the salesman. "Poor guys – I mean, after all they did for Tommy, Melissa and me –"

"I hope and pray that it is not," solemnly observed the Storied Watcher. "And neither I, nor my, ahh, 'children', heard any death-cry... although if we were too far distant, when such a tragedy would have transpired..."

She turned to address the cook.

"Sir," she asked, "How is it that you heard of these events in this fortress named 'Knox'?"

The man was half-overcome by the alien-girl's poorly-suppressed beauty and exotic demeanor. He hesitated for a moment and then replied, "Why... on TV, of course, Ma'am. Was just on the news earlier tonight, matter of fact... bunch of guys shot their way into the Fort Knox awhile ago... for what it's worth, there sure *was* some cheerin' in these parts, whatever the hell they called themselves – oh, yeah, *now* I remember, the 'Mars Gang' or somethin'. Nobody likes a banker... or them fancy-ass politicians back in D.C., you know. Why's this all so important to you, anyway?"

"Oh... just catching up on current events," nonchalantly answered the salesman, with a long-practiced, insincere smile. "Hey there, buddy," he continued, "Has there been any more about this on Neo?"

The cook shrugged and offered, "Nah... I don't use that thing much, mind you, but my son does, and he said the Feds are purgin' pretty much anythin' that's got 'Fort Knox' in its name, from them computer networks... even the tourist pages are down. You can't even plan a trip anymore, 'cause some stretches of highway have just vanished from the maps –"

"Which ones?" pressed Billings.

"How would *I* know?" countered the guy behind the counter. "Like I said, I hardly know how to turn on, one of those damn things –"

"You got a computer or a Neo terminal in this building?" asked the salesman.

"Not 'round here," answered the cook. "Think there's one in the office upstairs, but that's all locked-up this time of night, and I don't have the key to any of those rooms... if you wanted to use it, you'd have to talk to Boss Hislop tomorrow mornin', and by then you might as well just go find yourself a ho-tel with a connection. Listen – really – what's this all about?

"Bob," evenly remarked the alien-girl, "I have to, ahh, find the ladies' room... would you mind waiting here, for a few minutes?"

"Of course not, my dear," he unctuously replied, with a rapid-fire eye-wink.

"Just around the corner," added the cook, pointing a finger to his left.

The salesman caught a whisper that sounded like "*Ahn'jë*", as Karéin-Mayréij hurried off in the recommended direction and then vanished from sight, in the shadows.

Billings turned to address Tommy, Ramirez, Saquina White and Melissa Claremont.

"Let's wait for Sari outside... shall we?" he suggested; and, with some perfunctory "thank you" smiles, they filed silently toward the door.

Damn, he reflected, *I never realized how long that other crap goes on, when all you want is a re-run of the 6 o'clock news.*

They had been cooling their heels for perhaps twenty long minutes, with Saquina White pacing around frantically. All the while, they watched the last of the ballroom-dancers head slowly for the exits, thence for vehicles and the driveway out of the yacht-club.

Billings was amazed that not a single one of those leaving the area, seemed to notice the hulking mass of the *Mailànkh Express*; of course, by now it was near-pitch-dark outside those parts of the place that were lit by overhead lights, and the evening Mississippi mists had drifted in off the bayou.

Finally – as the door to the dance-hall closed, revealing the white-smocked figure of the cook, who was evidently assigned the task of closing up for the night – they heard the girlish, pleasant voice of the Storied Watcher, who appeared suddenly, directly behind her boyfriend's body.

"I am back," she pointlessly announced. "And there is quite a story to tell, although, unfortunately, a great deal of relevant information on these com-pu-ter networks, seems to have been deleted, by the American government."

"Shouldn't we do this back in the *Express?*" suggested Ramirez.

"Yeah... we got *company*, Karéin," added Saquina White, just before the cook advanced to a position within human earshot.

"Hey, folks," accosted the cook, "Lodge's closed now. You all better get along, now."

Nervous glances went back and forth, among the more-than-human troupe.

"We were, uhh, gonna call us a cab," prevaricated Billings. "But would you believe, none of us remembered to bring a communicator? You wouldn't happen to have one we could borrow, would you?"

The cook just stood there staring at them for a moment or two and then said, "Look – I've been around the bush long enough to know when somethin' *funny's* goin' on – and I'm damn sure this is one of those times. My communicator's in my car, as it happens."

He shook an accusatory finger at the group. "Now you *git* – and don't try nothin'. This-here place got surveillance-cameras all over –"

"They have all been disabled, sir," interrupted the Storied Watcher, as she moved forward without moving a muscle, allowing a small measure of her human-guise, to drop; her face was had a soft glow, as if it was being illuminated from a light-source below her chin. "As has been, everything else akin," she added, "But fear not. We mean you no harm... as long, that is, as you will *coöperate*."

Clearly frightened now, the cook reflexively stepped backward, but found that he could no longer move his feet, nor, indeed, any part of his body, except for his lungs, his eyes and the muscles in his face.

"What the...f..." he stammered.

"*Relax*, mister," reassured Tommy. "My Mom isn't going to hurt you, and neither am I. Want to know how you can be sure I'm telling you the truth?"

"Uhh... sure, kid," grimaced the cook.

"Because if I was mad at you," matter-of-factually explained the boy, "I'd already have blown you to bits."

"*Enough*, young prince!" castigated Karéin-Mayréij. "You will frighten this poor, honest working-peasant-man, yet more. Sir... may we sit down with you, on and around yonder stair-step, to have a quick parley?"

The cook winced once more – a gesture which the alien-girl took as a "yes", so she gradually released her telekinetic iron grasp and allowed the befuddled, fearful man to slowly retreat to the stairs leading up to the dance-hall.

She sat down next to him, and in her friendly, engaging voice, stated, "Obviously, it will be of no use to flee... so would you mind answering some more questions? Then you may go."

"Who *are* you?" he demanded.

"Yo, ain't there somethin' 'bout '*we's* the ones aksin' the questions'?" teased Melissa. "Kinda *like* bein' on th' other side, if y'all understand what ahm sayin'."

Again, the Storied Watcher had to remonstrate her followers. "Melissa, my sister – it is no sign of nobility, to taunt the weak and unenlightened."

"Yes'm," resentfully grumbled the teenager.

"What's it worth to you, for me not to tell your Mom?" quipped Billings.

"That's easy, Mista Billins'," smartly answered Melissa. "If'n y'all promise not to tell her, ah promise not to lift y'all few thousand foot up, then let go. Sound good?"

"Deal," muttered the salesman. "And I feel sorry for Whitney, by the way."

"Friends, I salute your wit," commented Karéin-Mayréij, "But we should not keep Charles, here, waiting, overlong –"

"How you know my name?" he worriedly interrupted.

"Oh... I know *many* things, including secrets far more well-hidden than what is in your mind," coolly noted the alien-girl. "But there is much that I do not know... and I was hoping that you could help me, with that."

"Why should I?" he countered.

The Storied Watcher produced three, small, yellow-colored coins from a hidden pocket. She placed these in the palm of her hand and displayed them.

"As pure gold as you will find, on this planet," she declared. "Worth many thousands of your dollars. Would that pay for some simple truths?"

"Can I see?" he asked.

"Certainly," she agreed, handing him the coins.

The man held one up to the light coming from the lamp illuminating the now-locked doorway to the dance-hall. He put it coin in his mouth and bit down.

"*Damn*," he gasped. "That's *gotta* be the real thing. Okay, lady – you's *on*."

"Tell me everything – no matter how seemingly-inconsequential – that you have seen or heard, over the past fortnight or so, regarding these so-called 'terrorist' incidents," requested Karéin-Mayréij. "Especially, concerning the whereabouts of these, ahh, 'terrorists', and of the President of the United States, himself."

"Well... sure, lady," complied the cook. "Tell you the truth, it's all folks have been talkin' about, lately – since that 'comet' business, and then that damn UFO that smashed up D.C., I mean; I'm not much up on it, all I can offer you is what I see on TV and some rumors and stuff."

"How would you say it, Bob?" answered the alien-girl. "Yes, I know – 'try me'. May I correct you on one thing, however? Whatever can be said about who was the cause of those, ahh, 'issues' in yonder capital-city... she is, in fact, *quite* well-'identified'."

The children laughed a bit, upon hearing this *bon mot*.

"Okay... anythin' you say," he acknowledged. "So, first thing that happened – and this was, oh, I don't know, maybe a week ago – was, we had some tornadoes on a highway up north of here, of course *that's* nothin' unusual... but then, before the government was able to yank it, there was this crazy footage of a twister headin' right for a bunch of cars 'n trucks that were stuck in a traffic-jam, and... well, I don't know how to describe this, exactly, but, see, this weird-lookin' UFO-type-thing went shootin' up from the ground, it flew all around the funnel-cloud, and then... the damn thing just *disappeared*, in a big snowstorm... don't think I have to explain how we don't get much of the white stuff this far south, this time of the year."

"'Less my husband's in your hood," interjected Saquina White. "And if he's still... alive..."

Ramirez offered the astronaut-wife a friendly hug, which was gratefully accepted.

"Huh?" replied the cook. "Well, anyway, a lot of people on the road dodged the bullet, when that tornado vanished. It gets crazier yet – right after that, there was this, uhh, 'news conference' right out on the Interstate, featurin' some guys who said they were them astronauts who went to Mars – *that* can't be true, obviously, because the government told everybody that they'd died of some damn disease – and they were claimin' that they had super-powers now, and that they were gunnin' for the President himself, on account of him havin' been behind some nasty business –"

"You ain't just whistlin' 'Dixie', there," morosely offered Billings.

"I can only tell you what I *heard*, mister," continued the cook. "And well, as you can imagine, that didn't go down too well with the government, which set a price on their heads... we didn't hear anythin' more about these 'super-astronauts' for a little while, although there *was* word of some kind of a shoot-out – never saw much in the way of details about it, mind you – up Missouri way, shortly afterward. That might have involved them or it might not have... can't say."

"Missouri?" wondered Ramirez, out loud. "What's with *that*?"

"Go on," directed the Storied Watcher, her tone cool and analytical.

"Anyway," said the cook, "Next thing we hear, these 'astronauts', now callin' themselves the 'Mars Gang', I believe, show up at Fort Knox... that place's pretty well locked-down, but they seem to have got into it easy, and then they basically started issuin' the same kinds of demands against the President that they'd done back on the highway – but they was uppin' the ante, like, callin' for him to be impeached, or some crazy-ass idea."

"What happened then?" asked Billings.

"Well, this 'Mars Gang', they said they wasn't budgin' from the Repository, but then, 'cordin' to what we saw on the news, Air Force bombed it into ratshit – sorry for my language there, but that's what happened," noted the cook. "Government said it might be *weeks* until they dig out whatever's left of them that was in there. News networks been yellin' their heads off for more information, of course... but Army's got everythin' for miles around, cordoned off. Or so we're told."

"Mom... does that mean that Captain Sam, Cherie, Brent and Devon are... *dead*..? whimpered Tommy.

Saquina White sat down on a stair-step, some distance from the dance-hall-cook, hung her head and began to weep.

"Hate to say so," grimly commented Billings, "But it sure *looks* that way."

The remark was ill-advised, as, upon hearing it, Tommy's poorly-suppressed anger immediately came back to the boil. He clenched his fists and his eyes took on a sinister, dull-red glow, while an ominously-low-pitched variant of his war-song began to play and a wave of cold fear washed over everyone in the area. All of the more-than-humans, save the Storied Watcher herself, reflexively cringed, under this oppressive display.

"I'll *kill* that fucking President!" hissed the boy, through bared teeth. "I'll kill the government! I'll kill *all* of them!"

The panicked cook jumped backward, trying and reflexively try to flee into the dance-hall; however, the door was locked, and he couldn't locate his key.

"Wait, *wait* – all of you!" cautioned a worried Karéin-Mayréij. "Terrible news is this, but only if it be more than foul rumor-and-hearsay! Tommy – keep your *Fire* under control – that is an *order!*"

Gradually, the boy's power-manifestations ebbed. With slumping shoulders, he walked over to the Storied Watcher, hugged her and, whimpered, "Mommy... there's so much hate in me... I promised not to lie to you, and I won't... I really *do* want to kill them... how much do they need to *do* to us, before..."

"I know, I *know*, dread young prince," she gently counseled, planting a kiss on the top of his head. "And you have my word – if this 'President' is responsible for the murder of my first-kin from *Mailànkh*, after he is brought to us in chains, you and Bob shall cast lots for the right of first revenge. But we know *nothing*, right now. We only... suspect. We must have proof. Oh-kay?"

Tommy mutely nodded.

"I don't agree with that, Karéin," spoke Saquina White.

"Why not, my sister?" asked a surprised Storied Watcher.

"'Cause if they killed Devon, I'm gonna do that motherfucker myself," vowed the more-than-a-woman. "I'll sink all of D.C. into the Potomac River!"

"Get in line, my dear," sourly offered Billings. "Why don't we see who can do it most *slowly*."

"*Jesus, Mary and Joseph*," gasped the cook, as he pointed at the alien-girl with a trembling finger. "What... what name did she call you by?"

"The same one that you *think* she called me by," said the Storied Watcher. "Your surmise is correct, Charles Chambers, of Del Norte Circle, Pas-ca-goula, Mississippi. I am *her* – the eternal Destroying Angel of the Many Worlds – and you are in my presence, now... also, that of my most mighty-and-noble brothers and sisters. Consider this to be the luckiest day of your life. Now... please continue with the story of recent events, if you please."

"Uhh... okay," the nonplussed man forced out. "About them 'Mars Gang' guys... we didn't hear from them no more, after the Fort Knox thing, I mean...

but now, there's reports of somethin' goin on in Tennessee, and maybe another one somewhere in Virginia. I don't know *what* to believe, since them boys back in Washington all lie like a sidewalk."

"No shit," miserably observed Saquina White, through tear-filled eyes.

"But," continued the cook, "Government's imposed this damn curfew everywhere east of the Big River, and they're really crackin' down on what gets put on the TV news... like, for example, just before all this 'terrorist' shit went down, there was a lot on about the Army tryin' to take back Los Angeles from them gang-bangers... now, all you get is sports games and bullshit about that 'Blaine Maine' kid runnin' wild all over the place, you know?"

"Right," grunted Billings. "Listen... are these 'Mars Gang' people, the only uhh, 'super-terrorists', who you've heard about? Did anybody else like them show up anywhere? A.P.B.'s, 'Most Wanted' announcements... you know."

"Very good question, Bob," interjected Karéin-Mayréij. "That is exactly what I was about to ask."

It is like you are reading my mind, my love, she sent, to Billings' considerable gratification.

"What?" responded the cook. He paused and pondered for a moment, and then offered, "Uhh... not really, mister... oh, wait a minute... yeah, like, there was an announcement that showed up on the news a few nights ago, something about some 'traitor', or some-such crap... they were sayin' that this guy was Public Enemy Number Six or somethin' after the members of the 'Mars Gang', and there's a big reward for turnin' him in. This is on top of the list of druggies and crooks that they put up at the end of the news, every night, of course. That what you were lookin' for?"

"Maybe," said the salesman. "They give a name? Of this 'traitor', I mean."

"Sorry... if they did, I don't remember it," answered Chambers.

"Mom... why don't you just pull it out of his mind?" coolly asked Tommy. "Or just... you know, like Captain Sam said you did to that CIA guy down under the island – before I got out of the jail-cell and then I –"

"That is an episode of which *neither* of us should be proud," remarked the alien-girl. "You ask why we refrain? I will tell you : because we must respect his privacy, because we must not hurt him without a very good reason, because we – though far more powerful – are not his masters, and because we do not want cruelty to shame ourselves, as does this gutter-tyrant called 'President'... are those enough reasons, my son?"

"I... *guess*," reluctantly retreated the boy.

"Did they say anything about where this 'traitor' is said to be living?" inquired Karéin-Mayréij.

"Think he escaped from jail, somewhere up in, uhh, Philly... or was it Pittsburgh?" said the cook. "Sorry... didn't pay much attention, at the time."

"We could just go an' aks a whole bunch more people," suggested Melissa. "One of 'em prolly know."

"We will so do," agreed the Storied Watcher, "But, what with the way in which this 'President' deals with crimes against the state, it would be unwise to assume such. Listen, Charles Chambers – has there been any talk of others, of our ilk? Specifically, of 'wanted persons', formerly of the eff-bee-ai police force, or, perhaps, a scientist?"

"Don't know what you're talkin' about, lady," argued the cook. "I ain't heard nothin' about anyone like that."

"What 'bout where the President's at, these days?" maliciously asked Saquina White. "Like, maybe where he's givin' his next speech? I'd like to reserve myself a place in the crowd, don't y'all know."

"Like I *said*," ruefully mentioned Billings, "You'll be about number 999 in line."

"You gotta be *kiddin'* me," nervously chuckled Chambers. "He ain't shown his face in public, for weeks and weeks now. Yeah, there's a speech that shows up on TV now and then, with the old windbag bitchin' about 'America's many enemies, foreign and domestic', and about 'how we've all got to tighten our belts' – well, mine's about as tight as it can get, I'm two months behind on my mortgage – but everybody *knows* he's hidin' out somewhere... probably in, like, Alaska or Hawaii or somethin'. He sure ain't been in the White House, if what they say on the networks is true. Mind you – they're still fixin' that up – after the UFO-business I mean... so I don't really blame him."

"As I believe that I stated before, sir," corrected the Storied Watcher with a mild smile, "That object has, ahem, been 'quite well-identified'. Very well, then... now, I have a, ahh, 'business proposition', for you. Would you hear of it?"

"Yeah... I guess," he responded.

"It is simple – 'five down, and ten later'," she said.

"Five of *what?*" asked the cook.

"Five coins, like the three you already have, for your silence to the authorities, in this affair," clarified Karéin-Mayréij. "Ten more, if you will assist us, in whatever way that we ask, when called upon to do so, within this month, and the next. Do you consider that to be a fair exchange?"

"Well... I don't know... are you folks, like, on the run or somethin'?" questioned Chambers.

"*Somethin'* like that," breezily offered Melissa.

"What if the government comes lookin' for you? Or for me?" warily asked the cook.

"Oh, that's easy," defiantly stated Saquina White. "That happen... we gonna blow 'em to Kingdom Come. 'Matter of fact, we're fixin' to do somethin' pretty much like that, anyways."

"But you're just six people –" he protested.

"We are – ahh – somewhat more than 'people'," calmly responded the alien-girl. "As that large obelisk in the President's capital city, found out, to its misfortune. Sir, the fact is... if the government of this country persecutes you on account of having encountered us – as it could do, though we have been as circumspect as possible, in making our re-appearance here – you would be far better-off being under our protection, rather than not. I hope that you will never learn that this is true... but I cannot guarantee this. What say you?"

Chambers pondered again for a few seconds, and then said, "What I got to do?"

"One – say nothing – nothing at all, about what has transpired on this night, no matter who asks you, and no matter how they press you... save to warn them that they court death, by doing you harm," explained Karéin-Mayréij. "Two, if someone comes to you asking for refuge, and he or she provides clear proof of endorsement by myself, or by any of my brothers and sisters... open your heart and your home. Three, pay close attention to the news, especially to developments associated with these 'terrorists', not to mention about the one whose title is 'Storied Watcher'. Finally... await further instructions, and obey these both in letter and spirit, when and if they are received. Do you understand?"

"Yeah," he replied. "But, lady... why me? I'm just a *cook*, you know."

"Not true," she asserted. "As of a few moments ago... you are become much more."

"Him *too*, Karéin?" asked Saquina White. "Y'all just *met* him!"

"He accepted my friendship," noted the alien-girl. "That blesses him with a morsel of it. Perhaps there shall be more, later on. The Gods only know it."

"Don't follow you," argued Chambers. "What you *talkin'* about?"

"Ahh... but if you are wise," smugly claimed the alien-girl, "So *will* you follow me, soon enough. Now, if there are no more questions, I would counsel you to make your own way home, for my friends and I need to conduct further discussions. Oh-kay?"

The cook stood up and said, "You mean... I'm free to go?"

The Storied Watcher advanced up the stairs, stood close in front of him – at which distance, he was unmanned totally, by leaking hints of her godly presence – and then moved to embrace him.

"Of *course* you are, and... good luck, my brother," she gently spoke. "I pray that the next days may find you happy, healthy and, above all else... *safe*."

At a loss, Chambers mutely nodded, scooted down the stairs and trotted over to the parking-lot, stopping twice on the way to glance over his shoulder, as if seeking validation that the experience had, in fact, not been a dream. He clambered into a beat-up-looking '20s-model Patriotic pickup-truck, gunned the engine, and drove down the driveway leading out to Martin Street.

"Y'all gonna need a computer to keep track of all these folks you recruitin', Karéin," sniffed Saquina White.

"The greatest power in the universe, next to that of love... is that of friendship," obliquely replied the Storied Watcher. "More friends are always better, than fewer. Now... let us decide next moves. Before I suggest anything, I would hear your wisdom."

"'Wisdom'?" quipped Billings. "Only had that in my molars, and they got pulled years ago."

"Huh?" asked the perplexed alien-girl. "How does one find wisdom, in tooth-enamel?"

It's just another name for the teeth in the back of your head, Mom, sent Tommy, to the Storied Watcher, who sighed and rolled her eyes.

In that case, she mentally deadpanned, *mine own fangs would count as 'genius-level'... would they not?*

Tommy's face showed a broad grin, upon perceiving this.

"Later, honey," parried the salesman. "Anyway... assuming – and yeah, I *know* all about 'assume' – that Jacobson and his astronaut-friends are, uhh..."

"Don't *say* it, Bob," pleaded Saquina White.

"I know," sympathetically acknowledged Billings, "And for what it's worth, Saquina... it sucks – the kid and I, not to mention Whitney, Melissa, Curtis and Elissha, all owe our *lives* to your husband and the rest of them, after all. Which leads me to what I was going to ask... namely, if they're, uhh... 'no longer with us'... wouldn't we have a duty to continue their work?"

"What you mean?" asked Ramirez.

"Well," offered the salesman, "If what we suspect is true, *is* true... Jacobson and crew issued the government an ultimatum – that is, they tried to bargain – and the favor was repaid by having bombs dropped on them, one or more of which, sadly, may have struck home. If *that's* the case, the mistake on Sam's part was in even attempting to reason with that sonofabitch President, as opposed to just smoking his treacherous arse... 'shoot first and ask questions later', kind of thing. Maybe, if for no reason other than to honor Jacobson And Company, and finish his work... that's exactly what we *should* do."

"Why would they not have called for me, in their hour of need?" pointed out the Storied Watcher. "They know my names, as do you all – and like you, they know how to chant for me to come. Yet neither I, nor my war-children, have heard a cry for help. Sam and Cherie, Devon and Brent, Wolf and Misha too – they are proud, and would not do so for any trivial reason... but neither are they fool-hardy. If their lives were in mortal danger, they would not hesitate. This I believe."

"What if they didn't get a chance?" commented Billings. "Like, they got dusted by some bomb, before they could open their mouths, or something?"

"But we don't know *what* happened to Minnie, Otis, Will, Jerry and Sylvia," argued the former JPL scientist. "What if –"

"What do you *think* happened to them, given the fact that there's been no news of them?" glumly countered Billings. "If any of them are still alive – which, frankly, I doubt, given the fact that they were planning to just show up and say 'hi, I'm a space alien, let me have a friendly chat with the President' – they're probably somewhere like where we found Tommy."

Immediately, a cold pall of fear, mixed with rage, washed over the group; but the boy's surging aura was quickly stopped by a cautionary finger-wave on the part of his adoptive alien mother.

"That's *speculative*, Bob," stated Ramirez. "But look – even if it *is* true – and God willing, it isn't – if the government was able to beat Commander Jacobson, considering his abilities, not to mention those of Cherie Tanaka and the rest of them... what makes you think that we're going to do any better?"

"Well, I'd say that poor Jacobson, and the rest of 'em, were holding a bunch of jacks to queens," commented Billings. "I got four aces standing next to me, and she trumps whatever the government's got... wouldn't you say, sweetheart?"

"Yes, Bob," quietly admitted the Storied Watcher. "But you know that I abhor violence, especially if one's ends can be achieved by other means. *Yet...*"

There was a pregnant pause, after which Saquina White spoke up.

"Yet... 'what', Angel Lady?" she inquired.

"By now, it is no secret to you that I love brave and ever-loyal Minn-ee, as woman loves and pleasures woman, scarcely less than I do the same with my beloved first-mate Bob, here," observed the alien-girl. "The safety of all of you is of paramount importance to me... hers, perhaps even more. And as you also know, while I refrain from the political affairs of man, if Sam Jacobson and his adventure-party, or Minn-ee and hers, have fallen to such a cruel fate – something that I pray with all my heart is not true, but if it is – then again is a blood-debt raised between me and the 'President'. In that sad event I swear : *this* time, I will not relent, until his head lies cleft from its neck, at my feet."

"Yeah," spat a red-eyed, devil-faced Tommy. "Oh... *yeahhh!*"

"Tommy, bro'," carefully remarked Melissa, "Y'all *scares* me, sometimes."

"Good," growled the boy, from under furrowed eyebrows.

The flying-teenager wisely did not pursue the discussion, and at length, Ramirez said, "God forbid that any of this is right, Karéin... but if we find out that something, uhh, *happened* to Sylvia and that little calico pup of hers – I'd like your help in identifying who did it. Leave the rest to me."

With glowing eyes and his war-song carried on the burgeoning winds, he stretched out his arms, bringing them below his waist; he looked up at the sky, for a moment or two, and it seemed as if a gale had come from nowhere, blowing off the water and whipping up fallen leaves and other debris. Then Ramirez looked down and extinguished his power.

The breeze ebbed to nothingness; and all was as before.

"You know," he observed, in a flat, analytical voice, "I've been practicing – on a small scale, mind you – how to create my version of a cumulo-nimbus cloud. I'm pretty sure that I can get work its polarity into a strong negative-based electrostatic-discharge... and I'm working on the positive, too. Now that I can get up there, all on my own I mean... I figure I can induce a few hundred kilo-amperes, for sure."

"What's he talking about, Sari?" complained Billings.

"Stand out in the open, when powerful Hector crafts his art, and you would find out, to your disadvantage, my love," smartly answered Karéin-Mayréij.

"Yeah... right," warily grunted the salesman. "Well, as for me, I'm kind of old-fashioned. All I need is a .45 and two bullets."

"Why two?" asked Saquina White.

"One for his balls, say, five minutes before I point the barrel at his head," shrugged Billings. "I can make it ten, if you want a longer rock-video."

"Make we not blood-vows, until the cause for these be writ large and plain," requested the Storied Watcher. "If that fateful time *do* come, not least among you shall be I, in exacting holy revenge. Now... a more basic question confronts us : namely, 'where next shall we go'?"

"Yeah... good question," admitted Ramirez. "I suppose we *could* show up at Fort Knox, but that'd be sort of like sticking our heads right into the hornet's-nest."

"Gonna be pretty hard hidin' our rig, *wherever* we hang out," mentioned Saquina White. "I'm surprised that nobody seen it yet, but it's dark, and all that fog was comin' in off the bayou, 'leastaways until Mister Hurricane there did his huffin' and puffin'. Point is... that thing's the size of two school-buses. You put it down anywhere there's a camera, and cloakin'-tricks or not, somebody's *bound* to mark us, eventually."

"Hmm... unless I were to stay with the *Mailànkh Express*, that is certainly a possible risk, and we cannot allow any Earth-government, let alone the American one, to capture her," allowed the alien-girl. "I had been considering as much, on our way in from Bouvet; we will need to pick a landing-place where we can leave the vessel safely unattended, for some time."

"We'd pretty much have to bury her," noted Ramirez. "Which doesn't leave us an easy way to move around, except if we..."

"Oh, *no*, you don't," instantly disputed Billings. "You *know* how I feel about heights, and I can barely *float!*"

"Come on, Bob," teased Melissa. "Y'all doin' *real* good – ah seen it! Y'all jus' gots to let go of that 'feets-on-th'-ground' kinda thinkin'!"

"I'll rent a car," he argued. "Or I'll take the bus. I'll damn well hitch-hike, before –"

"Anyway," interrupted Saquina White, "Where we goin', whether we're ridin', flyin' or walkin'?"

"This 'Fort Knox' place is likely to be dangerous, that is without doubt," observed Karéin-Mayréij. "But the surrounding areas are where any survivors of Sam Jacobson's team, would have been driven, after losing such a doomed battle. We should at least try to come to their rescue, forlorn hope though that may be. The only better alternative, it seems to me, would be to go directly for wherever the American President resides... but we do not know where that is. Do any of you have a, uhh, 'better idea'?"

Blank stares confronted her from all directions.

"Anybody remember where Fort Knox is?" asked Ramirez. "Tennessee?"

"No – it's in Kentucky," corrected Billings. "Just south of Louisville, as I recall. Went to a trade-show there, once. Did my whole quota for the year in one sale to some guy who was re-tiling the entire Army-base... bingo!"

"Yeah, right... 'bingo', Mista Billins'," sighed Melissa.

"I suggest that we should take the *Mailànkh Express* to the environs of this 'Fort Knox' place, and cruise discreetly around that area – avoiding confrontations if at all possible – while searching for our brothers and sisters," proposed Karéin-Mayréij. "We can use our hiding-skills to steal among the war-vessels of the President's armies, and there, perhaps my war-children and I can, ahh, 'tap in to' some of his plans and deployments. Of course, there is always the chance that we might be discovered, or intercepted. In that case, the subterfuge would be of little additional use, and we would have to boldly declare our presence here, if for no reason other than to advise our kin of the *Fire*, of the same. In spy-craft and war-craft, ever are these the risks."

"*Well* now," mischievously observed Saquina White, "Ain't *that* just gonna be the news that the President's lookin' forward to hearin'."

"I could give him worse news," evenly added a stone-faced Billings, to Tommy's obvious enjoyment.

"Now as to this, 'Fort Knox'," continued the Storied Watcher, "Though I dislike mentioning it, the task that may be of substantial risk, is the most unpleasant one : we must determine if the terrible thing just discussed, has indeed befallen brave Sam Jacobson, dear Minn-ee and the others of the *Khùl-Algrenàthi'i Srelkh –*"

"The... *whaaat?*" interrupted Melissa.

"A title of great nobility, little sister," explained the alien-girl. "It means, roughly, 'Those Newly Raised High, Of The *Fire*'". Thus it means... *you*."

"Much 'bliged," demurely replied the teenager.

"One of the arts that I least enjoy deploying," continued the Storied Watcher, "Though a great and subtle one, it is... I can tell if the spirit of a mortal being, has departed from this plane, if I am sufficiently close to the place where such a fateful event occurred. If the boasts of the American President are correct, if we were to enter this 'Fort Knox' fortress, and if I could spend a short while scouting it... I could tell if Sam, Cherie, Devon, Brent, Wolf or Misha took their last breaths, there; in which case, on that spot, I would lead all of you in a solemn pact of blood-revenge. If not, then we would rejoice, and ponder how to find where they have gone."

"Sometimes y'all don't really want to know the answer to such things," morosely remarked Saquina White. "'Cept to pray to the Lord that you'll hear what y'all *want* to hear. Truth is, Karéin... there've been times when a bunch of us have been prayin' to you. Or did y'all know that, already?"

"I did, and I heard, and go ahead and *do* it, my sister," gently replied Karéin-Mayréij, as she offered the astronaut-wife a brief embrace. "I seek not mortal-worship; but your love fortifies me, in ways that I hope, some day, you will understand... and may it be that the divinity that burns so brightly in you, shall also bless my poor soul."

She offered a respectful head-nod and hand-clasp, then looked up and, in a loud, strong voice, called out,

"So, ye of the *Khùl-Algrenàthi'i*... that is, those who wish not to try their flying-skills, all the way to the Fort called 'Knox' – go now, to the *Express!*"

Don't Look Under That Tarp

The astronaut's wife looked over her shoulder, for a second; then she put her eyes back on the road ahead.

"At least they're sleeping," she offered. "Even Roofer."

The dog lifted its head, stared back at her for a second, yawned, and again closed its eyes.

"Yeah," agreed Boyd, with a more lengthy glance of his own. "Don't mind saying, 'I envy them'. Although I sort of don't need it – sleep, that is –"

"What do you mean, 'you don't need it'?" asked the wife. "Oh, yeah – the 'alien' stuff... right?"

"Yeah," admitted the ex-astronaut. "Damn hard to describe... psychologically I need it, but physically... I don't. It's like when I'm flying around up there – the 'alien' part of me is fine with it – like swimming, once you get the hang of it; but the 'human' part of me is, well, 'scared shitless', is how I'd put it."

"Well, for that little 'human' hiding inside of Brent Boyd – join the club. About being scared shitless, that is," ruefully commented the wife. "Are you *sure* it was a good idea getting back on the highway?"

"I'm not 'sure' of anything, these days, Laura," replied the ex-astronaut. "Except that I love you."

He got an affectionate smile and head-nod – the kind that comes not after a year of marriage, but after a decade or more – as the wife drove on through the night.

They had gone no more than another two or three minutes, and there had been little further discourse, because Boyd insisted on near-silence; when his wife asked about the 'whys and wherefores', he had replied with some inscrutable talk about "maybe I can hear something on the side-bands, if you turn the radio between these two stations".

But despite his wishes, the ex-astronaut apparently hadn't picked up much new information. All that came to his ears – human and Mars-variety, alike – was non-stop hillbilly- and country-music. He longed to hear some news, but there either was none at all, or, for all he knew, they might have been past the top of the hour.

The car was entering a long, gently-southward-curving stretch of the highway, and Boyd's defensive instincts were already warning of trouble.

"Hey... slow down," he requested.

"Sure," answered the wife, as she immediately complied with the order. "What is it... oh, God, Brent, don't tell me you're going to jump out and take off –"

"Don't know," he said. "But you'd better get used to it... gotta keep that mobility up..."

He put his fist under his chin while intently studying the surrounding landscape, particularly, the roadway.

"Damn," muttered Boyd. "I sure don't like this."

"Don't like *what?*" quickly inquired the wife. "Should I stop?"

"Be ready to," he cautioned. "Did you notice?"

"Notice *what?*" she replied.

"We've been going for quite a ways now, and no traffic coming in the other direction," observed the ex-astronaut. "Maybe I had better – *whoa!* Okay, honey – pull her over, *now!*"

The SUV slowed and pulled up to the right, although there wasn't really enough of a shoulder in these parts, to get completely off the highway.

"What *is* it?" demanded the fearful wife. "So dark out there – I can't see anything ahead of us – "

"There's the difference between 'Mars eyes' and the Earth variety," phlegmatically noted Boyd. "Roadblock, way up there... at the limit even of my eyesight. Highway's completely blocked... now *that's* strange – got a glimpse of someone in *Um'nàhr'é*, but doesn't look like –"

"What did you say?" queried the exasperated wife, while her husband stared intently forward.

"Oh... that's Karéin's word for, 'seeing in the near infra-red'... like, the heat-waves given off by things like human bodies..." absent-mindedly explained the ex-astronaut.

"Woww... Daddy, you can do *that*, too?" gushed a small voice from the vehicle's back-seats.

"Sure *can*," replied Boyd, never taking his eyes off the scene in front of the SUV. "Listen, Laura... I'm going to have to go forward and check it out... and no, I don't think I'll do any flying here, at least not if I don't have to –"

"Awww, Daddy, we wanted to see you –" persisted a boy's voice.

"Believe me, son," mentioned the former Mars mission pilot, "You'll get to see more of *that*, than anyone should have to deal with, soon enough. Listen – you, Wendy and Nicky keep your heads down, and keep Roofer's trap shut... you hear?"

"Yes, Dad," came the elder daughter's voice.

"I'll be back in a few minutes," announced Boyd, as he unlocked the passenger-side door and exited the vehicle before there could be further argument. "One long flash of light means, 'drive forward', two means 'turn the car around and beat it, as fast as you can, away from here'... got it?"

"Yeah," sighed Laura Boyd.

Cautiously, Brent Boyd walked westward down Interstate 64, keeping his body as close as possible to the concrete median-barrier that separated the highway's eastbound and westbound lanes.

Ever-mindful of the need to balance 'not wasting time' against the possibility of walking into a trap, he had advanced to a distance of about two hundred feet from the roadblock, when he stopped, pushed his senses to the limit, and carefully surveyed the situation.

Damn, reflected the former Mars mission pilot. *Thought there was a roadblock here...*

I was half-right. There was *one... but most of the barricades have been smashed to bits, busted wood all over the place... judging from the damage, I'd say it got hit by a bomb or a RPG, but something doesn't quite fit... shit...*

Well, there's *why I didn't pick up anything with the warm-sight... residual heat-signature of a human body, no longer living...*

Boyd walked forward, at a brisker pace now, over a distance of about ten more feet. Then – out of the corner of his left eye – for a split-second, he thought he detected movement; but whatever he might or might not have seen quickly disappeared to the west, behind a battle-scarred automobile and a pile of wood-debris.

The ex-astronaut froze, intently scanning the scene. He crouched beside the median-barrier, hoping to make himself a less conspicuous target. And he energized a fraction of his dark-cloak, using just enough *Amaiish* to avoid that damnable war-music, from doing its surprise-ruining best.

I can easily zoom up, up and awaaay, he mused.

But if there's a lot of them on the other side of that bend, I'll likely have to shoot immediately, if we're to make it past here and on the way to Fayetteville... more corpses to my credit, and I'd have to leave Laura and the kids, for a moment or two... don't like that idea –

Boyd's introspection was abruptly brought to an end by a gruff – yet, somehow, familiar-sounding – voice, barking at him from behind the remains of the barricade.

"Whoever you are – better get your ass *out* of here, dude!" called the unseen antagonist. "You may *think* you're hiding, but we got you marked... give you thirty seconds to turn around and scram!"

I know *that voice,* something told Boyd. *That is... I think I know it... but if I'm wrong... and how the hell is he seeing me?*

It's damn-near pitch-dark out here to begin with, and I've got enough of the 'shroud' going to make it like a shadow, even in broad daylight... Army must have some funky new IR.

Better remember that, for the next time I think I'm sneaking up on them...

"I don't know who you think you are," counter-accosted the ex-astronaut,"But I can and *will* kill you with ease, if you don't get out of my way! I have to get my car past this roadblock. *You* got ten seconds, and when you hear some fast-paced music, you better get your ass out of here, or I'll –"

"Music?" came back the incredulous retort. "You said *music*, man?"

"Yeah, that's *exactly* what I said," stated Boyd.

"Let me hear it!" demanded the hidden voice.

"Most who *do* hear it," warned the ex-astronaut, "Don't live long enough to tell the tune."

But what's the harm? he thought. *Might put a scare into this strutting, blustering little G.I. or hillbilly-cop... might save some lives.*

Okay, then...

Boyd called on the power and allowed the luxurious, enervating thrill of the *Fire*, to course through his bloodstream; the first few notes of his war-song began to issue up from the ground below, and even more, down from the skies above.

"I can't – I can't – fuckin' *believe* it!" screeched and interrupted the voice. "Maybe there *is* a God... Brent – that *you*, man?"

The ex-astronaut quickly suppressed his surging energies, as well as the psycho-music and the already-weak dark-cloak.

"Yeah but who are – wait a minute, *now* I know – *Hendricks? Will* Hendricks? You *gotta* be *kidding* me – what are you doing –"

"One and only, man!" came back the overjoyed response. "Otis – get your butt *over* here! We just ran into Brent Boyd! Hey, Brent... where's the rest of 'em? Like, Jacobson, Tanaka and –"

Boyd arose from his crouch and ran forward at a quick trot. In a few seconds, he was close enough to clearly make out the third ex-FBI agent's lanky, tallish, red-haired figure; although, strangely, both he and his big, African-American counterpart, who was racing up from behind the debris-barrier, were decked out in backwoods-clothes, as if they'd just returned from a hiking-trip.

"They all went west to Texas, to rescue the Commander's family," said the ex-astronaut, as he offered a handshake – which was enthusiastically-received – to both Hendricks and Boatman. "My wife, Laura, my three kids and my dog, are in our car, a few hundred feet back – they've been through hell, the government's hunting for everyone and anyone related to any of us –"

"Got you beat on that one," ruefully interjected the third agent. "The 'hell' part of it, I mean."

"How so?" inquired Boyd.

"Reason we're here," said the big, black ex-agent, "Is, President had us pushed out of that damn plane of his, at ten thousand feet mind you, without a parachute or even a Bible. Somehow – thanks to young Will here's quick thinkin', and maybe some of this 'alien' stuff that she's got us doin' – we managed to survive that... don't ask me *how* we did... but we did."

"*Wow*... hat's off to you, and I'm very interested in the story behind that... it's fantastic to meet up with you guys," observed Boyd. "Just a sec..."

He held up his left index finger and let it glow brightly for two seconds, then extinguished the *Fire*-shine. After a few seconds, he saw the SUV begin to slowly roll in the direction of the barricade.

"Good man to have around, when I'm short a flashlight," quipped Boatman.

"Listen, guys," continued the ex-astronaut, "I'm taking my wife and kids back to Fayetteville – some miles to the west of here – because that's where Sam was supposed to return to pick us up, in a stolen Army V/STOL transport, by the way. As you know, Devon's family is safe, but the government almost got mine, they're after Jacobson's, and unfortunately, they've already grabbed Cherie Tanaka's mother... you can imagine what the Professor's going to do, about *that*. Where were you two heading off to?"

"Anywhere we *can*, man," replied Hendricks, with a half-grimace. "We approached this roadblock from the other direction, got stopped. State Troopers and Army tried to arrest us... after that, it didn't go too well, you know?"

"You can say *that* again," sadly commented Boatman. "May God forgive me, what I've done today..."

Boyd surveyed the scene, taking note of the mangled bodies lying in various places.

"Yeah," he quietly remarked, "Pretty much like how things haven't been going too well for the rest of us, I'd say. I ran into the Agency further east on the Interstate... they threatened my family. Not much left of them, I'm afraid."

Then his Mars eyes again noted, and focused on, the signature of a "live one".

"Look out!" he exclaimed, "We're being *watched* – behind that burned-out squad-car –"

"Oh... *him*? Don't sweat it, Brent... that's just Dorsie," reassured the third agent. "Good guy. Local guy. Helped give us a lift here, down from the mountain that we landed on, when... well, you know about that, now."

He turned his head and called out, "Hey, Dorsie! You might as well show, man – this-here guy's Brent Boyd... he's one of 'us'."

Slowly, suspiciously and cautiously, the mountain-man crept out from behind the wrecked vehicle. He approached the three more-than-humans and asked, "That boy... he's like y'all is?"

"Oh, even *worse*, man," diffidently answered Hendricks. "His 'specialty's' firing, like, photon-beams at things... kind of like a death-ray, but you're blind by the time it cuts you in half... hey, Brent, did I get that right?"

"Pretty much so," maliciously confirmed Boyd. "Did I tell you that I'm flying all by myself, these days?"

"Get *ouut*," responded an instantly-jealous Hendricks.

"Yep," said the ex-astronaut. "Piece of *cake*, once you get used to it."

"But she never taught you how to..." inquired the third agent.

The ex-astronaut saw a subtle, *Fire*-powered glow, appear momentarily in Hendricks' eyes, as the third agent spoke his words.

"She didn't *have* to," confidently answered Boyd. "What was it they said? 'Necessity's a mother', or something like that? *Amazing* what you can do, when your life depends on it."

"Gonna need some *lessons*, man," pressed Hendricks.

"Sure, in the fullness of time," stated the ex-astronaut.

Addressing the mountain-man while offering a handshake (the gesture was cautiously accepted), he added, "Pleased to meet you, Dorsie... but did they explain what you're getting into?"

"More or less," grunted the hillbilly. "Not like I got much *choice* in th' matter... these two boys kinda dropped in on mah kin, Billy-Ray 'n me, when we was brewin' some product, up on th' mountain. Since then, things gettin' *strange, real* fast, an' Billy-Ray had 'nuff of it... he took th' truck and went home. Reckon there's a price on mah haid now, or will be, soon... might as well run with y'all, 'least that make it interestin', when we's fixin' to shoot it out with them Fed-ral boys, y'know?"

"I'm trying to do as little 'shooting' as I can," replied Boyd, "But when and if I do – if you hear the same war-music that was playing a few minutes ago, especially if you hear the word 'Shine' – make sure to close your eyes... okay?"

"Found out all 'bout that damn 'music', aready," ruefully commented the mountain-man. "Saw your two friends doin'... well. Ain't *human*, what they did."

"Not *human*?" chuckled the ex-astronaut. "Yeah... you could say that."

At this point, his wife's SUV rolled up close enough to be in easy earshot.

She leaned out of the driver-side window and called, "Brent? Who's this?"

"Laura," he announced, "I'd like to introduce Will Hendricks and Otis Boatman, formerly of the FBI. They're well-acquainted, both with Karéin, and with her *Fire*. This other fellow is 'Dorsie'... he's a local guy who – lucky *him* – has somehow ended up with the two of them. Will, Otis, Dorsie – this is my wife Laura, and in the back are my kids, Wendy, Brent Junior and Nicky, in order of age. Oh, and my dog's in there, too; his name's 'Roofer'."

"Great to meet you, Mister Hendricks, Mister Boatman," greeted the wife. "You too, Dorsie."

"Much 'bliged, Ma'am," courteously responded the hillbilly.

Addressing her husband, she asked, "Brent... what do they, uhh, '*do*'... if you know what I mean?"

"I'd prefer not to go into that, Ma'am," offered the big, black ex-agent, looking momentarily down at his feet. "Because I've done some pretty awful things with it, lately. I'd say 'I wished she'd never given it to me, in the first place'... but I s'pose if she hadn't, well, I wouldn't be here talkin' to you all."

"I... *see*," she quietly replied.

"Well, as for me," remarked Hendricks, "I do a *lot* of things... kind of a 'jack-of-all-alien-trades', I guess you'd say – long on breadth, short on depth, but I get by. Nice to meet you, Missus Boyd... join the club."

"Wish I didn't have to," she complained.

"Y'all got *that* right, lady," grumbled the mountain-man.

"You two – uhh, you *three* – want to tag along with Laura and me?" offered Brent Boyd. "Only thing is, I don't think we could fit you all in there –"

"We've almost got that Army wheeled APC over there, started up," interrupted Hendricks. "Stripped the weapons and a bunch of other stuff from the... uhh... those who didn't make it. It'll hold lots of people, runs on either gas or diesel... nearly a full tank in her now. Most of the squad-cars are pretty banged-up, thanks to Otis' little special trick, but there's one ghost-car parked back behind the APC that looks like it escaped most of the shrapnel. You said you're going to Fayetteville... right?"

"Yeah," confirmed Boyd. "Commander Jacobson and I already set the *rendez-vous* point. Listen, guys – we'd better get going, sooner rather than later... in a situation like this, military and police detachments are supposed to check back with local headquarters on a regular basis, and their failure to do so is going to make the higher-ups, *suspicious.*"

"You got it," agreed Boatman.

He asked the hillbilly, "How far's this 'Fayetteville place'? Can we get there easy – you know, without runnin' any more of these damn roadblocks?"

"Decent 'nuff drive from hereabouts," replied Dorsie. "Maybe fifty mile or so. Y'all kin get there on th' Interstate, an' y'all got to go on it fer a ways regardless, but when y'all get to the junction, I'd take th' Midland Trail west, then Ol' U.S. 19 south. Bit longer, but less lights... prolly less po-lice, neither."

"Hmm," considered Boyd, "Fifty miles... sure makes the idea of just flying there, seem a lot more attractive."

"'Long as you can *stay* up there, once you find yourself in the clouds, Major," wryly mentioned Boatman. "As for me, well, I prefer lookin' beneath my feet, and seein' something nice and solid, down there."

"Don't blame you for that," remarked the ex-astronaut. "Because it's how I felt, up to a few days ago. Okay... Will, you think you can drive that APC?"

"Pretty sure I can," said Hendricks. "After having to steer that effin' bus of hers, all the way from Canada to Amchitka, at God-knows-how-many-thousand feet and God-knows-how-many-thousand miles per hour, mind you... how hard can it be?

"Point taken," said Boyd. "I'd come along in there so we can catch up on current events, but I can't leave my family... tell you what... why don't I ride on top of the APC – Laura, you and the kids follow behind, and don't worry, even if you can't see me because I have my darkness-cloak up, I'll still be able to see you – we'll take the back-roads up to Fayetteville; and if we run into any serious opposition, I'll attack from above, while you guys grab a gun, and –"

"Don't need no 'gun', any more," softly interjected Boatman.

"Really?" responded the former Mars mission pilot.

"Don't be anywhere in front of me, Major Boyd," warned the big, African-American man. "If I look like I'm about to... you know... *defend* myself."

"*Seriously*, don't," added Hendricks. "Remember how she said, he could, like, disintegrate stuff?"

"Yeah," said Boyd. "That she did."

"I think a bit of it's riding on that earthquake, or shock wave, or whatever the fu – sorry, whatever the H – he sends out," explained the third agent. "Want to see what it does? Take a look at what's under that tarp, over there."

"Thanks, but I'd prefer not to," grimly replied the ex-astronaut.

"You sure *don't*," sadly stated Boatman.

"Oh, and... Brent?" repeated the third agent.

"What?" replied Boyd.

"I didn't tell anybody except *her*," confessed Hendricks, "But when I was back at the camp, I was, like, *studying* things... you know? It's frustrating, I feel like ninety-five per cent of it's just past my grasp... but I *did* get a handle on, like, maybe a hundredth of Mr. Bounty-Hunter's mojo. She said something about 'if you would learn from your brothers and sisters, valiant Will, start with those things that are most simple, such as the ordinary elements and energies; behold how the *Fire*, begets the Flame'. So if you see me lit up like a Roman Candle... don't sweat it, man... it's all good, okay?"

"I can see how that could be one bad-ass power she gave you," observed a clearly-impressed Brent Boyd. "*Nothing* you can't do."

Hendricks winked an eye and smiled proudly.

"Look," proposed Boatman, "How about Dorsie rides along with young Will there, in the APC, while I go out ahead of everybody, in that unmarked police car, that is... your wife and kids can be third in line, in the convoy."

"Wouldn't you be a little safer inside the 'carrier?" asked the ex-astronaut. "It's armored, after all – though not against anything more than rifle-rounds."

"'Member your Commander's little 'gift'?" returned the big black guy.

"He's just about indestructible," commented Boyd. "Back at Fort Knox, I saw him taking auto-cannon shells dead-on... didn't like the impact-shock, of course, but otherwise... not so much as a scratch."

"Well, I guess I know something of how he feels," said Boatman. "It stings, and I'm still coverin' my eyes... but I think I'll be okay, drivin' out front."

"*Neaaat!!*" came a boy's voice, from the back-seat of the Boyd vehicle.

"Keep it down back there, Brent," demanded the father. "You'll have plenty of time to get to know Mister Boatman and Mister Hendricks – and Dorsie, too – once we get some down-time."

"Listen, Brent, this sounds like a plan," observed Hendricks, "And it's the best one we got... but, like, there's still one thing that's still bugging me, you know?"

"Yeah?" inquired the ex-astronaut.

"Well... what if Jacobson doesn't show?" asked the third agent.

Boyd just shrugged, holding his palms upward in a "got no idea" gesture.

"Brent dear," spoke up the wife, "Isn't that more or less what you said, when I asked you, 'what if something goes wrong, with the trip to Mars'?"

"Pretty much so," he admitted.

"Well, then?" she persisted.

"Trip's not over, yet," said Brent Boyd, with a weary, rueful smile.

Let's Make A Deal

Minnie Chu was, by now, thoroughly frustrated with being confined to the pseudo-prison of a single chair in the airborne command post's security section.

She had expected to have been dropped off, undoubtedly to then be sent to some dungeon akin to those with which she was by now familiar, long ago; but instead – though the aircraft had, in fact, landed and again taken off, at least three more times since her *contra-temps* with the President and his advisers – somehow, for some unknown reason, she was still... *here.*

Thank God for small blessings, morosely mused the former FBI team-leader, as she stared absent-mindedly out of the porthole-sized cabin-window at the burgeoning dawn.

At least they let me take a shower, and gave me a change of clothes... don't I just look the part of an unranked junior Air Force officer?

Well, I'd resign my commission... if I could, she said to her self, with a half-suppressed, miserable chuckle.

What the hell did I think I'd be accomplishing, *anyway?*

The fucker's incorrigible – I should have known that, from the start.

Sam did *know it... didn't he?*

No need to dwell on it, Minnie – you'll just make yourself even more depressed –

Just then, her heightened hearing gave her a half-second's advance warning that the locking-assembly on the door leading to the command-post's inside corridor, was being disengaged.

Chu expected to see one of the hulking, taciturn Secret Service agents returning to spell the one who was lounging in the rear of where she was now at; but instead, she was confronted by the Brylcreemed, leather-faced, civilian-business-suit-garbed figure of the Presidential Spiritual Adviser.

"Good morning, Missus Chu," he smoothly announced. "How we doin' today?"

"It's 'Ms.' – I'm not married yet, because you kidnapped my fiancée... remember?" she retorted. "And I'm fine... whatever 'fine' means, under the current circumstances."

"Why, I guess I forgot about that... 'fact you're *engaged,*" unctuously stated the preacher-man.

He turned to address the Secret Service agent (a muscular, brush-cut, Caucasian guy) in the back of the room.

"I got some, uhh, *private* stuff, to discus with Ms. Chu here," he said. "Would it be okay for us to be alone in here, for a few minutes?"

"Hmmph," complained the agent, "Against protocol for this area, or her, to be unaccompanied... but as you're with the Big Man's personal team, I'll let you away with it this time, sir. All the systems are locked down – don't be touching anything on the control-panels or inside the desk, you hear? Doing so's a felony, and I'm afraid I couldn't –"

"Oh, you needn't worry 'bout anything like *that*," reassured the Spiritual Adviser, with a thin smile. "Ms. Chu and I, we're just gonna have a little *talk*... that's all. Isn't that right, Ms. Chu?"

"Beats talking to myself, all day," replied the former team-leader, with a bored shrug. "Though I have no idea what you'd have to say, that would be of any interest to me. *Sir.*"

"Well... we'll *see* about that," he countered, with another insincere smile.

"Fine," grunted the Secret Service agent. "Twenty minutes?"

"Should be enough," agreed Brother Harold.

"Okay then," said the agent, as he went for the doorway. "Opportunity to go forward and snitch some *real* coffee, as opposed to the instant shit we get out of the port-a-brewer back here. See you in twenty."

With that, he exited, closing the door behind him.

"Mind if I take a seat?" said the smiling Spiritual Adviser.

"Can't stop you," replied Chu. "Matter of fact... seems I can't do much of *anything*, these days."

"Oh... I wouldn't say *that*," he stated, while draping himself across a seat that was uncomfortably close to Chu's own, artificial prison-chair.

In a minor breach of the rules, he put his feet up on a third seat, turned and looked the team-leader right in the eyes and said,

"In the interests of time, I'll get right to the point... okay, *almost* right to the point."

"Yeah?" she said, with a dismissive shrug.

"I'd like to ask you, Ms. Chu," he inquired, "Why you think you're still on-board this-here airplane... after that little, uhh, *incident*, that you had with the President? Ever been wonderin' about that?"

"As a matter of fact, I *have*, sir," politely responded the team-leader. "I was expecting to have been dropped off on our next landing, then taken to some holding-facility. I was quite surprised when that didn't happen, particularly the second time. I can only assume it's because we weren't near enough to a suitable jail. Oh well. Doesn't matter much to me... only a matter of time, I suppose."

"Got nothin' to do with that," disputed Brother Harold. "And you're wrong on both – no, 'scuse me, three – counts."

"How would that *be*, sir?" bemusedly spoke Chu. "Three? Not following you."

"Well, first," he replied, "You ain't gettin' off this plane. Second... the *reason* you ain't, is because I had to pull some strings with some pretty important folks up front – I think you know who I'm talkin' about – to make that happen. I s'pose I shouldn't be tellin' you this, but, there was a *real* lively discussion 'bout all of it, up in the executive suite. As a result of that, we seem to have lost dear old Mr. Bezomorton from the President's team; he was sent away as of our last brief landin'. I'm sure he'll be well looked-after, of course."

Immediately, Chu's interest-level – along with her warning-senses – began to surge.

"Want to know what the third one is?" he teased.

"Sure... yeah," stammered the more-than-a-woman.

Brother Harold leaned forward, with the faintly-alcohol-besodden scent of his breath unappealingly-evident to Chu's nose, and whispered,

"I know what you *are*... little Ms. *half-alien*, slave of the Devil-Girl... I've known it all along! Gotta give you credit – that's quite an act you've pulled on the rest of 'em up here... but you don't fool *me!*"

He's bluffing, thought the former FBI team-leader.

He can't *know... can* he?

Wait a minute... she told me, 'when peril is near, you shall know of it'... right? That's got to be why the hairs on the back of my neck are standing up straight!

Shit... but how could *he... not important, now.*

What the hell does he want, *anyway?*

Trying to keep a poker-face, Chu answered, "Oh, for God's sake... sorry, forgot you're a man of the cloth. Look, sir... we've already been over that idea and talked it to death, several times now, but since I've got nothing better to do except sit here and watch the clouds go by, let me humor you for now – let's say you're right about me. If I'm some super-duper follower of Karéin-Mayréij – given her well-known antagonism with the President, and all the rest of it... why on *Earth* do you think I'd let myself get stuck in this bloody chair, for days on end, when I'm close enough to the Big Man to, uhh, 'end the whole thing', all by myself? I bet I'd go right to the head of the devil-worshiping first-grade class... I'd get enough alien Brownie Points for the best of her Martian merit-badges."

She let out a mock-contemptuous laugh; unfortunately, the Spiritual Adviser did not seem to be deterred by it. His purposeful stare still had Chu, mightily worried.

"You and I both know that's a lie!" persisted Brother Harold. "I got no idea about what perverse things she did to you – and I don't care. It ain't important, whether or not you admit to what you are... if it means anythin', if I were you, I'd do that, down on your knees, prayin' to the Lord, real soon... might save you an eternity in the warm place, you know. Just in case your time of reckonin' might be a little sooner than you anticipate."

"We all have our personal belief systems, sir," offered Chu. "Mine probably differs somewhat from your own. And as for how this government deals with 'traitors' – real or imagined – I'm very well-aware of that. Like how it probably dealt with my two fellow-agents, Will Hendricks and Otis Boatman. May they rest in peace..."

"Like I said... not important," went on the Christian leader. "Any of all that. Want to know what *is* important, Ms. Chu?"

"Since we're talking speculatively... sure," she responded, with a *faux*-smile.

"So," he explained, in a cold, flat voice, "Here's how it is. Very soon, Ms. Chu, this-here airplane's comin' down... and I don't mean, in a nice, three-point landin'. A lot of folks – a *real* lot of 'em, almost all with no foreknowledge of what will be goin' on – will meet their Maker, at that point. And you're the only person on this Earth, who can stop it."

Chu's mind was reeling from the shrieking warnings of the alien danger-sense, as she mumbled,

"If this is a joke, sir – it's not funny! I mean... you can't be *serious*... right? What are you *talking* about? And if, God help us all, you *are* serious... why would you tell *me* about it, instead of the President?"

"It's no joke, and I won't go into details, beyond what I've already said," he answered, in the same, smoothly-controlled, detached manner. "But on your last point... see, here's how it is. I know a *lot* about you, Ms. Chu – I've had special access to some, shall we say, 'privileged' information, and I know, for example, that if you want her to, the Devil-Girl *will* show up here... come to your rescue, that is. Get her to do that, and we'll take it from there."

"What the *hell* – and yes, *sir*, I *do* mean to use that word – is *that* supposed to mean?" angrily retorted Chu. "How would Karéin, you and I, 'take it', anywhere?"

I call upon the power, she furiously pondered.

Fire, tell me if he's on the level – tell me what to do!

A burst of ideas, from she knew not where, popped into her head.

Yes.

More to it than he says.

Up to you.

Thanks a fucking lot! she mentally replied, with her face twisted in a grimace.

"Okay – *okay!*" desperately exclaimed Chu, her mind racing near-out-of-control. "I'll make you a *deal!*"

"I don't do, 'deals', Ms. Chu," smirked the Christian man. "'Specially not with me bein' where I am, and you bein' where you're at. But just to be polite... what you have in mind?"

"If I level with you – if I tell you the truth, the *real* truth," she stammered, "And if I keep your, uhh, 'secret', which I have a duty *not* to do, but anyway – I need your assurance that it'll stay between you and me."

"That's not much of a 'deal', considerin' that anythin' you say, is gonna be laughed off as some kind of pathetic attempt to get attention and save you from what's likely to be an unpleasant trip to a jail, maybe a firin'-squad," he answered. "But... why not? Sure... you keep up your part of the bargain, and I'll keep mine. You have my word as a man of God, that I won't repeat what you tell me, to anybody outside this room."

She looked him over, once more.

He'll probably just run right to the Agency and turn me in, the minute that he's got a confession out of me... but... so be it.

The last glance that I take of this aircraft, as they take me away from it... I'll make sure that it's a mean one.

I'll pour every last ounce of Amaiish in my body, into it.

Hope you've got a laser-proof parachute, Mr. President.

"You want the *truth*, Mr. Crowford?" defiantly stated Minnie Chu. "Okay... here it is : congratulations – you got it in one. Am I a 'follower' of Karéin-Mayréij? You bet your *ass* I am, sir – more than that; in fact... I'm in *love* with her, she's in love with me too... and no, it's *not* Platonic."

The Spiritual Adviser's countenance darkened, and, while shaking his head, he remarked, "Mortal sin, on two counts : 'homosexual perversion of the flesh', and 'doin' it with a beast'... no, three. 'Doin' it with the spawn of the Devil', as well. You *do* know where you're goin', when you leave this world... don't you?"

"Well, sir, if it's of any consolation, we've *never* 'done it'... not yet, anyway," countered Chu. "Since I met Karéin, things have been rather 'hectic', and we haven't had a private moment; although when this is all over, I *plan* to, the first chance I get. There might be a few, uhh, *complications* there, considering that I'm getting married, and considering that she also has a boyfriend – this 'Bob Billings' fellow – and honestly, I've grown quite fond of him, too –"

"Nice try, distractin' me from the main issue, by paradin' all your sinful plans for promiscuity of whatever sort," he interrupted. "Now tell me about this 'alien' stuff – how it works, and what you can do. I need to know *all* of it... or else, I walk out of here and tell the President to have you shot. Got that?"

"Sir," prevaricated the former team-leader, "If I had alien-powers equivalent to those of, say, Sam Jacobson, or even Melissa Claremont... what do you think the chances are, of both you and the President, still being alive? But I promised you the truth, and you'll have it. You got a pen?"

"Yeah... here," replied the Christian man, producing a cheap gel-point.

"Put it on that notepad, on the mini-table, here... the one in front of me," she directed.

"Okay," he said, depositing the writing-instrument according to her instructions.

"Watch," suggested Chu.

Using a small fraction of her telekinesis – as little as possible, so that neither her war-song, nor the other outward manifestations of the *Fire*, would show – she made the pen position its sharp end on top of the paper. With careful concentration, Chu moved the writing-instrument back and forth, spelling "P E A C E O N E A R T H" in child-like, large, non-cursive lettering.

"See?" she offered. "*That's* what I can do. Satisfied, now, sir?"

"Oh my sweet *Lord*," he gasped. "Then... it *is* true..."

"These 'alien' abilities aren't all they're cracked up to be, I guess," disingenuously claimed the former team-leader. "When you hang around with the Storied Watcher, one person will get a smattering of it... the next will get the whole nine yards, and there's no predicting how or why. As for *me*, well, I suppose I've got enough of it to sign off on my death-warrant, without having to use my hands. Bully for *me*... right?"

"But you *can* call for her," pressed the Spiritual Adviser. "Don't lie about it. I *know* you can!"

"Sir... you *must* be aware," slowly observed Chu, "That if she shows up here... she very well might slice you in half, on account of having threatened me? To say nothing of what she's likely to do to the President, and perhaps half the others on board this aircraft. Why on *Earth* would you want to risk something like that?"

"That, Ms. Chu," he answered, with his composure rapidly returning, "Is for me to know... and for you not to worry about."

What's his game? she silently pondered.

Is he working with the President, to lay a trap for her?

Wait a minute... that makes no sense, either – they have to know that however many fighter-planes they've got keeping formation out there, they won't stand a chance against Karéin-Mayréij.

Maybe he's suicidal? Could be... a lot of these religious nuts are that way.

Or maybe he secretly believes in her, and wants to fall at her feet and worship?

Minnie, you've got to get inside his head – use the 'look' on him, no, not that one for God's sake, the other one – and make him spill the beans, find out what the hell's really going on, here... if not now, then... when?

Here goes...

Chu reached into the recesses of her recent memory, calling on the sequence of thoughts that she knew would energize the 'mind-fuck' thing; but as she was about to press home her attack, the Christian man flinched, rose rapidly from his chair, and angrily accosted her.

"What was *that?*" he exclaimed, shaking his finger at the more-than-a-woman.

Her own head in a momentary daze, Chu did her best (and, half-sincere) imitation of being genuinely startled. She answered, "What was... *what*, sir?"

"You *know* what I'm talkin' about!" he barked. "Some darn thought in my head – not my own –"

"Very sorry about that," hastily dissembled the team-leader. "Sir, I forgot to explain... some of the, uhh, 'arts' that the Storied Watcher gave us, seem to be latent – that is, we don't even know that we *have* them. It's possible that this was one of them... I was trying to remember how to call out to her. Are you okay?"

"I'm... fine," uneasily stated the Spiritual Adviser. "Now you listen, because I've heard, and felt, more than enough of this devil-stuff, for one day... one *lifetime*, in fact. The deal is, you get her here, and you give me an hour's warning of when she's going to show... in exchange for that, I'll make sure that you keep those pretty little lungs breathin', all the while. Speak one *word* of what we've been discussin' here today, to anyone 'cept myself, and my next call's to the head of the Agency – with whom, incidentally, I've lately formed quite a good workin' relationship – and I don't have to tell you what happens, if you end up in *his* tender care. You understand, Ms. Chu?"

"But *sir*," she pleaded, "I'll do my best to call her, but I can't promise five minutes' worth of warning, let alone an hour's-worth –"

"Just *do* it," he growled. "Unless you'd like to join your two former Bureau friends. Did I mention what happened to them, by the way?"

"No," quietly replied Chu.

"Seems they got pushed out the back cargo-door, and somebody forgot to give them boys a parachute," remarked Brother Harold. "But it wasn't *all* bad."

"What do you... *mean*, sir?" said the team-leader, with distress all over her face as waves of heartache beset her.

"I heard that this 'Boatman' fella was a Christian, and he would've had ten thousand feet in which to say his prayers," observed the Spiritual Adviser. "Better than a quick bullet in the head with no warnin', I reckon."

With tears streaming down her cheeks, she stared blankly at him for two or three seconds, then whispered, "I'd like to be alone, if you don't mind."

"Alright," he said, walking out the door.

Down the corridor a bit, she heard him saying to some unseen third party, "I tell you... *women*. There's a *reason* why the Good Book tells 'em to obey their husbands, you know... she's still in there, bawlin' her eyes out."

And on one count, at least, he was right; because a grief-stricken Minnie Chu, was doing exactly that.

Farmer Jones, You've Just Met One

Despite her otherwise formidable skills (both mundane and sublime), Cherie Tanaka was anything *but* used to driving a vehicle like the one she had just stolen from the Agency; as a result of this, when she took the black, partly-armored SUV off the road, it almost keeled over on its side upon hitting a divot in the usually-arid Texas turf.

That – and the rattlesnake that made its presence scant yards away uncomfortably evident, shortly after the former Mars mission science officer stepped out of the driver's-seat – was enough to convince her that this stop-over had better be an abbreviated one.

With the percussive *thump-thump-thump* sounds of explosions, coming from some as-yet-unknown battle somewhere off to the east, she hurried over to the side of the vehicle. Unfortunately, this – like the reinforced steel partition between the driver's-compartment and the rear holding-area – securely sealed shut. The same turned out to be true for the rear doors.

Shit, she angrily considered. *I could easily blast the damn thing right off... but who knows what might happen to the prisoners on the other side.*

But maybe if I just use a little of it, say on the hinges and the handle – isn't that how an arc-welder works, after all –

Door to force body stick iron my be open, came a small voice, speaking into the back of her mind.

Okay, Little One, mentally replied the former Mars Science Officer, *give me a crowbar –*

At that moment, Tanaka was forced to pay attention to something startlingly-different; in the first instant, she perceived the grinding, clanging, guitar-rock sound of the bounty-hunter's war-song, and then – encased in a meteor of smoke-trailing flame – he streaked over Texas State Route 195, about 100 feet above the highway, heading due north. About three seconds later, came the ominous turbine-infused roar of military jet engines, apparently headed in the same direction.

Damn, damn, damn! pondered the former Mars mission science officer. *Why couldn't he just have –*

Oh, forget it... we had a deal, after all... Jacobsons, I pray you'll be safe!

Vîrya Sài'ymë – we fly to the rescue of our brother... full power!

Tanaka felt the thrill of the *Fire* excite every nerve and sensory-system in her body, as, with her eyes glowing, her trunk protected by an ethereal breast-plate, her entire being protected by her "bubble" force-field and her exciting, inspiring psycho-music urging her on, she rocketed upward in the direction of the overhead commotion.

She didn't have to wait long to be in the proverbial "thick of it"; the nature of the battle was instantly evident.

Wolf – who was being pursued by four single-engined fighter-planes (older ones, apparently without much stealth ability) – had executed a tight turn-and-climb maneuver, which put him on a collision-course with a bad weather front, that was approaching from the western horizon. But the bounty-hunter's airspeed wasn't up to that of his assailants, who were closing the distance rapidly, with their auto-cannons firing intermittent bursts.

Okay, fuckers, thought the more-than-a-woman, *maybe I'll just take out the two of you on the flanks, leave the rest for Mister Hot-Head to deal with...*

But her plans were interrupted by *Vîrya Sài'ymë*, whose child-like, alien-yet-endearing voice warned,

Behind from us more evil two chariots-air mother valiant!

Uh-oh – downward at tree-top-height, to the east, Little One – let's at least lead them away from Wolf!

So – although she had been pulling over a dozen positive Gs and was therefore climbing rapidly – Tanaka did a very rapid course-change of her own and dove toward the ground.

The living-armor's little voice again called out an alarm.

Arrows-war, us behind!

The former Mars mission science officer's *Fire*-song echoed across the central Texas plain, as she poured energy into her protective bubble and momentarily turned to face dead-astern, while continuing to hurtle forward, to the east. She unleashed a sweeping, conical spread-pattern of lightening-bolts, at anything and everything behind her.

The maneuver was effective; one fighter-plane, and two missiles, were struck by her attack, with the latter exploding immediately and knocking two more AAMs out of the sky.

Suddenly, to the west, the sky lit up with a series of brilliant, orange-red flashes.

Go get 'em, Wolf, she mused.

The second fighter-plane found a way to quickly recapture Tanaka's attention, as it unleashed a fusillade of auto-cannon-shells accompanied by yet another missile. Most of these were aimed high, but three or four of them struck home near the top of her protective "bubble", and a half-second later, there was a powerful warhead-explosion, coming from the same direction. The impact was considerable, and though no shrapnel penetrated, the former Mars science officer was flying so low that – driven downward by the shell-strikes – she clipped the tree-tops, thereby being sent careening, arse-over-teakettle-style, toward the ground.

She caught a glimpse of an unpaved driveway passing underneath, hit the gravel at hundreds of miles per hour, bounced back upward over a side-road, smashed through more trees and, while desperately trying to regain control, saw a large building looming right in her trajectory. *Amaiish*-enhanced senses and reflexes were of no use, here; there was no time to avoid it, and she struck dead-on.

There were the sounds of splintering wood, shattering glass and structural destruction of various other, confusing types. Marveling at the fact that, though shaken, she was apparently otherwise unhurt, Tanaka managed to apply enough braking-thrust to sort of stabilize herself and finally stop altogether, albeit in a half-prone position.

As she cautiously dropped enough of her protective shield to allow sound-waves through, the more-than-a-woman righted herself and took stock of her situation.

What's that smell? pondered Tanaka.

Oh... shit, she realized. That's *what it is. In both senses of the word...*

She was standing what was left of a chicken-coop, looking at the western face of a barn, through which she had smashed a jagged, charred hole at least ten feet wide. To her relief, her dramatic entrance had not resulted in fatal damage to any of the residents, though several of them did seem to be nursing feathers both ruffled and singed.

The former science officer looked around.

Mooo, came the call, from the left-hand side of the building.

You're damn lucky I didn't hit over there, Bluebell, Babs, or whatever they call you – or there'd be hamburger on the menu tonight –

Burger inform what Mother ham this is wise inform thee please?

Later, little one, mentally replied the more-than-a-woman. *But something that if you're a cow, you aspire not to be...*

Voices were coming from outside.

"Ah think it's in th' barn, Billy!" shouted a male one. "Lookee there – done busted right through – damn! Git mah gun!"

"No need for that!" she quickly exclaimed, in reply. "Just one of me, in here! I'm coming out – no shooting!"

Tanaka suppressed as much of the *Fire* as she dared to, considering that she was still in a combat-zone. She used her arts to float over the chicken-enclosure, while avoiding getting any more of the crap on her shoes, and approached the barn-door, which unfortunately appeared to be locked from the outside.

"Could one of you please let me out?" she implored.

"Who the hell's 'you'?" came back one of the male voices.

"Sounds like a woman," observed another, younger-sounding one.

"Yeah, I'm female," remarked Tanaka. "And if you don't let me out, right now, I'll bust out on my own, and in that case, you'd better get your arses about a mile away from here, before the Air Force –"

There were sounds of an old-fashioned key being used to decouple a lock, along with a warning to "not try nothin'".

The barn-doors swing open, revealing a wizened, elderly, Stetson-hatted Texas farmer standing out in a barnyard, while a younger man – probably a son – pointed a shotgun at the former Mars science officer.

"Who the hell are *you?*" the man asked.

"Ever seen a super-heroine, sir?" amicably replied Tanaka.

"What's *that* got to do with anythin'?" he grumbled. "And... of *course* I ain't... because there ain't no such thing."

"Oh yes, there *is*," purred Cherie Tanaka, First Of The *Fire*, as – to the astonishment of the two rural Texas men, her "bubble" re-constituted itself, her eyes began to glow and her war-song's exotic beat began to enervate human and more-than-human psyches, alike.

"There *is* at least one," sang Tanaka, "Her name is 'Thunderchild'. And you've just *met* her," she added, a half-second before she again soared into the Texas night sky.

Every Place Has A Back-Door

As the convoy – with a purloined airport-limousine (this, the product of a tripartite scam : Kaysten's fast-talking as a distraction, some locking-system-jamming on the part of *Vîrya I'ëà'b*' and illusions, courtesy of Sylvia Abruzzio), in the lead, with Sullivan's vehicle following close behind – turned south-east within Dupont Circle, the ex-President remarked from the black-painted luxury-car, "Never thought I'd see D.C. again... and I sure didn't imagine seeing it, like *this.*"

The streets of downtown Washington, though they did accommodate some foot-traffic, seemed unusually barren of pedestrians, food-carts, vendors and general population, compared to what would normally have been the case. As the two vehicles approached the vicinity of the White House, there were grim reminders of battles only recently-past : there were broken windows on some buildings, and the upper floors of several displayed hastily papered-over scars of impacts by errant missiles and by heavy-caliber gunfire.

Evidently, nobody had yet figured out how to get the huge top of the Washington Monument, out of the White House lawn; there it remained, a mute testament to battles lost.

Kaysten, who was in the driver's-seat and who had somehow snatched a chauffeur's-cap to look the part, grinned as he responded, "Makes two of us, sir... believe me, there were times down there in L.A. – or should I say, up *over* L.A. – when I thought I wasn't going to see this town, or *anything*, ever again."

"Yeah," morosely grumbled the former U.S. leader. "Listen, Jerry," he asked, "Sylvia tell you about how she plans to actually get us *in* there?"

"Sort of," answered the ex-Chief of Staff, with an insouciant shrug.

"Well, that's not much of a plan, you know," complained the First Lady.

All this got in return, was another shrug, on Kaysten's part.

"She's supposed to be, like, 'alien-smart', second only to Her Comet-Smashing Highness, that is," he offered. "Sure hope that's true."

They turned due south. The ex-President asked, "Where are we now?"

"Going down 17th," said Kaysten. "Eisenhower building – the tunnel in the basement, emerg egress from the White House... remember?"

"Clark, this is a *crazy* idea," complained the former First Lady. "Didn't they say in those the briefings we got when we first arrived here, that it's sealed shut?"

"Yeah," confirmed the ex-President, his eyes never leaving a continuous scan of the streets and surroundings, "That, it certainly *is*. Reinforced concrete, in fact – Secret Service has to set of a bursting charge, to blow it outward..."

"Well, then?" persisted the wife.

"You haven't seen 'Daughter Tornado Diamond-Curtain' at work, Ma'am," cheerily riposted Kaysten. "Little bugger could saw through a *mountain*, if she put her mind to it."

The former First Lady sighed, rolled her eyes, folded her arms in front and settled back into her seat, while her two children beamed wide-eyed excitement.

"I'm sure that between *Vîrya I'ëà'b'* and Sylvia's 'now-you-see-'em, now-you-don't' stuff, we can get into the building through the provisioning-dock entrance and down into the basement... she thinks that she can knock out the intrusion-detection circuits, guess we'll have to take her word for that... but what about the guards, sir?" asked the former Chief of Staff. "Supposed to be one from the Service and one Marine, at least, on duty at all times..."

"Leave *that* one to me," replied the ex-President. "Either I convince them, or I don't. Oh, and none of those alien-bafflegab tricks of yours, if we run into them, if you don't mind, Jerry. It wears off after a while, anyway... isn't that right?"

"Honestly don't know, Mr. President," evaded Kaysten. "Just because I'm using it, don't assume I know how the H it really *works*... when we were up at that campsite, she tried to explain the theory behind it, but I kind of got lost after the first two minutes, you know?"

There was a giggle from the daughter, as her father looked to his left. The elaborate, French Second Empire edifice of the Eisenhower Executive Office Building, loomed ahead.

"There we go – pull up right in there, side-entrance driveway, don't go to the main stairway – good... like I suspected, they're short-staffed, must have pulled most of the Service and guard duties back to George's homes away from home," directed the former President. "Be careful – the fact that we drove here in a limo probably got us past the curfew-checkers, but they might not be so easy on somebody who's just walking around on the street."

Ever playing the part of professional chauffeur, Kaysten slowed the car, signaled for a left-hand turn and then gently brought the vehicle up into a short driveway leading to the north-west corner of the Eisenhower Building, stopping short of the guard-post further up the driveway, closer to the building-walls. Sullivan's car followed behind and came to a stop behind the limousine.

The ex-President momentarily closed his eyes, then stared straight ahead, upon re-opening them.

"You know," he ruefully muttered, "I had figured that the next time I got to Washington, my biggest challenge was going to be having to deal with the *Democrats.*"

Private First Class Homer Maloney, U.S. National Guard Reserve, yawned, checked for stubble on his sallow, nineteen-year-old cheeks – sadly, there was none – and leaned back in what passed for a reclining-chair, in the Security Office on the first floor of the Eisenhower Executive Office Building.

He unwrapped another candy-bar, reminded himself about the diet, and promptly ignored the advice. But at least his aim was true, when he chucked the wrapper into the trash-bin; this was no mean feat, considering that the thing was already well over full.

Since the tourists had all but stopped coming, after the 'excitement' of a few weeks past (secretly, he wished that he'd been at his post for *that* undoubtedly historic event, but, truth be told, he only narrowly missed being called out for AWOL, after a two-day drunk in Bethesda), as well as the more recent after-dark curfew, the job had ended up being even more boring than it had previously been.

The current ennui-level *had* to be some kind of a record, as his duties, even in those halcyon days, consisted largely of filling out paperwork which the computer system somehow "lost", patrolling empty corridors and occasionally standing for hours on aching feet, when the Rent-A-Cops at the front entrance ticket-booth, failed to show up for duty.

Wish they hadn't kicked all the girls out of this unit, he morosely reflected.

Like that Monita from the Silver Spring barracks... big hips and not so hot to trot, but I could have worked on her, what with nothing else to do, hours, days, weeks on end, stuck in this miserable rat-hole.

Now, all I got is the porno Ultra-Ray video discs, and I already watched all of 'em... six times each, or more.

I hate this job.

He had almost completely dozed off, when, out of one barely-opened eyelid, he noticed that one of the status lights on the building perimeter control console, had changed from its usual "everything is peachy" green, to the orange color that – or so his perfunctory, one-hour training course upon being assigned this duty, had instructed – indicated "data loop failure".

Back to sleep, he resolved, and again shut his eyes.

After a few seconds, however, a warning thought got Maloney up again.

Didn't Sarge say something about, "two weeks without pay, if you don't clear those status lights in twenty minutes"? he pondered.

Shit.

Where's this one, again?

He took a closer look at the status panel.

Basement Lower Level 3-D, Corridor 15, East Side... what the fuck?

There's nothing *down there... haven't checked it in two months, and last time I did, about a third of the lights were out, some fucking SNAFU about "item too old to be sourced through requisition, gotta special order"... ah, fuck it, let's get down there, visual inspect... wait a minute... what if the fucker's really shot? I don't know shit about how to fix it, and all the electricians are over at the White House, wiring things back up... fuck!*

Okay, wait *a minute... what about that GrayWar guy, the one up in Records? He said he did electrical, before the second Pakistan thing went down and the Army had to back-fill with the mercs.*

Bit of a dick... but best bet I've got.

He hit a button and a few keys on his mobile communicator.

"Rizzo?" said the private. "Yeah, it's me... what? You know, Maloney, down in the Security Office. Oh, come *on*, man, you remember me – you know, scored you that synth, two months ago?"

A reluctant acknowledgment came back, from the other end.

"Listen, man," continued Maloney, "Got a job for you – meet me in the basement, five minutes from now... okay?"

An irritated Maloney had already been waiting at least an extra minute, maybe two, by the time that the other man – a pudgy, pock-marked Italian-American guy in his mid-40s with curly hair and a half-week beard, wearing only part of his regular GrayWar Legion uniform, finally showed up and got off the elevator. He was carrying a tool-chest and had a wide leather belt with various types of screwdrivers, crimping tools and other similar gear, arrayed upon it.

They were in a nondescript basement corridor, several levels under a point just north of the Vice-President's Ceremonial Office, that could accommodate perhaps two grown men walking side-by-side. In better times, the walls, ceilings and especially the floors, would have been kept spic-'n-span, but standards had obviously not lately been obeyed : many of the overhead florescent lights were either flickering or out entirely, and even in this less-than-brilliant illumination, as they stepped forward, they could see faint footprints in the dust that lay all over the floor.

"You call the Service?" asked the GrayWar guy.

"No, I didn't call the *Service*," peevishly replied Maloney. "No point – there's only a few of them left here in D.C., and they're all spoken for, last I heard, from higher up. Besides, if I called them for every goddamn alert I get on the panel, they'd have to pitch a sleeping-tent here. That thing's a piece of shit, it's always acting up... *you* know that."

"Yeah," agreed Rizzo. "How about the Marines? Protocol, you know."

"No fucking *way*," said the private. "Called them on a bomb scare just after I got stuck on this stupid assignment, they got pissed that it was a false alarm like the twenty others, grabbed me, stripped off my pants and threw them over the fence... had to fetch them in front of the tourists. Ain't *happenin'*, dude."

"Well, can't blame you for *that*," concurred Rizzo. "Hey – this fuckin' place looks like it ain't been swept in, like, six years," he unhelpfully added.

"What'd you *expect*, with ninety per cent of everyone being sent overseas, or off to do, I don't know what?" replied Maloney. "Anyway... don't tell Sarge, or he'll have me down here cleaning up from now to Doomsday."

"What's it worth to ya?" maliciously answered the other man.

"Easy... I don't tell nobody about all that blow you got in the locker, upstairs," countered the private.

"Deal... I guess," snorted Rizzo. "Come on... let's get this bullshit *over* with – All-Star Wrestlin's on, over Neo, in twenty, and my favorite, 'Ball-

Crusher Bill', he's takin' on all comers. You see what he did to that nigger, 'Pimp King Paul', last week? He's singin' three pitches higher up the scale –"

"Think you can fix the fucker, in that amount of time?" interrupted Maloney, as they proceeded down the corridor, heading southward underneath the east side of the Eisenhower Building.

"Depends," explained the GrayWar guy. "If it's just the relays that are shot, that's easy... I'll just clean 'em up, usually it's corrosion that gets 'em, no biggie. If a wire's shorted out in the wall, then you can call in the crew and get *them* to deal with it – I only do the simple stuff, for what they're payin' me – *whoa–*"

Involuntarily, both men came to a rapid stop, raising their flash-lights as they surveyed the scene that confronted them, about twenty feet further south, down the corridor. At that point, the left-hand wall appeared to have simply been removed; about an inch up from the floor and down from the ceiling, extending to a width of about five feet, there was a dark hole, leading eastward to who-knows-where. There was a spall of what looked like dried dirt, at least a half-foot in height, all over the corridor-floor, right in front of the opening.

"What the *fuck?*" breathed Maloney. "The damn thing just... *collapsed?*"

"*Looks* that way," agreed Rizzo. "Except for how straight those edges are... funny. Better check it out, don't you think?"

"Well, yeah," said the private. "But HQ is gonna throw a shit-fit over this, I can tell you."

"You first," suggested the merc.

Maloney surveyed the breach, with a sense of trepidation gnawing at his consciousness. He used the flashlight to illuminate the wall-sides just inside the hole, and was disturbed to see that not only had at least a foot of solid concrete wall been, well, simply sliced as cleanly-flat as your best high-end kitchen-countertop – and more foreboding still, the opening did not end immediately; instead, it continued into the blackness beyond, past where his unaided eyes could see without good light.

"Jesus," he inveighed. "I dunno about this, man... it's like somebody's building a fuckin' *tunnel* – and that's the direction of the White House, isn't it –"

"Yeah," confirmed the other man, as the two stepped gingerly into the breach.

"Hold on – need the light, I'll shine it down there –" requested Maloney, after only a couple of steps into the tenebrous beyond.

"Shut up," demanded Rizzo. "Think I *hear* somethin' –"

After a few seconds of concentration, the private realized that the other man was right.

There was a weird, buzzing, whirring sound coming from a distance that had to be fifty to a hundred feet down the tunnel. Every five seconds or so, this was supplemented by the noise of something being dumped, and Maloney also thought that he heard subdued human voices, in the direction of the other sounds.

Whispering over his shoulder, the GrayWar guy warned, "This's *gotta* be terrorists, or some shit like that – we'd better get our asses out of here, go get reinforcements –"

"That wouldn't be a good idea," came a firm-but-pleasant, woman's voice, from out in the corridor, behind them. "Would you mind coming back out here, so we can have a quick chat, gentlemen? Oh... and keep those guns down, if you don't mind. Raise them, or raise an alarm, and I'm afraid I'll have to kill you."

"What the *fuck*," cursed Maloney, under his breath. "Rizzo – you see anybody back there?"

"Back... where?" stammered the bewildered mercenary. "No, for fuck's *sake* – there's nobody there!"

"I heard that – and you're hurting my *feelings*, calling me 'nobody', you know," remarked the female voice, which seemed to be coming from behind and to the right of the two hapless soldiers. "I went to way too many high-school dances, being called that. Would you do me the courtesy of getting your asses back here, please? I don't have all *day*."

"What should we *do*, man?" cringed Maloney.

"What she says, I guess," shrugged Rizzo. "They got us in a cross-fire... probably, like, twenty of 'em with them night-sights further down this tunnel, with a bead on us already."

He turned and called out, in the direction of the corridor, "We got to put our hands up, or something?"

"Oh, no," reassured the woman's-voice, "That won't be necessary – just keep them away from those guns, please. Now... come on! Time's a-wasting!"

Blanching, the private reversed course and took a tentative step toward the breach.

Fearing this moment would be his last, he stuck his head out of the opening and carefully surveyed the area that they had just come from.

"Psst – *Rizzo!*" he whispered. "There's fuckin' *nobody* out there –"

"This 'nobody' thing's getting quite annoying," complained the female voice, which was – as Maloney could now see beyond any doubt – was originating from a section of the corridor, outside and to his left, that was utterly devoid of human habitation.

It was like he was hearing some unseen ventriloquist.

"Keep the hands away from the guns," repeated the voice; and what the private saw next, had his jaw dropping in astonishment.

The corridor-wall seemed to slowly dissolve, sort of like the fade-out effect caused by a computer slide-show presentation.

After perhaps a half-second, it revealed an average-sized, reasonably (but not overly) attractive-looking, young-middle-aged, flat-bosomed, olive-skinned Caucasian woman with curly black hair. She was wearing a conservative, mid-length, dark-green skirt and Ludlow blazer, a tan shirt of some kind, standard panty-hose and flat, casual shoes.

Except for an odd twinkle in her eyes, she was exactly the sedate, plain kind of person that you'd expect to see in a university librarian.

By now, Rizzo had also crowded into the opening between the corridor and the tunnel.

"How'd... how'd you *do* that, lady?" stuttered an incredulous Maloney.

"She ain't got no gun," whispered the mercenary, into the private's one ear.

"Well, gentlemen," replied the newcomer, "As to your question... let's just say, 'it's all done with mirrors', kind of thing. Oh... and I *heard* that, Mister GrayWar Person. Thing is, firearms are *so* 'last-century'... you know? Especially when one can cripple or kill with just a *thought*. But full disclosure, here – I'll do my level best not to unleash my own power on you; because, although you'd be instantly incapacitated by the radiation, it'd likely take you a few minutes more to actually die. All that flesh melting off your bones and your blood flowing out of every body-orifice... messy, *messy!* I think having your heads instantly sliced off, would be *much* easier... wouldn't you say?"

"That ain't funny, lady," nervously bluffed Rizzo. "You ain't got no –"

"Is that right?" calmly replied the strange woman. "Why don't you try moving your feet forward, toward me? See how that works out for you."

Where's that funky pop-rock music, coming from? wondered Maloney.

But he had other things to worry about. Though he could easily move his feet back and forth within his boots, and could otherwise bend and twist to his heart's content, the boots themselves felt like they were welded to the floor.

A quick look at the mercenary's face revealed that Rizzo was in similar straights.

And a return-glance at the woman's own visage showed that her eyes were... *glowing*, like two miniature, multi-colored kaleidoscopes.

"Let you in on a *secret*, boys," she taunted. "You're close enough, and weak-willed enough, that I can easily lock on to your clothes and gear... not to mention your guns. You couldn't lift and fire them if you *tried!*"

Reflexively, Rizzo tried to do just that; but the stranger's admonition, wasn't an idle one. Not only couldn't he get his sidearm out of its holster, but it felt like the damn quick-release catch that secured the holster's retaining-flap, was glued shut.

"So," continued the bizarre, rainbow-eyed intruder, "You're not going *anywhere* – that is, if I don't want you to... and on top of that, you've managed to stumble on the most important impromptu Washington tourist-expedition, in history. That's a *problem*, unfortunately."

"Got no idea what you're talking about, lady," protested Maloney. "And we got *orders* about what to do when there's, like, an incident, you know. Right from the government, that is!"

"Well," offered the woman, with a wry smile, "Don't I just know all *about* 'orders' and 'incidents', involving the 'government', now. Matter of fact, getting the 'orders' straight – from the right 'government', that is... that's sort of what this whole thing is about."

"So what the hell you want us to *do*, anyway?" interjected Rizzo.

"Why don't you just relax for a second, and listen to what I've got to say," requested the librarian-lady. "See... I've got a little 'proposition' for you."

Texas Shootin'-Gallery

To Cherie Tanaka's dismay, as she had just begun to gather speed in her zoom-climb over the central Texas plains, a second flurry of loud, fireball-like explosions appeared off in the distance, just ahead of the incoming cold-front. The roaring sound was akin to – but different from – the thunder that was rolling in, along with the darkening western clouds.

Accepting the risk of an undetected attack, she hovered at an altitude of about a thousand feet and directed both her own sensory-abilities, and those of *Vîrya Sài'ymë*, to a carefully-focused survey of the far west.

There was no sign of the bounty-hunter; but – ominously – Tanaka could see the heat-signatures of at least two fighter-planes, as they exited the battle-area to the north-east, seemingly of their own accord.

It was difficult to see because of the failing natural light and the worsening climate, but she thought that she detected a pall of smoke over the distant battlefield.

They get him? worriedly mused the former science officer.

I don't hear his war-song... but that might just be a 'out-of-range' thing...

Well, I had better go and tend to the Jacobsons –

Is but Fire of One the kin ours, came the child-like voice of the living-armor.

So are they, honey! sent Tanaka.

Is hurt he, argued *Vîrya Sài'ymë*.

How do thou know? demanded the more-than-a-woman.

Pain feel his I Mother beloved, responded the other.

Shit! pondered Tanaka.

If anything happens to Sam's family...

Okay – fine.

We do this fast... off we go, then!

It did not take long to reach the area where Tanaka figured the explosions had taken place.

She dove down from altitude, and at a vantage-point about two hundred feet overhead, saw a burned-out impact-site – at least thirty feet across – in the middle of a fallow-field, with a farm-house a few hundred meters off to the west and an *arroyo* just to the south.

The smoldering, smashed remnants of a fighter-plane had made an even larger crater-and-burn-mark a half-kilometer to the east, and in the center of the still-smoldering scorched-area, an apparently groggy-headed Wolf was coming slowly and unsteadily to his knees.

Worryingly, there were signs of activity around the farm-house.

There he is... damn you, Wolf, turn it off – if I can see you with the warm-vision... so can they, mused a worried Cherie Tanaka, as she executed a sort-of-controlled crash to earth, landing close by.

Immediately, she was confronted by her more-than-human "brother's" infernal aura, which was waxing with each passing half-second (although, the bounty-hunter's war-song – normally so evilly-entrancing – wasn't to be heard). The heat was – mercifully enough – partly offset by the burgeoning wind and by the first raindrops of the approaching storm, which were now beginning to fall in the vicinity.

"Ohhh...." moaned Wolf, as Tanaka – now with feet planted on ground – fought against the heat and tried to approach him.

"How badly you hurt?" she inquired, noting with alarm that his clothes were ripped to shreds in several places, in a few of which she could see bloody wounds.

"Don't... know..." he slowly mumbled. "Took on three of them fuckers... or was it four?" he related. "Blew one to bits, mid-air... knocked down another – crashed back yonder – third of 'em must've got a clean shot..."

He tried to rise up, but then fell back to his knees.

A second later, he collapsed, head-first, into the corn-stubble.

She could hear fitful breathing coming from his direction, but nothing more.

Brother – can you hear me? she sent, directly to his mind.

There was no response.

"*Wolf!*" cried a worried Tanaka. "Wake up! Your *Fire*'s too – uhh – *hot!* If you don't dial it back, I can't get close enough to help you!"

But the bounty-hunter just lay there, prostate and apparently unconscious.

I can use the force-field, she reasoned.

That should keep his damn personal-oven-aura away from me.

But if I drop it and try to touch him –

She heard voices coming from the west, toward the farm-house; and to her dismay, Tanaka noticed a group of three Caucasian Texans – a grown man in his mid-40s, accompanied by two others who looked like a lanky, tallish, acned young teenage boy and his slightly-younger, delicate-framed, freckled and red-head sister – running rapidly across the field, toward the crash-site. All were dressed in variations of standard farm-denim overalls, with half-soiled t-shirts and sneakers that had seen better days. The humans had just entered the field.

Goddamn, she sourly mused. *More witnesses... more potential victims...*

Wolf, she sent, trying to target the broadcast as narrowly and directly as possible, *turn it off – I can't lift you to safety with your heat-shield going... and out here, we're sitting ducks for –*

Her apprehension was unfortunately prescient; for, in the next half-second, Tanaka's mind was overtaken by a near-panicked warning on the part of her strange, bio-mechanical alter-ego.

Attack above any from second Mother beloved comes now – time none away fly! shrieked *Vìrya Sài'ymë*.

Instantly, Tanaka – with the fast-thinking invoked and her war-song ringing all over the cornfield and beyond, while her force-field was pushed to maximum-power – held her hands at about a 60-degree angle and swept a large section of the visible sky with crossed arms, sending a lethally-brilliant barrage of *Amaiish*-powered lightening-bolts upward.

Boom! came a devastating, fire-infused explosion, at an unnervingly-low altitude.

We Mother beloved it felled! congratulated the living-armor.

Hoping that she had correctly-recalled the thought-pattern to allow sound temporarily through her bubble, Tanaka yelled at full volume, "*Get down! Incoming!*"

Somehow ignoring her more-than-human-brother's hellish aura (or having it partly-abated by her own force-shield), Tanaka dove over top of Wolf, hoping to protect him from downward-onrushing shrapnel. And none too soon : she felt multiple, high-velocity impacts on the top of her bubble, as shards of whatever had been directed against them, rocketed hither and yon.

A few of these – or perhaps just the shock-wave – must have made it as far as the farm-house, because sounds of broken glass came from that direction.

Oww – shit! her mind reflexively protested, not only from the bomb-fragments above, but also from the furnace coming up from below.

There were screams from the west, and the rain was now starting to really come down.

Damn... shrapnel might have gone right through the poor guy...

In the next few seconds, the heat from Wolf's essence – even through the force-field – became very uncomfortable, so Tanaka righted herself and tried to re-survey the situation.

Vìrya Sài'ymë, she communicated, *do thou see any more attacks coming?*

Far off more no than five so or minutes bang-sticks their us assail may, warned the war-child.

But then – unexpectedly – came another demi-human thought, akin to – but somehow different from – what Tanaka was used to, from *Vìrya Sài'ymë*.

Hurt master Wolf-man mighty, advised its crackling, sputtering, hissing, utterly-alien-but-girl-child-like mental voice.

I him heal try, humans there over but bleed lives their away.

Who the hell...? wondered the professor.

Even more difficult to understand than Little One – no insult meant there, darling – but anyway...

Can thou defend him? she sent, not knowing if the message would get through.

Try I, Fire-The-First-Of Honored, came back the response.

Two cheers for effort... whoever thou are, ruefully mused the more-than-a-woman, as she turned her attention to the west.

To her dismay, she observed two children yelling in panic, while a woman raced from the farm-house toward where the youngsters were standing while being drenched in the downpour.

"Dad's hurt real *bad!*" shrieked the male teenager.

"Mommy!" cried his sister.

Tanaka saw the woman fall to her knees, screaming and moaning with her hands held over her head in disbelief.

We can't do anything about this, the former Science Officer tried to resolve.

First the Wades – then Sammie – then Sam's family – we can't take the whole fucking country along with us, every time that the government –

"Noooooooooo!" wailed the girl. "Daddy – Daddy – get up – *get up!!*"

Tanaka's eyes were wet; and it wasn't from the rain.

Whatever you're going to do, she realized, *better do it* tout de suite... *heat-signatures way off to the north-east – Little One isn't kidding...*

So – with a breaking heart and with fear for the fallen Wolf nagging at her psyche with each passing second – she powered up the *Fire* and rocketed across the field at shoulder-height, coming to a stop-and-landing about ten feet from the distraught (but astonished) Texas farm-family, which had gathered at a point about a hundred meters away from their home.

"You've *got* to get *out* of here!" warned Tanaka. "There's another Air Force attack on the way!"

"Who... who... *are* you?" stammered the teenage boy.

"Jimmy... oh... *Jimmy!*" moaned the woman.

"Let me see," requested the former Science Officer, as she temporarily suppressed her external *Fire*-manifestations and rushed over.

One look at the woman's former mate was all Tanaka needed to realize that even Whitney Claremont's now-legendary skills wouldn't have been any help, here.

The poor farmer had taken a large piece of shrapnel right in the forehead; part of this was still sticking out, while the bulk of it had gone deep into the brain.

It must have killed him instantly.

"Oh my *God,*" gasped the grimacing more-than-a-woman, "I'm *so* sorry! Your... *husband?*"

Hoping that they couldn't or wouldn't notice, her telekinesis forced the dead man's eyelids shut.

"*My Jimmy!*" sobbed the farm-wife.

"*Daddy!*" added the wailing girl-child.

"Are any of you hurt?" asked the professor.

"Nope... Dad told me to duck, and then he covered Kerri with his body," explained the boy. What are you *doing* here, lady?"

"It's a long story," evaded Tanaka. "I – uhh – showed up here to rescue my friend, who's lying, badly-wounded, out in that field. I've got to get back to him in the next couple of minutes, or –"

"We saw explosions in the sky," interrupted the teenager. "Something – looked kinda like a scarecrow on fire – fell out there... Kerri and me, we went out to see. Then... all *this* happened."

"I'm truly sorry, son," offered a horrified, repentant Tanaka. "The Air Force and all the rest of the damn government, they're hunting us – I only shot down their last missile, or bomb, or whatever it was, at the last minute... which is why it exploded so close to all of you. But neither Wolf – he's my friend, by the way – nor I, thought they'd try to bomb us, so close to... *civilians.* Now listen – you've got to get out of here, or –"

She suddenly found herself being pummeled by the small fists of a hysterical, 13-or-so girl.

"*You* brought them here!" angrily cried the child. "They were trying to get you – and they killed *Daddy*, instead!"

The professor was now openly crying, herself, as she passively absorbed the punishment (and silently instructed her armored *alter-ego* not to retaliate) and replied, "Yes... I... we... did, honey. God help me – I did *not* mean for anything like this to happen... neither did Wolf."

She grabbed the girl by the shoulders and then said, "There's nothing I can do to help your father, now, dear; he's... *gone*. All I *can* do, is to try to protect you, your brother and your mother. You understand?"

Tanaka released her grasp, but the child just stood there, looking down at her feet and bawling in a manner that would break the hardest heart.

Even *Vîrya Sài'ymë* began to sob, in her own inscrutable way.

Dying what dear is Mother? innocently asked the war-child.

Know it of I not.

Something very sad – the end of mortal life, Tanaka tried to reply.

And I pray that never will thou know of it...

"Look," she warned, in a trembling-yet-ominous voice, "I'm not kidding about the danger, here! *I* can survive another hit by their bombs – *you* won't – they'll splatter you all *over* the place... and they're on their way, right now! If you don't want to leave him lying here, then start moving your father back to – uhh... okay – under those trees up north of us... the ones between the house and all those bales of hay, see –"

Best I can think of, she reflected.

Next to no cover around here... nowhere to hide...

"What you *talkin'* about, lady?" incredulously demanded the boy. "Livin' through having a *bomb* dropped on you? And we got to take Dad back to the house, call the doctor... or... somethin'..."

"*Listen* to me, son," sympathetically counseled the former Science Officer, "Go in that house – or in a car, or in anything around here where the Air Force thinks that my friend Wolf or I might be hiding – and your lifespan from then on will be measured in seconds to minutes! They'll simply blast *everything* around here, hoping to get a lucky hit on one or both of us. You *got* that?"

"Well – what're we *supposed* to do?" managed the wife, between anguished sobs and embraces of her late husband. "Just sit out here in the rain, without even takin' Jimmy's body anywhere?"

Cherie they Mother only a away minute are! ominously advised Vîrya Sài'ymë.

Out of the corner of her eye – and to her immense relief – Tanaka saw that the bounty-hunter had suddenly sat up, though he was still looking dazed and half-aware of what was transpiring.

"Wolf!" yelled the professor, "Attack – incoming – any second now! Can you use your powers?"

"Whaa..." stammered the big more-than-human. "Man... thought I was a 'goner' there... shit got past my thick skin... Magic-Candle-kid melted it out... attack... attack? Oh... yeah... right... *think* so –"

"Wolf – we've got *civilians* over here – one dead from the last attack, and three others – can you protect them? Can you fly?"

He was standing now, albeit in wobbly, "half-with-it" fashion. Tanaka could see that his clothes were ragged, having been shredded all over their front and left side.

J.H.C., she considered, *How the hell did he survive an explosion like that...*

Seconds few only a! warned the living-armor.

"*Defend them, brother!*" she shrieked, as her eyes lit up, her force-field came to power and her war-song roared through human and extra-human minds, all about.

Trusting on the special sight to guide her through a rain-storm near-totally-opaque to human eyes, Tanaka streaked skyward.

She had gone less than three hundred meters upward, when the Um'nàhr'é-sight revealed a huge "bloom" of heat appearing in the farmer's-field; that this was not accompanied by an explosion, she took as a positive development.

But there was no time for reflection, for the former Mars mission Science Officer quickly had her hands full with her own problems : as she scanned the surrounding airspace for threats – using all of her sensory-abilities to their limit – instead of detecting the expected signatures of fighter-planes, what she detected was unfamiliar.

There were fleeting glimpses of delta-like shapes – dozens, perhaps scores of them, each one no more than a third the size of a F-32E, obviously too small to have contained a human pilot – and they were coming at her *fast* from all sides, no more than a kilometer away in any direction.

Let's hope we can lead them away from Wolf, she confided to *Vîrya Sài'ymë.*

He's less able to deal with them than are we – that is, I hope we are...

In the next instant after that, Tanaka's 'bubble' was struck dead-on, by something that dazzled her eyes into near-blindness; she felt an infernal heat – very different in nature from that exuded by the bounty-hunter – assail her through the force-field.

Ee-owwww! moaned the stricken more-than-a-woman, as her exposed skin immediately felt like it had been on a Florida beach for a day without sun-block. Her 'bubble' was evidently stopping some of what was being directed against her... but not all of it.

I'm burning up!

What the hell – feels like when Minnie gave me a taste of her 'gaze', back in the woods – but she was at minimum-power – these are anything but –

Little One – let's get out of here!

Pushing her flying-ability to the limit, Tanaka rocketed upward into the cloud-layer, a move that thankfully bought her a few seconds' respite from the maddening, Devil's-searchlight-like laser-beam weapons being fired by whatever was chasing her.

Mother us at dear war-arrows come! warned the living-armor.

Can't track them precisely in these clouds, replied the ex-professor.

And it's damn hard to lock on – some kind of stealth-technology, no doubt...

Karéin said that they can't maneuver properly in the upper stratosphere... that had better be true, thought Tanaka.

And I hope those lessons that she gave me about "breathing the Fire, *instead of air", will pay off...*

She felt this same *Fire* surging through her veins, accompanied by a thrilling, enervating war-song that echoed throughout the heavens, as the more-than-a-woman streaked into the upper atmosphere, into the Texas night-sky far past the cloud-layer.

Allowing herself the briefest of glances downward, she saw a swarm of tiny heat-signatures, inexorably tracking her every move.

But her mechanical tormentors – the most sophisticated war-drones that the United States Air Force had yet been able to construct – hadn't been designed to cope with what came next.

To my arms and also my feet, do I call the power! she resolved, while starting to spin on her vertical axis, all the while continuing to soar upward at nearly a thousand kilometers per hour.

Sword! broadcast Cherie Teruko Tanaka to no-one except faithful *Vîrya Sài'ymë,* as a spiral cascade of *Amaiish*-energized lightening-bolts – looking like a weird booster-rocket-discharge issuing from every one of her limbs – showered lethally down from above.

The bounty-hunter – though still proverbially "dazed and confused" – was enough wits-about-him to know that Tanaka's warnings weren't idle ones.

Fuckin' rain, he mused.

Should feel good... somehow, just feels... itchy, or somethin'...

Still in pain all over his wound-inflicted body, he stumbled toward the farm-family, which was still clustered over the mortal remains of their late father and husband.

"Hey –" he started, upon approaching within speaking-distance; but they blanched and moved back.

"What's your *problem?*" he interrogated.

"Your eyes... they've... uhh... *red,*" responded the teenage boy. "And it's starting to feel hot around here –"

"It's the *Devil,* come to claim Jimmy's soul!" exclaimed the panicked, bereaved wife, who – after a bit of fumbling – retrieved a crucifix from a chain hanging around her neck. With trembling hands, she held it out in front, evidently hoping to drive off the sinister denizen of the Underworld named "Darryl Bennington".

"My – oh... *yeah,*" acknowledged a grimacing Wolf. "Listen – it ain't what you *think* – I ain't no Devil, but don't I wish I was, 'cause then I'd –"

His explanation was interrupted by the ominous thunder of powerful explosions taking place, inside or above the overhead rain-clouds.

"*Shit!*" shouted the alarmed bounty-hunter. "They're gunnin' for us – okay, for me – again – feel it comin' back fast, but I can't fly out of here yet... you folks got a car, a truck, or –"

Boom! sounded a loud, ground-level impact, several hundred meters distant, with Wolf between the detonation-point and the farm-family.

"*Hit the deck!*" he bellowed, while crouching but not falling to the ground. "And baby – *light my fire!*"

To his immense relief, the flame-screen roared into being, a split-second later : and none too soon, as it was immediately impacted by scores of small projectiles, each much too lightweight to have done him much harm, but each conversely at least as potent as a low-grade pistol-bullet.

"*Fuck!*" he cursed. "Cluster-bomb, I reckon – folks... *folks?*"

"Kerri's *hurt!*" called a male voice.

The little girl was howling in pain.

"Cover up that wound in her arm!" screamed the farm-wife.

Tamp it down, Little Hot Stuff, he silently commanded.

They're scared enough as it is.

'Least, keep it from roastin 'em until the next round of shrapnel shows up...

There's more where that fuckin' bomb came from, grimly realized Wolf.

If the Air Force drops 'em all 'round, one or two directions will hit for sure, and if I put these people inside my little protective bonfire, they'll likely be toast of a different kind –

Moving faster than any human could do, he charged toward the farm-family, doing his best to tamper-down his infernal aura while he went.

He saw the body.

Poor bugger, thought the bounty-hunter.

'Least he went fast...

Fuck you, Mr. President! This the way you treat the poor-folk?

Don't answer that – don't waste your breath, before I catch up and waste you!

Got to get him out of here, so they'll come along too... if I drop the Fire *to grab 'hold of him the old-fashioned way, we'll all be sitting ducks... but if I don't, he'll likely start to burn the minute I touch him.*

That probably won't win me a lot of friends, 'round here.

Okay... what about this damn 'mind-grabbin' thing that they was all fiddlin' with, up at the camp?

Never was very good at it... but hell – any port in a storm...

He concentrated hard, as the Storied Watcher had instructed him to; and, miraculously, it proved extremely easy to "lock on" to the unfortunate dead-man's mortal remains. He thus began telekinetically moving the corpse, trying all the while to suppress the sinister, orange-red *Fire*-glow that came to his eyes; but the reactions of those around told him that he wasn't completely successful at this.

Oh yeah, mordantly recalled the bounty-hunter.

She said somethin' about, "a living being, if its will actively resists you, is much more difficult to grasp with the force of your mind".

Well, I guess he ain't doin' much of anything, these days... 'cept in the next world, I hope.

Funny how being mistaken for the Old Boy From Downstairs, makes you think about stuff like that.

"What's... *happening!*" gasped the farm-wife. "What are you doing with Jimmy!"

"Gettin' his body *out* of here, so it don't get shredded by the next cluster-bomb that them Air Force fuckers drop on our heads," grunted Wolf, as he levitated the remains about a foot off the ground and began a fast trot toward the driveway leading from the nearest arterial road, to the farm-house.

"And if you don't want to get blown to smithereens neither – you'll follow me," he added.

"Leave my husband's body alone!" cried the woman. "Have you no *decency*, you follower of Satan –"

Secretly elated that he had mastered a modicum of telekinesis so easily, the bounty-hunter looked straight ahead as he forced the dead man's mortal remains forward, toward a clearing just to the north of the farm-house.

The teenage boy shepherded his wounded sister, who was crying in pain from a severe laceration in her upper left arm, to which a crude bandage made out of ripped shirt-cloth, had been applied.

"I'm just tryin' to get him somewhere he can have a decent burial – *Christian* burial, if that means anythin' to you, lady," grunted Wolf. "And for the record... I was never much up on religion, anyways. God never done *shit* for me, and that goes for His Infernal Whatever-ness down below, too. Guess I'm in both their bad books..."

They had reached the clearing. A tractor was parked beside a nearby pile of hay, and there was a beat-up-looking pickup-truck stationed in front of the house.

"You want me to put him in the back of the truck?" asked the bounty-hunter. "'Least that way, you can get him to a funeral home... or something," he added.

"Anything – as long as you release him!" pleaded the farm-wife.

"How are you *doing* that, mister?" demanded the boy.

"Doing what?" replied Wolf.

"Levitating Dad's body," pressed the teenager.

"Oh... *that*," muttered the bounty-hunter. "Long story... well, I'm kind of a super-hero, 'spose that's what you'd say – it's like movin' your arm or leg, you sort of – *shit – hit the deck!*"

There was another thunderous explosion, this time to the north. Whatever the offending projectile was, it had hit – and instantly shredded – a stand of two or three trees, and then it sent a murderous hail of shrapnel rocketing across the Texas plains in all directions.

As Wolf (and his extra-dimensional *alter ego*, the two of them working as one) instinctively raised a wall of fire to block the incoming projectiles, he – and the cowering, mud-smeared human family – perceived a second, even more powerful blast, coming from considerably further overhead.

Shortly after this, they heard airplane engine-parts grinding and coming apart, and there was a brief glimpse of something burning and exploding, crashing to the south of the *arroyo*, resulting in a third, even more puissant detonation.

At this point – much to Wolf's relief, though he tried hard not to give it away – they heard Tanaka's exciting, fast-paced war-song. A half-second after this, the more-than-a-woman burst through the rain-clouds, coming to a rapid landing near the pickup-truck.

"Wolf!" she called. "Thank God... you're okay, now?"

"More or less," he evaded. "Think I'm good to fly, but not too fast, and don't get me mixin' it up with them fighters... rain's fuckin' up my style, it's like it sucks the *Fire* out of my flame, if that makes any sense... that and gettin' my *corpus delictus* half shot-through in the last one – it's kinda got me a little gun-shy... you know?"

"Can't blame you," reassured Tanaka. "Last wave was drones – like what you ran into up on Amchitka, but worse, much faster and more firepower – combined with about six conventional fighters. I shot down more than twelve of 'em and I think they're done for now – but we've got to scram, before they send ten times more our way. How are our new, uhh... 'friends'?"

"None too friendly," offered Wolf, with a shrug. "Can't say I blame 'em. Girl took one in the arm – not sure how bad it is."

"Here, honey," proposed the former science officer. "Let me have a look at it –"

The mud-encrusted child flinched, but was obviously too overcome by the pain and the novelty of Tanaka's glowing-eyed, imposing presence, to put up much resistance.

A soft, purple-and-white glow issued from the fingertips of the one called *First of The Fire*, and it brought succor to the wound, which – though not fully-healed – appeared to no longer be reducing the little girl to total helplessness.

"Listen – all of you," she instructed. "You've got two choices : stay around here and take your chances with the government; or – come with us. I'd strongly suggest the second, but it's up to you."

"Who's 'us'?" asked the farm-wife. "And I ain't going nowhere, without seeing Jimmy properly buried. You've got a lot of explaining to do – whoever you are."

Tanaka walked over to the woman and embraced her. The gesture was evidently unwelcome, but there seemed to be no way of avoiding it, as the farm-wife was unable to move in that moment.

"You're right," acknowledged the science officer, "We *do* have a lot of 'explaining' to do – and it breaks my heart, what's happened to your husband and family, Ma'am. If it's any consolation, many of my team and I, have suffered similar outrages... or worse. We're followers of Karéin-Mayréij – the Storied Watcher, who saved our planet from the 'Lucifer' comet – and we'd be honored to welcome you into our group, as brothers and sisters –"

The children stared in wide-eyed realization.

"Uhh, Cherie," interrupted the bounty-hunter, "You *sure* about that? I mean, we're overloaded with 'civilians', as it is, and I don't think –"

"We'd be *happy* to welcome them... wouldn't we, Wolf?" she persisted. "Especially after having indirectly caused the wrongful death of their husband and father."

"Sure... fine... *whatever*," he muttered, unsubtly throwing up his hands and rolling his eyes as well.

The rain was pouring down, now, turning the Texas dirt into a mud-bath.

"As to your late husband," continued Tanaka, "Unfortunately, I don't think we can take him with us – it will be a challenge to get you all to safety, as it is. But I *can* make a half-decent grave for him, right here... if you want to say a few words, after we lower him into it."

"You're *crazy!*" retorted the farm-wife. "It takes two grown men an *hour* to dig a grave!"

"I'm not a man... or a human, anymore," replied the science officer. "Just point to where you would like to see him laid to rest. Be quick about it – we could come under attack at any moment."

The bereaved woman did not reply; instead, she just mutely shook her head.

"Then I'll have to choose the spot," stated Tanaka, "Wolf – help me with the grave... use your telekinesis to propel the dirt out, as I tear up the ground and pull it upward. Ready?"

"No," complained the bounty-hunter, "I hardly got a handle on that shit, but go ahead – just don't bitch if it ends up all over you."

"One – two – *three!*" counted the former science officer, as – with the customary *Fire*-manifestations of glowing eyes and war-song, paralleled by Wolf's own – she pointed at a spot of earth next to a tree with a rope-and-board swing hanging from one of its branches...

And *fired*.

The farm-family dashed fearfully for cover, as Tanaka's lethal lightening-bolts drove deep gashes into the Texas earth. This form of improvised excavation (aided by an improvised, spade-like appendage appearing from *Vìrya Sài'ymë*) appeared to work well enough at first, but she noticed that only a very small amount of mud was, in fact, being removed from the putative grave-site.

"Pick it *up*, for God's sake, Wolf," complained the more-than-a-woman, "I'm doing all the work here!"

"Then hold off with the light-show, Cherie," he retorted. "Lockin' on with this tele-whatever shit's hard enough as it is... with you firing them damn electro-bolts, it's like tryin' to tickle a fish with a blind-fold on. And my personal cookin'-stove's gettin' doused damn good, by all this rain."

"Okay," she responded. "Don't like doing it down here, anyway – might attract *attention*."

The lightening-attack came to an abrupt end, as the bounty-hunter walked up to the side of the grave.

Show me how to do it... if you know yourself, honey, he silently requested of his alien *alter ego*.

Try will I, replied the Little Burning One, *drains sky-water me the but*.

The task turned out to be much more difficult than had been the one of moving the man's corpse.

Though – to his elation – Wolf felt his telekinetic abilities flowering rapidly, the rain-soaked ground seemed to evade his mental lock-on at every turn, as if there was some natural disaffinity between his flavor of the *Fire* and the muddy composition of the dirt.

He improvised by casting a continuous shower of flame over the grave-site, a move that, mercifully, dried out the ground faster than the rain could again soak it. Tanaka jumped in, with her force-field defending her from the conflagration, and bade *Vîrya Sài'ymë* to form an ethereal pseudopod into a replica shovel.

After several minutes, the two had excavated a furrow of perhaps three to four feet in depth. Tanaka self-levitated out and stood beside the bounty-hunter.

"Ain't six feet... but it'll have to do, I reckon," he pronounced. "'Least until a proper one gets dug, and we ain't worryin' about being bombed any minute."

"We can't just put Jimmy in that, without something to wrap him in," argued the farm-wife.

"You got a tarp in the barn, or anything like that?" asked Wolf.

"Yeah... for the horses," said the teenage boy. "I'll get it."

"Make it fast," ordered Tanaka. "I'm scanning the sky... nothing yet – but that could change any minute."

For a short while, they all just mutely and somberly stood there, with Tanaka and Wolf voluntarily allowing themselves to be soaked by the downpour, though they both knew that their alien-powers could easily keep them safe and dry.

Eventually, the boy returned with a horse-blanket, easily big enough to completely enshroud the fallen farmer. Both the more-than-humans levitated the man's body, while the grieving family wrapped him from head to toe. Then he was gently deposited into the grave, which was already starting to fill with muddy water.

"Anybody want to say any words?" asked Wolf. "If so, you better do it quick – we'll have to put the dirt back in soon, or you'll end up with a swimmin'-pool in there."

For God's sake, brother, sent Tanaka, *can't you use a little tact?*

"Sorry, Cherie," he mumbled. "Guess I seen a lot of death, lately... kinda forgot that it's a hell of a thing, for folks like this."

"I could go get our Bible," offered the boy. "Not sure where we put it, though. You know, Mom?"

"No... forgot where it is, myself..." sobbed the overcome farm-wife.

"Ma'am – you want to say a prayer, or something?" inquired the former science officer.

"No," was all that the wife could manage to say. "Can't..."

"Then... *I* will," softly responded Tanaka.

Her eyes were glowing, again.

From all around – but more from above than below – there began to play a strange, mournful variant of the former science-officer's war-song; much more subtle and gentle than what an immediately-impressed Wolf had been accustomed to, it was replete with long, crying electric guitar-chords and the sounds of ethereal violins playing from above the clouds.

"Lord," she quietly implored, "Please receive the soul of this beloved husband and father... and bring peace to his family, from whom he has been so cruelly- and unfairly-taken. May your angels accompany him on his journey to a better place; and may your grace protect and comfort his loved-ones, in the days and weeks to come. We ask that you show my brother Wolf and I, how we can make amends for this tragedy... how we can show this family how terribly sorry we are for having brought this calamity upon them. We are *so* much more powerful than mortal humans... but we are still, 'mortal' – and at times like this, we cry the same tears as our human brothers and sisters. Never let us lose sight of that – and never let us forget the vows we pledged, to your good Earth's Guardian Angel... amen."

"Amen... I guess," muttered the bounty-hunter, as the sounds and Tanaka's *Fire*-manifestations subsided.

"Why the 'I guess', mister?" asked the teenage boy.

"Well, let's just say," remarked Wolf, "That when I finally get put where your Dad is now... whoever's sayin' *my* eulogy – he's gonna have a lot more 'explainin' to do... music ain't gonna be near as good neither, I reckon. You don't want to *know*, son."

Again, the scene fell silent for a few seconds, with the tears of the farm-family mixing into the miserably-cold downpour.

Then – at length – Tanaka commented, "Wolf... after we pour the earth back in, we'll need a cross..."

"Iron picket-fence over there," he replied. "I'll weld something together."

"I'll inscribe a name," responded the former science-officer.

She shot an interrogatory look at the farm-wife.

"Jimmy," said the woman. "Just... 'Jimmy'."

Every One's Got To Count For Two

"So what we got?" asked General Blanshard, his tough, bull-necked presence broadcasting clarity-of-purpose to all those in the Air Force One Command HQ.

He bent over the situation-display, which showed an infinitely-zoomable, high-definition digital-display map of Southern California.

It was set to view a large part of eastern Greater Los Angeles.

"Traces... it's been moving, evidently," replied a lesser-decorated, male, Caucasian officer, probably a brigadier-general or colonel. "As near as we can tell."

"I thought we had – or were about to have – a fix," complained the newly-promoted Chairman of the Joint Chiefs.

"We're doing the best we can," remarked a guy dressed in a white, information-technology smock. "We've only got residual-stuff, and at the ranges that the sensors are deployed – like, a half-mile up on a 'copter and so on – a lot of the returns we're getting are almost certainly false-positives... things like hospital radiology-gear and so on. Plain fact is... if we *really* want to zero in on the damn thing, we're going to need precision-equipment – boots on the ground, with the gear in a truck – and they'll need to be much closer than anything we got now."

"*How* close?" inquired Blanshard.

"Can't give you an exact distance, General, because it depends on how well-shielded it is... bunch of other factors as well," explained the scientist. "But I'd say no more than a kilometer at best."

"Situation down there's *very* chaotic," warned the other senior officer. "Gang-violence on a level we've never *seen* before – our ground-forces have actually lost some battles with this goddamn new Latino gangster-army that seems to have sprung up from nowhere. Even with offloading as much as we can to GrayWar, we're *desperately* short of both air-support and grunts down there, sir – if we could just pull say a division's-worth and a few wings from the Central Front –"

"That's out of the *question*," brusquely interrupted Blanshard. "You *know* why."

"Sir," interrupted an Air Force lieutenant, "Report from the East Texas area – we've got an *engagement* –"

The senior general's eyebrows raised and he sent the understudy a long look.

"TacEval?" demanded Blanshard.

"Agency was doing a rendition... not sure of the circumstances involved with that," returned the lieutenant, "Appears they ran into terrorists or something – they called in air-support. We had a composite wing operating temporarily out of Tinker AFB, up on CAP over the area; they were first to intercept, although we also got a bunch of drones from Dyess in there a few minutes later. Ran into at least one bogey... maybe more."

"Status?" asked the general.

"Incomplete as of now, sir," came the answer, "But we have at least five fighters and twenty-two drones down... and from what I'm told, hostiles may still be in the area."

"How many hostiles?" demanded the senior officer.

"We think one or two, sir," stated the lieutenant. "Very small size, extremely maneuverable, with stealth-abilities and a lethal, ranged energy-discharge attack, capable of splashing a fighter from about a kilometer away."

"For God's sake... I knew that Anderson wasn't that on top of things," muttered Blanshard, "But we threw *dozens* of his pilots at a couple of hostiles – and we *still* don't have local air supremacy? I goddamn give up... okay. We got any intel on these things – satellite pictures, gun-camera shots, *et cetera*?"

"We don't have very much, sir," admitted the understudy. "Weather in the area's completely socked-in, so the overheads are coming back empty, except for a brief blip where something looked like a SAM going up... but then it just reversed course and dove back under the clouds. For what it's worth, we *did* get some imaging-IR-signatures at relatively close range, but the returns don't make a lot of sense –"

"What do you mean?" inquired Blanshard.

"I know how this is going to sound, sir," sheepishly offered the lieutenant, "But the hostiles look like... uhh... kind of perfect *spheres,* as near as we can tell. They're about two or three meters in diameter... at times we observed that one of them seemed to have a much more prominent IR-sig than the other... but except for that – and for differences in the, uhh, music that the pilots reported hearing during the engagement – it's pretty hard to tell them apart."

The general fell silent for a second or two. Then he commented,

"A... 'sphere', you say? *Interesting.*"

"How so?" asked the lieutenant.

"Just like the *alien,*" remarked Blanshard. "Corresponds perfectly to the descriptions that we had of it, on numerous occasions – for example, during the engagement over the North Pacific."

"You mean... that little bitch is back to fighting us, now?" interjected the information-technology-man. "Didn't we have intel that it had flown off somewhere?"

"Maybe," evenly replied the general. "Or maybe it's taught its tricks to its followers... I had suspected something like this after the fiasco over Missouri – but now, I'm 99 per cent certain. Either way, gentlemen – I think we're facing a new threat of very serious proportions. I'll have to inform the President... *that's* for sure. Are we pursuing the hostiles?"

"Yes, sir," eagerly confirmed the lieutenant. "We're reinforcing the South-West Front with everything we can get into the air... but it'll take some time for the rest of the fighters and drones to arrive at the engagement-area. The other thing is... uhh... we've kinda lost track on the two bogies –"

"Jesus H. *Christ!*" cursed Blanshard. "I thought –"

"They just... uhh... dropped completely off radar, sir," apologized the understudy. "We think they've landed, or something –"

"Well then... bomb the *piss* out of wherever they did!" demanded the general.

"Not to worry, sir," confidently replied the lieutenant, with a cheerful grin. "Three strikes already inbound. When they get there... East Texas's gonna look like the dark side of the moon! Only problem is, we're running low on ordnance – as you know, we used up a lot of it against the Fort Knox Repository. We got enough for maybe two or three more full-scale carpet-bombing attacks, or six or seven smaller ones. After that... we're waiting for the factories to come through for us, sir."

"That's the bottom-line?" asked Blanshard.

"'Fraid so, sir," confirmed the junior officer.

"Then let's make every damn bomb, count for two," ordered the general.

The Shattering Shield

Billings was – to say the least – nervous, as he and the others waited impatiently in the jury-rigged semi-space-ship named *"Mailànkh Express"*, which had been secreted by the Storied Watcher in a clearing next to a dense stand of forest, about a kilometer to the west the Fort Knox Repository – or, more accurately, what little was left of the latter.

He had learned that in the most cursory of briefings provided by his alien girlfriend, just before she again flew off – her light-bending-skills at full-power, with only a few uncommon wave-lengths left to leak through the 'bubble' with which to navigate – toward the grim remnants of the former monument to lucre.

"Stray you not from the *Express*," she had warned. "And make no light or commotion. Night has fallen and I chose a secluded nearby spot, where our landing would not smash any trees... but there are many American army-men in these parts – and they will not hesitate to shoot at you."

There they waited, for almost an hour.

"Listen, everyone," declared the Storied Watcher, upon her return, "At length, there will be time for explanations and evaluations – but presently, I have some very important news for all of you."

Saquina White – a grave, fearful expression on her face – requested, "Give it to us straight, Karéin. Whatever it is... I want the *truth... y'hear*?"

"Glad tidings – or, at least, the absence of sad ones – bring I," proudly declared Karéin-Mayréij. "For in my travels through this 'Repository', as it is called, never did I detect or overhear convincing evidence of the defeat – still less, the demise – of Sam Jacobson or the others of his brave questing-party. *Surely*, this should lighten our hearts."

White sat down on one of the exit-steps going from the *Express* to the ground, hung her head and began to quietly weep, mumbling "Thank you *Jaysus*", along with other similar invocations. She was immediately comforted by Melissa Claremont, who stood alongside and embraced the astronaut's-wife.

The Storied Watcher came over to the folding-staircase, put one foot upon it and began to elaborate her address to the others.

"What else did you find out, Mom?" asked Tommy, looking up.

"'Mom'... 'Mom'," murmured the Storied Watcher, quietly cursing her sentimentality as she wiped a tear and planted a quick kiss on the boy's head. "Keep saying that until the end of days, sweet prince," she whispered.

Now speaking with regained composure, she went on, "As I had promised to, I flew over these parts, searching against hope for any signs of Sam Jacobson's team... alas, I found none. If they were hiding around here at one time... they are now long gone."

"Not much of s'prise there," offered Saquina White. "Y'all knock over a bank, it's ain't a good idea to hang 'round afterwards."

"I should caution all of you," stated the alien-girl, "That I was not able to reach the depths of this 'Repository' because it is now very heavily-guarded – there are American war-soldiers everywhere – and curiously, it appears that there was a massive explosion in the nethermost reaches of the fortress, which collapsed much of the structure in on itself; this not only made it impractical for me to stealthily venture there, but – to the consternation of many of the leaders whose conversations I overheard – it has also melted and made unusable, most of the gold-stocks which were stored therein."

"Ha ha – smart move there, Jacobson," commented Billings, with a cynical smile. "Hit 'em where it *hurts*... in the ol' bank-account."

"There wasn't anything about – uhh – 'recovering bodies'... or anything like that...?" uncomfortably inquired Ramirez.

"No – and if even one or two had died there, my arts would have told me," advised the Storied Watcher. "Indeed, the army-men seem to be most confounded as to how the, ahh, 'Mars Gang terrorists' – for such is how Sam's party seems now to be called by those who rule this empire – could possibly have eluded demise, or capture."

"Yeah, but Karéin," inquired Melissa, "If they didn't get smoked in there, an' they ain't there now – what they 'zactly do to get out? Catch a cab or somethin'?"

"Wolf and those dogs wouldn't fit in no car, anyways," wryly commented Saquina White.

"It seems that Sam and his friends *were*, at one point, besieged within said fortress," noted Karéin-Mayréij, "Yet – escape... they did. I cannot explain this – within their number when they were transported back to this 'America' place, only Cherie was able to take flight – and none of them had the hiding-arts available to myself, Bob and my war-children. Our sister Sylvia has a measure of the latter ability; but she, of course, is with dear Minn-ee's group. Certainly... this is a mystery."

"Better a 'mystery', than a funeral," grimly mentioned Ramirez.

Nodding acknowledgment, Karéin-Mayréij revealed, "And there are several *other* odd things that I learned in the brief time that I had to do – ahh – rek-kee, on and around this area. For one, these speak of the 'Mars Gang' including many more people than the six of Sam's group, who I deposited in the southern-province of Flo-ri-da. This does not make sense, unless he is trying to recruit an army of his own. And for another, there is now a full-scale war going on in this empire's far west, in the city of 'Los Angeles', between American imperial forces and the brigand-forces with whom our comrade Sebastiàn – may the Gods watch over him – would be well-acquainted. This is *also* good news... that city has not yet been demolished by the atom-splitting-bomb that latterly was detected there."

"Yeah, Angel Lady, it's always a good day when y'all know they ain't set off any H-bombs in your 'hood... you got *that* right," mordantly quipped White.

"It could have gone off at any time," observed Ramirez. "And *still* might. After having barely dealt with that one up north, I'm not keen to repeat the experience."

"Hear, *hear*," interjected Billings. "Anything else?"

"As I noted... I dared not tarry there overlong, if for no reason other than not to leave all of you alone," replied the Storied Watcher. "I had my war-children, uhh, 'suck up' as much com-pu-ter data as was practical, while I was in proximity to the American army data networks. Lamentably, almost all of this is scrambled so as to make it impossible to understand, but I have asked *Vîrya Ahn'jë* to work on it and perhaps derive some wisdom therefrom. She has so far had only limited success – this task is still quite difficult for her – but she is trying very diligently. In the interim, the only other thing of interest is talk of 'terrorists using poison gas, having abducted the former President'; they say that so far the public is unaware of this event, and a massive search is now underway to recapture –"

"Whoa!" exclaimed Saquina White. "What y'all say – the *President?* Where? How? By Sam 'n his folk? Why you not tell us that up front –"

"She said, 'the *former* President'," corrected Ramirez. "Not the jackass who we've got running the show now. But *that* doesn't make any sense, either... why would anyone *do* something like that? And chemical weapons – that gangsta we left back in L.A.'s the only one of our team who had *that* power, so it *can't* be one of us... right? Besides, the current Administration certainly isn't going to give in to blackmail... they'll just sit back, watch these 'terrorists' slit the poor guy's throat, then use that as an excuse to get rid of whatever civil rights we have left. It can't *possibly* work!"

"I concur," agreed the Storied Watcher. "Those who rule this empire seem not to care, even when one of their own number are at risk; I saw this first-hand, in the case of our friend Jerr-ee Kay-sten."

"You think that it was Jacobson and his pals who pulled off this 'abduction', Sari?" inquired Billings.

"I cannot say for sure – but I would doubt it," returned Karéin-Mayréij. "Such tactics are unlike what I would expect from Sam himself, and I do not believe that our brothers Brent or Devon would countenance them. As to the location, all that I have is something about a 'guarded retirement community' named 'ARN', which seems to have a lake in or around it. But no co-ordinates or map locations were given... so this could be almost anywhere."

"Hmmph," grunted the salesman. "Well... so some 'terrorist' greases the former President –no skin off *our* ass, I'd wager. And maybe it will keep the bastard who's now running the show, occupied while we do, uhh... whatever we're going to do. Just out of interest, Sari – what *is* our next move?"

The Storied Watcher's face showed one of her now-familiar pursed-lips, bemused-to-exasperated expressions.

"There is not much that I *can* do," admitted the alien-girl. "I *could* mind-call out to *Vîrya I'ëà'b'*, wherever she may be... but that art does not work over the distances that may separate us, at least not here on a planet with so many other intelligent minds about, to confuse the, ahh, 'signal'."

"Wish you'd have given all them folk who set out on these-here 'quests', a cell-phone to call us with," complained Saquina White.

"These are naught but an easy way for the seeking-death-bombs of the American empire to find us," reminded Karéin-Mayréij. "Even a Russian one was used in this evil manner, back in the Tucson Hotel, when this entire sad affair was in its nascent stages. My war-children and I have already had enough of a challenge in defeating all these ingenious tracking-systems available to the President, as we travel across the skies of this land; scarcely, then, do we need to make his task that much easier."

"Yeah, well, 'don't call us – we'll call you'... that's how it goes... right?" quipped Billings. "So what do we do, Sari... just lay low for a while? Maybe wait until Jacobson or somebody else makes another move that ends up on the evening news?"

There was an embarrassed stare on her face.

"'Lay low' means, 'hide out and be inconspicuous'," tactfully interjected Ramirez.

"Oh... of *course*," sheepishly answered the Storied Watcher.

She turned around and sat down on the stairs, her infernal aura seeming to have neither an effect on whatever substance made up the shell of the *Express*, nor on the being of Tommy George, who placed himself right next to his adoptive mother.

Karéin-Mayréij pondered for a few long seconds, and then said, "Ach... somehow, doing thus seems futile and shameful to me. Bob, my love – this is the same situation as I encountered shortly after you, Tommy, Melissa, Whitney and Curtis had been kidnapped by the spy-torturers of the American empire... the trail goes cold. We could undertake more exploration – ask around, see if anyone in this region has seen or heard of Sam and his team –"

"Well, at least you aren't threatening that asshole in the White House, with burning down the whole *country*, if you don't find what – excuse me, *who* – you're looking for," chided Billings.

"A vow such as that is made only in defense of those who one loves most dearly," she countered.

"Point taken, honey," retreated the salesman, "And like I mentioned back at my house in Tucson – that is, while the damn thing was still there in one piece – it's great to have the big guns on my side, for a change. But use a little common sense, Sari... Jacobson's not stupid : he's made himself scarce for the very good reason that if he hadn't, he'd be wearing every smart-bomb that the Air Force has left in its arsenal. Even with *your* skills, we'd likely have next to zero chance of finding him."

"Bob's right," added Ramirez. "This is a big country, and Sam and his team are obviously pretty good at staying one step ahead of the authorities, or they'd already have been caught by now –"

"Maybe they *have* been, and we just don't know about it," unhelpfully commented Billings.

"Don't *say* stuff like that!" protested Saquina White.

"If I know anything of tyrants," offered the Storied Watcher, "The capture of rebels such as Sam and his adventure-party, would be swiftly announced to the peasantry of this empire – as if any prison built by mortal man, could hold our friends, in any event. You all know of their powers of the *Fire*... you know this to be true."

"They couldn't even hold *me* – not now," hissed a scowling, devil-faced Tommy. "I'd like to see them *try*, with Captain Sam, Ms. Tanaka, Major White, Major Boyd, Wolf and Misha! You know back at the camp, Mom? I went off with Wolf and he showed me – and Mr. Hendricks, too – what he could do. He melted this big rock, it was granite I think, into a pile of –"

"Son," cajoled Karéin-Mayréij, "It is said that we should be judged by what we can build and create – not by what we can ruin and destroy; though, these days, I must confess that I sometimes find that wisdom to be wanting."

"Look," argued Ramirez, "These two ideas aren't mutually-exclusive; why don't we just find a safe place to stay under the radar-screen, make ourselves comfortable for a while, and do some searches on NeoNet and the news-media, or something like that? If we go floating around Kentucky looking for Jacobson or for trouble, we'll probably find it sooner than we want to. Sam's bound to make a move in the near future – don't forget, his whole plan was to flush the President out into the open. That's got to mean something spectacular is going to happen soon. We simply wait for it to show up on the news and then act accordingly. But let's not get on the news ourselves, first... you know?"

"Doing so is against my will, my training and my instincts," unhappily offered the alien-girl, "Especially because while we sit in forlorn idleness, our brothers and sisters may be in danger... in need of our help. And there would be practical issues : we would have to hide the *Mailànkh Express* very carefully – we dare not let her be captured by the American army, lest the secrets of her construction thus be revealed to them – and we would have to find an alternate living-place where we would not, ahh, 'stand out' inordinately, at least for a short while. This is a substantial challenge. Do any of you believe that we can accomplish it?"

"Well, before we get to that... you didn't mean around *here*, did you, Karéin," queried Ramirez. "You said yourself that it's *crawling* with soldiers and police..."

"Aye," said the Storied Watcher. "We would have to pick another location – preferably somewhere near the mid-part of the American empire, so our travel-distance to wherever we hear of Sam or Minn-ee, ahh, 'surfacing', should be as short as possible."

"Fort Knox isn't bad for that," remarked Billings, "But it's still sort of 'hot', obviously. How about, uhh... Nashville? Nice place, small place, kind of out of the way, and not that far from here... nobody'd look for us there, I bet."

"As good as anywhere, I suppose," she agreed. "But..."

"Yeah," confirmed the salesman. "But, *what?*"

"Where are we going to put our sky-ark?" asked the alien-girl.

Billings shrugged.

"Not sure," he evaded, "But there's lots of run-down places downtown in Nashville.. junk all over the place, piled nearly as high as a house in some parts. They haven't carted it away for years – we're probably safe for a while yet, I'd imagine."

Tommy started laughing.

"What's so funny?" inquired Melissa.

"I can just imagine them trying to load the *Express* into a garbage-truck," smirked the boy.

"The truck would indeed be at a loss," added the Storied Watcher.

"There are also some decent-sized rivers that we could sink her into," observed Billings. "Although that might cause more trouble than it's worth... especially trying to get her back out."

"Oh... I don't know 'bout that, Bob," countered Saquina White, with a brief flash of the *Fire* coming to her eyes.

"Sorry... *forgot*," grunted the salesman.

"I suppose that we will have to take our chances in finding a suitable hiding-place for our ship, in or around this 'Nash-ville'" declared Karéin-Mayréij. "But that leaves us with the question of where we all shall stay, and not, ahh, 'make a spectacle of ourselves'."

"Don't see why that's gonna be a problem... long as y'all don't mind hangin' out in some mo-tel watchin' TV all day," said Saquina White, with a smile. "But it'd have to be a low-rent one, 'cause anywhere worth stayin' in, they don't take cash, it's all credit and computer-chips and so on... you know, 'Real ID verification'. The Man'd catch up with us in an hour or so."

"Yeah... I'd stay away from hotels altogether," suggested Billings. "Only reason we got away with it while heading down to Tucson was that most of the computer networks were out at the time. A B&B'd be a lot better."

"A... uhh... 'bee and bee'?" awkwardly asked the Storied Watcher.

"An ordinary house that someone rents out rooms within," explained Ramirez. "They tend to be run more informally than conventional hotels and motels... less high-tech stuff for payments and so on. Which would be good for us."

"We might even be able to rent a whole house, all to ourselves," proposed the salesman. "As long as the landlord will accept a few gold coins as the down-payment."

"Do you all endorse this plan?" asked Karéin-Mayréij.

"Do you?" countered Saquina White.

"I, uhh... asked you first," returned the alien-girl.

"But you all's in *charge* here," said the astronaut-wife.

"No, I am not – I am the *servant*... not the master," claimed the Storied Watcher.

"We could hold a vote," proposed Billings. "Hands up, everybody who's for rentin' a room – or rooms – somewhere, and waiting until all hell breaks lose."

He put his hand up; it was matched by Ramirez and Saquina White, while Melissa Claremont, the alien-girl and her adoptive son remained silent and unsupportive.

"Does that mean you vote 'no'?" asked the salesman.

"No," she replied, "It means that I choose not to vote. I will be governed by whatever the rest of you should decide."

"Well, for th' record," grumbled Melissa, "I'm all for flyin' up there an' doin' a bit more lookin', before we crib out somewhere."

"Hope your force-field is in better shape than mine," commented Billings. "Because flying up where their radar can tag you, reminds me a lot of sticking your head out of a foxhole on the front lines."

For this, he got a tongue-out-of-the-mouth on the part of the Claremont girl.

"Mom," asked Tommy, "Do my, uhh, 'war-brothers' and 'war-sisters' get a vote? Because if, like, *Vîrya Ahn'jë* and *Væran Ss'éth'ch'* joined you and me, and if only one of the others voted 'no', then –"

The Storied Watcher looked upward at an apparently-unoccupied spot in the night sky, paused for a couple of seconds and then spoke to the boy, "You heard that... did you not, young prince?"

"*Sure* I did," he peevishly answered, "But come *on*, guys – what's all this about 'you don't know what it means to vote'? How can you know all this stuff about, like, computer-networks, and not know about voting? I learned it in third grade!"

"They've had an, uhh, 'sheltered upbringing', you know," mentioned Billings.

"My love, your step-war-children have been in mortal combat – or the threat thereof – well-nigh since the hour of their coming into this world," patiently observed Karéin-Mayréij. "As have been dear Tommy and little Elissha so far-away – hardly can this be considered 'sheltered'... at least in one sense of that Eng-lish word."

"One of these days, Sari," mumbled the salesman, "You'll have to explain to me, how you, uhh, 'gave birth' to all these, uhh, 'kids'."

"It is, ahh, a 'long story'," she responded. "They have always been with me, since my earliest days – but not in corporeal form; you see, and... but I digress. This is a subject best discussed under other circumstances, do you not think?"

"I want to learn!" pestered Tommy.

"Y'all be learnin' 'bout all that stuff sooner than yo' Momma want y'all to, if'n y'all anythin' like mah brother," quipped Melissa. "She tell Curtis – an' me –

'somethin' real *bad* gonna happen if'n y'all keep watchin' them dirty movies on Neo. Momma was right... ah gots to give her that."

"Much suffering and woe has indeed come your way," quietly remarked the Storied Watcher, "I doubt that watching a vid-e-o on the gentle arts of love and pleasure would be the cause, but to the extent that it was due to my advent here, I accept responsibility and humbly pray for forgiveness. But... it has not been *all* bad... has it?"

"Well," offered the teenager with a warm smile, "Back in th' old days in De-troit, only 'flyin' ah'd get to do, was with a kite that was made out to look like a seagull or somethin'... ah'd look up there at it an' 'magine what it be like to be a bird, clouds under mah feet an' all that. Wasn't just a dream 'bout flyin' – it was also 'bout gettin' somewhere else than that hot, dirty ol' city. But since y'all dropped in, up there on th' island ah mean... things's been goin' in an upward direction – y'understand what ah'm sayin'?"

The alien-girl nodded agreement, and then – to the undisguised delight of Melissa Claremont – asked, "Tell me, my noble young sister – do you feel ready to escort a Storied Watcher and an air-ship, as they cruise in stealthy-guise, toward the fair metropolis named 'Nashville'?"

With excitement immediately apparent in her voice – and the beat of her personal war-song somehow infusing every syllable that she spoke – Melissa replied, "Y'all *bet*, Angel Lady!"

A second later, however, she wore a crestfallen look.

"But... Sari," hedged the teenager, "All ah can do is fly – real fast, tight turns 'n such, an' my bubble gettin' wicked strong, y'all saw that up north – but ah cain't, uhh... *hurt* nothin'. What good ah'm gonna do, without no *firepower?*"

With a regal expression on her face, Karéin-Mayréij stood up, moved so as to be directly in front of the Claremont girl, put one flaming hand on the latter's shoulder and advised, "Are you *sure* of that, young princess?"

A wide-eyed Melissa, still surprised that nothing hurt, answered, "*Shore* I am."

"Come over here with me," directed the Storied Watcher. "Away from the others and from our ship. For a threshold of great and sinister portent, shall you soon be the first to cross, on behalf of your brothers and sisters of the Holy *Fire.*"

"*This* should be interesting," mentioned Ramirez to Billings, *sotto voce.*

The salesman nodded.

The flying-teenager and the alien-girl proceeded rapidly until they were about fifty feet away from the cadre of travelers and from the *Mailànkh Express.*

The Storied Watcher moved so as to interpose herself between the teenager and the group of travelers, whispered something to *Vîrya Quü'j* and then placed the necklace-and-amulet over Melissa's neck.

"*Oh... woww*," breathed the teenager. "Hey... Grandma... damn straight meetin' y'all..."

"I will count to three, and the Venerable One will also do so in lock-step, within your refuge," instructed Karéin-Mayréij. "Upon one, energize your bubble; upon two, make her to wax as if to be proof from the strongest peril or from the rush of the winds that come when you hurtle at top-speed; and finally, upon three, let your *Fire* run wild, according to the mind-trigger that my eldest companion shall send you... and commit that war-thought to memory. Do not worry about anything else – I will protect as needs be. Are you ready, mighty young *Vìrya* Melissa Claremont?"

They had expected a typically awkward, bashful answer; instead, what came back was, "Ah'm ready, Karéin... *Sensei*."

You look... awesome, broadcasted a visibly-impressed Tommy, as he observed the Claremont girl's demeanor beginning to show a fraction of her mentor's godly presence.

Miz Cherie done taught me 'bout the 'Sensei' thang, came back a quick response, though Melissa was concentrating on something entirely different.

Ah feels her inside me... just like y'all, Angel Lady...

"One," spoke Karéin-Mayréij.

Okt'á, sent *Vìrya Quü'j.*

With her eyes glowing, the *Fire* burgeoning in her chest and her newly-exciting, faster-paced war-song starting to play, Melissa considered,

That must mean 'one', ah guess...

"Two," counted the Storied Watcher.

Her own force-field was now manifest, although it was strangely-deformed, being flattened so as to deny line-of-sight from the Claremont girl to the air-ship.

Ym'ë, transmitted the weirding-amulet.

Several of those at the doorway retreated back inside the *Mailànkh Express*, although Tommy only crouched behind the folding stairway.

A dimly-apparent, translucent bubble surrounded the teenager, as her battle-music lit up the nerves of all around. From inside, Melissa could see the Storied Watcher's lips move, but could hardly hear a sound.

"Three," came the silent count, echoed by "*Zjù!*" on the part of *Vìrya Quü'j.*

The teenager felt a sudden, overwhelming rush of power, accompanied by a sound like far-off thunder and a brilliant flash that temporarily obscured everything outside her bubble.

Through the latter, she could barely see some kind of translucent distortion in the atmosphere that seemed to be receding from where she stood. It was mostly deflected by the Storied Watcher's force-field, but it nevertheless struck the far bow- and stern-ends of the *Mailànkh Express*, which rocked mightily on its longitudinal axis (Tommy was nearly crushed under the staircase, but was saved by the appearance of his own protective-field; the Storied Watcher seemed unfazed by all this), bringing cries of panic from inside the air-ship.

The shock-wave then hurtled into the tree-line, whose outermost examples, alternately shattered, splintered or at least lost their leaves and needles, according to each tree's durability.

Immediately, Melissa – reacting out of panic – powered down her bubble, extinguished her personal *Fire* and called out, "Oh mah *Gawd* – y'all *okay?*"

"Never better," grumbled a disheveled Billings, dusting himself off after having been knocked flat on his back just inside the entrance-way to the *Mailànkh Express.*

"Tommy?" he asked, with a mild tone of worry.

"Fine, Mister Billings," came the voice of the boy, as he peeked out from behind the folding-staircase. "What *was* that? Felt like... uhh... like... like and earthquake, or one of those missiles going off, when I was with Mom, over the ocean –"

"Indeed," came the voice of Karéin-Mayréij, her own protective bubble now lowered. "*Vîrya* Melissa has learned how to make her shield into a bludgeon. For proof of this... observe yonder forest."

Her commentary was apt; Melissa's new-found attack had almost completely smashed all the trees on the outermost periphery of the forest – snapping the trunks of many at about a person's waist-height – and had subjected those in the second and third ranks to progressively less damage, including some sort of thermal-effect that had charred the bark and leaves off them.

The teenager stared in wide-eyed disbelief.

"Y'all mean... I done *that?*" she gasped.

The Storied Watcher approached Melissa, put an arm around the teenager's shoulder, and in a motherly, instructive tone, counseled, "Yes, my sister – you *did!* This is a war-art that my kin term *'T'à'b'-ak'ài'*... the word means, roughly, 'The Shattering Shield'. Many of those who can call upon the *Fire* can use it, although for some, it manifests to no more than a loud shout or noise; for others who are more puissant, it can deafen nearby enemies or send them careening... however, your own bubble is already very strong, and when you use it in this dread manner – well, you can see the results for yourself. Impressive... do you not think?"

"Y'all can say *that* again," stammered Melissa.

"Just don't tell Curtis how to do it... okay?" quipped Billings.

"Y'all can be shore of *that*, Mista Billins'," wryly responded the teenager. "He loud 'nuff, already."

"And this means, perforce," continued the Storied Watcher, addressing Melissa, "That you have been entrusted with a power that can crush and blast the very *lives* of mortal enemies who we may yet encounter, on our journey. You can snuff out their existence with naught more than a *thought* – that is, the one that the Venerable One has just taught you. How does knowing this, make you feel?"

Melissa stopped and pondered for a couple of seconds, and then replied, "'Lot of thangs, Karéin... firstly, it *scary* – I ain't ever even fired no gun before, y'all understand? An' Momma done tell us, 'y'all ever kill someone, y'all more'n half-way to th' hot place when y'all pass 'way'... so ah don' want to do that – *never*. But..."

"'But', *what?*" asked Ramirez.

"Well," admitted the teenager, "Ah just wish ah'd had this thang back down in th' jail up there in 'laska... if'n ah had, maybe Momma still have her tongue, y'know?"

"A *lot* of things would've been different," chimed in Billings, looking wistfully at Tommy. "Like, if I had been able to... before they... *you* know..."

"Don't sweat it, Mr. Billings," consoled the boy. "They got what they deserved... *eventually*."

"Mighty powers require the restraint of true nobility," observed Karéin-Mayréij. "And now, dear sister Melissa, you must learn these ways, yourself."

"Ah'll *try*, Angel Lady," said the teenager. "Ah *swears* it!"

"Oh-kay," serenely responded the alien-girl.

"Karéin," inquired Ramirez, "Many of the rest of us have been working on our, uhh, personal force-fields, since at least as far back as our camping-trip up there in Canada... after all, you instructed us yourself on how to do it. Is Melissa the only one who can use this, uhh, 'yab-akai' thing?"

"No," answered the Storied Watcher.

"So who else can use it?" asked Billings.

"Theoretically... *all* of you," evenly replied Karéin-Mayréij.

"Well, then?" pressed Saquina White. "When's the lesson? And why didn't y'all teach us before?"

"There are many reasons," explained the alien-girl. "Foremost among these are, one, you had to learn how to safely control the, ahh, less 'indiscriminate' powers, before you acquired this one; and, two, this can be a *highly* dangerous attack; it affects everything and everyone – friend or foe, guilty or innocent, harmless or dangerous – unlucky enough to be nearby, when your own *I'à'b'-ak'ài'* is triggered. This is doubly-perilous, because its effects are particular to the *Khùl-Algrenàthi'i Srelkh* who uses it; one person's attack may be relatively easy for the rest of you to resist or survive, while that of the next may be deadly and may slay all for many paces distant. There are other reasons, beside..."

"I want to *learn*, Mom!" demanded an instantly demon-faced Tommy. "I'll get them to close in on me, and then –"

"Okay, Sari... I see what you mean," grunted Billings, looking dismissively at his adoptive son. "Kid's already got an alien machine-gun... no need for him to have an alien Claymore mine, too –"

"Y'all been *playin'* us, Karéin," complained Saquina White.

"What do you mean?" deflected the Storied Watcher.

"For starters," interjected Ramirez, "Why wouldn't you have taught this nice, destructive little trick to – at least – Minnie and her group, and Sam and his?"

"Yeah," added Saquina White. "What with what they up against... they sure could use it, I'd reckon."

"The arts that they can already deploy, are very potent," claimed Karéin-Mayréij. "These should be more than enough to achieve their objectives – those of both parties."

"But your holding out on them like this," pressed Ramirez, "Might endanger their lives. What if their 'ordinary' powers aren't up to the job, and they need to fight their way out of – I don't know – say, some kind of prison like they were stuck in, up there on Amchitka? How can you know for *sure*, Karéin? For that matter... how can *we?*"

The Storied Watcher stood silent for a few long seconds, and during that time, her acolytes worried that this line of questioning might have antagonized her.

But presently, she again spoke up, and her voice was soft and contemplative.

"Have you considered, dear friends," she counseled, "That I might have done this – oh-kay, that I might have *refrained* from doing this – out of fear?"

"*You? Afraid? Get ouut!*" taunted Tommy.

"Not for myself," said Karéin-Mayréij, "For the people of this world."

"What do you... uhh... *mean?*" nervously asked the Tex-Mex scientist.

"When one possesses *Amaiish*," solemnly explained the alien-girl, "It is crucial that one's wisdom – one's compassion for one's fellow-beings – should wax, in like measure with the potency of one's powers. All of you are yet very new to these weirding-arts... and they are already growing in you, substantially faster than memory tells me, has ever previously been the case, in the Many Worlds. Venerable *Vîrya Quü'j* confirms this, and her recollection far surpasses my own. I fear that the balance between your recourse to the *Fire*, and your ability to regulate its destructiveness, is falling out of alignment. Even more so with those pledged to brave Sam Jacobson... since they are further along in this process."

"So y'all afraid they might kill a bunch of folks, if they get cornered again?" advanced Saquina White.

"I saw the results at this 'Repository' place," observed the Storied Watcher. "Much of it has been shattered, and by an explosion from the inside out. Perhaps Sam's compatriots already *have* learned of this dread art."

"Ahh... what you warned me about, way back in Tucson," phlegmatically remarked Billings. "Remember how you said, 'don't be anywhere near, when I have to defend myself'?"

"Aye," confirmed Karéin-Mayréij. "And this is only one of several... each equally – or more – deadly... and all just as indiscriminate. Remember the refulgent burst of sun-fire that destroyed the comet, that saved your planet, and that almost killed me? Imagine something like that... only somewhat less potent."

An awed Ramirez shook his head and commented, "I can't *begin* to imagine the amount of energy that you're talking about here, Karéin... I take back what I just said about Sam and Minnie. Allowing ordinary people – like us, for example – to possess this kind of destructiveness... that's an *insane* idea! Sooner or later, somebody's *bound* to use it – and I don't think I have to explain what the likely consequences will be, if any innocent bystanders happen to be around. Can't you, uhh, 'order it back', or something?"

"No," quietly countered the alien-girl. "Like other blessings of the *Fire*, this is a path that cannot be traveled backwards. But if it is of any consolation... you and your brothers and sisters are nothing like, 'ordinary humans'... not *now*."

"You didn't tell us about this back in the canyon, when you enticed us into this high-falootin' alien lifestyle, you know," complained the Tex-Mex scientist.

"You would not have *understood*," deflected the Storied Watcher.

"I *guess* not," ruefully offered Ramirez.

"Okay... you're saying that I can do this kind of 'alien-suicide-belt' crap myself... do I have that right, Sari?" interjected Billings.

"Aye," repeated his erstwhile girlfriend. "Though it will manifest differently. It is your destiny. Do you remember how I told you that 'the American President would be *insane* to fight me'?"

He let out a resigned-sounding sigh.

"How could I ever *forget*," muttered the salesman. "You have a talent for understatement."

"You were frightened enough of me, at that time," noted the Storied Watcher. "I sought not to magnify your anxiety; nor, in so doing, drive you away from me. And do you know what is ironic? I will say it : now, the President and his war-legions must fear *another*, who equally can blast enemies into nothingness, with naught but a thought. To whom do you think I refer, my love?"

"Swell," muttered Billings. "Another way to slaughter people... just what I *needed*. *Jesus*, Sari!"

"I believe that this 'Jesus' of yours eschewed violence," wryly observed the alien-girl. "That is an ideal to which I would also strive... when this is all over."

"Okay, we *get* it, Sari... but if this thang's so dread, why y'all teach it to me?" asked Melissa Claremont.

"Presumably, you will only use *I'à'b'-ak'ài'* when you are high in the atmosphere above... that is, far away from bystanders," offered the alien-girl. "And whenever something new is tried, one person is *always* first, after all."

"Guess we'll find out, one way or 'nother," observed Saquina White. "I just hope nobody got to die, doin' that."

"May it be so," added Karéin-Mayréij, briefly bowing her head and clasping her hands, as she spoke.

There was another long silence, and then Ramirez spoke up.

"We should get going," he said. "Setting off a bomb – alien- or human-variety – is likely to set off somebody's motion-sensors... especially this close to something like the Repository."

The Storied Watcher nodded affirmatively, and turned to address the teenager.

"The time to fly approaches, young sister," declared the alien-girl. "Are you ready?"

Melissa stepped away, with clenched fists, with traces of the *Fire* evident below her clothing and with a dim glow in her eyes.

In a voice still her own, but somehow echoing with a new-found, siren-like quality, Melissa replied, "Yes I *am*, Karéin – let's... *fly!*"

And with that, Melissa Claremont, encased in an almost invisibly-translucent bubble that could now destroy as well as protect, soared into the air, coming to a hover at an altitude of about a hundred feet.

Karéin-Mayréij turned to look at the others. Without another word, she extended and then elevated a mail-clad finger, pointing at the door to the *Mailànkh Express*; the gesture was not lost on her more-than-human acolytes, who immediately re-boarded the air-ship.

The doorway closed.

In another couple of seconds, the Storied Watcher – her own powers surging in familiar fashion, had pulled the *Mailànkh Express* straight upward, so its stern-end was in front of the teenager, at an equivalent height.

We will cruise at a few hundred meters' altitude, at a speed of about four hundred kil-o-meters per hour, so as to be inconspicuous to the President's air-spies; and you should stay just outside my cloaking-field, behind this ark within which reside our beloved, soundlessly instructed Karéin-Mayréij.

I will make it so that you can see the hind-parts of the Express *in one kind of* Um'b'as'ài, *as long as you are dead-astern of her. In this way you can easily follow; yet, neither will it be easy for the President's air-warriors to detect or track us. Do you understand?*

Think ah does, Karéin, mentally responded Melissa. *Yeah... okay... ah sees that 'really dark purple' sh... ah means, 'stuff'. But... just one thang...*

Yes? patiently answered the Storied Watcher.

What if they does *catch us, 'spite everythin'?* asked the teenager.

Then, we try to fly away, sent Karéin-Mayréij. *Allowing for the fact, of course, that we cannot man-oo-ver very well, with the* Express *in tow. The rapid-turns needed to dodge the guided war-arrows fired by these 'fighter-planes', would instantly kill a normal human... and they would likely injure even our brothers and sisters within the sky-ark.*

So what we do if that *happen?* pressed Melissa.

I would have thought that this would be obvious, the alien-girl sent back.

Uhh... hesitated the flying-teenager. *Guess ah ain't much on riddles these days, Angel Lady. Mind tellin' me what ah's s'posed to do?*

Easy, responded Karéin-Mayréij. *In that case... you fly by yourself, as fast and high as you need to do – always keeping watch on where I have gone, all the while – and you chase down our assailants.*

Then... you blast them out of the sky.

Right, grimly resolved Melissa Claremont, as she brought her *Fire* to full-power.

Scalps At Arrow And Sierra Madre

The scouting-expedition had taken longer to get going than had been planned, of course; some of the communications-gear had been balky, and one of White Terror Leader Clayton Lomass' fellow-warriors had insisted on "having a little fun" with a few of the female Latino captives from the dungeons under the golf course bunker, before setting out. (This, of course, ended up with two fewer living slaves, plus another two scarred and crippled for life.)

None the less, by the late morning on this day, Lomass had a string of six black- and brown-colored ears hanging from his black-leather-and-chrome belt.

As he walked slowly and attentively down the sidewalk beside the Los Angeles area Arrow Highway, with his M-240LNG machine-gun at the ready (of course, it was a point of pride to fire the thing from his hip), the hulking, shaved-head, elaborately-tattooed Whiteman strike-force leader felt uneasy. His victories so far had mostly been lower-level Latino and African-American street-runners, and three out of the six had been shot in the back – hardly good sport, after all... and not much of a challenge for an self-respecting Aryan warrior.

Still, he reassured himself, *an ear's an ear. It's all good.*

Along with the other two equally big-and-mean, sweating skinhead warriors who were covering him as the group advanced eastward, having just made their planned turn at the junction of Arrow and Grove, Lomass was taking it slow.

After all, the area was teeming with ruthless, well-armed Latino and black gang-bangers, and just collecting dried-out ears, scalps, girl-nipples and boy-dicks – usual trophies of the Aryan Nations – wasn't the objective, *this* time. So he just took the ears; he left the other, severed and blood-smeared body-parts, stuffed in the lifeless mouths of those foolish or unlucky enough, to have been in the proverbial wrong place at the wrong time.

You gotta advertise, after all, he reasoned.

And there's our "trademark".

There was a familiar sound : the staccato *crack-crack-crack* of auto-rifle-fire, about a block ahead. Instinctively, the Aryan Nations West Front commander sent a hand-signal to his two compatriots, and then quickly raced to crouch beside a nearby privacy-wall, which separated a now-abandoned bungalow from the street.

For perhaps five seconds, the sounds continued; then there was a short pause, during which Lomass again began to cautiously rise and advance; then the weapon-fire returned, with multiple combatants evidently involved.

Another signal from the Terror Leader brought the other two over to his immediate vicinity.

"Yeah?" asked Little Joe Hale, a brush-cut, blond-haired monster of a man, taller than Lomass by at least an inch and a half and heavier by fifty pounds. The swastika tattoo on his biceps twisted out of shape, as he flexed his muscles. "Don't tell me it's the fuckin' go-home alarm... we just got *out* here, and I'm startin' to have some *fun*."

"Nah... showin' green, no need to head back yet... it's just some fuckin' *putos* up ahead," explained the commander. "Heavy business. But I can't tell who they're shootin' it out with."

"Niggers, maybe?" offered Buzz Blackworth, a tight-muscled, dark-haired guy of about Lomass' size, with a goatee and cruel, shifty, almost black eyes.

"Dunno... probably," indicated the Terror Leader.

"Well, let the fuckers do each other," proposed Hale. "Who *gives* a shit?"

"Yeah... I got plenty of ears already," snorted Blackworth.

"Problem is, them scumbags is right across our path, and we've doubled back pretty far east... which was always the plan," observed Lomass. "Can't rule out the possibility that it's AB'ers they're up against, or if the *objective's* bein' used in the fight – in which case, you *know* what we gotta do. Let's recce it out... if it's them fuckin' Bloods, Crips or El-Rukn's, without what we're lookin' for, we leave 'em be and hope they smoke the *tamale*-fuckers... and vice-versey. Got it?"

Rueful grunts of acknowledgment came from the other two Aryan warriors, as they released their safeties and prepared for full battle mode.

With Blackworth and Hale about ten feet behind, Lomass approached the intersection of Arrow Route and Sierra Madre Avenue, moving cautiously and looking carefully in all directions, taking stock of the situation with each foot-step. He crept forward on the south-west corner of the road-junction just north of an abandoned doctor's-office-building, trying to keep under cover, although the desiccated remains of the trees and shrubs in the front lawn of the building didn't provide enough to hide his extra-large frame as much as he'd have preferred them to do.

This area was no stranger to gang-fights, a fact mutely attested to by the broken glass and chip-marks made by bullet-impacts against nearby windows and concrete walls – not to mention the turf-marks and other graffiti that emblazoned most of the surrounding vertical surfaces.

Suddenly, a fusillade of gunfire erupted from the smallish house on the other, south-east side of the street – no, on second thought, *not* from the house, but from a position behind its far side – then from the house one spot further east, down Arrow Highway.

By counting the number of discrete firing-positions and by his own estimation, Lomass figured that there had to be at least three and probably four groups of concealed gang-bangers on the southern side of the street, and for a second or two, the Aryan warrior was actually concerned for his own safety. However, with relief, he noted that the shots were not directed against him or his two soldiers. Rather, they impacted all over the window-openings of a similar bungalow on the north-east side of the intersection, from which a few shots – many fewer than had come from the southern house – issued in return.

To his alarm, he also realized that the northern house was being fired at from several concealed points on the north-west side of the intersection.

Shit – if them that's up there look south, there's a clear shot, at us...

Guttural taunts in Spanish came from the southern group of belligerents.

Fuck, he thought. *Latino putos... a lot of 'em, judgin' by how many guns.*

We could take 'em – but not now, not 'till that fuckin' thing shows – and there's more of the fuckers on the other side of the street, they got us flanked. How'd that happen, anyway?

Fuck!

He waited for a few seconds, while the gunfight continued.

Funny, considered Lomass.

If it's niggers in that other house... they're the quietest ones I ever seen. Usually them porch-monkeys is yellin' curses like no tomorrow, when it gets hot.

The next events – which transpired in only a few short seconds – left the Aryan leader shaking his head with wary amazement.

There was a chorus of ululating cries in some foreign tongue that Lomass didn't recognize coming from the north-east bungalow, and then a barrage of gunfire erupted from the place, mostly directed in poorly-aimed but continuous fashion at the south-east house, but with at least one hidden gang-banger firing westward across Sierra Madre.

Out of a corner of his eye, the White Terror Leader saw an oddly-dressed gangsta, charge out of the bungalow's hastily opened-and-closed front door; at first glance, this guy looked Latino, but he had a long, black beard and was wearing a white, body-length robe, with a bulky-looking belt and some kind of red-and-white-checkered handkerchief wrapped around his head.

What the fuck's he doin? incredulously considered Lomass. *He's either the bravest mofo I ever seen, or he's fuckin' loco – he ain't even packin' –*

Shrieking incoherently while he dashed across Arrow Highway, stooping down so as to avoid the occasional shot coming back at him – a tactic that worked until this crazy-man got almost up to the low, screen-mesh fence that surrounded the south-east house, as he took one in the thigh, dropped down for a second, and then charged forward, leaving a gushing trail of blood behind him.

The white-robed guy was now right in front of the doorway to the south-east house. Still yelling something that Lomass couldn't begin to understand – although he could tell that it certainly wasn't Spanish – the bleeding, crazy-man took a green-covered, gold-embroidered book of some kind out from under his robe, waved it around while sending a wide-eyed, berserk-looking, leering grin right at the Aryan leader, and then...

BOOM!

A tremendously-powerful, fiery explosion radiated outward, from where the white-robed crazy-guy had just been standing. Windows in every direction shattered, as did almost everything else that was anywhere near the blast-point.

Reflexively, Lomass hit the ground; good that he did, because it was a fraction of a second before a hail of shrapnel rocketed over his head. This was followed by a billowing dust-cloud that covered everything near the intersection, with a thick, suffocating layer of sand-colored dirt.

Half-stunned from the shock-wave that hit him like the impact of a wrecking-ball, the Whiteman felt a trickle of blood from deep inside his left ear, and another one from one of his nostrils. To his relief, though, he could still hear the sounds of utter chaos going on around him, even over the dull ringing that now beset his head. His body was also scarred and aching from the buckshot-like impact of small pieces of debris that he hadn't been able to dodge. The pain from this was, however, manageable.

The Aryan Brotherhood leader managed a half-roll so that he could look backward, and immediately he felt a surge of regret, pity and hatred. Hale was dazed but he was still operational.

Blackworth hadn't been so lucky; he had been thrown against a stucco-wall and was now seated with his back against it, with blood pouring out of his mouth and from his neck, which had been almost severed by a flying piece of jagged metal. There was also some other piece of junk lodged in his right eye, from which blood was gushing.

Reflexive nerve-responses told of the unfortunate warrior's last moments, as Blackworth's dirty-covered body twitched and shook, while pouring its life-force out on the dry earth.

Lomass felt like screaming in fury, but he knew that his group – already badly-outnumbered – had just had its numbers reduced by a third; so, despite the urge, he held his tongue.

There's this wall between us – even poor ol' Buzz, what's left of him – and them fuckers north and north-east, he reasoned. *Sit tight, at least we get a good shot, if they come for us...*

Hunkered down, he forced himself to look due east.

Where the south-east house had stood, there was now nothing but a flame-infused foundation, consisting of charred, splintered wood-remnants and crumbled, haphazardly-strewn bricks; the building, along with those who had been in it, had been completely destroyed, as had been most of the houses immediately to the place's east on Arrow Highway and south on Sierra Madre.

The place on the north-east, from which the late crazy-man had issued, was missing its front door, many of its roof-tiles and anything that had been around its windows, but was still standing.

There was confused shouting in Spanish from the north-west side of the intersection; after five or six seconds, this ebbed, and it sounded like whomever had been shooting at the suicide-man's hideout, had retreated, although Lomass didn't know in which direction.

They could be right behind us, for all I know, thought the frustrated Whiteman, as he silently motioned for Hale to advance. The other man did, albeit on his belly, all the way.

"What we gonna do with Buzz?" whispered the dust-covered big guy, as he approached his commander from behind. "He deserves a decent –"

"*You* know the rules," interrupted subdued-voice Aryan leader. "Soon as we can do it without bein' noticed, we strip his gear, much as we can carry, get some rocks, build a cairn. Now cork it – I hear *talkin'!*"

Indeed, he was right. A group of three thugs, dressed in street-clothes although still somehow different-looking compared to what you'd have expected of a standard bunch of, say, *Mexican Mafia* types, had come out of the north-east house. Unlike their now-departed compatriot, they very obviously had guns at the ready, as they cautiously explored the remains of the devastated south-east-corner bungalow.

Through pain-throbbing, encrusted-bloody ears, Lomass strained to hear what was being said. Much of it was in the strange language that had formed the suicide-guy's last words, but occasionally these out-of-place gang-bangers reverted to English. The Whiteman leader made out a lot of back-and-forth along the lines of, "blessed be Brother Mumtaz, he is now in Paradise". Then he heard something that immediately brought both interest and worry :

"The way is open to the objective... where is that... yes, if the map is correct, that 'Empire Lakes' golf-course... it *must* be somewhere in there," stated one of the strange group of gangsters. "We will soon be close enough to use the homing-device."

"But what of the buzzing horror, which took Brother Ali?" argued another. "It also looked to be heading straight toward the objective. If we do not detour, we shall likely encounter it, again."

One of the gang-bangers – a tall guy – reflectively stared off into space and only said, "Insh'allah."

What the fuck? silently pondered Lomass.

What are them camel-fuckers doin' down here? And why are they headin' back to the Lictor General's bunker?

Either way... better tail 'em... and waste 'em, before they get anywhere near. And if I get lucky... there's my shot at this fuckin' weirdo puto weapon.

He waited, listening to the rest of the conversation – about ninety per cent of which was unfortunately in whatever damn guttural language that they actually spoke – and then stayed down, as the Muslim gang headed southward on the east side of Sierra Madre Avenue.

As the last of them was almost out of sight, Lomass muttered to Hale,

"Two minutes to deal with Buzz... don't forget his string of ears. Gonna add three more camel-fucker ones to 'em, before this day's over."

"I'm gonna be shootin' just to slow 'em down, 'least at first," offered Hale, as he set to work.

"Why the fuck would you do *that?*" countered the Aryan leader, while wiping away caked blood and trying to get at the dead man's ammo-belt.

"Goin' for scalps this time, and when I do it," methodically replied Little Joe, "Gonna take them sand-niggers *alive*. Gonna use Buzz's huntin'-knife."

"*Now* you're talkin'!" grunted a grimly-determined Clayton Lomass.

Hot Red, Hot-Head Bubble

The effort at leveraging her telekinesis had been Herculean; Tanaka's throbbing, pounding, insufferable headache was unrequited testimony of that.

She knew that she could keep the damn thing airborne, as well as heading eastward at a smart clip; but with Wolf having taken the beating that she had just witnessed – and what with his personal alien-power being sapped that much more, by the driving rain coming from the low clouds – there couldn't have been a lot of reserve left for fighting.

Well, the former science-officer ruefully said to herself, *better me than him, in front, doing the tow.*

Put him up there as lead dog on the sled, and these poor people would have a blowtorch on their windshield.

I guess that makes him what counts as 'top-cover', around here... at least I can sort of tell where we're going, despite this area having nothing but the occasional side-road as a landmark... must be another one of those 'mundane-arts', as Karéin described 'em...

Undoubtedly, the grieving, numb-with-loss Texas farm-family – or what was left of it – would never have consented to the trip, had they known how it was to be conducted. They had merely assented to the more-than-humans' suggestions to "get into the truck – then we'll figure out where we go from there", only to be terrified half to death when the vehicle simply... *took off,* being transported at a height of a couple hundred feet.

At least, it *appeared* to be about that far off the ground; it was almost impossible to judge precisely, because the truck was encircled by some kind of strange effect similar to looking through a thin pane of beer-bottle-glass.

"Where's that guy with the devil-eyes?" asked the boy, from the half-seats behind the front cab.

"Hope I never *see* him again," spat the farm-wife in the drivers-seat, her head still hung low.

"But Mom... he said that he wasn't a –" argued the wounded little girl, in the front passenger-seat.

Her voice was interrupted by panicked yelling from all three of them, as the truck suddenly careened downward, leveling out only when to have gone any further would have put them below the tree-line.

"Oh wow – you see *that?*" shouted the boy, who was now staring at something going on behind and above the truck-cab, through its rear-window. "Must be a missile – big flame comin' from behind it – look *out!*"

BOOM! came the sound of a powerful explosion, which was accompanied by a big fireball, somewhere to their hind-quarters.

Fuck! heard – or, perhaps, felt – Tanaka, coming from places to the aft. The invective was accompanied by a wash of pain and fury, both prominent signs of Wolf's surly personal signature.

A half-second later, it seemed like half the sky behind the airborne-truck lit up, as a barrage of the bounty-hunter's errantly-aimed fireballs seemingly made contact with one of whatever had been pursuing the fugitive group.

"Cherie!" he shouted, from his rear-end vantage-point, "Think I got tagged again – can we put down?"

Shit, angrily realized Tanaka, *He's the proverbial marked target...*

"We're almost there!" countered the former science officer. "Hold 'em off until I can ditch the truck and maneuver again!"

And indeed she was; the Jacobson vehicle – or what she supposed was it – was just below and to her left.

But if I land us too close, and they attack – they might hit that Agency SUV... okay then – right here...

Abruptly – as another flurry of fire-bolts streaked upward at their tormentors, with at least one shot striking and destroying an aircraft or drone – Tanaka dove downward at a sharp angle. The maneuver was met with shouts of dismay from inside the truck, and the former science officer silently prayed that the seat-belts would hold.

Whatever was left of what had been pursuing them, roared overhead, rapidly heading eastward.

Bet you they'll be back, grimly mused the more-than-a-woman.

In the next couple of seconds, the truck landed to a hard, suspension-and-bone-rattling stop on the muddy Texas plains, about three hundred feet from the captives' vehicle. Tire-tracks born of the sudden change in motion, extended over several car-lengths.

Never letting her feet touch ground, Tanaka darted around to the back of the pickup. She saw a badly-bloodied – but still-defiant – Wolf, whose face and upper-body were cruelly-riddled with yet more shrapnel.

"God help us, Wolf!" consoled the former science officer, "You gonna *live?* I can try to heal you again, but if it's your eyes –"

"Stow it, Cherie," gruffly responded the bounty-hunter. "Taken enough today to kill six normal men, I reckon, and I can *feel* that shit in me – big as buckshot meant for a damn *dinosaur* – but Miss Magic Candle 'n me, we got things worked out, by now... stand back!"

Tanaka could feel the heat surging.

"You'll roast our passengers in the cab!" she warned.

With a silent nod, Wolf – a cushion of fire underneath his feet – levitated a few feet into the air, then traveled about twenty feet away from the truck. His sinister, pulsating, crackling war-song began to play with renewed vigor, and – only slightly to her amazement – Tanaka watched with fascination as the bounty-hunter's wounds began to ooze out something that looked very much like molten metal. As this fell under the force of gravity, it solidified, resulting in a rain of reconstituted lead and steel underneath.

How the hell isn't it burning holes in his clothes? she wondered. *And how is it that it didn't kill him already?*

But how glad I am, that my brother is oh-kay!

Oops... sorry, Karéin. Didn't mean to steal your meme...

Wolf now looked profoundly more healthy than he had even a dozen seconds before. Most of the flesh-marks had vanished altogether, although his clothes still were rent and torn where the shrapnel had impacted.

He closed his dull-red-glowing eyes for a second or two, as if concentrating on something. When he opened them again, the shine was brighter, and he was encased in an almost-invisible, red-tinged bubble. Rain-droplets hissed and evaporated, upon coming into contact with it.

"Oh... *wow*," breathed Tanaka. "Like mine?"

"You fuckin' better *believe* it!" came the proud, self-satisfied reply.

"And you know *what*, Cherie?" he added.

She shrugged.

"*They* better believe it, too – got a *score* to settle!" growled Wolf.

With a moon-rocket's-worth of fire propelling him, the bounty-hunter streaked upward through the rain-clouds, turning to the east.

Their Masters' Voice

The burrowing-work had come to a pause, as the sound of a substance more solid than just packed-earth, came into contact with the sharp edge of the living-shield. With her characteristic collection of high-pitched, almost-inaudible chirps and whirring-noises, she communicated to Kaysten and Abruzzio that "is ahead wall something like".

"Don't try anything like 'running away', boys," commanded the former JPL scientist, her eyes glowing malevolently in the dark of the narrow, hewed-from-dirt tunnel behind Maloney and Rizzo, as she edged past them. "You might get two or three steps back, before I can lock on to your shoes."

"They're gonna mark us AWOL, you know," complained the GrayWar guy.

"Fuck it, man," caustically whispered the junior soldier, to his compatriot. "She can fry *your* nuts, for all I care... she ain't gettin' a shot at mine."

Rizzo grunted.

"The 'AWOL" issue's something that I should be able to excuse you for," offered the ex-President with a wry smile, "Provided that... well, *you* know."

"Would you mind standing aside, sir?" asked Abruzzio. "*Vîrya I'ëà'b'* has done most of the heavy-lifting... but I'll need to knock out what remains in front of us."

"How do you propose to do *that?*" nervously inquired the former First Lady. "I can see a light – a little hole – but there's concrete or something all around it. See?"

She had been holding a flashlight, and its light-beam revealed that she spoke the truth. Behind the crumbling dirt was something definitely man-made.

"I'll show you," confidently purred Abruzzio. "Out of the way in front, everybody –"

The ex-President, his First Lady and the rest of them, quickly retreated.

"Give it a good shot, and I'll take a run at it," requested Kaysten, who was now standing beside the scientist, about ten feet from where the Storied Watcher's girl-shield had stopped digging.

"You sure?" she hesitated.

"Go for it," he insisted.

Abruzzio shrugged, and immediately, the glow in her eyes, along with the subtle background-hymn of her susurrating war-song waxed perceptibly; it was joined, in the next second, by Kaysten's own *Fire*-signs.

With fingertips facing upward and her palms facing the wall, the JPL scientist made a pushing-motion, and – with a shock-wave that rattled everything around, causing an alarming cascade of dirt and dust to fall on the group's heads – much of the wall cracked, with a jagged, foot-wide vertical hole opening up at the center-point of where Abruzzio's invisible telekinetic attack, had struck home. The area behind this was well-illuminated, as light flooded from there back into the tunnel.

A split-second later, Kaysten – with an almost-invisible, silver-blue glow encasing his figure – raced forward, reaching impossible speeds from a standing-start. He impacted with the opening, whose formed-concrete edges shattered as if penetrated by a cannon-shell, and rocketed past, out into the open-area beyond. In so doing, he had forced open a breach large enough to easily accommodate at least one person going through at a time.

Those in the tunnel heard a very firm, male voice shout out, "Whoever you are – *freeze!*"

Another voice, also male, barked out the word, "Terrorists!"

"Hey – hey – don't *shoot*, man!" came back Kaysten's reply. "I know this was kind of an, uhh, unexpected entrance... but we're on your side!"

Both war-songs abated to nothingness.

"Get down, with your hands behind your head!" came back the order, from the unseen new voice. "You have two seconds, before I fire!"

There was the sound of a door being slammed shut.

"Okay... *okay!*" muttered Kaysten. "Just let me *explain*, if you don't mind?"

"Mr. President," whispered Abruzzio, "I should go next... I'm the only one among us – other than for *Vîrya I'ëä'b'* of course – who can withstand gunfire... I'm sure you understand why I don't want *her* to go out there head of us."

"I sure *do* understand, Ms. Abruzzio," he replied, *sotto voce*. "But I have to do this. I'm well aware that you – and she – can easily kill everyone who Jerry has encountered. That's precisely why it has to be me. Would you please stand aside?"

Kaysten, meanwhile, seemed to be arguing with whomever he had confronted; he was pleading – apparently to little avail – that "I'm the Chief of Staff... your *boss*, you know?"

"And if they just *shoot* you, sir?" pressed the former JPL scientist. "What do we do then?"

"I honestly don't know," whispered the ex-President, "But in that case, I suppose I won't have to worry about it."

"*Clark!*" exclaimed the First Lady, in an uncautiously-loud voice. This outburst was joined, a second or so later, by an equally-uncalled-for "yip" on the part of Abruzzio's puppy.

"It'll be okay, Ma'am," reassured Moira Sullivan, who had otherwise been as quiet as the proverbial mouse. "It always *is*, with Sylvia."

Owe you one, came an unrequited thought.

"This is the rightful and duly-elected President of the United States now addressing you, gentlemen of the Secret Service," called out the former American leader, from inside the tunnel. "I'm unarmed. I'll come out into the open, in three seconds."

"Exit the tunnel with your hands in the air," ordered the unseen, police-type voice.

"Certainly," said the ex-President, as he complied, forcing his way through the breach that Kaysten and Abruzzio had made in the outside retaining-wall, with his arms held as far up as the confines would allow.

Abruzzio – though not the others, save the living-shield – could hear gasps of recognition, coming from what she could now see was a lavishly-equipped meeting-room, with leather-bound seats arranged around a long, oaken table, with computer-screens and maps on every part of the walls surrounding the table.

"Stand down, gentlemen," demanded the ex-President. "Yes... it's really me."

"You *could* just be a stunt-double," argued a guy, who – while she was still hiding in the shadows – Abruzzio could tell must have been a Secret Service agent. "If you're really – uhh – 'real'... I assume you heard about that little incident that happened here, with the alien and your stand-in, sir?"

"Yeah... I did," confirmed the U.S. leader. "Much more to that – for example, as you can see, Jerry Kaysten's still very much with us – than you've probably been told," offered the U.S. leader. "Oh – and... Command ID code Oscar Alpha, Eight-Fourteen."

"Challenge word Tango Zulu, Thirty-Seven," said the agent, using some form of internal U.S. government cant.

"Confirmation word, Papa Bravo, Zero-Three," confidently provided the ex-President.

"*Shit*... that's a match," Abruzzio heard someone else say. "Okay... okay. Don – get the DNA-tester. Come *on!*"

"It's in the case," a third voice replied. "Just a sec... yeah... here. Got it. Mr. President – hate to ask you, but can you please open your mouth... you can put down your arms, now, sir."

"Oh... no problem," the U.S. leader stated.

There were more fumbling-sounds, and then Abruzzio – who had, by now, been joined, in tight proximity, by the former First Lady and her two children – heard, "Mr. President – sir – with all due respect... what the hell's going *on*? Why are you – uhh – busting into the Situation Room, through a *wall*?"

"That's a long story, Agent... let me see... oh yeah, Agent 'Kortish' – that's *Curt* Kortish... right? Of course, I remember you," smoothly explained the ex-President. "Curt, didn't you sign on to the White House detail, shortly before the 'comet' business started up? Remember... you had just transferred in from the Rowley Center, and you wanted me to autograph a letter for your son?"

There was a long silence, and then they heard the befuddled agent reply, "Jesus... it's *gotta* be him – *nobody* else knows about that! Don – cancel the alert, and the perimeter integrity-alarm, too. We'll need to get the contractors in here to fix this thing up... can you call –"

"Just a couple of things, first, if you don't mind," requested the former American leader. "One... can you please get those handcuffs off of my Chief of Staff. And two..."

"What, sir?" asked the agent.

"I have a few friends and family, who'll be coming out of that tunnel," said the ex-President.

Please... No More Funerals

Keep him safe... give him victory, Destroying Angel, silently prayed Cherie Tanaka, as she flew quickly to the pickup-truck's driver-side, landed on the running-board and then opened the door. Inside were three profoundly-terrified humans, each of whom looked like they had not taken well to the ride of their lives.

Her left hand gave a "come out" gesture, but no movement seemed to be forthcoming on the part of the passengers.

"L-lady – your *eyes...*" stammered the little girl.

"Ah, yes," answered the former science officer. "Like Wolf's... but different 'color of the *Fire*', is how our mentor – the mighty Storied Watcher – described this feature, to us. You'll just have to get used to it, I guess. Now... *please* get out of the truck! While we were airborne, we were being pursued by fighter-planes, or something like that, and they might have seen where we came down. If they come back around at us, this vehicle is going to have a big bulls-eye on it."

"Where we supposed to go?" asked the boy.

"Over there – several hundred feet, not a long run," responded Tanaka. "There's a SUV over there, big enough to hold those who are already there, and the rest of you, as well."

"Who's that?" mumbled the farm-wife.

"Friends... I hope," offered Tanaka. "Now come on!"

To her relief, the three stirred, after quickly rummaging around for the few belongings that they could carry. In a minute or so, they were all sprinting across the sodden Texas field, toward the Jacobson SUV, with the former science officer's force-field doing an inadequate job of shielding them from the rain-storm.

About halfway, Tanaka's special hearing detected the low, percussive "booms" of explosions, somewhere far off to the east.

Well, Wolf... if there's anyone to 'give 'em hell'...

Upon arrival, the SUV looked pretty much exactly as it had, when she had reluctantly left it there, a short while ago.

Odd... no noise from inside there – didn't they notice anything was amiss? If they're still alive, of course... damn it, Cherie – don't think like that!

Vîrya Sài'ymë... if thou please – give me a crowbar!

Instantly, a translucent, hard-to-see-in-the-darkness pseudopod, extended from the surface of the living-armor.

"Holy – what's *that?*" exclaimed a wide-eyed farm-boy.

"A child, like you – uhh, okay, *not* quite like you," mumbled Tanaka.

She couldn't figure out how the thing had got past her outer layer of clothing, without ripping a large hole in the latter; her war-child's essence seemed to "ooze" through, as if it were water going through a cheese-cloth. It formed into a straight appendage very much like a steel pipe with a double hook in its end, but – unfortunately – *Vîrya Sài'ymë* had formed it rather too close to her *ersatz* mother's waist, so Tanaka had to slightly levitate to get the thing wedged against the rather formidable-looking bar-lock that the SUV's former Agency owners, had affixed to the vehicle's rear-doors.

The more-than-a-woman used judicious amounts of her lightening-attack on the hinged attachment-points for the lock, while simultaneously fixing her telekinetic powers on the object and twisting on the long axis of *Vîrya Sài'ymë*'s contrived "crowbar".

The lock split apart just after it flew off its hinges, to Tanaka's satisfaction. The door appeared not to have been separately-locked (or perhaps this had been disengaged, in the sound and fury back near the bridge), and it opened easily.

The former science officer's enhanced vision disclosed a scene that immediately made her heart sink, as her war-child retracted the "crowbar" into nothingness.

Inside a paddy-wagon-like enclosure, with Army-style metal sitting-benches on either side of the cabin, were five forlorn, trussed-up, slumping figures : two smaller ones, two adult-sized but slender ones, and a rather more substantial one, furthest away from her sight. All of these were in the now-infamous U.S. government "rendition" garb, namely orange prison-suits, cheap sneakers with no socks, hoods that completely covered the head, and handcuffs on both wrists and ankles.

Five of them... wait a minute... Sam's family is only four?

Ominously, the prisoners made no sound and did not stir, although – thankfully – Tanaka could somehow hear heart-beats and could tell that the captives were still breathing.

"Thank God – looks like they're *alive!*" exclaimed the former science officer.

"Who's, 'alive'?" asked the wounded farm-girl.

"Friends," responded Tanaka. "Family of my former boss – at least that's who I *hope* they are. Stay outside, and keep your eyes peeled for signs of the military coming back our way – airplane engine-noise, lights in the sky, that kind of thing. If you see anything... yell!"

Ever-mindful of the possibility of another attack from above, she darted into the cabin and went to the largest adult figure, pulling the hood off the latter in a swift motion. This was an average-looking white-haired, Caucasian woman in her late-forties or early-fifties.

Well... I remember her, from the pre-launch cocktail-parties at NASA, ruefully acknowledged Tanaka.

Now all I have to do is figure out how to explain that I've been helping her husband to cheat.

"Yvonne? Mrs. Jacobson?" she spoke, while gently prodding the captive on the shoulders. "It's me, Cherie Tanaka, from the Mars mission – do you *hear* me?"

But the woman's head just lolled back, as if she were unconscious. This prognosis was confirmed a second later, when Tanaka used a combination of finger-tips and telekinesis to open the captive's eyelids, revealing characteristically-dilated pupils and a complete lack of response to having light shone into them.

Shit, realized the former science officer, *they must be drugged – and with something pretty damn potent. I can* smell *it on them... ugh...*

Could try the same thing as I did on Melissa and Whitney, back in that accursed prison... but they were New People.

Didn't Karéin say something about "the mortal mind is a fragile thing – to abruptly force it back from the dream-world, risks leaving some of it behind, never to return", in one of those sessions back at the camp?

But it was draining to me, and there are five *of them – it would take too long, anyway.*

A voice sounded from outside. It was the boy.

"Lady," he remarked, "Those people are dressed up in, like, prison-uniforms. Doesn't that mean they're criminals or something?"

"No – far *from* it," replied Tanaka, not returning the boy's glance as she spoke. "The Government was trying to use them as hostages, against Sam Jacobson – he's the former commander who I told you about – and me. Can you come up here and help me for a minute, please? And bring your sister too."

The boy shot a stare at his mother.

"'Zat okay?" he asked.

The farm-wife just mutely nodded, while staring into space. It was a demeanor that Tanaka recognized.

Just what I need, she mused.

Five drugged, immobile and utterly helpless prisoners to defend... and a woman slowly going into traumatic shock, as well.

The boy and his younger sister clambered aboard the SUV; the thing's roof was high enough that neither really had to stoop, unlike the former science officer.

"Why are they... tied up so much?" warily asked the girl.

"They were kidnapped, by some very bad, mean people," said Tanaka. "The same people, incidentally, who were dropping bombs on us, back at your ranch –"

Momentarily, she stopped talking, as her enhanced hearing picked up more explosive-sounds; these were perhaps further away, and more to the north, than the last set had been.

"What?" pressed the girl.

"Nothing... *nothing,*" responded Tanaka. "You and your brother – you didn't see anything out there, a minute ago... did you?"

"Uh-uhh," came back the answer, with a negative head-shake.

"Well then, I'm hoping we have at least a few minutes, before we get more bombs dropped on our heads," muttered the more-than-a-woman. "Here – Vîrya Sài'ymë and I will try to get those damn – excuse me, 'darn' – shackles, off their hands and feet, and you two try to –"

"Who?" inquired the boy. "Who's this other person? There somebody else around here?"

"Who... you mean – oh... *right.* Well, that's – uhh – 'complicated', I guess – I doubt you'd understand about her... Vîrya Sài'ymë, that is. She's kind of my – uhh – 'child'... except you can't see her."

"What?" asked the dumbfounded girl.

"I *said*, 'I didn't think you'd understand'," grumbled Tanaka. "Long story... I'll fill you in later."

With that, she set to work, requesting that her war-child produce a pair of pincer-like appendages which – when assisted with small amounts of telekinetic force, to the wide-eyed amazement of the two human children – made methodical short work of the arm- and leg-restraints that had been afflicting the captives.

In no more than another minute or so, all of the prisoners had been freed, after a fashion; but to Tanaka's disappointment, all of them were also in the same somnolent state as was Yvonne Jacobson.

The former science officer recognized one person – it was her old boss's son, a callow-looking boy in his early teens – and there were three girls, one of about the same age as the farm-boy and two older ones, whose age and physical appearance reminded Tanaka more or less of the Storied Watcher herself (although one of the teenage girls had dark, almost black hair).

Didn't Sam say that he only had one *daughter in college?* she mused.

Well – whoever you are – apologies in advance.

"You're in for a hell of a ride," she absent-mindedly murmured.

"You say somethin', lady?" inquired the farm-boy.

"No... nothing," demurred Tanaka. "Just talking to myself, I guess. Can you call your mother, please?"

"Sure," he replied, jumping to the ground from the SUV's tailgate.

The former science officer heard the boy imploring the farm-wife, multiple times, and eventually, she seemed to snap out of her stupor. She came around to the back of the vehicle.

"Yeah?" said the farm-woman.

"Okay – we've done all we can for the Jacobsons, for the time being," announced Tanaka. So –"

"'Jacobsons'?" interrupted the farm-wife. "Who's that? And what're they doin' in a big black truck like this, all trussed-up 'n such?"

"Like I said to your son, Ma'am," responded Tanaka, trying as hard as she could to be polite, "It's a long story – they're the family of a very close friend of mine, and he's on his way here now, but –"

"So you sprung 'em from jail?" pressed the farm-woman. "Don't tell me you didn't – I know what them clothes they're in, are all about."

"You don't know the whole *story*," argued Tanaka. "They were illegally-captured, not by the police, but by the Agency – that's the CIA, by the way – and they didn't *do* anything; the Agency wanted to use them as hostages against Sam, me and the rest of us. If I hadn't gotten here when I did, well, you don't want to know what the Government was going to do to them, just to get back at us."

"Oh... I got an idea," countered the farm-wife. "Same as they do to folks 'round here, when they get caught brewin' up meth or synth. Anyway, lady... if you got a gang and you're runnin' against the law, I guess I got no choice except run with you, until they get you cornered. That happens... you gonna let Chris, Kerri and me get out of all this? Or are *we* hostages, too?"

With compassion in her voice, the former science officer answered, "Of *course* not... uhh... what did you say your name was, again?"

"My name's 'Cassie'," said the farm-wife. "Cassie Young."

"Nice to meet you and your family – well, no, it's never 'nice' in circumstances like this," abashedly offered the more-than-a-woman. "My name's Cherie Tanaka... my flying, flaming friend is a former bounty-hunter named 'Darryl Bennington', but don't call him that – he prefers to be called 'Wolf', you know?"

"How you *do* that, lady?" asked the farm-boy. "Flying around and firin' those lightening-bolts and stuff. It's *so* cool!"

"I'd lose it in a heartbeat, if doing so could bring your father back, son," spoke Tanaka, "But yes... it *is* pretty amazing... isn't it? Wolf and I use a supernatural power called '*The Fire*', which we were given by Karéin-Mayréij, the 'angel' who you may have seen coming back to life on Mars –"

"Is she... *real?*" inquired the girl. "The... 'angel', I mean."

"*Very* real," answered the former science officer, bending over to look the farm-girl in the face. "Karéin is now one of my most near and dear friends... in addition to being the most powerful being ever to show up on this planet. And if you hang with us, there's an excellent chance that you'll get to meet her."

"*Really?*" said the wide-eyed, instantly-excited child.

"Nothin' but *devils*," muttered the farm-wife. "Like that guy with you..."

"Neither Karéin, nor Wolf, nor I, have anything to do with evil," countered Tanaka. "We had to take a pledge to fight it, to be allowed to use the *Fire* in the first place, as a matter of fact. Once you get to know the Storied Watcher and myself a little better, I think you'll come to understand that, Ma'am; and as for Wolf, well –"

Her extra-sensitive ears noticed the bounty-hunter's sinister-yet-inspiring war-song, off in the distance, and she remarked, "Looks like you'll soon get a chance to ask him yourself."

The sound of Wolf's coming waxed, to the point where even the apprehensive humans could hear it; there was a brief increase in luminosity overhead, and then both the sound and the light diminished rapidly.

Where's he going? thought the former science officer.

But before she could ponder the subject any more, the bounty-hunter's light-, heat- and song-signature returned.

With a pillar of flame underneath his feet, Wolf alighted on scorched ground, about thirty feet away from the SUV. He then pointed both arms directly up, and fired two brilliant fireballs, directly into the vertical.

"*Wolf!*" shouted an alarmed Tanaka. "What the hell are you *doing?* You'll lead the whole *Air Force* to us!"

"Took care of all them fighter-plane mothers 'round here, already," nonchalantly replied the bounty-hunter, as he strode confidently up to the vehicle, while tamping down his fire-shield as well as extinguishing the red glow in his eyes. "Took a page out of Little Miss Nuclear Angel's playbook – didn't flame their parachutes. Admit to bein' sorely tempted, though. But that ain't why I did it, anyway... it's so Mister Diamond-Ass and them in the plane, can find us –"

At this point, the barely-visible outline of a large-sized aircraft, flying almost at tree-top-height, roared by. In similar manner to how Wolf had just done, it overshot; but – while the plane appeared to be banking, somewhere to the west – something the size of a big man, almost the height of the bounty-hunter but more heavily-built (and oddly light-reflective), dropped out of the sky, as if it had been jettisoned out of the back of whatever had just flown overhead.

The figure landed upright, with an impact appropriate to something much heavier, producing a substantial mud-splash and an unusual, musical echoing-sound. Tanaka caught a brief glimpse of a shimmering, multi-faceted protective-screen being dissolved; then her face lit up upon recognizing the familiar visage of her former Mars mission commander.

"*Sam!*" she exclaimed. "So glad to see you've been able to drop in!"

Wolf groaned and rolled his eyes.

"Happy to see both of *you*, too," responded Jacobson.

The aircraft was now in sight, and it began to slowly descend with its VTOL jets engaged, about a hundred feet away.

"Mister?" addressed the farm-boy.

"Yeah?" answered Jacobson.

"You just... *jumped* out of a plane?" remarked the boy.

"Yeah," repeated the former Mars mission commander.

"How come you didn't, like, get *killed* or something?" pressed the farm-boy. "That was a hundred feet at least, you fell down!"

"Probably more like three hundred or so... what's your name, son?" countered Jacobson.

"Chris... Chris Young, sir," offered the boy.

"Well, Chris – my name's 'Sam Jacobson'," spoke the commander. "And as to jumping out of airplanes, that's *nothing*... wait until you see me jumping a half-mile or so, *up* to one."

He turned his attention to Tanaka.

"Cherie – where *are* they?" he demanded.

She pointed to the open back-doors of the SUV.

"They're in there, Sam," she indicated. "Oh-kay, as far as I can tell – but they're drugged, and –"

Not to her surprise, Jacobson shot past her in a single leap into the back of the vehicle, which shook from side to side under the impact and weight, until its shock-absorbers again stabilized it. The rest of them heard the former Mars commander pleading with his wife, saying something like, "Yvonne... oh *God*, Yvonne... Riley, come *on*, son, wake *up*..."

The V-37 had now landed, facing them, and from its hind-parts issued a number of debarkees, including Donny Wade, the Russian and, of course, Wolf's two dogs, who traveled across the sodden Texas field in quick-time (the wounded one was notably slower), to rejoin their grateful master.

"Who's all this?" warily inquired the farm-wife.

"Friends," sideways-answered Tanaka.

She saw the figure of Devon White, who had levitated himself to a position on top of the aircraft, scanning the sky, undoubtedly for signs of enemy activity. He briefly waved to her. She returned the gesture.

"Those dogs are... breathing *fire*," gasped the farm-girl.

"Uh-huh," confirmed the former science officer, with a nod. "The female's name is 'Boob', the male is 'Tube'. They're like their owner – they look scary, but they're actually not hard to get along with, once you –"

"I *heard* that, Cherie," called Wolf, from a distance. "Mars ears... remember?"

"You just burn me up," quipped Tanaka.

"Hope to," he parried.

"Jacobson's folks – they okay?" asked the truck-driver, once he was within earshot. "Oh... and 'hi there', Mister Barbecue."

Wolf's face showed a sinister, proud smile.

"Sort of," answered the former science officer. "They've been heavily-sedated by the Agency... Sam's trying to bring them around, but even *I* couldn't do that – or at least not within the amount of time that we probably have, around here. You guys are a little late – what *happened?*"

"We were intercepted by American fighter-aircraft – it was over Arkansas, I believe," explained Misha, "And we were only able to evade our assailants, with considerable difficulty. They near-missed us with at least two heat-seeking missiles, before Major White was able to use his, ah, 'powers', to properly disguise our infra-red signature, and thus allow us to escape. We were heading for the agreed-upon destination, but Wolf flew up in front of us and guided us here. The aircraft has suffered some damage... nothing that would stop us from taking off, but we have lost pressurization and the use of one fuel tank."

"Any Air Force on your tail right now?" anxiously asked Tanaka.

"Not as far as we know," indicated the Russian, "But we intercepted a lot of radio-traffic on military bands, and it is clear that much of your country's military is now actively looking for us, Professor. They will likely not abandon the search until they have a 'validated kill' registered against us. I think we should load Commander Jacobson's family on to the V-37 as quickly as possible, and then get airborne immediately after that. But..."

"Yeah?" asked the former science officer, with a quizzically-raised eyebrow.

"I hate to be so – uhh – 'direct'," said Misha, while pointing to the remnants of the farm-family, "But who *are* these people?"

"They got caught in an engagement between me, Wolf and the Air Force, Misha," stiffly responded Tanaka. "They bombed the area indiscriminately. The children's father – the woman's husband – was killed in the crossfire. I couldn't do anything for him. I think you can imagine how I'm feeling about all this."

She hung her head.

"*Shit*," muttered Donny.

He turned to address the farm-family.

"Listen," he offered, "My name's 'Donny Wade'... trucker by profession, but not any more, I guess. Me and my folks, we nearly got smoked like that, back Missouri way – my Uncle Callum and Aunt Marie, they just lost their farm they worked on for the past forty years – their horses, their cows... everything, not to mention my rig, which I still owe thousands on. And neither them nor me, really has a *clue* about what the hell's goin' on. Tell you what... why don't I take you all back to the 'plane – introduce you to 'em. Maybe between us, we can figure out what we do next – or at least we can trade stories of what a shitty situation this is turnin' into... okay?"

The farm-wife just stared for an uncomfortable few seconds, but eventually, she said, "Why not... got nothin' *better* to do, I suppose."

She motioned to her children, who accompanied her as the trucker led them around to the back of the V-37.

Thank you, brother, sent Tanaka. *I owe you one.*

She said that not all great powers, come from the Fire, you know...

"Yeah," mumbled Donny, though he was out of human earshot. "Gettin' tired of seein' folks all shot-up, on account of this little joy-ride we're takin', you know," he added.

As she glanced at the retreating group, Tanaka took note of a new development; White's figure, encased in a dimly-blue-and-white colored, translucent cold-shield, had levitated or flown to a position at least a hundred feet above the aircraft's dorsal surface.

Wow... he's been working on things, too, she mused.

With one crisis temporarily under control, the former science officer turned her attentions again to the kidnapped family in the SUV. Jacobson was in there, still trying to cajole his somnolent wife into consciousness; he had been joined by the Russian, though Wolf – near-totally absorbed in re-acquainting himself with his two hell-hounds – stayed a distance away, sitting on the back of the pickup-truck as the dogs pranced and bellowed sparks at his feet.

The former science officer joined her Mars commander inside the SUV's prisoner-compartment.

"Any luck, Sam?" she inquired.

"Not... really," the frustrated more-than-a-man, heavily replied. "We got any idea what those sonofabitches in the Agency, used on them?"

"Didn't see anything so identified, in here," she offered, "But I was acting in a hurry, as usual; I intercepted this car as part of an Agency convoy on a bridge – the one that's had half its span knocked down, back a way from here. They were heading straight for the airbase and tried to fight it out – let's just say it didn't go well for them... but it could have gone a *lot* worse."

"Thank you *so* much, Cherie," came back Jacobson's emotive reply.

"Well, look at the bright side of it – they're alive, and they're all here... right?" she remarked.

"Yeah," confirmed Jacobson, never taking his eyes off his wife and family. "Yvonne... Jenny... Jean... Riley... there's also one other – that girl over there – who I've never seen. Whoever she is, I surely do regret getting her caught up in all this... but I guess that's out of our control. Listen, Cherie... think you can help me levitate them back to the V-37?"

With a faint hint of her war-song starting to play in the background, Tanaka's glowing eyes fixed on one of the teenagers, whose unconscious figure lifted off the vehicle-floor by an inch or so.

"Piece of *cake*," said the former science officer. "Not even standard human resistance to locking on – they're asleep, so they can't fight consciously fight it. Since Devon's standing guard over the plane, did you want me to call Wolf to help? He seems to have learned a bit of telekinesis, over the past few hours, by the way."

"No, if you don't mind," grunted Jacobson. "He'll probably roast them, while trying to –"

A small fireball, the size of a Roman Candle firework, whizzed past the open rear-door of the SUV.

"Mars ears," they heard the bounty-hunter taunt.

"I just meant, 'you're probably busy with Boob and Tube," deflected Jacobson.

"Love you *too*, Mister Space Man," came back the inevitable reply.

"Don't be too hard on him, Sam," counseled Tanaka. "Wolf took a lot of tough hits from the Air Force, while covering me – he's not scared of *anything*, as far as I can tell. It was really good having him on my side, up there."

"Can I say 'I love *you*' as well, Cherie? Or that gonna get my face slapped?" quipped Wolf.

"It's genuine, but just platonic," she answered, with a wan smile.

"Come on," directed the former Mars mission commander, "Let's get my family – and that other one, God help us – the hell out of here."

As two subtle, all-but-suppressed war-songs played, Sam Jacobson put his arms underneath his unconscious wife's shoulders (although the gesture was completely unnecessary, both he and Tanaka felt compelled to undertake it, as the scene of a beloved family-member unsupported by anything visible, was too disconcerting for either to countenance), while Tanaka did the same for Yvonne Jacobson's hindquarters.

While they gently maneuvered the woman's limp body out of the vehicle and then toward the V-37, Jacobson again spoke to his former understudy.

"You *do* know, don't you," he offered, "That it'll be all but *suicide*, flying back the way we came? The transport's not meant for maneuvering combat in the first place, it's been shot up a fair bit on the way over here, and we were already nearing full load, with all of us on board. Now, we've got three more civilians, plus the five of my family, to carry. The Air Force will have every fighter in the continental United States, patrolling over our route back to the *rendez-vous* with Brent. How we're going to manage this... I haven't got a *clue*."

"Ahh... we'll cope *somehow*, Sam," philosophically reassured the more-than-a-woman. "We always *do*, you know. But lately..."

"'But'... what?" asked Jacobson, as they had almost reached the V-37's rear loading-ramp.

"I've come to know," quietly remarked Tanaka, "What the 'alternative' is. To 'getting by', that is."

"There's an 'alternative'?" inquired the puzzled former Mars mission commander.

"What I mean is, Sam," said the science officer, "Please, *please*... no more funerals."

A Son For Desperate Times

By now, Minnie Chu – perpetually at odds with herself, in the Air Force One visitor's-lounge that doubled as her solitary-confinement-cell – had lost track of the number of the airborne command-post's take-offs and landings. The pattern of these was irregular, although the frequency seemed to be slowly increasing.

The team-leader was almost always alone, during this time; but she was never unsupervised, whether this was by check-ups on the part of silently-glowering Secret Service agents, or by the baleful eye of the two video-surveillance cameras in the lounge-room.

She had, mercifully, been freed of the restraints that had previously confined her to one of the aircraft's reclining-chairs; but the door to places outside the lounge remained locked.

Her only chances to move outside came with thrice-daily, brief, escorted trips to the washroom. She treasured these, not just for the obvious biological reasons, but because some kind soul had stocked the toilet-side magazine-rack with recent copies of Disney News' flagship publication, *Timeweek* (all other reading-material had, churlishly, been removed from the prison-lounge).

Other than for sleep – of which Chu had more than enough – only three things intermittently broke the boredom : one, faint, far-off conversations about "how we're losing the fight against those fucking Mars terrorists"; two, fleeting glimpses and mental-images, as if in a daydream, of a small boy calling for his mother; and finally, random visits (there had been four so far) by the unctuous, slick-haired "Presidential Spiritual Adviser", whose presence would have been crazily-annoying, had it not been one of her very few meetings with other people within recent hours.

Each time that Mr. Crowford had come to call, he had been increasingly impatient, over what he claimed was Chu's "foot-draggin', in callin' for the Devil-Girl"; and no matter how patiently or earnestly the team-leader tried to explain about the fickleness of this particular alien-skill, her entreaties made little difference to the man's sweaty-faced, near-maniacal obsession about the Storied Watcher.

And besides... sure, I know how to call for Karéin, the former team-leader had silently mused.

I could just repeat her name, like Bob did – but over my dead body, I will!

Go call her yourself... and you had better hope she doesn't hear you.

His last visit had ended badly, with him shouting incoherent warnings about "this is your last chance, honey – better be careful, or we're gonna put you in the middle of a field tied to a stake, set it on fire and then see if your whore witch pays attention, *then*".

Oh... by all means, go ahead, she had thought, while carefully hiding her inner rage.

I've got some Fire, *too.*

Try something like that... and you'll find out all about *it.*

Chu had also noted, with mild interest, that the Spiritual Adviser always seemed to have the same military-guard – a tallish, pasty-faced guy with a nervous, jumpy comportment, who for some reason seemed a half-size too big for his Army-fatigues – accompanying him, when Crowford dropped by to bother the imprisoned team-leader.

Privately, she was beginning to wonder if he was right.

What's Karéin doing, anyway?

She's dropped off the face of the Earth, as far as I can tell... I know she said that she didn't want to get involved in this stupid race between me and Sam – a race that I'm certainly losing, if I haven't already lost – but isn't she at least interested in what's happening to me?

Well... after all that's happened, I can't really blame her for that...

Face it, Minnie – you'll have to fight your own battles.

Funny thing is... I can blow this rig out of the sky, anytime I want; but I don't see how that advances my cause... except, of course, to avenge poor Will and Otis, God rest their souls.

What's the point, if I die too... and my story – the truth *– dies with me?*

Is this how a super-heroine is supposed to feel... the proverbial pitiful, helpless giant?

She tried to go back to sleep, but she needed even less of that now than she ever had done; it was a futile venture. She noticed herself absent-mindedly stroking the little aquamarine pendant that hung between her breasts, underneath her blouse, and tried to clear her head from a confusion of odd, unexpected thoughts.

Chu got up, stretched her legs, and looked out of a nearby window. It must have been just after daybreak, because the sun was rising above the cloud-tops, far in the distance. She paced back and forth in her stocking feet, up and down the lounge-room's carpeted floors, longing for diversion of any kind, to break up the monotony.

So this is how we used to break 'em down, back at Bureau H.Q., she reflected.

Just stick 'em in a room by themselves... and let 'em get bored out of their skulls.

Pretty damn effective – even the meditation-stuff that Karéin taught me back at the lake, is beginning to wear a bit thin. Don't know how much more of this I can take...

Resignation to tedious fate overcame the team-leader, and she again tried to relax in a reclining-chair that had been opened as far as it went, almost to the point of being cot-like.

She closed her eyes and began to count sheep.

One sheep... two sheep... three sheep... four... five...

Me Mommy hear thou do?

What? thought a perplexed Minnie Chu.

Who?

Me, came back a thought – a meek, sad-sounding little one, that was unmistakably not her own.

Who is 'me'?

Am I. Mommy thou mine are?

Huh? What? Who are you?

Who is this, in my head?

Though everything was going on in her head – she could tell that the room was utterly silent, to human-ears at least – the team-leader heard a bizarre, heartbreaking, sobbing-sound.

Mommy not mine are then thou...

Being for me forgive in mind thine, lady gentle.

Myself by hide will I. Away go.

Alone scared and.

Alone.

Alone...

Wait!

Don't go, little voice! shouted a panicked Chu – her maternal instincts immediately surging past all caution and common sense – out loud.

For a few seconds, she held her breath, both out of fear of having driven off the *something* in her head, and out of apprehension that her outburst would attract the attention of the Secret Service.

But nobody opened the door.

Oh-kay, came a thought, with the same bashful little-boy cadence.

You are... alone, little voice-in-my-head?

Alone, came back the answer.

Up woke. There talk nobody to.

Dark... dark only.

Sound none, voice always none... quiet.

Lonely so...

By now – for reasons that she dared only guess at – the only thing that mattered to Minnie Chu, was keeping this unseen entity, talking, or thinking, or... *whatever*.

Despite wiping a tear, she could still see and hear perfectly; but somehow, the mundane world around her in the Air Force One lounge-room seemed distant, unreachable, not-quite-there.

No, little voice – you are not *alone, any more.*

I will keep you next to my heart, as long as I will live.

Though she knew not how, Chu sensed happiness, relief and someone's guard being partially-lowered.

What is your name?

That is what... name?

It's what you are called... the unique word that distinguishes you from everyone else – given to you by your mother and father, when you are born –

Have not do, timidly responded the voice.

Forever since I alone been remember that.

Me name nobody a gave.

You don't have a name?

No.

My name is "Minnie". Oh... that's my first name, for me specifically. My second name – for everybody in my family – is "Chu". Do you understand?

So think.

May I give you a name, then?

Please... please... please...

The team-leader pondered, not knowing if what she was thinking would be visible to the unseen voice.

Boy's names... boy's names... at least I hope *he's a boy... let's see*, furiously considered Chu.

How about "Will", or how about "Hector"... after all they – no, scratch that, can't name him something that might confuse everyone... think, Minnie, think – damn, drawing a blank...

Okay, how about something from an old TV-series, like they're endlessly re-running on Neo... how about "Beaver"?

No, not dignified enough.

This little guy must be from... wait, what about the father?

What was his name, again? W... W... Ward? But that's a short-form, isn't it?

Got it... "Warden"!

Hey, little voice... how about "Warden"? Would you like that?

"War...den?" responded the unseen entity.

Name mine that?

Yep – if you will accept it from me, mentally answered Chu.

There was a long pause, and for a moment, she was gripped by an inchoate fear that she had somehow offended her private companion.

But at length, he – or it – sent back,

Thou if me name give a... mother my must be thee?

I'd be honored to be your mother, little voice, she instantly replied.

And then you – as my son – will be called, "Warden Chu".

You will be in my family, forever and ever.

Thee then call familiar-like I... Mother-Honored?

What?

You then call familiar-like I... Mother-Honored?

"Familiar-like"? Oh, wait – right, pronouns... for sure, little voice! No problem! Call me anything you like... I mean, that thou likes... I mean...

Her mind perceived a giggle.

Good is anything.

Thank you, little voice.

An irrational feeling of love, trust and protectiveness washed over the team-leader. She was about to continue the conversation, but at that point, there was a brief rap on the door leading from the lounge to the rest of the aircraft, and her attention turned from inner thoughts to the mundane world.

"Ms. Chu? Ms *Chu!*" came a semi-familiar, brusque voice.

It was one of the Secret Service agents – a big, muscular, brush-cut, Caucasian guy – whose clean-shaven, dour face, appeared in the opened doorway.

"Who... oh... Agent Mitchell... right?"

"Yeah, Mitchell – that's me," the man confirmed. "Get up. President wants to see you."

"The '*President?*'" said Chu, with feigned disinterest and a raised eyebrow. "I was told that he was finished with me, and –"

"I got no idea," parried the Secret Service agent. "All I can tell you is that we got you covered by three guys, counting yours truly... so no funny business! Come *on*. He's waiting."

"Just got to put my shoes on," pleasantly answered the team-leader.

The agent was staring to one side, and he didn't notice how the shoes seemed to arrange, side-by-side, all by their own, just before Chu slid into them, stood up, coiffed her hair and strode outward.

Mitchell hadn't been bluffing; while he took the lead as they walked forward down the carpeted hallways of the airborne command-post, there were also two other Secret Service guys – an Italian-American guy with greased-back, black hair and another Caucasian, somewhat taller and leaner than the others – following behind.

The sections of the aircraft through which she was traveling looked oddly depopulated; many of the civilian hangers-on and non-military staff of the 747-derivative, seemed to have been disembarked, or, at least, must have been in another part of the plane.

Mommy... warning-danger why sounding is? came a burst of little-boy, mental counsel.

I don't know, Warden, silently responded Chu, *but I feel it too.*

If you can help – without giving yourself away – Mommy would like you to.

Oh-kay, he answered.

Little minds dumb now around all here, now hear I, think I, at.

Do to hard they are because closed to me all.

Asking but keep I.

Speak to me maybe will they?

That's fine, little one, she advised, *but don't tell them who you are.*

Mommy always do you what say.

Chu reflexively smiled for a half-second, then went back to poker-face.

They had passed the meeting-room from which she had earlier been unceremoniously uninvited, and she wondered where, exactly, she was being taken to.

Fear suddenly gripped the team-leader's mind, as she remembered what had been done to Boatman and Hendricks, only a few days before. But the Secret Service team was not going toward an exit; instead, they led her to a point about midway in the aircraft, stopped outside an intricately-locked portal, entered a code and spoke a key-word into an embedded microphone.

In a couple of seconds, the portal opened, and Chu was ushered into an area about ten feet wide by thirty feet long, with dimmed lighting and computer-consoles, displays and control-panels, to both the left and right. There were four uniformed military staff, each seated in a well-padded reclining-chair, attending to these communications and surveillance systems.

"Wow," she whispered. "A *lot* of high-tech stuff in here... I thought this place was on the upper level, behind the cockpit...?"

"Had to relocate it, a few refits back," responded one of the Secret Service men. "Needed more room for the comms-gear."

At the far end of this room was the usurper-President, accompanied by Blanshard of the Army, the rotund, shifty-eyed Warnock, and two armed military police (these men, both Caucasian, were prominently armed, though their guns were holstered).

The team-leader suppressed her initial surprise at what she saw, when she had a second or two to look directly at the President. His dark-ringed eyes were bloodshot, and the wrinkles on his elderly, sweaty face seemed deeper than she remembered from her last encounter with him. His shirt was creased and there were perspiration-stains at the underarms.

The same air of overwork and sleep-deprivation appeared on the other members of the Executive Branch staff, albeit, to a lesser degree.

"Yeah... so *there* she is," he sneered. "Okay then – let's get going."

"Sir?" warily spoke Chu.

"Get your ass over here," he commanded. "We've got a *job* for you to do."

"Uhh... okay, sir," she answered, stepping forward until she was about five feet away.

From this distance, Chu could easily smell the booze on the man's breath.

"You called, Mr. President?" came a voice from behind.

It was Crowford, whose Brylcreemed, preacher-man face appeared in the doorway that provided the only apparent way out of the area. He didn't seem to be accompanied by the lanky, awkward-looking soldier that she had noticed in recent encounters.

"Yeah," called the *faux*-American leader. "Catch her if she runs."

"Oh... no *problem*," airily replied the Spiritual Adviser. "I'm sure these fine Service agents on either side of me, will see to that. By the way... nice to see you again, Ms. Chu."

"Likewise... I'm *sure*," reflexively sent back the team-leader.

The alarm-bells went off in Chu's head, and she honestly couldn't tell if they were sounding an alien or common-sense-human warning. Her psyche was being bombarded by similar shrieks from her weirding alter-ego, but she managed to filter them out, at least for the time being.

"Why... why would I run out of here, sir?" she politely inquired. "Where would I run *to?*"

"*Nowhere!*" he retorted. "And that's where you'll *be*, if we don't get *full* cooperation out of your pretty little face."

"What would you like me to do, sir?" asked Chu.

Not now, Warden, she inwardly resolved.

Mommy's really busy.

"I'll explain," interjected Blanchard. "Stand over here, so you can see this high-res display clearly."

He pointed to a large, circular computer-screen, perhaps two by two feet in size.

"Of course," she said, with an unconvincing half-smile.

Chu bent over to study the display more carefully. It seemed to have a map of the central United States – somewhere in Kansas or Missouri, possibly, judging from the nondescript terrain-features and lack of large cities – as background. Superimposed on this were a number of military unit-symbols in various bright blue, green, yellow and white colors.

Of these, about half the blue and green symbols – mostly triangles but also a few arrow-signs – seemed to be converging on a red circle in the center of the display, which was almost in the middle of the screen as it slowly moved from the bottom-left to the top-right. The white markers seemed to be avoiding the center of the map, as if they were detouring around it.

There was also a single odd-ball symbol – one with a magenta-to-violet diamond – that was following behind a group of blue triangles, at a distance, as near as could easily be judged, of about five centimeters.

"Okay... so here's what's going on," described the general. "What you're looking at is a combat situational display of roughly five hundred miles, representing airspace over east Texas, Arkansas, Oklahoma and northern Louisiana. That built-up area there, to the top right, is Little Rock. The symbols here, and here," – he pointed at the blue and green ideographs – "Are our fighters and drones, respectively. Yellow symbols are other military aircraft, while white ones are civilian air traffic, which has been ordered out of the engagement-area."

"I think I understand," offered Chu. "I did have to take basic air traffic control terminology at the Bureau, so it's not completely new to me. But what are the red and violet symbols, sir? The red one that seems to be in the middle of the display, that is."

"The red marker represents a bogey that Continental Air Defense is currently pursuing," evenly stated Blanchard. "We believe it to be an aircraft commandeered by this 'Jacobson' guy and his so-called 'Mars Gang'."

"I... *see*," she quietly acknowledged. "So you're tracking it, then?"

"Very definitely," he said, nodding confirmation with under-stated pride. "It's been a challenge, because Jacobson and his crew have been making things difficult for us; he's certainly a resourceful traitor – I'll give him that. We've already had scores of casualties. But *this* time... we've got a good track on him."

"Well then," stiffly observed Chu, "Please forgive me for being direct, sir, but... what do you need *me* for?"

You can't let this happen, *Minnie!* her conscience cried out.

Wait a minute... calm down... think it through...

There must be some reason *why they're involving me in this.*

Like – they don't have a clue *how to get at Sam.*

They'd have to get Cherie, Devon and Brent first... let's see 'em do that. If they could have shot Sam down by now, they would have...

Stall... delay...

The *faux*-President now joined Blanshard on the other side of the tracking-display. He leaned forward too, with his craggy, wizened face illuminated malevolently from below, as the day-old whiskey-smell issued from his mouth.

"See... the thing is, girlie," he leered and hissed, "So far, this 'Jacobson' motherfucker, has managed to shoot down half the fucking *Air Force,* that we've sent up against him – the more we send, the more he knocks out of the sky. I'm about to run out of fighter-pilots – at least, pilots who have the balls to climb into a cockpit and fight for good old Uncle Sam...and after the fuck-up at Fort Knox, the economy's teetering on the brink of total bankruptcy. He's heading northeast, maybe to knock out D.C., maybe New York, maybe both of them, and it's all getting *old*, my dear – it's getting very, very, fucking *old!* You understand what I'm *saying?*"

"I... uhh... understand you perfectly well, sir," gulped Chu, while trying to keep competing emotions of fear and rage, under control. "And for the record, I think it's, uhh, shameful, what Commander Jacobson has done, if he has in fact done all of what you've alleged, but –"

I could try to vex him... make him into my nice puppet, she mused.

But there are too many other people in the room here.

It would be noticed, instantly.

"Oh, spare me the tears and the hankie, honey," growled the *faux*-American-leader. "You don't fool *me* – you don't give a *shit* about loyalty to your country, or about anything other than your now-over-with career and that little whore alien popsy who you want to hop into bed with – yeah, the good Reverend Harold told me all about it, so don't try to claim otherwise –"

Chu turned her head and stared at Crowford.

"I thought we had a *deal!*" she angrily called out.

Brother Harold nonchalantly shrugged, with a smug smile on his face.

"It's my *job* to alert my Commander-In-Chief to the presence of sin in his proximity, my dear," he purred. "Oh – but if it's any consolation... I *did* also advise the President, of how a good man, might set you straight, in all this, in a nice, old-fashioned way. You know?"

A few of the lower-ranks chuckled, while the team-leader glowered.

"What I know, sir," she shot back, "Is that you have no *right*, making my personal life an issue, in all of this. And that's the *last* time that I ever –"

"Okay, look," interrupted the *faux*-President, "Enough about your slutty sex life, honey – not what we called you up here for, anyway."

"And what, sir," said a furious Chu, "*Was* I called up here for, exactly?"

"Well, you see," spoke up Warnock, "We've got a theory, Ms. Chu, that we're going to give you a chance – and only *one* choice, mind you – to validate, for us."

She stared at him, as the hand-picked FBI Director continued,

"The thing is," he said, "We think that, given the extensive amount of time that you spent with this 'Jacobson' and his gang of traitors... you actually *do* know of what their weaknesses are – that is, how the Air Force, and the government's other coercive assets – can most effectively target Jacobson And Company, so as to ensure a clean kill. So out with it, Ms. Chu – what is it? What are they vulnerable to? Microwaves? Poison gas? Attacks from underneath? From above? You need to tell us... *now!*"

The team-leader hung her head and wearily replied, "Oh, for God's sake... not *this*, again! I've already *told* you, sir... I never found out –"

"*Every* military asset has had an exploitable weakness, since the dawn of Time," interjected Blanshard. "Like, for example, a weak-spot in the armor, of even the best-designed tank; or a limit in the amount of G-forces that a human pilot can endure, in a fighter-plane. So far, we've lost *way* too many good men, trying to figure out what Jacobson's Achilles Heel is. Let me echo Mr.

Warnock, Madam – in the time that you spent with these guys, you *must* have seen something. I'm asking you, in the name of the Joint Chiefs, to reveal it."

"No more evasions, no more double-talk," unhelpfully added the FBI commandant. "We need to find out what's Kryptonite to this crew. Or... *else.*"

"Or else – *what?*" she spat back.

"Then, my dear," mentioned the *faux*-President, with a cruel smirk, "You'll be of absolutely no more use to us... and we'll rid ourselves of you. *Got* it?"

"The way that you 'rid yourselves' of Will Hendricks and Otis Boatman, sir?" coldly asked Chu.

"Oh... I'm sure we'll figure something *suitable*, out," smoothly responded the usurping American leader. "Probably something even less pleasant than for them – like a good, old-fashioned bullet in the back of the head. Now... *talk!*"

Help can Mommy I, came the child-like voice-in-the-head.

You protect –

Mommy can use all the help she can get, little one, answered Chu, while trying to keep her attention focused on the physical goings-on.

But not until I say... okay?

Oh-kay, came the response.

"Having my life threatened is something that I expected from you... *sir,*" stiffly remarked the team-leader. "And if it's of any interest... I anticipated this line of questioning. So I'll keep this brief, and tell you everything that I know. First off, Sam Jacobson has an altitude limit as to how far he can leap; I'm not sure what it is, but it's probably less than a kilometer. Secondly, Cherie Tanaka – like Karein herself – has a limited ability to endure explosive shock-waves, even if these are deflected by her force-field, so if you hit her with enough force, you might be able to knock her unconscious... or worse. Devon White's ability originates from elemental cold, so he is vulnerable to fire, and –"

"This is all crap that you told us before," complained Warnock. "It's in the reports."

"That's because it's all I *know*, sir!" protested Chu. "These 'alien-powers' don't come with a specification-sheet or an owner's-manual! They don't say, 'if you fire your lightening-bolt with more than this number of Watts, you'll short yourself out', for Pete's sake!"

"Wait a minute," requested Crowford, from his vantage-point, near the door. "There's a way to test this. Why don't we just have *her*, direct the attack? Like, tell them fighter-planes of yours, how to hit Jacobson where it *hurts*."

"I beg your pardon?" said a startled Blanshard.

"What I mean is, General," offered the Spiritual Adviser, "If she knows how to bag this gang of criminals, and sets us up to do it... then she gets a medal and a nice retirement-party, somewhere. If she *doesn't* know – or if she *does* know and turns traitor on us – that gets her a funeral, instead. Either way, we get to the bottom of it, *real* quick. Wouldn't you say?"

"Mr. Crowford, with all due *respect*," stammered Blanshard, "I can't put the Air Force under the control of a potentially-disloyal individual – one with zero military experience, to boot! What if she deliberately sets them all up to be compromised, and then be *clobbered*? I can't accept the risk of –"

"She can't do much worse than we've been doing so far... *can* she?" sarcastically commented the *faux*-President. "She gets them all whacked... then we go to Plan 'B' – which we were going to do, anyway. Nothing really to lose."

Plan 'B'? pondered Chu.

I don't like the sound of that...

"Mr. President, sir, I don't think –" argued the general.

"Okay, honey," motioned the impostor-leader, with a hand-wave, "Get your ass over here... your time to shine, or to sign your last will and testament. Sit down right there, in front of the display."

A sullen Blanshard muttered something under his breath, shook his head and pulled the reclining-seat out, so Chu could sit in it.

She reluctantly complied.

"You'll... you'll have to help me here, sir," she uneasily requested. "While, as I mentioned before, I'm somewhat familiar with the unit-symbols, I've never had any training on how to actually issue orders."

"Just tell me what you want each unit to do," instructed the general. "For example, this blue symbol is a formation of three F-32E's; this one over here is a drone squadron. You can have them attack from any altitude, using any of their weapons – which you can see by pressing your finger down on the symbol... see the pop-up Order Of Battle listing? If you have more extensive orders, describe these to me, and I'll enter them with the head-set, over on this side; they'll be transmitted exactly as you specify. By repeatedly pressing on this symbol on the side of the display, you can superimpose various additional information artifacts on the map; for example, by pressing twice," – he did so – "You can see the meteorological display, which shows that Jacobson's outrunning a cold-front, coming in off the Rockies. Understand?"

"I suppose that'll have to do, sir," stated the team-leader. "Alright... let's start with this group of fighters over Oklahoma, and this one to the south, over Texas; can you move the first one to here," – she indicated a point just behind and to the north of the Jacobson aircraft-symbol – "And the second one to... here." (She pointed to a spot behind and to the south of the Jacobson ideograph.) "Have the aircraft that are ahead of the, uhh, 'bogey', do the same thing, but with equivalent positions, so the Jacobson aircraft is bracketed in all directions. The fighters in the north should fly higher – say at 5,000 feet – while the ones in the south go in lower, like, 1,000, or something. From what I see, the, uhh, 'stolen' aircraft's pretty low already – seems to be about 2,000. Is that right?"

"Yes, but why are you... oh, never *mind*," muttered an obviously-frustrated Blanshard.

He picked up a headset with a microphone extending from one side, and repeated some kind of military jargon into it.

After a delay of five or six seconds, Chu noticed that the fighters were inching slowly toward their assigned positions.

"The squadrons are following your orders, Madam," noted the general. "Please complete the tactical-instructions."

"Sorry?" asked Chu.

"The *load-out*, Ms. Chu – the weapons, I mean," said Blanchard. "You have to tell them what to attack with, and what to follow up with, in the event that the first salvo isn't combat-effective."

"Oh, right – the *weapons!*" skated the team-leader. "Well... what do I have at my disposal?"

"Latest and greatest, Madam – advanced third-gen multi-role medium-range missiles, your choice of fully-active radar-homing, heat-seeking, optical-imaging, plus track-on-jam, except that so far, we aren't detecting any significant emissions from the Jacobson plane; not surprising, really – he *is* a former Air Force pilot, after all... he's undoubtedly in strict EMCON-mode. We can also attack with a heavy-caliber Gatling cannon on the fighters. The drones have basically the same load-out, but they carry less ammunition and have smaller guns. On the other hand, they can be ordered to collide with the target, then set off their internal self-destruct charges. Please tell me the order in which you want to attack, and which weapons to use at each stage."

Think, Minnie – think! she desperately pondered.

Does Sam know that they've got a bead on him?

He can't – otherwise why would he be flying in such a straight line?

Dear noble Mommy, came the private voice, *big with can connect I eye glass front in.*

One the little pictures color on.

"Is that it?" she stalled. "What about, uhh, surface-to-air missiles, attack helicopters, Army-units –"

Okay, little voice... see what you can find out. Can you shut it down?

Hard that really do to. Protections many it on.

Maybe eye glass but big make fuzzy go.

Do your best, Warden!

"They're mostly located at Army and Air Force bases, due to the size of the engagement-area and lack of mobility," countered the general. "Not relevant to this discussion, at least until Jacobson over-flies one or more of these bases... which he's so far been careful not to do. Proceed."

"So these fighters and drones are all we've got?" she persisted. "What about those super-duper hypersonic spy-planes that we keep hearing about?"

"What do you think's providing the tactical-display, Ms. Chu?" he sneered. "*Proceed!*"

"Ah, I – uhh – *see,*" she answered. "Can I ask you a question, General?"

"About what?" he retorted.

"Given what you know about whatever aircraft that Jacobson is now flying," she inquired, "Is it armed – like, with missiles or guns of its own, I mean – and how close would the fighters have to be to it, to be clearly seen from inside the plane?"

"I have no idea what you're talking about, Madam," officiously replied Blanshard, "But to answer your question... we believe that it's a medium-sized military vertical-takeoff transport-plane, with limited maneuverability and no self-contained weapons, unless of course Jacobson and his gang have rigged some up themselves. Visibility in the engagement-area is poor, first of all because it's night-time, but also because of the low clouds that Jacobson's hiding in, as he travels cross-country. Our fighters would have to close to a proximity of no more than about a thousand feet... probably less. Doing so would be *extremely* dangerous, because in the past, something – or some*one* – from the Jacobson craft has intercepted us at much greater distances; we've lost a lot of fighters and drones. We need to attack from beyond visual-range... which we can easily do. What's your *point?*"

Hit it with whatever you've got, Warden, she silently pleaded.

Mommy trying, came back a meek voice.

But the tactical-display looked just as sharp and functional as ever.

"Get *on* with it, honey," barked the *faux*-President. "You either find a weak-spot to aim at... or we aim at your weak-spot... like, 'right between your eyes'."

"*Look,* sir," argued Chu, "I'm just using common sense, here : what I propose to do is to completely encircle Sam's aircraft with so many fighters that he can't *possibly* shoot them all down before one or two of them gets a missile in; we make that state of affairs obvious, by closing in from all sides. Then we just wait until he runs out of fuel. He'll *have* to land, at that point, and you inform him by radio, just before he does, that he has to surrender, 'or else'. If you want, I'll convey the message personally; I'll even tell him that I've joined up with you and will protect you from him. He may not be in a mood to negotiate with yourself... but it may be different with me."

"From what you've been tellin' *me*, girlie," commented Crowford, from one side of the exit-portal, "You couldn't protect the President from a shavin'-cut... much less a monster like this 'Jacobson' fella. You ain't much cut out for lyin' convincingly, I'm afraid."

A couple of long seconds of so-thick-you-could-cut-it tension passed by.

Chu tried not to sweat, but failed, as her alien danger-sense re-started its peals of psychic alarm.

"For fuck's *sake!*" suddenly cursed the impostor-American-leader with a look of just-released, latent fury on his face, "Are we back to 'negotiating', now? I *told* you – stupid bitch – I want Jacobson and his crew... *dead!* Time's up for talking with him... and time's up for *you*, my dear!"

"Yeah... I'd say so, sir," gratuitously agreed Warnock.

"But sir, what about the military situation –" Blanshard tried to interject.

Damn it, realized Chu, *I can't beguile all of these guys at once... fine bloody power you gave me there, Karéin...*

The imposter FBI-director gestured to the two military police.

"Take her out of here – give her five minutes... then *shoot* her!" he hissed.

The two burly gendarmes at the far end of the chamber began to walk forward.

Though she had been at risk of her life umpteen times over the last few days, for some reason, this very personal threat seemed far more direct and ominous.

I don't want to kill anyone – but my life's in danger!

Should I try to beguile them? she pondered.

No – too many – can't do them all at once, and even if I convince one of them, there are plenty more to pull the trigger...

What about all those martial-arts maneuvers that Karéin taught us back at the camp? She said, "even without the Fire, *these can easily cripple or kill any ordinary human"...*

Could try them – but in a confined space like this, there's hardly any room to move... I'm facing multiple assailants, each of whom are a lot bigger and heavier than me, they're probably all trained in hand-to-hand combat, and many of them have guns...

Chu – her face blanching, despite best efforts – pressed her back in the chair, while her panicking mind tried to recall the commands that would uncage her inner *Fire*.

"Before you take me... *out*," she gasped, "Can I ask you one last thing?"

The military policemen paused their advance.

"Sure," cruelly allowed the *faux*-President. "As long as it isn't 'asking for mercy'. You'll get none around here – I can *assure* you of that."

"I... I didn't *expect* any," she stammered. "Anyway... what I wanted to know... just curious, I guess, is... you know that violet symbol on the display, General?"

"Yeah," answered Blanshard. "What *about* it? For the record, Ms. Chu... my regrets. I'm sorry we have to do this – but this is a *war* we're in, nowadays; and war's a harsh mistress... it involves *casualties*. You're just one more among way too many that we've had, so far. If that *means* anything."

"Thanks... I guess," slowly replied Chu. "What I wanted to know is... what, exactly, does that symbol, represent?"

"You mean you haven't guessed by now?" sneered the usurper-U.S.-leader. "God, you're *stupid*. Certainly no loss to the gene-pool, in snuffing you out."

"Odd kind of 'last wish'," said a nonplussed Blanchard, "But that's your choice, I guess. To answer your question, Ms. Chu – the violet diamond-shape is an aircraft carrying a 'special weapon'... about four hundred kilotons worth on a long-range, loiter-capable cruise missile, that is. You won't live to see it, of course – but since you've so obviously failed in trying to find an end-game scenario against Jacobson that doesn't involve using this weapon, we've really got little choice but to wait until he lands somewhere; then, well... I'm sure you know what comes next."

"What if that's in a *city* or something, you *monsters!*" exclaimed Chu, passion and swelling anger, overwhelming the fear that had afflicted her, a few seconds earlier.

"We're assuming it won't be," elaborated the general. "But that's not entirely up to us – just to preclude any disruptions in the chain of command, the launch-conditions are pre-programmed and automatic, based on how close this 'Jacobson' traitor gets to either the aircraft you're now on, or to other important targets, like for example Washington D.C., or if he tries a return-visit to Fort Knox. We can cancel or over-ride it with a coded message from the President via the communications-console... but I guess that's a moot point as far as *you're* concerned, Ms. Chu."

Shit – if Sam flies over a city – an even-more-panicked Chu realized.

Mommy ooh, came an awed mind-voice, *surging I Fire Holy, wave a mighty like!*

"Okay – this little tutorial's *over*," commanded the *faux*-President, with a feigned yawn. "All wasted effort, on a dumb little whore like her... who shortly won't be around to remember it, or to trouble us any more. Stand up, dearie... and spare us the indignity of these fine men having to carry you out, sniffling and wailing."

"I'll *do* that – with *pleasure!*" riposted Chu, as she came to her feet, shoulders straight, with a defiant, at-last-resolved look on her face.

The *faux*-President was Blanshard's right, with both of them to the right of Chu, further into the chamber. The Secret Service agents were with Crowford, near to the entrance-door.

I call upon the Holy Fire – **full power!** inwardly-invoked the team-leader.

A subtly-stirring set of musical chords with a rapid, exciting beat, began to reverberate from the communications-consoles, from earphones... from the very air-molecules.

Chu's voice now carried a Stentorian air of authority, as she shouted, "You two MPs – everyone around here – stand back and keep your hands off those guns – or I'll *kill* you!"

"With *what* – harsh language and a dirty look?" quipped Warnock.

"You don't know the *half* of it!" spat Chu, through clenched teeth.

Her back was turned to Crowford and the Service agents; she had to trust her alien-senses to warn of an attack from that direction.

The MPs – their faces stonily impassive – strode forward. In another three seconds they would likely be close enough to grapple Chu.

I'm surrounded, feverishly realized the team-leader.

I can take one group with me – but the other one's going to get a clear shot, no matter what –

Power mine flourishes also Mommy beloved, came a reassuring thought.

"*No further!*" bellowed Chu, at the military policemen.

She held an opened hand up at them, in a gesture similar to the familiar one for hailing a taxicab.

To the shock of the onlookers, her eyes were now starting to glow unmistakably, and electric-discharges of the *Fire* danced underneath her business-suit.

Shit, she mused, *I'm throwing enough at them to stop a dump-truck – but can't quite lock on –*

The MPs continued to advance, but much more slowly, in a pained manner, as if every step was mightily straining their muscles.

"What the *hell*...?" gasped one of them, through a grimace. "Can hardly *move!*"

"What you *waitin'* for!" she heard Crowford ordering. "Can't you *see* what's goin' on here? Shoot her – while you still *can!*"

"Shoot her!"

The *faux*-President dashed away from proximity to the team-leader; he went to the far corner of the chamber and echoed the Spiritual Leader's demands.

"The bitch is an alien *spy* sent by Jacobson, to get at *me!*" he yelled. "*Shoot* her, for Christ's sake! Use your *guns* – that's what they're *for!*"

*"Shoot her! **Shoot her!** **Kill her!**"*

She saw the military policemen reaching for their guns, and though Chu's *Fire*-energized, fast-thinking telekinesis tried again and again to lock on to their holsters and the weapons themselves, she found it impossible to direct her attack against both at the same time; the instant that she established a firm grip on the one, she felt her grasp on the other loosening.

She had perhaps another four seconds before the gendarmes would have their arms raised high enough to aim and fire.

The warning-sense in the back of her mind, surged off the scales.

From behind – watch out! it screamed.

Reflexively (and faster than the most lithe human acrobat could have done), Chu pivoted in place – she was now facing away from the MPs, toward the exit at the far end of the chamber – and crouched down into a squat, hoping to get out of the line of fire.

But the desperate maneuver, though it did save her from some of the bullets sprayed in her direction by the Secret Service agents to Crowford's right, wasn't completely successful : the terrified team-leader felt three burning, suffusingly-painful impacts against her flesh – one on her right shoulder, one just below the right collar-bone and a third one that felt like someone had run a hot razor-wire, across the rightmost outside part of her neck.

The sounds of ricochets came to her ears, for a micro-second. Other bullets hit the communications-console, shattering the video-display and wrecking various pieces of electronics.

*Hurt hurt **hurt!*** wailed the little inside-voice.

*I'll take you **motherfuckers** with **me!*** furiously resolved the pain-shocked more-than-a-woman.

Both sick with fear and enraged by the belief that she'd been mortally-wounded, Minnie Chu called upon the power, washed her stare from left to right at the three Secret Service agents beside Crowford, and...

Fired!

The warbling, sizzling, orange-red-hued energy-beam blazed from her eyes, striking the hapless big, Caucasian agent on the far left, instantly vaporizing most of his lower torso and upper abdomen, while burning right through the wall above and behind him, traveling some unknown distance beyond.

A feeble croaking-sound issued from his glassy-eyed, dead-man's face, as the now-unsupported top of his body, along with auto-pistol still grasped in mortified fingers, collapsed and fell forward.

Conveniently, the super-heated energy transmitted by the deadly *Gaze of the Khùl-Algrenàthi'i* cauterized the gaping wounds on this victim; so not *too* much blood splattered out, as his corpse hit the floor.

The second agent – the tall white one – didn't fare any better; for some reason, Chu's death-gaze didn't do as much obviously-catastrophic damage to him, or to the wall behind him; but she *did*, literally, burn his heart (along with most of his right lung) out of his body.

He, too, toppled over, his smoldering corpse rolling pitifully over and over until it came to rest.

The third Secret Service agent got off "lucky"; the team-leader's death-ray only disintegrated all of his right arm below the elbow, while simultaneously melting the gun that the man had been wielding, into popping, exploding metal-slag.

He fell to his knees, screaming and sweating, thrashing and kicking in agony, while Crowford – no fool he – dashed out the door, with the speed of a man justifiably scared within an inch of his life.

From outside in the corridor, there were shouts of alarm, including words to the effect of "put out the fire in the ceiling!", "there's been a bombing – the wall's blown out!" and "reinforce the window – it's almost melted *through!*"

With super-human speed, a brilliant-eyed Chu sprang to her feet, levitated until she was about six inches off the floor, and stared regally down at her erstwhile tormentors.

Wow, she mused, *I couldn't really fly, while I was up at the campsite... but now... I wonder...?*

When did I learn to do that?

Her war-grade *Fire's* telekinesis came down on the two MPs like a ten-ton weight, and both of them found it next to impossible to even *breathe...* let alone raise their guns to an elevation where they could fire and hit her.

The *faux*-President had somehow dodged the hail of bullets and was cowering in the far corner, behind his two deranged military policemen.

The unfortunate Blanshard hadn't had the same luck; he had apparently been shot by the barrage meant for Chu, having taken a round to the chest and at least one more to the thigh.

Blood was pouring out of the former wound, while the general lay moaning on the chamber-floor.

"Make *one* fucking move," angrily inveighed the triumphant team-leader, "And I'll pour even *more* power into what I hit you with – I won't leave enough of you to fit into a fucking *ashtray...* you *got* that?"

Wait a minute, came a hesitant thought.

I got hit by three bullets... I must be dead... *right?*

She ran her hands over the impact-points. Each touch hurt like hell, and a sidelong glance revealed ugly, black-and-blue bruises where she had been hit. But there was neither a perforation in her skin (though, there were certainly bullet-holes in her clothes), nor was there any trace of blood.

Protect Shield-Fire Mommy your I you helped to, murmured Warden.

Was our help did I Mommy enough?

She openly cried as she said out loud, "Yes, you *did,* dear son... you *did!*"

Chu stared balefully at the two MPs.

"I'll release you, on the condition that you drop your guns... throw them underneath me," she demanded. "Then attend to the General – see if you can stop the bleeding... make him more comfortable. One false move, and I'll fucking *vaporize* you – *understand?*"

Despite their bodies being encased in a crushing, invisible giant's-fist, the two gendarmes managed to nod in agreement.

Gradually, Chu dropped her telekinetic pressure, and the two men hurried over to Blanshard, using a portable mini-medical kit to try to treat the stricken general's wounds.

"The rest of you – guys at the consoles, and Mr. Jackass J. Warnock, who I just relieved of his position in the Bureau – get over there in the back, with your wonderful fucking 'President', after leaving your sidearms at my feet," demanded the floating, glowing-eyed team-leader. "Same rules apply. I have *more* than enough power in me, to disintegrate every one of you. All I have to do – as you've seen – is to *look* at you. Don't make me have to *prove* it!"

"What... what the hell *are* you?" stammered the imposter-U.S.-leader, as the rest of the inhabitants of the communications-chamber, including a shaken Warnock, reluctantly complied with the demand.

"Someone much more powerful than you can possibly imagine – who you've pushed *way* too far!" sneered Chu.

To emphasize the point, she cast a glance to the doorway, and – though it was at the outside edge of her reach – the team-leader's telekinesis forced the hatch shut, while locking it a second later. In so doing, the door pushed one of the corpses over to the left-hand side of the chamber, leaving a grisly trail of charred flesh, military-clothing and blood, across the floor.

Then, though still levitated a half-foot off the floor-surface, Chu floated gracefully and deliberately over to a point about three feet away from the *faux*-President.

Her war-music ebbed greatly, until it was just a faint, rhythmic beat, somewhere in the back of the onlookers' minds.

"I guess your in-house preacher didn't mention *this,*" – she used her index fingers to point at her still-brightly-glowing eyes – "*Did* he? *So* sorry that you all missed *that* important little bit of intel! How's it go, again? Wait – don't tell me, *I* know – 'sucks to be *you*, dude'... that's how my dear, late friend Will Hendricks, would have put it. *You* remember Will and Otis... don't you? They're the totally innocent Bureau agents of my team, my friends and brothers, who you cruelly *murdered*, a day or two ago... you vicious, worthless son of a *bitch!*"

"Are you going to *kill* me?" he weakly gasped.

"Not *immediately,*" coolly ordered the team-leader, rotating slowly in place to address all within the chamber, "Unless you, or anyone else around here, does something *stupid*... like heading for the door, trying to attack me, or calling out for help... not that there's any around here, that would have a snowball's chance in *hell*, against me!"

The *faux*-President just stared upward at her.

Fuck, silently pondered Chu,

Is he the only one who can cancel that launch-code?

"Now listen up – this goes for *all* of you!" she demanded. "*Nobody* moves from where you are currently located, without specific authorization from myself. The first time you try it, I'll aim for an arm or a leg; if losing either of those doesn't smarten you up, my next shot will be... well, just have a look at those three, over by the door. *Got* it?"

Mutely, all of the junior-officers and communications-technicians, nodded acknowledgment.

Chu gradually lowered herself, until her feet again were supported by the chamber-floor. She spoke to one of the military policemen.

"I think you've done all you can for the General," she advised, looking at the at-best-semi-conscious man, whose breathing was strained, and whose face was ashen. "He's going into shock; I'll try to use my abilities to help – no promises, though. Get over there and do what you can for that Service agent whose arm felt the kiss of my *Gaze*. But don't try for the door... you won't go very far, without any legs beneath the knees."

Wisely, the gendarme didn't reply, but just walked quickly over to the stricken, agonized victim of the team-leader's lethal attack.

Chu took a long look at Blanshard.

"Not such a bad guy – just working for the wrong boss," she sourly observed.

How did Cherie and Whitney do it? she pondered.

Any of it rub off on me, maybe?

The team-leader knelt, extended her hands over the General's failing body and tried to concentrate on healing. But the effort seemed unsuccessful; Blanshard's outward appearance didn't change, and after about thirty seconds of effort, Chu arose, shaking her head in recognition of defeat.

"*You* two," she indicated, pointing to a couple of fit-looking, male Air Force technicians on the right-hand side of the chamber. "Today's your lucky day. Your General's suffered some serious wounds... and unfortunately, I don't seem to have inherited even a smidgen of the healing-arts that some of my half-alien brothers and sisters have in abundance. He might die anyway, but if he stays here... he's a 'goner', for sure. So one of you get his arms, another get his legs, and I'll levitate him as far as the door, for you; then you'll have to take him to the aircraft's sick-bay."

"You'll... 'levitate' him?" said one of the technicians.

"Just one of the many alien-powers to which I have recourse," matter-of-factually offered the team-leader. "This one's telekinesis... kind of like an invisible, 800-pound gorilla bending iron bars and tossing cars around, on my behalf. Your two MP friends can tell you what it feels like, when I use it on you."

"That true, man?" one of the staffers asked the MP who was still crouched down beside Blanshard.

"Felt like my whole body was inside a fuckin' *drill-press*," he muttered.

Chu again addressed everyone within earshot.

"And what you've seen so far, is only a *subset* of my powers," she warned. "You have virtually *no* chance of surprising me... or of overcoming me. So make it easy on yourselves – no 'funny business', and nobody gets *hurt*. That clear?"

Again, the onlookers, who were confronted with a situation far outside their training, could but nod silently in acknowledgment.

She locked on to the out-of-commission Blanchard, lifted him up to a height of about five feet, and waited until the two staffers grabbed on. She followed behind them to the doorway, opened halfway it without touching it (taking care to stay behind the hatch, so she couldn't be seen from the corridor), directed them to leave, then re-sealed the portal and came back to the middle of the chamber.

"Okay," started the team-leader, "I'd like to explain what's –"

Her directives were interrupted by a loud pounding on the outside of the sealed-shut hatch leading to the rest of the aircraft.

"Open the door – *now!*" barked a determined, angry-sounding voice.

"*Took* you long enough," she diffidently responded. "This is Minnie Chu, formerly of the Federal Bureau of Investigation, now working – *ahem* – as a private investigator. I'm in control of everything and everyone – including the pathetic son-of-a-bitch who you've been calling 'President', plus our friend Warnock and several other people – in here; and if you want to see any of them live past the end of this day, you'll behave *very* carefully, from this point on. Who am I talking with?"

"This is Major Todd Brown of the U.S. Marine Presidential Guard, Ma'am – and I'm authorized to use lethal force to compel the safe release of the President, and all others who may now be held hostage. If *you* want to live, Ma'am, you'll surrender... *immediately!*"

Chu threw back her head, let out a contemptuous chuckle and powered up her *Fire*, causing the background-music to appreciably increase its volume.

Her presence was intimidating, to all those who beheld her; she looked like a sort of petite demonic warrior in a partly-shredded women's business-suit.

"'Lethal force'... well – that's a game that *two* can play!" taunted the team-leader. "So let me give you a tactical evaluation of where we're both at, Major. You've probably got a small army of Marines, Secret Service Agents, military police and a cast of thousands of others out there, all of them with itchy trigger-fingers, eager to be the one who gets the first crack at Ms. Me –"

"That's largely correct, Ma'am," he interjected. "And we're *very* well-trained to deal with situations like this. You have no *chance* against us."

"No... *chance*," she smugly repeated. "Now... let's see how things add up... *shall* we? I have the might of an *angel* flowing through me – God, you can't possibly appreciate how *powerful* I'm feeling, right now – and not only can I vaporize any one, or any hundred, of you, just by *looking* at you... but I can also slice this aircraft in *half*, in pretty much the same way. *I'll* survive... but unless you're wearing one of those 'para-choots' – that's Karéin's way of saying it, cute, wouldn't you say – *you*... won't!"

I hope, she found herself reflecting.

I can levitate six inches.

I wonder if I can do it down from 30,000 feet...

"I can give you another minute or two," he threatened. "After that, I have authorization to attack."

"Well then let's cut to the chase, 'Major' Brown," she defiantly riposted. "You so much as fire *one* bullet at that door – or do something equally stupid like pumping gas through the ventilating-system – and in the next second, I'll reduce both the so-called 'President' and Warnock, to ashes; then I'll pour every last *ounce* of energy into my attack, firing at random so I blow this airplane to bits. Let me apologize in advance, not only to the poor Secret Service agents who I had to kill, in defense of my own life, but also to all the ordinary Executive Branch personnel, who had no part in this affair, and whose lives might thus get snuffed out. I don't *want* to cause your needless, senseless deaths – let *that* decision be on the conscience of our fine 'Major' out there."

"Is that all?" he asked.

"Pretty much," she replied. "If you give me some time, 'Major'... I'm hoping that we can negotiate a mutually-acceptable solution to this little – *ahem* – 'misunderstanding'. By doing that, you not only save the lives of your

'President' and the guy calling himself 'FBI Director', but also your own and those of scores of innocent government staff. Pretty good deal, if you ask me."

"Don't *listen* to her!" she heard Crowford's voice, counseling. "She lied through her *teeth* to me. You can't believe a *word* she says!"

"Hey there, Mr. 'Spiritual Adviser'... how's your *day* been going?" cheekily called Chu. "For the record... did I 'lie' to you? Well, apart from having forgotten five or more of the Ten Commandments... you neglected to make me swear to tell the whole truth, and nothing *but* the truth... *et cetera*. You asked a question and I told you the truth about that ol' telekinesis thing, I mean – I just left a little bit out. Oops! I'll try to be more, ahh, *forthcoming*, next time."

"You may *think* you're in the driver's seat here, girlie," he growled, "But you ain't! I'll *see* to that."

Damn, mused Chu, why's my danger-sense going off the charts?

There's nothing that this half-rate televangelist can do to me, that the Marines and all the rest of those nice big men with their guns, can't do much better... is there?

Well... at least as long as he's talking... maybe that buys me a bit more time, before this 'Major' starts shooting, and thus forces me into backing up my threats.

People-humans these all not you kill Mommy would? came an innocent-feeling thought.

It's... complicated, Warden, she answered.

Mommy desperately doesn't want to do anything like that.

But if she's forced to – especially as the alternative is that you and I both die instead... yes, God help her – she will.

Be ready to help Mommy defend herself, at any time... okay?

Oh-kay, came the re-assurance.

Oh, Karéin – why did you give me the power, to end up in this place!

I was just a team-leader... I wanted to have a career, have a nice house, maybe enforce the law... I didn't want to pronounce life or instant, senseless death, over people who I don't even know!

"Well if it's of any interest, Mr. Crowford," continued Chu, "You'll be glad to know that I *have* been keeping up the other side of our little bargain... but no answer yet, that I know of. And as a matter of fact I'll go you one better – if I don't have to reduce this plane to wreckage in the next few minutes, I'm planning to call out to Sam Jacobson and Company, as well. Originally I had no plan to do so, but what with the way things are now... what do I have to lose?"

Evidently those outside weren't taking her superior hearing into account, because she could hear the Marine Guard-leader whispering to the Spiritual Adviser, "About these threats to destroy the plane – is she armed with an explosive device or something that could really take us down, here?"

Chu heard Crowford reply, *sotto voce*, "I'm afraid, Major, that she's armed with somethin' *much* worse – namely, the hateful power of the Devil himself! I saw what she's capable of... cut a man clean in half with some kind of hell-fire, comin' straight out of her *eyes*. So yes, I'd have to say that she *could* do that – but stand your ground. We got an ace up our sleeve that this damnable little bitch doesn't know *diddly-squat* about – one that can take her down and send her back to Hell, *whatever* these accursed 'alien-powers' she's boastin' about, might happen to be. And it's almost ready to go. I just need a bit of *time*... that's all."

"I'm not reading you here, sir," complained the Marine Guard-leader. "If it's a weapon, it needs to be under *my* control –"

"Leave that to *me!*" cryptically called out Crowford's receding voice.

Chu heard his footsteps heading off toward the back of the aircraft, while – silent but supernaturally-alert – she pondered what to do with her captive, self-styled "Leader of the Free World".

Ramòn's *Mordedura*

The mystical force that led Sebastiàn inexorably on through the lengthening shadows of the South California late afternoon was beckoning ever stronger, and – somehow, though by a sense or a sensation that he didn't quite understand – he knew that he must, now, be *very* close.

Yet, he was uneasy; despite having a ghetto-born mega-gang numbering in the thousands – one whose ranks blanketed every street in nearby Rancho Cucamonga – over the past day and a half there had been disquieting reports of mysteriously-slaughtered *compadres,* far inside his army's outer perimeter. When the corpses were shown to him, they were missing various body-parts, typically, ears, noses and eyes.

Trademark of them puto AB'ers, grimly noted the former *Mara* lieutenant, as, perched on top of a burned-out courier-van in the dwindling light of a Greater Los Angeles late afternoon, he carefully scanned in all directions, over the battle-scarred surroundings of Sixth and Hermosa.

'Specially when their boobs, balls, 'n dicks get sliced off an' left in their mouths.

I been fresh all the time – some bueno yayo *we scored in them apartment-buildings back there, just like a fuckin' breath of fresh air* cada vez, compadre – *shouldn't have let* mi ejército *sit 'round here yesterday, havin'* una fiesta an' *catchin' up on their* comida, their *sexo an' their sleep.*

Claro que si, me divertí un poco con unas chicas, pero... *whole 'time-off' thing makin' us a sittin' duck for them fuckin' skinheads... whoever the fuck he is, he fuckin' good, an' he pickin' off* muchachos uno tras otro.

He checked for signs of movement, off in the distance.

There wasn't much good cover here, at least not right at street-level; the area was mostly warehouses and low-rise office-buildings, though these were almost all deserted.

Gonna find whoever did that, he resolved.

Gonna let mis pequeños amigos *eat him nice and slow.*

These musings of *El Nuveo Diablo De Los Angeles* were interrupted by Ramòn's familiar voice.

"*¡Hola, jéfé!*" exclaimed the second-in-command. "We takin' a break from scoutin' duty, anytime soon? *Compañeros* all strung out. *¡Hemos estado bailando durante cinco horas hasta el momento!*"

Sebastiàn delayed his response for a few seconds while stroking his goatee beard. He noticed that Rodrigo was approaching, and then said, "For *una hora, no màs*. We leavin' ourselves wide open, by stayin' in one place. How many dead?"

"'Least twenty on our side," uneasily stated Ramòn. "We done bagged 'bout seven or so of them nigger Crips, plus a bunch of other fuckers."

The ex-*Mara's* cruel, unnerving stare froze the under-study in place.

"What the *fuck?*" complained Sebastiàn. "How we lose more than them *putos? ¡Mi ejército es imparable!* Thought we was on a *roll!*"

"*Sì señor,*" hastily cajoled Ramòn, "But you gotta *understand...* somethin' else's been pickin' off *nuestros compañeros*, one by one, real sneaky-like. We ain't been findin' *los cadáveres* 'till roll-call after a battle. They cut up real bad... AB'ers, *sin lugar a dudas.*"

"*Él está diciendo la verdad, jéfé,*" broke in Rodrigo. "Fucker waits 'till we gettin' off the gate with, say, them 18th-Streeters... takes out our shot-caller in, like, two or three seconds... gotta be that because most of the time, still hot rounds *en su nueve*, but it ain't been fired. We only findin' it out *cuando hayamos terminado el baile*, we get back there, and poor hermano's *cojones stickin'* out his mouth. Whoever this *puto* is, he's *good...* he's operatin' way behind the front."

"Well, what the fuck you *doin'* 'bout it?" challenged the former *Mara*.

"We got more patrols goin' out –" started Ramòn; but his voice was interrupted by distant shouting and the sounds of gun-shots, coming from a side-street going east, just north of where he stood on Hermosa Avenue.

"*¡La fiesta está terminada...* gonna deal with this fucker *myself!*" growled Sebastiàn, as he took an impossibly-long leap off the van-roof and on to the pavement. "*¡Sígueme!*"

He dashed northward, with Ramòn and Rodrigo, plus another three tough, battle-hardened *compañeros*, who had overheard parts of the discourse, huffing and puffing far back, as the distance between the more-than-human leader and his lesser followers, quickly widened.

In less than thirty seconds – though by now he was completely alone – Sebastiàn made a right-hand turn and began to head down a tree-lined *cul-de-sac*, which opened out into a wide parking-lot halfway-through and which was surrounded by four large, low-rise industrial office buildings.

A subconscious command focused his superior eyesight down the street, and immediately *El Nuevo Diablo* discerned a scene of mayhem; four or five bloody, mutilated corpses lay piled, one upon another, almost exactly in the middle of the circular paved area at the end of the *cul-de-sac*.

Una trampa obvia, he mused, while coming to a temporary stop near the half-desiccated tree-trunk. *Bueno... let's do some color-changin' and* – mierda!

He had tried to dodge but a well-aimed bullet – fired from some unidentified assailant, evidently in a hidden firing-position – had clipped his left arm just below the shoulder, slicing through his bicep at an oblique angle while leaving an ugly, profusely-bleeding flesh-wound.

Grimacing in anger and pain and muttering various Spanish curses, he ducked behind the tree; it was an opportune move, because it saved him from the next three rifle-rounds fired by his unseen tormentor (although, two high-velocity rounds struck the trunk, sending wood-splinters hither and yon).

The ex-*Mara* cautiously peeked between two stripped-down, abandoned cars, straining to determine where the shots were coming from; and as three more shots whizzed past, he realized that he was facing not one but at least two snipers, given the criss-crossing trajectories involved.

"¡Hey, *jéfé!*" called out Ramòn's voice, evidently from behind the building-corner.

"Stay back!" shouted Sebastiàn, calling out backward, over his shoulder. "*Puto's* got a scope or somethin' – set us up good. You come 'round, he smoke you, *por supuesto!*"

To his relief, *El Nuevo Diablo* didn't see any familiar faces peeking around the corner; but his attention to this scene was quickly pre-empted by more rifle-shots, including one that, to his dismay, somehow struck home against his upper thigh. The pain was horrendous, but – somehow, in a way that he was sure he couldn't have done, even a couple of weeks ago – Sebastiàn managed to steel himself, and ducking, weaving and bleeding, he dashed back to the sheltered location where his two subordinates were waiting.

"*Jesús, María y José*," gasped Ramòn, upon seeing his limping boss. "*¿Qué pasó?*"

"What's it *look* like?" retorted Sebastiàn. "*Puto* laid one on me... *pero voy a estar bien*. Now listen up fast and listen up good. I'm goin' up – over the building – I'll draw the fucker's fire... *los más pequeños me protegerán*. Get down on the ground *y prestar atención a lo que está pasando*, an' when I get close an' they ain't payin' no attention back here, you two jump out an' shoot the *fuck* out of 'em. *¿Lo entienden ustedes?*"

"¡Sì señor!" immediately echoed both of the lieutenants.

"*Bueno*," said the ex-*Mara*. "Now stand back."

Both Ramòn and Rodrigo knew very well what *that* meant; so they quickly retreated to a safe distance of perhaps ten feet.

The move was none too soon, because faster than could have been anticipated – to the humming, susurrating accompaniment of Sebastiàn's oddly- and hypnotically-beautiful-yet-ominous war-song – *they* came, encasing the more-than-human man's figure in a buzzing, throbbing carpet of tiny, shimmering, multi-segmented bodies.

Dios mío, silently considered Ramòn, *I was* inside *that!*

And what's even worse *is... it wasn't so bad...*

Now, while the war-song sounded ever louder, the one man – and the other, who knew himself to be slightly more – saw the amorphous, swarm-like mass that hid *El Nuveo Diablo De Los Angeles* within its midst, gradually lift off the pavement and soar skyward, at no more than the speed of a slow walk at first but then with increasing velocity, until it cleared a height of about fifteen feet and went over the roof of the building behind which Ramòn and Rodrigo were secreted.

Sebastiàn hadn't gone much more than six feet over the roof-line before he became the target of a multitude of rifle-rounds. Loud Spanish curses issued forth, although he continued to float to the east. To their dismay and try as they might, neither of the two understudies could clearly see where the shots were coming from; so, while praying that the gambit would be successful and that the hidden sharpshooter's attentions were duly distracted, they cautiously crawled forward on hands and knees around the building's south-west corner, trying to keep well below any likely line-of-sight.

The insect-encased ex-*Mara* passed out of eyesight, and Ramòn subconsciously flinched, as he heard a couple of sharp, barking-explosive sounds, and then received a primitive, agonized psychic impression, coming from exactly the direction that *el jéfé* must have been in.

¡La mierda!... they screamin' in pain... he still alive? considered the slightly-superhuman man. It was all he could do to keep going, as the bizarre, indirectly-inflicted discomfort flooded through his mind.

But there was no time for sentimentality, because, to his dismay, Ramòn heard the sounds of a crowd of his fellow-gangsters, coming up hard on his heels, behind and to the right.

The appearance of the first ones brought a predictable response, and again, both Ramòn and Rodrigo ducked as a fusillade was unleashed over their heads. They heard screams and moans, as some of the rounds had undoubtedly struck home, though the two dared not turn to see or to try to help out.

There was, however, at least one hard-won benefit : the snipers had been distracted, and now Sebastiàn's sub-commanders had a relatively undisturbed crawl forward; the tension as they had to traverse the driveway behind the office-complex was gut-wrenching, but mercifully, they weren't targeted for the five or six seconds that this required, and soon they had reached the dried-up remains of a low hedge that separated the building's rear parking lot from the main part of the *cul-de-sac*.

Creeping ever lower with bellies right against the ground, the two edged ever-so-carefully eastward, until they were at the far corner of the parking-lot. Knowing that the slightest apparent movement might result in a bullet between his eyebrows, Ramòn edged up to the desiccated hedge and peered through it.

"Hey —" whispered Rodrigo; but he was silenced by a quick hand-gesture by his compatriot, whose head and shoulders were already inside the bushes.

Straining his eyesight to a newly-empowered limit, Ramòn surveyed the scene in front of him, and to his simultaneous elation and trepidation, he noticed two separate sets of gun-flashes – one at ground-level and another from the roof – coming from a smaller low-rise building, diagonally across the *cul-de-sac* from the one to their backs.

¡La mierda! he mentally cursed.

Fuckers got easy shot at us – we'll never get close enough, without bein' –

At that moment, a familiar ominous, buzzing, energizing sound, coming from above and behind, took the under-study's attention momentarily away from the semi-hidden snipers, and immediately the gunfire was directed at the insect-shrouded Sebastiàn, who seemed, as near as could be determined, to be continuing despite being repeatedly struck.

While Ramòn silently wondered how *el jéfé* could withstand such punishment and still be alive – never mind, still stay airborne – he heard a mad cacophony from the intersection of Hermosa and the *cul-de-sac*. A brief glance over his shoulder verified that a large group of *hermanos,* who had evidently heard of the fire-fight, were pouring around the building-corner. The crowd surged forward, seemingly oblivious to the fact that the Latino gangsters within it were now completely exposed to the snipers.

He caught a glimpse of Sebastiàn – who was still the singular target of both the semi-hidden assailants – above and to the right. As the more-than-human man and his insectoid shield took hit after hit, Ramòn finally resolved,

¡Basta! It gettin' off the gate now, o nunca!

At first to the astonishment of a wary Rodrigo, who none the less followed after a second's hesitation, hot on the other semi-human's heels, Ramòn burst out from underneath the bushes. Faster than he could have imagined possible, he charged across the *cul-de-sac*, hurtling over one side of the pile of mutilated bodies in the middle of the circle with a newly-empowered long-jump. In only a few seconds, he had dashed up to a point with a clear view of the broken ground-floor window, behind which this one of the two accursed snipers had secreted himself.

For a second – even under the influence of battle-rage, adrenaline and some other, new, drug-like, enervating feeling, coming from he knew not where – Ramòn could not help but slow down and flinch at what he saw ahead of him. Though he could only observe the guy's skin-shaved, *swastika*-tattooed head and shoulders, this was the kind of enemy that, scant days beforehand, could have torn a Latino gangster like Ramòn limb from limb : the hulking, Caucasian *hijo de puta* looked as big a *mountain*; and he was not only obviously armed with a smoking-barreled auto-rifle, but also had some kind of body-armor.

Seeing that an enemy was now within a couple of second's distance, the sniper started to aim his rifle at the hard-charging gangster.

In a split-second, as sounds of a furious battle upon the roof of the building began to issue forth, Ramòn's desperate mind could think of only one tactic.

¡Saltar por encima de esa cosa!

While almost-perfectly-aimed rifle-rounds screeched scant inches from him on either side, he compressed his legs and rocketed forward and upward, covering a distance of at least twenty feet in a manner that no ordinary human Olympic athlete, could possibly have accomplished.

In a split-second, he had smashed through the remnants of the plate-glass window just to the gun-man's right, and though Ramòn suffered a couple of bloody gashes in so doing, the gesture momentarily stunned the astonished AB'er, who was hit on the right shoulder and thrown backward and down by the impact. Even better, the man's grip on his rifle had been broken by the unexpected assault, and the weapon went careening off to one side, sliding out of reach toward an inside doorway.

¡Cholo! yelled the voice of Rodrigo, which, judging from the volume, couldn't have been more than five to ten seconds further back.

But there was no time to wait for reinforcements.

A gut-wrenching fear came, as Ramòn realized that he could no longer feel the presence of his pistol under his belt : the damn thing had probably hit something and been wedged free, while he had been leaping over the window-wall.

The Aryan warrior – all six-plus-many-inches of his muscular bulk – was fumbling for a hand-gun of his own, but there was something wrong with the holster, and the mountain-of-a-man missed a crucial second or two, while trying to draw.

Ramòn charged, again picking up speed faster than humanly possible. Though much shorter than the AB'er, the Latino gangster lieutenant was strongly, stockily-built, and had been street-fighting since the age of eight, so he knew where to aim; he punched for the guy's crotch, missing only slightly and striking just above the pubic bone, with a force and violence that surprised both of the tumbling, sweating, opponents.

Curses and growls in both English and Spanish echoed throughout what, at one time, must have been a company cafeteria, as the two men punched and kicked at each other with mortal-combat viciousness. The skinhead warrior's upper-body strength was enormous, and as he struggled to keep the *puto*'s hands away from his still-available pistol, Ramòn realized that even with the strange empowerment newly come to him, eventually, the AB'er was bound to grab the gun. Punches and kicks flew aplenty, while the two combatants rolled back and forth, each grappling for some slight advantage while sending tables, chairs, plates and dinner-cutlery, falling and shattering, all about.

And then – loud enough to get the momentary attention of even men locked in savage combat such as this – there was *another* sound; they saw a huge, combat-geared figure (though, one suffering horrendous, bleeding wounds, over almost every square inch of his body), crashing to the ground, right outside the smashed windows that Ramòn had made his entry-point.

Considering the distance the man must have fallen – twenty feet for sure – it would have been a feat to have just survived such a mishap, never mind the battle-scars; but, amazingly, after only a second or so, he was back on his feet, just in time to meet the on-rushing Rodrigo, who managed to get at least one shot off before being attacked by the fallen thug.

What was going on outside, however, was, right now, the least of Ramòn's worries, because the big AB'er had managed to get one of his hands free; the Latino felt an agonizing pain in his upper back. He had been stabbed by a hidden fighting-knife, and as the blood gushed out of the wound, Ramòn realized that if he didn't do something dramatic, and quickly, the next stab would be to his neck or heart. Yet he couldn't get near his own *cuchillo*, stuck as it was on the outside of his pant-leg.

So he did the only thing he could think of : he bared his teeth and bit the Aryan *puto*, hard, on the man's knife-wielding right arm, just above the wrist. Only a few drops of blood ended up on his teeth and lips, but the taste was oddly exciting and empowering.

He tried to avoid wondering why.

For a second or two, the struggle continued and Ramòn feared that he would shortly lose the fight; but then, something profoundly unusual happened – the grip of the AB'er's right hand began to weaken, and he groaned as if in severe pain.

Though he only caught the briefest of glimpses, it seemed to Ramòn that a greenish-gray, varicose-vein-mimicking discoloration had begun to spread around the bite-mark, and in the next half-second, he found himself being first kneed in the groin and then kicked hard in the teeth by his hulking, but pain-grimacing and sweating enemy, who had clamped his left hand over the wound on his right arm (which was hanging almost limply) and who managed to get to his feet, making rapidly for the inside doorway and parts unknown, further inside the building.

While the half-stunned Ramòn spat out blood and silently wondered why his opponent hadn't immediately gone for the kill, the Aryan thug paused only for a second to grab his auto-rifle and then staggered out of the doorway, disappearing into the interior darkness.

The Latino gangsta – though bleeding profusely from the stab-wound in his back and still "seeing stars" – stood up and was about to pursue, but he hesitated for a moment upon seeing a dense insect-cloud completely obscure his view of what was going on outside. That might have been a blessing, because what he heard was appalling, even to his hardened ears.

First, there was the obligatory and foreboding buzzing, humming noise, but whomever Sebastiàn had been pursuing evidently wasn't immediately caught, because there were the sounds of mayhem further back into the *cul-de-sac*; Ramòn thought he heard a brief outburst of defiant English-language cursing, followed by gunshots, screams of defiance and then just blood-curdling, unnatural screams, eventually trailing off and being over-ridden by Spanish-language crowd-babble.

He hurried to the broken-in window, looking periodically over his shoulder, ever mindful of the possibility that the Aryan warrior that he had just fought, might suddenly re-appear. Ramòn could only catch fleeting glimpses through the gangster-throng that had encircled... *whatever*-it-was, but the picture wasn't pretty : lying on the ground, some ten to fifteen feet from the window-ledge, was the mangled corpse of someone who, at one time, might have been a pretty big fellow, over six feet for sure.

Not a square inch of the remains looked undamaged, and the poor bugger's skin – plus at least the top layer of his flesh, underneath that – had been completely eaten away, except in a few odd places. The wounds went down to the bone at the ribs, on the skull and in all the limbs. All the metal fittings – a belt-buckle, a finger-ring, several fighting-knives and a still-warm auto-rifle – seemed to be mostly untouched, however.

"What you all *starin'* at?" bellowed the familiar, gruff voice of *El Nuevo Diablo De Los Angeles*. "*¡Eso es lo que le sucede a todos los que me desafía!*"

Warily, the crowd backed off, giving Ramòn a briefly improved view of the opponent's mauled body-remnants. Trying not to stare – but unable to resist, as the sheer extent of the damage had a certain, eerie fascination – he addressed Sebastiàn, whose frame was no longer adorned by the insect-cloud, and who was bleeding from several serious wounds of his own.

"*¡Jéfé!*" shouted Ramòn. "*Bailé con un hombre aquí,* but he's movin' – might be out back settin' up for another shot... *big* fucker, AB'er for *sure*."

"*¿Estás herido?*" came back the reply.

"*Sì señor,*" admitted the understudy. "Got me in the back with the knife. *Me duele como el infierno, pero puedo manejarlo.*"

"Bueno... get your ass back here," ordered Sebastiàn.

"But he's gettin' *away* –" argued Ramòn, while taking another backward glance at the cafeteria-door.

"Rodrigo – Miguel – Felipe – *ustedes tres* take over for him –" directed the *jéfé;* but he was interrupted by Ramon's hulking, sweating friend.

"Miguel took one in the head, back at the corner," advised the Latino thug.

"Emilio still breathin'?" asked a frustrated Sebastiàn.

"*Sì señor,*" called a different male voice. "*Voy a ir con ellos.*"

Rodrigo led this guy – a thin, wiry, shaven-headed fellow – along with another, taller man (who sported long, black pony-tail and a goatee beard), at a fast trot around the side of this building, toward what appeared to be an open storm-sewer, just to the east.

"*¡Tráeme su cabeza cortada!*" gruffly demanded Sebastiàn.

The pain in Ramòn's upper back was now severe, and the slightest abrupt movement pushed it close to sheer agony; but, worried that the might run into a half-crazed Aryan warrior if he tried to detour through the building to get back to the *cul-de-sac*, he somehow mustered the strength and fortitude to hop up on the window-ledge and then back down to dry dirt.

"*Te ves como una mierda,*" grimly quipped *El Nuevo Diablo De Los Angeles*. "*Como yo.*"

"Shit, boss," gasped Ramòn, upon seeing the *jéfé*'s battered body, which bore at least four more savage bullet-holes, not counting the one that had been taken early in the encounter. "You're *bleedin'* –"

"*Sí, yo lo sé,*" replied Sebastiàn, more wearily than usual. "*Tu también.* Need some down-time."

So that was what the two did, while the rest of *El Posse Del Nuevo Diablo*, set about to the ever-grim task of cleaning up.

They heard one of the more businesslike of the ex-*Mara*'s followers, issuing instructions to someone in the crowd.

"*¡Hombre!*", the guy shouted, "*¡Ve a buscar algunos cubos, por favor!*"

Breaking In... And Breaking The News

The former President's family had emerged from the rift in the wall, one by one; and their appearance had quenched any doubt among the local Secret Service agents, as to the authenticity of their unexpected new company.

However – despite the fact that *Vìrya I'ëà'b'* had (on Abruzzio's orders) remained hidden – suspicions among the American Praetorian Guard were still high, especially when the ex-JPL scientist and the rest of the entourage joined the U.S. leader in the White House Situation Room.

"So we *get* it, that you're the former President of the United States," complained the first agent who they had heard while waiting in the tunnel – he was a hulking, brush-cut Caucasian guy – "But if you don't mind my asking, sir – what the hell are you *doing* here? We'd been told that you were, uhh, on medical-leave or something... and we're now taking orders from the former Vice-President, as I'm sure you're aware. And then, there's the issue of how you managed to break through a reinforced concrete wall with your bare hands... not to mention how you dug out a tunnel to even get *down* here."

"I can *explain*, Curt," replied the ex-President.

"You'd damn well *better*," challenged the agent. "Because I have standing orders to detain, and if necessary shoot, anyone who attempts to undertake unauthorized access to these premises. If you're interested, the orders were issued by the current President, immediately after the alien showed up here and – uhh – was seen to murder Mr. Kaysten."

"Yeah, well," grumbled the former Chief of Staff, "I'm just thrilled to re-acquaint with *you*, too, Mr. Kortish. And – for the record – Little Miss Nuclear Angel sure *did* lay a bite on me... but 'that which doesn't destroy me, only makes me stronger'... at least, that's how I *think* it goes."

"Where'd you learn that?" whispered Abruzzio.

"Wolf," responded Kaysten in a low voice, with a wry smile. "He's really big into the whole 'tough-guy' stuff, you know."

"Okay," remarked the ex-President, "I'll tell you... and Agents Spick and Credoe too – 'hello' to both of you. Also to Mrs. Butkowski and Mr. Fallon, who I see over there on the other side of the table."

He was referring to a taller, thinner Caucasian agent, blond-haired and younger than the leading one, and an average-sized, darker-skinned, mid-30s guy who was probably some mixture of African-American and Hispanic. The two civilians were a middle-aged Caucasian woman and an elderly guy, probably in his 60s or older. All were dressed in conservative business-suits.

"Great to see you again, sir," came back the obligatory – though, markedly uneasy – replies, from the others who had been addressed.

One of them (the older one), added, "Sir... we're already familiar with the First Lady – and it's great to see you back here, too, Ma'am – as well as with your family and the Chief of Staff. But who are these other folks, if you don't mind my asking?"

"Oh... no problem, Bert," crisply replied the ex-President. "I'd like to introduce you to Sylvia Abruzzio, of the NASA Mars mission team, and her personal friend, Moira Sullivan. Also to Homer Maloney, of the National Guard, and – do I have this right? – Giuseppi Rizzo of, uhh, GrayWar."

"GrayWar *Legion*, sir," unhelpfully corrected the disheveled, not-ready-for-parade-duty, Rizzo. "They even let me carry a gun."

"Right," offered the former U.S. leader.

"Thanks for the information, sir," inquired Kortish, "I can understand why you've got a military escort... but what about the civilians – what are *they* doing here? Not to mention the dog."

Rainbow let out a pathetic-sounding sigh, which was rewarded by bemused laughter on the part of several onlookers.

"Ms. Abruzzio and Jerry, not to mention Ms. Sullivan, were instrumental in – ahh – getting my family and I, safely to D.C.," tactfully offered the ex-President. "We couldn't have done it without them. Even little 'Rainbow' helped a bit, if you want to know the truth. For the record... initially, I didn't want to come here... to do what I'm now set to do. But given the threat to the country – which I'll describe shortly – I realized that I couldn't, in good conscience, not do this. Which is why we're having this discussion, I suppose."

"What you mean, sir?" skeptically asked the senior Secret Service agent.

"So, gentlemen and ladies," recounted the American ex-leader, "Here's where we're at, right now... and this is the *highly* abbreviated version. First of all – as you can see with your own eyes – there's *nothing* wrong with me, health-wise... there never has been. What you've been told, in that respect, was a cover-story cooked up by the former Vice-President, along with the leadership of the Agency and some in the military – not to mention a few disloyal elements of my own inner circle – to engineer a *coup d'état* against me specifically, and against the legitimately-elected Executive Branch, generally."

"They told us that you had requested to be relieved of office, yourself," noted Kortish.

"That, Curt, was a lie," countered the ex-President, "Like almost everything that you and most of the country have been told, lately – starting with what's been said about the alien... that is, this 'Karéin-Mayréij' that you've no doubt heard so much about. The only reasons why I didn't immediately fight what George and his crew had cooked up, were, at the time, they were threatening Kathy, Matt and Clairie – I was in Air Force One at the time, and had no way of physically protecting them; and the alien was flying all over the country, doing things like wrecking national monuments and threatening my life. George's stab in the back took me completely by surprise, and I didn't want to have the government fighting against itself, while the alien – not to mention a couple of loose nukes, which as far as I'm aware, are still out there somewhere – were threatening national security. If you know where to look, this is all well-documented within the Executive Branch's internal records."

"There's *another* one... over and above the one in L.A.?" whispered Kaysten, to Abruzzio.

"Seems so," she whispered back. "He tell you where it is?"

Kaysten shook his head.

"Go on," requested the Secret Service agent. His arms were crossed in front, and his body-language was defensive, but was perhaps a bit less so than a minute before.

"And why *don't* you tell us about the alien, while you're at it?" he demanded. "Know what? The current President *warned* us, that she might use you as a way to take over the government, again. 'Mind-control' and all that, sir. How can we be sure that she isn't standing right beside you? She can become *invisible*, you know... or so the military reports suggest. And it'd explain how you got through that wall."

"By all means," answered the ex-President. "First of all... from my point of view – and that of anyone who's interested in preserving Constitutional government in this country – I *am* 'the current President'. Secondly, about the alien... you're absolutely justified in being afraid of her – I won't dispute that. If anything, you don't know the *half* of it, Curt – from what Ms. Abruzzio here tells me, the Storied Watcher could easily reduce this country to ruins, if she so chose to do. But she isn't here right now, and my aim is to ensure that she doesn't show up in the U.S. again... at least, not until we've worked out some way of peacefully coexisting with her. How can you be sure of that? Easy... if Karéin-Mayréij *was* here, I can assure you that I wouldn't have to explain anything to you or negotiate with you, because if you were to fight her, you'd be d –"

"Mr. President – that's *very* unfair!" interrupted Abruzzio. "Not only is Karéin not into murder, but – as we've discussed – she has *repeatedly* told me, and many others, that she has no interest whatsoever in getting involved in human political disputes. And for your information, Agent Kortish – this applies not only to you, but also to everyone else at the White House and the Executive Branch – I'll save the President some time in explaining all this. Is the Storied Watcher here, today? No; but *I* am – and not even counting Jerry, I'm more than a match for all of you put together... and *then* some!"

"How would *that* be, Ma'am?" politely asked the third Secret Service agent. "Far as I can see... you aren't even armed."

With a saturnine – but foreboding – smile, Abruzzio answered, "'How', you ask? Well, it was *me* who knocked that hole in the wall, simply with the force of my mind... using an alien-power bestowed on me by Karéin-Mayréij herself. That's only *one* of the highly destructive abilities at my disposal; I honestly hope that you'll never be on the receiving-end of these, because I don't want to hurt *anyone*, if I can possibly avoid it. And no – neither the President, nor anyone else in this room, is under any form of mind-control – he hasn't even *met* the Storied Watcher, although both Jerry and I, also my puppy-dog, *have* done so. The entire project of getting the rightful President in here, was *my* idea. With me so far?"

"I was kind of wondering what a dog was doing down here," quipped the blond, younger Secret Service agent. "Assuming we believe all of this, though... what, exactly, do you want? What's the goal, here?"

"May I, Ms. Abruzzio?" peevishly inquired the former U.S. leader.

"Oh.. for *sure*, sir," responded the more-than-a-woman.

"You're taking orders from her?" demanded Kortish.

"I sure aren't," quickly interjected Kaysten. "Sorry, Sylvia."

"Oh... I can't make you do anything you don't want to do," demurred Abruzzio.

"Absolutely not the case, Curt," countered the ex-President. "Ms. Abruzzio and I have a certain commonality of interest – that's the extent of it."

"About what?" pressed the agent.

"You seen the news lately?" asked the former U.S. leader. "About this 'Mars Gang' at Fort Knox, and so on."

"How could we *miss* it?" remarked the third Secret Service agent, with a wince. "We're getting briefings almost by the hour... it's one hell of a mess!"

"Well, gentlemen," announced the ex-President, "That's actually the main reason that I'm here to take back leadership of the country... before George and his crew of mutineers, make an already-bad situation, uncontrollably worse. Mind if I ask you a question?"

"Go ahead," indicated the senior agent.

"What do your briefings tell you about the abilities of this 'Mars Gang'?" knowingly questioned the former U.S. leader. "And what do they say about the effectiveness of our efforts to stop them?"

"That's classified information, sir," argued Kortish.

"Not if I'm your Commander-In-Chief... which I am," insisted the ex-President. "And besides, I've been getting these briefings anyway – one of the few perks that George let me retain, after shipping me off to the gilded cage in which the redoubtable Ms. Abruzzio, and Jerry, found me."

With obvious suspicion, the Secret Service agent stared at his former boss for a few seconds; but eventually, Kortish offered, "Then you should already know, sir... situation's extremely grim. This asshole 'Jacobson' guy – and the rest of 'em, we don't know exactly how many there are, but it's more than five for sure – they took over Fort Knox, we sent in three full mech-infantry battalions from the local garrison... Army got its ass kicked into next week. I saw some of the casualty-reports... they were... uhh... *appalling*, that's the only way I can put it... like, '90 per cent KIA or MIA', for some companies. It was like we were fighting guys with ARs, and we had nothing better than slingshots. They can only identify some of the deceased, with dental-records."

"I know," softly observed the ex-President, "And Jacobson's going to have to answer for what he and his crew have done to our soldiers."

"I don't know how you're going to accomplish that, sir," disputed Kortish. "Because the current President's thrown everything we've *got* – short of nukes, that is... and the rumor's that's next, soon as we can get some fully-operational – at the Mars Gang –"

Abruzzio's face turned ashen, while that of Kaysten wore an equally-grim look.

"*Please* tell me that you're making that up!" she angrily demanded.

"Lady... I don't know you from a hole in the ground," sneered the Service agent, "And I don't owe you the time of day... but just out of personal interest... what's it to *you?*"

"What *is* it?" growled an instantly-furious Abruzzio.

Her war-music began to echo from the four walls, and her eyes began to dimly-glow, causing an immediate startled reaction from the White House humans, who reflexively backed off, while the agents among them slowly reached for their guns.

"I'll *tell* you!" she hissed. "Would it help to know that the fucking government already *dropped* an H-bomb on a bunch of Karéin's friends – including myself, Sam Jacobson and most of those in this 'Mars Gang'? I fucking know how it *feels* – heat and radiation that'll send a human being to an agonizing death – you better hope it's a quick one... and I can *assure* you –"

"Calm *down*, Ms. Abruzzio!" ordered the ex-President. "You're *frightening* them!"

A glowering Abruzzio slowly and unwillingly tamped down her *Fire*. But she added, "Just be very glad, that I don't give you a small taste of what the son of a bitch who's now running the Executive Branch, tried to do to all of us."

"It's going to your *head*, Sylvia," grimly advised Kaysten. "Remember... she warned us about letting it get the better of you. Learned that myself, back at the Reservoir... if that means anything."

Abruzzio nodded in acknowledgment, at him.

"What's he *talking* about?" asked the second, younger agent. "And... you said you had a *nuke* dropped on you, Ms... uhh... 'Abruzzio', is it? That's pretty hard to believe, given that you seem to still be alive."

"It wasn't for lack of trying, on the part of the government," countered the former JPL scientist, "And did you catch the part about, 'it would have killed a human being'?"

"Yeah," he said.

"You aren't talking to a human being, now," she proudly declared, her brown eyes staring forcefully at him. "I survived a nuke – okay, a *near-miss* from a nuke, but all the same – and I'm still here. Stop to think about what that says about you guys and your friends, successfully fighting me... or Sam Jacobson, and the five or more of them who have powers equivalent to mine. Can we say, 'death-wish'?"

The Secret Service agents mutely exchanged wary glances, as Abruzzio concluded,

"And *that,* folks, is why you had better listen to the rightful President of the United States, who's standing next to me. You either support him – and have a chance at reasoning with Jacobson And Company, not to mention with Karéin herself – or you throw your lot in with the insane megalomaniac and war-criminal, who's flying around in Air Force One, watching the country get blown to bits by a force that he can't *possibly* defeat, but with which he's incapable of negotiating. What'll it *be,* boys?"

There was another prolonged silence, and then Kortish spoke up.

"So what, exactly, did you want us to *do?*" he asked.

"That's easy," offered the ex-President. "All you have to do... is to watch my back."

He paused for a second; then he added,

"And accompany me to the Oval Office... I have an *announcement* to make."

A Whiff Of Death

"*Sígueme, cholo!*" was what they heard *El Nuevo Diablo* casually demanding of his wounded under-study, never mind the fact that the short guy had obviously just been stabbed in the back in a way that likely would have killed many others, outright.

Yet, *el jéfé* did not seem in the least perturbed about all this. He had just gone up to the stocky little gangster named "Ramòn", spat on both of his own hands, rubbed them over his gasping, crippled deputy's wound, and then shrugged with a bemused smile.

After this, Sebastiàn simply walked away, toward the gangster-army convoy of commandeered trucks and vans.

"He leavin' Ramòn to die *en la calle*?" whispered one of the convoy-girls, to another. "That ain't *right –*"

¡Cállate! responded the other one. "He can hear shit that nobody else can – an' anyways – *look* at Ramòn now, *chica –* "

The little guy – though still obviously groggy and worn-out from his recent battle – had somehow gotten back on his own feet.

But that wasn't what got attention from all around.

Ramòn's eyes had a dull, sinister, green glow in them; and his demeanor was a snarl personified.

"Ohhh... *me duele la espalada*," he moaned. "*¿Que pasó?*"

"You smoked that 'Aryan' fucker... or just about," congratulated Sebastiàn. "*¡Buen trabajo, soldado!*"

"*Esa pieza de la mierda –* he get me with that fuckin' knife," explained Ramòn. "He get me *good*. Why I no *dead?*"

"Because you one of *us* now!" said Sebastiàn, with a sinister smile. "*¡Eres el esbirro del Diablo, muchacho!*"

He let out a sinister, bellowing laugh that sent a chill through everyone around – with the exception of Ramòn, who was breathing deeply, and – seemingly – recovering more and more, with each inhale and exhale.

"You need a few hours for it to take hold," advised Sebastiàn. "I don' want to waste any more time – but I need you *fresh, cholo!* You rest up... *me escuchas?*"

"*¡Claro que si!*" answered the second-in-command.

Ramòn looked over his left shoulder.

A small bug – a cockroach or just some kind of beetle, perhaps, but one with an oddly-iridescent hue to its carapace – had come to rest on it.

Oddly, he had no inclination to brush it off. Instead, he just shot a quick glance at the tiny creature and winked at it, while a grin came to the face of Sebastiàn.

The gang-leader turned to his followers. He pointed at his understudy.

"*Si mi vida llega a su fin*", announced Sebastiàn, "*¡Él será su nuevo líder!*"

Meanwhile, the *jéfé* had other business to attend to, in the meantime.

The two *muchachos* who had been sent out in search of Ramòn's tormentor, had come back empty; they had followed the blood-splattered floor-stains out of the building and into the street, but the trail had gone cold after that point.

For this, their reward had been being ordered to stand in front of the rest of the group; Sebastiàn's baleful glare had transfixed the two, while he casually sliced off the distal portions of their little fingers with his hunting-knife.

The local feral dogs had appreciated the unexpected protein-treat thus forthcoming.

"*¡La próxima vez... esto será la mitad de tu pene!*" he had grimly warned one of them.

The lesson was obviously not lost on the other, nor on the crowd.

He turned to the onlookers.

"*¡Ustedes han visto lo que les sucede a los que fallan!*" he threatened. "*La próxima vez...* I ain't gonna go so easy on whoever fucks up. *¿Lo entienden?*"

Grave nods of acknowledgment came from the Latino gangster-army.

"*Bueno,*" continued the more-than-human *Nuevo Diablo*. "We holdin' here for a while. But... this is our last lay-over, 'cause when we get goin' again... we ain't stoppin'!"

He turned to Rodrìgo.

"Make sure every one of 'em, got three full clips," demanded *el jéfé*.

He stopped for a second, and added,

"And a knife. Whoever that *puto* is... *quiero su cabeza ... y sus bolas!*"

Unhappily, most the entire night had by now been frittered away, and – with the first rays of sunlight appearing on the eastern horizon – *El Nuevo Diablo* had decided that the waiting-time was over.

Fortunately, there had not been any more "attrition" among the soldiers and hangers-on of his personal army – unless one were to count two dead as a result of a "misunderstanding" between members of formerly-opposed gangs, over ownership of convoy-girls and speed-pills.

Sebastiàn had solved the former dispute by awarding the *chica* involved, to the *muchacho* who had survived the *ad hoc* battle.

He solved the latter, by confiscating the *drogas* for his own personal use.

In any other context, this would likely have led to another gunfight. But one stare with is foreboding, green-glowing eyes, were enough to deter even the thought of mutiny.

As the order to break camp and move out had been given, Ramòn – now seemingly "one hundred per cent", though his shirt still bore the open gash made by the AB'er's dirk – approached.

"*Entonces, jéfé,*" advanced the understudy, "Where 'zactly is it, that we goin'?"

"Forward," replied Sebastiàn. "*Por ahí.*"

"But what's so important over there?" pressed Ramòn."

"*¡Algo que es grande, chico... algo que es muy grande!*" cryptically replied the gang-leader.

"*Bueno...* you the shot-caller," obliged the second-in-command, who had visibly recovered from the stab-wound at an astonishing rate. "But can't *usted* give us just a little hint 'bout what we chasin', *jéfé?*"

"Not right now," parried Sebastiàn, "But when we get there – *esto es mío... es demasiado grande para ti o para cualquiera de nuestros muchachos*. And when I do what I gotta do – you hang back and look after all them – *lo que pueda pasar*. If somethin' happen to me... the torch passes to you. *¿Entiendes?*"

"*Si señor,*" gravely acknowledged Ramòn, "But how close *is* we?"

"*Estamos muy cerca, ahora... puedo sentirlo*," replied the gang-leader. "In my *bones*. The little ones say so, too. *Debes estar listo en cualquier momento, cholo* – 'cause when we gettin' off the gate... it goin' down *realmente rápido*."

He stopped for a second, sniffing the air, in a weird way that they had seen him do, once or twice before.

"*Está allí*," announced Sebastiàn. "Get your fuckin' boots on, *compadres*... destiny awaits us!"

Double-Bogey

"Corn Eagle Five, requesting tactical," sounded the narrow-band local comm-link, in the dimly-lit, computer-display-replete fighter-wing-commander's cockpit.

Already half-annoyed at the breach of protocol, Major Earl Sednik answered, "Cornhusker Eagle One, rodge – what *is* it, Gene? You *know* we're supposed to be maintaining radio-silence, except for situation-changes."

"Don't want to talk out of turn, sir," asked the subordinate F-32E's pilot, "But we've been tracking the damn thing for almost two *hours*, now – why don't we have authorization to engage? We're *way* under super-cruise... but even so, we're gonna be near fail-safe fuel-status, soon."

"Don't know," parried the wing-commander. "I repeated the request ten minutes ago... no response from H.Q.. I'll *admit* it's damn strange, because they're still transmitting, and the IFF's nominal... I'd have expected at least an update. ACP may have gone to EMCON Status 3 or higher, due to some local airspace threat, I'd assume – that's SOP, anyway. Anyway... we've got *orders* – pursue, prevent egress, maintain station at optimal sensor-range – and await further instructions from C-in-C. We'll execute our orders to the *letter*. That clear?"

"Rodge that," muttered the frustrated under-study. "It's just that we've got a tight track, good lock... the works. And the bogey's on an almost straight course. We could *easily* down the damn thing, once and for all... and after that bullshit over East Texas –"

"Yeah, yeah... I know," said Sednik. "Look... let me get confirm from on high. Stand by."

"Rodge that," repeated the other fighter-pilot, as the squadron cruised eastward, just under the speed of sound.

The wing-commander had, by now, been trying to make contact for ten minutes or more.

He flipped a switch which enabled encrypted, ship-to-ship talk, audible to all the fighters in the formation.

"Now hear this," announced Sednik. "I'm informing you all, that I seem to be unable to contact either General Blanshard, or anyone else in the C-in-C plane. I say again... 'no contact with Top Dog'. Do you acknowledge?"

"Acknowledged," came back the response, from several of the fighters.

After some incoherent babble, one voice seemed to take over the discourse.

"Corn Eagle Two, here," spoke the pilot. "What you think's going on, Major? They *crash* or something?"

"Negative that," replied the commander. "Their transponder's still good, and they're still maintaining their previous track... no delta in altitude or direction. But they're not responding to queries – I'm not getting static or a comms-out status... so the link seems to be nominal. They just aren't picking up the phone... that's how I'd put it."

"So –" the other pilot began to ask, only to be cut short by his superior.

"So you know the drill," explained Sednik. "Local control, which means, I guess... yours truly's in charge – lucky *me*. Okay. Fuel-check, please? I got the ship-to-ship numbers from the tac-link, but you *know* that damn thing lies like a sidewalk, and I gotta figure out best place to *rendez-vous* with the tanker so we can stay up here, while these assholes in the bogey start runnin' dry. Each driver check your status locally... sound out."

"Corn Eagle Two, 52%," called out the first to respond.

"Corn Eagle Three, 47%," replied the second.

"Corn Eagle Four, 61%," came the third answer.

The fourth fighter-pilot was about to quote a per centage, when he, too, was pre-empted by the wing-commander.

"Just a sec," interrupted Sednik. "Sensor-return from two of the ships behind you – IR-trace, faint but it's there... hmm. Crossing south to southwest track, behind the vanguard and flank formations, but in front of you and the guys in back... low, but... whoa! 492 knots, at 4250 *feet?* And it's about the size of a drone... no, wait, bigger signal... now it's back to... size and shape of a *balloon?* What the *hell?* Maintain position... I'm hailing this new contact, now, on all civilian frequencies."

"Say again Commander," requested the voice of a different fighter-pilot. "I thought I heard '492 knots'. Activating tac-link... yeah, goddamn, there it is... sir, that can't be a *civilian* aircraft... not at *that* speed and that altitude – right?"

"Your guess is as good as mine, Corn Eagle Three," offered the perplexed fighter-wing-commander. "Looks like we got another bogey... *stupid* fuckers – don't they *know* we've got 'shoot-to-kill' rights on everything in the exclusion-zone?"

There was a brief period of silence, then Sednik again spoke up.

"No response, on any frequency – or from the secret IFF back-doors on the standard FAA nav-suite," he muttered. "We're getting that even from the main bogey... but not *this* one. Peculiar..."

"Corn Eagle Four here, sir," came another voice. "'Scuse my French, but... what the fuck *is* it? Wasn't that gear supposed to be *mandatory*? And what about the differential returns?"

"Damn straight," replied the wing-commander. "All planes since about '20, for the transponders, as I recall. Listen... this could be one of those Brazilian spy-drones... or... okay, look – Corn Eagle Three, Five, Six – new orders... peel off, intercept-course, establish visual on the new bogey, force down at nearest large airport, notify local LEA for arrest on grounds of violating no-fly-zone regulations. Three shots with tracer – then you have authorization, shoot-to-kill. Confirm."

"Rodge that," the two other fighter-pilots, said in chorus.

A second later, afterburners roared and blazed through the continental American night, as two F-32Es executed a hard bank and streaked westward.

Intercepted

In her few lapses of concentration (which were quickly corrected by mental cautionary-notes, apparently sent by her alien mentor, out in front and below), Melissa Claremont found herself alternately astonished and terrified by the reality of what she was, in fact doing : specifically, "propelling herself, by means of some unseen force that she still scarcely understood, through the freezing-cold, pitch-dark, clouded skies, thousands of feet above Middle America".

The Claremont girl's new-found, magic "bubble" was now strong enough to keep her relatively warm, to prevent her from hypoxia and to deflect the hurricane-force, on-rushing air-stream; but the experience was – as Karéin-Mayréij had nonchalantly mentioned, just before take-off – "not exactly like flying in an air-o-plane First Class lounge-seat".

Billings had wise-cracked about "when did *you* ever fly on a plane, dear?", to which his distaff alien companion had smartly replied, "does an 'Airborne Command Post', with a smashed death-ray-gun in its front and much re-modeling now needed to its interior, count, my beloved prince?"

Once or twice Melissa had faltered, as the human side of her psyche imposed an inchoate, primal fear, not just of falling, but also of the utter impossibility of what she was doing; yet – somehow – a split-second later, some *other*, as-yet-unfamiliar ability automatically took over, and the exercise seemed as straight-forward as doing a lazy front crawl through a swimming-pool.

How ah doin', Angel Lady? she sent, to the narrow gap in the weirding dark-cloak that otherwise enshrouded the entire *Mailànkh Express*.

Excellently well, newly-mighty, noble Vìrya *Melissa!* came back the encouraging answer.

How does your Fire *burn inside, young princess? Do you yet tire?*

Nah... ah'm fine, modestly responded the teenager.

Prolly good for 'nother hour or so... then ah'm gonna want somethin' large to eat, if y'all don' mind too much.

Oh... I am sure that can be arranged, reassured Karéin-Mayréij.

I am in hiding-mode, so my senses are constrained; but when we land, then I will go looking for one of those 'Dar-ee Queen' places... Bob says that they have many nice sweet-things there.

Are you partial to these?

Why, yeah, eagerly sent back Melissa.

But back in De-troit, we couldn't get none, 'cause they was all in the suburbs, an' –

Abruptly – upon being washed over by the wake of something big and *fast*, crossing just behind her – she stopped the mental chit-chat and broke formation, reflexively propelling herself upward at break-neck speed.

A couple of words from Karéin-Mayréij's last message got through :

Melissa! What is –

The flying-teenager – following instructions previously-communicated by her alien mentor – pushed her extra-senses to the limit, while slowly rotating in complete circle, first left-to-right and then (though still hurtling upward), head-over-heels, eventually returning to being perpendicular to the surface of the Earth far below.

What that... oh mah Lawd! she exclaimed to herself.

Them Air Force jet-planes – two of 'em, one goin' west, one goin' east –

Let's get 'bove 'em...

So Melissa darted up and to the north-west, in so doing, losing any obvious trace of where the Storied Watcher was guiding the *Mailànkh Express*.

Wonder if they can see me...

The answer came quickly, with a spray of orange-colored cannon-tracer-rounds from a third fighter-plane. One or two of the shells clipped and deflected off her bubble at an oblique angle, and the resulting impact-energy sent Melissa careening, almost out of control.

Shit!

One of 'em done sneak up on me – and that shot was ten times what Curtis 'n me felt from them drones up on th' island....

Got to fly!

Though pleased at the increased speed that she had somehow been able to call upon, there was no time for the teenager to self-congratulate; she had to dodge another two rapid-fire bursts of cannon-shells from a pursuing fighter-plane, whose stealth-masked outline Melissa could still only barely see with her "Mars eyes", in hastily-taken glances during evasive maneuvers.

Again implementing tactics that Karéin-Mayréij had taught, the Claremont girl started to fly a cork-screw path upward, away from the former course of the air-ship, with each successive rotation being slightly wider than the previous one.

The counsel had been wisely-given, for – along with the spotty cloud-cover present all over the battle-area – it not only threw off the fighter-plane that had first assailed her, but also exceeded the turning-capability of the two short-range air-to-air missiles that one of the other aircraft had just launched against her.

They tryin' to kill *me!* realized a frightened Melissa.

What I done to them, *anyways?*

Oh yeah... jus' bein' who I is... forgot that.

Bein' a black girl, or bein' a half-alien black girl... take yo' pick.

Outta here!

Ever-higher, and ever-further to the north-west, flew the teenager, until she seemed to be out of the danger-zone; no fighter-planes, nor cannon-shells, nor missiles, followed her above the clouds.

As near as she could tell, she had probably gone four or five miles away from the original point of intercept, before the sound and fury of the engagement had abated enough to justify slowing down and doing another slow, senses-maximal review of the surrounding airspace.

Coming to almost a dead stop – and hovering in place – Melissa scanned the area. At first, surveillance was made next to impossible because of the clouds, but a few judicious course-corrections brought her below the bottom of the cloud-deck, and from here, she had an uninterrupted view for many miles.

Fear borne of isolation momentarily overcame her, but left as quickly as it appeared – only to be over-ridden by even worse apprehension, when Melissa realized what was going on, several miles away.

Her special-sight could just – barely – detect the receding narrow-beam heat-signature of the *Mailànkh Express*, which had three fighter-planes about a mile behind, and closing the distance rapidly.

Why ain't Karéin turnin' 'round an' knockin' them dudes out of the sky? mused the teenager.

She could easily *do that... maybe she jus' don' see 'em?*

But her Mars eyes is way *better than mine... what goin' down here?*

They gettin' away... ah better catch up.

Making sure that her force-field was boosted as much as she could muster while retaining enough *Fire* to propel herself, Melissa set out on a collision-course with the battle-area, which was receding rapidly to the north.

As she started to close the distance (the effort in doing so was considerable; both the *Express* and its pursuers were flying at high speed), it became immediately apparent why there did not appear to be any counter-measures from either Karéin-Mayréij or the ship that she was dragging through the skies : there were two fighters about thirty degrees off the port side of the *Express*' center axis, with the other one a bit closer-in, on the starboard.

Must be like lookin' through a straw for her, Melissa realized.

They so far off-center, she can't see nothin'.

But then... how the hell they trackin' her?

She was still pondering this issue, when – to her immediate consternation – she saw a fusillade of tiny, spark-like motes of orange-colored light, issue from two of the fighters, directly at the stern of the cloaked air-ship.

They shootin' at her!

Can't hurt Miz Atomic Angel none, ah reckon... but if they hit th' ship –

Melissa poured her supernatural powers into her propulsive and protective abilities, streaking through the Midwestern skies faster than she had ever done; the fact of this was made evident by a split-second of violent turbulence, a loud crashing-sound, and then a significant decline in the noise-level outside her bubble.

She was rapidly closing on the *Mailànkh Express* – which now seemed to be slowing and losing altitude – when she observed the stern-most fighter-plane loose two air-to-air missiles at the air-ship.

That one gonna go right up they ass –

Instinctively, she dove, aiming at a point between the leading fighter, and the stern of the *Express*, while frantically calling forth a lethal trigger-thought, earlier committed to memory, yet locked away in the back of her consciousness.

Melissa's intercept-course crossed the path of the fighter-planes, and that of the receding missiles, only for a brief split-second; but that was time enough.

Boom!

Out Of Gas... Out Of Luck

"How's the fuel-situation looking?" asked Jacobson, not turning his head to address anyone in particular.

His attention was mostly devoted to the heads-up display in front, as they cruised perilously close to the tree-tops, following the terrain over the Appalachian mountains and through the corresponding valleys, while trying to evade the seemingly-omnipresent Air Force fighters and attack-drones.

Despite the possibility of being tracked by it, the V-37's radar-altimeter had to be left on, or the chances of crashing into a side of a mountain in the darkness would have been huge – even with enhanced, 'Mars senses' assisting the pilot.

All in all, Jacobson frankly couldn't believe that their pirate air-transport hadn't yet been blown from the skies. The brief episodes of sleep that he had been able to steal here and there – a psychological need, not a physical one – had been dominated by nightmares of just this.

"Not so good, Commander," advised the Russian, who was sitting in the co-pilot's seat, on his shift, having relieved White of the duty, some ten minutes earlier.

The turn-coat SVR spy had proved an excellent pilot, despite his lack of previous familiarity with the controls of this American V/STOL transport.

"*How*, 'not so good', Misha?" pressed the former Mars mission commander.

"Given that the left rear fuel-tank was perforated on the inbound trip, and that it continues to leak at the current rate," explained the Russian, "We might just be able to land in the small town – what was its name again – ahh, yes, 'Fayetteville', *that* is it – where we were supposed to meet Major Boyd. Unfortunately, it is more likely that we will be fuel-critical shortly before that, and we *certainly* would not have enough to become airborne again, at our current weight. This assumes no more abrupt maneuvers and a steady cruise."

"Devon," called Jacobson, "You come up with anywhere that we could put down and refuel?"

"*Lots* of places," replied the African-American ex-astronaut, "But 'member that radio-chatter we picked up, down over Arkansas? They got everything locked up tight under this 'martial law' thing... down to even some grass airstrips for them flyin'-clubs. There's five or six local airports ahead of us in the next fifty miles or so, but we'd be takin' a chance of runnin' into LEA or the National Guard, the minute we land. Didn't make too many friends with that fun time we did in Fort Knox, I guess."

The commander was about to say something ungentlemanly, but at that moment, the more-than-human passengers aboard the transport-plane briefly perceived Tanaka's not-quite-completely-suppressed war-song, and then heard the pre-arranged four rapid fist-strikes against the outside of the Kingfisher II's side entrance-hatch.

Despite the prominently-displayed, stencil-writing warnings on its inside surface to the effect of 'leave locked while in flight', the altitude was low enough to make breaking such rules, safe to do; so the door was quickly opened, in came the bright-eyed Tanaka and the hatch was closed behind her, with little effect on inside air-pressure.

"Devon... you ready to go on top-watch?" she requested.

"Yeah," he confirmed, with a shrug. "Would've been scared shitless 'bout doin' all this a week ago... just *amazin'* how flyin' 'round a tornado or two, changes a man's frame of mind. That... and learnin' how to lock on to this crate so I can shag behind her. I've been practicin' lettin' go and seein' how long I can stay in formation, with that nice jet of frost under my feet... but two or three seconds and I gotta lock on again, or I'd be down in moonshine country *real* fast. Oh well... took me awhile to figure out roller-skatin', too."

Tanaka sent him a wryly-appreciative smile.

White's eyes began to blaze with a blue-white shine, as he opened the entrance-hatch once more, energized his alien-powers (with muted, accompanying war-music), then darted outside and topside, despite the onrushing exterior air-stream.

"Just don't mention it to Saquina... okay?" was what they heard, before, again, the door was closed.

"So how many you bag this time... leave any for me, Cherie?" mordantly joked the bounty-hunter, as one of his dogs (the male one) reinforced the comment with a low, spark-inflected bark.

"None – and that's the *weird* thing," replied the superhuman ex-professor. "I checked in a spherical radius of at least three kilometers in every direction, centered on this aircraft. There are *dozens* to *scores* of them out there, all over the place, and even more drones. I have to assume that at least *some* of them must have detected me – but none of them fired, or even broke formation."

"Well then – that's a *good* thing... ain't it?" offered Donny, who was – along with his girlfriend-of-convenience, 'Sammie', and his aunt and uncle, plus the recently-acquired Texas farm family – sitting on a bench-seat on the starboard side of the V-37.

The still-somnolent Jacobson family was arrayed to port, securely strapped into place in semi-reclining positions.

"I'm not sure it is," answered Tanaka. "It's like they're *escorting* us, or something. Why aren't they attacking, when they easily could do that?"

"Well," phlegmatically remarked the trucker, "*Not* gettin' shot at by the government, beats the alternative, in *my* book."

"You can say *that* again, pardner," ruefully added Wolf.

"'Least you can give 'em back better than they're givin' you, Mr. Barbecue," enviously commented Donny.

"I s'pose that's right," laconically agreed the bounty-hunter, "But you know... when I lit it up – that Mars *Fire*-shit, I mean – when I turned it all the way up, back there over Texas, I felt like some kind of fuckin' *god*... I mean, I was shootin' hundred-million-dollar fighters out of the sky like you'd do skeet-shootin' at a rifle-range – but I *still* nearly got my ass handed back to me. Ever take a grenade – or maybe buckshot from a shotgun – at, say, fifteen yards'-range? I had *that* much iron shot through me – no idea at all, how it didn't end up in my skull as opposed to my chest – but somehow, my flamin' friend and me, we melted it out... and I'm here to tell you."

"It *is* truly amazing," observed a plainly-jealous Misha. "Your powers have evolved into something quite awesome."

"Yeah – and thanks, *amigo* – but," admitted Wolf, "Point is... sittin' here as a human – or as someone who *thinks* he's still sort of human – flyin' around out there and takin' on the whole fuckin' *Air Force*... just seems completely *insane*. It's like when I turn it on... it's another 'me' who's in charge, is the best I can describe it. If that makes any sense at all."

After a brief, reflective interlude, Jacobson asked the Russian, "Location-check?"

"Coming up on... just a moment... the city called 'Bowling Green' – that is in, uhh, the state called 'Kentucky'... right?" Misha responded, after a quick look at the moving-map display.

"Yeah... can we put down there and refuel?" queried Jacobson.

"'Put down'... oh, yes... you mean 'to land'," said the Russian. "Well, there are three local airfields around there showing up on the map... but the RWR is detecting military radar-emissions from all of them, especially from the main one that is actually in the southern part of that city. We would likely have a 'warm reception', were we to try to land there, I am afraid."

"So that's a 'no-go', I suppose," grumbled the former Mars mission commander. "I guess we push on. What's our next option, to the east?"

"There is a paved airstrip of reasonable size to the south of the small city of London, Kentucky," stated Misha, "And as near as I can tell from the rudimentary countermeasures-equipment on this aircraft, it does not *appear* to be guarded – of course we will not know for sure until we actually land –"

"Then that's where we go," determined Jacobson.

"If we lose mobility, we will be – how do you say in English – oh yes... a 'sitting duck'," protested the Russian. "These fighter-planes that encircle us – what do you suppose that they will do? Or have you forgotten the video-feeds about what happened back at the Repository?"

"*I'll* deal with them," savagely vowed Tanaka, with a grim shine in her eyes.

Now Donny – who had been passively listening to the conversation – spoke up.

"I'm sure you *will*, Miss Thunder-Thighs," he started, while Wolf grinned maliciously.

"It's 'Thunder-*Child*'," corrected Tanaka, with a bemused look on her face.

"Yeah... whatever," grunted the trucker, "Anyways, like I said... I got no doubt that the Air Force'll have a bad day, if you fly off at 'em with blood in your eye – all the more so, if you take Mr. Gas BBQ out with you. But look back there, lady – we got a plane-full of *civilians*... uhh, *humans*, with us; and the slightest thing goes wrong – like them Air Force boys get a lucky shot in – and this rig's gonna end up in a million pieces all over the Great State of Kentucky. Judgin' from what went down back at that restaurant, I'll likely survive that... *they*, won't – and we got no *right* to put them to such a risk."

"I guess you're entitled to your opinion," politely responded the former Mars science officer.

"Bet I got a few others to back me up on that," he offered.

"Hear... *hear!*" instantly came the supporting calls from the Texas farm family, joined by Wade's aunt.

"Look, Donny," interjected Jacobson, "My family's in the back of the plane there with you – they're the most precious thing in the world to me and the last thing in the *world* that I want to do is to put their lives in danger... but we're running out of fuel. What would you have us *do*?"

The trucker looked down, shuffled his feet and admitted, "I don't know, Mr. Space Man... I don't *know*. I'm just a worker-bee... not management, if you know what I mean. All I *do* know is that puttin' down there with a big bulls-eye on our backs, and half the Air Force pointin' missiles at us, seems like a damn reckless thing to do. Only slightly *less* reckless than gettin' my aunt 'n uncle, and my Texas friends there, involved in all this, in the first place."

"We had little choice in the matter," countered the former Mars mission commander. "And we don't have the time to recriminate : London Airport is coming up fast. Either we put down and try to refuel as quickly as possible – get airborne again, immediately after that – or we continue on as far as we can, stop off briefly at Fayetteville and then crash-land somewhere in eastern Kentucky or West Virginia. Those are the facts, ladies and gentlemen... whether or not we want to face them."

A few seconds of strained silence ensued, and then, eventually, Tanaka offered, "Misha... you're capable of flying the plane by yourself... you could land her at the London Municipal Airport – isn't that right?"

With reluctance obvious in his tone, the Russian replied, "Allowing for the fact that I am much more familiar with avionics instrumentation that is denominated in metric, with labeling in Cyrillic... yes. I have been observing the take-off and landing-procedures, and they are not too different from what I learned how to do back home. But do not count on me, if something, ahh, 'unexpected', befalls us."

"Well, about shit that we've 'expected' on this damn trip – name *one*," snorted the trucker.

"Ya *tell* 'em, Donny!" echoed Sammie, from the back of the cargo-compartment.

"I've been to Mars and back, and it's been one nice little alien goddess surprise after another, all along the way," countered Tanaka. "But what I mean is... Sam, if Misha flies the plane, and you, me, Devon and Wolf do top-cover – I bet we could set up an effective layered defense. Wolf and I each take a hemisphere – say, me in the front, him in the rear – and anything that comes at us on an intercept or attack course, we shoot out of the sky, at the maximum range possible. Devon's the second layer; he catches anything that gets by us. You're the last-ditch defense – if a missile or some cannon-shells evade Devon, you, uhh, whack 'em –"

"You want me to detonate an AIM-145 AAM, within arms'-reach... do I have that right?" incredulously remarked Jacobson. "I can use my telekinesis to stay in tow with the airplane, and I'm pretty confident in my force-field... but maybe not *that* confident. The warheads on those missiles are meant to shoot down stealth-bombers, I'd remind you. If one of them goes off within a couple hundred feet of this aircraft –"

Several of the humans in the rear of the plane blanched and cast apprehensive stares back and forth.

"Believe me," interrupted Wolf, "Bein' anywhere *near* one of them fuckers when they blow, is something you gotta be *insane* to do, whether you're Mars or plain old *Homo Sap... Sap... Saphead...* or *whatever* the fuck it is. He ain't kiddin' about it – like I said, I got no *idea* how I lived through that shit. *And*, I mostly set 'em off, like, a mile away from me. *Mostly.* One that got closer... well, that's how I ended up in that cornfield back there... remember?"

"Yeah... you *were* in pretty bad shape – I'll concede you *that*," acknowledged the former Mars mission science officer. "But, Sam, if the rest of us do our jobs properly, they should never get close to the V-37... furthermore, we'll only have to do this until Misha can get us landed, fueled and back on course to Fayetteville. If the Air Force is foolish enough to attack us, they'll lose so many planes in the first five minutes that the rest of them will *have* to break off the engagement."

"However," observed Misha, "There are many other possible outcomes – for example, Professor... what if one of the fighter-planes or drones, gets a, uhh, 'lucky shot' against either yourself or Wolf, not only disabling you – or worse – but also leaving us without a mobile defense in either the front or rear hemispheres?"

"Chance I'm willing to take, because I don't think we have another viable alternative," smoothly argued Tanaka. "Unless you count 'crashing in the Appalachian woods', as a 'viable' option. I just wish we had Brent to help us."

"Heard from him?" idly asked the bounty-hunter. "Bad enough us bein' all hunted by the *Federales*... I'd sure hate to do it as a single man – or whatever the fuck we *are*, these days."

"Nope," mumbled Jacobson. "Not that he has an easy way to communicate with us, of course. But if I know Major Boyd, he'll be okay... he's an expert in military tactics, to name only one thing."

"Excuse me, Commander," interjected the Russian, "But I have this 'London' airport in sight, on the display. We need to start our descent –"

"Take over the controls, Misha," responded Jacobson, as he left the pilot's-seat. He motioned to the trucker as the Russian put on a pair of bulky headphones and started adjusting some console-switches and dials, while maintaining a tight grip on the aircraft steering-control.

"Donny – can you sit yourself down here, please?" requested the former Mars mission commander.

The trucker moved forward through the aircraft at a smart pace, although while striding toward the bow he offered, "You guys *know* that drivin' a rig is a bit different from flyin' a plane... don't you?"

"*Could* be worse," said Tanaka with a wry smile. "Wolf, Sam – come on – let's all line up by the door, so we can get deployed outside as quickly as possible."

"How you figure *that*?" grumbled Wade in Tanaka's direction, as the trucker fumbled around for the pilot's-headphones. "What's worse than bein' asked to fly a plane that you ain't never even *seen* before, with no trainin' whatsoever... while the whole Air Force's gunnin' for you?"

"We *could* have asked you to fly a *spaceship*," quipped the glowing-eyed science officer.

"Starting our descent," announced Misha, as the V-37 began a gentle slope downward. Ladies and gentlemen... now is the time to assume your defensive positions."

Tanaka nodded affirmatively; aided by a subtle head-shrug-gesture, her telekinetic powers disengaged the door-locking mechanism, while her living, weirding armor-suit appeared to encase her torso and two other war-songs began to hum in the background.

In another couple of seconds, the egress-hatch opened. Jacobson's big, muscular, diamond-enshrouded arms grabbed the inside top of the portal and he flung himself outward and upward into the jet-stream, landing on the top of the aircraft with a resounding reverberation; he was followed in turn by Tanaka and then Wolf, whose rocket-backwash almost set the back of both pilot's-seats on fire, along with singeing the back of Donny's hair.

"I *hate* this fuckin' job," muttered the trucker, to the Russian. "Mind tellin' me where's the gas-pedal and the brake on this thing?"

Pit-Stop, With Incoming

The Corbin-Magee Field Municipal Airport – its main landing-strip being clearly-illuminated despite the erstwhile blackout – was in plain sight as the V-37 descended on a steep angle, aided by its STOL thrust-vectoring engines.

At first, Tanaka, White, Wolf and Jacobson breathed a collective sigh of relief, as the menacing fighter-escort that had pursued them for hundreds of miles, roared off in a straight line to the east. In fact, the stolen transport-aircraft, having ignored repeated demands to self-identify from the local control-tower, had actually landed and had taxied about halfway to the airport's darkened, apparently-closed maintenance-hangars, when the more-than-a-woman's countenance turned to one of alarm.

"Something's *wrong*, Sam!" she shouted, while hovering about a hundred feet overhead."

"What *is* it?" called back the diamond-enshrouded man, his feet planted firmly on the V-37's dorsal fuselage. "They didn't engage us on the way down..."

"*Vìrya Sài'ymë* says that they're coming back around," warned the former Mars science officer. "We must have temporarily dropped off their radar when we started to descend –"

Jacobson was about to say something else, but a second or so later, Tanaka let out an even more impassioned advisory.

"*Incoming!*" she cried, followed by, "*Vìrya Sài'ymë* – **full power!**"

With her exciting war-song echoing everywhere, she streaked upward, followed a half-second later by a different war-song and a pillar of flame that must have been the bounty-hunter.

"Devon – cover our top-flank!" ordered Jacobson.

"Roger that!" agreed White, who – to his former commander's admiration – had a jet of ice-particles under his feet; the more-than-human's body was encircled by a shimmering, blue-white bubble of ice-crystals, as he took a station at approximately the same point that Tanaka had maintained just before.

"I'll cool out the air above us," he added. "Might fuck up their IR, don't you know."

Instantly, Jacobson – even through his protective diamond-shroud – felt a chill, as White's elemental power did its work overhead.

The former Mars mission commander, invoking his personal *Fire* to boost his protective force-field as much as possible, caught a limit-of-vision glimpse of something breaking through the fence surrounding a large parking-lot, way off to the south-east. It looked like a wheeled army-vehicle of some sort, possibly an armored personnel carrier.

A quick scan of the surroundings revealed that the APC wasn't alone; a column of similar vehicles was approaching northward on a road to the right of the parking-lot, with another group approaching on the left.

Shit, he inwardly cursed, *classic flanking-maneuver.*

They're going to surround the terminal and the hangars – and even if Cherie and Wolf knock down everything launched by the fighters, we can't refuel while being shot at...

Bright flashes – accompanied by percussive thunder-sounds – from far above, provided grim confirmation of the gravity of the situation.

The inner aircraft-marshaling-strip, leading to the airfield's main hangar-building, was in plain view. Whoever was running this installation either hadn't heard of the blackout, or was imperfectly implementing it, because the maintenance-hangar's cavernous interior was still dimly-lit, with one fully-illuminated duty-station – staffed by a couple of workmen – visible near the back of the building.

Jacobson pulled back an access-panel, pressed an enabling-button and spoke into a built-in exterior-microphone.

"Misha – Donny – come in!" he demanded.

"Yes, Commander?" crackled the Russian's reply.

"We got *trouble!*" cautioned Jacobson. "Fighters must've gotten permission to fire – and there's an Army-group approaching from the south-east, on the ground."

Jacobson had expected to hear cries of fear from inside the V-37, but then he realized that the conversation was only audible on the pilot's and co-pilot's headphones.

"Understood," came Misha's voice. "How many in the ground-contingent?"

An explosion went off overhead, at lower altitude than the previous ones; and though this did no real damage, it shook the taxiing aircraft, causing the panic that the former Mars mission commander had anticipated, as well as sending the two aircraft-technicians in the hangar running forward to see what was going on. He could hear Donny shouting for calm.

"Hard to tell," advised Jacobson, "But at least a couple of platoons... maybe a full company. Light wheeled AFVs – I don't see any tanks. They're trying to flank the hangar and the terminal-building."

"Should we turn back and try to become airborne again?" asked the Russian.

"And go *where?*" peevishly argued the diamond-encrusted-ex-astronaut. "You *know* our options – or more precisely, our complete *lack* of them. Keep driving toward the fueling-station... stop when we're a safe distance away, so a stray round won't set off the gas and catch us in the explosion. I'll try to deal with our Army-friends. I'll try to hold 'em behind the back of the hangar and hope they don't try to shoot right through it."

"Acknowledged," said Misha.

No longer marveling at how easily he was able to do it, Jacobson crouched down slightly, tensed the muscles in his legs, and released. He sailed through the air like a crystal missile launched by some unseen catapult, towards the roof of the hangar.

Now on top of, and close to the edge of, the hangar-building, Jacobson was aware of furious mayhem happening above and behind him, even though he tried to keep his attention focused on the ground-based threats unfolding before him.

As near as he could tell, the bounty-hunter and Tanaka had engaged the fighter-escort, and judging from the receding sound of the many explosions now ongoing, it seemed like they were trying to lead the air-battle away from the airstrip.

Better hope that Devon can stop any that leak through, he nervously mused, *because with Wolf and Cherie heading off to the north... we got no other top-cover around here...*

Though night had fallen long ago, and despite the recently-announced curfew, the prospective battlefield was more than well-enough lit to make it plainly visible to human senses, never mind Jacobson's enhanced ones. Floodlights marked the periphery of the hangar at roughly thirty-foot intervals, and there were also bright lights and corner-reflectors on the roof where he was standing, undoubtedly to mark it to aircraft on their landing-approaches.

Hate giving away the element of surprise... but I owe it to these guys to warn them what they're in for...

He could easily have just hopped over by a few yards and physically grabbed the thing, but instead, Jacobson stared at the closest roof-light, focused his telekinesis on it, and yanked it skyward, its power-cable trailing behind. In a half-second, his hulking, translucent, diamond-encrusted figure – with eyes glowing ominously behind the multi-faceted force-field – was brightly illuminated from the fixture's light-beam.

Nothing like Brent could fire up, mused the former Mars mission commander... but you'll have to do.

Jacobson could see that there were at least five APCs in the flanking-columns and probably ten more, with one that looked like a command-vehicle, in the center-column.

He waved his arms frantically, but there seemed to be no reaction from the Army component, which continued to slowly advance on all headings.

"Hey, you! Hey, *you!*" he tried to call. But the vehicles were still several football-field-lengths away, and evidently his voice wasn't carrying.

Hmm... I could just leap down there, it's only a hundred feet or so, down... holy crap, Sam... have you listened to yourself, lately?

A hundred feet, just like hopping over a crack in the pavement... how far we've come...

Let's try pushing the envelope – how did she say to do it, again? Like she did, right after smashing through the ceiling, up on Amchitka... oh yeah – "think of a hurricane in your upper-body, and then let it out" –

He took a deep breath in, tried to force the *Fire* into his lungs, opened a modest-sized hole in the part of his force-field protecting his mouth and then, while exhaling all at once, he bellowed,

"You in the Army! Stop!"

Jacobson was amazed by the roaring, bull-horn-like volume-level that his voice had gained; it seemed to wash over everything immediately in front of him, causing two of the center-column armored personnel carriers to stop. Loading-ramps dropped from the rear-parts of both of these vehicles and out issued around twelve to sixteen well-armed soldiers, each garbed in combat-gear, pointing auto-rifles and – ominously – larger weapons which were probably anti-tank-missiles – in his direction. It was also notable that at least three of the other personnel-carriers had the now-familiar "GrayWar Legion" logo prominently displayed on their sides.

The APCs on either flank continued on course for a few more seconds, albeit at even more reduced speed. Then they, too, came to a halt, still quite a long way from actually reaching either the left or right sides of the hangar-building.

He tried the same *Amaiish*-trick again, using the alien-power to boost the volume and presence of his voice.

"This is Sam Jacobson of the Mars-Gang!" he shouted. "Our purpose here is peaceful! Hold your positions!"

Initially there was no response, although Jacobson's enhanced eyesight noticed that one man from the second APC in the center column, had raced inside the vehicle. In a few seconds, he had come back outside, with a megaphone in hand. He stood a foot or two off from the side of the APC and spoke.

"This is Major Baldwin Kramer of the Kentucky National Guard," came the metallic-sounding voice of the apparent leader. "We have orders to occupy and secure this facility – and also to place anyone violating the curfew, under arrest. Stay where you are and await the arrival of our soldiers. Do not offer any resistance and you won't be harmed. Is that understood?"

Jesus, silently inveighed the frustrated Mars mission commander, *not this*, again.

Don't these guys ever learn?

By now, he had figured out how to boost the timbre and volume of his voice in consistent fashion, and Jacobson loudly replied,

"I say again, 'the purpose of my group here is peaceful' – just give us ten to fifteen minutes, refrain from hostile moves against us, and *you* won't get hurt – is *that* understood, Major Kramer?"

"I have a full reinforced infantry company at my disposal," argued the National Guard leader.

"Is that right?" countered Jacobson. "Well, I've got five or six super-humans – not least of whom is 'yours truly' – at *my* disposal, Major; and any *one* of us can utterly vanquish your company, like we did to those stupid enough to attack us at Fort Knox and thereafter. I'll say the same thing that I did there – for God's sake, man, don't do something *stupid*; just wait it out for a few minutes and let us be on our way. We don't want to hurt anybody under your command, but we *will* defend ourselves, with lethal force, if necessary. Got it?"

Even at this distance, the former Mars mission commander could hear the sounds of dissent and confusion, breaking out within the Guard-company. While the leader of the contingent was preoccupied by calling his HQ for further instructions (Jacobson noted, with grim satisfaction, that while the soldiers had been told to "secure the airport", the higher-ups hadn't bothered to explain what to do, if the "enemy" actually showed up), there seemed to be two or three hot-heads who were eager for a fight; these were being strenuously argued against by most of the other troops, who – having seen the reports of what had happened at Fort Knox, and elsewhere – were anything *but* enthusiastic about being used as cannon-fodder.

Good, he reflected. *Keep 'em talking... every wasted minute works in our favor. I hope Misha's got the gas flowing into our tanks...*

So Jacobson just stood there, mutely observing the confusion in the ranks of the National Guardsmen, counting off the seconds against his mental estimates of how long the refueling-process would likely take.

At least thirty seconds, then forty, then fifty, passed; but at shortly less than a full minute, the interlude was abruptly cut short by an alarmingly-close set of explosions overhead.

He caught a glimpse of a fighter-plane approaching at low-level from the south. It started firing its auto-cannons so as to strafe the tarmac, a tactic that was – thank God – negated by White's quickly-raised ice-screen; but the aircraft – pursued by Wolf and shot down by him a couple of seconds later, crashing in a thunderous fireball in the nearby fields – survived long enough to loose a stick of high-explosive bombs. These had been aimed at the V-37, but the unfortunate pilot overshot his target, and the projectiles (a couple of which were deflected, somehow without exploding outright, by striking the ice-screen at an oblique angle), were now heading straight for the top of the hangar and for Jacobson himself.

Shit! he cursed, *I can withstand cannon-shells... but a whole stick of half-ton HE bombs?*

No way!

His battle-instincts reflexively taking over, the former Mars mission commander launched himself high into the air, on a course that would take him right over the entire Guard-column.

Halfway through the leap, he looked behind and below him. It was an ugly scene. One bomb had clipped the top edge of the hangar, approximately where he had been standing a second or two ago, and had exploded a few feet away from the building, causing severe damage to the hangar, caving in part of its roof and its south-facing wall.

But far worse had been inflicted on the hapless soldiers in the Guard-columns; at least two bombs had missed the hangar entirely, but had hit the pavement just in front of the APCs.

A huge shock-wave struck the lower parts of Jacobson's force-field, propelling him even further away from the hangar than he had planned to go, and as he applied telekinesis to slow and control his descent, he looked back on a scene of carnage.

Three of the leading APCs had been severely damaged by the bomb-impacts; the vehicles had been flipped on their sides and were burning brightly, with the sounds of ammunition-rounds cooking-off adding to the chaos. At least twelve soldiers lay dead or dying, with twice or more that number having suffered crippling wounds.

Without really considering what he was getting himself into, Jacobson initiated a smaller, lower-arc leap. He landed next to what was left of the former leading APC, which was now little more than a piece of burning, smoking metal-junk.

Cries of *"medic!"*, intermixed with whimpers of fear and moans of pain, accosted his ears.

"Listen," he said, in somber tone, to a nearby Guardsman who seemed to have insignia of higher rank on his uniform, "We have people who can help with injuries, back in our plane... you got anybody trapped in the wreckage? I can help get them out –"

"Oh, *sure* you do, after you killed half our guys... you fuckin' weirdo *freak!*" angrily shouted the Guardsman. "So go ahead, do *me* too, asshole– what're you *waitin'* for?"

"No, no – that was the Air Force, trying to target *me* – they just missed!" Jacobson tried to explain. "And they might be coming back around for another pass. They've probably declared this whole airport a 'free-fire zone' –so if you don't want to get hit again... get your asses *out* of here, while you still *can!*"

As if to reinforce the point, there were more explosions overhead, intermixed with the faint, far-off sounds of both Wolf's and Tanaka's war-songs.

All the while under the sullen, suspicious stares of the Guard-soldiers and apprehensive about the very real possibility of another air-attack, Jacobson set to work retrieving the bodies of those who still seemed to be alive, using a combination of telekinesis and plain manual effort to pull these unfortunates out of wrecked personnel-carriers. He took six or seven direct hits by cooked-off rifle-bullets, but these, of course, bounced off his force-field with negligible effect.

Christ, he unhappily mused, *most of these guys are just kids, who probably signed up just for a bit of extra income, or to play soldier on week-ends.*

Maybe Donny's right... everything we touch, everywhere we go... just death, death and more death... where's the end *of it?*

In less than forty seconds, he had deposited ten bleeding, crippled soldiers – overwhelmingly young Caucasians, although there was one guy who might have been Hispanic or maybe of Italian ancestry – in front of the command-APC. Out came the leader with whom Jacobson had initially exchanged challenges.

"*Proud* of what you've done here?" spat the man.

Jacobson noticed (without particularly caring) that there were several MPs and other bodyguards, who had emerged from all directions, and who were pointing automatic rifles at him.

"Neither I, nor anyone who answers to me, did *anything* to your forces, Major," countered the former Mars mission commander. "You got bombed by the *Air Force* – and the only thing that's keeping them from doing it again, are the efforts of Professor Tanaka and others of my team, who are flying top-cover, over this area. For the record... though it wasn't our doing, I'm *horrified* at the loss of life, here; and I'm afraid there'll be a great deal more of it, unless somebody higher up stops the use of indiscriminate firepower against my group. All that's been coming of it, is massive amounts of collateral damage... as you can see."

"What you *mean* – 'flying top-cover'?" demanded the Guard-commander. "So now you've got your own air force?"

"In a way of speaking... yes," answered Jacobson. "Without giving away too much intel on the subject, let me warn you, that my group can –"

His voice was cut off by a furious argument breaking out in the soldier-ranks behind the row of bodyguards.

"We're gonna get *raped* out in the open like this – you hear more planes, man?" shouted someone.

"Fuck this! I'm *outta* here!" called another voice.

Although it would have been impossible for a normal human to have seen in the darkness, Jacobson caught a glimpse of the "GrayWar Legion" insignia on the uniforms of the men involved.

"Who's with us?" asked the first voice. "Army and Guard's led us into a *trap!* They're probably working with them 'Mars' terrorists – get our asses kicked, then blame it on us – I'm fuckin' off, right *now!*"

"Legionnaires, you *will* carry out your mission!" yelled a different voice, from yet further back. "Turn around, *immediately!* That's an *order!*"

Pandemonium broke out, along with rapid-fire gun-shots coming from the area of the argument; the Legion-commander, or those still loyal to him, seemed to be firing wildly. Evidently the mutiny had included a large number of GrayWar mercenaries, because they were running in all directions except ahead, toward the hangar.

Initially, Jacobson dodged the shots (the Guard-commander wasn't so lucky : he was hit around the right knee, and dropped, screaming in pain, to the ground), but then the former Mars mission leader heard, "*There's* the enemy – hit him with everything you've *got!*"

A fusillade of poorly-aimed auto-rifle fire came at Jacobson, with one or two rounds striking his force-field, although the barrage proved murderous to the hapless soldiers standing in the vicinity; most of them were cut down, with only a few managing to get out with superficial wounds.

He crouched down, hoping to assist the fallen Guard-commander; but in the next second, an errantly-targeted anti-tank rocket or missile hit the command-APC, blowing it to bits, and instantly killing everyone, including Kramer and his entire bodyguard, in the immediate vicinity. The blast was so powerful that – despite his hopefully-impenetrable force-field – it sent Jacobson himself tumbling, end-over-end, away from the center-column of AFVs.

The shock of the impact was merely unpleasant, but somehow he knew that it would have crippled or killed a normal human being.

Ouch, he thought, *so that's what it feels like, to get hit by what Cherie took, down at the bottom of the jail in Amchitka...*

Remind me not to do that *again!*

Another heavy-weapons projectile whizzed over his head, and – to his dismay – Jacobson saw that it had completely missed everything in the area; instead, it exploded on impact with the what was left with the hangar's southern wall, blowing a huge hole in this and causing a partial structural-collapse.

Oh my God, he realized, *if the V-37 was in the line of fire from that HEAT-charge –*

Now the gunfire was being directed at him in a sustained, co-ordinated manner, coming from every direction except from that of the hangar-building. Another anti-tank-projectile streaked in, missing the former Mars mission commander but striking an APC filled with soldiers, whose death-screams simultaneously nauseated and enraged Jacobson.

Where I come from, assholes, that's a firing-squad offense – I don't know who you are... but I'm going to make you pay *for that!* he seethed, while his pounding, adrenaline-pumping war-song began to roar.

Following a gesture that he had been taught back at the camp (but that he had been loath to use, and had tried to purge from his memory), Jacobson crossed his hands in front, poured his personal *Fire* into them, and then unleashed his power with a pushing-motion, as if he were trying to fend off a grappling-attempt.

He was both delighted and terrified with what he saw happening as a consequence of this : an invisible but thunderous shock-wave, manifesting in a broad conical area of effect, smashed into the rear of the middle row of APCs, sending these flying backwards and to the sides like they were childrens'-toys. Several soldier-figures were at the periphery of the shock-wave, and they were tossed dozens of yards up and backwards.

When they landed... they didn't get up.

Another war-song – deep-pitched yet exciting and ominous all at the same time – invaded Jacobson's psyche. It was the Russian's.

The former Mars mission commander looked all around, yet couldn't see anything; he chided himself at forgetting that one of the SVR-spy's abilities was partial invisibility.

Then Jacobson, reflexively checking for incoming airstrikes, glanced upward. To his amazement, he saw Misha "blinking" in and out... while levitating, feet-downward, through the air at an altitude of fifty feet or more. The Russian was being orbited by his two throwing-knives, which were revolving around him, one at a 45-degree inclination, the other at about 135 degrees.

A few rifle-rounds came up at him, and even though the aim of these was off by a mile, they drew a savage reaction : one of the knives – whose faint silver-and-yellowish-tint looked slightly brighter than the other's subdued green – rocketed downward at the APC that had evidently been in front of the enemy firing-position.

This sinister, alien-crafted missile hit the vehicle's upper deck at an oblique angle, throwing off a brilliant shower of sparks and lightening-charges as it ploughed right through the armor-plate, exiting on the hidden side of the APC to the sounds of screams, further gun-shots and then... silence.

The former SVR spy landed next to Jacobson and came into full view, even to mundane eyesight. The dagger that had been launched a few seconds ago flew back to the Russian's grasp; he did not seem at all fazed by the powerful electric current that Jacobson could sense flowing through the weapon.

"I came out here when I heard the sounds of battle," explained Misha. "Donny has almost finished fueling the aircraft – but we are in serious danger, every second that we stay here, Commander. Major White has already shot down one fighter-plane and three incoming missiles, but he is warning us that he cannot target more than a couple at a time, so –"

"Yeah... I know," interrupted Jacobson, who was scanning in every direction for signs of incoming gunfire, though he found none. "So when did you start – uhh – flying?"

The Russian offered, "Why... about five minutes ago; but it is more like 'floating' than 'flying', I must confess. I have trouble maintaining a constant altitude and speed... though, I *am* improving. And Commander – when did you start using that 'thunderclap' power?"

With a wry smile, the former Mars mission commander provided the inevitable reply, "About five minutes ago, of course."

Misha looked at the devastation arrayed in the direction that Jacobson had unleashed his powers against.

"A *highly* effective attack," he observed.

"As is that dagger of yours," carefully stated Jacobson. "What do you call it, again?"

"That one was *Væran Ivan*," said the Russian. "His abilities – like those of his, uhh, 'brother' – have been developing rapidly, lately."

"He can penetrate armor-plate, now?" uneasily asked Jacobson.

"Yes," confirmed Misha.

"How did you know?" pressed the former Mars mission commander. "That he could... *do* that."

"He *told* me," noted the Russian.

"Oh... *right*," said Jacobson.

The two more-than-humans stood there for a second or two, each one at odds as to what to do next.

"Well... not much more to do here anyway, I guess," remarked Jacobson. His voice was sad.

"Yes –" started Misha; but then the attention of both was immediately drawn to new sounds of mayhem – gunshots and crashing-noises – coming from inside and around the hangar.

The Russian took off immediately, heading toward what was left of the building at about the speed of a fast bicycle, while the former Mars mission commander made it through the rift in the hangar-wall in about a hop-and-a-half.

The interior of the building was a scene of chaos, although – to Jacobson's immense relief – the V-37, which had been parked just outside the hangar-doors, still seemed fully-intact, with White's frost-clad figure hovering several hundred feet above it. Two business jets that had evidently been in the hangar for repairs were now little more than burned-out hulks, and there were pieces of jagged, torn metal strewn haphazardly all over the place.

Mercifully, there wasn't any sign of human casualties, although he could somehow sense the presence of two terrified aircraft-mechanics, cowering behind an interior wall in the office-space section of the hangar, at its south-east corner.

The trucker sprinted out one of the V-37's side-entrances, racing over to Jacobson's vicinity at well more than the speed of the fastest human sprinter.

"Listen, Mr. Space Man," shouted an alarmed Donny, "Don't know if you been followin' current events – but we're gettin' *bombed* out here! Sno-Kone boy up there took a pretty big one side-wise against his screen, he's sayin' that if another hits straight-on –"

"He ain't shittin' y'all, Commander," came White's far-off voice. "Hit it with a cold-shot before it got near – think I fucked its fuse – but it still damn near broke through my ice – remember, I got no time to do that 'face-hardened' shit... all I can put up's the regular stuff. I seen Cherie and Wolf flyin' every which way up there and lettin' loose big-time – hope it's them doin' the chasin' and not the other way around – but we're a sittin' *duck* down here!"

"I know – I *know* – but are we refueled yet?" pressed Jacobson.

"Much as I could do," confirmed Donny. "Ran the nearest hook-up dry, asked them guys in the hangar, 'where's some more', they said 'you gotta taxi over to the other side of the airport', I said, 'fuck *that*'. We got a lot more gas than we did before... but probably not a full tank."

"Shit," complained the former Mars mission commander. "Well... it'll have to do, I guess. Okay – but let's try a rolling take-off, save some fuel by going STOL as opposed to VTOL."

"Affirmative, Commander," called out the floating Misha, who had appeared as if out of nowhere. He landed by the aircraft's side-entrance. "Donny, can you assist?" he requested.

"Damn straight," agreed the trucker, who dashed back to the V-37 at a better-than-Olympic-medalist pace. "Barely can fly the fuckin' thing... I was afraid he'd ask *me* to do it."

"I just hope that Wolf and Cherie notice that we are –" started Jacobson; but he was interrupted by a final comment on Donny's part, before he disappeared inside the transport-plane.

"Oh... and by the way, Mr. Space Man," advised the trucker as the V-37's engines began to power-up, "I think them folks of yours, is comin' *to*."

An Address From Your Last and Next President

The relatively short trip from the bowels of the White House to its much better-known upper-levels, had taken much longer than any of the party – especially, the former President – had first counted on.

There were two encounters with suspicious Secret Service agents, and another with even more wary Marine guards, on the way up; each of these had required its own identity-verification routine, and one had actually resulted in shots being fired.

Had it not been for quick bullet-deflections on the part of *Vìrya I'ëà'b'* as well as Kaysten's "silver tongue" being used at an opportune time, this incident might have deteriorated into an ugly exercise in bloodshed.

Happily, cooler heads prevailed, and the much larger combined group had – with some internal misgivings, and a side-trip to a closet that luckily still contained some of the President's business-suits – proceeded as far as one of the inside entrances to the Oval Office.

The former leader's family, along with Kaysten, Abruzzio, and two Secret Service agents, clustered in the President's vicinity, while Sullivan (in charge of "Rainbow"), the two *ersatz*-soldiers from the other building and most of the accumulated White House military guards, stayed back, guarding avenues of ingress.

Meanwhile, the living-shield had been dispatched to stand guard over the White House, lest it become the target of retaliation, be that in the form of smart-bombs or just an old-fashioned attack by armed assailants.

"Just like old times... right, Jerry?" gamely offered the former President from behind the Oval Office desk, as he bent forward to let his wife run a comb through his hair.

"You *got* it, sir," compliantly responded Kaysten. "Oh... except for, we couldn't find any of the real-stuff makeup back in the *en-suite*. What we got on you may not hold up – so just try not to sweat too much."

The former Chief of Staff paused for a minute or two, and then softly offered, "You know, Mr. President... wasn't long ago, that I was in here with your 'stunt-double', and with... *her*. Seems like a lifetime, though – and it was... I'm a whole new man. Except... I'm not..."

To a half-suppressed, wary stare from the ex-President, Kaysten's voice trailed off.

"Okay," Abruzzio called out to the Marine guards down the back-hall, "You guys – yeah, you – up here, *pronto*, if you don't mind... right behind the President, to the left and right, please!"

Two burly, stone-faced, assault-rifle-toting Marines, bedecked in their navy-and-white parade best, duly complied and moved to positions to either side of the ex-President, while Kaysten fiddled with the building's video-camera controls in a console on the far side of the room.

"We ready?" said the U.S. leader.

"On my count," affirmed Kaysten, "But don't forget, sir – I'm using the 'National Security Bulletin' over-ride; and although I'm sure it's going to get on the air over top of whatever's playing right now on Disney and the rest of 'em, there's no guarantee about how long you'll have before George The Turkey gets the Agency – or the Puzzle Palace – or someone else, to over-ride you. Talk as long as you want – but get the gist of it over with right up front... okay?"

"Noted," replied the President. "I've been memorizing what I'll say, on the way up here. Bit different from all those on-the-spot speeches that I had to do on the campaign... but I'll manage."

"I've got Moira monitoring the channels in the back-room," remarked Abruzzio. "She'll let us know if we get cut off. And you know that if *Vìrya I'ëà'b'* comes crashing through a window or something... it's time to hit the floor, then beat a quick march downstairs... right?"

"Understood," said the U.S. leader. "Trusting our lives to that th – I mean, *her* – well, I guess I can get used to *anything*, these days. Proceed."

Another flick of a console-switch dimmed the lights everywhere else in the room, with the exception of the ex-President, who was illuminated by klieg-lights at his desk.

Except for the lack of TV-grade makeup, he looked exactly as he had, in his first addresses to the nation, prior to incidents with comets and godlike alien-girls.

"Five... four... three... two... one..." counted Kaysten. The red "live" indicator at the back of the room, lit up.

Staring deliberately and confidently forward, the U.S. leader began to speak.

"My fellow Americans," he intoned, "Tonight, I'm addressing you from the White House, on a national-security matter of great importance to our country. I'll get to that in a minute; but first, I must address some of the questions that will be in your minds, after seeing me again in the Oval Office after my recent absence.

"Now," he stated, in the fatherly, business-executive voice that had won him so many nominations and elections, "Many of you must be wondering, 'where did he go, and why'. Well... the details are complicated, and I'll explain them in more depth at another time, but briefly – the stories that you may have heard about me 'resigning voluntarily for health reasons' are wholly untrue. In fact – and I'm sorry but there's no other way to put this – I was *forced* out by a conspiracy that included some of my closest and most trusted advisers, including even some members of the Cabinet."

"At the time," he continued, "I vigorously resisted these illegal and absolutely unconstitutional actions; but to avoid division, instability or the appearance of weakness in the government while the alien called 'The Storied Watcher' was attacking the United States, as well as to ensure the safety of my family (who were, unforgivably, also being threatened), I allowed the former Vice-President to temporarily take over from me, as President. I will repeat : this decision was made under severe duress, and it did not legitimately reflect my intentions – either then or now."

"Subsequently," he elaborated, "In a *flagrant* and criminal abuse of his authority, my family and I were placed under house-arrest by the former Vice-President – a situation from which I have only just escaped, with the help of members of your government, including many in the Armed Forces, who still respect the rule of law. I don't think I have to tell all of you out there, how much I value and respect the loyalty of these brave Americans, who have joined me in this noble venture. And I'm calling, here and now, for every one of our citizens – young and old, men and women, of all races, creeds and backgrounds – to join us as well."

The President paused, took a deep breath and explained, "Another question that most of you are probably asking yourselves is, 'why *now*'? That is... why would I take the risk of escape from what was – as I do have to admit – a comfortable existence, to return to the Oval Office and address you tonight? One reason's obvious : it's time to restore Constitutional government to America. But there's another, more pressing issue – and it's why I have had to step in now and take over, from those falsely representing themselves as the leadership of our country."

"Specifically'" he announced, "However much the current, illegal Administration has tried to cover it up, we currently have a very dangerous and quickly-worsening national security and public safety problem associated with the so-called 'Mars Gang', headed by the former astronaut Sam Jacobson. This group has been causing mayhem throughout the eastern United States, including but not limited to a violent attack on the Fort Knox Gold Repository that must have cost the lives of many of our law enforcement and Armed Forces personnel."

The U.S. leader's visage and tone of voice darkened markedly, as he gravely related, "Without revealing any classified information, I must inform you that the extent of the damage caused by this criminal gang is much more serious than the current Administration has revealed; and – even worse – it appears that the 'Mars Gang', which seems to have access to some of the supernatural powers possessed by the alien called 'The Storied Watcher', has actually been *prevailing* in battles against our Armed Forces."

"When we consider," he said, "That the 'Mars Gang' has threatened the personal safety of the current President – my illegitimate successor – as well as my own, it's obvious that this is an untenable situation. We cannot allow this group to devastate the entire country, in its obsession with revenge against individual members of the government. I am telling you now, my fellow Americans, that I intend to put a *stop* to all of this, before an already-bad situation becomes completely unmanageable."

There was a steely, composed determination on the U.S. leader's face, and Abruzzio – for all her alien-intuition-skills – couldn't tell if it was feigned.

"Now," he said, "I'm sure you're asking yourselves, 'how is he going to succeed in stopping the 'Mars Gang', where the Air Force and Army have so far not been able to do so?' There are two reasons. First, I'm acknowledging – here and now – that although none of these justify what they have done, Mr. Jacobson and his group *do* have some valid grievances against the government. I take full personal responsibility and accountability for these, even though some of the decisions involved were undertaken without my full knowledge or authorization, and though many of these actions were irresponsible and ill-considered ones ordered by my illegitimate successor."

"So," he proposed, "I'm challenging Jacobson and his group to immediately stop their program of wanton destruction and come to the White House, where they can lay their issues on the table in front of the legitimate, Constitutional leadership of our country. I'll answer for any decisions that I've made, in front of a court of law; I expect Mr. Jacobson and his crew, to do exactly the same. If he has the *slightest* loyalty to his country... now's his chance to prove it."

"The second reason why I'm willing to extend this offer of a truce and discussion," disclosed the President, "Is that Mr. Jacobson is not the *only* American citizen who has inherited some of the powers of the alien being named 'Karéin-Mayréij'. Without getting into the details, I can reveal tonight that several of these individuals are with me here in the White House; and – as true American patriots – they have pledged to defend me and the legitimate Administration, against the 'Mars Gang' or anyone else, should they decide to use violence to press their demands. Of course, I don't want a confrontation; but should one be forced on us, your government *does* have the ability to defend itself."

A nonplussed Abruzzio suppressed a gasp.

She whispered, *sotto voce,* to Kaysten, "Goddamn *liar* – what the hell's he *talking about,* Jerry? I never promised to fight Sam on his behalf – and, no offense but you'd last ten seconds against Cherie, Brent, Misha, and –"

With a bemused smirk, he replied, "Oh, *c'mon,* Sylvia... haven't you ever played poker, before? He's just trying to keep Sam guessing. Such a thing as bluff... you know?"

"*Right,*" sourly replied the former space scientist.

"And I bet you'd fight for me, if Sam went after either or both of us," he unhelpfully added.

"Never found out if microwaves can get through his force-armor, before he body-slams me into the next world," she grumbled. "Not going to find out, if the experiment might cost me my life."

"Therefore," stated the President, "I am making the following promises to each and every one of you."

"First," he declared, "I *am* the legitimate President of the United States, in full charge of the Executive Branch, and I'm calling on our citizens – especially members of the intelligence community and the Armed Forces – to give me and my Administration their full and loyal support. This means that the authority of the former Vice-President is hereby revoked; you should no longer obey orders issued by himself or by anyone invoking his leadership. Failure to do so will be considered treason against the Constitutional government of the United States and will be dealt with accordingly."

"Second," he went on, "To Mr. Jacobson and to individual members of the 'Mars Gang', the time has come to stop your rampage, come to the White House, have a fair hearing and submit yourself to lawful authority. I'll do the latter myself, and I will be accountable for any mistakes that I – or those reporting to me – may have made in the past. I give you my personal assurance that you'll not be attacked while you travel here; and the Armed Forces, the intelligence community and law enforcement should take this as a directive from the Commander-In-Chief to refrain from hostile actions against the 'Mars Gang', until I state otherwise."

"Finally," the President added, "I want to address Karéin-Mayréij personally (and I should mention, she has not surfaced lately, although we have no reason to believe that she has permanently departed from our planet). Madam, I'm also holding *you* accountable for the damage inflicted by the 'Mars Gang'; it was *you* who decided to bestow upon Jacobson and his group, the supernatural powers that they have used to bring ruin to parts of the United States. This was an *extremely* irresponsible move that hardly supports your reputation as some sort of a 'goddess'; you seem have nothing like the judgment that I'd expect of someone of your self-declared divinity. *Shame on you!* If you have a good explanation for this tragic episode... I'd love to hear it!"

The President paused and finished with, "I'll conclude by stating that we must look to each other and pull together, in this hour of crisis. The situation is serious, and it could become disastrous; but it *can* be overcome if all of us – especially Mr. Jacobson and his group – respect Constitutional authority, remember the values that made our country great and refuse to settle for anything less. I'll issue updates to all of you as circumstances dictate – but until then, my fellow Americans, God bless each and every one of you... and God bless the United States of America."

After manipulating the console-controls, Kaysten turned off the video-feed and exclaimed, "*Bravo*, sir! You really hit that one out of the *park!*"

A voice – Sullivan's – from down the hall announced, "Still on the air, as of now... we're getting those 'talking-head' guys from the news media, chattering on about 'this shocking, unexpected new development', *et cetera, et cetera.*"

"Oh... *really*, Jerry?" complained a visibly-annoyed Abruzzio. "Mr. President – with all due respect, I never volunteered to serve in your army – least of all, to fight on your behalf against Sam Jacobson and his five or six super-powered *confidants* – and on top of all *that*, you've thrown in a gratuitous personal attack against the Storied Watcher herself! Frankly, sir... what could you possibly do for an encore!"

"Ms. Abruzzio," diffidently replied the U.S. leader, "While I'm grateful of course about what you and Jerry have done for my family and I so far, everything that I said in this speech was meant to make Jacobson And Company listen to reason... before he wrecks the entire country. To do that, I've got to convince him that I have something to bargain with, even if that's – *ahem* – a bit of an exaggeration. Secondly... what do you suppose George is going to *say*, about what's actually motivating my re-asserting control over the government? I'll save you the trouble – it'll be, 'he's just a puppet of this alien-person'. I need to demonstrate that your 'Karéin' and I have some real differences of opinion... fortunately, that's *not* much of an exaggeration. You following me here?"

"Yeah – I understand what you're doing," she countered, "But this kind of dishonesty... I can't endorse it! Especially considering where it's gotten the government, so far. I'll have you *know*, sir – while I'll do my best to defend you and your family, I *won't* tell lies on your behalf – neither will I try to kill other followers of the Storied Watcher... let alone, Karéin herself. Optimistically, I'd last two *seconds* against her!"

"Even if that means that I might get killed myself?" offered the President, to the obvious distress of the former First Lady.

"We've already been *over* that," parried the ex-scientist. "I *might* have been killed, multiple times, since this entire fiasco got rolling. Like, when your Air Force, dropped a hydrogen bomb on myself, Jacobson and many of the rest of us. Being almost vaporized – and surviving only by one's own arts – *does* change one's attitude on things, you know."

"Well then... I think we understand each other... don't we?" neutrally remarked the President.

"*I'd* sure say so," sighed a frustrated Sylvia Abruzzio.

Stop The Convoy, Grab A Table

Everyone in the convoy – with the significant exception of the mountain-man, though he was still plenty-disoriented by what he had lately-seen – was amazed that not only had they not run into any more roadblocks, but, in fact, other than for a couple abandoned cop-cars, they hadn't seen *any* LEA in these parts, all the way to the outskirts of Fayetteville.

That was a *good* thing, considering the curfew and considering the dire "National Guard has the right to shoot prowlers, on sight" warnings, which, along with fragmentary reports of more "terrorist activity" to the west, had come over the radio at intermittent intervals; these abruptly interrupted the country hurtin'-song music that had been playing otherwise.

Eventually Brent Boyd – paranoid at being tracked via the equipment – had ordered the radio turned off altogether.

But the trip had proved surpassingly-unnerving for Dorsie and Laura Boyd, none the less. Her husband had insisted on having the lead-vehicle (an unmarked police-car, with the big, black former FBI-agent as driver) to go at speed, around cliff-side mountain roads, with its headlights completely off; and the ones further back in the convoy were only allowed their dew-lights, so from the perspective of the human travelers, the trip was made in near-total darkness.

Boatman, for his part, was phlegmatic about it; his wry comment was, "I can see just *fine* with these Mars eyes; and anyways... after bein' thrown out of a plane at ten thousand feet... how much worse it gonna be, goin' off a five-hundred-foot cliff?"

So thus, Boyd had led them off Route 19, into a secluded, relatively-dark spot in the north-west corner of the vast parking-lot of a Wal-Target store, with their line of sight to most of the rest of the lot blocked off by a parked tractor-trailer. The stop was not particularly voluntary; it had been forced by determined hammering and shouts from inside his family's SUV, since several of his children were demanding a rest-stop.

The convoy pulled to a gradual stop, with the APC closest to the edge of the lawn at the periphery of the parking-lot, with Laura Boyd's family-vehicle and the unmarked police-car closer to the store-entrance. The arrangement seemed to work, as no on-lookers curious at the advent of a military vehicle appearing on-scene, showed up to complicate matters.

The area – especially the several fast-food restaurants on its western-side, nearest the highway – was surprisingly busy considering the lateness of the hour, with many families coming and going in vehicles of all shapes and sizes. Evidently, either these locals or highway-goers hadn't heard of the curfew, or had decided to ignore it.

One by one, the human convoy-travelers clambered out to stretch their legs and to answer the call of nature, behind the bushes that surrounded the extent of the lot.

"Don't *you* have to go, too?" idly asked Hendricks, of Brent Boyd.

"Funny now you ask," replied the former Mars mission pilot, "But the honest truth is... I haven't taken a real dump in three days. Don't even have to piss. Feel fine, though."

"Yeah," acknowledged the third agent. "Me neither."

"Well," observed Boyd, "I seem to remember that we asked Karéin – this was while we were coming back from Mars, mind you – about the same thing, and she said this was another way in which 'your bodies will become more robust, and these natural functions will no longer beset you so much'... or something like that."

"I just hate to think of where it's going... you know?" quipped the other more-than-human. "I mean... Minnie always told me that I was full of it, but..."

"If you've been eating as little as I've been, lately," noted Boyd, "Maybe there isn't very much in the first place."

Now Boatman, accompanied by Laura Boyd and Dorsie the mountain-man, had approached the two. The woman kept one eye on her children and the dog, as they 'did their business' behind the bushes.

"What you all chattin' about?" asked the black agent.

"Oh... just some random shit," answered Hendricks, with a wink and a smirk.

"Anyway," said Boyd, "We'd better take this opportunity to figure out what happens from this point onward; I had originally wanted just to push right on to Fayetteville... but maybe it's better doing things this way."

"I was meaning on asking you all 'bout that," remarked Boatman. This 'Fayetteville' place – it's just up Route 19 over there… right?"

"Yeah… that's right," confirmed the former Mars astronaut.

"How big *is* it?" queried Boatman. "The city, I mean."

"Oh, I don't know… maybe four or five miles, end to end," answered Boyd.

"And the plan's for Mr. Jacobson and this-here airplane that you all stole off the Air Force to come land somewhere up there, and take us all off to safety… where *was* that, again?" inquired the agent.

"Well… not *exactly*," dodged the astronaut.

"Not 'exactly'… *what*?" pressed the former FBI agent.

"Not 'exactly', as, 'we never really worked out where in Fayetteville that our transport was supposed to land," sheepishly admitted Boyd. "We had to move fast, once we realized that our families were in danger, and I guess we kind of missed some of the details. I sort of figured that when I saw the V-37 circling overhead, I'd just fly up to greet her; that's still the plan, unless you've got a better one."

"Don't you think you'll – uhh – *stand out* a bit… 'specially in this deep dark night we got 'round here?" observed Boatman.

"They got to be able to *see* me, after all," explained Boyd. "And I can't just radio them – they'll be flying under emissions-control to avoid being tracked by the government… which is why I never brought a unit along with me."

"Okay – so you're shining like a thousand suns, and they let you flag 'em down," interjected Hendricks. "Then we all load on to this rig – hope it's got enough seats for us – and then we go… where?"

"Plan had been to – ahh – pay a friendly little visit to the White House," evenly responded the former Mars mission pilot.

"*Whoa!*" exclaimed Boatman. "Brent, you all can't be *serious* about that! 'Specially after Her Martian Highness whacked the top of the Monument into the South Lawn, that place will be defended like all get-out –"

"I already *told* my husband that this is a *crazy* idea," mentioned Laura Boyd. "Especially with the kids along with us. It's like driving them right into a war-zone."

"Not, 'like'," unhelpfully added Hendricks. "That's *exactly* what he's planning to do. By the way – over L.A., Otis and I had a taste of what the Air Force is willing to throw at anybody who gets on their shit-list. We only barely got out of it with our skins intact… and that was with Sylvia and Little Miss Angel running interference. I'm not keen to try *that* again, I can tell you!"

"Yeah – we *talked* about that, dear," peevishly spoke Brent Boyd, in the direction of his wife. "And you remember me pointing out, that the only alternative is to try hiding out somewhere, until they get lucky and track us down and then drop everything they've *got*, on our heads. I've been on the receiving end of it too – if it's of any interest, that's when I learned how to fly, because I'd be *dead* if I hadn't – and I'd far rather face them with Cherie,

Devon, Sam, Wolf and Misha to back me up, than trying to do it just with yours truly and you two... no offense meant, of course."

"Oh... none taken," politely responded Boatman. "I can't fly, not so much as jump for more than hop-scotch. All I can do is clap my hands."

"Don't be out in front, when he does," warily advised Hendricks.

"So where's this leave all us human-folk who's taggin' along fer th' ride, 'gainst their better judgment?" asked the mountain-man. "Yer missus's right, Mr. Space Man – treatment them Fed-ral boys gonna give us, gonna make 'Bonnie 'n Clyde' look like a Sunday-School picnic. Maybe we should just give up, an' hope fer only ten years or such."

"I don't suppose I have to remind you all that you're fingered for the murder of several law-enforcement officers?" noted Boatman. "That's a federal death-penalty offense, you know."

"*If*, they do it quick," commented Boyd. "Up in Alaska, I saw what it looks like, when they do it slow. Believe me, Dorsie... you *don't* want to know. If I were you, I'd take a nice fast missile over D.C., any day of the week, over what they're going to do to you – to all of us – once they get us in captivity."

Upon seeing the look of anguish on his wife's face, the former Mars astronaut embraced her and whispered some words of reassurance to her. The others, however, could still see the tears that had stained her cheeks.

"That isn't going to *happen* – I'll melt everything in D.C. that's more than a foot high, before I let it happen," Boatman and Hendricks heard him say.

"Well now," the black former FBI agent muttered to the other one, "Ain't *that* just nice and reassurin'?"

"*If* you don't disintegrate it all first... right?" countered Boyd.

"Yeah," ruefully acknowledged Boatman.

By now, the Boyd children, with dog in tow, had returned from the bushes.

"Daddy," pleaded the eldest one, a skinny, off-blond-haired girl about 9 to 11 years old with big eyeglasses, "You need to take us over there to Bobby's Family Restaurant. Right *now!*"

"Why's *that*, sweetheart?" inquired the mother.

"I can't 'go' out there, behind the bushes," complained the daughter. "It's yucky! And we're all hungry and thirsty. Brent Junior finished off the last snack-bar a half hour before we pulled off the highway. He had the last soda pop, too. There's nothing left to *eat*."

"Wendy," cautioned the ex-astronaut, "We talked about that in the car... remember? Bad men are looking for Daddy and Mommy – and maybe for you and your brother and sister as well. It's not safe to go anywhere that we might be recognized. Right?"

"But we're *hungry!*" protested the child. "And why can't Mr. Boatman, Mr. Hendricks and Mr. Dorsie, take us over there? Nobody's looking for *them!*"

With a gentle chuckle, the big black ex-agent remarked, "I think she's got you there, my friend. Perfect plan – 'ceptin' for the fact that Will and me, we're a little short of cash these days."

"Oh no," countered the mountain-man, "Y'all ain't gettin' me *nowhere* near someplace them Fed-rals gonna I.D. me... specially without no kinfolk there to cover fer me!"

"We're wanted for *murder*," noted Hendricks. "Showing our faces in public isn't a great idea, you know."

"Yeah, but we're s'posed to be *dead*," countered Boatman. "That should keep us off the database, least 'till they figure out what happened back there at the roadblock. I guess if we can get some spendin'-money to cover the cost of whatever the young'uns want to eat, we could chance it. As long as – mind you – it's for take-out... not eat-in."

"Brent," worriedly stated Laura Boyd, "I don't like the idea of *anyone* other than you or I, being in charge of the children. What if the police are in there, and recognize Wendy, Nicky or Brent Junior? What if they try to apprehend them? What if –"

"Ma'am," interrupted Boatman, "They're completely safe with Will 'n me around. Only risk, frankly, is to anybody who gets in our way. As – may God forgive me what I done – those Troopers found out back at the roadblock. I'm sure hopin' that we just get in there, get our food and drinks, then get back over here with no fuss and no muss. But if we run into *trouble*... we're ready for it."

"Yeah – he's right about that," reluctantly added the third agent. "I'm not afraid of anything less than a tank-company, these days; problem is, if we get into a fire-fight with the government, that – or something worse than that – is *exactly* what they'll throw at us. It's no place for civilians and a bunch of kids to be caught in the middle of. So let's do what the big guy says... not waste any time in there, and hope for the best."

"*I* trust Mr. Boatman and Mr. Hendricks, Daddy," chirped the elated pre-teen girl. "They're your friends with the *Angel*, after all."

"Yeah... well, Wendy," Boyd wearily mentioned, "I just wish the Angel was here to lend a hand... no reflection on Otis and Will, of course. Laura – you got any cash?"

"I can spare about seventy-five dollars or so," offered the wife, as she glumly fished the money out of her purse and billfold. She handed forty to Boatman and the rest to Hendricks.

"So how many we got?" asked the big black agent. "Two, and... here, honey," he added, as he scooped up Nicole Boyd in his long, muscled arms.

"Let's go, Uncle Otis!" chirped the child.

"This is going to be *fun*, man," unenthusiastically said the third agent, as they set out across the parking-lot.

"Cheeseburger, if'n y'all don't mind," called out the mountain-man.

"Make that two," requested Brent Boyd Sr., with a wry smile on his face.

The five of them – Boatman with the littlest girl cradled in his arms, and the other two tagging along either side with Hendricks – had an uneventful walk across the wide expanses of the parking-lot, and had now arrived at the entrance to Bobby's All-Time Family Restaurant.

The doors to the fast-food joint were in constant use and Boatman was only able to squeeze through one of them with all his new-found agility.

For a second or two, he panicked, upon losing sight of the two elder Boyd children; but it turned out that Hendricks had taken the girl by the hand and had put the boy on his shoulders – a maneuver that almost came a-cropper when, due to the third agent's lanky height, the kid had to bend way forward to avoid hitting the door-jam.

The place was decorated with typical cheap-plastic-and-stainless-steel modernist *kitsch*, replete with flashing holographic advertisements hawking a variety of sugary drinks and high-carbohydrate pastries.

The restaurant looked as if it hadn't been substantially cleaned in the last decade and was crowded, almost to overflowing, with people of every size, shape and description – a few of them local but many more obviously not – milling around everywhere.

All the tables were full and there was nowhere to sit, although periodically one or two did become available, only to be immediately snapped up by some lucky family.

There were line-ups of between fifteen and twenty individuals waiting to place an order at every one of the three available serving-counters.

Somehow, the smell of over-cooked French-fries and greasy hamburgers seemed more pungent than he had ever remembered it having been.

Well, thought the big black former FBI agent, *at least I can catch up on the sports-scores, courtesy of those two 3-D televisions on either side of this restaurant.*

'Cept I can't hear a word they're sayin' over all these folks tryin' to order food... hmm... but I wonder, if I just fire up these 'Mars ears' and focus 'em, like she told us how to do, up at the camp...

Yeah... that's *got it.*

Hooray – Cardinals are second in their division... only one game back.

What I wouldn't give to sit in on a tailgate-party or two... like old times...

Hmm... news on in 5 minutes, would be worth it to see what they're tellin' –

The line-up moved slowly forward.

With a wary gaze cast in the direction of the bathrooms all the while, Boatman ushered Wendy Boyd off to the women's room. It was a six- or seven-minute wait just for her to get in, but eventually the girl came back with a "mission accomplished" look on her face.

"Mr. Otis," interrupted a Boyd child's voice, "Can I have a milkshake?"

"Yeah," added the second one, "I want one too! The 'Triple-Sugar Mile-High Treat' one!"

"Now, you all listen," cautioned the big man, "Your Daddy done told me, it's 'burgers 'n fries' that's on the menu, and we haven't got hardly enough money to –"

As the children pouted and whined, Boatman pressed his sensory abilities past what could have done as a human man, yet not nearly as far as he somehow knew he could do.

Though he was still aware of the maddening din of a hundred pedantic conversations, the former FBI agent found himself able to isolate individual ones, by concentrating on these and mentally tuning out everything else. There was the usual talk about local affairs, including (apparently) an upset in a high-school baseball game and about various other miscellany such as changes in the garbage collection schedule; but also, Boatman noticed a few people discussing more serious matters.

Hmm... "Air Force engagement against as-yet-unidentified intruders, over the central United States"... that's gotta be Jacobson and Company... hope that poor man didn't get his ass short down... let's listen some more...

The black former FBI agent tried to synthesize the upshot of three similar conversations that were all going on at once, and though his efforts were only partly successful, the results produced a puzzled expression.

Now, that doesn't make any sense, pondered Boatman.

What's this about "Air Force lost two fighters, in the fight against the second unidentified aircraft"?

Didn't Brent say that Jacobson only stole one *plane, from the Army?*

Remind me to ask –

"Hey Mr. Boatman," interrupted Wendy Boyd, "It's *our* turn next –"

"Shushh!" cautioned the agent, *sotto voce.* "Remember honey, we're in public... so it's 'Mr. *Bartman*' –"

The girl had been right; the family just ahead of the two former FBI agents and their young charges squeezed awkwardly through the crowd to Boatman's right, and he was now next to be served by the sweaty-faced teenager at the burger-joint checkout-counter.

He hoped that nobody else had heard, and fumbled for his cash and change.

Boatman and Hendricks had somehow managed to order the prescribed food in the pre-stipulated amounts, flavorings and configurations, and both were proud of the fact that they had done it with at least a dollar-fifty to spare, when all was said and done.

There were even two milkshakes, although the sharing of these would no doubt be a contentious thing.

The more-than-humans' arms and hands were fully-occupied with carrying the foodstuffs, meaning that the two could no longer keep control of the Boyd children, who had been ordered to "hold on to my pants or something, and don't you all stray". The directives were obeyed for approximately ten seconds; then Hendricks – to his chagrin – realized that he had lost track of the Boyd girl.

In a panic – forcing himself to overcome the overload of sensory information that immediately assaulted his mind, upon activating the "special sight" in such crowded circumstances – the third agent quickly spotted Wendy's unique heat-signature over to his right.

She was sitting with her back to the wall at a side-table which had just been vacated by some Latino family, and had strategically deposited her hairband and glasses so as to preclude the three remaining seats (one more on the wall-bench, two more as individual chairs arranged around the eating-table) from usurpation by other passers-by.

"Wendy – *Wendy!*" he called, to no avail.

The girl was sitting there at the bench and table, studiously avoiding his glance and willfully refusing to acknowledge his entreaties.

Rapidly, while holding the remaining kids firmly in-grasp, Boatman led the group over to the table.

He confronted the girl.

"Young lady – what you think you're *doing?*" he spoke.

"I want to have my cheeseburger right here!" she answered.

"You *know* that's not possible," he argued. "Your momma and daddy said –"

"There's lots of space – I saved you all a spot, each one," persisted Wendy.

"We *can't*, honey," countered Boatman. "The more time we –"

"Please... *please*, Mr. Boat-uhh-Bartman," interrupted the girl, with tears welling in her eyes. "We've been running for a whole *day* now, and those bad men almost *killed* –"

Instantly, Hendricks sat down beside her, motioning with finger-in-front-of mouth for silence.

"Look, Otis – let's just sit down... get this over with as quick as we can," he proposed. "I don't think we need a *scene*... you know?"

The black former FBI agent spent a second-and-a-half considering his options.

He nervously scanned back and forth.

"Okay, *okay*... fine," reluctantly retreated Boatman. "Yeah, I reckon a 'scene's about the last thing that we need... *that's* for sure. But listen, young lady – if your daddy asks, 'why are you folks all so late'... I'm not coverin' for you – you *hear?*"

"That's okay," Wendy replied, her countenance immediately more cheery as she retrieved her personal belongings and put her glasses back on. "Daddy will understand. *Mommy* might not. Nicky – you sit next to me, right here."

As the little one complied and the rest of the group arranged themselves into the available seating (Boatman took an outside chair, which accommodated about three-quarters of his *derrière*), Hendricks commented, "Kid reminds me of Cherie or maybe Sylvia – real '*organizer*', you know?"

"Hey – enough with the names," cautioned Boatman. "Walls have *ears*."

The third agent shrugged phlegmatically. He said, "So... small-size burgers are for you kids... other ones we'll keep in the bag. Don't feel like eating right now. You want one, Mr. 'Bartman'?"

"What? Oh... no," responded the black former agent.

His demeanor was absent-minded, as his attention had been pre-empted by a discussion going on over a mobile communicator's holo-display, amongst a five-person Middle American Caucasian family at the next table over.

He didn't have to use his 'Mars ears'; the tables were so close that conversations were easily audible even by the *hoi polloi*.

"So what's the latest?" asked the middle-aged white guy, probably the father, at the table with the holo-display. "They gonna let us on to I-64 after all?"

"Showing 'closed off', on the map," advised a frumpy-looking woman, likely the man's wife or better half. "Might have to take the state roads. Networks are acting up again... I can't get updates from 'em. All it's saying is this stupid message about "two terrorist aircraft intercepted over the Missouri-Arkansas-Kentucky-Tennessee area, all travel to or around strictly prohibited"... it just repeats. I don't *know*, Jack. We might have to grab a room around here for the night, but I can't use the communicator to find hotels... it's not *working*."

"Well, it's gonna be hard for us all to sleep in the car," observed the father. "You get a brochure or something with local accommodations on it?"

"Picked over, sold out – whatever you want to say, there ain't any more of 'em in that stand by the door," said the woman. "We got to drive around, I guess, but I don't fancy doin' that in the dark –"

Now one of the kids – a mop-haired, slightly-overweight Caucasian girl close to Wendy Boyd in age – leaned over to address Boatman's table, to the thinly-disguised horror of the black FBI agent.

"So where are *you* staying tonight?" she interjected.

"Now, *now*, Dais," chided the mother, "We don't *know* them folks. Sorry! My daughter's just a bit 'outgoing', if you know what I –"

"Oh... no *problem*," quickly responded Hendricks.

"We're going to Washington, D.C.!" proudly chirped Brent Boyd Jr..

"I don't *think* so, son," remarked the father at the other table, with a bemused smile. "Newsman sayin' capitol's now *totally* out of bounds – roadblocks on every route in there, since all this latest 'terrorist' stuff started going down. And there's somethin' goin' on about that big plane that the President's flyin' around on... they're tryin' to cover it up, but there's rumors all over NeoNet. Didn't you *hear*?"

"What my young – uhh – 'nephew' means is," semi-stammered the third agent, "We're just heading off to a place in Fayetteville, where we're planning to stay until we get our plans for – uhh – visiting relatives in the D.C. area, all sorted out."

Damn, he mused, *too bad that Karéin only gave the 'alien-power of bullshit', to that Kaysten guy.*

And to Minnie, wherever she is – Lord keep her safe...

"You don't *say*," responded the mother. "Where, exactly? Like... a hotel? Is it very expensive? You think they'd have space for Jack, me and the kids?"

Hendricks and Boatman spoke at nearly the same moment.

The big black agent said, "Oh, well, it's actually a campground –", while the third agent offered, "It's a B and B, and last I heard, they're –"

The two stared uneasily at each other.

"You go ahead," proposed Hendricks.

"Oh, no... this one's *yours*," demurred Boatman, while the Boyd children began to break out into open laughter.

"Umm... what my friend here *means*," the third agent tried to explain, "Is that it's kind of, like, a *private* bed-and-breakfast with a place to park your RV out back; and you have to book well ahead of time. So I don't think –"

"*Figures*," interrupted the father. "You need a private reservation... right?"

"Yeah... something like that," evaded Boatman.

"I get you," said the father. "Probably they don't have any space for us – guess that's a chance we'll have to take – but is it okay if we follow you folks as you go in to this place? Least we can do is ask, and we could sleep in the car without being ticketed –"

With a pained look Hendricks replied, "I... uhh... I don't think that'd be a good idea. Sorry."

"Well, you got their phone-number?" persisted the mother. "We could just call 'em – that is *if* these communicators are working, which I wouldn't bet any money on, mind you."

The third agent and his black companion stared in bewilderment at each other.

"You got it, Will?" pleaded Boatman.

"No... 'fraid not," spoke Hendricks. "Didn't Brent say that he had dropped in there, and then right after... uhh... well, *you* know – some *explaining* to do, is what I mean –"

"I'm sure my Dad – that's 'Brent' – would give you the number, if you come back with us when we're finished dinner," offered Wendy's annoying, "too-smart-by-a-half", little voice.

"Hey – that's *my* name!" protested the boy.

"You're just 'Brent *Junior*'," taunted the Boyd girl. "Daddy's the *real* 'Brent'!"

"Is *not!*" retorted the younger "Brent".

Boatman – seeing the signs of pandemonium about to break out – stared in menacing manner at the two youngsters.

With a cautionary wag of his big finger, he warned, "Now you two *behave* yourselves! You *know* what your Daddy done told you about making a scene in here –"

"She *started* it!" pouted the boy.

"I don't care *who* started it," demanded the black former FBI agent, "I'm endin' it... right here, right now. You *understand* me, young lady... young man?"

"Oh, sorry – we thought they were *your* kids," apologized the wife at the next table, "Oh, uhh, *his*. So this 'Brent' guy's their dad? How come he isn't taking them out, himself?"

Boatman and Hendricks did another shared-frustration back-and-forth stare.

"He's, uhh, gettin' gas for his car," prevaricated the black agent. "Should be back there in the parking-lot, any minute now. And we're, well... we're these kids' 'honorary uncles', is kind of what it is. Listen, Will – you think it's time to go see if our man Brent has got that car all gassed up, yet?"

"Oh, yeah – *definitely*," nervously responded the third agent. "Finish these burgers *en route*... too crowded in here. You know I'm claustrophobic... right?"

"Then how did you survive on that 'Magic Bus', 'Uncle Will'?" pestered the Boyd girl. "I mean, Daddy told us, while we were driving here, about what went on, Ms. Sylvia told him, that it was *filled* with people, when it went flying –"

"That's *enough!*" reprimanded Boatman, with a forceful stare in the girl's direction.

His tone of voice was almost angry.

Sullenly, Wendy looked down and went into a pout.

"'Scuse me," interrupted the father at the other table, "But did the young'un there say, you had been on a bus that 'went flying'? Man – you was *lucky* there! Accident like *that*... seen too many of 'em... like there was one where a bus went off a bridge, three weeks ago, and they were all killed... *terrible* thing, no doubt about it. So I guess you two must've just had a short fall, like five feet, or –"

"Honestly, sir," faked Hendricks, "Neither Otis – that's my friend over there, nor me – we don't really like thinking about it... you know?"

"Oh, sorry!" retreated the husband, "Didn't mean to upset you –"

"Uncle Will and Uncle Otis, they fell out of an *airplane!*" blurted out Brent Junior.

"My, *my*," bemusedly remarked the wife at the other table, "You two *have* had a bad time, lately... now haven't you?"

"Young man's got quite an imagination," claimed Boatman. "As you can see."

"Oh... for *sure*," she answered. "I think you mean that your 'uncles' here went skydiving – with a parachute – right?" she asserted, in the boy's direction. "Now mind you... that's nothing that I'd ever do – afraid of heights, you know."

"No parachutes," quickly stated the Boyd boy, "They just –"

"I done *told* you – *both* of you!" interrupted a clearly upset Otis Boatman.

"Yeah... that's *it*, kids," added Hendricks, as he rose from the table while starting to collect what food-stuffs remained; much to Wendy's chagrin, he yanked a half-eaten hamburger right out of her grasp.

"That's not *fair!*" she loudly complained.

"Yeah, well, we got a plane – no, a bus – no, not one of *those*, either – to catch... or something," muttered the exasperated third agent, a stony expression on his face. "Come *on*."

Reluctantly, the elder Boyd children complied and joined the two former FBI agents (Boatman carried the youngest) as they moved towards the exit-doors.

Hendricks and his more-than-human companion noted, via some special "eyes-in-the-back-of-the-head" sixth sense, that the TV-displays in the place were showing a "Stand By For An Announcement From The White House" message; but both of them were now committed to herding the Boyd kids out of the restaurant and – despite intense curiosity – could not reverse course.

That's all *we need,* Boatman silently reflected, *Havin' Brent's kid sayin' some smart things about the White House, in front of a crowd of twenty-odd folks, lookin' right at us...*

They had made it all the way out of the building and were starting out into the parking-lot, when – to his dismay – Hendricks' Mars-senses compelled him to look behind; and his eyes were confronted with the sight of the family from the other table, following them, about fifteen paces back.

Boatman stopped and turned around.

"Can I *do* something for you folks?" he interrogated.

"Oh, well... we was finished anyways," noted the mother. "Just wanted to get that phone number from this 'Brent' fellow, if you don't mind."

"Well, no offense meant, Ma'am," parried the black former agent, "But, matter of fact, I do mind. See, thing is –"

"Look – you aren't doin' anything, well... *illegal*, or *wrong*, are you?" asked the husband. "We don't want any trouble... so if that's what you're up to, we'll just turn around and head right back. Although, you shouldn't have all these kids caught up in it..."

"I'd *hope* not," added the wife, "I used to work with Minnesota Family Services, you know, and it just drives me crazy to see kids being dragged into bad situations – I'd have no choice but to report it –"

"No... uhh... no, nothing like that," dodged a wincing Hendricks, "It's just that we're, uhh, in a big hurry... you know?"

"We'll just get that phone number and be right off," proposed the mother. "We wouldn't want to hold you up."

The two more-than-humans, cursing the immaturity of the "mind-talking" skills that the Storied Watcher had latterly tried to educate them about, tried to whisper to each other; but the restaurant-family was so close that even human ears could undoubtedly have partially overheard.

"What the fuck we do *now*, Otis?" desperately queried Hendricks. "We can't take them back there... Brent will be royally pissed off, and can't say I'd blame him."

"Yeah, and if we try to push these folk back, we might be makin' even *more* trouble for ourselves... what if they run off and 'report' us, like she's saying?" mentioned Boatman. "We got enough trouble as it is. Well... if our friend Brent Senior lays one on us, I'm just gonna tell him, 'it's your own loud-mouthed kids' fault' –"

"I *heard* that!" whined Wendy Boyd. "I didn't tell them anything – all I did was tell Brent Junior that he –"

"Tell it to your Dad, kid," demanded Hendricks. "I'm sure it's old news to him and your Mom."

He turned to address the restaurant-family.

"Okay... look, folks," declared the third agent, "So... here's what – the truth is, there's nothing 'illegal' or 'unethical' going on here, and if you really want this phone number so badly, I guess there's no harm done in us introducing you to Brent, who's the leader of our, uhh, 'private self-help group'. It's just that he's kind of suspicious of outsiders, because membership's by invitation only; we don't recruit among the public, and we kind of keep to ourselves, so if you can keep the number of questions to Brent, to a minimum... that'd be really great. That work for you?"

For a second or two, the husband-and-wife team stood transfixed, and then the man offered, "Sure does... and much obliged."

Boatman and Hendricks did a mutual double-take.

Well... maybe studying Jerry's bullshit-talking, up at the camp... maybe it did me some good, after all, ruefully mused the third agent.

Up And Over

Tommy was the first one to have noticed that something "outside", had gone wrong.

This time, he had been chatting with his adoptive mother's hot-dagger (it had apparently been whining to the Storied Watcher about privileges previously extended to its freezing-cold "war-brother", so she had let it substitute for the latter, taking a place inside the *Mailànkh Express*), holding the thing – semi-incandescent in its flame-bedecked, infernal heat – without apparent injury.

The two had been in a kind of trance for nearly an hour, mentally conversing about something-or-other, when, all of a sudden, Tommy shouted out, nearly at the top of his lungs, "*Væran Ksé'l'ch*' says, 'hold *on* to something'!"

The warning was an apt one, because in the next half-second – barely enough time for even the enhanced reflexes of those on-board to react – the air-ship was struck from directly behind, by something loud and powerful. Its shock-wave – accompanied by multiple, smaller impacts sounding like rifle-shots – reverberated from stem to stern, propelling the hot-dagger forward-wise, out of the boy's hands and alarmingly-close to Billings' left ear, before it stabilized in mid-air.

Immediately after all this, there was an even more powerful booming-sound, coming from a point that must have been a fair distance behind the air-ship.

Despite all else that was going on, the salesman somehow found the time to think to himself,

Damn, that's hot – and take it as a compliment, 'Væran'-*whoever-you-are.*

He heard a weird-sounding, crackling voice reply – not in English, but in her crazy-ass language that he didn't at all understand, though he still got the drift of it – *Portal where is? Join to Mother noble need war in! Open must!*

Billings managed to respond, *Oh no, you don't – you blow that hatch, kid, you'll depressurize us – and those of us made out of flesh and blood need air to breathe –*

"Mom says, 'hold on *tight!*" shrieked Tommy. "She's gonna pull an 'up-high evade'!"

Oh shit – that damn 'halfway-to-the-moon' maneuver she told us about – realized Billings

The bow of the *Mailànkh Express* tilted abruptly upward, its angle at least 45 degrees to the vertical.

Here we go...

The only one to (relatively speaking) cope with what came next was Ramirez, whose alien-powers propelled him into a seat, before the air-ship began to streak upward at rocket-like speed; the rest of the passengers, conversely, tumbled, head-over-heels, to be unceremoniously deposited in an uncomfortable jumble of knees, elbows and body-contortions, at the stern of the *Express*.

Upward and upward they went – judging from the G-forces and the incline, it must have been a very rapid ascent – and to his alarm, and despite the noise of rushing air outside, Billings' enhanced hearing detected an ominous "hissing"-sound coming from the rear bulkhead.

Faint emanations of what looked like steam were coming from three or four places on the bulkhead, and upon closer inspection, there appeared to be small, almost-round holes corresponding to the location of each steam-puff.

"Goddamn – they must have shot through the outside of the hull!" he yelled, while slamming his hands over two of the perforations. Two others, however, were substantially out of his reach.

He noticed Ramirez' eyes starting to dimly glow, as the Tex-Mex scientist stared deliberately at the points of Billings' concern. The "hissing"-sound abated to nothingness.

"Okay – I think I got it – re-pressurized the whole back bulkhead," explained Ramirez, while the angle of ascent (though not the *Express'* airspeed, which they could tell was even faster now) seemed to be leveling off. "You can let go – it won't leak out any more... at least not while I'm awake. But Holy Crap, Bob – that *was* a close one, especially with us going as high as we're at now –"

"*How* high?" uneasily queried the salesman.

"Not exactly sure," offered Ramirez, "But I can sort of 'feel' what the air-pressure is, outside... and it sure is getting thin. We're above fifty thousand feet, for sure – maybe a lot more... that's my guess."

The yellow-orange-dagger had self-propelled back into Tommy's out-stretched hand, and the boy added, "Mom's saying, 'we are above the most-part of this blue world's sea of air; and shortly, we must plunge back down, like a fire-stone from the Heavens' – whatever *that* means."

"It means, 'almost in outer space', kid," suggested Billings. "As in, about to play 'meteor'."

Silently, he marveled at the concept of his elfin 'girlfriend', hefting a several-ton-weight airship thousands of feet, up into the Earth's outer atmosphere.

I'm dating a chick who looks like a teenager... but who has the power of a thousand moon-rockets, lurking under that perfect, delectable skin.

And one who disintegrates comets the size of a mountain.

Yeah... what she is... that slipped my mind, for a minute...

"Oh my *Lord!*" exclaimed a shocked Saquina White, "What 'bout Melissa?"

Tommy's brow furrowed as he momentarily closed his eyes. Then he said, "She's okay... Mom's saying that she's, uhh, 'latched on' to the back of the ship. With her *mind*, I mean... only managed to do that at the last second she could. But she's been saying some things to Mom that Mrs. Claremont would wash her mouth out with soap, for."

"Like what? idly asked the salesman."

"Like... uhh... 'Karéin, it's fuckin' *freezin'* up here, and I can hardly *breathe*, even with mah 'bubble' and even by suckin' yo' *Fire* into mah lungs'... something like that," explained the boy.

"Sorry about the cuss-words," he obligingly apologized, to bemused grins and chuckles coming from the other passengers. "Oh – and by the way – Mom's saying, 'going down'".

The advisory was only too apt, because just as suddenly as it had started on its upward trajectory, the air-ship reversed this, hurtling downward and, apparently, to the right. Frantically, the passengers grabbed for hand-holds, or for anything that could be even a poor substitute for one.

Billings, for his part, ended up wrapped uncomfortably around the supporting-pillar between one of the *Express'* seats, and its floor.

Even through the several layers of protective alien force-fields arrayed outside the air-ship's hull, all aboard could hear the roar of the winds, as the *Mailànkh Express* rapidly picked up speed, plunging through the mesosphere at a very steep angle.

This second half of the roller-coaster ride went on for about two-and-a-half minutes (though to some it seemed much longer), and then, finally, the air-ship seemed to level off. It gradually came to a full stop, then resumed descending, albeit at a considerably slower and more gentle pace.

"I wish I knew what the hell she's doing... where she's taking us," grumbled Billings.

"We're low now – air-pressure's almost normal," observed Ramirez. "I'll release my block on the holes. I don't think we need it any more. By the way... near as I can tell, we've been going east."

After perhaps another two minutes of downward motion, the *Express* came to an abrupt stop with a "thumping"-sound coming from directly below.

"Mom says that we've landed," announced Tommy.

Billings still couldn't believe that he could touch that damned flaming-dagger... much less, grasp it firm in his hand. Yet the boy seemed to be almost *caressing* it.

The door to the outside opened without any of the normally-expected air-egress, probably due to the perforations in the rear-bulkhead having already equaled-out the air-pressure.

The passengers stumbled out, one by one. They were on a lawn behind what might have been a warehouse or grocery-store to the west, judging from the many big trucking rigs parked at loading docks leading into this building. To the left of this place was a retail shop of some sort (Billings guessed that it was a women's hairdressing salon). A line of trees restricted vision to the north, south and east. The lawn where the air-ship had landed was scorched from the heat of recent battle.

To the dismay of all three of Billings, Saquina White and Ramirez, the air-ship wasn't cloaked or otherwise hidden, and disbelieving stares were coming from perhaps seven to twelve onlookers – mostly warehouse-workers, supplemented by ordinary people in cars – arrayed randomly to the west, north and south.

A shivering and wide-eyed – but otherwise apparently physically-unharmed – Melissa Claremont broke a vise-grip on the hind-parts of the *Express* and gingerly hopped to the ground, stepping forward to meet the others.

The Storied Watcher was there, in full war-gear, just outside the *Express'* exit-hatch.

"Sari... what the fuck's going *on* here?" demanded the salesman. "The ship's right out in the open –"

"I know it," she acknowledged. "*Most* unfortunate. I was concerned that one or more of you – especially young Melissa, though thankfully I see that is not the case – might have been seriously injured in the latter-most engagement. So I landed, uhh, 'ay-sap' to validate this, as soon as I could be sure that we had evaded those damnable fighting-planes; and I am at a loss to understand how they detected and tracked us, thence to attack. Some of the weirding-mechanism that obscures the vessel – that is, the part of it which is independent of my own abilities – seems to have been damaged in the engagement, though it was still intact enough to evade the ray-dar trackers that are all over the local airport. I will need more time than we likely have at our disposal, to fully fix our hiding-tricks. *Væran Ksé'l'ch'* believes that everyone is, ahh, oh-kay... is that true?"

"But these-here folks," – Saquina White motioned at the onlookers, who were cautiously advancing on this amazing sight, from three directions – "They gonna *see* you, Karéin!"

"Yes?" diffidently replied Karéin-Mayréij.

The others – despite their arts – were at a loss to tell if her *sang-froid* was real, or feigned.

Saquina White's warning was nothing if not apt, given the several sets of dull-glowing, alien-powered eyes (including her own), that – though efforts at suppression were being attempted – made the newly-arrived a painfully-obvious novelty-sight.

"You sure *were* ragging on me back there in Nowheresville, when I decided to go exploring," complained Billings. "What's good for the gander –"

"Angel Lady... didn't y'all tell us, back there in L'wesiana, that is... that we was s'posed to be, uhh... 'incognito'?" added Melissa. "Couldn't y'all have put us down outside th' town, or somethin'?"

"Well, brave Melissa," replied the Storied Watcher, "I landed the ship in the first place that I could find, caring little for who would descry us; and my war-children were telling of strange chatter, among the ray-dee-oh waves, of 'who is the President now'... I thought it appropriate go to a place where we might avail ourselves of the truth about this. Anyway... I would have thought that you would have been the first to understand why hiding ourselves is no longer a realistic option. Or have you so quickly forgotten what just transpired, up there?"

"Y'all mean, 'wid them fighter-planes'?" continued the Claremont girl.

She stared guiltily at the ground.

"Yeah – ah gets it. What ah *done* to 'em. Lawd *forgive* me!" whimpered Melissa.

With a quick embrace – somehow, the flame-aura of *Vîrya Ahn'jë* was either suppressed, or it no longer bothered the flying-teenager – Karéin-Mayréij comforted her under-study.

"You did what you *had* to, little sister," counseled the Storied Watcher. "To protect and save those who you escort through war. And that is all that *any* of us can do, when so called upon to do. Do not blame yourself – I do not, and if this 'Lord' of yours is any 'god' worthy of worship, he will not sanction you for defending to the utmost, those who you love. The accounting for it – if there will be any – that will come later."

A sad-eyed Melissa mutely nodded.

"But we're right out here in *public*, Karéin!" protested Ramirez. "In another minute or so these people all around are going to get a good look at us – including with their communicator-cameras. Are you *trying* to get us on the evening news? I thought you said we should avoid –"

"'Trying'?" she haughtily responded. "No. Do I *accept*, a changed set of circumstances, which was not of my doing... just like I so accepted, when it was apparent that the Holy *Fire*, was spreading, yet not by my own volition? Yes. Think on it, brother – after the fight-in-the-sky just finished, undoubtedly the American government knows of our return to this continent. The refulgence of Melissa's dread attack lit up the very heavens, for many leagues from the scene of the battle, after all. Should not the President's peasant-citizens know the same as their king? Why is their right to know, the less than his?"

"So... you're planning a press-conference?" grumbled Ramirez. "You'll *involve* them," he cautioned. "In all of," – he waved his arms back and forth, over the air-ship – "This. *We*, can barely survive the government's repeated attacks. *They*, are going to get blown to *bits*, the next time that the Air Force comes after us. Which may be, 'already'. It's *wrong*, Karéin!"

Unusually for her, the alien-girl did seem taken aback at the Tex-Mex scientist's words. She fell silent for a moment or two, and then offered, "So... what would you have us do, my brother? Where should we fly –"

But the question was too late; the curious, rapidly-growing crowd had now approached to more than easy viewing-range, encroaching on the more-than-humans' preferred boundaries.

"That-that's *her!*" excitedly exclaimed someone.

"But I thought she was *dead*," countered another.

"They're all dead," mentioned still another. "At least, that's what them news-guys been sayin'."

"Look at their *eyes*," half-whispered yet another. "They look like *demons* –"

"No 'demon' am I," defensively parried Karéin-Mayréij. "For if I were, surely you would be dead, consumed, or... worse. At grievous risk have I slain many of the likes of these, and I can *personally* attest that –"

Her explanation was cut off, leaving the alien-girl uncharacteristically flustered, by a confused babble coming from three directions.

Deciding to literally 'rise above' the crowd to get everyone's attention, her soles had just left the ground, when she heard an unexpected comment.

"Hey lady... you're showing up now – that's because of all that's going down in Washington... right?" said a man in the crowd.

Never one to admit being caught by surprise, the gradually-self-levitating, fire-bedecked and (if any had the perception to notice) lightly-blushing Storied

Watcher responded, "Uhh… 'Washington'? Oh… yes, my… *my!* How *could* I have failed to so acknowledge! Why… of *course!"*

"So you gonna take him up on his offer?" persisted the voice from the crowd.

The alien-girl, now floating high enough so that her knees were roughly the height of her boyfriend's eyebrows, stared deliberately at the guy in the crowd, for a long second.

With consternation appearing on her face, she quickly changed her gaze to the circle of friends and confidants just below her.

"Quickly… what do you think? *Should* we?" she shot downwards.

"'Should we'… *what?"* whispered an irritated Billings.

"Go to parley with the President – in Dee Cee," she whispered back.

"But wasn't y'all gonna off him –" argued Melissa Claremont, a bit more loudly than she had likely wanted to do.

"No… not *that* one," stammered Karéin-Mayréij, "The *old* one… the, uhh, 'original' one, who now apparently resides again in the capitol city. There apparently was an announcement on the vid-e-o, a few minutes ago –"

"How y'all *know* this shit?" interrogated Saquina White.

A second later, realization coming to her while the Storied Watcher phlegmatically tapped an index finger against the side of her own head, White retracted with, "Oh… wait… yeah. Okay then… *I* get it."

"What the *hell?"* complained Billings. "What happened to this other guy… the old Vice-President, I mean? How's *he* not in the picture, any more?"

"If I read the thoughts correctly, and it was at the limit of my range… I believe that he still *is,"* explained the alien-girl, *sotto voce.* "There seems to be a power-struggle –"

"Well?" called several voices from the crowd.

"You gonna promise what he's asking for?" demanded one person.

"What's *that?"* whispered a frustrated Billings, in the alien-girl's direction.

Addressing the crowd rather than her boyfriend and using a tone of feigned confidence, Karéin-Mayréij announced, "I always honor an honestly-raised flag of truce, so that discussions can proceed without either party fearing safety of life or limb, on account of the other. Beyond that… I make no promises, either for good or ill. We shall see what he has to say… and that, is all that I have to say. Now – if you will please – move away from our air-ship here, as its departure may be hazardous to those who come too close. Thank you!"

"Sari… what the hell is going *on?"* implored an agitated Billings.

As the Storied Watcher drifted downward, to alight in the middle of a dense crowd of onlookers (both human and extra-human), with a slow, deliberate stare, she said,

"To those of the *Mailànkh Express…* did all of you remember to pack some nice clothes – the likes of which one would wear, on a little social call to the House of White?"

Wake Up, Yvonne

Despite all odds, the V-37, though having to fly low over the mountain-tops, given its multiple-perforated pressure-hull and over-full passenger-load, was still on course for Fayetteville.

A weary and bloodied Tanaka – having shot down three more fighter-planes on the escape-route out of the London Airport – puzzled about the facts of the last few minutes, while recovering from the battle as best she could.

It was no longer amazing to those around, to see her concussion-wounds slowly shrinking, millimeter-by-millimeter, as her dimly-glowing inner *Fire* did its magic.

"Devon's confirmed it – he observed the same as I did, when he relieved me topside," she spoke to the Russian, trying to keep her voice low enough to be drowned out by engine-noise, at least as far as human ears were concerned. "Makes no sense at all... but I'll *take* it, I guess. I gave them the pasting that they deserved, but they just kept on coming. *Bastards...*"

"Why the whispering, Professor?" asked Misha.

"All those explosions back there must have helped to wake up Sam's family," she replied, "But I'd prefer to give him a few minutes to level-set with them, before they find out that we've been fighting against the whole damn Air Force."

She glanced over her shoulder at her former Mars mission commander, who was near the other end of the aircraft, gently counseling an obviously-still-groggy extended clan, with the help of the elder two of the Wades as well as of the Texas farm-family.

"Hmm," the Russian ruefully acknowledged, "I suppose that we *should*, bestow that courtesy upon him. But I will grant you that I cannot explain this development... why would they break off from the battle? From everything that I know of American air-engagement tactics – not to mention Russian ones – pressing one's attack until the target is destroyed or neutralized, is an absolutely mandatory objective. Let us be specific... exactly *what* did you and Major White observe?"

"They just... flew away... that's about it, Misha," she sighed. "I knocked down six of their AAMs, but at least one or maybe two – don't know, it's all a blur – detonated *way* too close, my *Amaiish*-shield and *Vìrya Sài'ymë* protected me from the heat, the shrapnel and the DU-bursting local radiation but the damn shock-wave threw me around like a rag-doll... when I got my wits back, I saw them all breaking formation. I think they went off to the north... or possibly the north-east. I *was* a little disoriented, after all. So I dropped back to the top-hull and asked Devon to take over. He saw the same thing as I did. That's about it."

"Strange, indeed," he observed. "Particularly since they undoubtedly still have a continuous target-lock on us. But as you implied... it is better to not be shot at, than the alternative. We should keep our guard up, none the less."

"Well... Devon told me he's good to stay up there, for the duration," noted Tanaka. "I owe him one for letting me take a breather."

She paused for a couple of seconds, then asked, "How much further to Fayetteville?"

The Russian turned to Donny.

"I believe that we entered the way-points into the flight-path-computer... correct?" said Misha.

"Yeah... and ain't been much evadin' goin' on, since all that shootin' back there," remarked the trucker, who was manning the controls, "So I think it's still more or less on-target. What's this... yeah... well, if I'm readin' it right, we got another twenty minutes... maybe a few more. I'll let you know when it's in sight. Damn – if I ain't gettin' the hang of flyin' this thing, too, y'know! Easier than parkin' my old rig in a loading-dock, I'll tell you *that* much."

"Works for me... just hope that Brent's there," offered Tanaka. "We sure don't want to go searching for him, with all this –"

She stopped, having caught a glimpse of a "come-hither" gesture on the part of Jacobson, in the rear of the plane.

Suppressing a gulp, she stepped backward into the cargo-hold.

The aircraft, though large enough quite easily accommodate all those now within it, did not take long to traverse, and in a second or two the Mars mission science officer was there with her former commander.

"Cherie... *you* know Yvonne, from those pre-launch parties back at Canaveral – right?" introduced Jacobson.

"Oh... of *course*," replied Tanaka, with an obligatory, weak half-smile in the matronly, dull-eyed woman's direction. "Wonderful to meet you again, Yvonne! Oh... I'm Cherie Tanaka, if you didn't remember."

An extended hand was limply shaken by the woman, who, obviously straining with every word, replied,

"Nice... to... meet you, too, Cherie," she managed.

They're still half-out from the damn drugs that the Government injected them with, when they were first abducted, silently sent Tanaka to Jacobson, accompanied by a deliberate glance.

He nodded in acknowledgment, while his wife just stared forward.

But it appeared that others of Jacobson's family were recovering more quickly.

One of them – an elfin-slim, brown-haired girl in her early teens – was struggling with the orange "rendition-suit" into which she had been forced, a few hours ago.

"Get it off... get it *off!*" she angrily wailed, while – like several of her youthful peers – she was consumed in frustration at the thing's many, cross-interlocked belts, clasps and restraints.

"Hey – *hey* there, Jeannie," consoled Jacobson. "Let me –"

But Tanaka beat him to the punch.

She took one step to position herself directly in front of the young teenager and then, with a brief eye-glow, energized a minuscule portion of the *Fire*, using her telekinesis to rapidly free the girl from the hated prison-garb. Its catches and clasps were either instantly disengaged or simply ripped asunder, as if by some unseen giant's-hand.

Jeannie stared in disbelief.

"How... how'd you *do* that?" she stammered.

"It's... uhh... *complicated*," said the more-than-a-woman. "Sam – did you tell them –?"

"I told them a bit," he responded. "Let's give them a little *time*... okay? It's a lot for them to take in... especially given what they've just been through. Come here, Jeannie, sweetheart."

He embraced his daughter, who was now entirely out of the prison-garb. Her under-clothes, after the orange suit was removed, were a mauve-colored pair of relatively-thin pajamas, with slippers on her feet.

"You're Ms. Tanaka... right?" inquired Jeannie, while still in her father's arms. "Who went to Mars, along with Dad..."

The rest of Jacobson's children – plus one other female teenager who neither he nor Tanaka immediately recognized – had now shed their prison-clothes and were listening in on the conversation.

"Yeah... that's me," confirmed Tanaka. "Just call me 'Cherie'. And of course I wasn't the only one – if you remember, we also had Brent Boyd and Devon White, plus Sergei Chkalov in the mother-ship, orbiting overhead. We're heading to a place called 'Fayetteville' to pick up Brent and hopefully his family as well; Devon's gone topside, but he's with us here, you'll get to meet him in a few minutes –"

"*Wait* a minute," interrupted the teenager. "Did you say, 'topside'? What's that *mean?* There's only one level on this plane... right? So –"

"That's complicated as well, honey," deflected Tanaka. "Devon's on the top of this aircraft – on the outer hull, that is."

"What?" replied a perplexed Jeannie. "That's on the *outside*... isn't it? What's he doing there?"

"He's – uhh – protecting us from attack," offered Jacobson. "Sweetheart, there's a lot that you, your Mom and the rest of our family don't yet know about –"

"They're all, like, 'super-heroes', or somethin'," unhelpfully interjected Sammie, with a mischievous wink at most of the Jacobson family.

"Huh?" spoke another one of the former Mars commander's offspring, this time a somewhat older teen-aged girl, also brown-haired but more full of figure. "*Super-heroes? What?*"

"Sure *are*," continued the street-walker, much to the obvious consternation of both Jacobson and Tanaka. "That lady yer talkin' to, she flew hundreds of miles, all by herself, and rescued you all from them government bad-guys. Fried a bunch of 'em – not to mention a lot of fighter-planes – with lightenin'-

bolts that she can let loose with anytime she wants, too... least, that's what *I* heard."

"Gee... thanks for letting me tell my own story, Sammie," complained the former Mars science officer.

"Well, sorry, Cherie," came back the smart-ass comment, "But *you* was the one who invited me on to this crazy train... y'know?"

"But is it... *true?*" pressed the elder teenager.

"Yes... it is," plainly answered Tanaka. "You must be... Jennifer... right?"

"Everybody calls me 'Jen'," noted the girl. "I can't believe it, though..."

"You *saw* what she did to my prison-clothes," argued Jeannie. "Didn't even touch me, but –"

"Are *you* a super-hero now, Daddy?" demanded a dark-haired young man, probably around twelve or thirteen years of age. "Like Ms. Tanaka? Like... flying all over the place, and –"

"No... not *exactly* – I mean, yes, but... *look*, everybody," pleaded Jacobson, "We're going way too fast here; Riley, Jeannie, Jen, Yvonne – I'll fully explain what's going on later, but for now, I think we need to just take a deep breath and try to relax a bit. *Please.*"

The younger daughter gave a wide-eyed nod, and was joined in embracing a grateful Jacobson by her elder sister.

His wife, now somewhat more lucid, spoke up.

"Sam," she slowly forced out, "What's this... all about? Who... *did* this... to us? *Why?*"

Jacobson took hold of her hand and replied, "We don't have all the facts by any means... but – sad to say – we're pretty sure that you were abducted by our own government's intelligence-agencies. They –"

"Why would they *do* that, Daddy?" demanded the older teenager. "We haven't *done anything!*"

"To get at *us* – Major White, Major Boyd, Cherie and myself," evenly stated Jacobson. "*That's* why. We're too powerful for the government to kill... though that's not for lack of trying on their part. So like the cowards they are, they did the next best thing – namely, go after our families and loved ones. Had it not been for Cherie's heroism – for which I'll forever be grateful – in finding and rescuing you at the last minute, they'd likely have taken you off to some well-hidden prison where we'd *never* have found you. It was a very close thing, honey."

"So... she did just – uhh – *fly* to where those black cars that they put us in, were, and she... *what?* Like... *shot* them, or something?" persisted Jen.

"Yes... that's *exactly* what I did," proudly confirmed Tanaka.

There was a serene, half-smile on her face.

"Get *ouut!*" jealously teased the Jacobson boy. "How? They had *guns!* Did you have a gun, Ms. Tanaka?"

"Nope," answered the more-than-a-woman. "I didn't *need* one; I had... *this.*"

She held out her arms in front, with fingers spread out and palms facing each other, as if to embrace someone.

Her eyes briefly glowed, the first chords of her war-song began to issue from all around, and a barrage of evidently low-voltage electricity-discharges jumped back and forth, from one hand to another. After a couple of seconds of this display, she powered down her *Fire* with a bemused wink at the young man.

"*Wowww...*" breathed the awed boy.

"I had a lot of help from my friend Wolf over there, by the way," noted Tanaka. "As your father knows, we owe him our thanks as well."

The big man – who had been reclining, half-asleep, on one of the opposite benches, close-up against his two hell-hounds – smiled and gave them an insouciant casual-salute, via a flick of outstretched palm from side of forehead.

"He flew with you?" asked Jeannie.

"Wolf flew a bit behind me," explained Tanaka. "We have different powers; mine's lightening – *his*, is fire."

Wolf – his eyes still half-shut – held up one index finger, which became enveloped in a flame for a brief moment, after which the fire was quickly self-extinguished.

"I can make it a lot bigger and hotter than that, of course," he drawled, "But Ms. Lightenin'-Thighs there told me not to, 'less I wanted to set off this crate's fire-extinguishers. Didn't want the pups to end up all wet – that 'wet-dog-smell', don't you know – so I went along with her."

"Love *you* too, brother," Tanaka quipped back.

The male dog let out a friendly, smoke-infused "woof", to the amazement and excitement of the Jacobson offspring.

"Daddy," implored Jeannie, "Show us what *you* can do!"

"Just a little, uhh, *shielding*," demonstrated the former Mars mission leader, while holding out both hands and allowing his diamond-*Fire*-armor to encase them. "I don't fly, either... I just hop."

They heard the Russian – who, although still assisting Donny with the aircraft-controls, had been listening all the while – call out, "I would advise you young ones to respect your father, none the less. In our last engagement, I saw him defeat an entire army-battalion, essentially by himself. He has a deadly attack and is a *formidable* opponent... you should be grateful that he is here to defend you."

"Is that *true*, Daddy?" pressed the elder teen-aged girl.

"Being able to kill people and to destroy things isn't something of which I'm proud, Jen honey," reluctantly mentioned Jacobson, "But... yes, it *is* true. All of us were given these powers by our friend Karéin-Mayréij – the alien who we first met on Mars and then transported back with us in the *Infinity*."

Now the woman from the Texas farm-family spoke up.

"But why'd the government go after you, Mister?" she asked. "We all saw that trip you made to Mars – 'till the comet showed up, you were the biggest thing on TV. I'd have thought they'd give y'all a ticker-tape parade, or whatnot."

"*You* tell *me*," he ruefully answered. "Because that's exactly what *we* expected... things didn't turn out that way, unfortunately."

"President said 'jump' and we didn't immediately say 'how high'," added Tanaka. "That didn't get us off to the best of starts."

Jacobson paused for a second or two, then explained, "As you no doubt saw from the media after the 'comet' episode, Karéin ended up in the United States and things sort of went downhill from there; for reasons we still don't understand, the President tried to kill her the moment that he knew she was here. Obviously, that didn't turn out too well... she's *far* too powerful to fall victim to human-invented technology. Cherie, Devon, Brent and I have been imprisoned and then hunted by the government ever since then, but – due to these 'alien-powers' that Karéin bestowed on us – so far, we've come out on top."

"Sam," spoke up his wife, "This is really starting to *scare* me... we were at home, Jen had Ammy here for a sleep-over, we got a call from some random guy who didn't want to give his name and he warned us that 'the Men In Black are coming' and then less than a minute after that, the windows shattered, something got thrown through them into the house... don't remember much after that. I don't understand why the government *hates* us so much! We haven't done *anything*... and I'm married to a *space-hero!*"

"I know... I *know*, dear," responded Jacobson, holding Yvonne's hand tightly. "Little of this makes any sense to us, either. If it's any consolation, you aren't the only ones... they've been targeting Brent's family, Devon's and Cherie's, too –"

"Blew up mah whole damn farm, for the 'crime' of puttin' your crew here, up for the night," muttered Callum Wade.

"My truck, too," called out Donny, from the pilot's-seat. "And it ain't nowhere *near* paid off yet."

"Well," sniffed Sammie, "These 'Mars-Gang' folk aren't *all* bad... got me away from my – uhh – 'manager', back home. He's *mean*... and he had it out for me. I'm better off here with you all and Donny, that's for sure."

"We're hoping that Brent has got his family with him in Fayetteville," continued Jacobson, "Devon's family is – uhh – elsewhere; we're pretty sure that they're safe. But Cherie's –"

"We had an inside source tell us that the government has already abducted my mother, who was living on the West Coast," interrupted Tanaka.

With a glowing-eyed scowl that impressed and intimidated even her post-human companions, she savagely spat, "And I've already made it clear, that if they touch so much as a hair on her head – and sorry for the language, kids – I'll lay this entire fucking *country* to *ruins!* The President's reward for abusing my mother – like we've already caught him doing to thousands of others, including helpless children – will be a country reduced to flaming *rubble!* I'll start at one coast and not stop until I hit the other, with everything behind me, on *fire!*"

"Sam," whispered Yvonne, "Is she... capable of *doing* that? Does she have the power to *do* what she's saying, I mean?"

"Yes, honey," he replied in an even, matter-of-fact tone of voice. "She most definitely... *does.*"

Yvonne's face blanched as she stared momentarily at Tanaka.

"And if she goes that route... she'll have some help in doin' it," idly mentioned Wolf.

He opened one eyelid wide enough to show his red-tinted, *Fire*-infused eye-glow, while holding up an incandescent hand for a second or two before self-extinguishing its flame.

"President's an ass, cheatin' at a poker-table, with a hand of deuces that he's callin' aces," warned the bounty-hunter. "Seem to remember from them Westerns, that usually don't turn out too good, if the other guy's gun's got a round or two in the chamber. Well... Miss Lightenin'-Thighs here's 'Number One With A Bullet'... and yours truly's 'Bullet Number Two'. 'Sides... a nice big fire's a *pretty* thing... you know?"

"Lord Above," exclaimed the wife, "If I wasn't scared enough, before..."

"Daddy," plaintively demanded Jeannie, "Are we the 'good guys'... or the 'bad guys'?"

"I can only speak for myself, sweetheart," replied Jacobson, "But I'm just out for justice – whatever *that* word means, these days. As to the rest of it... that's really up to the President and the rest of the government. We'll soon find out, I guess, because after we pick up Brent... we're heading for the White House."

"The *White House?*" gasped the other teen-aged girl (a somewhat more buxom, dark olive-skinned one, with crazily-tinted red-and-blue hair and a nose-ring) of roughly Jen's age. "Isn't that where the *President* lives?"

"That'd be it," philosophically confirmed Jacobson. "By the way, honey... I don't think we've been introduced?"

"Oh... I'm Amina Khapadi, sir," explained the teenager. "Jen invited me over to her place for a sleep-over, before... well, *you* know. Everybody just calls me 'Ammy', though."

"Nice to meet you, Ammy," offered Jacobson. "Although I wish it wasn't because of events like this. I'm truly sorry for what's been done to you – not to mention what's been done to some of the others around here."

He nodded in the direction of the bereaved Texas farm-family.

"Well... nothing *exciting* used to happen to me, back in Texas," commented Ammy. "Guess *that's* changed... hasn't it?"

"Yeah," sadly remarked Cassie Young, "It sure *has.*"

"Hey... 'Sammy and Ammy'," cheerfully chirped the streetwalker. "I *like* it!"

"Thanks," politely stated the teenager.

"But *sir*," she challenged Jacobson, "When we get to the White House... what are we gonna tell the President?"

"The *truth*," answered the former Mars mission commander. "About what's happened so far to us, and about what counter-measures we've taken, with what justification. We'll expect no less from him, in return. He'll have to tell it to the whole country, so there can be none of the government's usual lies and back-tracking, later. It's the only way to end this, without an outcome such as the one Cherie's prepared to deliver."

"And if he don't wanna *do* that... what happens *then?*" asked Callum Wade.

"Then... God help *him*," grimly warned Jacobson. "We'll have no alternative to wage a full-scale war, with our goal in that case being to simply overthrow the government and rule the United States, all by ourselves. It's the last thing in the world that I want to do – but if we're backed into a corner, and the President refuses to negotiate in good faith, it'll either be *that*... or us all being captured, tried in front of a kangaroo court and then murdered –"

"If you're at all interested in hearin' this," noted a still-half-somnolent Wolf, "Little Miss Nuclear Angel told us – it was back in L.A., as I recall – that there's pretty much no way for a regular human bein' to off one of us 'New People' just by hangin' us, or the 'lectric chair, or just by that good ol' firin'-squad... 'long as we're not totally out cold, beforehand. Somethin' about 'natural defenses' or such, showin' up automatically to save the day. I'm inclined to believe her... which means, if the Army don't smoke us in some big fight with tanks 'n missiles 'n whatever – and that's possible, I'll admit – they can march us in front of all the rigged-up trials that they want, but when it comes time to carry out the sentence... 'all dressed up and nowhere to die'... you know? Works for *me*."

"I heard that counsel as well," interjected Misha, from the front of the aircraft. "And though I have no reason to distrust what the Storied Watcher said to us... it is not wise for us to put this theory to the test. Large nations like the U.S. or Russia can be very creative in devising methods of 'liquidating' enemies of the state, after all."

"I have no intention of giving them that chance," declared Tanaka. "As Wolf knows, we've had some close calls fighting the Air Force... but I'm betting that they'll run out of missiles and fighter-planes – not to mention pilots who are willing to get into one, to go up against me – long before I'll run out of lightening-bolts. After that, well... let's see them *try* to arrest me!"

The conversation came to a halt, as the Jacobson family – not to mention the other civilians in the V-37 – pondered the magnitude of the situation of which they had just been informed.

The silence was quickly broken, however.

"Well... just in case the Air Force has a warm welcome planned for us over Fayetteville," committed Tanaka, "I'd better go topside again."

"But you just did a shift...?" challenged Jacobson.

"Yeah... tired as hell," she conceded, "But I don't want Devon handling an ambush, all by himself. What if they, like, found out about the plans, set up a missile-battery in there, and told it to fire the moment they get a line of sight?"

"I do have to admit that the Professor has a point," interjected Misha. "We all hope that this will not come to pass... but it is better to be prepared. Cherie... for the record, if you get into trouble – call on myself. You will find that my ability to defend us, has... *improved*, lately."

"Sam...?" she questioned.

"He's not kidding," confirmed Jacobson. "Those two daggers of his... not quite up to Karéin's ones... but catching up fast, if you know what I mean."

Misha's face showed a satisfied half-smile.

They heard a thrice-repeated knocking-sound coming from the upper fuselage, and then the trucker in the pilot-seat announced,

"Fayetteville just a few ridges away, folks – we're within twenty miles. Seat-belts, no smokin' – yes, Mister Gas Barbecue, that *does* mean you and them hot-dogs too – and last stop before Truth or Consequences, D.C."

Overtaken By Events... So Taking Over

This was a nameless, near-featureless place; its gray, subterranean concrete walls – whose extent receded in a straight line, past the limit of eyesight, to the left and right – bore almost no distinguishing-marks. The air here was obviously well-filtered; it had been passed through several stages of scrubbers, before being circulated.

The floor was also of concrete, although in a faint concession to style over substance, these were at least painted blue-gray (with a central, highway-like yellow dividing-line, running into the distance) and were polished to a shiny quality. There was no dust, even though nobody could possibly have been there to do any cleaning.

The Agency director – one of the very few living human beings who knew of the place's existence, never mind its location – was alone, standing in the tomb-like silence, in front of a stainless-steel door. He waved his right hand at the thing, and though there was no obvious electric-eye or other surveillance-device, the biometrics worked well enough and the door opened with an almost inaudible sound.

He walked, at a steady, deliberate pace, into the room beyond. Formerly dark, its ceiling- and wall-lights illuminated automatically, bathing the director in a soft, subdued glow.

The room was unfurnished; there was nowhere to sit, nor, indeed, was there much of *anything* in here. It would have reminded most onlookers of a maximum-security isolation-cell, except that it was too large for a single person.

"Enable," his voice – anodyne, inexpressive as ever – announced.

A large, million-color flat-screen display appeared in the opposite wall. It showed a static image of the Agency logo, superimposed on a plain, royal-blue background.

"This is Top Dog," he announced, toward the screen. "ID-value is Molehill 461, Lotus 95, Trapezoid 3F. Do you copy?"

"Copy, voice signature and ID-value confirmed," came back an electronic-sounding response. "ID value here for HQ Gopher is Paperweight 7C97, Dog-house 16, Duo 7E18. Do you confirm, sir?"

"Confirmed," said the director. "And down to business – immediately."

Untypically, his voice rose by a small decibel-fraction.

"I need a tactical assessment," he requested. "No, on second thought... I want a complete situational review! I've had no updates for six *hours* – and I was due to be on the line to the Old Man about releasing our special airborne assets against the Jacobson group – but the ANHQ's not responding. What's going *on*?"

The other voice hesitated for a half-second and then said,

"I'm afraid we really don't know, sir; we had a normal status-check from our primary deep-cover source on the plane about eight hours ago, and there was another one due about two hours back... but we received no data."

"You *know* the protocol," retorted the director.

"Yes, sir," apologized the voice. "We tried the backup – an orderly, by the way – but haven't been able to get through to *him*, either. I consulted with the Palace to see what they can patch in to at their end, but although their main sensors seem to be operative, what they've got makes no sense –"

"What do you mean?" interrupted the director. "What *have* they got?"

"Just a few garbled captures, sir," the voice tried to explain. "There may have been an *incident* on board the aircraft, as near as NSA can figure out... they've heard people calling for Marine guards and the Service, for example. However, the plane's still flying on its normal course, and there haven't been – hold on... something's coming in..."

With his usual impassive expression, the director waited.

After a lapse of six or seven seconds, the remote voice again spoke up.

Its tone, though still computer-modified, was distinctly nervous.

"Sir... some – uhh – unanticipated information here," it said. "NSA's getting COMINT indicating that there may have been a fire-fight – a shoot-out – on-board –"

"Between who and who?" interrupted the director.

"Uhh... not sure, sir," replied the voice. "There's talk of 'terrorists using energy-weapons', and –"

"Just a second," pre-empted the director. "What did you say about 'energy-weapons'?"

"That's all the Palace has been able to ascertain, sir," the voice responded. "They've only been able to identify one terrorist – a female, apparently – but she's heavily-armed... there's a stand-off, she's taken hostages..."

"What about the President and the command-staff?" pressed the director. "What's *their* status?"

"No information on that, sir," stated the voice. "The only senior-circle voice-signature that NSA's been able to validate over the past couple of hours, has been that of the President's Spiritual Adviser... Mr. Crowford, that is.... and wait, sir – *here's* something really odd – the intercepts having him declaring, '*I'm* in charge here, now'. That doesn't make any sense at all – he's just –"

"Way ahead of you," interjected the director; had there been anyone in the room, they would have seen an upset, worried furrow on his usually-impassive brow. "Get me the manifest of who's on the aircraft – immediately – and make sure it's accurate, including all comings and goings in the last 24 hours. Highlight anything unusual or unplanned. *Now!*"

"Yes *sir*, sir!" reflexively responded the remote voice.

After a delay of seven or eight seconds, a list of names associated with military rank, on-bording and off-boarding time-stamps and a brief functional description of each staff-role, appeared on the screen. Its top-row scrolled slowly upwards, so as to allow data to populate upward from the bottom of the screen. Four of the rows, distributed randomly throughout the 85 that collectively made up the entire database, were highlighted in dimly-glowing yellow text-color.

The director's eyes carefully surveyed the information, line-by-line.

"Okay... stop there," he ordered. The scrolling halted.

"Mattheney – communications tech, TI-HP... on-board to fix Mark LXV Mode 7 transponder... cross-check with records validates... okay," he mumbled. "Then there's that 'Chu' woman, played around with the alien – bad idea, from the start – know all about *her*... some low-ranking guy named 'Grassleigh' – now *that's* interesting, explanation and trace on physical movements don't match up... what's *he* doing there... and finally a GrayWar guy, who... oh, right, he's one of ours, under cover."

His voice fell silent, while he pondered the meaning of the data just provided to him.

"Sir," offered the voice, "I've got some additional information. It just came in –"

"Yes?" cut in the director.

"It – uhh – appears, that the President and General Blanshard, and many of the command-staff, are among the hostages," uneasily stated the remote voice. "There's also damage to the aircraft... fortunately, it seems to have been temporarily repaired, but they've had to go on a gradual descent, in case –"

"The... *President?*" incredulously exclaimed the director. "And *Blanshard?* What about... uhh... what about Warnock? Or Bezomorton? Or – is there any sign of the alien being involved here? On-board the aircraft, I mean..."

There was the genuine sound of panic in his voice, and if any had been present, they would have seen a sheen of sweat on his brow.

"I'm sorry, sir, but I have no data on that," evaded the remote assistant. "Although I'm pretty sure that NSA would have so reported, if the alien had appeared in person, up there. Also, of the command-staff, the only one who's accounted for is the Spiritual Adviser. Should I see if I can get a communications-link with him?"

"Yes... no... I mean, 'yes'... but later," said the director. "Not right now – too much else to do. Okay... please inform the Agency Extraordinary Emergency Actions Group that based on the information that you've just provided me with, we must assume that the National Command Authority has been incapacitated or compromised; and given that set of circumstances, I have no option but to invoke Agency Contingency Plan Memorandum CA-199, Revision 2. Ensure that DeWitt and Bezomorton have been de-provisioned from the special assets chain of command. I want the Emergency Actions Group to meet at the substitute HQ bunker here with me, ASAP, as we will need a full team. This is a Class 'A' confidentiality operation and there are to be *no* onlookers to the travel and location plans. Do you copy?"

"ACPM CA-199R2, full team, absolute lock-down on logistics... copy that, sir," noted the remote voice. "Do you have the necessary command-infrastructure and the new activation-codes?"

"Yes," dispassionately confirmed the director. "I have the suitcase and the snap-cards close by; please have them activated immediately. As you know, the most important asset that will now be under my control, is the one that was meant to be deployed against the Jacobson traitor-group. Can you get a command-channel directly to the launch-vehicle?"

"I'll *try*, sir," pledged the voice. "That's on a dedicated Air Force link, and we'll have to over-ride their controls – but doing so was in the plan; so it should take only a short while, maybe an hour at most. After that you can target and fire from the suitcase. Not only *this* asset... but all the other ones that would ordinarily have responded to a command-channel from the aircraft, as well."

"Acknowledged," responded the director. "I'll need a status-update on any other special assets. For example, on any newly-constituted weapons, or the missing Barksdale one, or the one being pursued in the L.A. area. What are our sources saying?"

"Mixed results on those, sir," carefully noted the remote voice. "From our sources inside the military, although they're working 24-by-7 to reconstitute as many as they can, the ETA to that is still at least a full week away, unfortunately. We think we've got a reading for something that *could* be the Barksdale item going through Madison, Wisconsin – it tripped one of our embedded nation-wide under-road surveillance sensors at an interchange with Interstate 90 – but due to current events, when we got a team up there, whatever it was... was long-gone. If it's any consolation, our embedded deep-cover people with the Southern California initiative, are reporting better results. The Army-sensors are showing close proximity to the box – but their problem is, they don't know what parties have physical control over it. They're undertaking flanking-maneuvers to isolate the unit and were planning to launch a vertical-envelopment operation, but then the chain of command failed, so they're basically waiting for orders. That's what we've got so far, sir."

"So what you're telling me," interrogated the director, "Is... I've only got *one* at my disposal. And two others, in the hands of parties as yet unknown."

"I'm afraid that's the case, sir," offered the remote voice. "Of course we're doing everything we can to get good intel on the other assets. The minute we get updated information, you'll have it."

There was another short pause, for perhaps two or three seconds, and then the remote voice asked, "Sir... you still there?"

"Yes," came back the passionless answer.

"What are your supplementary orders, sir?" inquired the other.

"Two things," evenly remarked the director.

"Yes, sir?" said the remote voice.

"One," stated the director, "Get the Emergency Actions Group to the selected location, on the double."

"Communication is already on the way, sir," obliged the voice. "And your other order, sir?"

"Let the rest of the Agency know," the director said, "That we've got a *country* – and a military – to run, now."

Flight-Plan And Bad Outcome, Confirmed

She had expected an attack at any proximate time – and had repeatedly consulted her mysterious, apparently-alien-crafted *alter ego* for signs of just such – but it had been well over forty minutes since Minnie Chu had her last, stiffly-tense conversations with what remained of the military, on-board the aircraft.

Amazingly, she had been able to suppress the nauseating sense of guilt that beset her, upon seeing the destruction that her alien-powers had inflicted on her hapless opponents.

You taught me well, Storied Watcher – taught me how to kill, and how not to puke my guts out, in so doing.

Bully for you!

Though Chu was amazed (and, frankly, gratified) that no more assaults seemed to be forthcoming, there was, all the while, a nagging and steadily-growing sense of foreboding; and – strangely – it had nothing to do with that "Brown" guy who had claimed to be the leader of the Presidential guard-force.

Rather, all that she could see in her mind, on those fleeting moments when she took her focus off the door and concentrated on the special sight, was the scowling face of Crowford, the religious-adviser.

He's just a corrupt, self-promoting, dime-a-dozen preacher, she reflected.

I could beat the crap out of him just with the martial-arts training that Karéin taught me, never mind with the Fire...

Why does he give me the Willies, so much? Makes no sense...

Anyway – so let's think this through, one last time... damn it anyway, I never planned to take over the bloody airplane, and now I've got to figure out what to do with it... fucking President and his toadies are cowering in the corner, like the nice little pricks they've always been, deep-down... got the remaining Air Force boys bringing the comm systems back on-line, that one over there's saying that they should have minimum capability in a minute or two, but of course I got no way of knowing if what's being shown is all faked... guess I'll just have to trust my instincts, and Warden's... what's that?

Yeah, son, I know... Mommy is making this up as she goes, but don't worry – we'll be okay...

Just wish I could say that for the rest of them...

Now as to plans... yeah, that's the only way... bring her down to a safe landing somewhere far away from population-centers or risky areas like refineries or power plants – but where?

"Hey... you!" she called out to one of the Air Force flunkies, a nondescript white guy with auburn hair in a brush-cut and a hint of freckles.

Isn't he the guy who let me use his communicator? she tried to remember.

"Yeah – *you!*" she directed.

After a second or two of the "deer-in-headlights" look, the man responded.

"What you want, Ma'am?" he said. "Just don't shoot, okay?"

Damn... if they aren't all terrified *of me,* Chu noted, with a sense of grim satisfaction.

So am I...

"I need to know the complete picture," she demanded. "Altitude, speed, heading, fuel remaining to 'Bingo' – the works. And a damage-report, please."

"I don't think I can –", the man started; but one quick stare by Chu's malevolently-glowing eyes set him to rights, and he quickly circled and began to work the console.

"The systems got impacted by – uhh – that recent incident," he claimed, "And I can't access some data, like the damage-register – looks like it's been re-routed, which shouldn't be a surprise, Ma'am... that's what they *do*, you know. The Service, I mean."

Is he telling me the truth, Warden? she inquired.

Thinks he so, came back the answer.

"*Sure* it's what they do," she persisted. "And you saw how well that worked out for them, against Yours Truly. Don't tell me what you *don't* know – tell me what you *do* know."

"Uhh... right," nervously replied the Air Force worker. "So... here's what I've got : heading 102 degrees east by south-east, 380 knots airspeed, we're at 36,200 feet and slowly descending from that, bit less than a hundred feet per minute... not sure why but it might be damage-control – lessen the structural load on the pressure-hull, you know –"

"Wait a minute," interrupted Chu. "Where are we now? And where will our course take us? Oh – and do you still have a track on the Jacobson aircraft?"

"Working... working on it... controls are unusually slow to respond, Ma'am," the guy evaded. "There it is, assuming that the GPS isn't being spoofed – looks like we're over, uhh, Ohio... between Dayton and Columbus, specifically. We've got fuel for at least another 12 hours airborne, if we don't hook up with a tanker. What was the other thing...?"

"The course – where we're going," impatiently prodded the more-than-a-woman. "And the Jacobson plane – where is it, and where's it headed, now?"

"Oh – right!" he unhelpfully answered. "Our course will take us – now *there's* an odd one – right over D.C., in a little under an hour or so, assuming that our airspeed and direction don't change. Normally that's prohibited, of course, but we're the Old Man's ship, so I guess we get a 'bye' from the special airspace rules. As to the Jacobson one... just a minute, got to update the track... there it is, and... uhh..."

Chu's psychic alarm-bells went all-at-once ballistic.

What the hell? she pondered.

Omigod – did they shoot him down?

She half-sprinted, half-levitated over to where the Air Force man had been working at the console. The big, circular display to which the unfortunate Blanshard had introduced her was still working, albeit with a large crack in its transparent outer-surface and with occasional bursts of static that intermittently obscured much of the imagery.

"What's going on with it – the Jacobson aircraft, that is?" she half-shouted.

"Nothing," the guy replied, "Although it looks like it got in and out of a couple of big fire-fights – Holy Crap, lady, look at the count of our airborne assets left, we've lost, like half our fighters, and now the Air Force is preparing –"

"That's *classified* – shut your *mouth!*" came Warnock's unrequited voice, from his wallside place at the other end of the room.

In the next second, the *faux*-FBI-head was struck hard by a burst of *something* – it might have been pure psychic hate, but was more likely a shock-wave of air compressed by Chu's *Amaiish* – leaving Warnock bowled-over and gasping for breath, as if the wind had been knocked out of him.

"That was the *weakest* attack that I can use," loudly growled Chu. "Any *more* smart-ass challenges to my authority here?"

To nobody's surprise, there did not appear to be any.

"Okay, buster," the more-than-a-woman pressed, "What are you seeing? I need *everything* – now!"

He cowered for a second and then explained, "The – the Jacobson aircraft seems to still be airborne but at a pretty low altitude, just enough to clear the tops of the mountains in fact, to the south of Charleston, and it's heading on a course over central West Virginia – see here, on the display?"

He pointed at the "red circle" icon that was in the middle of the view-field.

"Yeah," said Chu, "So what? I've seen that before."

"It's... not *that* one, Ma'am," the Air Force guy commented. "See this one, over here?"

Shit – the "special weapon" that Blanchard told me about, before all the shooting started, she recalled.

The one marked with the purple diamond... wait... icon looks different...

"You see how its heading has changed, to intercept the Jacobson plane? It's about 400 kilometers to proximity, assuming that both planes maintain their current courses and airspeeds," he nervously remarked. "And that little check-mark inside it? Inside the diamond, I mean?"

"Yes," she confirmed, with both a human sense of dread and the special-senses, ringing mental alarm-bells.

Damn thing's much closer to us than it is to Jacobson, she silently mused.

"It means, 'the weapon's fully armed', Ma'am," carefully stated the Air Force guy. "435 kilotons maximum selectable yield, 250 standard. It can be fired at any time."

"What the *hell?*" Chu angrily exclaimed. "It takes the *President* to do that!"

She turned her gaze to the former Vice-President, his back to the wall next to the slowly-recovering Warnock.

"Was it *you?*" she spat. "Some kind of secret order? To launch it at Jacobson? I swear to God, *this* time, I won't do you the fast way – I'll fucking burn your corpse to *ashes*, inch by inch, until –"

"*No – no!*" the terrified man stammered. "You've been here all the time – you've *seen* me! The plan was always to use it against Jacobson if he got too close to Washington or New York, and anyway... it *can't* be armed just on a verbal command – it takes, like, those key-cards in the 'football' and so on!"

Warden... same question as before, Chu quickly requested.

And the answer was the same.

Scared make up story too is he, the little voice opined.

"Well if it *wasn't* you, asshole," interrogated the more-than-a-woman, "Then who *did* give the order to arm a nuclear weapon and prepare it for use, right over the continental *United States?* Answer me *that!*"

"The – the only person that I know of who could do that," the *faux*-President claimed, "Would be my predecessor... Clark, that is. He's the only one who'd have the codes, and whose authority would be recognized. But... he's, uhh, 'indisposed' – he's not in a position to communicate with the Air Force in this way... I made *sure* of that."

"That's a non-answer," countered Chu. "Either you're lying – surprise, surprise! – or you don't have a clue about how the system really works, and there's some other way to do it. Fine, then… how do we turn it off? Abort the launch, I mean."

The Air Force guy at the sensor-display spoke up.

"That requires a countermand order, on a special secured channel, from the President, as well, Ma'am," he offered. "But it's only good until the weapon is launched. After that, the only way to stop it is to *shoot* it down – and because it has a proximity shock fuse, not a good idea to be anywhere nearby, when that happens. We had to set them up this way to stop the enemy from neutralizing all our weapons, just by spoofing the President's countermand. I'm sure you can see the logic in all this?"

"That kind of 'logic', mister," retorted an aghast Chu, "Might just get millions of people *killed*, tonight! Look – I want you to set up the 'countermand' channel from this plane… from here, in this room. Get working on it – right now!"

"I'll *try*," he pledged.

Under Chu's baleful supervision, the Air Force staffer worked feverishly for a minute or two, manipulating various dials and controls while occasionally entering what appeared to be codes on two nearby, specialized keyboards.

Then the man let out a loud "sigh" and leaned back in his shock-absorbing chair.

"What is it?" demanded Chu.

"Dead-end, Ma'am," he muttered.

"What do you mean?" she pressed.

Throwing up one hand in a gesture of frustration, he replied, "So… here's how it is. Normally, our S.O.P. is to enable the encrypted, point-to-point command-link to the launch vehicle – a stealth-bomber, in this case – and then the Commander-In-Chief – that is, the President over there –"

"Don't flatter him with that title," interrupted Chu. "Soon his only 'title' will be on a prison-suit."

"Whatever you *say*, Ma'am," the Air Force guy continued, "The thing is, he'd have to enter his ID-code, along with biometric validation, and then he'd have to issue a personal code to take the weapon off-line. It's quite a bit easier to do that, than it is to authorize launching one, for obvious reasons. What's happening *here* is… I've got the command-link sort of working – had to re-route it on a different channel, the primary's damaged and not responding – but something's blocking the unlock-sequence at the other end. So even if the… uhh… 'President' there were to do his part – no dice, I'm afraid."

"That's not *good* enough!" the more-than-a-woman shot back. "How the hell can it be 'blocked at the other end'? Who could do that? *Answer* me, or I'll –"

The man put up both hands in a "surrender"-gesture.

"*Look*, lady," he protested, "You can kill me or everyone here if you want… but it's not going to change *anything*. I got no idea what's blocking it – near as I can tell, something, or someone, has changed the preliminary access-codes to the countermand subsystems – if it's of any interest, that's *supposed* to be impossible, outside of the normal change of Commander-In-Chief functions when there's, like, a new President or whatever, from what I've been told. There's nothing that you, I or the President can do, to stop this thing. Other than to get physically on top of the weapon, open it up and pull the right chips out of its arming-circuitry – and if you pull the *wrong* ones... well, I'm sure you can guess what happens *then*."

"Yeah," ruefully acknowledged Chu, "I sure *do*. Okay, then – we're not finished with this, not by a long-shot, and I want you to keep me informed on a minute-by-minute basis if anything changes in what we see going on with this damnable 'special weapon' or its launch-vehicle – but in the meantime, open a communications-channel to the Jacobson plane –"

"Cancel that order!" angrily interjected an apparently-recovered Warnock. "There's to be no communication with that gang of traitors!"

Chu strode over to a spot about six feet from where Warnock was slowly coming to his feet, with a look of defiance on his face.

"You're in no position to issue orders – or to cancel them," she growled.

And in a warning-gesture taught to her back in the Canadian forests, she energized the *Fire* and caused a red-glowing pencil-beam of hot (but not lethal) energy to project from her shining eyes, right at Warnock's heart, she hissed, "I can cut you in half, with just a *thought*, you know."

"Then why don't you *do* it?" he challenged. "Must be easy for you?"

"Because – unlike you – I'm not into murder," admitted Chu, as she extinguished her latent attack. "I don't wantonly slaughter people just because they annoy me. At least... I'm not doing so... *yet*. That doesn't mean, however, that I won't kill, in self-defense. As you've no doubt seen."

The imposter FBI-director wisely refrained from any more repartee.

After a second or two of tense silence, the Air Force guy at the console interjected, "I don't think I can raise them, anyway. Comms-link is working okay... but they're rejecting all hails. We're calling, but they ain't answering. Considering that they've been under attack, I can't really blame 'em... the traffic could be used as a homing-beacon for an ARM-shot."

"Don't we have any way of over-riding that?" demanded a frustrated Chu.

"Not from here, Ma'am," he explained. "If we get within about 30 kilometers, line-of-sight, we can try a focused, directional transmission-beam into their analog backup radios... even if the digital primaries are switched off, we could get a few quick voice messages to play over their internal speakers, before they physically disconnected those. We can also try to force short digital messages – like, maybe 80 or so characters per transmission – into their on-board air-data status-displays, from further away, like about 60 to 80 clicks or so. Jacobson would have to disable those systems entirely to avoid seeing them, which wouldn't be a good idea, because they're the same ones that tell him, for example, if the engines are still working. But that's risky because the status-display might topple if we overload its buffer. In that case it's borked until they land, power it down altogether and then reset it. And..."

"'And'... what?" asked the former FBI team-leader.

"Well, Ma'am," the Air Force guy pointed out, "Remember what they've got pointed at them. If it went off anywhere near their ship, with us only 30 kilometers away – we *do* have full EMP-shielding on this airplane, but we might not survive the heat-flash and the blast-wave from a weapon like that, especially if it's turned up to maximum yield. And we've taken some damage from the, uhh, 'fire-fight' that just happened here... our structural-integrity's probably already been compromised. Getting close enough to the Jacobson plane would be *very* risky, if the weapon's released against them."

"That's a chance we'll have to take," grimly resolved Chu. "Set a course."

"You're i*nsane – nobody* can survive a nuclear explosion!" caterwauled the *faux*-President, from his wallside cowering-place.

Chu did not have to walk far, to confront him.

"*I* did," she proudly offered, with a faint *Fire*-glow in the back of her eyes. "Admittedly, with a little help from my alien-friends, Sylvia Abruzzio in particular. And I'm stronger – *much* stronger – now, than I was then. I can't survive right next to Ground, or Air, Zero – that I'll admit – but I *can* put up with being far closer than what would kill a normal human being. Oh, and I'd bet you good money that if this aircraft comes apart, I can just float slowly down to Earth, none the worse for wear, parachute or none. I suspect that Sam and his group are the same way. I just have to warn them in time, so they can prepare themselves."

"Well thanks for the kind consideration, Ma'am," complained the Air Force guy. "If all that happens... what are the rest of us supposed to do? Flap our wings, or something?"

"That's *your* problem, I guess," insouciantly parried Chu. "Maybe you should have thought of it, when you decided to camp on with Fearless Leader, here."

She did a head-gesture toward the *faux*-President.

"I *knew* you were a spy, and a traitor, sent here to do Jacobson's dirty work!" he accused. "This just *proves* it!"

"You're completely wrong about that," she countered, "I started out on my quest trying to *oppose* Jacobson, for all the good it did me. But go ahead and believe whatever you want to believe."

She turned her attention to the Air Force guy and repeated, "Set a course."

"Want the good news or the bad news, Ma'am?" he answered.

"Both," she requested.

"The *bad* news is," he explained, "There's no way to fly the plane from here, at least not with the auto-pilot systems over-ridden the way they are – Secret Service probably did that. To change the flight-path you'd have to be up front, sitting in the Captain's chair. To do *that*, you'd have to get past the Marine guard and the Service, who'd be between you and the cockpit... maybe you *could* do so, but your, uhh, 'death-ray' might either shoot out the main flight deck controls, or breach the forward windshields, or both. Either of those would crash us almost immediately. So..."

"And the *good* news...?" asked the more-than-a-woman.

"Well – again, assuming that nothing changes," the Air Force guy elaborated, "Our present course will take us pretty close to them – certainly within 100 kilometers to the east of them, possibly a lot less than that – it all depends on if they stay airborne or put down temporarily, which we've seen them do before."

"Swell... I *think*," mordantly commented Chu. "What happens if this 'special weapon' launcher sees this plane in close proximity to the Jacobson one? Wouldn't that prevent it from firing? I mean – don't we have some kind of kill-switch built into this airborne command-post?"

"No," stated the *faux*-President, from his hiding-place. "I ordered the military's command-and-control systems to assign top over-ride priority to eliminating Jacobson's 'Mars Gang'. Blanshard and DeWitt didn't like that, because it also over-rides the 'no-shoot' gizmos that they've got on this plane, and in the White House too, for that matter. But it was a national priority... and still is, in my opinion."

Staring into space, Chu offered, "You really *are* one vindictive son of a bitch – aren't you? Is there *anything* in this world more important to you, than slaughtering the passengers in Sam's plane? I wonder if your fingerprints will work for the biometric stuff, once I shoot your hand off at the wrist..."

The *faux*-President didn't reply.

"Okay... so here's where we are, as I see it," opined the more-than-a woman, to no-one in particular. "You're all my hostages here, and I can blow this plane to bits any time I want, but I can't change its flight-plan without convincing our pilots, who no doubt have the guns of the Secret Service pointed at their heads. There's a nuke armed and ready that might be fired at the Jacobson aircraft – or at us, for that matter – at any time, and if it goes off while Sam's plane or our own, happen to be flying over a city, 'bye-bye city', *et cetera*. Have I missed anything?"

"Yeah," mischievously asked the Air Force guy, "Assuming that we're stuck in here for the duration... what if we gotta use the bathroom?"

"Ask the Secret Service to deliver a bucket, and a privacy-screen," replied Chu. "Did I mention that the Storied Watcher taught her followers how to 'hold it', almost indefinitely? As long as we don't eat or drink a lot, while so doing."

"Super-power, Ma'am," he commented.

"While you're working on what we were just discussing," directed Chu, "I want you to get all the communications-systems working. I want to be able to speak with anyone and everyone – and I *do* mean, 'everyone', particularly whatever's left of the military chain of command, like, DeWitt and so on – the minute that I need to do it. Understood?"

"Yes, ma'am," he courteously agreed. "And for what it's worth, I don't think that'll be as much of a problem as the, uhh, 'other thing'. A few circuits are blocked but I should be able to route around 'em."

"Well then, I guess you've earned your pay, quantified in 'hours more to live'," coolly offered the more-than-a-woman.

Then, there was a knock on the door leading to the outside corridor.

"Who is it?" called Chu. "No 'surprises', please... unless you'd like to be quickly vaporized."

"Well, my dear," came the ominously-smooth voice of Harold Crowford, "'Surprise' or not... I think it's more *you* who should be worryin' about that... not lil' ol' *me*."

The Hendricks Finger

There had been a lively debate in the far corner of the shopping-center parking-lot, after a frustrated and abashed Boatman and Hendricks had finally managed to lose the annoyingly-inquisitive family from the restaurant. The two former FBI agents had argued for running with lights out, but had been tutored otherwise by Boyd, who quipped, "boys... when *I* turn it on, you'll be wishing that all you were staring at, was somebody else's high-beams".

That – and the risk of being mistaken for booze- and drug-runners, as noted by Dorsie – convinced the agents that they'd be better off just driving to Fayetteville like everybody else did.

In any event, it was a short drive to the settled parts of the town, and soon, on Boyd's directions, they turned right on North Court Street, headed left on Fayette Avenue, and then – just as the others were starting to worry that the former Mars mission pilot had somehow lost his bearings – they were directed to take a right on to Sarah Street; about 30 seconds later, Boyd brought them to a stop in a wide-open, park-like area.

He stepped out and surveyed the scenery.

A second later, his children heard one of Boyd's rarely-used curse words.

"Shit!" he complained, looking to the north. "I thought this place would be dead, what with the curfew – but there's a baseball-game going on, at the farthest-away of those three diamonds up there to the north."

"Hard to miss with all those lights illuminating the field, dear," patiently observed his wife.

"I took you all to the Fayetteville Huse Memorial Park because I figured it would be an easy place for Jacobson to land, Laura," he replied, "Assuming, of course, that his airplane's still in one piece. And we're kind of at the edge of town, so hopefully less, uhh, 'disturbance factor'. Sam would probably reason the same way – at least that's what I was hoping. But *here*... damn, I don't know. Maybe the game will end soon..."

"Daddy," whined one of the Boyd children, "Don't *like* it here! It's a cemetery*!*"

"We won't be here very long, Nicky, hun," he parried. "And I figured that we'd have a little more privacy here."

Both Hendricks and Boatman, just debarked from vehicles, strained their Mars eyes.

"Hate to burst your bubble, Brent," remarked the third agent, "But the sign up there on the baseball field says 'Third Inning'..."

"Yeah," admitted Boyd. "Well... we're here now... might as well make the best of it."

The mountain-man, Boatman and Hendricks looked back and forth among them.

"So... what's *that* mean, man?" insouciantly asked the third agent.

"What do you *mean*... 'what's that mean'?" retorted Boyd.

"What I mean is... 'what do we do *now*, dude'?" asked Hendricks. "Like... just sit around and wait until Mr. Jacobson the Mars Mission Spelunker, somehow finds us down here, 50 feet from the headstone farm?"

There was an uneasy silence for a few seconds, and then Boatman spoke.

"Now Brent," inquired the big black agent, "I know we done talked about this before, but... I guess you all never *did* have a good plan about hitchin' up with Jacobson and this-here 'airplane' of his... did you? What I'm sayin' is... the man might have already landed somewhere else in this town already for all we know. Unless we want to get back in the car and hunt down each and every street, lookin' for some damn vertical take-off plane parked in the back of a lot... well, *you* get the idea. But we gotta *do* something... don't we?"

Again, the "you-go-first" looks went back and forth, a state of affairs that was ended when the ever-helpful Hendricks suggested, "So Brent – didn't you tell us that you'd, uhh, 'go topside', to check things out and to guide Sam and his crate, back to where we're at?"

"Yeah," agreed Boyd, "I did."

"Well?" teased the third agent.

"Well... *what?*" parried the exasperated Mars mission pilot.

"So show us what you've got... you know, 'up, up and awaay' kind of thing," demanded Hendricks. "Just look down and you're bound to see a parked plane somewhere in... where *are* we, again... oh, yeah... in Fayetteville."

"But –" started Boyd.

He was interrupted by Dorsie, who quipped, "Aw, come *on*, boys... 'man flyin' off into the sky, all by himself – whoever *heard* of such a thang, anyways? Didn't y'all figure out that he's shittin' ya?"

Stung by the smart-ass needling, Boyd countered, "Okay, okay – I *get* it! But... uhh... listen guys... we'd better make plans, because when I power her up – enough to get airborne, I mean – it's going to attract *attention*, and you had better have a good story cooked up when the Great Unwashed come running up asking 'what the H was *that*'... you know? I'll slink off to the other end of the park and try to take off from inside that stand of trees – hope I don't cream myself on a branch, on the way up – but when and if I guide Sam and the others back here, well, at that point, we're going to have a crowd-control issue for sure. Understood?"

"Could be worse… we could be doin' this in Times Square," noted Boatman.

"Daddy – are you going to *fly*? Up in the air?" shouted an excited Wendy Boyd.

"Yes, sweetheart… I am," he confirmed, with a smile and a nod of the head.

"I want to come *with* you!" she demanded.

"I'd love to take you," he demurred, "But it's *much* too dangerous – I might run into some of those bad men with the guns, and it's also quite cold up in the night sky, Wendy dear. So it'll have to be some other time –"

"I was meaning on asking you about that," asked a jealous and fascinated Hendricks. "How come you don't freeze your balls off up there? I mean, Otis and I nearly did, and we were just dropping down –"

"Honestly don't know," shrugged the former Mars astronaut. "I *do* feel it a bit when I'm just speeding up, and then… hard to explain… it's like something just kicks in… and then I'm okay. I think she said something back in the camp, about 'your personal weirding-shield' or whatever?"

"It's all bull-crap, anyways," grunted Dorsie. "Only way that boy's gonna get into the sky, is if somebody loads him into a big ol' cannon and points it upwards."

"Want to bet on that?" challenged Boyd, with a determined look in his eye.

"Since all that shit went down back there, I ain't got nothin' left to bet *with*," ruefully acknowledged the mountain-man. "But if I did… I'd bet y'all a case of my finest 'shine, that y'all can't go no further than a man can jump off his feet."

"Tell you what, Dorsie," proposed Boyd. "I'll give you credit for that moonshine, and I'll put up a case of Jim Beam, from any local liquor store, to cover my bet. Deal?"

"You're on, Mister Space Man," said Dorsie.

"Better start brewin', my friend," counseled Boatman with a wry smile, as Boyd hoofed it in the direction of the woods at the far end of the Fayetteville Huse Memorial Park.

About thirty seconds later, the convoy-members heard Boyd's exciting, pounding war-song – acoustically far-off, yet somehow, intuitively right next to them – and saw something that looked much like a yellow-white Roman candle streaking skyward up to an altitude of a few thousand feet.

The glowing-thing – which illuminated the otherwise-dark overhead sky as if five full moons had suddenly appeared – leveled off and began flying an expanding, circular pattern, which activity continued for almost a full minute; it paused for a few seconds, as if surveying the situation, and then, with the same war-song playing but in subdued fashion, came straight for the convoy, stopping about fifty feet above.

Nervously, Boatman glanced over at the baseball-game. His worries were justified; the game had stopped in mid-inning and a few of those who had been watching from outside the protective mesh-screens surrounding the diamond, had started trotting toward the former FBI agent and the other travelers.

The others had to squint and partially cover eyes with hands, to even be able to comfortably look at Boyd.

His figure, and demeanor, was overpowering. Every inch of his skin was glowing, as were his eyes in even more brilliant fashion, and he was surrounded by a shining aura that made many think of the Heavenly Host.

"Tell Dorsie that he owes me some moonshine," amiably quipped the flying-more-than-human, from his aerial vantage-point.

"I ain't *never*..." gasped the mountain-man. "How the hell you *do* that, man?" he called back.

"How do you get up on your feet and walk to the kitchen for breakfast?" returned Boyd. "About the same thing... give or take a few hundred miles per hour and a few thousand feet."

"Oh my *God*, Brent," echoed his wife. "It's... *true*, then?"

He nodded, regally.

"But remember what I told you, Laura," he added. "About... *us*."

It was her turn to mutely nod acknowledgment, mixed with fear of the unfamiliar.

"Wow, Daddy – *wow!*" gushed Wendy Boyd. "You're *flying!*"

"When this is all over, I'll take all of you for a ride – *promise!*" the former Mars mission pilot pledged. "Anyway... I can see that you're going to have some company soon – tell them whatever you need, to bafflegab 'em – but I looked pretty much everywhere that a 'plane could be hiding here in Fayetteville, Mars eyes and Earth eyes together... nothing."

"You think he could have beaten us here, seen nobody waitin' for him, and then high-tailed off for wherever?" asked Boatman.

Like most, he was craning his neck backward to look upward.

"Or, maybe the Air Force finally got them, once and for all," ominously added Hendricks.

"Anything's possible," observed Boyd. "But knowing Sam, Wolf, Devon and particularly Cherie as I do... I refuse to believe *that* outcome."

"So what we do now?" asked the third agent. "Like maybe you sit up there glowing like the Mother Of All Patio-Lanterns, and let Jacobson and Company home in on you?"

"Over my dead body," countered Boyd, "And that's probably how it would end up – it wouldn't be Sam homing in on us... more likely that it'd be the whole damn Air Force! I *obviously* can't expose Laura and the children to that kind of risk, to say nothing of being a sitting-duck target, giving up the element of mobility I mean. Tell you what – I'll fly a search-pattern centered on Fayetteville, high enough so that I can get a good vantage-point on air traffic in the vicinity. I'm pretty sure I can distinguish the IR-, radiation- and magnetic-signature of the V-37 from other airplanes – particularly, civilian ones. If Sam's rig is anywhere within a hundred miles, hopefully I'll see it... and then I'll guide him back to Fayetteville. Okay?"

"Well, what're we s'posed to do, while this's all happenin' up there, Mister... uhh... Mister Lighthouse?" complained the mountain-man. "Them folks from the ball game's gonna be here in less'n a minute. We s'posed to bake 'em a cake or somethin'?"

"Let you in on a secret, Dorsie," confidently expounded Boyd. "My nick-name's 'Sunburn'... not 'Lighthouse'. You can call me that, or just 'Brent', either will do –"

"Shit's goin' to his head," muttered Boatman, in Hendricks' ear.

"He probably heard that with these damn Mars ears, you know," the third agent whispered back.

"No offense taken, and super-powers well under control," Boyd amiably called back. "Laura – can you get everybody back in the cars and head to the Morris Harvey B&B that you were originally going to meet me at? Provided that the VTOL stuff is still working, there are parking-lots around there that the V-37 can just fit in to... and that place is at West Maple and Harvey, so it's a decent distance from where we're at now, just for safety's sake."

He looked backward, pirouetting effortlessly in mid-air.

"Oops – they're almost here," he warned. "Better get going – head away from the Harvey House at first, so they get mixed up if they try to follow you," he directed.

"Okay, kids – you heard what Daddy said," instructed Laura Boyd, as she began ushering the wee folk back into her car.

"But I wanted to tell those people that Daddy's a *superhero!*" whined the younger Master Boyd.

"They already *know*, dear," reassured the mother, as she double-timed the task of clipping them into car-seats.

The former Mars mission pilot began powering up his inner *Fire* in preparation for full speed, a move that brought his electro-rock war-song to nearly maximum-volume; it was accompanied by his aura waxing to overwhelming brilliance.

"Hey, Mister 'Sunburn'," shouted a plainly-envious Hendricks (whose eyes were locked in an odd stare at the flying ex-astronaut), "How long's this all going to take? Like... how long are we waiting at this 'Harvey House' place?"

"Take as long as it takes," shrugged Boyd. "Longer, if I have to knock down some fighters – shorter, if not. Leave some space in the lot for an airplane, bring a good book to read, and lie convincingly if anybody asks what you're doing."

"God keep you safe, my love," whispered his wife, as Brent Boyd rocketed upward at scarcely-believable speed.

Boatman had taken the wheel, and he almost hit two pedestrians from the baseball-game as he hurtled out of the cemetery street-system. The maneuver had been necessary, however, to keep the convoy all together, with Laura Boyd's SUV in front, the APC in the rear and the commandeered police-car in the middle.

The big black former FBI agent was mumbling discord as he navigated through the dark streets of Fayetteville, mimicking the turns and driving-tactics of the two leading-vehicles.

"I don't know, Will," he remarked. "Don't think it was a good idea to put Dorsie all by himself, in that-there squad-car. He bolts on us... yes, we *can* stop him – but I don't want either another human life on my account, not to mention a big ol' mess to get the local police on our backs, and then maybe yet more of this 'alien' shit, and yet more dead bodies..."

"He'll be *fine* – don't sweat it, man," claimed the third agent. "He knows perfectly well that he gets caught as a fugitive murderer driving the same wheels as his cop-victims – they *ain't* gonna read him his rights, before they fill that car full of lead. He parks it and runs... his chances aren't much better. *You* know how the game's played."

"Well, you better hope you're right," grumbled Boatman. "Anyway – why was it so important for you to hop aboard this-here Army-rig, in the first place? You just sick of how that boy smells or something?"

"Nope... nothing like that... but I wanted you to be the first to know," mysteriously offered Hendricks. "Just our little secret, kind of thing."

"What you *talkin'* about, Will?" complained the black ex-agent. "I had enough riddles and secrets goin' on this week to last me a lifetime and a half, you know."

"Keep your eyes on the road," requested the third agent. "While I show you something."

"Okay..." obliged Boatman, as he turned a corner in lock-step with the stolen squad-car ahead.

"Need somebody to light your way?" maliciously commented Hendricks, as he held up an index-finger.

Its yellow glow, extending from the fingertip to the knuckle, illuminated the interior of the APC, as if someone had just turned on a small flashlight.

A Friendly Chat About Armageddon

The Oval Office was no stranger to atmospheres of tension and crisis, of course; but what was going on now, was one of the foremost examples thereof.

As he had been doing for well over an hour, the President paced back and forth behind the Resolute Desk, stopping every second or third trip to steal a quick look through the curtains, to the dimly-illuminated lawns outside.

"You shouldn't be *doing* that, sir," reminded Abruzzio. "Dangerous. Somebody could take a *shot* at you."

"*Everything's* 'dangerous', Ms. Abruzzio," he parried. "Some things... just a little more than others, and I'm sure that the top of the Monument that she dropped in the White House grounds – damn her anyway – will nicely block the line of sight. Anyway – there's been *plenty* of time, by now. Where the hell *is* this 'Jacobson' guy? All he has to do is find a phone, and –"

"Well, the military *has* been trying to *kill* him, for the past few weeks running, you know," she pointed out. "That might make him a little, uhh, 'cautious' about giving them an easy way to pin-point him... don't you think?"

"No, I *don't*," he testily replied. "If he heard the speech then he knows that the miltary's been told to stand down, at least for the time being. This is his one chance – he'd better take it."

He quickly glanced at his wrist-communicator, then sent an interrogatory look at the Secret Service agent-in-charge.

"Any news, Curt? Anything *new*, I mean?" asked the U.S. leader.

The Service man started to shake his head, but abandoned the motion halfway. He called down the hall, in the direction of the communications-center.

"You *got* something?" he called.

"Yeah," came back a voice. "An intercept... seems to be from the, uhh, old President's ship, over Ohio right now. I'll patch it through."

"*This* will be fun," muttered the President, "But I suppose I'll have to confront George at some point... might as well be now."

At first, what they heard was just static, and this lasted an uncomfortably long time – probably twenty to thirty seconds, prompting bewildered gestures from the President – at length, they heard a distorted though still understandable, female voice.

"Mr. Secretary," it went, "It's *imperative* that you get the military to deal with this, *immediately!* If not –"

"That sounds a lot like Minnie!" whispered Abruzzio to Kaysten and the President.

"What do you want me to *do*, Madam?" retorted another, male voice. "I *told* you –"

"That's Arthur... the Secretary of Defense," noted the President, while trying to keep half his attention on the conversation.

"He on our side... I mean, *your* side, sir?" asked Sullivan.

"Don't know," responded the U.S. leader.

"Rainbow" let out an enthusiastic "yip", which brought out a few smiles, even from the Service agents.

"I can't stop the damn thing, from where I'm sitting – something's jamming the command-signals," continued the stressed-sounding female voice. "I even got your former 'President' to try to enter his codes, but they aren't working either. Mr. Secretary... if they launch it and you can't issue an abort, it's going to home in on Jacobson and it *will* detonate, wherever he happens to be at the time. Do you understand? *Do you understand!*"

"Jesus, Joseph and Mary!" gasped Abruzzio. "I don't like what I'm hearing..."

"*Look*, Madam," growled the male voice, "Let's be blunt about this... shall we? I'm talking to a *terrorist* who – by her own admission – has just *murdered* several members of the Airborne Command Post's crew, who then hijacked the plane, and who comes to me with pleas to spare Jacobson's gang of traitors, who – if what she says even *is* true, and of *that* I'm far from convinced – from a nuclear missile that may or may not be targeted against them. Why would I give you the time of *day*, Madam – much less, the ability to over-ride our most important military command-codes?"

"Can we break in to the dialog?" shouted the President. "Do it *now!*"

Kortish repeated the instruction to his contact down the hall.

"It's point-to-point," called back the communications-expert in the office. "I'll try to force it into a multi-cast, using the speakers and microphones in the Oval Office... either it works or it doesn't... here goes..."

The static sounded louder for a few seconds, and all around – save Abruzzio, who was staring straight-forward with a multi-colored back-light in her eyes and her war-song playing at very low volume – worried that the signal had been lost entirely.

"Did it drop? Get it *back!*" demanded the President.

"Still there, sir," pre-empted Abruzzio. "Give them a second or two – I can feel the data-streams merging – I"m giving them a boost –"

"How is she *doing* that?" whispered an amazed Presidential daughter.

"Oh... we've all got a few little alien-tricks up our sleeves, you know," smirked Kaysten.

"Okay – they're all one stream now – go ahead, Mr. President," instructed Abruzzio.

"This is the President of the United States, speaking from the Oval Office in the White House," he forcefully spoke. "I urgently need to talk to you. Can you both hear me?"

Again, there was a slight delay, but after a second or so, two responses came back.

The female voice said, "What? Who *is* this? How are you..."

The male voice said, "Mr... Mr. *President? Wait* a minute – assuming that this isn't disinformation... you were relieved of your position and your duties!

The President's on the Airborne Command-Post, but he's being held hostage! I can't –"

"For Christ's sake, Arthur – shut up and *listen*, for two seconds... okay?" demanded the President. "I assume that neither you nor whomever else is on this line, saw my address to the nation, a few minutes ago –"

"No," interrupted the male voice. "We've got our hands full right now, but I can't tell you –"

"Fine, then... I'll talk to *her*, instead," growled the President. "Madam – who are you? *Where* are you? What's this about murder, hijacking the Presidential aircraft, and a nuclear weapon?"

"Mr. DeWitt has a point, sir," offered the female voice. "From my point of view, you're simply somebody who's hacked in to the conversation that I was having with the Secretary. What we're discussing is *extremely* sensitive... I can't disclose it without knowing for sure, who you are."

"That's right," added the male voice. "This circuit is protected only by standard ciphers. An experienced attacker could probably break it in a few minutes."

"What the hell do we do *now*?" groaned the President. "She's *got* to –"

"This is Sylvia Abruzzio," called out the more-than-a-woman in the room. "I'm here with the President – Minnie, is that you?"

"Sylvia? *Sylvia?*" came back the astonished response. "*Wait* a minute... not good enough – not good enough by a longshot! You *could* just be someone impersonating her. How would I know..."

"*Really*, Minnie?" riposted Abruzzio. "Here – I'll show you, sister... listen to your headphones – and to your heart!"

Abruzzio's war-song began to wax, and its power and majesty awed even the Service agents. Its graceful, exciting chords came from everywhere and nowhere; they somehow blended with the communications-streams, sounding simultaneously in remote places.

Now another song began to play; it was Chu's equally-impressive one.

After a few seconds, both war-tunes began to ebb.

"*Nobody* else – not even the Storied Watcher herself – could recreate that, and have it sound perfectly like the original," came back the remote female voice. "Mi*god*, Sylvia – it's *so* good to hear from you again! Are you really with the former President? Tell me the truth – because *millions* of lives might depend on it!"

"Yes, I am," answered Abruzzio. "I've also got Jerry Kaysten, Rainbow, *Vîrya I'ëà'b'*, the President's family, and a bunch of other people here with me. I'll fill you in on the story later – but what's going *on* up there?"

"Long story here, too, sister," stated Chu, "I'm on the Executive Branch Command-Post airplane, flying currently over Ohio as I've been told. The son of a bitch who's been calling himself 'President' up here, issued orders to have Otis and Will *murdered*, by throwing them out of the plane at thirty thousand feet. He was about to do the same to me, and... well... I didn't let that *happen*... you know?"

"How would she have *done* that?" whispered the President, to Kaysten. "There's no *way* to smuggle a gun on board that plane!"

"Remember how Little Miss Nuclear Angel, sliced the top off the Monument... you know, that ol' 'shootin' death-rays out of your eyes' stuff?" shrugged the former Chief of Staff. "Well... Minnie's got it down straight, sir."

"*Jesus*," muttered the President.

"I saw her fire it," added Kaysten. "You sure wouldn't want to be in the way, when she lets loose. Not a lot left of you to bury, sir."

Tears were streaming down Abruzzio's face.

Her chin trembling, she softly spoke, "Will... Will, and Otis, too? Are you *sure*?"

"Yeah," came back the equally-subdued answer. "I didn't see it... but I spoke to a bunch of people who did. If it's of any consolation... a few of them that participated in this murder, aren't *with* us, any more. I'm sure you know what I mean."

A grim-faced Abruzzio turned to address the President.

Her eyes were shining ominously, as were "Rainbow's".

A couple of the Secret Service agents moved hands closer to gun-holsters.

"Those were two of the most loyal, patriotic and professional FBI agents that you or I will ever meet, Mr. President!" she angrily remarked. "Their only 'crime' was to have met Karéin, or to have been traveling with Minnie... or with me. They were good men... they were our *friends!* And *this* is how the government thanks them? If you think that I'll –"

"I have it on good authority that there are six or seven dead by this individual's hand, on the Command Post," countered the male voice on the radio-link. "Not counting the scores more that Jacobson and his crew have already murdered. All of *these* were loyal military and Secret Service staff, too."

The President did an exemplary job of suppressing the sweat on his brow, as he tried to head off this line of conversation.

"Ms. Abruzzio, I share your distress at hearing this sad news," he deflected, "And I'll assure you – if crimes were committed here, they'll be prosecuted to the full extent of the law. A *lot* of innocent people have been dying lately, and from what we heard earlier, if we don't act now, we could be facing something *far* worse. Who's your friend? The one who you've been speaking with?"

"I'm Minnie Chu, former FBI team-leader, in charge of the 'Red Rover' project, sir," replied the remote female voice. "And assuming that you're really the President – or *a* President – here's the situation. Like I said, your counterpart up here – the former Vice-President, plus that weasel Warnock who got dropped in over Cesar Ochoa – tried to have me killed; I defended myself with the alien-powers bestowed on me by the Storied Watcher, and in the crossfire, unfortunately, a number of other people died. I feel sick about all this, but if you want someone to blame... talk to the bastard who cruelly murdered Otis and Will, and who then ordered my own pre-meditated murder, for no reason other than 'he doesn't like me'."

"We'll deal with those issues later, Madam," broke in the President. "What else is going on?"

"Well, sir," mentioned Chu, with an unmistakable air of confidence (mixed with trepidation) in her voice, "I'm now more or less in charge of this aircraft, with the significant limitation that I can't change our flight-plans, since I'm barricaded in the communications-shack and not the cockpit. The Marines and Secret Service have announced that they're going to shoot me if I venture forth; I'm not worried about that, because they don't have a *chance* against me, if I decide to unleash my full powers against them. Unfortunately... if I *do*, there's also a very good chance that I'll blow the plane to bits. You with me so far, sir?"

"There's much that I can and will say to you about this, Madam," he seethed, "But do continue. You mentioned something about a nuclear weapon?"

"Yes, sir," she said. "Just before the, uhh, shooting started, I was advised by General Blanshard – by the way, sir, he was wounded in the engagement but was alive the last I saw of him – that under the ex-President's orders, a stealth-bomber equipped with a nuclear-tipped cruise-missile has been readied for use against the small Army transport-plane that Sam Jacobson has been using to travel across the country, in. It looks like the warhead's been armed and all that has to happen is for the bomber to get within firing-range."

"*Armed?* What the *hell*?" stammered the President. "*Who* gave the order to do *that*?"

"We don't know, sir," answered Chu. "Your successor up here swears on a stack of Bibles that *he* didn't issue the order... for whatever *that's* worth. We're trying to over-ride it, but something's blocking us. Mr. Secretary, would you like to give your perspective on this?"

"I *told* you," came back the male voice, "That I can't confirm the identities of anyone on this call –"

"*Stow it*, Arthur!" interrupted the President. "Use your voice-print authenticators if you want, I don't care... but at least tell me – is what she's saying, accurate?"

There was a prolonged silence, and then DeWitt spoke up.

"I'm on shaky grounds in assuming that you have authority to ask, but... unfortunately," he said, "It *does* appear to be. National War Command Control has been re-vectored to a bunch of non-DoD endpoints that we have no control over and which don't show up in our trusted inventory. We're trying to do a trace and de-commit but given the complexity and diversity of the systems involved, that could take days to weeks. In the meantime... if the weapon *is* launched... there's no way that I know of, to stop it."

"My *God*," gasped a horrified President. "Arthur... do you have any idea of where the intercept-point might be? Where it might go off, that is. And is this the only one?"

"I suppose I'll be court-marshaled for divulging this information over a not fully-secured channel," sighed the Secretary, "But our best guess right now, given Jacobson's last-plotted flight-route and optimal intercept-course for the bomber, would be somewhere between Harrisonburg and Manassas, Virginia. Could be *anywhere*, however, if he changes course. And other than for one other device – Mr. President, I think you know which one I'm referring to here, and I can't say any more in a meeting like this – the one on the bomber is the only one that we have ready for deployment. We're working on several new ones, however."

"Well isn't *that* just wonderful – the 'several more bombs' part, that is," said Sullivan, *sotto voce*.

"Manassas... that's in the suburbs of D.C.... isn't it?" observed Abruzzio.

"About ten miles or so, from here," noted Kaysten.

"How powerful is the warhead?" quietly asked the President.

"Can be anywhere from 200 to about 430 kilotons, sir," stated DeWitt. "That's between 10 and 25 times the yield of the Hiroshima bomb, basically."

"Sylvia... didn't you say that up on the island, you..." started Kaysten.

"Yeah, Jerry, I did – but I had many other people to help me, and remember, I can really only stop most of the radiation and some of the heat... not the blast-wave," she cautioned. "And I was protecting a *much* smaller area than what we're talking about here. Remember what we told you happened to the GrayWar guys that got caught out in the open, up there?"

"Yeah... you sure *did*," he ruefully admitted. "Well – can you at least protect the President and the rest of us?"

"I can *try*," she pledged. "But if it goes off too close – you'd need Karéin's powers, or better still, to save you, I think. Not something that I want to experiment with."

"Listen, Sylvia," came Chu's voice, "There's more."

"More...?" uneasily replied Abruzzio. "What more could there be?"

"I just had a visit from that 'Crowford' guy... you know, the religious nut," explained Chu. "And my 'danger sense' lit up like a Christmas Tree, on me. He wouldn't be specific but he issued me a vague warning about 'if you don't call the Devil-Girl' – by that he means Karéin, incidentally – 'right now, you and everyone aboard this-here plane, will go to the Lake of Fire, all by yourselves, and I'm the only one who can decide if you live or die'. He said that I had at most another hour, and then 'I'll have no choice but to do what has to be done, and that will be the end of *you*, whore' kind of thing."

Kaysten spoke up.

"Minnie... I'd just ignore him, if I were you," he advised. "Harold was *always* full of shit – we only brought him aboard to keep the voters in Dixie happy, after Billy jumped ship and went off to parts unknown. He's just bluffing... that's all."

"Jerry? Jerry *Kaysten?*" came back the gratified reply.

"The one and only," cheerily responded the former Chief of Staff.

"Thank God you're safe!" remarked Chu, "But Jerry – you remember how she told me, 'the warning of peril that comes to you, is metaphysical, it's always true and it can't be fooled'?"

"Yeah... that she *did,*" he acknowledged.

"Well, whenever I'm around Crowford, it goes *crazy,*" she cautioned. "An '11' on a scale of '1 to 10'. It doesn't make any sense... but I'm really worried!"

"This is another one of these 'alien-powers' that were bestowed on you, Ms. Chu?" inquired the President.

"Yes," she confirmed.

"If it's some kind of supernatural power... doesn't it tell you *why* it's warning you about the Spiritual Adviser?" he asked. "And why isn't it warning you about the bomber with the nuclear missile? Or when George was about to have your two friends, killed?"

"I don't know, sir," offered Chu. "It doesn't work that way. It just tells you that some*one,* some*thing* or some *situation,* is dangerous, to me personally. Apparently Karéin evolved the ability to detect traps on some long-lost world that she lived on, eons ago... or so she told me. If it had warned me about Will and Otis I *assure* you that the Vice-President and anyone around him, would be dead by now."

"That's great," he complained, while noting cries of distress from somewhere in Chu's vicinity.

"Mr. President," explained Chu, "Neither Sylvia, nor Jerry, nor I, completely understand how these 'alien-powers' really work. We just know that they *do* work, although sometimes not exactly how we'd want them to. They can be very hard to control – for example when I had to, uhh, 'defend' myself recently, even though I tried to fire it at minimum-power, my *Gaze* nearly shot out a window, which would have depressurized the plane and could have crashed it. That's also why I don't want to rush the cockpit. I'd *certainly* win any fire-fight with the remaining guards, but I might make the plane unflyable in so doing –"

"You'll do no such *thing!*" the President immediately shot back. "This situation is already *enough* out of control! Do you *understand* me, Ms. Chu?"

"Sir, you're in no position to order me – or Sylvia or Sam, for that matter – to do *anything,*" she countered. "Jerry I can't speak for, since I guess he sort of answers to you officially. But with that having said... as matters stand now, I have no intention to act in a manner contrary to your request – on one condition."

"Let's have it, then," he grimly demanded.

"Sir – we *have* to warn Sam Jacobson and his team!" Chu pleaded. "We *can't* let him just fly blissfully forward, while a hydrogen bomb is homing in on him!"

"You have my permission to do so," said the President. "Ask him to fly out to sea, as far as his aircraft can go, to minimize casualties if the weapon goes off. We'll have the Navy and Coast Guard search for survivors."

"Most military aircraft – including the type that Jacobson stole – do have over-water survival-gear," added DeWitt's remote voice. "They should be able to last quite a long time, if they do a controlled-ditching."

"Wonderful idea, Mr. President... but I can't call him from here," argued Chu. "Sam's got all his radios turned off, to avoid the Air Force from using them to target a missile on him. I'm told that I might be able to over-ride it with the systems in this aircraft... but we have to be within about 30 kilometers to do that, and to get there, I'd have to change my own plane's flight-direction – and to do *that*, I'd have to get into the cockpit. The pilots are apparently on a slow descent to the Washington, D.C. area – some airfield where they can land the plane and surround it with armed soldiers, probably – and they're ignoring my requests to change course to intercept Jacobson. Can you hail him from your end, sir?"

"On the way to D.C.?" uneasily remarked the First Lady. "Clark – what if she tries to crash it, into the White House –"

"Minnie would *never* do something like that!" quickly reassured Kaysten. "I *know* her, ma'am!"

"We'll try every trick in the book to contact him," pledged the President. "Curt – pull out all the stops... see what you can do. Arthur – can DoD over-ride the radio-silence on the Jacobson plane? Or just get one of our aircraft close enough to do what Ms. Chu's describing?"

"That's a 'negative', sir," demurred DeWitt. "We've been trying for *hours*, just to tell Jacobson and his crew to land to avoid being shot down. Incidentally, we're also being stopped from directly contacting the flight-deck of the, uhh, Vice-President's plane; it looks like someone's interfering with communications to *them*, as well. And I'd note that any aircraft that's gotten too close to the stolen V-37 has been attacked and destroyed by, uhh... we don't know *what*, exactly –"

"Spare you the trouble," spoke up Abruzzio. "Cherie Tanaka, Devon White, Wolf, Misha – any of them – would be more than a match for a single fighter-plane... maybe a whole squadron. They have *godlike* powers, after all."

"Like *you*, lady?" asked the Presidential son.

Abruzzio – her eyes still glowing with a dull kaleidoscope effect – just nodded.

"So even if the plane I'm currently on, got close enough to Jacobson's one to send the message," observed Chu's remote voice, "There's a chance that Cherie, Wolf or one of the others might blow us out of the air, before we could say a word. And I sure don't want to get too close to an aircraft that has a nuke pointed at it, in the first place."

"Listen, Minnie," remarked Abruzzio, "I've learned how to fly, after a fashion – might it be possible for you to do the same? That is... just leave the Airborne Command Post and fly over to Sam's plane, and warn him in person?"

"You've learned to... *what?*" responded an astounded Chu. "How'd you do *that?*"

"Easy – because I *had* to, sister," serenely replied the other more-than-human woman. "You can too... just *believe* in yourself!"

"Well, I... umm... look, Sylvia, let's be *practical* here, if you don't mind?" a flummoxed Chu answered back. "What you're asking me to do is, 'jump out of this aircraft without a parachute and then fly, using some alien-power that Karéin never told me about and that I've had no training on at all, several hundred miles in the dark, finding an aircraft that I've never *seen*'! If I'm lucky, I'll get to deliver the bad news to Sam and his team ten seconds before the nuke catches up with me – that is, if the Air Force doesn't track me down in mid-air and blow me out of the sky, *en route!* You've *got* to be kidding me, sister!"

"Yeah, Sylvia," chimed in Kaysten, "I mean... *you* might be able to do all that, but I can't do so much as float an inch off the ground – and I, uhh, got the full bite from Little Miss Alien Angel, so you'd think that if *anybody* could do it... *I* could. You're asking an awful *lot* from Minnie. If I were her, I'd sure be wearing a parachute before trying something like that."

"You're right, Jerry," commented the President, "No offense I hope, Ms. Abruzzio... but this isn't a practical idea, however much I'd like to see Ms. Chu off that airplane. And speaking of her – Ms. Chu, can I ask you to please put George, that is my former Vice-President, on the line?"

"For a brief time... yeah, fine," she guardedly replied. "And no coded messages between you and him, sir. Without getting into details... I have *ways* of detecting that kind of thing – and I can assure you that I won't react well to it. Understood?"

Be on your guard and tell Mommy if they are sneaky-talking to each other, she silently thought, to her *alter ego.*

On it thinking, came back the message.

Detect if tell ay-sap.

"Understood," reluctantly assented the President.

There was a slight pause, and then those in the Oval Office heard the sound of heavy breathing, over the communications-link.

"This is... George here," said a new voice.

"You don't sound very good," mentioned the President.

"I'm *not*, Clark," grumbled the *faux*-President. "*You* wouldn't be either, if you were stuck up here with *her*, me and Warnock."

"What's the situation?" diplomatically inquired the President.

"Well, to put it briefly," the other explained, "Along with six others, I'm sitting here as a hostage of this... *person*, who has threatened to kill me, several times. And from what I've seen so far, she's more than capable of doing it. *Jesus*, Clark – if you had *seen* what she did to those three Service agents that Harold dragged in here – fucking cut them in *half*, with one shot of that accursed death-ray –"

"I'm aware of that – and I'll hold her accountable for it," cut in the President. "Do you know if Blanshard is still alive?"

"He was, as of when they carted him out of here... that was some time ago," confirmed the *faux*-President. "He took a bullet –"

"Which was aimed at *me*," interrupted Chu. "As were two or three others, which hit me fair and square. It hurt like hell – but I'm still here."

"How did she –" whispered the President, to Kaysten. "Does that mean that Ms. Abruzzio and you, can also withstand –"

"You know how Little Miss Angel, has been able to shrug off hits by bombs, missiles and cannon-shells, sir?" answered the former Chief of Staff, while nodding his head. "It's some kind of 'invisible personal alien body-armor'. She told us that we *all* have it, to one degree or another, but it doesn't come at first– too bad, since the Agency wouldn't have been able to lay a *scratch* on Karéin's family, if that had been the case. As for getting shot... well, that's not something that I'm eager to try out... but a 'nice to have', you know?"

The President momentarily rolled his eyes and sighed, while Abruzzio's face showed a wan smile.

An unfamiliar thought invaded his consciousness.

Still *want to fuck around with Karéin, Jacobson and the rest of us, Mr. President?* it taunted.

The U.S. leader, trying to maintain his composure, continued, "George, can you confirm what Ms. Chu and Arthur have said? About the nuke, that is."

"Yeah... what they're saying is more or less true... as far as I know," grunted the *faux*-President.

"Did *you* order the nuke to be fired against Jacobson?" demanded the President. "Over *American soil?*"

"What I *ordered*, Clark," riposted the other, "Was to have Jacobson and Company brought down by any and all means possible, particularly if they got too close to either D.C. or New York... or any other place where they could do the kind of damage that we saw at Fort Knox. Which is exactly what *you'd* have done... right? But no, I didn't order it to be fired yet, because –"

"Oh – *please!*" angrily interjected Chu. "You tried to have me *shot*, when I refused to play along with your plans to use it against Sam, you fucking *liar!*"

"You can kill me any time you want... but do you mind if I finish my conversation with Clark, Ms. Chu?" complained the *faux*-President.

"George... don't *provoke* her!" warned the President. "Ms. Chu, can I please ask you to let the Vice-President and I continue? You might *learn* something about running a country."

"I've learned all I need to, about how the two of you have been doing just a smashing job – pun intended – of it, sir," sarcastically responded Chu. "But don't let little ol' *me* get in the way."

"Come *on*, Minnie," spoke Kaysten. "He's a good man... who's trying to deal with a shitty set of circumstances. Cut him some *slack!*"

"Largely of his own making," argued Chu. "But go ahead, sir."

"Thanks... I *think*," said the President. "So George – I'll bring you up to speed on what's been going on, down here. I'm back as President, and I'm not leaving again – at least not while I'm still alive. You and your co-conspirators going to *answer* for that little caper you and the Agency pulled to force me out – but I'm prepared to be lenient, if you make a public statement resigning as President, officially ceding the Executive Branch and control of the military and making it clear to the country that we've got *one* President... and that's 'me'. We can't afford a divided government, with Jacobson on the prowl and a hydrogen bomb aimed to go off at any moment! Well?"

"Go *fuck* yourself, Clark!" spat the former Vice-President. "If it hadn't been for you... Jacobson, the alien, the Muslims and all the rest of them, would've been taken care of, the 'old-fashioned way', *long* before things got out of hand. You waited – you *hesitated* – you were *weak* – and now everything's an effin' *mess!* We'll *see* who gets to be President, when all this is over –"

"There's an easy way out of this, Mr. 'Real' President," ominously interrupted Chu. "Why don't I just *kill* him? Then we've only got one President, once and for all."

"That's *enough*, Ms. Chu – I'll hear *no* more talk like that!" furiously shouted the President. "Whatever George has done – just like whatever your friend Jacobson has done – there's a legal process to deal with it. We both know that I can't stop you from murdering him... but I'm appealing to whatever humanity is left in you, not to take this step! *Please!*"

"Just like you showed 'mercy' to Karéin's *son*, Mr. President?" commented Abruzzio. "Heaven help *you*, if you try this kind of hypocritical bullshit with *her*, standing in front of you, listening to it."

"Gee... thanks for the kind words, Sylvia," grumbled Kaysten.

"You're right, sir," came Chu's voice. "I *could* reduce this cruel asshole that I have next to me, to a pile of ashes, in about a tenth of a second, if I so desired... and there's nothing that you, or anyone on this Earth – except maybe Karéin herself – could do to stop it. But for now... if only to keep us all talking, I'll refrain from doing so – *except* if I see any aggressive move made against me, either by him, by anyone else in this room or on this aircraft. In that case, I'll have no option but to defend myself, with the most lethal weapons at my disposal. Do we *understand* each other, sir?"

"Yes... damn you," said the President. "George – you had better watch your step here, and not just with Ms. Chu – but also with me. I'll give you some time to reconsider your last statement on this matter... at least if you want to get out of prison while you're still alive."

"You *heard* me, Clark," countered the *faux*-President. "I've got nothing more to say."

They heard yet another remote voice, now; it was that of a male, speaking in Air Force-cant.

"Excuse me, Ms. Chu," it said, "But... remember how you had asked me to alert you, about changes in the tactical situation?"

"Yeah," Chu replied, "What do you have?"

"TACEVAL via NAR Continental Defense sensor-array is showing something really unusual – here, look at the tactical-display... see it for yourself."

There was a slight pause, and then Chu's surprised voice was heard to remark, "What's *that*? Judging by the color on the icon, I'd say it's an 'unknown'... wait a minute – it just disappeared! Is something wrong with the system?"

"No ma'am," the Air Force voice answered. "It's like it's jamming us or using stealth-technology or something, but our computers are predicting its track and velocity based on previous IR-emissions, and are concentrating sensors on its expected location... we can over-ride its stealth, at least for a few seconds, until it goes dark on us again. But look at the *speed*, ma'am! Have you ever seen anything like *that*?"

Again, Chu's voice paused, but there was a tone of concern when she spoke.

"If I'm reading that right," she was heard to say, "It's going at least 3,000 kilometers per hour. Could it be... uhh... one of the Air Force's secret spy-planes? You know – the ones that fly faster and higher than anything else?"

"No ma'am," contradicted the Air Force staffer. "All of them are accounted-for, and none are currently in the area. I ran an IFF-check as well... no response. Our sensor-returns on this thing are *very* weak – it might be using radar-absorbing shielding – but they don't look at all like any U.S. military aircraft in our inventory... it looks almost like a missile, although with an unusually low length-to-diameter ratio, if it *is* a missile. Whatever that is... it's *not* one of ours."

"And," Chu ominously remarked, "It's heading on a course straight for the *White House*, in Washington, D.C.!"

"Ms. Chu –" sounded the legitimate President's voice, over the communications-channel back to the White House; but he seemed cut off in mid-phrase, and the line suddenly went to static.

"Get that *back!*" demanded the former FBI team-leader.

"Will do, but –" the Air Force guy started speaking.

The Air Force Two radio-shack was reasonably well-shielded from the outside; none the less, Chu's attuned ears were easily able to pick up the calls of panic that seemed to be issuing from the aircraft's internal intercom system.

"Attention! Attention! Emergency!" she overheard, followed by,

"Service and Marine support, to bow – Call-Code 18B – I say again, Call-Code 18B – *shots fired in crew-cabin!*"

A Whiteman Is Disarmed

Though his earliest memories were of repeated beatings at the hands of a drunken step-father – and though the wounds of scores of brutal street-fights, showed all over his sweating, dirt-smeared, hulking, muscular body – Clayton Lomass had never, *ever*, felt pain like *this*.

He had been bitten by a decent-sized Pacific Western Black rattler once, and he had never forgotten the burning pain caused by the serpent's flesh-destroying venom (dozens of snakes after that day, had been shot dead by the whiteman, for no reason other than that they reminded him of the incident).

But what was afflicting him now, was like he had been struck by about *twenty* vipers, all at once.

That little wetback son-of-a-bitch with whom Lomass had exchanged blows back in the building, had managed to bite the Aryan warrior just above his right wrist, and an overwhelming wave of agony, far in excess of what human teeth could be expected to inflict – and which would certainly have incapacitated any man less battle-hardened than him – began radiating from that point.

He had lost control of his right hand almost immediately.

Worse still – as the AB'er saw, to his dismay, upon cutting away his tunic-sleeve with his Bowie knife – his flesh was literally *rotting* away; it was degenerating into a stinking, deliquescing, greenish-white mess, which had – in less than five minutes of desperate running from the scene of his wildly-outnumbered battle against the mongrel-race hordes – almost completely encircled his forearm.

It was rapidly advancing on his elbow-joint.

The only "good" thing about the weirding-wound – if one could call it that – was that it didn't bleed. This, and jury-rigged bandages elsewhere, had at least served to cover his trail somewhat.

With nightfall rapidly approaching, Lomass had sprinted to the east, further into the industrial-park.

At first, he could still just hear the aggravating shouts of the Latino gangster army, seemingly inexorably advancing, from the west. But then – for some reason he couldn't fathom – the noise had died down, and, much to his surprise, the expected follow-on-assault, never happened.

Lomass called on his inner strength to negate the damnable light-headedness that had – atypically – come to oppress him.

He stumbled, gasping for air, across a narrow, tree-lined street in what must have been an industrial-park; then, using his one good arm, he used the butt of his sniper-rifle to smash in the plate-glass in a set of double-doors leading to the reception-area of a very large, nearby warehouse.

Put some distance between me and them chili-shitter cunt-muffins, he considered, *Now I can't hear 'em anymore – but they'll be comin' soon... no doubt of that.*

And I'm gettin' dangerously near our bunker in the golf-course – it can't be more than about four or five long blocks off to the east.

Which means... there can't be any more "retreatin'".

Introspection wasn't really Lomass' "thing"; but, none the less – possibly because of being dazed from the wounds – he found himself engaging in a bout of it.

How the hell did things get this way?

Why ain't there no reinforcements around here? I'm practically on top of it, and there ain't no white faces nowhere around here!

What'd I do wrong?

Fuck! I didn't do nothin' wrong!

Greased dozens of them fuckin' beaners, but so many more of 'em... and then, there's that fuckin' insect-plague thing – that was a man inside it – I saw it, with my own two eyes! What the fuck?

So did poor Little Joe... a second or two before he...

Get a hold of yourself, Whiteman!

'Sentimentality'... that's just another name for 'cowardice'... you know that, don't you?

Our Lord And Savior, Adolf Hitler, didn't sit around, complainin' about how tough life had been on him – like the noble, white warrior-king that he was, he stood alone and stared death right in the face... and, with steadfast defiance, spat in its eye!

If you call yourself an "Aryan", Clayton – how can you do any less?

This is a blessing... not a curse!

Behold your chance to reach out and seize the final glory – the Viking berserker, savagely fighting the defilers of his race, to his last breath – all the way to Valhalla!

Better to die on your feet like a real Whiteman, than to slink away and avoid fate... like some stinkin' cowardly nigger or Jew!

He looked down at his arm.

The burgeoning, "gangrene-on-steroids" thing was now halfway up his forearm; and – with barely-suppressed panic – he noticed that there was now next to no rigidity left, in the parts of his flesh that it had overcome. What was left of his hand was hanging limply, as if his radius and ulna had been turned to some kind of foul, barely-solid jelly.

The pain was agonizing; although, somehow, he had managed to get it under control.

Okay.

Let's think this one out... everything below the elbow's gone, anyway... and if we don't deal with it, this fuckin' disease – or whatever the fuck it is – will eventually get into my neck, torso and, eventually... my... head.

Game over... slowly.

I don't do, "slowly".

Military problem... *military* solution!

With maneuvers practiced umpteen-many times before, his still-good left arm reached into his backpack and retrieved the miniature, Sterno-fueled cooking-element located there. Upon placing it on top of the reception-area coffee-table, he flicked a side-switch on the mini-stove, and this instantly lit up with a pale, blue-and-white, alcohol-based flame.

After ripping off another piece of hopefully-uncontaminated shirt-fabric, balling it up and forcing it into his mouth, the AB'er produced his Bowie knife and thrust its big, deadly-sharp, black-tinted blade, into the flame, waiting until the knife was hot enough to be giving off a faint trace of smoke.

Lomass looked upward, taking note of the sun that he could just see behind the clouds, through the windows.

Send me courage, O my Savior Adolf Hitler and the mighty ancestors of the noble Master Race, he prayed.

Send me the triumph of the will, to take it like a man – like a true Aryan warrior, worthy of my pure, white heritage!

Yet...

A muffled scream, still did pass his lips.

Unfriendly *Fire*

At first, the airborne, incandescent, *Fire*-supercharged Brent Boyd, had despaired at being able to locate or identify Jacobson's plane.

He's intentionally trying to make himself scarce, ruminated the former Mars mission pilot.

Which is exactly what I'd do, given the same circumstances.

Better to think that way, than the alternative... that is, 'that he's been shot down'.

Weird thing is – that might have happened, and at least the 'more-than-humans' in Sam's crew, including Jacobson himself, might still have survived... but they'd be stuck somewhere between Texas and here.

That doesn't do me, Laura, the kids, Hendricks or Boatman, or that backwoods-boy, much good... now does it?

Following the plan that he had outlined to the others back in Fayetteville, Boyd began to fly a slow, circular path over the town, staying high enough to (he hoped) be difficult for a ground-borne human to clearly distinguish his body-shape.

Throughout the process, he energized his "Mars-senses" as far as they could safely be pushed, scanning the nearby airspace for signs of aerial traffic.

Of which, he noted, there was very little; and there was certainly no sign of anything resembling the Jacobson airplane.

A few high-flying airliners, maybe on flight-plans that couldn't be changed, he reflected.

Amazing how I can make 'em out, at such great distances... gogo Mars-eyes...

There's a long-cabin helicopter, looks like it's heading to the hospital... nothing special there... suppose I shouldn't really be surprised – there is a curfew theoretically in effect... and it would be easier for them to enforce in the air, than down on the ground... hospital-craft must be exempt, I guess...

Hmm... some far-off, faint Um'nàhr'é-signatures to the north and the south, close to the western horizon... hard to make 'em out, but looks like they're moving quite fast... that might be a "concern"... need a better look, I think.

So – still half-believing that he could, in fact, do so – Boyd re-energized his propulsive-powers and soared ever higher on an inclined course to the south-west, until he judged his altitude to be somewhere between 10,000 and 15,000 feet.

This is completely insane, *Brent old boy,* he found himself thinking.

I'm hovering in mid-air, tens of thousands of feet off the ground, with no apparent means of lift or propulsion – certainly, nothing that I can easily describe – and as far as I can tell, there's no reason for me not just to keep flying upward... to the Moon, or beyond... yeah, let's not push our luck...

No wonder Laura's a bit scared of me... truth is... I'm afraid of me.

What the hell am I doing up here, anyway?

There was a nervous smile on his face, as he suppressed feelings of panic from his human-half.

The shores of the Atlantic were just visible, far to the east, and despite the intermittent cloud-cover, the lights of many large cities – particularly the D.C. area in the north-east, and Columbus and Cincinnati to the north and west – were also discernible.

Again, he looked in all directions, before concentrating his attentions on the western skies.

Good – nothing seems to be targeting on me, he concluded.

I can see – okay, maybe "sense" would be a better word – quite a few more jet-liners and (maybe that's what they are... not sure) big cargo-planes on high-altitude tracks, from up here... hmm, that one far to the north-west's interesting, smaller heat-sig than it should have... maybe it's military? Anyway... too far away to bother with.

And hey... it should be freezing effing cold up here, and I should be a bit short of breath... but I'm not.

I can feel how it's cold – and how the air's thinning out – but it's like those things hardly affect me... same thing with air-resistence as I speed up – I'm maybe feeling a tenth or a hundredth of the discomfort that I should be experiencing...

Damn, Karéin – but doesn't this 'alien' stuff, grow on a guy!

He regarded the airspace leading into the continental U.S., to the west and south.

Okay, now I've got a slant-angle on them... uh-oh, that doesn't look good... even at this distance, and it's got to be nearly hundred klicks or more, those IR-signatures have got to be something military – there's no way that there would be ten to twenty of anything else flying in formation, and... hmm, that's odd – half are peeling off to the north-east and the other half are heading south-east... that might be a flanking-maneuver.

Let's hope that none of them turn a sensor-array against Yours Truly...

He activated his "shadow-power", leaving only his eyes un-shrouded by the darkness.

Wish I could fly and fight with this dark-stuff masking me, Boyd inwardly complained, *But it cramps my style and cripples my light-attacks... also seems to be harder to fly and turn.*

Oh well... it's sure more than I could lay claim to, before we set out for Mars...

He further considered the situation.

Those Air Force jets – if that's what they are – seemed to either be retreating... or they're trying to outflank and surround, something. *They were on a course in Fayetteville's general direction, that is, to the north-east. If they're trying to encircle the town, that's likely a prelude for an attack – they might have somehow figured out it's where Sam's heading, and then got orders to flatten the whole place – which I can't let happen.*

But they're still a long way off... and if they were going to bomb Fayetteville... they could just fly straight to it. In which case, they'd run into Yours Truly, and that "flash" would be the last thing that they'd ever see.

Either something's going on that I completely don't understand... or they're chasing something – and I'm betting that's Jacobson.

I'd better go see...

Dropping as much of the dark-shroud as he could manage and still maintain speed, forcing the darkness to be above him, Boyd accelerated on a gradually-declining-altitude course to the south-west, aiming for the area in between the two groups of "bogies".

By now, he had figured out how to use the reflections from his infra-red light-beams against the ground as a kind of crude altimeter and airspeed-gauge (judging his relative height and speed by parallax) and – after diving very close to the tree-tops – he leveled out and tried to hold a constant 500 to 700 feet over ground-level, a height which he was pleased to note kept him substantially below the dark, brooding mountain-ranges to the north-west and south-east.

Okay – down to about 200 knots, that should give me a bit of time to see anything the size of the V-37, before it's in front of me – thought Boyd.

He cast his gaze forward, assuming that he was low enough so that any other airborne object would have to be higher, and thus be silhouetted against the sky's dim back-light, above the horizon. His path was not straight; he deviated by about 15 degrees to either side of center as he flew, hoping thus to maximize his field of vision.

He flew this way for perhaps a minute, keeping a careful watch out for signs of military assets; there were none.

Then – with zero warning – Boyd's senses, particularly the ones associated with pain-reflexes, lit up in true "life-or-death" mode.

There was a flash – brilliant like his own, but different, somehow – and an impact of shocking *power*, which struck him a glancing blow at an oblique angle, from ahead and to his right, sending him careening, feet-over-head, on an uncontrolled impact-trajectory with the forest-top.

Somehow, Boyd knew that whatever had hit him, would *certainly* have killed a normal human being... or would have blasted an ordinary aircraft into smithereens.

*Mother**fucker!** he inwardly swore, as he desperately fought to regain control.

What the fuck *was* that – *some damn new Air Force laser, or –*

Wracked with pain from a right shoulder that bore burn-marks as if it had come into contact with a high-voltage wire, Boyd's mind blanked out for a second; but then – using some scarcely-understood alien fighting-power – his wits came back. It wasn't enough to stop him from involuntarily descending into the forest, but he managed to pull up just before he hit a large conifer.

Recalling his years of experience as an aggressor fighter-pilot, skyward he rocketed, determined to build speed and maneuvering-energy as he reversed course, to tail-chase whatever had struck him.

Whoever or whatever you are, Boyd grimly pledged, *you're fucking* dead! *Too bad if you're a living pilot... this is* war, *my friend... my enemy!*

Where the fuck is *it?* he angrily reflected.

Something with that kind of energy-output – got to be bigger than a breadbox – quick, Brent, quick, scan your front and your six –

Wait – there it is – port-side... damn, that's small, must be some new kind of drone...

Holy shit, *look at it accelerate – where's its IR-plume –*

Need to damage its flying-capabilities, before I close in for the kill... got it tagged, but can't lock on like Karéin showed me back in Canada, fucking stealth-field's throwing off my aim – now or never – **uh-oh!**

Frantically – using all the instant-maneuvering tricks at his disposal – he dodged another energy-shot coming from his unknown assailant; the shot missed by a hair's-breadth, and for the first time, realizing its ferocious potency (the enemy-attack hit the forest and blasted a huge, burning gash in it), Brent Boyd, who had faced death so many times before, was genuinely afraid.

He reacted in the only way he knew how to do – by counter-attacking with everything he had.

Fire, *unleash yourself for me now, war-song and everything!*

Rack and ruin!

Shine!

Energized by his now-pounding, echoing battle-song, Boyd fired a barrage of his own, lethal beams of super-charged light, in a spreading pattern designed to saturate the entire area of airspace in front of the "bogey".

The sky over the West Virginia countryside momentarily lit up with the brilliance of his assault.

Which had, fortunately... struck home!

Whatever had been firing at him was caught squarely by one of Boyd's light-beams and was at least grazed by one other. There was a loud, cracking "bang!"-sound, followed by a shower of sparks, like a shell self-disintegrating against a robust piece of armor-plating. The *thing* was sent cartwheeling backward on an erratic course, and Boyd thought he detected signs of fire or smoke trailing behind it for a second or two.

Then – though with a distinct wobble in its flying at first – it seemed to regain its bearings, and began to streak skyward, with an odd sound, more like some warbling kind of music than that of a jet-exhaust.

What could the Air Force make, that could take a direct hit from one of my full-power shots? his panicked mind told him.

I experimented at the camp – I shot a granite boulder clean through, and melted two more behind it! There's nothing except –

Oh... shit!

Don't tell *me* – the mother *of all fuck-ups* –

Then – if she thinks that I'm –

Cursing himself for taking his attention off his opponent even for a split-second, Boyd quickly did a scan downward and backward. He saw the oblong, aerodynamically-mediocre shape of a medium-sized transport-aircraft, with an oddly-heat-poor spot directly on top of it, on a straight course for Fayetteville, about a thousand feet below him.

His tactical-skills came immediately to the fore; this was fortuitous, since another lethal energy-burst cleft the night from above, again missing him by the most narrow of margins, and only because he dodged to a randomly-selected side, a split-second beforehand.

Only one thing I can do will show them who I am, he realized.

Risky, because it's like a big "Bomb Me Please" sign for the Air Force – but even that's gotta be better than a duel with her, with either or both of us going down in flames – okay – here we go –

Trying to restrain its potency, Boyd unleashed his flash-attack, sending rays of brilliant – though not otherwise dangerous – visible-spectrum light, from every direction out from his body.

For perhaps a full second, the equivalent of daylight came to the Fayette river-valley, an event that brought astonishment and fear to everyone around, not least among these, Boyd's family and friends back in the town. Then he reversed course, plummeting toward the newly-discovered transport, while trying to force all his power into skyward protection, both from his personal force-field and from the dark-cloak above it.

Keep the plane on a LoS to her, with me in the middle... compensate for forward airspeed... betting she won't fire, if it might hit them instead...

The next few seconds were gut-wrenchingly long ones, as the former Mars mission pilot considered the possibility that he'd be blown to pieces by a fusillade of lightening-bolts. But fortunately these never came.

Soon, he was only about a hundred feet from his original quarry.

As he neared the V-37 – which, he silently noted, had obviously taken a good deal of battle-damage, he saw Devon White, encased in a frigid, translucent ice-shield, hovering about twenty feet above the transport's dorsal-surfaces. The more-than-human's own war-song, was murmuring in the background.

"Brent... that you? Y'all fuckin' *nuts*, man?" Boyd heard. "What you *doin'*, shootin' at the Professor? And y'all damn near *blinded* me there!"

Before he had a chance to reply, Boyd noticed that the transport was now starting to descend. Fayetteville was in the distance, probably no more than two or three minutes away at current speed.

Then they both heard Tanaka's exciting, inspiring (though strangely faint-sounding) war-song, and in no more than two seconds, she had dropped to a position above both Boyd and White. They noticed that her flight was erratic and that while she hovered, she was unstable, as Boyd was when first he had learned how to fly.

There was a sick feeling in the former Mars mission pilot's stomach, as Tanaka dropped enough of her force-field to let her two former compatriots have a good look.

Her hair was singed – in fact, it was still lightly-smoking – and there was an ugly, blood-splattered scar across her midriff, bearing ugly burn-marks to either side of it. Burn-marks were evident elsewhere on her garments, too. Her right arm was hanging limply by her side.

A weird, other-worldly child's-voice – crying distress and alarm – invaded their psyches.

"Devon... *Vîrya Sài'ymë... help!*" gasped Tanaka, just as her powers failed, and she began to plummet.

"*Lock on her!*" shouted a panicked, shame-addled Brent Boyd.

All Aboard For Parts East

"Damn... he's been gone a *long* time now," opined a worried Otis Boatman, speaking in Hendricks' direction, in a secluded, dark spot on the other side of the street from the Morris Harvey Bed And Breakfast House. "Didn't he say something about, 'I'll be back in five minutes'... or some-such thing?"

"Wasn't really paying too much attention to that," answered the third agent, and anyway – there's clearly *something* going on up there, from the look of all the fireworks we just saw, off to the west. I just hope that –"

"Has my Dad been in a *battle?*" interrupted the little boy, while tugging on Hendricks' sleeve. "Did he get a lot of bad guys? You think he used his super-powers – like you, I mean –"

The third agent bent over, to address the child on more or less his own level.

"Listen, kid," he said, in an unusually-serious tone of voice, "Brent – I mean the older one, since that's your name too – your Dad – he wouldn't do something like that, unless something really *serious* had happened... like, 'he got attacked'. None of us use these 'alien-powers' unless we really have to... they're, uhh, *dangerous*... you know?"

"Have you ever... *killed* someone with your powers, mister?" pressed the boy.

Hendricks shot a pained look at Boatman and then admitted, "Yeah... I think so. I'm not sure, but it was one of those 'life-or-death' things, and I hit him with everything I had. He didn't get up. And you know what, kid?"

"No... what?" asked a wide-eyed Brent Boyd Jr..

"It *sucks, big*-time," plainly offered the grim-faced third agent. "You don't ever want to do anything like that, if you can possibly avoid it."

Boatman silently nodded agreement.

"Okay, young man," intervened the mother, "That's *enough*. Leave Mr. Hendricks alone now."

She said, "I hope he isn't bothering you too much, Will... the kids are all just *excited*. Too much going on too fast, I guess."

"Yeah... and not just for *them*," ruefully remarked the third agent. "Some of us post-humans are wondering when *we* get off the crazy-train, too. Did Brent or anybody tell you, back in the day, Otis and I signed up for a simple old field-assignment, with this trainee team-leader... and they told us, 'oh, just the occasional drug-bust, lots of fraud investigations, paper-work kind of thing'? Well, a funny thing – like 'comets, impending world-destruction, alien-goddesses and becoming some kind of also-ran alien-god yourself' – happened on the way to the old Bureau desk-job... you know? As for yours truly, I'd have settled for just being able to watch a ball-game all the way through, without having to worry about all this crap. Not meant to be, I'm afraid..."

"You got *that* right," echoed Boatman. "'Least your husband and them Mars-folk *volunteered* for all this 'alien'-stuff. As for Will and me – not to mention Sylvia, Minnie and a bunch of other people – we sort of got 'volunteered' by Her Alien Highness, without a lot of choice in the matter."

"You mean you don't *like* being a 'superhero'?" inquired Laura Boyd.

"It's kind of like, 'not liking' how tall you are, or whether you've got freckles," mentioned Hendricks. "You can like it or you can hate it... but you can't ignore it... or change it."

"Wow," was all that the wife could say.

"And speaking of that –" started the third agent.

"What *is* it, Will?" asked Laura Boyd.

"I think... hold on... yeah... Otis – you hear it too?" said the third agent.

"No... *wait* a minute... yes – man, that's *dread*," confirmed the big, black agent. "Like when we heard it, far-off, up there at the first camp in Canada, before she took off to – listen, Will, we'd better get everybody off to the side, for when they come in –"

"Now how did she say to do it – like Brent told me – just point it downward, and push off the ground," mumbled a determined-sounding Hendricks, as he stared downward.

They noticed that an ethereal beat was starting to whisper from the local environment, and that the third agent's eyes were starting to dimly glow.

To everyone's amazement, and to "oohs" and "aahs" on the part of the Boyd children, Hendricks began to lift off the ground. He hovered uncertainly at a point about two feet from the ground for four or five seconds, momentarily looked as if he was about to come crashing down, then seemed to regain control, and resumed levitating.

After perhaps another six seconds, he had gone high enough to easily see over the surrounding roof-tops. The third agent, who had turned so as to face the south-west, began frantically waving his arms (a jealous Boatman noted that all of Hendricks' finger-tips were now glowing like low-voltage pen-lights), shouting, *"Here! Here! Hey Brent – you guys – over here!"*

Unfortunately, these gestures seemed to have affected his concentration, because in the next seconds, Hendricks was heading rapidly downward, and the others noted with fright that he had been more than high enough to do serious damage upon high-speed impact with the parking-lot pavement.

They rushed to break his fall, but the efforts were unnecessary; he slowed down at about man-height and came to a perfectly-acceptable, if wobbly, touch-down.

"Everybody get out of the way," he warned, "If that's Jacobson's plane – and I'd bet you good money, I see three weird-looking folks on top of it – it's coming straight in."

Laura Boyd quickly ushered her children out of the parking-lot, a move that was mimicked by Dorsie the mountain-man, who followed the woman to the street separating the parking-lot from the bed-and-breakfast hotel on the other side. Boatman and Hendricks high-tailed it to the far side of the lot.

Less than five seconds later, a very loud roaring-sound was heard, as the V-37's hulking form appeared close overhead, initially slightly over-shot its intended landing-space, then reversed its swiveling jet-engines and slowly lowered itself into the middle of the parking-lot.

It was a tight fit; the transport was barely able to land upright, with its forward-cockpit facing the street; two of its extensible wheels struck and badly damaged parked cars, before sliding off and stabilizing on the pavement.

To his elation, Boatman saw the figures of Brent Boyd and Devon White – their *Amaiish*-shields still raised, against the potential of an Air Force attack – on the dorsal hull of the transport-plane. But to his dismay, he also saw a prone figure, also field-shrouded but much weaker-looking. From his ground-borne perspective, it was impossible to tell who the apparently-wounded person was.

"Hey, guys," called the third agent, "Great to see you but... what *happened* up there? We need to watch out for Air Force attacks comin' at us?"

The rear loading-ramp of the transport was starting to open.

"Don't know," came Devon White's normally-cheerful voice, this time colored by concern. "I'm hopin' that them mothers have backed off a bit... haven't seen 'em up close for a few hours. But the Professor's hurt *bad* – can y'all help us get her down?"

"*I* can do that," offered Hendricks.

"Okay," White replied, "But y'all watch out when you approach her. That damn 'war-kid' that Karéin fixed her up with... it's actin' like a pet Rottweiler whose master just got knocked down, and it don't know who's to blame."

The third agent used his new-found levitating-skills to rise to the top of the aircraft, and looked down. Immediately he realized why White was worried.

A half-conscious, badly-wounded Cherie Tanaka lay on the V-37's dorsal-plating; she was moaning in pain, and evidently couldn't even get up.

Boyd – for his part – seemed strangely silent. He nervously wiped his hand across his mouth.

"Well don't just *stand* there, Brent my man!" implored White. "Come on... we can get her down there, if we both just –"

At this point, Jacobson himself appeared on the top of the aircraft, having come thence via a short leap from ground-level.

"*Cherie!*" he cried, as he bent over to comfort her.

Turning to the three others, he demanded, "Who – *what* – *did* this? Oh, and by the way – nice to see you, Will. I see you've been... *progressing.*"

While Hendricks smiled, Boyd spoke up. In a low, guilty tone, he admitted, "*I* did. I was heading towards the plane, and she must have mistaken me for a drone or a missile or something; she hit me with a lightening-bolt – damn near *killed* me – and then I made the same mistake... I hit her square-on. *Fuck!*"

"Well you sure did a *number* on her, Brent!" growled an upset Jacobson.

"I *defended* myself!" argued a frustrated Boyd. "Just like *you'd* do – like you've done – like we've *all* done! For the record though... I'm *sorry*. It's pitch-dark up there, we've got no fucking IFF, and both Cherie and I have a half-second at most to decide whether to shoot or hold our fire... get it wrong once and we can easily wake up crippled or dead. Frankly it's a *miracle* that something like this hasn't happened already."

Several of them looked him over, taking note of his badly-wounded shoulder.

"Holy *shit* – I see what you *mean*, about getting hit," remarked Hendricks. "You *okay*, Brent?"

"Only hurts when I laugh," responded Boyd, with a grimace. "Let me give you a little advice – 'don't get hit by one of the Professor's lightening-bolts'. She didn't hit me dead-on; which was damn lucky, because if she had, I'd probably be just... 'dead'."

The former Mars mission chief just said, "Alright... let's all lock on her and lower her to the inside of the plane, where hopefully we can at least make her more comfortable."

"Sorry, but... uhh... I haven't learned how to do much in the way of this 'telekinesis' stuff," demurred Hendricks. "But I *can* levitate, now... I'll get underneath her, maybe support her a bit. Nice seeing *you*, too, Commander."

"Yeah," obliquely acknowledged Jacobson, as he, Boyd, White and the third agent, worked together to get Tanaka's wracked figure down to the interior of the aircraft.

An energy-discharge of some kind – accompanied by a weird, angry-sounding, extra-audible chirping-sound – arced at Boyd. He dodged it, but only marginally.

"Looks like *Vîrya Sài'ymë* isn't very happy with you," observed Jacobson. "Better lay off on helping, so we don't make an already-bad situation, worse. It's okay... we can get her down, with just the rest of us."

Boyd silently nodded. It was clear he was anguished about the situation.

They were greeted by Boatman at ground-level, whose demeanor visibly changed when he saw the Professor's state of health. Misha, for his part, volunteered to stand guard against potential aerial attack and immediately flew up to a position high over the junction of the V-37's wings and fuselage.

Wolf – upon seeing what had been done with Tanaka – unleashed a suspicious stare at Boyd, along with a barrage of swear-words; but the former Mars pilot put up stoically with the abuse, and didn't respond.

They laid the still-groggy Professor down in the middle of the aircraft's cargo-hold, tending to her as best they could, considering that the standard U.S. Army medical-kits seemed to have little to no effect on her wounds. Boyd's wife rushed to his own aid and insisted on cleaning off and dressing his shoulder, which – happily – had begun to self-heal at its expected rapid rate.

With some trepidation, Laura Boyd, her children and the mountain-man, approached the V-37 and became acquainted with its passengers, exchanging stories of amazement, pride, grief and disbelief amongst each other. At first, there was real hesitation on the part of the Boyd family and Dorsie about approaching Wolf's two hell-hounds; but fortunately the animals responded well to doggie-treats, and even got along with the Boyds' own dog.

After a few minutes, the reunited group observed a small (probably less than ten currently, but steadily-growing) crowd of local onlookers, gathering in the surrounding streets and alley-ways.

White tried to deter this as he had done back at the scene of the tornadoes on the highway, by raising walls of ice that blocked foot-borne access at all convenient ingress-points; luckily, the Boyd family SUV and the stolen police-car ended up inside the protected-area, although the purloined APC was outside the perimeter.

But it was obvious that they *had* been seen – the Russian, floating thirty feet up, in mid-air, not to mention White's ice-barriers, guaranteed attention – and that sooner or later, either media-attention, or an Air Force attack (or both), could easily be forthcoming.

Laura Boyd's mobile communicator – which, she believed, had been powered down – somehow turned itself back on, and then began buzzing with an incoming call. But the originating number was an odd one, all "1s" and "0s", so she promptly hung up and turned the thing off again.

At length, the more-than-humans, accompanied by family-members and other fellow-travelers, gathered at the lower-end of the loading-ramp. After a few minutes of excited, intense chit-chat, Jacobson's calm, authoritative voice was heard over the din.

"Listen, everybody," he announced, "First, I want to give those of you who haven't been with her lately, an update on Cherie Tanaka. The Professor took, uhh, quite a hit –"

Boyd winced and hung his head, while his wife held his arm and whispered encouragement to him. Again, her communicator started acting up. She reached in to her purse and powered it down, a second time.

"But," continued Jacobson, "As near as any of us can tell, she seems to be out of danger, and she's resting comfortably. So thank God for that. However – as many of you who were on the trip to Texas and back with us already know – Cherie was our first line of defense against the Air Force, and they might come back at any time... we're now short one of our most powerful friends. Does anybody volunteer to take the Professor's place, if and when that becomes necessary?"

"As if I have much of a *choice*," glumly offered Boyd, as he raised his hand. "Most of you know the story... my fault... so, my responsibility."

"Yeah, well," menacingly commented Wolf, "I've been flyin' with Ms. Lightenin'-Thighs, myself – we're like 'this', you know – and I ain't tagged her yet... nor she, me. You and I end up, up there," – he pointed to the sky – "And if I was you, Mister Mars Man... I'd give yours truly a *wide* berth... get what I'm sayin'?"

"I certainly *do*," evenly replied Boyd. "But it was an *accident*, for Christ's sake! She hit me *first*, you know!"

"Then you'll excuse me if 'accidents' happen at some other time," the bounty-hunter shot back.

"Gentlemen," admonished Jacobson, "I don't think we're getting anywhere with this... fine, we have a commitment on Brent's part to fly top-cover until the Professor has recovered enough to take over again... let's leave it at that. Now, on to other, more important things. I have to be a little careful in how I say this – we can't be sure that somebody out there doesn't have a long-range mike pointed at us, after all – but the bottom line is, the V-37's overloaded as it is and we're short of fuel. I'm counting around 24 people here, and that's over the plane's designed safe carrying-capability. We could probably take off with all of you on-board, but we'd be unstable and could hardly maneuver. So we simply can't safely accommodate everyone who's now here, in the plane. Nor would we *want* to, because –"

There was an odd, significantly louder noise coming from Laura Boyd's purse. It was garbled, but sounded like somebody shouting, "Hey, man!" over and over again.

"Listen, Ms. Boyd, if you don't mind... can you please shut that thing off?" requested the former Mars mission commander. "It's *very* distracting."

"Oh, sure – sorry," she apologized; but as she fumbled for it in her purse, the noise changed, and those with Mars-ears heard, "Important message for the Mars-Gang!"

"*Uh-oh*," warned Boatman. "Probably traced by the Company or the Palace or one of the other 'agencies'... they might have you folks tagged, and the longer it's on, the easier to zero in on us. You want me to smash that thing?

"No... it's okay... *sort* of," commented Jacobson. "Damn guys sure don't waste a lot of time... do they? Here... give it to me."

Uneasily, Laura Boyd passed the communicator over to him.

"This is Sam Jacobson," he spoke.

"Oh, thank God we finally got *through* to you, dude!" came back a ghostly, distorted-sounding voice. "My name's 'Ben Dover', by the way."

"Ben... *Dover*," chuckled Hendricks, in White's direction. "Wish *I'd* thought of *that* one. Who the H *is* this?"

"Bunch of hackers callin' themselves the 'NRA' – yeah, I know how stupid that sounds – that somehow tracked us down, way back," explained White, *sotto voce*. "They've been useful, though... gotta admit that much."

"You're on a normal phone, you know," advised Jacobson. "We've probably got two or three minutes at most, before the agencies can latch on to the signal."

"Yeah, well... keep it short as I can, man," said the remote voice. "We've been doing a lot of traces on the government-feeds since we last hooked up back west, and a lot's changed. Here's the bullet-point version : somebody's apparently hijacked Air Force One, or Air Force Two, or Air Force Whatever, with the 'new' President and everybody else, aboard – it's heading for D.C. as we speak, but we got no idea who the hijackers are, or what they want. There's been orders given to the Air Force to shoot it down if it gets too close, but they've been walked back by the 'old' President, who's showed up in the White House... he's claiming that he's back in charge. Not sure if that's true, though. You gonna take him up on his offer?"

"*What* 'offer'?" asked a perplexed Jacobson.

"You mean you ain't *heard* yet?" said the hacker.

"Heard... *what?*" countered the former Mars mission commander.

"The Old Man's been on TV, earlier tonight," explained 'Ben Dover'. "A lot of what he said was about 'the shitty things that my old Vice-President's done to me', and 'the government's under *my* control now, and ignore anything that the other guy tells you to do', but also, he said that 'if the Mars Gang comes to meet me here in the White House, I'll tell the military to lay off 'em'. He seems to be pretty spooked by you folks, honestly – basically said that the military can't handle you and it's time to negotiate... there was also a lot of legal-sounding shit in it, like, 'I'll let myself be judged by the courts, if Jacobson does the same', kind of thing. Thought you'd like to know... for what it's worth."

"*Damn*," breathed White, "Maybe we *was* makin' an impression, after all."

"Thanks for the update," mentioned Jacobson. "Anything else? Particularly, any signs of an impending attack on us? I'm not going to say our location out loud, but no doubt both you and the government already know it."

"Not as such, man," declared the hacker, "But there's a lot of, uhh, *unexplained* shit... you know? Like, in this speech he gave, the President said he's got some 'super-persons' fighting on his side – well where'd *they* come from? And don't want to rattle you none, but in that transmission about the hijack, we thought we heard talk of a nuke bein' 'all ready to go'... but the link dropped before we got the details. Oh... and we've been pickin' up conversations referring to 'possible Mars-Gang sightings in, like, Chicago, and then in Bowling Green, Kentucky'... but you're clean cleared out of those places... isn't that right?"

"Affirmative," stated Jacobson. "We never went that far north, and we never went to Bowling Green... although we considered stopping there. Peculiar, I'd agree – I can't imagine any follower of the Storied Watcher willingly taking orders from either of our 'Presidents' –"

"*I* can," countered Misha, speaking from on high. "Ms. Chu, specifically. She has taken an oath of loyalty to the U.S. government, after all."

"So have we," disputed Hendricks, "And look where it's gotten us."

"Yeah," agreed Boatman. "Minnie just wouldn't *do* somethin' like that. You just don't know her like we do."

"Either way," remarked Jacobson, "I don't like the sound of a nuke being out there... but we had better get off the line, now. Thanks for the call. Stay safe. Mars-Gang, out."

He switched off the communicator and waited for a second or two to verify that it didn't self-power again; fortunately, no signs of this happening, appeared.

For another moment, he remained silent, just staring forward at the throng, though not at any particular person.

Then Jacobson said, "So... what do you all think of that?"

"Didn't we hear that he had been, uhh, 'replaced', or something?" observed the usually-taciturn Callum Wade. "As in, 'under guard' or whatever."

"That's true," affirmed Yvonne Jacobson. "There was an announcement from, uhh, the guy who used to be the Vice-President. He said, 'I'm in charge, now'. It was on TV."

"Well then... how'd the old guy, get back in the White House?" asked the farmer.

"No idea," deflected Jacobson, "But he couldn't have done that by himself. He *must* have some level of support within law enforcement, the intelligence-agencies, the military or all three. What it means, for us, is that part of the government might be loyal to him, and part of it might still be loyal to the other guy. We'll have to take that into account for our own decision-making."

Wolf cracked his knuckles and threatened, "Well, if either of them assholes want to make it that much easier for us to get there and grease 'em... who're *we*, to turn 'em down? Save the asses of a bunch of little soldier-boys who'd otherwise get in the way. Get within a mile of where he's at, flame the whole thing, get the hell out of there... 'mission accomplished'."

"He's talking about a flag of *truce!*" argued an annoyed Boyd. "The convention is that you don't attack someone who offers you that... at least, not right then and there."

"Guess I ain't too 'conventional', then," snorted the bounty-hunter, to scattered chuckles amongst the crowd. "And you don't even know if the President – whichever one we're talkin' about, incidentally – is gonna *be* there, in the White House I mean, when we all show up. What if it's just a big fuckin' trap and all you run into's one of his 'stunt-doubles', five seconds before some hidden bomb goes off under our feet?"

"Or," warned Hendricks, "A nuke gets dropped at the front door. Been through one of those... got no interest in doing it again."

"But that would wipe out the whole *Capitol*... wouldn't it?" interjected Yvonne Jacobson. "*Surely* the President wouldn't *do* that!"

"The government's surprised us before, with things that we thought it wouldn't do," noted Boatman. "Like, 'throwin' young Will 'n me, out of a plane, without a parachute, at ten thousand feet or so'."

This remark won the black ex-agent a number of stares both incredulous and envious, but the conversation went on.

"I wish the Professor was 'with it' enough to add her two cents'-worth," commented White, "But... isn't an invitation to the White House, what we was out to do, when we started out on this whole thing? I mean... 'least this way – if what the man's sayin' is true – it solves one big problem, namely, 'how the hell do we track him down'. I gotta admit, though... Mister Gas Barbecue there, he's got a point. We shouldn't risk everybody goin' down there and potentially gettin' trapped, or worse. If you want, I'll volunteer to check it out alone – see if we're bein' set up. If so, I'll make an iceberg out of the whole damn place and then get back to the plane to warn y'all. If not, I'll wave y'all on down. Make sense?"

Uncertainty reigned for a few minutes, as arguments for and against were passed back and forth. Finally, Jacobson's voice again was heard over the din.

"We have a proposal on the table," he said. "Specifically, for at least some of us to head to the White House, in Washington, D.C., to confront the President – the original one, that is – about the crimes he's committed, about how the government has persecuted us and our families, and about how he's going to clean up all of this, in some halfway-fair manner. Devon has volunteered to be our scout, to avoid falling into a trap, as best we can. Are there any other proposals? If so... now's the time to bring them before everybody."

Judging from the silence, it was clear that no-one else had thought through a viable alternative.

"Seems we're in too deep to really think of doin' anything else," opined Boatman, "But... I think you owe it to everyone who's listenin', to explain to us, what you're plannin' to do with the President – if things don't work out, I mean."

"I'd have thought that had been clear from the start, if you remember our discussions in the 'Council of the Woods'," replied Jacobson. "We give him a fair hearing – let him state his case – and then I guess we vote, just among us I mean, about what to do at that point."

"You should be more precise, Commander," came the Russian's overhead voice. "What do you *mean*... 'what to do at that point'? This situation that Mr. Boatman describes – it would hardly be an appropriate place or time in which to be making decisions... how does one say it in English... oh yes... 'off the top of one's head'."

"You know... I've been thinking of this, in the limited amounts of free time that I've had, on the trip to and from Texas," disclosed the former Mars mission commander. "The whole, 'what to *do* with him', issue. We can't be completely sure of what we'll be faced with, when we get there, and we don't know what the President's going to say. But if a suitable deal to pardon us all and correct the wrongs that the government has so far done, isn't offered... then we'll have three basic options : namely, 'surrender and take our chances with the courts', 'leave him alone, but declare war and try to take over the country ourselves', or... 'either take him hostage, or kill him'. Obviously, I'd far prefer to work this out peaceably – but the government's track-record isn't good, and we have to face the possibility that the President will try to double-cross us, yet again."

"Brent... you aren't seriously thinking of going to *war*, against the entire *Army, Navy and Air Force*... *are* you?" asked Laura Boyd of her husband, in an inopportunely-loud voice.

"Yeah... I guess I *am*," he reluctantly admitted. "Not that I *want* to... not that the Commander does, either; but you have to *understand* –"

"Speak for *yourself*," chided Wolf. "Some of the rest of us, are kind of itchin' for a chance to 'make it some hot' against old Uncle Sam, lady."

"I don't know who you are," retorted Laura Boyd, "But that's *very* irresponsible talk! My children and I were nearly *killed* by agents of the government, the moment that all this 'Mars-Gang' stuff started up. While you were having your wet dreams of 'wars against the entire government', did you maybe think – just for a second or two – about what the government might do back to ordinary civilians like us... or like Yvonne's family... or the Wades... or these folks from Texas? Or just other people who get caught in the cross-fire? You know – people who don't get to fly around with these 'alien-powers'... who don't have force-fields to protect them?"

"Lady... I ain't got nothin' against you personally," offered the bounty-hunter, as amicably as he was able, "But that's what happens in *any* war. And it's what was happenin' to yours truly – always bein' exclusively on the receivin' end of shit bein' fired in my direction, by the government – until I got a little of Miss Nuclear Angel's mojo. If I was you... I'd spend less time worryin' about gettin' smoked as 'civilian collateral damage', and more time figurin' out how to hook up with Karéin and, uhh, gettin' to the next level, like the rest of us."

"Okay, *look*," intervened Jacobson, "That's another one that we aren't going to resolve here and now... except, we *do* have to figure out how we're going to protect our extended families against government retaliation – remember, if what we just heard is true, even if the President issues an order that we aren't to be harmed... there's no guarantee that the military and law enforcement will necessarily obey it. We can't possibly carry everyone in our families – not to mention others like Sammie, the Wades and the Youngs and so on, even if we wanted to... and it'd be *crazy* to bring them along with us to the White House, where we might end up in a high-intensity shooting-engagement."

"So I guess what we have to decide," he went on, "Is – basically – 'who should stay here, or at least stay somewhere safe, who should protect them, and who should head on to D.C.'. I think at the absolute least, Brent, myself, Devon, the Professor when and if she's able and maybe one or two more fully-combat-ready persons, should continue on the the White House. Any volunteers?"

"For doin' which of those?" snorted Wolf. "You already know what *my* choice is. I'm in for D.C... whether or not I'm invited."

"Why doesn't that *surprise* me?" evenly responded Jacobson. "Consider yourself 'invited' – but for God's sake, man... try to keep it under *control*, and don't start shooting until it's clear that there's no other choice, if you don't mind?

I know we have to be ready for a war – but let's not *start* one, without a damn good reason. Do we understand each other?"

"Yeah... I s'pose," grudgingly agreed the bounty-hunter. "Just as long as you realize, Mr. Space Man, that the government's likely to give us all plenty of them ol' 'good reasons'. Based on what we've seen so far, that is."

"Can't reasonably argue *that*," offered Jacobson. "Let's hope they have an attitude-adjustment, before we show up there. Anybody else?"

"I would certainly want to go," sounded Misha's voice, from above. "If for no reason to be able to truthfully say that 'I have been in the White House'... one moment before it is reduced to rubble. By the way, Commander – I have noticed an increasing number of people beginning to gather outside these ice-walls created by Major White. There are some police-cars, as well, and they seem to be speaking on mobile radio-equipment. We should consider how long we have here, before the authorities try to break through... or they call in the Air Force."

"They want our *asses*, y'know," warned the mountain-man. "'Less y'all want all us poor-folk to end up in some jail – or jus' shot daid – y'all better leave somebody behind who's got some *firepower*."

"Point well taken," acknowledged the former Mars mission commander. "I certainly can't leave Yvonne and my family in an unsafe situation, and I'd imagine that's also true of Major Boyd –"

"*Damn* right," interjected Boyd.

There were calls along the line of "Daddy, I want to go along with you," from multiple members of the Jacobson and Boyd families; but these were quickly deterred by firm refusals on the part of both former Mars astronauts.

"And we have a moral responsibility to protect all the other, uhh, 'civilians', as well," spoke Jacobson. "So with *that* in mind... who do we have left? Will – Otis – what's the state of your alien-powers?"

"Relative to *what*?" Boatman answered back.

"Relative to, say, 'a tank-battalion or two'... or maybe a squadron of fighter-planes," elaborated Jacobson.

"Uhh... well..." stammered Hendricks.

"Not that far, yet?" half-teased the Mars mission commander.

"We took on a bunch of State Troopers, backed up by a few National Guard, back there on the highway," explained the black former agent, "And I'm not proud to say that not many of 'em came away from that, alive. But a real Army-formation, or the Air-Force... I don't know, Jacobson... I don't know. Sure not somethin' that I'd like to try out, and find out I'm not up to the task."

"Didn't she say something like, 'and when the hour is dire, that's when your arts will come to full-flower'... or some-such shit?" observed the third agent. "But I'm backing Otis up on this one, Commander. I'm good against a guy – or even a few guys – with guns; but *tanks*? *Fighter-jets*? Count me *out*, man! I'm half-alien – that I'll admit – but I'm not *stupid* half-alien... you know?"

"So what you want to do, Commander?" remarked White. "'Less Donny there wants to volunteer –"

"Oh *no*, you don't!" called out the trucker, shaking his head and holding his hands up in the air. "Only 'power' I seem to have, is 'gettin'' shot and gettin' better afterwards'... and okay, I *can* throw a punch or two, but I doubt that's gonna do much against a tank. I'll try to defend Uncle Callum and Aunt Marie – but you'd better get somebody else, if you're takin' on the Army or the Air Force... not to mention them Marines, neither."

"So *that's* out, I guess," continued White. "Look – she might *kill* me for suggestin' this, but... could we maybe leave the Professor back here, to protect them all? I know she took a damn bad shot up there, but last I checked – and that was a few minutes ago – she's been healin' up about as well as we could expect. I'll admit that I don't like goin' in to D.C. without her flyin' top-cover – but we got Brent to do that now. The Man prolly think that we're all goin' to D.C. together anyway... so he'd target everything on us and Cherie would only have to deal with, like, local LEA or such. Donny 'n Will 'n Otis can hold 'em off until she's 'with it' enough to chuck a few lightenin'-bolts at 'em. What you think?"

Jacobson hesitated. Then he said,

"Geez, Devon... I don't know... Cherie's been such an integral part of our team, right from the start – wouldn't it be unfair to deny her the chance to confront the President, face-to-face, as we're all planning to do? That's above and beyond the question of whether we can safely do without her assistance, if we run into trouble. Brent, Misha, Wolf... what's your opinion?"

They all tried to talk at the same time but eventually Boyd was able to say, "For my part... I think the Professor deserves a little R and R, before she has to start fighting again. She also, uniquely among us, has *Vîrya Sài'ymë* as an extra line of defense. Maybe that – excuse me – 'her', was what saved Cherie's life. Of course, my POV is a little colored by... uhh... recent events. I just wish I could be here when she comes to... so I could apologize."

The Russian stated, "I feel my own powers increasing rapidly; none the less, we are engendering a significant risk in leaving the Professor behind. Would it not make sense to ask her – or someone else in the group that she is guarding – to monitor media reports of what is happening at the White House? If we are forced into a fire-fight, and she observes it occurring, perhaps she could fly there, to reinforce us."

Wolf commented, "Doubt that anything will be left for her to zap, after *I* get finished with it... presuming, of course, that Mr. Presidential Jackass is stupid enough to jerk our chain. But I think I'm with Mr. Flyin' Shiny-Pants here. Cherie's taken some hits... I'd give her a rest. My pups can guard her stretcher."

The two hell-hounds seemed to agree, by simultaneously sending out throaty, flame-and-smoke-belching growls. This duly impressed all around, while causing alarm to the Boyd mutt, who had been sitting rather too close at the time.

By the look on his face, Jacobson seemed genuinely torn.

Eventually he said, "I'm reluctant to do so... but we've got to face *facts*. The Professor's still wounded and she can't effectively help us right now. Hopefully she'll self-heal quickly, but we don't know how long that will take... and given the media-presence here, it's probably not a good idea to just sit around and wait until she's fully recovered. So yes... I'll go along with this plan. Are there any objections... especially, from Otis, Will or Donny? After all, you'll have to defend our families and the others, until Cherie can take over."

"Considerin' the alternative – which isn't much of one, mind you," offered the big, black ex-agent, "I guess I'd have to say 'yes'. I sure hope it won't take very long for your 'Professor' to get back to speed... because if we have to deal with anythin' more than a few policemen – and may God forgive me if I have to... uhh... *you* know – well, I can't *guarantee* anythin'. You understand?"

"Yes... unfortunately," confirmed Jacobson. "Will... what about you?"

"Pretty much like Otis said," responded the third agent, "It's going to be dicey until Tanaka can give us some real bang for the buck, but I'll do my best to keep your folks, and *these* folks, safe. By the way, we found some guns in that APC... I stashed about half of 'em, plus lots of ammo, in the back of the cop-car. I'd suggest that we give 'em to Dorsie, Donny, Mr. Wade and anybody else who's willing to shoot, if necessary."

"I ain't lookin' forward to doin' anything like that... but I s'pose I will, if I have to," pledged Callum Wade, "But ain't you forgot one little thing?"

"Uhh... what?" asked Hendricks.

"Well... if it's too risky just to sit here," noted the farmer, "Then, where you want us to go, *to*?"

"Good question," conceded Jacobson.

He looked up and addressed the Russian.

"Misha," asked the former Mars mission commander, "You think they can hear us, from the other side of those ice-walls?"

"They are too far for human-hearing," stated the levitating more-than-human, "But you might be picked up by a directional microphone. I would suggest that you discuss this somewhere with more privacy."

"Let's *do* that," agreed Jacobson. He motioned the others to follow him, and went inside the aircraft, sitting down beside the somnolent Tanaka, on her stretcher.

With the others arrayed around, he said, "Okay... so we've got to figure out where those who won't be going to D.C., can hide out – and how we're going to get them there. As I mentioned earlier, it's going to be a challenge getting the V-37 airborne with all these people on board, but we can lighten the load by having Brent, Wolf, Devon and Misha fly alongside; we can probably accommodate everyone that way, at least for a short distance. The obvious question is, 'to *where*'. Anyone got a map?"

Quickly, Donny fetched the one that he had been using, while flying the aircraft.

"We've got some constraints," explained Jacobson, while studying the map. "We're very short of fuel – only enough for a one-way trip to D.C., basically, with a small safety-reserve – so if we're going to transport the 'stay-behinds' on the V-37, and still go to the Capitol, we can't deviate too far off a straight line north-east; doing so would run us completely out of gas. Secondly, wherever we deposit our families, has to be relatively out of the way and not easily-accessible to law enforcement – a defensible location, in other words – so it's hard for them to find in the first place, and difficult to attack, even if discovered. Remember that if worst comes to worst... you only have to hold out until we get back here to deal with whoever's after you."

"Don't spend too much time on the tourist sights in D.C.," grumbled Boatman.

"Other'n scribblin' my name on that big fuckin' thing she dropped into the White House lawn," quipped Wolf, "You got my word of honor on that."

"We'll try to be back as quickly as possible, if we can't get the President to order the military and LEA to leave you alone," promised Jacobson. "But about where you go... my problem is, I really don't know these parts that well... I'd just be guessing as to where the best spot would be. Anybody know better?"

"Yeah... *I* do," spoke up Dorsie. "Y'all get over the state line, Virginny-way I mean, an' it's gonna be hard to avoid bein' noticed... highways, lots of traffic, lots of people... that means 'lots of po-lice'. But up 'round here'" – he pointed at an area around Route 219 – "Top of Cass Mountain, that is, mah cousins Ezra 'n Cooter hang out there all fall 'n winter, because they can sell th' product at this-here 'Snowshoe' resort over the ridge, where all the rich-folk go... late in th' season, so they might or might not be there – and if they is, y'all be careful how y'all introduce yourselves, 'lessn y'all want two barrels of buckshot up your ass – but I reckon that'd be right up your alley. It's way up th' mountain an' there ain't but one dirt road leadin' up there, an' it gits snowed in a lot of the time. Ain't never seen no law up there, neither."

"Everybody – what do you think?" asked Jacobson.

"Looks like it's almost right on our flight-path to D.C.," observed Boyd. "That's a *big* advantage. If we stage it right – that is, cruise at an altitude as close to level with where we'll be landing, take as little time as possible to drop people off and then again be on our way, it might look to the Air Force that we didn't stop at all, or just hovered temporarily. They might think it's a primitive attempt to throw off their pulse-Doppler moving-target-trackers. I'd recommend that we do so at a couple other points on the route, just so they have more places that they have to search, if they decide to do so."

"Well... we've already had one little taste of mountain-man hospitality," ruefully commented Hendricks. "At the point of a shotgun, like Dorsie warned us about. As long as he's with us to do the introductions... I can't think of anything better. We got anywhere else to go?"

No alternate proposals were forthcoming, so Jacobson declared, "So... I think it's 'Cass Mountain or bust', folks. Any objections?"

"We've only been together again for a few hours... we've hardly had a chance to catch up!" protested his wife. "Sam, I don't like the idea of you going off like this, and we might never *see* you again. Can't it wait just a *little* while?"

"Exactly what *I* was thinking," chimed in Laura Boyd.

"I know," sadly acknowledged the former Mars mission leader, "But honey, we've learned the hard way on this trip, about staying too long in a single location, thus allowing the military to target us. I *swear* to you and the kids, that I'll be coming back as soon as possible – after taking care of this situation, once and for all – and then our times apart from each other, will be *permanently* over with."

"Laura," added Boyd, "I make the same promise to you and our family. This B.S. was *forced* on us – we had little to no part in it, initially – and the Commander's absolutely right... we've got to end it, one way or another. And anyway... if what the hackers are saying is correct, the President's cooling his heels waiting for us to show up and have a friendly little chat. We're wasting time as it is. If we delay too long, he might give up on the whole idea – and then we'd be in a war, for *sure*. It's not fair... but it's the facts."

"Well," remarked Boatman, "A damn *lot* of things haven't been 'fair', lately. Like, 'bein' thrown out of a plane without a parachute' and such. I think you folks had best get goin'... gettin' in a war against my own government... that doesn't fit in with my plans, you know?"

"*Definitely* not," said Hendricks. "When I started out this trip, I figured that 'cheating on my Bureau expense reports' was gonna be my biggest fight with the government... 'getting in a *war* against them', wasn't on the ol' radar-screen... you know?"

Jacobson – perhaps recognizing the portentous nature of the discussion, and the responsibility that he had to assume – seemed lost in thought for a few seconds.

Then he arose, standing tall and in command, as he spoke up.

"Friends – family – brothers and sisters," he declared, "Our struggle to bring justice to this country, is either about to end... or it's about to get much, *much* tougher. For those of you who believe in the power of prayer... now's the time to put it to the test."

"Amen to *that*," offered White. "I believe we got an angel on our side... but it won't hurt to have the Lord there, too."

"Alright, then," said Jacobson. "Gather what you need from the cars – as little heavy-stuff as possible – and then... 'all aboard for parts east'."

To Join Our Fuehrer In Hell

Another muffled explosion thundered overhead, followed by six or seven more, mostly to the east. They weren't loud enough to drown out the recorded Nuremberg Rallies speech by Adolf Hitler, playing in "repeat mode" in the background, over the internal PA system; but *these* blasts sounded much closer than before.

"Any word from Clay?" asked the Aryan Nations Lictor General, his yellowed, tobacco-stained teeth prominent as he barked out the inquiry.

Even in the basement redoubt of the 2020's rebuilt golf-course clubhouse, the temperature was uncomfortably warm, after the A/C had failed; the white warrior's leader was naked from the waist up.

His presence wasn't made any more appealing by the fact that it had been almost a week and a half, since he'd had a shower.

"Hasn't reported in twelve hours," answered his bald-headed, tattooed, six-foot-four, 275-pound deputy. "Nothin' since he ran into them fuckers at the intersection... where Buzz went down. Radio might be out, I guess."

The building shook, having been impacted by the shock-wave of a too-near miss by something large-caliber. Plaster came spalling off parts of the ceiling, although the structure of this converted, former golf-chalet seemed to be more or less still holding up.

The hulking form of the east-front lieutenant appeared in the doorway leading to the command-center. The man was bleeding from at least three wounds and had suffered burns to quite a bit of his left bicep and shoulder.

"What are *you* doin' back here?" peevishly demanded the Lictor General. "You said you could hold the Army –"

"Ain't *them*," replied the man, through strained breathing. "It's niggers – fuckin' *hundreds* of 'em! We took out a big advance by the Army, set off some of them rigged trucks we was talkin' about... smoked about a hundred – that sent 'em scurryin' – but then, on our right flank, up comes this mob of them jungle-bunnies... looks like all their tribes, or whatever, got together, 'cause they ain't shootin' at each other the way they usually do, and some of 'em was wearin' red and others blue... you know?"

"What's the *situation?*" gruffly pressed the whiteman leader.

"I personally took out at least eleven – might be twelve or fifteen... don't know, exactly," answered the lieutenant, "And the rest of our soldiers are proving again and again, that one white man's worth at least ten niggers. But the truth is... I honestly don't think we can hold 'em. We were outnumbered four to one by the Army as it was, and now... *this*. I figure we got a day, at most, before they get here. Maybe less."

"You *will* fuckin' hold them off, whiteman – is that *understood!*" angrily retorted the Lictor General. "We're not fuckin' *ready*, here!"

After a couple of seconds of silence (except for the sounds of more nearby explosions and gunshots), the east-front lieutenant slowly stated, "I ain't afraid to die – *you* know that. And if it means headin' back to the front, just get me some full clips... I'll go with my boots on, like a white warrior's supposed to. But I'm tellin' you the *truth* – for every AB'er out there, he's holdin' off five or six of them spooks... not to mention the Army and them fuckin' border-bunnies... they're still around. You can like to hear it, or not like to hear it, boss. That's the *situation*."

The Lictor General sent out one of his trademark, cruel-eyed stares, a gaze that had spelled death for uncounted victims, over past years.

Yet – as much as ever was done, within the Aryan Brotherhood – he *trusted* this particular lieutenant.

If the guy *said* something was so... there was a good chance, that so it was.

"Look," added the east-front lieutenant, in a quiet, pensive tone that was most unlike him, "How much time you need?"

"For *what?*" answered the whiteman leader.

"*You* know what," said the lieutenant, with a shrug in the direction of a specially-guarded, locked room at the end of the underground hallway.

"'Nother eight – maybe ten – hours," indicated the Lictor General. "Then – they tell me – she'll be rigged 'n ready... although they don't understand half the fuckin' electronics in it, and they just left those all alone... they set up a bypass. Command-fuse and a delay-fuse, supposedly up to an hour– but once you set *that* one, there ain't no turnin' back. They're sayin' they need extra time to run 'diagnostics' and test the circuits, or the fucker might not fire at all, if and when. Oh, and by then, 'copter'll be ready, too."

"The plan...?" asked the lieutenant.

"You know that fuckin' 'insect'-thing that Clay was after?" responded the leader.

"Yeah," affirmed the east-front warrior. "Maybe it *got* him. That'd explain why he ain't called in."

"I don't *believe* that," argued the Lictor General, "I think Lomass is still huntin' it. Don't know how... but I just *know,* somehow. If it's still out there – I'm gonna find it myself, lookin' down from above... I'm gonna lead it to where I want it, and then I'm gonna ride our little surprise-package, all the way down its fuckin' throat, or up its ass, or *whatever* the fuck it's got... you *understand?*"

The east-front lieutenant mutely nodded.

"What can you do to buy us some *time,* soldier?" demanded the Aryan leader.

"Well," mentioned the other AB'er, "For what it's worth... you pick up that broadcast from back east? The 'President', I mean."

"Came over the radio," noted the Lictor General. "Didn't pay much attention – I was havin' some fun with two of them beaner bitches the boys brought in last night. Left their bodies out on the burnin'-pyre in the back yard – got fresh ones for tonight. Do your duty... I'll share 'em with you. Let you have your pick of the prettiest ones. Or the youngest, if that's your thing. We've got the virgins in a special holdin'-pen, you know."

"Doubt I'll live long enough for that... but thanks anyway, boss," observed the east-front captain, "As to the 'President' – I only heard half of it myself, I had to take down two niggers that showed up as I was listenin' – but near as I can make out, there's some kind of power-struggle goin' down... at the top, I mean. The original fucker's back there – or so it seems. We noticed the Army layin' back a bit, just after that. They might be wonderin' who they're actually reportin' to... that might get us a few hours... at least for the guys who are facin' off against them."

Then he slowly added,

"Listen, boss... Mike Spencer and Big Ax Jake – they can hold off the spooks just as well as I can, and they're already on their way over to the front – they volunteered soon as they saw me. So... I was wonderin'... if that's what you want to do... and you could use someone as guard... and I know how to fly one of them crates – learned it on tour in Paki-fuckin'-stan. Gotta stay low, to keep off the Army's radar, like, "between the buildings", or we might wear a missile up our assholes before we get to where we're goin'. But I took that 'terrain-avoidance' training... think I can do it."

For a second, the Lictor General's brow furrowed in anger, upon thinking that he'd seen a hint of cowardice.

But then he flashed a cruel, satisfied smile.

"Of *course* you can," he agreed. "Even let you hit the button, if you want."

"The final honor – to join our Fuehrer in *hell!*" pledged the other man, with his fist clenched at the end of that hallowed old stiff-arm salute.

Not Who You Had Counted On

"*Damnit*, Ms. Abruzzio," growled the President, the fatigue and stress of the situation starting to show plainly on his face, "I'm beginning to think that George – despite his treachery – had it right about Jacobson. Why haven't we seen him... or at least *heard* from him?"

"Last track from the Air Force that I got when I went back to the comms-center," observed Kaysten, "Had Sam and the rest of them over southern West Virginia... and they seemed to be sort of heading towards D.C, albeit slowly. You want me to see if there's an update, Mr. President?"

"Yeah, if you don't mind," directed the U.S. leader. "What about that, uhh, *other* target?"

"Dropped off radar, about ten minutes ago," Kaysten replied.

"And this 'Chu' woman on the National Command Post?" queried the President.

"Not sure, sir," came the voice of one of the Secret Service agents. "We're trying to get the channel back... there was some kind of packet-storm of garbage data and the feeds completely dropped, including the one for the Secretary. Ms.. Ms... uhh, 'Abruzzio' – that's your name... right? Is there any way that you can help us?"

"I have nothing coming in from your radio-feeds, to force into the stream," demurred the former space scientist. "The moment that you get either signal back, please let me know."

"Bloody hell," muttered the President. "What a time to have these systems go down!"

"Mr. *President*," came the worried-sounding voice of another Service agent, "I really *have* to insist that you get out of this building... or at a minimum, retreat to the White House survival-bunker. I checked with the Air Force and that other track looked a lot like a stealth-missile – possibly a scramjet or sub-ballistic one. It might impact here at any time, and it could easily be targeted right for the Oval Office! Sir, I *beg* you –"

"He may be right, sir," added Abruzzio. "There are probably elements of the military that are still loyal to the former Vice-President. It's consistent with his behavior so far, that he might have issued some kind of secret order to attack the White House if a 'challenger' ever showed up here. They could be jamming our feeds to Minnie and DeWitt, so they can't warn us either. If we take a missile – even one with a conventional warhead – *Vìrya I'ëà'b'* and I can't guarantee to protect –"

"I've already *told* both or you," countered the President. "I appreciate your concern... but this is where I'll stay, until the matters-at-hand are dealt with. If God means this to be my time... then so be it. Kathy – is there *no* way I can convince you to take Matt and Clairie, to the bunker? Curt and Ms. Abruzzio do have a point, you know. I'm here only because it's necessary."

"This is where *I'll* stay, Clark," firmly replied the First Lady. "I've been at your side since the start, and this is no time to change."

"Yeah, and besides, Dad," commented the President's teenage daughter, "This is where it's all *happening*... you know?"

A wry, fatherly smile came to the U.S. leader's face.

"*Thought* you'd all say something like that," he said. "Love you."

For this, he got a hug from Clairie, along with a "thumbs-up" gesture from his son.

"Well... okay then," the President addressed to the Service agents. "We may not be able to deal with a missile... but what's the situation outside? The Avenue and surroundings, I mean."

"I've been in contact with the Capitol Police, sir," mentioned the Secret Service captain. "They seem to be loyal enough – or, at least, they're not rushing to dispute your leadership. They've got a perimeter of about a city block set up in every direction, although they're having problems with those damn video-feed micro-drones that Disney News keeps sending past the boundary... every time we shoot down one, another two show up to take its place. We've warned them that they'll be prosecuted for doing it, but I guess they're willing to take that chance, because this story is getting blanket coverage on all the news-networks. Oh, and by the way – the Capitol Police have been warning us about problems with GrayWar personnel who claim that they have the right to pass the perimeter. They've reached out to Mr. Duke to try to resolve these issues... but he doesn't seem to be answering their calls."

"GrayWar, *again*," sighed the President. "I'm *so* sick of *that* word, you know... alright. Keep trying to get through to Duke, and if you do, I'll talk to him for a minute or two. Given how joined at the hip the military is with those clowns, I don't think we can afford to ignore them."

"Just one of the million things that the Old Man has to deal with, that you probably didn't know about," opined Kaysten, in Abruzzio's direction.

"We all have our little issues... don't we?" she deflected.

A second later, a look of alarm showed on her face, as she bolted for the door to the left of the President's big, hardwood desk, throwing it open and dashing outside.

"*Vîrya I'ëà'b'!*" shouted Abruzzio, up to the sky, past the huge, awkward shape of the top of the Washington Monument, in the South Lawn. "Where *go* thou? Is an attack coming?"

Kaysten caught up with her a split-second later.

A quizzical look overtook him.

"Did I hear... 'Mommy'?" he said. "Where the hell'd she *go*? Oh – wait, *there* she is, but what's that she's heading toward – oh, *fuck!*"

A stirring, portentous war-song – familiar to some, but just amazing and exciting to the others – began to sound in the background; its tempo and volume was waxing quickly.

Using a small fraction of his speed-skills, Kaysten reversed course and suddenly appeared next to the President.

"What's that noise... that music?" warily asked the U.S. leader. "Is it your, uhh, 'war-song'?"

"It sounds *so* cool!" gushed Clairie.

"Wow... what a *beat*, man!" added the President's son. "I feel like dancing... or fighting... or both. Like a drug..."

"Not... *exactly*, sir," answered the former Chief of Staff.

Abruzzio's face – showing a mixture of elation, awe and fear– appeared in the doorway.

"We – uhh – have *visitors*, Mr. President," she announced.

"Well... I suppose, 'better late than never'," grumbled the President. "Can you please show Mr. Jacobson in? I'd prefer just to speak with him alone, at first –"

"Sir," interrupted Sylvia Abruzzio, "It's not the 'Mars-Gang', with whom you now must contend."

The President looked stunned.

"What... what do you *mean*, Ms. Abruzzio?" he nervously asked.

"Prepare yourself; because in a minute or so, sir," she ominously declared, "You'll be dealing with someone… far, *far* more powerful and dangerous, than poor old Sam Jacobson."

Fear Her… But More, Fear Her Family

The President, after straightening his tie and wiping his forehead, moved to a position just in front of the Resolute Desk.

"Sylvia," requested Kaysten, "Would you mind doing the Old Man and I a big favor?"

"What?" she asked.

"Stand on the other side of him, in front of him, while I stand on his right," said the former Chief of Staff.

"Why's that?" she inquired.

"So she can't take a shot at him without hitting either of us, first," remarked Kaysten.

"I very much doubt she'd do something like that," countered Abruzzio, "Certainly not before talking to him, first. And did you forget her power of invisibility? She could already be standing behind us right now, you know."

"*Clark!*" cried the former First Lady.

"Stay *out* of this, Kathy!" demanded the President. "That goes for *all* of you – Matt, Clairie, Ms. Sullivan, Curt and the rest. This is between me, and the alien. Whatever she does… I don't want anyone to antagonize her. Is that clear?"

"Yes, sir," said Moira Sullivan and the two Presidential offspring, almost in unison. The Secret Service man began a protest about "Sir, we're obliged to protect you – " but his commentary was abbreviated by a "knock, knock" sound outside the Rose Garden door.

"This is the President of the United States," called out the U.S. leader. "Come in."

They had expected to see a mighty alien-queen, bedecked in lethal fighting-gear, flying through the threshold; but what in fact stepped lightly into the Oval Office was a strikingly-pretty, green-eyed, slim young Caucasian woman with long, straight, off-blonde hair cut into a teenager-style bang over the forehead, wearing vaguely-tropical-looking, elegant civilian-clothes, complete with a pair of slippers on her feet. The only (slightly) unusual things about her, other than her physical attractiveness – and you had to be looking specifically for these – were her incisor-teeth, which were perhaps a bit more prominent and pointed than would be those of a normal young human woman.

She was holding hands with a rather less-stylishly-dressed, dark-haired and tan-skinned young boy of about eight to ten years of age. The child had the expected wide-eyed amazement about being here, but there was something unnerving about his demeanor, none the less.

The weirding-music had faded, but none the less, the fingers of the Secret Service agents felt for gun-holsters.

"See," they heard her whisper, "This is the throne-room of the American kingdom, of which I have told you, dear son."

Abruzzio and Kaysten, evidently abandoning their recent plan, rushed forward to greet the Storied Watcher and her son, about six paces inside the Oval Office. They were rewarded by warm embraces on the part of the alien-girl, and polite – though clearly grudging – hand-shakes on the part of the boy.

A second or two later, clearly to Abruzzio's distress, her dog seemed to appear as if from nowhere, at the Storied Watcher's side.

"Ah – Rainbow – stealthy little one!" exclaimed Karéin-Mayréij with a wan smile, bending down to pet the mutt, "I see that you have learned much from my sister Sylvia... has she profited also, from your own teachings?"

Rainbow gave a satisfied "yip" and then ran back under one of the nearby stuffed-chairs.

"Couldn't have done it *without* her," quipped Kaysten.

"Karéin," began Abruzzio, "What brings you and Tommy here, tonight? Are you two here alone? I thought you were going to, uhh, stay out of all this?"

"Many things, both personal and of the affairs of kings, bring us hither," answered Karéin-Mayréij, in an even tone of voice. "Principally – we respond to the direct challenge from the President, that we have recently heard, indirectly, from the tee-vee. The *Express*, I have brought with us; she lies, half-cloaked, behind the, ahh, little 'gift' that I had deposited in the lawn of this palace, some time ago. Within her have come brave Melissa, wise Hector – these two, along with my joyously-reacquainted war-child, *Vîrya I'ëà'b'*, hold above, lest an air-attack come upon us; sea-loving Saquina is guarding the *Express*, while my love and mate, Bob, is outside... Bob?"

Billings' familiar face – he apparently hadn't shaved recently, and was wearing a badly-creased sport-shirt and jeans – now appeared in the doorway.

"Oh... hi, Sylvia... Jerry," he said. "Mind if I come in?"

"By all means," gestured the President, trying to sound as welcoming as possible.

Billings entered the Oval Office. He had left the door open, but a second later, it seemed to close and latch all by itself.

The President stepped forward and extended a hand.

"Nice meeting you, Ms. Mayréij," he said.

The Storied Watcher just stared at him, coolly, and did not accept the handshake-invitation.

"Physical contact with her can have *unpredictable* side-effects," whispered Abruzzio, to the President. "She's not being impolite."

"It is actually 'Karéin-Mayréij'," advised the Storied Watcher. "I do not have a name such as you humans do. If you want... you can just say 'Karéin'. May I call you, 'Mr. President', sir? Though... I believe that we have met before... after a fashion. If you recall that conversation while I was on your aerial death-ray-plane."

"Of *course*," he answered, with a forced smile.

"These two of my beloved," – Karéin-Mayréij waved her hand at Tommy and Billings – "Are my son Tommy and my mate Bob, whose stories I am sure that you already know and about which, we will shortly speak. Others among my party are, as I have earlier informed, outside. I will usher them in as well, as soon as we can be certain that we will not be attacked. I am acquainted with my sister Sylvia and my brother Jer-ee, of course; but who are these others?"

The President noted, to his dismay, that most of those who he had demanded to decamp to other parts of the White House, had trickled back in to the periphery of the Oval Office.

"Oh... well, let me introduce," said the President, "My wife, Kathy; my son, Matt, and my daughter, Clairie. My U.S. Marine guard and Secret Service detail, led by Agent Kortish, is over there, and just to one side, that's Moira Sullivan – she's one of Ms. Abruzzio's best friends – and then we have servicemen Maloney and Rizzo, of, uhh, GrayWar Legion –"

"GrayWar Legion?" interrupted the Storied Watcher, in her now-standard, even, dispassionate tone. "As Sylvia knows... we welcomed two of your mercenary-army, into our ranks, up on that island in Alaska. A 'promotion', as one might call it."

"What 'island'?" whispered the Presidential son, to his distaff sibling.

"The same one where the government dropped a hydrogen bomb, on us," commented Abruzzio.

"The same one that *blinded* me, for a while," came Tommy's seething little voice. "That killed all those soldiers who were on the island."

The Storied Watcher – her presence growing with each passing minute – walked calmly over to where the First Lady, along with her two teenaged children, was standing.

The alien-girl did one of her odd-looking, half-bow, half-curtsy gestures, while the President's family tried to maintain their composure.

"Madam Kathy... young prince Matt and princess Clairie," she addressed them, with a saturnine half-smile. "May our dealings ever be friendly ones... regardless of what else that the Spirit of Fate may come to declare."

The two teenagers stared uneasily at each other.

"Thank you," was all the first Lady could think of to say.

The Storied Watcher also called out to Abruzzio, "Sylvia... let you, I and your friend spend some time together, when this is all over. Moira – nice to meet you, new-found sister."

"You too," uneasily answered Sullivan.

"Would you like to sit down?" asked the President.

"Certainly," she obliged, directing Tommy to one side of her, with Billings on the other. Kaysten and Abruzzio, for their parts, flanked the President on the opposite Oval Office sitting-couch.

The President hesitated for a couple of seconds, but – wanting to avoid a frosty atmosphere, and also desiring to guide the conversation – he decided to speak up.

"So... did I get it correctly, that you had heard my recent address to the nation?" he asked.

"Not initially," she corrected. "My fellow-travelers and I were, ahh, 'conducting other business' – we were flying through the skies – when we were attacked without warning or cause, by your Air Force. In that engagement, though we were victorious, our air-ship, whose name is the *'Mailànkh Express'*, was damaged; so we landed to see if it would be safe to carry on. However where we came to ground was an inhabited place, and it was there that we first heard that such a speech had been made. We resolved to come here, and on the way, my war-children and I used our arts to, ahh, listen to your... what is the word..."

"TV-broadcasts," assisted Abruzzio.

"Yes... to your tee-vee broadcasts," said the Storied Watcher. "So by this, we learned the import of your messages, both to ourselves and to Sam Jacobson and his friends, who you have called the 'Mars-Gang'. The latter is up to Sam and his people; but as to the former – and to other things, which to us are more important still – those are why we now are here."

"I... *see*," he neutrally offered.

"Before we discuss any of this... I *do* have a question, however, sir," stated Karéin-Mayréij.

"Go ahead," he indicated.

"My understanding of your message to your subjects is, that you have those of my own kin – that is, those who have inherited the Holy *Fire* – who are pledged to war, on your behalf. This sounds strange to me, sir. Unless someone has come to the knowing of *Amaiish* without mine own doing of it –"

"He means, 'Jerry and me', Karéin," broke in Abruzzio. "We tracked the President down to where he was being held against his will, freed him and the First Family and then got them in here. I can't speak for Jerry, but I told the President that I'd ask you to at least *listen* to his explanations for what's gone on with all of us, over the past few weeks... so consider yourself 'asked'. But as for *fighting* you – or Jacobson, for that matter – on his behalf? I think you know the answer to *that*, already."

"Jer-ee?" pressed the Storied Watcher, with a searching gaze in Kaysten's direction.

"You know me... I'm a 'lover', not a 'fighter'... you know?" he evaded. "But to tell you the truth, Karéin," he went on, sounding more serious as he spoke, "I'm *conflicted*, big-time, about this thing. I'm with you – *you* know that – but I've been with the Old Man here, almost since I got out of university. I *owe* him my loyalty, come what may. I just want to see everybody work it out... without it escalating into something more than talk."

"Wise is the person who does all to avoid war; less wise is he or she who persists, when war comes, none the less," cryptically replied Karéin-Mayréij. "And I can see that this claim – that is, of an 'army of super-people, pledged to fight to the death in the service of the American Empire' – well, *that* one is worth about as much as many of the other promises that were latterly made by yourself, sir, some time ago... when I was thought to be weak and gullible, and Bob and Tommy here were languishing in your dungeons. Is it not?"

A perceptible chill came to the surroundings.

Tommy's cold stare caught the President dead-on.

Billings had a "cat who ate the canary" look on his face.

The President cast his eyes downward.

Oh shit, thought Abruzzio, *I thought she'd wait just a little while, before – I had better deal with this fast –*

As the President stood up and walked around to the back of the couch on which he had been sitting (although he kept looking at the Storied Watcher), Abruzzio jumped in to the conversation.

"Karéin... Bob... Tommy," she implored, "I *know* why you're angry with the President and the government – God knows, you have ample *right* to be, as do every one of us who ended up on Amchitka – but *please* let him tell you his side of the story, before you... uhh... *do* anything! The story's more complicated than I think you yet understand."

The First Lady's lips were pursed and the color had almost completely left her face, while her two children shared frightened glances.

"What's 'complicated' about, 'torturing kids', Sylvia?" unhelpfully remarked Billings. "Not to mention... 'torturing, *me*'."

"Look, Bob," stepped in Kaysten, "We went over this up in the woods... remember? And there's more – this miserable stuff was all *George's* idea –"

"Who is 'George'?" asked the Storied Watcher.

"The former Vice-President, who took over the government in a *coup* against the President," whispered Abruzzio, to Karéin-Mayréij.

"Ah," the alien-girl remarked, "A knave, who seeks to become king –"

The President was now standing behind the couch upon which Abruzzio and Kaysten were sitting.

The U.S. leader interrupted,

"No, Jerry... the responsibility for this, is mine... and mine alone. I invited Karéin here knowing that from the start. All I would ask, Madam, is that before you try to judge me – or the government of the United States generally – that you at least *listen* to our side of the story, and – if it's at all possible – try to understand what this has looked like, from the perspective of my office."

"Oh... by all *means*, sir," coldly and precisely answered the Storied Watcher. "And we shall see how well *you* 'understand' how it has all looked like, from the perspective of a small boy being tortured – or that of my beloved, orphaned little daughter Elissha, who – while being tormented in similar cruel manner – watched her brother die an agonizing, premature death, inflicted for the amusement of your kingdom's monstrous jailers, alongside her."

"Yeah," growled Billings. "Did I mention, I can send the entire experience your way, just with a *thought?* I guarantee it's something you'll never forget!"

Now it was the President's turn, to acquire a sudden pallor.

"*Jesus Christ,*" he muttered. "Jerry... what's she *talking* about? *Surely* we didn't..."

"I... I don't know what to *say*, sir," Kaysten, now staring downward himself, forced out. "She... uhh... adopted a little girl who the Jacobson party found deep in the Agency's Amchitka prison, while on the way to free Tommy. I have to assume that what Sam and his friends said about it, might be correct... I felt sick when I heard the story. But it was the *Agency*, dammit! We can't take the fall for what those assholes were doing –"

"Jerry – let *me* speak to that," requested the President.

His face was grim, yet composed and determined, as he said, "Karéin – Mr. Billings – young man – let me first apologize, in the most sincere terms, for the intolerable cruelties that were inflicted on yourselves, as well as on other members of your families. Jerry's correct in saying that these disgraceful actions were undertaken by the Central Intelligence Agency, as well as other branches of the U.S. intelligence community; and for the record, they were unknown to myself, until well after the time when you – Storied Watcher – appeared on the scene... that is, after the incident with the comet, when you landed in the United States."

The U.S. leader continued, "But I *should* have known that they were going on, and I *should* have put a stop to them, the moment that I found out that they were happening. I hesitated; I didn't do that. I *failed* you; I failed my *country*; and most of all, I failed *God* and my own *conscience.* There's no other way to put it... and that failure is something that will shame and haunt me until my dying day."

The Storied Watcher stood up, on her part; Billings and Tommy also tried to do so, but were motioned by their mate and mother to remain sitting.

There was a look of cold contempt on her face.

"Well... *curse you!*" she spat, while moving away from the couch, to a point to Abruzzio's right, with a direct path to the President. "*Indeed*, pathetic is a king, who pretends not to know what his hired-brutes are doing to poor, helpless peasants, in the bowels of a dungeon. Many of your kind, have I met across empires and worlds uncounted... and what they all have in common is, 'they all fall to deserv-ed ruin'. Now you know – or *should* know, if Jer-ee and Sylvia have so disclosed – that within me is the ability to lay open your mind, with or without your assent, to force out the truth behind what you say –"

"*Trust* me, my friend," Billings commented, "She ain't kidding about this! She tried it on *me*, back in Tucson... and it was almost as bad as dealing with what your 'doctors' in the jail, put me through. And I'm supposedly much better set up to deal with it, than a human is. If I were *you*... I'd tell her nothing but the full truth, from here on in. You *don't* want Her Alien Highness fucking around inside your head – that is, if you want to have a mind *left* –"

"Leave him *alone!*" shouted the First Lady, rushing to the President's side.

"But I... will *not*, do this thing," softly spoke the Storied Watcher, with tears in her eyes.

"*Why* not?" challenged the President. "We both know, Madam, that you can do anything that you want... right here, right now. We all know that your powers would overwhelm my guards, which is why I'm reminding them to stay at their posts and not intervene. You want to *kill* me, or just cripple me? Go ahead – now's your chance."

"I will not," quietly retreated Karéin-Mayréij, "Because it is *shameful* to me, to beset a helpless opponent – even one who has, like yourself, greatly wronged me – in cold blood. I realize that this is my personal code of honor, and that you may not understand it, but –"

"No, Karéin," he contradicted, "I understand, *perfectly*. And... 'thank you'. I've made many mistakes along the way, and I'm prepared to own up to them, and to make amends for them, to the extent I'm able –"

"Your cute little 'amends' don't count for Jack *shit* around here," warned Billings. "*She*, may decide to act 'nobly' and give you the benefit of the doubt... as for Tommy and I, well, let's just say, 'having your veins filled with acid and being almost burned alive in a torture-chamber... that changes your perspective on life, a bit'. Kind of lessens the attractiveness of 'second chances'... you know?"

Wisely, the grave-faced President silently nodded acknowledgment.

"Mommy – he's here – so are we – and he *did* it! Let me *kill* him – *please!*" shrieked a devil-faced, red-eyed, agitated Tommy, who came immediately to his feet.

His electrifying – yet frightening – war-song, began playing as if out of nowhere.

The President – though clearly believing himself to be living out his last seconds – did not move; he sent another wave-off to the Marine guards and Secret Service agents, all of whom were a split-second away from charging forward.

Both Abruzzio and Kaysten immediately arose and blocked the boy's line-of-sight to the U.S. leader.

Worryingly, however, Billings stood up beside Tommy.

"Tommy," demanded Abruzzio, "Stand *down!* This is *not* the time and the place for *murder!*"

"Miz Sylvia," hissed the boy, "I don't want to hurt you or Mister Jerry – but you're in the *way!* He *deserves* it! Don't you *care* about what he did to me, to Mister Billings, to Elissha... to Korey?"

"Of *course* we do, little brother!" she tried to cajole, "But your Mom is right – and you need to listen to her! Killing people in a war, who are trying to kill you first... that's *different* from what you're proposing to do, here! You're just lowering yourself, and all of us along with you, to his level –"

"Sylvia... why don't you just stay out of this?" accosted Billings. "This isn't your fight, and with all due respect, you don't have the *slightest* fucking idea of what was done to us! The kid's right – the son of a bitch *deserves* it, in *spades!*"

"And you or Tommy kill the guy behind me... and what happens *then?*" angrily retorted Abruzzio. "Think it through, for God's sake! Are you planning on running the United States, all by yourself? What's your fucking genius plan for the bloody morning after, Bob?"

The Storied Watcher had now moved a substantial distance away from the two sitting-couches in the middle of the Oval Office.

"I don't know – and frankly, Scarlett, I don't *give* a damn!" grunted the salesman, whose eyes were now starting to glow an ominous green-color. "Not my *problem*. Give it back to the Indians, sell it to the Gypsies... all the same to *me*."

Billings' war-song began to merge with Tommy's, in some foreboding way.

"Mr. President," called out Agent Kortish, "Please move back, away from these individuals. This is an unsafe situation!"

"You're not just fucking whistling *Dixie*, it's 'unsafe', whoever you are," growled Billings. "You want to *die*, more painfully than you can possibly imagine... you raise those guns against us!"

"My responsibility is to protect the President, sir," replied Kortish. "That's what I'll *do* – have no doubt!"

Sullivan and the two GrayWar guys tried to hide behind furniture, although there was little to use for this purpose.

"Curt," demanded the President, "You'll take *no* aggressive action against them, under *any* circumstances – *is that understood?*"

"Sir –" the agent tried to say.

"*Karéin!*" implored Abruzzio, "Tell them to back off! *Surely* you can't approve of this!"

With a sad look on her face, the Storied Watcher replied, "Sylvia... I promised that I would not slay this man, except in heat of battle. I said nothing of imposing the constraints of my own honor, upon *others*. This doom may come from events set in motion long ago, within which I had no part. It is between my greatly-wronged family, and your 'President'. It is not *my* war."

"Didn't you say something about 'not ignoring a war, when it shows up at your doorstep'?" disputed a frustrated Abruzzio.

"Leave my Dad *alone!*" cried Clairie. "Doesn't it *matter* to you, that *George* and the CIA were the ones who did these awful things to you?"

"Oh... I got *nothing* against your Dad, my dear!" retorted Billings, "Other than he was – you heard him just say it himself – in charge of the whole sorry show, while my fingernails were being pulled out, and my flesh was being Julienned by the Agency's dull razor-blades. As to this 'George' guy... there's *always* somebody else to point the finger at, so it's 'not my fault'. Sorry that it's your Dad who's gotten in over his head on this one, kid... maybe he should have thought about that, when he got the body-count reports back from Amchitka. Them's the breaks. Sylvia – Jerry – stand aside!"

"Go *fuck* yourself, Bob!" inveighed an uncharacteristically-livid Kaysten, whose own eyes – like those of Abruzzio – were now starting to glow, along with their own, burgeoning war-songs.

"Don't be an *idiot*, Jerry!" countered Billings. "She told us that our attacks would probably overwhelm your defenses. You're holding a paper shield, and the kid and me are here with guns. You're asking to get *hurt*... or worse!"

"Yeah, well," argued the former Chief of Staff, "Last I heard, nobody – particularly not your girlfriend – appointed you or or your step-son, unofficial state executioners, or tourist assassins. If you're up for *murder*... then go ahead and add me to your head-count, along with the only man who can still save the country from anarchy, as well as your 'sister', Sylvia. Just one other thing, though."

"Yeah?" said Billings.

"Don't *miss!*" threatened Kaysten.

His demeanor was completely at odds with his usual chipper self; there was a cold anger in the former Chief of Staff's voice.

"If you *do*," he spat, "Get ready for a fucking high-speed impact!"

"*Karein!*" shouted Abruzzio. "*Help!*"

The Storied Watcher – with tears now flowing down her cheeks – just mutely stood there.

*Bob – Tommy – **please!*** she sent, *Find another way... I beg you!*
Cold blood, even justly spilt – it brings hot blood later, ten times ten over!
I feel us all, falling into darkness!
Turn away from this dread path!

"Maybe *you've* lost your nerve, honey," spoke Billings, aloud, "But 'Mr. President' and me here... we got *business!*"

"Mister Jerry," added Tommy, with his hands and fingers held out in menacing claw-fashion in front of him, pointed in the general direction of the President behind Abruzzio and Kaysten, "I can't *control* it that good – if you stand there, you might get hit! Get out of the way – *please!*"

"No," said Kaysten, with utter obduracy. "Son... I hope you know what you're doing, because it will stay with you... *forever.*"

His body began reverberating, moving quickly back and forth, so that his very image became indistinct, at the edges.

What happened next, occurred in a fraction of a second.

The Storied Watcher flew towards the President at unbelievable speed, from a standing start. Something moving too fast for human eyes to track, shattered the top-part of one of the Oval Office windows just behind the Resolute Desk and kept on its inward trajectory, rocketing into the room.

One of Tommy's screeching, brilliantly-shining, projectile-like death-shots, screamed outward from his finger-tips. It was aimed squarely at the President, just above his waistline, but struck a glancing blow against Kaysten's right-hand side, deflecting off at an oblique angle.

The attack still seemed likely to hit the American leader in the lower chest, but it did not impact him. Instead, it struck the hurtling Karéin-Mayréij, who had interposed herself between the President and the couch. The boy's attack was clearly lethally potent, since there was a loud "bang" accompanied by a hail of sparks and the unfortunate alien-girl was thrown head-over-heels backward, smashing into one of the office's peripheral walls at high speed.

The President did not get away scot-free, however; as the Storied Watcher was sent off-balance, part of her stricken body hit his own, sending him to his knees, moaning in pain.

The Secret Service disobeyed their orders and charged forward, forming a human-shield around him, while the First Family and others in the room, cowered and crouched.

While this was going on, Billings loosed a greenish-yellow lightening-bolt that was probably also aimed at the President, but looked like it would instead strike Kaysten. The former Chief of Staff tried to dodge, but Billings' attack covered too large a target-area to be avoided.

Yet Kaysten suffered no damage from this; instead, the lightening-bolt hit *Vìrya I'ëà'b'*, who had re-entered the Oval Office through the broken window behind the desk. The sentient-shield was also sent flying, and it went careening high into a side-wall, embedding itself in the latter not far from where the Storied Watcher herself had crashed.

Vìrya I'ëà'b' reverberated as she struggled in frustration to free herself.

Billings suddenly disappeared from human eyes, but Kaysten had a clean fix on the ex-salesman's last position, and ruthlessly took advantage of it. The wounded – but still operational – former Chief of Staff, achieving a substantial fraction of the alien-girl's rocket-like velocity, ploughed directly into an apparently empty space, body-slamming its invisible inhabitant backwards into the opposite wall of the Oval Office at a speed that would certainly have killed or crippled an ordinary human being. Billings' body was smashed at least a half-inch into the wall, crushing gypsum-board and splintering wood all around.

A shudder from the impact, echoed through the entire building.

A badly-hurt Billings came partially into view, and he and an also-wounded Kaysten began struggling, with blasts of yellow-green energy and impossibly-fast hand-blows, being traded back and forth.

Tommy prepared another attack, but was deterred by the now-fully-powered Abruzzio, who – accompanied by her dog – had encased herself in a multi-colored, shimmering 'bubble', and who moved right in front of the boy, with her hands pushed forward, palms-upward.

"*Stop it now – all of you!*" she yelled. "Or Rainbow and I will pump so much *Amaiish* into our microwaves that the ones who die *quickly*, will be the *lucky* ones!"

"You wouldn't *do* that..." challenged Tommy.

"Wanna *bet?*" she furiously retorted. "Tommy – you leave me no *choice!*"

Abruzzio leaned forward and, working in unison with the dog, directed her invisible attack toward the boy, ramping up the strength of the *Fire* in it on a logarithmic scale per second.

The Rad-Haz badges on the Secret Service, started to change color.

"*Oww – it hurts – it **hurts!**"* wailed the boy.

Somehow, Abruzzio intuitively knew that Tommy's healing-abilities were being stretched to their limits; she was using a level of power that would be instantly fatal to any normal human.

She silently prayed that he *could*, in fact, recover. She also prayed that he wouldn't or couldn't counter-attack, since there would be no dodging at this close range.

The protests of pain were echoed by the now-visible Billings and Kaysten, who were more or less in the conical line of fire extending out from in front of Abruzzio's hands. The two – already bruised and bloodied from only a couple of seconds of close combat – crawled away, attempting to catch their breath and recover from the ordeal.

"*Jesus,*" gasped the ex-salesman, "Whatever that was... got through my hidey-cloak... damn you..."

Abruzzio's lethal energy-field slowly powered down.

The paint of an area of the Oval Office wall, directly in line of Abruzzio and the dog and roughly where Kaysten and Billings had impacted in their abortive fight, began to bubble, smolder, crack and fall off. The damage seemed to go at least an inch into the drywall behind, which was crumbling into dust.

A three-foot section of the couch behind Tommy, had changed color to a blanched white and it, too, was starting to disintegrate.

The Storied Watcher – obviously hit hard by her erstwhile son's explosive-blast – slowly staggered to her feet, wheezing and coughing out acid blood, as she arose. A second or two later, *Vîrya I'ëà'b'* dropped down from her impact-spot and landed on Karéin-Mayréij's arm.

Abruzzio, now also crying openly, dropped to one knee and reached out to embrace the boy, who seemed dazed and possibly going into shock.

"Tommy... *stay* with me, for God's sake!" she implored; the entreaty seemed to work, as he opened his eyes and stared at her. "Son, I'm *terribly* sorry that I had to do that – but it's what happens when adults get in a real war. It's not a video-game... and you *don't* get a 'replay' when you get killed. Hold me now and draw strength from me, if you need to."

"I'm... *sorry*... Miss Sylvia," whimpered the boy.

In a half-second, the Storied Watcher – though clearly still badly-hurt herself, with an ugly, baseball-sized, bloodied wound in her midriff – had dashed over to the two.

She laid hands on Tommy, who was 'woozy' and half-aware.

"He will survive," she counseled, to Abruzzio's immense relief, "Though he urgently needs to rest, so as to direct all his arts to recovering."

"Mom," breathed the boy, "Did I... *hurt* you? I didn't *mean* to!"

"It is oh-kay, young prince," she replied, with a forced, pained smile, "Although I should not want to repeat that experience. Your attack is *most* potent. Daughter Tornado Diamond-Curtain attests the same, for that of my mate and your father. Her mind was filled with foul thoughts, which she struggles to expunge... though I will ensure that so she does."

"Jesus *Christ!*" came Billings' voice, "What the hell was *that?* It felt like I was being electro-shocked and roasted, all at the same time!"

"Oh... *man...* I'm going to *puke!*" groaned an ashen-faced Kaysten.

He bolted for the door to the Rose Garden, apparently only just making it outside before unpleasantly proving his remark a prescient one.

"Mr. *President*," called Abruzzio, while still holding the boy close to her body, "Are you *alright?*"

His voice came back from inside a scrum of Secret Service bodies.

"I... I *think* so," he gasped. "I got hit hard by something, but I don't think I'm seriously wounded. Curt – can you get the team off me, please? I want to try to stand up."

"Sir –" protested Kortish.

"I think the shooting's over, for the time being," argued the President. "Ms. Abruzzio... am I right?"

"As far as Tommy's concerned, 'yes'," she answered. "Bob?"

"I guess he's safe for now, as long as he has you to protect him, Sylvia," threatened Billings. "Goddammit Kaysten... that felt like being hit by a dump-truck. And thanks for the wonderful support... 'sister'. Did I tell you... I have a long memory?"

"Seems short to *me*, Bob," she contested. "I saved your *life* up on Amchitka. No thanks for the 'gratitude'."

The First Lady, assisted by her son and daughter, took the President's arm, as the Service agents began to un-cluster from around him.

Sullivan, throwing caution to the winds, came over to crouch by Abruzzio.

Tommy seemed to recover from his radiation-bath, with remarkable speed.

"I don't know who you *are*," angrily accosted the First Lady in Billings' direction, "But you're trying to kill the wrong man! It's a *miracle* that nobody else around here was killed! For the love of God... leave us *alone!*"

"Don't know if you overheard, ma'am," grunted Billings, who was still feeling his body for burn-marks and self-healing multiple bruises, contusions and fractures, as he struggled to his feet, "But the name's 'Bob Billings', former flooring-tile and kitchen-reno salesman extraordinaire, former U.S. government torture-experiment non-volunteer, now a half-alien with a chip on shoulder. You want me to lay off your husband? Fine, then – get me some *evidence*, that he's just a little lost lamb who had nothing to do with what's happened to Tommy, Elissha, her late brother, or myself. Until then... he had better watch his *back!*"

"You're a *monster!*" she spat.

"Yeah, well... being tortured for days on end and then being turned into an alien with the ability to kill by just wanting to, *does* funny things to you... try it some time and you'll see," he sourly replied. "As to being a 'monster', well... I'll leave it to others, to figure out who that best refers to."

"Mom," half-whispered Tommy, "Are you just going to let the President get *away*? After what they *did* to Mister Billings, Elissha, Korey and me? Don't you *love* me, Mommy?"

The Storied Watcher hung her head and began to softly weep.

"Tommy... that's *really* unfair!" protested Abruzzio. "Your Mom is trying to avoid getting more people hurt or killed... she's trying to prevent a *war!* What happened to you and your family was utterly, disgracefully wrong, it was tragic... but it can't be un-done, by yet more violence. Don't you understand?"

"No," he flatly replied. "They made us hurt *so* much... they *killed* Korey, and he was the most important person in the whole world, for Elissha – and you're wanting them to get *away* with it, Miz Sylvia!"

"Is this... *true?*" spoke up the previously-quiet Sullivan.

She crossed herself.

"Yes, new sister Moira... it *is*," quietly confirmed Karéin-Mayréij, "And though the damnable intent behind these atrocities was never mine own, the blame lies also with me... because I *failed*... I was *late*, in finding and rescuing my then-helpless kin, who suffered this on account of me."

"Karéin – it's *ludicrous* to blame yourself for any of this!" argued Abruzzio. "*You've* been a victim of the government's cruelty too. So have we all. Only the method, and the severity, differs between us. The responsibility is theirs alone... not ours."

"That is human-thinking, beloved sister," claimed the Storied Watcher. "Not how *I*, think... not how my principles, guide me. And Tommy's plea is valid. His life-path, and that of my other children, is forever scarred.. forever, *changed*, by these experiences. The balance of the Heavens is upset... it must be made right. Thus..."

She arose, with the majesty of her power, refulgent and awesome to all.

Her eyes glowed bright, as the weirding-shield left her arm and went to assuage Kaysten (this gesture on the part of *Vîrya I'ëà'b'* was gratefully accepted by the wobbly-kneed, greatly-weakened former Chief of Staff).

Slowly and deliberately, she walked on a reverse-course back to where the President and the First Family, were standing together.

"My soul-wounded son speaks the *truth*, not just on his behalf, but for that of his absent sister, and her brother, who died in agony, at the hands of your lackeys," solemnly declared Karéin-Mayréij, addressing the U.S. leader, directly. "While it is shameful to strike you down... scarcely less, is it to leave you untouched by all that has happened. I spared your life, at risk to mine own – Tommy's attack would not just have killed you, but indeed would have spread the remnants of your body all around this room – because for you to die in this way... it would not be *right*. Unfortunately, I do not know exactly how to say this in Eng-lish, in a manner that you would understand."

"Not... 'right'?" complained Billings, from the other side of the room. "Well, just let *me* get a clean shot at him! *I* can put it 'right' – I'll give you a money-back *guarantee!*"

The Secret Service tried to form a wall in front of the President, but he directed them away, so as to confront the Storied Watcher directly.

"So what exactly are you proposing to *do*, Madam?" he challenged.

"The balance of celestial justice is badly in deficit," explained the alien-girl, "On account of the cruelties done to my son and daughter. And even if we seek not to avenge the dead – while still we mourn and remember them – and even if we ask those such as my beloved Bob, to endure the unendurable and to forgive – *still* the balance is failed, for Tommy and Elissha and little Korey."

"I'm sorry, Madam," said the President, "But I'm not following you."

"My *God*, Karéin!" exclaimed Abruzzio, "No, no... **no!** You can't be seriously *thinking* about doing this! Please, in the name of mercy and all that's holy... I'm *begging* you!"

"What are you so upset about?" whispered Sullivan to the former JPL space scientist.

"Moira," breathed Abruzzio, *sotto voce*, "If you know how... say a prayer for those poor two kids."

"Which ones –" asked Sullivan.

"In *my* world," evenly expounded the Storied Watcher, "The way how *I* think – I have two children, who, though still living, were tormented in bestial fashion; and I have the man who accepted, ahh, 'ownership', for this. I am forestalled from crushing him – as he would otherwise deserve – for reasons that have already been stated. But... this man... this *guilty* man... he *does* have, two children, of his own."

Her gaze – regal and terrible, yet, somehow, sad and sympathetic at the same time – fell upon the two First Family teenagers.

"Don't you *dare!*" screamed the First Lady. She tried to slap the alien-girl (who just stood impassively in place, while being assaulted) across the face, but on contact, there was a bright flash, accompanied by an energy-discharge which sent the woman crashing to the floor.

"*Kathy!*" cried the President, as he rushed to comfort her.

"Hey... did we forget to warn you about that happening, to people who try to hit Sari?" taunted Billings. "Son of a *bitch*, eh?"

"Fuck off, Bob... and spare us the 'tough-guy' bullshit," swore Kaysten, who had re-entered the room. "She's just an old *lady*, for God's sake!"

"Do not worry," reassured Karéin-Mayréij, "She is not badly-hurt; I reduced my self-defense to a minimum. But she waxes and wanes according to threat. Your bodyguards should take this into consideration."

Clairie and Matt were white-faced with fear, and they tried to step backwards, toward one of the doors leading from the Oval Office to other parts of the White House.

"Come... come now, young princelings," unctuously cajoled the Storied Watcher. "Why so soon to leave us?"

"Karéin," pleaded a grim-faced President, "Now *I'm* begging you – if you're out for revenge... then take *me!* Matt and Clairie had nothing – absolutely *nothing* – to do with this! It was all *my* fault... I *admit* it! Kill me if you want blood on your damn 'cosmic weigh-scales'... but leave my family *alone!"*

"Madam," added Kortish, "We can't let you do this –"

With a perfunctory gesture of her left hand, the alien-girl's telekinetic attack sent the agent flying head-over-heels to the far end of the Oval Office.

Kortish hit part of the wall below the windows looking outside; he appeared to have the wind knocked out of him, but otherwise did not seem seriously injured.

"This is not between you and I, nor the bodyguards and I, nor your American President and I, any more," sniffed Karéin-Mayréij. "It is between a prince, and a princess, and I."

The teenaged girl stepped defiantly forward.

"If you're planning to *kill* me," she called out, "Then go ahead... I'm ready."

"I prefer to go down fighting," added the Presidential son. "Get me a gun, a sword... anything!"

The First Lady was crying profusely, with her husband's arms around her.

"Not in *here*," contradicted the Storied Watcher. "Not in front of these others. Now Matt – Clairie – I regret that your fortunes, heretofore so easy, are about to... *change*. If you value the lives of your father and mother, you will accompany me to elsewhere in this building, where what is... *necessary*, will be done. Either that... or I authorize my mate Bob and my son Tommy, to enact revenge, as *they* conceive of it."

"Tell her 'no' – *please!"* maliciously exclaimed Billings. "Can we say, 'I'm itching to go'?"

Kaysten – strangely – seemed unperturbed by all that was going on.

"All this really *has* made a monster out of you, Bob," castigated Abruzzio. "Not to mention of our wonderful, 'angelic' mentor. *Damn you, Karéin!* You talk of 'lowering yourself'... well, you couldn't get 'lower', if you joined the Agency, tomorrow. I'm ashamed to be associated with you... and I want nothing more to do with you or your poisoned, accursed super-powers!"

"Perhaps some day, as your own powers and responsibilities wax, Sylvia," quietly responded the alien-girl, "You will come to understand why I think, and act, as I do. Judge me not, until again comes the dawn."

"Holy Mary, Mother of God, save us all, from this foul sin," chanted the ex-scientist, while fingering her crucifix.

"No... no... please *God, no...*" whimpered the First Lady.

"Mom – Dad – I love you," spoke Clairie's trembling voice.

"Me too," echoed Matt. "Dad... I want you to know, I'm proud of you, and of how you've run the country. And I'm proud to be your son."

"I thought *better* of you, Madam," spat the President, "But you really *are*, just the mortal danger to the peace and safety of this Republic, that George warned me about. I welcomed you into this office to make peace, and you repay my trust, by trying to kill me and then murdering my *children!* I can't defeat you... all I can do is pray that Almighty God will, in His own time, eventually strike you down. *Curse you to hell!*"

"Make no predictions about the future, sir," elliptically offered Karéin-Mayréij, "For it will never come to be, as you suppose."

She sternly motioned to the two teenagers, as the door to which they had been moving, suddenly flew open.

"Goodbye," sobbed Clairie, as she and her brother – followed by the Storied Watcher – exited the Oval Office.

"Let me go... I want to *see!*" growled Tommy.

"No, son... you *don't*," quietly said Abruzzio.

Her shoulders slumped and she began to cry.

The three – with the two teenagers, each lost in what they believed to be final thoughts, in front of the alien-girl – walked at a slow pace down the carpeted halls of the White House.

Eventually they came to a corner-office. "CHIEF OF STAFF" was emblazoned on a brass-plate adorning its oaken-door.

A few Secret Service agents appeared far-away, down the corridor going off to the right. But neither of the Presidential offspring, perhaps resigned to their fate, called out for what would certainly have been a futile battle.

"How... *appropriate*," murmured the Storied Watcher. "I remember this place... as, no doubt, would Jer-ee."

From out of nowhere, there appeared a very sharp-looking sword, its blade glowing in an ever-changing mixture of green and red.

"*Væran Fàiagàryuu*," she directed, "Guard thee the door, and let none – even others of the *Fire*, neither yet mine own kin – into this place."

A weird, other-worldly growl was heard, as the sword, levitating in place, went into the hallway.

The Storied Watcher's telekinetic powers forced the door open, and also propelled the sullen boy, and his trembling, scared-stiff sister, into the room. The interior was still in fairly rough shape from events recently past, although at least the window leading to the lawns beyond had been temporarily repaired.

The door shut behind them, leaving the sword outside.

"This will do nicely," she said, while laying a couple of pillows taken from a sitting-divan, on the floor, and arranging a pair of state flags, which had previously been arrayed on a wall, in parallel fashion below the pillows.

"I want to die on my *feet*, damn you!" spat the boy.

"I'm not lying down," said Clairie. "I just want a chance to say my prayers and ask God for forgiveness."

There was a wry smile on the alien-girl's face.

"Who said anything about 'dying', young man?" she countered. "Certainly not *me!*"

An astonished, unwilling-to-believe look came over both of the teenagers.

"You *told* our Dad, and our Mom – and Ms. Abruzzio –" started Clairie.

"No... I most definitely did *not!*" contradicted Karéin-Mayréij. "All that I did, was to allow them all to *infer* this... and for the purpose currently at hand, nor did I reveal what fate that I actually have in store for the two of you."

"Which *is*...?" warily asked Matt.

"I informed to your father that the balance is in deficit, on account of my tormented children, and that his own children would be forfeit, in the stead of Tommy and Elissha... and those words were entirely true," explained the Storied Watcher. "Something unanticipated – and unwanted, to say the least – came upon my beloved children; and their lives will never be the same... *so*..."

They noticed that her fangs were starting to extend.

Again, Clairie blanched.

"You're going to *torture* us?" she wailed. "Or *bite* us to death?"

"Ach! Child – you know *so* little, of how I work!" complained the alien-girl. "I said, 'changed'... *not*, 'hurt' or 'made to suffer'. Now listen closely; for this is the *only* way out for you and your father... perhaps, for your country, as well. For if you refuse me, my next move is to simply say, 'have your way with the President, and all who guard him', to my sorely-wronged and anger-filled mate, Bob Billings. He is more than capable of laying waste not just to your father, and to these 'Secret Service' guards, but indeed for many leagues in all directions... so provoke him not! Do you see my teeth?"

"Yeah," cautiously answered the boy. "Are those, like... *real*?"

"Very," confirmed Karéin-Mayréij. "They bear many venoms, of diverse purposes, and I can choose which will come to them, at any time. One of these – which any mortal should crave above all other things – I call 'the Kiss of Fire'. I mean to bite each of you with it, provided that you will swear an oath beforehand."

"What... does this thing do?" demanded the boy. "Like... make us into some kind of alien zombie?"

"You will fall into a deep sleep, and you may be ill of stomach when you awake, which will be a few hours later," described the Storied Watcher. "As to being a 'zombie'... well, no, young man, and I have seen many real ones of this sort, and necromancy is not something that I dabble in. No, Matt... the Kiss of Fire does something much, much different... much, *better*. Specifically, it give you the knowledge of *Amaiish*... it turns you, into one of 'us'. Like Jer-ee, Sylvia, Bob and Tommy."

"Uhh... not following you," complained Matt.

"Your own powers – and your own war-songs – will come," explained the alien-girl. "You will live long years – many more so than for normal people of your race – and many other blessings will equally be bestowed upon you. But... listen carefully to me now, princelings – with all this, comes *responsibility*; you will be in the service of others, to the end of your days. You will automatically become far better than humans, physically, and mentally... but you will have to *learn* how to be better than these lesser beings, ethically and morally. This challenge will not be easy; you will have to work to achieve it. What *say* you?"

The teenagers were utterly perplexed, exchanging wide-eyed glances.

Eventually the girl offered, "Well... that sounds a lot better than being killed... or than Dad or other people getting killed. What you think, Matt?"

"I bet it's just a way for her to control our minds," he responded with suspicion.

The Storied Watcher stared into his eyes.

No, son, came an unanticipated thought,

This, *is how I plague and control human-minds.*

Immediately – somehow being unable to regulate his nerve-reflexes – Matt began to spasm and jerk as if overcome by palsy. He drooled, grimaced and jerked aimlessly on the floor, and was beginning to asphyxiate due to lack of lung-control.

"Stop it! *Stop it!*" shouted Clairie.

The boy's spasms abated and he got to his knees.

"How did that feel?" disingenuously inquired the Storied Watcher.

"Fucking *miserable*," mumbled the boy, still trying to regain his composure. "I'm lucky I didn't piss my pants... I *think*."

"Human-minds are weak... nearly helpless," remarked the alien-girl. "I would wager that you *hated* me doing that to you... am I correct?"

"Yeah," disclosed Matt.

"Want to learn how to resist me, so I cannot again dominate your mind?" she cajoled. "Want to be *powerful*, beyond human comprehension... to make a *difference*, in the future of your kingdom... of your *planet?*"

"Will I still be... *human?*" plaintively asked Clairie.

"Clairie," softly and earnestly spoke Karéin-Mayréij, "I want you to become my 'little sister of the *Fire*'... and where *I* come from, one does not mislead one's kin, or one's kin-to-be. So I will say the truth : no... you will *not*. You will be less than I am... but you will become much, *much* greater than any human. You will have to find your own way in the world, thus set; and you will have to serve others and use your new-found powers to help them, because time after time, there will be no-one else who can do so. Fear it not, little sister – for it is a great blessing... a great honor! And do you know what else it is... perhaps, most important of all?"

"Uhh... no... *what?*" asked a befuddled Matt.

The Storied Watcher – tears in her eyes – hung her head.

Then she quietly explained,

"It is a way *out*... for me. That I would preserve my honor, and in some way, avenge the wrongs done on my children... yet without hurting you or your father, nor without starting a war that would bring terror and ruin, to your kingdom. Your father... *he*, begged me. Now it is time for *me*, to do the same, in front of you."

She knelt submissively in front of them.

"I *can* force," she said, "But I will, instead... *ask*, humbly and sincerely, with all the hope in my heart that you will trust one who has given you fair reason, not to. Help me to find a way to *peace*. Far too much innocent blood has been spilled, already! Its stench poisons my soul, it *disgusts* me... and the curse fixes to spread. Help me to *stop* this!"

Matt and Clairie looked at each other, then knelt beside the alien-girl.

"Karéin," said the Presidential daughter, "What's this 'oath', of which you spoke?"

It had taken several minutes for the survivors of the fire-fight in the Oval Office, to gather their wits and take stock of the situation.

While Billings, accompanied by Tommy, reclined sullenly at the far end of the damaged sitting-couch – a substantial part of which, afflicted by Abruzzio's radiation-burst, had disintegrated entirely – the ex-JPL space-scientist, flanked by her puppy and Sullivan, had sat down opposite the salesman and the boy, the better to intercept any aggressive moves against the President.

The two GrayWar guys had actually done something productive, by stepping out into a nearby office and brewing up some coffee for the First Family (or what was left of it); the gesture was well-appreciated.

Kaysten, for his part, had gone over to comfort his former boss and the First Lady. Unfortunately, the two of them were inconsolable.

"She's gone now," prodded the now-recovered, but bruised, Agent Kortish. "Sir, we've *got* to get you out of here! Let us protect you while we head for the door to the Rose Garden... I can get the Capitol Police to escort you to a safe place. It's the only course of action that makes any sense, now!"

"You do *that*, chum, and you'll be wearing six to sixteen of my lightening-bolts, before you step through that threshold," warned Billings. "Did I mention that they apparently drive you insane, one second before they blow you to Kingdom Come?"

He winked and pointed at his "Mars ears". The humor of the gesture was lost on Kortish, not to mention on the President.

The Service agent was thinking of an alternate plan, when there was the same light knocking-sound on the door to the White House interior, that they had heard before tonight's disasters had come to pass. The door opened and through it, stepped the Storied Watcher.

She was alone.

For a second or two, there was an aghast silence.

Then a still-angry Abruzzio managed,

"So what *now*, Karéin? How about we call Hector and Melissa down here, so you can show off your fine 'accomplishments' for the night?"

"I asked them to hold above and outside, regardless of what they might detect going on in this place," replied the Storied Watcher. "Happily, they obeyed... only *Vìrya I'ëà'b* chose to abandon her post, though," – she spoke to an apparently-empty part of the Oval Office ceiling – "I will not hold that against thee, my war-child."

"Leave us *alone*, for the pity of God!" sobbed the First Lady, who was sitting on the carpet, her head nestled next to the President's chest. "Or kill us. What does it *matter*, anyway!"

Karéin-Mayréij came over to crouch beside them.

"Woman," she said, in a firm but kind tone of voice, "Actually... it matters, *greatly*. Go now to the office of the 'Chief of Staff' – latterly that of Jer-ee here, as I recall – and there you will find your children, laid out on the floor. I know not what your customs are... but I would ask that you bring them back here. You can get some of these fine guardsmen who cluster 'round, to assist you."

"For *what?*" spat the President. "So you can hang them on the walls, as some kind of fucking *trophy? That's it!*"

He lunged at the oddly-impassive Storied Watcher, not caring about her already-demonstrated close-range defenses, but – to everyone's astonishment – he somehow was able to land a very hard punch against her jaw, sending the alien-girl staggering backwards, while acid blood appeared on her lower lip.

Tommy and Billings energized their *Fire*, and were about to unleash double, lethal attacks in the President's direction, when he found himself held immobile in an invisible grasp of iron, though his hands were still around her throat.

His face was less than six inches away from that of the Storied Watcher. Her big, doe eyes were glowing and it was very evident that she could easily vaporize her over-matched assailant, with the proverbial thought.

But instead, the alien-girl whispered, so softly that even Mars-ears overheard, only with difficulty. Her voice was kindly, friendly and reassuring, despite the assault to which she had just been subjected.

"Go retrieve your children, man!" she counseled, "And then come to me, knowing what has been done to them – all by their own assent, freely given. I have ordered my war-child, *Vœran Fàiagàryuu*, to refrain and give you passage thence."

He released her – or, more likely, she released him – and he went back on his heels, with an utterly nonplussed expression on his face.

Without saying another word, the President dashed for the interior door, charging through it as if his life depended on the pace of his feet. The Service agents (all except two who stayed back to protect the First Lady), raced behind him.

Karéin-Mayréij closed her eyes, which, again, were wet with tears.

"Bob... Tommy... no more of this, I *beg* you!" she demanded.

They powered down, although Billings grumbled, "Sari... I'll never understand you, girl. Or maybe it's just, 'you don't understand us humans'... at least, those who still *are* humans. You do a man's kids... you'd better do *him*, too, or you're going to have him on your tail for what's left of his life. At this point, I'd bet he'd consider it a 'mercy-killing'."

"Why not just kill *everyone* who gets in our way, anywhere, anytime, Bob?" dejectedly spat Abruzzio. "I'm *so* disappointed in you, Karéin! I thought of you as an 'angel' – somebody above us humans, in every way – but you're really just like a psychotic mortal with lethal abilities. I'll hang around here until the President dismisses me... but that's the last you'll ever *see* of me, at least if I have any say in the matter. I'm ashamed that I ever called you a 'friend'!"

"Sylvia... I *pray*... say not things that you will later regret, in the haste of hot blood," responded the Storied Watcher. "The fortunes of battle, of honor, and of state... they take many twists and turns. You are new to war, and you do not yet understand. I will only say : 'never give up hope... not even, when all seems irretrievably lost'."

The usually-garrulous Kaysten did not voice an opinion; all he did was sit next to what was left of the First Family, staring vacantly into space.

"Miz Sylvia," spoke Tommy, "Mom only did what she did, to even it up... to get back at the President, for what he did to Elissha and me... and to Korey. If it was up to me, I'd have killed *all* of them –"

"You know *what*, Tommy?" interrupted Abruzzio, anger visibly rising in her voice and a cold, fed-up look on her face, "*Fuck off!* Yeah – you heard that right, you murderous, spoiled little *brat!* Many of us are sick to death, pun intended, of your, and Bob's, self-pitying excuses for inflicting horrendous cruelty on people who can't defend themselves! Do you have any *idea* of what's happened tonight... and what it means?"

The puppy, perhaps comically, also growled at the boy.

"Sylvia," cautioned Sullivan in a low whisper, "You *saw* what he can do... you better be careful what you say..."

"I don't fucking *care* what I say... or what he thinks of it!" retorted Abruzzio, standing up and walking away from the couch, over to the Resolute Desk. "He tries that 'magic bullet' thing on me, and he'd better not miss, because – and Tommy don't you *ever* think I'm bluffing – my counter-attack will have a hundred times the radiation that Bob and Jerry got a little taste of, there; and it *won't* be aimed... it will hit everything within a hundred feet of me! You *understand?*"

The others just stared sullenly and did not immediately reply.

"Don't any of you *see?* This isn't the end of it – it's just the *start* of it!" continued a desperate Abruzzio. "If I was the President, or his successor, the first order I'd give, would be for the Air Force to get the most powerful nuke that they can muster, and –"

The inside-door suddenly opened. Through it came the President, his arms supporting his limp and apparently-unconscious son's shoulders, while a Service agent carried Matt's feet; two other agents did the same for the daughter.

"Get off the couches – *now!*" he barked.

"What..." gasped the First Lady.

"They're... *alive!*" cried the President.

Death, En Route To D.C.

"Why'd they cut us off?" demanded a perplexed and apprehensive Chu, of the Air Force staff-guy who had been her proxy against the aircraft's array of communications-systems and other computer-gear. "Get them on-line – *immediately!*"

"I've tried three times now... no answer, ma'am," came back the pedantically-polite reply. They've closed the connection at their end."

"Well... what about that military guy... uhh... 'DeWitt', the Defense Secretary?" pressed the former FBI team-leader. "Did you try *him?*"

"Affirmative," stated the Air Force guy. "A number of the channels are blocked... and the weird thing is, it looks like the Secretary's one got multiplexed into ours, back at the White House end, by some technology that I don't recognize... must be something new and secret that they've got goin' down there. But when they dropped the connection they somehow tied up that particular channel. I'm trying on other ones... I'll let you know if I can raise him again."

"Keep trying!" ordered Chu. "And while you're doing it – don't take your one eye off the display that's tracking that plane with the nuke. Any change in its status, and I need to know *immediately!*"

"Yes ma'am," the Air Force man obligingly pledged.

A panel-light self-illuminated, and an all-too-familiar voice began to issue from the communications-room's speakers.

"This-here message is for that struttin' little pretty who's holdin' the President, the Director and others of our fine fightin'-men, hostage," came Crowford's over-confident tone. "I got a patch-in to the local mike in there, so you all should be hearin' this, although the rest of the plane's not gonna. Confirm that – right now!"

I shouldn't do him the courtesy, reflected Chu.

But he sounds really agitated... I could hear heavy breathing just in those few words.

What if he's got something cooked up... maybe fighter-jets heading our way?

Don't like that idea... maybe I can survive a fall from thirty thousand feet... but to do that, while being shot at by machine-cannons and air-to-air missiles?

"I doubt that you have anything to say, that I want to hear, Mr. Crowford," she pushed herself to respond, "But just to relieve the boredom... fine, go ahead."

"You had *better!*" he admonished, "Because, my dear... the situation has *changed*, quite a bit, from when we had our last little chat. I'm callin' you from the crew-cabin, which has been nicely sealed-off from the rest of this fine aircraft. I'm here with the navigator and the co-pilot, who are nominally in charge of the plane – although now, all the decisions about where we're goin' are mine –"

Migod, Chu immediately realized.

What the hell has he done?

"What do you *mean?*" she interrupted.

"Well," he said, undoubtedly with a smirk, "Let's just say that I showed up in the flight-deck, with admittance granted due to my Executive Office rank... there was a slight disagreement about our new flight-plan, and after all was said and done, the pilot had to go meet his Maker – but if it's of any interest, I *did* indeed say a prayer for the man, right afterward. Co-pilot's doin' a bit better – only took a round in one arm – and he knows better than to try anythin' stupid. I closed and locked the bullet- and blast-proof door to the rest of the plane, and ordered the Service and other guards to stand down; unfortunately they don't seem to be recognizin' my authority... but they *do* recognize what's likely to happen, if they rush in here."

"I don't *believe* this!" ruefully offered Chu. "You hijacked the plane, I take it? And you *murdered* the pilot, just because –"

"You're *hardly* the one to be lecturin' me about 'hijackin' or 'murder', my dear," he coldly observed. "But yes... my custom-throated and -ramped pearl-handled .45 is pointed just where it needs to be. To answer your next question, the Service had to hold off on rushin' the cabin because – apart from the door bein' in the way – there's a small device that I've got set up on the instrument-panel, which is set to go off the moment that my heart stops beatin' –"

"How in God's name did you get a *bomb* on-board?" again broke in Chu.

"Don't take the name of the Almighty in vain, honey," came back the retort, "And as for 'bombs' – you don't know the *half* of it. But *this* little guy... he's a lot more elegant than *that.* You heard of 'EMP', girl?"

"I *wish* you wouldn't use this demeaning language on me," complained the former team-leader, "But yeah... I know all *about* it. Don't forget, I got subjected to that, and much more, up in Alaska, when the government set off a nuclear weapon very close to me. An experience that I never want to repeat..."

"Well, you see," he snickered, "This fine airplane's very well-shielded against pulse-effects comin' in at it from outside... but they never planned for what might happen if, a blast of the stuff came from *inside*... right at the control-panel, which will be done better'n any chicken-fried steak you can get in Alabama. And since the plane's all computer-run, when that happens... down we go, real fast. You *followin'* me, girl?"

Shit, she realized, *He's going to crash the plane, just to get at me and Karéin! That's* got *to be his plan!*

"Crowford," came the Vice-President's anguished voice, "What do you think you're *doing?* You'll kill everybody on the aircraft – including yourself, Blanshard, Warnock and *me!*"

"My friend," smoothly responded the Spiritual Adviser, "We're all soldiers in our Father God's army; and sometimes – when the battle ain't goin' the way that the Lord wants it to – He demands a battlefield change of command... that's what I've had to do today. I want you to know that I have accepted this commission humbly – and that if the Lord calls me home in the furtherance of it... I've said my prayers and I'm eager to go. *You* should be, too. You got a Bible in there with her – or did she rip it up or burn it already?"

"He's fucking *nuts!*" Chu heard the *faux*-President whisper to Warnock, who grimly nodded affirmation.

"Clark was out of his *mind* to let this guy into the White House," the Vice-President sullenly added.

"Sir," she answered, "This is *insane!* I thought I already *told* you – using my alien-powers, I can almost certainly blast my way out of this aircraft and then drift gently back to Earth... I don't *want* to, because I don't want others to be killed when and if the plane crashes... but if it comes down to my survival you *know* that I'll do it – and I *won't* call for the Storied Watcher's help! You can't *possibly* come out ahead, by this plan!"

"Is that *right*, my dear?" he smugly inquired. "You're gonna bail, just like that... parachute or no parachute?"

"Of *course* it is!" Chu replied. "You've already seen a demonstration of my abilities. Why do you think I'm bluffing?"

"Well, you see," came back the ominous explanation, "I'm afraid if you do that... things won't turn out quite as well as you had planned, in the biggest of big ways. I now have this aircraft headin' straight for downtown D.C. – the White House, more specifically – and when it gets there, or indeed if you try any funny business past what you already done... you're gonna have another chance to repeat that Alaskan experience, that you keep talkin' about –"

"*Crowford!*" shouted the Vice-President, "What the fuck are you *talking* about!"

"I s'pose it don't matter none, if you hear the whole story," the Spiritual Adviser mentioned, "But... you remember how that nice big bomb went AWOL, from Barksdale Air Force Base, some time past?"

Chu shot a horrified, wide-eyed stare at the *faux*-President and Warnock, whose faces were both ashen.

To need fast here Mother leave, came a thought from little 'Warden'.

I know, sweetheart, mentally replied Chu. *But this is our* job.

I'm scared, just like you.

Hold tightly on to Mommy, while she holds on to you!

"Y... yes..." stammered the Vice-President.

"The Soldiers of God, actin' under my control, had to avail themselves of this implement, in the Holy War to send the Devil-Girl back to Hell, where she belongs," Crowford elaborated. "Many apologies to members of the Executive Branch – includin' yourself – who this may have, uhh, 'inconvenienced'; but it was necessary for God's divine purpose, for only the hottest fire, can banish the spawn of Satan back to –"

"He's *batshit*-crazy!" mumbled Warnock, to the Vice-President, while Crowford rambled on. "It was *him* and the other Bible-bangers, all along!"

"Does Clark know?" whispered the Vice-President.

"Don't think so," offered the *poseur*-FBI-director.

"I don't know which of you I despise more," spat Chu, "You're *both* murderers and authority-worshipers; he's at least sincere, but you're sort of rational, in your cruelty –"

"Now as to the present situation, girlie," declared Crowford, "Let me lay it out for you. Somewhere on this-here plane – modesty prevents me from sayin' exactly *where* – there's a device originally from Barksdale, and I'm told that its yield is *more* than big enough to wipe out a city the size of D.C.. Should you try somethin' stupid – such as, for example, tryin' to defuse it, or cut it apart – I think you can guess what's gonna happen. It's also got fuses based on impact, air-pressure and radiation, so if you just throw it out of the plane, or if we go down too fast, you had better be ready to meet our Lord and Savior Jesus Christ, in the next few seconds –"

"You've somehow smuggled a hydrogen bomb on-board, and it's rigged to go off if we tamper with it, or jettison it, or if we crash-dive the plane... is *that* what you're saying?" interrupted Chu.

"That'd be 'bout right," he confirmed. "'Cept, I'm told that she'll blow if we climb too fast, as well... not that that's likely to happen, of course."

"And you brought something like that – with hair-trigger detonating-fuses – on this plane, while everyone was just going about their daily business?" protested a frightened Minnie Chu. "Did you ever think of what might happen if somebody just *dropped* the damn thing, by mistake?"

"*More* foul language," pompously riposted Crowford. "But, girlie, just to set your mind at ease... *some* of these fuses, they'll set her off, straight-away; other ones – sorry but I can't say more – well, they might give you enough time to at least say the Lord's Prayer, maybe even a psalm or two, before... *you* know. I can get the firin'-sequence goin' from up here, any time I want to; and once I *do*, there ain't any power on this-here Earth – 'cept, of course, that of our

Lord and Savior Jesus Christ, and He's on *my* side – that can stop it. Oh – and I forgot to mention one other thing... try foolin' with it just a *little*, and you'll get such a dose of gamma-rays, that you'll be dead in a few hours, one way or t'other."

"How do I know that any of this is true?" challenged the former FBI team-leader. "You could simply be lying about it! Nice way to bluff someone much more powerful than you, sir."

"Oh... I'll leave it to yourself – and to anyone who you choose to inform elsewhere on this aircraft – to verify that I'm tellin' the truth," remarked the Spiritual Adviser. "Just a bit of advice, though... if you *do* find it – 'don't touch', 'less you've decided what to say to the Lord, when you're standin' in front of Him, tryin' to explain your many perversions of the flesh. 'Matter of fact... I'd start thinkin' about all that right now, if I were you."

I call upon the Holy Fire, silently invoked Chu, with her eyes momentarily closed.

Show and tell me that this peril, is a false one!

She concentrated for a second or two, then gasped in horror.

Chu's mind showed a scene of utter devastation – akin to what she had seen on Amchitka, but this time, as if she were standing in the rubble-strewn midst of what might have been a city.

Almost everything – including what must have been the bodies of people – was encased in flame. A gale roared overhead, driven by a nascent fire-storm.

O Lord – why have you forsaken us! came a scream from under a smashed, smoldering building, as the more-than-a-woman's mind came back to consciousness.

"Crowford... you *crazy* son of a *bitch!*" cursed the former FBI team-leader, out loud.

"Hey... you've *gotta* be right – he's just *lying!*" hopefully proposed the Vice-President.

"He *isn't,*" grimly returned Chu.

"How do you know?" pressed Warnock.

"I just... *know,*" persisted Chu. "The insight of an *angel,* bestowed on me."

She hesitated for a second or two, and then went on,

"Okay, Mr. Spiritual Adviser," she challenged, "You didn't do all this, just to set up a spectacular light-show over Ohio and Pennsylvania. If I assume for the moment that you really *do* have a usable nuclear weapon on board this aircraft – and that you somehow *can* set it off – what do you want from *me,* in exchange for not doing that?"

"See... here's the thing, my dear," he lectured, "If you had just called the Devil-Girl up here, when I first asked you to... this all would have been *much* simpler. But as you chose to disobey me, just like you've disobeyed your Lord and Savior, I'm afraid that I've had to turn things up a notch. I'm bettin' that both you and this space-harlot think that you can only be saved from a crashin' airplane, by her – 'scuse me, *its* – direct intervention. So at this point, it doesn't matter a hill of beans if you call for her – like you always were s'posed to – or if she just sees this-here plane headin' straight for the White House and then comes to the rescue of her partner-in-sin... or so she thinks –"

"Karéin doesn't even know that I'm *here!*" exclaimed Chu. "How can you *possibly* believe –"

"You believe what *you* want to... and I'll believe what *I* want to," countered Crowford. "My Christian beliefs tell me that my plan... is *God's* plan."

"But what can I do to make you *happy*... to give you what you *want?*" pleaded the former team-leader. "*Surely* there's *something!*"

"Honestly, honey... there's just about diddly-squat that you *can* do," taunted the Spiritual Adviser. "'Cept for 'stayin' put, on this-here plane'. If I catch wind of you fixin' to bail on us, I'll push the button in the next two seconds... no way for you to get far enough away to live through it. That goes equally if you come lookin' for me with those hell-spawned eyes of yours. I got *ways* to tell where you are... you won't take me by surprise – of that I can *assure* you!"

"But you just said that you're planning on crashing the plane into the White House!" desperately argued Chu. "And that the bomb is fused to go off in a steep dive! What are we supposed to do, to stay *alive?*"

"Why, Miss Chu... that's the whole *point,*" unctuously replied Crowford. "Christians – at least, the *real* fundamentalist kind like Yours Truly, as opposed to the apostates, lib-rals and traitors who reject the Lord's revealed word – they don't *fear* death; they *welcome* it! Death is just the first step in the redeemed sinner soul's journey to Paradise, at the right side of our Lord and Savior Jesus Christ. I've made my peace with my Father God; my conscience is clear, and so is my destiny. You – and this aircraft – will be the blood sacrifice demanded by the Lord, to redeem this perverted world, and to send the Devil-Girl back to the Lake of Fire, where she'll burn with Satan, in all eternity! *Hallelujah!*"

"I... *see,*" quietly commented a deflated Chu. "If that's the case... is there anything more for us to talk about, Mr. Crowford?"

"Don't believe so," he confidently answered. "Except to say two things : one, 'it's been nice knowin' you', and two, 'it's never too late to get down on your knees and beg God for forgiveness', Miss Chu... and it seems to me, that considerin' your sinful, lustful personality, you all got lots to be beggin' *for*. You're now livin' out the last minutes and hours of your life, girlie... I'd suggest you put that time to good use. That goes for everyone who's hearin' my voice."

"I like to think that there's *always* hope," she observed.

Then she gestured to the communications-technician to cut the connection.

"He can't hear us any more... right?" asked the former team-leader.

"Affirmative, ma'am," said the Air Force guy. "I saw an attempt to re-enable the back-up microphones in here, but I over-rode the command. Unless the Spiritual Adviser has his ear right up against the door leading to the corridor, whatever we talk about, stays in here."

"Migod... *migod*," quivered the Vice-President. "He can't really *do* all this... *can* he?"

"I'm afraid he *can*," disputed Chu, "And the Storied Watcher's arts have shown me what it will look like, when he does. Not a pretty scene, I can assure you."

"What the hell are we going to *do?*" persisted the *faux*-President. "Just sit here and wait to die?"

Chu – her mind reeling, while trying unsuccessfully to reject the enormity of what she had just heard – was lost in thought for a few seconds.

Then she asked the Air Force guy,

"What's our ETA to Washington, D.C.? Assuming current speed, that is."

Uncharacteristically, he looked up and back over his shoulder, catching Chu in a worried glance.

"A bit more than an hour, ma'am," he informed.

Sacrifices And The Second Test

The two Presidential offspring were duly laid on opposing divans, although Matt's legs were elevated by a pile of pillows that were placed so as to obscure and avoid the melted-spot caused by Abruzzio's radioactive-beam. The alien-girl tried to argue against this, on the grounds that "no more shall they fear the little particle-shine", but it was to no avail.

"Clairie... Matt... can you *hear* me?" implored the overjoyed – though still worried and desperate – President.

There was no response, except for deep-sleep breathing on the part of the teenagers.

The U.S. leader turned to address the Storied Watcher.

"They look so damn *pale!*" he observed. "And what's *that*... it looks like there's something inside them, and it's *glowing*... what the hell did you *do* to them?"

"I *took* them from you," diffidently replied Karéin-Mayréij; and it was hard to tell if she was simply stating a fact, or was gloating in some inscrutable way. "They will never again be the wastrel-children that they were, scant time ago."

The grimacing President grabbed his son by the shoulders and shook the boy.

"Matt... *Matt!*" he shouted. "Wake *up*, son!"

The Storied Watcher rushed over to kneel by the side of the couch.

"You should not do that," she counseled. "He has not fully... *changed* yet – he is still partly human... you might hurt him!"

"'*Changed*'?" shot back the President. "What do you *mean?*"

"She's turned them into *zombies*... under her *control!*" wailed the First Lady.

"Ma'am," intervened Kaysten, "Let's not be too hasty... okay? It's no worse than she did to me... and I feel *fine!* Oh, and by the way, Karéin – fuck off!"

"Uhh... you castigate me for *what*, brother?" returned a perplexed alien-girl. "Maybe for saving your President-liegelord from being annihilated? Or for –"

"For nothing in particular," chirped the former Chief of Staff, "Just so they know, that I *can* mouth off to you... like I've always been able to do. Point being, ma'am... if *I* can do it, and *I* can still think straight... so can these two."

"Well, just being able to insult someone, isn't convincing evidence that one isn't under some kind of mental domination," unhelpfully mentioned Abruzzio. "Although Jerry *does* happen to be right. As you've seen from my own comments, I have had my own differences with our alien mentor here. For the record, Karéin... that little display of theatrics was *totally* unnecessary! We all thought you were going to *kill* the President's children! What did you hope to accomplish, by all of this?"

"A way *out*," meekly replied the Storied Watcher. "As I told these two callow princelings, before laying the Kiss of *Fire* upon them. To preserve my honor – to avoid shame in the eyes of my family and beloved, for exposing them to pain and terror, by way of personal failure – but not to match grievous harm for unrequited cruelty... to prove that one can avenge – yet not in same kind. These two are forever changed... and there is no going back for them!"

"Yeah, but Sari," protested Billings, "Giving them the 'bite'... that, like, makes them 'super-people'... just like us! How is *that* 'revenge' for what was done to Tommy, Elissha and me? You're 'paying back' a fucking *outrage*, with abilities that most of us, had to work – and suffer – for!"

"Indeed your approval, and Tommy's, are necessary, to absolve me of my failure, my love," she replied, with big, searching-looking eyes. "I am asking you to accept what was done to Matt and Clairie, as blood-sacrifice for what was done to all of you. That you would accept and love them as brother and sister – that you would guide them in the path to true nobility, as newly-born of the *Khùl-Algrenàthi'i Srelkh*."

A totally-confounded Billings shot back, "And why would we do *that*? Uhh... the whatever-the-hell you're referring to. What's our alternative?"

"Our alternative is," she quietly responded, "Is that you reject this sacrifice, that I stand by and permit you and Tommy – yourselves – to slaughter them, while helplessly they sleep."

"Don't you *dare!*" screeched the First Lady; but the President constrained her from unwisely lunging at Billings and the boy.

"But *they* didn't hurt us," whined Tommy. "*He* did!"

"*He* did not do so, either, son," counseled the alien-girl. "At least not by *deliberate*, calculated will of cruelty. *He*, was given a chance to stop it, but he abjectly failed the test of judgment, and of wisdom... just like I failed all of you, when I left you back at Bob's home in Too-sawn. I promised not to force my intellect upon his, and so I have refrained to do; but my other arts tell me that he speaks the truth in admitting his stupidity and abdication of duty, in allowing these excesses to be inflicted on his subjects... including you, Bob and Elissha."

They mutely stared at her, somehow anticipating the challenge that was next to come, though not wanting to hear it.

"Thus you, dear son – and your father-by-declaration, too... you have a *choice* to make," offered Karéin-Mayréij, with more than a hint of her godly presence leaking out. "You have free will – and the knowledge of undeserved savagery that was inflicted upon you... and you have full and proper reason to pay this 'President', back in like kind."

Then she stared at them, again with watering eyes and quietly advised, "You come to a fork in the road; and once chosen – like the Kiss of *Fire* – it *cannot* be retreated from. You can demand, '*blood* for blood'... or you can offer up, '*love* for blood'. Choose *wisely!*"

An awed, teary-eyed Abruzzio gasped, under her breath, "Holy Mary, Mother of God... may they *hear* the voice of thy angel... and may I never again, fall into doubt."

Little 'Rainbow' murmured and licked her arm, as she crossed herself.

Billings looked straight at the President, and said,

"Do you understand what she's asking us to *do*?"

"No, Mr. Billings... I *don't*," calmly responded the U.S. leader. "Because though I hear the words... so God may help me, I'll never know how you and your son – and this daughter who she speaks of – have suffered, because of how terribly I failed, when most I needed not to. I can't ask you for forgiveness. All I *can* do... is to beg you to spare the lives of my *children*. If blood's what you want... what you believe you must have, to end all this... then here I am. Karéin – don't protect me again. If your husband –"

"We're not married," interrupted the ex-salesman. "At least... I don't *think* we are."

"I stand corrected," continued the President. "What I meant to say – and to Tommy, too – is, 'I'm offering my life in exchange for those of my children'. I understand why you want revenge. I can't say I blame you... it's probably exactly what *I'd* do, in your place. I've made my peace with the Lord... go ahead."

"Uncle Bob," muttered the boy, "What are we supposed to do *now?*"

"He could have *saved* you from this, you know!" glowered Billings.

"I *want* to blow him to bits!" growled Tommy. "I *want* to... I *want* to..."

"Do you remember the vows that we all took, when last we were all together?" cajoled Abruzzio. "Killing him when you don't have to, is a straight-forward betrayal of that oath. And you'd be lowering yourselves to his level!"

"Thanks, Sylvia," grumbled Kaysten, "I think..."

Wraith-like, the Storied Watcher slipped elegantly over to Tommy's side.

"Now... regard him," she advised, directing the boy's attentions to the President. "You have the power of life or death over this human who calls himself, 'President', son. You can kill him... and there is *nothing* that he can do back to you; indeed, all that he *can* do against yourself, has already been done; and though the foul memory of that will forever be there... you *survived* it! You *defeated* it, and in so doing... you *defeated, him!*"

"What do you *mean*, Mom?" uncertainly asked Tommy.

"Did you hear him say, 'I would certainly kill you, if I were in your position'?", she answered. *"That,* son – *that* is what makes *us,* different from these 'humans'. *That* is the difference, between greatness and pathos; between craven-ness and fortitude; yea – even is it the difference between nobility, and bestial savagery. Yes, you *can* kill him – but you have *already* triumphed, *over* him; and he will live out the rest of his natural life, always knowing that fact, but never being able to admit it, either to himself, or to his subjects and courtiers. His death will serve you *nothing* – except, blood on your soul, going to forever! Is that the path that you would knowingly choose, my son?"

She shot a scowl at the President.

"Is anything that I say, untrue?" she loudly challenged. "Do I mislead my son?"

"No," the U.S. leader evenly replied. "I *should* have stopped the Agency the moment that I heard about these activities. I did *not.* Tommy... Mr. Billings... and to all those who aren't here, to hear me say it – I am truly sorry, and I'll take anything that's coming to me. All I ask is, 'spare Matt and Clairie'. *Please!*"

Hearts sank as they heard the warning-signs of Tommy's lethal powers, being energized. But the war-song only reached a low level, and the boy's eyes only glowed dimly, before beginning to fade.

He dejectedly whimpered, "I *want* to... I *want* to... he *deserves* it... but I *can't!* It *hurts,* down here, when I get ready to... Mommy... why *can't* I?"

"Because, young *Væran* Tommy, prince-above-all," purred Karéin-Mayréij, with tears in her own eyes, "You pass the test of nobility. *Come* to me now, son – and let us sing in our hearts to Korey's spirit, and to all those others equally wronged, that they may by this sacrifice and forbearance, be avenged... and thus be made free, to go where the Gods may so will."

The alien-girl, tears streaming down her cheeks, tightly embraced the boy while Abruzzio mumbled something, fingering her cross all the while.

"I guess that leaves *me,*" unhappily offered Billings. "Well, I'm not going to spoil this nice little touchy-feely thing we somehow got going on... but, my friend, I'm putting you – and the whole damn government too – on notice. I think she said, 'wasting someone in a war, is different from smokin' them when you're armed and they aren't'... isn't that right, Sari?"

The Storied Watcher – lost in reverie and in a hug with her son – merely stuck out her arm and gave a "thumbs-up" gesture."

There was an odd, shocked, knowing look on Kaysten's face, as if he had suddenly come to a realization about something-or-other.

"So *that's* what it's all about..." he mumbled to himself.

Nobody else – except for a quick glance on the part of the Storied Watcher – paid any attention to this.

"I'll take that as a 'yes'," continued Billings, addressing his comments to the President. "So she's bending over backwards to give you the benefit of the doubt... 'bully for her and six brownie points with God, if she really *is* an angel". But as for Yours Truly, my friend... all I can say is, 'watch your step, and watch your back'. Tommy and I both experienced what the government – *your* government – does to people who can't fight back. Well – now we *can*... and at the first sign of back-sliding on your part, all bets are off. *Got* it?"

"I think you left off, 'asshole', Uncle Bob," chirped the boy.

"Thanks for catching that, kid," congratulated the ex-salesman. "You got it... *asshole?*"

"You mind your *tongue!*" admonished the First Lady.

"Mr. Billings," solemnly responded the U.S. leader, "You must know that I'm not used to being spoken to this way... but considering the circumstances, and considering what I've already admitted to, I can't say I blame you for feeling as you do. I'll do my utmost to ensure that these tragic events never happen again... and I hope that someday – even if that day is a long way off – we can even see each other as friends."

"Ha! *That'll* be the day!" taunted Billings. "I wouldn't bet any money you don't want to lose on it!"

"Stranger things have happened," observed Abruzzio. "Like, 'finding an alien on Mars, and having her save our whole planet'."

"Yes," softly reflected the Storied Watcher, while still wrapped around her son. "Like, 'this alien – this mountebank, this so-called 'angel' – whose powers once were so great that she could shatter a comet, and thus save an entire world; yet never could she even protect her own family against a gang of hired-thugs... and so all came to what we behold today."

"It wasn't your *fault*, Karéin!" said Abruzzio. "*Everyone* here, knows that."

"Yeah, honey," added the salesman, "Get that chip off your shoulder... you hear? Tommy and I know that it was *his* fault... not yours."

"Well, Bob," added Kaysten, "Even if you aren't going to be pals with him, maybe you should stick around here for a while... you might find out how being a 'President' – all that responsibility, and a gazillion lunatics running around out there, trying to kill you, and to blow up the whole country – that gives you a new perspective on things. I can tell you, I didn't understand it at first, either."

Billings was about to dispute the claim, but he was pre-empted by a shout from the direction of the communications-shack.

"Sorry to interrupt, Mr. President," came the voice of one of the lower-rank Secret Service agents, "But that lady from the airplane came back for a few seconds... I heard her saying, it's an 'emergency'."

"We've been having one out here too... or hadn't you heard," replied the flummoxed President. "Did she say what was the nature of the 'emergency'?"

"Well sir... I'll just read you what she said, before the channel dropped – doesn't make a lot of sense, but doesn't sound too good, either," said the agent. "Her exact words were, 'tell the President and Sylvia that it's an emergency, for *real*, now... I'm riding a bomb, straight *for* you'."

Knaves And Plans For A Massacre

The President reluctantly tore himself away from his two still-somnolent offspring, and dashed over to a point closer to the White House local communications-shack.

"*Hail* her!" he demanded. "I don't care *what* you have to do... get the channel back!"

There was a momentary delay, and then the answer came back.

"*Can't*, sir," said the staffer at the consoles. "There's some kind of analog interference on the line... it's like every time it re-establishes the connection, the noise quickly amplifies across all the usable bands and overwhelms the signal. It *can't* be accidental... it exactly coincides with the link-handshake."

"That's a standard Service technique, for jamming local communications, when we're taking you overseas, sir," interjected Kortish. "All the other government intelligence and protective agencies have access to different versions of it."

"Isn't there some way that we can over-ride it... turn it off?" the President asked.

"Not that *I* know of, sir," argued the Service agent. "I heard somewhere, that you could *theoretically* do it... but you'd need very specialized equipment that could broadcast an opposite signal, to cancel out the interference. It's the kind of gear that only a few of our agencies have, basically."

Abruzzio shot a glance at the Storied Watcher.

"Karéin... I can try by myself... but I could sure use some help..." implored the former JPL scientist.

"Who is 'the lady on the plane'?" inquired the alien-girl. "Wait... it comes to me, by my arts... 'Min-ee'? But which airplane? How does she come to be there? And... a *bomb*?"

"Long story," deflected Abruzzio, "But she's been fighting for her *life* lately... and if we don't get back in touch with her, things could become much, *much* worse, very quickly. Will you help, *please*?"

"Of *course*, sister!" obliged the Storied Watcher.

She came over to stand beside Abruzzio, taking hold of the ex-scientist's hand.

"Direct your power to the little particle-glow on paths of the ray-dee-oh," requested Karéin-Mayréij. "As it varies, so shall we both do with our own shining. It is not difficult... just the same as by which, I befuddled our fine President's ray-dar trickery, but in reverse. Ready?"

Two war-songs – both inspiring and reeking of latent power, the one more potent than the other – began to reverberate in the background of human psyches.

"As I'll ever be," answered the ex-scientist, with her eyes – like those of her alien mentor – beginning to dimly-glow, while staring straight forward. "*You* there! On three, then give it all you've got! One...two... *three!*"

"Engaging," called out the communications-technician. "Establishing... okay, there it is... interference ramping up... holy shit, what's *that* –"

"Have you got her?" demanded Abruzzio.

"Just a sec... voice-override... hello?" said the technician. "Yeah... wow... I got no idea what it is, but there's a compensating wave-form... two, actually –"

"Hello?" interrupted a remote voice. "This is Minnie Chu – who am I talking to?"

"This is the White House, ma'am," he stated. "I'll put the President on in a second, Ms. Chu, but you should know, someone's trying hard to jam this channel... we have two of your friends keeping the connection up, but it could drop at any time. I can't get DeWitt on, at all. Go ahead."

"*Two* of my friends?" came back the astonished reply. "Sylvia? Who's there with you?"

"I have a very powerful friend standing alongside me, sister," offered Abruzzio, with a wan smile. "I think you've met her?"

"*Omigod!*" shouted an elated Chu. "You don't *mean* –"

"Hi, Min-ee!" offered the Storied Watcher. "Perhaps the circumstances could be happier; still, with joy in my heart, do I hear your gentle voice. I am here with Bob, Tommy, Jer-ee, my war-children, Melissa, Hector and Saquina... the latter three hold guard outside this palace. We have had an – ahh – 'interesting' visit with the American President and his entourage, so far. They are all alive and well... though not for lack of recent misfortune. What is this news of a 'bomb'?"

"I can just *imagine* how your introduction to the President must have gone," observed Chu, "And you'll have to fill me in on the details – but in the meantime, it's *imperative* that you all listen closely to what I've got to say!"

"Please tell us *everything*, Ms. Chu," interjected the President. "Service – I need this recorded – every *word!*"

"Yes *sir!*" came the response from several directions.

"Okay... so here it is," resumed the former FBI team-leader. "Crowford's gone nutzoid – or, maybe he's just more batshit-crazy than he always was. He claims to have smuggled a nuclear weapon on-board the Airborne Command-Post, and he's hijacked the plane by shooting one of the pilots and locking himself in the cockpit. He also claims to have rigged an EMP-device up there, that will crash the plane by shorting out all the controls, if the Marines or the Service, try to force their way in –"

"He's *lying!*" spat Kaysten. "Harold was *always* full of shit! There's no way to sneak a *gun* on-board... let alone a *nuke!*"

"I wish I could believe that, Jerry," countered Chu. "Karéin – you gave me the power to be warned of danger... I used it, and the pictures that came to my mind... well, they were *horrific*. What does it *mean*? Is there any way that my intuition could be wrong?"

"Did you call upon the Holy *Fire*, in so doing?" asked Karéin-Mayréij.

"Yes," confirmed Chu. "And – thank God – she *did* come to me."

"Then your warning was a prescient one, sister," offered the alien-girl. "That it would show you what is to come, unless we act to prevent this. Mr. President – this weirding-art has kept me safe by forewarning, over centuries unremembered; it cannot be vexed or deceived. If Min-ee says that it tells her of one of these accursed atom-smashing bombs on the air-plane... you should believe her."

"I've learned the hard way, not to under-estimate these 'alien-powers' of yours, Madam," ruefully acknowledged the U.S. leader. "We have to assume that the Spiritual Adviser's threat is real, though what he's got to gain by it, escapes me –"

"For what it's worth, sir," interrupted Chu, "He's got it in his head that by threatening me with being blown to bits, he'll get Karéin to come and rescue me. I think his idea is to get her close enough to the Command-Post to set off the bomb and then take me, Karéin and himself – he goes up to Jesus and we get the Lake of Fire – out, all at once. By the way, he's saying that he can remotely trigger it... I get the impression that it might not go off immediately if he does that, although I sure don't want to find out how long a timer he's got on it. He's also claiming to have the bomb rigged so that if I leave the plane prematurely, or if I try to disarm it, or if the aircraft climbs or dives abruptly – *boom!*"

"Karéin," the President asked, "Do you think you could withstand that kind of explosion?"

"I do not know," evaded the Storied Watcher.

"What do you *mean*... ' I don't know'?" he pressed.

"It depends on many variable factors, few of which are currently within my knowledge, sir," the alien-girl deflected. "These 'bombs' of yours have different levels of destructive power... a small one, *perhaps*... a big one... 'not likely'. It would also depend on how close that I was to it, when it detonated. My safety-powers wax greatly, but I do not know if they are yet sufficiently robust. It is not something that I would want to experiment with... and even if I *did* know – I would *not* tell you."

"*Why* not?" he asked.

"Lest you turn around and use one of these weapons against me, latterly, sir," coolly responded Karéin-Mayréij. "Did you think that I would not consider this possibility? We *do* have a truce... but that is very far from trust and friendship, where I come from."

"But I thought... fine, *whatever*," grumbled a frustrated President. "Ms. Chu – is there any more?"

"Unfortunately... 'yes', sir," confirmed Chu. "Crowford says that he's got the Command-Post on a declining course to crash into the White House, in... just a minute... you there... how long 'till we're there?"

There was some back-talk evidently coming from the room in which the former FBI team-leader was located, and after a few seconds she continued, "About 35 to 40 minutes, sir. But we'll be close enough to downtown D.C. to kill hundreds of thousands of people, in no more than 20 to 25."

"Sir – if you don't come voluntarily, I'll have to invoke my authority as your bodyguard to *force* you to evacuate this building!" exclaimed Kortish. "Your life, and that of the First Family, is in *imminent* danger!"

"Not yet!" countered the President. "It's *vitally* important that we manage this situation!"

Kaysten's eyes began to glow and his war-song added itself to the background-track. In a half-second he had positioned himself between Kortish and the U.S. leader.

"We all understand what you're saying," remarked the former Chief of Staff, in the Service leader's direction, "But if the Old Man wants to stay... I'll make sure that happens. And for the record, sir – I'm here with you, whatever happens!"

"Thanks *so* much, Jerry," said a visibly appreciative President.

"Sari," broke in Billings, "If our – uhh – 'Old Man' here, wants to get himself vaporized... well, who are *we* to call him back on it? But we'd better get our asses out of here – *pronto!*"

"There's *more*, Karéin," came Chu's remote voice. "There's *another* nuke – about 400 kilotons, being carried by an Air Force bomber – it hasn't been launched yet but we think it's aimed at Sam Jacobson's aircraft, which, as I can see from the tracking-display that's in front of me, is also approaching the White House; the Jacobson plane's currently over northern Virginia, and –"

"*Wait* a minute– if you please!" interrupted a flummoxed Karéin-Mayréij, "*Two*, atom-smashing bombs? *Both* on their way here... and one of these, aimed to kill brave Sam Jacobson and his comrades?"

"Mr. President," interjected Kortish's determined-yet-restrained voice, "Just for completeness... there's a third one on top of that : remember the, uhh, ex-Pakistani weapon? The one that the Armed Forces had lost track of?"

"Yeah... foremost on our minds, before all *this* happened," acknowledged the U.S. leader. "I asked for continued briefings, but got nothing from George. Don't *tell* me –"

"It's been traced to the Rancho Cucamonga area just to the east of Los Angeles, sir," matter-of-factually interrupted the Service agent. "Army's trying to get a precise fix on it right now so the Delta Force can launch a recovery-mission, but they're in the middle of a pitched battle with a number of very well-armed criminal gangs, any *one* of which might have physical control of the device."

"What's the risk of it going off in the next few hours?" demanded the President. "And where *is* that again... 'Rancho Cucamonga', I mean."

"About halfway between downtown L.A. and San Bernardino, sir," responded Kortish. "As for the risk of detonation, well, for what it's worth... we think it's been down there for days to weeks... and L.A.'s still there."

"*Three* of these accursed bombs, now?" came the inevitable and somewhat-disingenuous protest on the part of the alien-girl. "By what madman's plot, does such come to *be?*"

Karéin, sent Abruzzio, *You've known about the L.A. bomb for many days now; why...*

He will complain that I did... and yet did nothing to stop it, came back the psychic reply.

And he was told of it by Min-ee, when she first flew with me.

Yet this 'American' government chose instead to spend its time persecuting us... especially, in vexing Sam and his friends.

Besides... what if this 'bomb' is now controlled or sought by our brother Sebastiàn, in his death-quest against the bandit-army who wronged him, a fortnight ago... and the President means to reclaim the weapon, by way of war? silently noted Karéin-Mayréij.

I will not war against my own kin; and I need not *such a problem, on the other side of this* continent!

How many of these atom-smashing bombs, must one Storied Watcher juggle into the silent heavenly void, at one time?

Better neither to falter... nor to let one of these, drop!

A giggle came from Tommy's direction.

"Welcome to *America*, honey!" sourly mentioned Billings, with equal guile.

"*I* invited Jacobson and his crew here, Madam," explained the President to the alien-girl, "In the hopes of working out his grievances with the government, before he wrecked the country venting his fury at us. I hadn't counted on *your* appearance, beforehand. Anyway – I suppose Jacobson and the L.A. bomb are the *least* of my worries, right now. Curt – do whatever you can to reach DeWitt or the military – we've *got* to shoot down the Command-Post, before it reaches –"

"Mr. President – *no!*" shouted Abruzzio. "You *heard* what Crowford told Minnie! She'll be –"

Voices on Chu's aircraft could be heard in the background; it sounded like cries of anguish from the former Vice-President and from Warnock.

"It's alright, Sylvia," came the voice of the team-leader. "I *knew* this was a dangerous assignment. I'll be *okay.*"

"No... no... *no!*" protested the former JPL scientist.

Now Karéin-Mayréij looked distraught.

"I'm sorry, Ms. Abruzzio... but *millions* of innocent lives are at stake, here!" argued the President. "Curt – get *going!*"

"Yes *sir!*" obliged the Service leader. The others heard him directing other agents to run elsewhere, in the hopes of finding alternate communications-channels.

"Clark – you've *got* to get out of here!" demanded the First Lady. "This 'alien' is bad enough – but *two* nuclear weapons coming our way? What about Matt and Clairie? What about *me?*"

"You're right," he agreed. "I'll stay at my post... but you and the kids need to leave, immediately. Can we get a helicopter?"

A voice – evidently one of the Marine guards – came from the direction of the communications-shack.

"Two already on their way, sir," the guard announced, "But they're both at least twenty-five to thirty minutes out. The stand-by 'copter at the White House was damaged in, uhh, recent events, so the former C-in-C had the backup-machines relocated away from Andrews."

"*Shit!*" cursed Kaysten. "By the time they get here – *damn* George!"

"Oh my *God!*" shrieked the First Lady. "We're going to *die –*"

"Don't you have some kind of, uhh, 'safe room' here?" inquired Moira Sullivan. "I saw a story about it on TV, once..."

"We do," confirmed the President, "Quite robust – but they told me that it wouldn't survive a direct hit... or even a near-miss."

"If what's on its way is anything like what we encountered up on Amchitka, and if it lands close to us, sir," ominously noted Abruzzio, "We'll *never* survive! I protected against that blast – but it was *miles* offshore!"

"Yeah – and it blinded me for *days!*" growled Tommy. "Serve you *right* to have one dropped on your head!"

"*Horrid* little boy!" castigated the First Lady.

Tommy stuck his tongue out at the Presidential wife.

"Sari – come *on –* we've *got* to bugger on out of here!" admonished Billings. "If you care about Tommy and me, not to mention Saquina, Hector and Melissa, out there –"

"Now about 33 minutes from the D.C. metropolitan area," warned Chu. "Sir... if we get too close, I intend to power up my force-field as much as I can, and then head forward to vaporize Crowford and his EMP-box before he can react. Please order the Marines and the Service not to contest my approach – since any shooting will spook him. The problem is... the plane may go into a crash-dive if my *Amaiish*-rays hit the flight-controls, and if Crawford's to be believed, he can set a countdown for the damn thing the moment he thinks he's being attacked, anyway. If *that* happens, I guess I'll find out if I can fly like Sylvia wants me to, but even if I can... he's probably right... I just won't be far enough away... when..."

"Min-ee... *no!*" exclaimed an ashen-faced Storied Watcher. "Your weirding-shield is not yet equal to one of these damnable 'bombs', so close to it! You will *never* survive!"

"Karéin... I love you, in every sense of the word... but you *heard* what I said to Sylvia... I'm at peace – *whatever* may happen," Chu softly responded. "It's been wonderful, tasting a bit of your *Fire*. I wouldn't change a *thing*... okay, maybe I *would* change what happened to poor Otis and Will. But *thank* you, teacher. Thank you – from the bottom of my heart!"

"*Curse* the day when I landed in this benighted kingdom!" wailed a frustrated Karéin-Mayréij. "Is there *no* day upon which some knave plans not some foul massacre?"

"If it helps," interjected Chu, "I've got the communications-arrays on the Command-Post, sending messages to the Jacobson aircraft's status-display, advising him about what's going on. Problem is... it's one-way traffic – I have no idea if Sam has even *seen* these warnings... let alone if he's going to *do* anything about them."

"Thank you, blessed sister," gratefully responded the Storied Watcher.

"Tommy... come *on*," directed Billings. "Let's get back to the *Express*... we gotta warn the others, at least. Sari – our life is in your hands."

The boy nodded and joined the former salesman in heading for the Oval Office's outside door.

"*Wait!*" called the Storied Watcher. "Sylvia – keep the interference at bay!"

"I think I have it figured out," pledged Abruzzio.

"The 'Express'?" asked the President. "Oh... right – the, uhh, space-ship that you came here in. Well... yes... maybe it *is* better that you get away, to somewhere safer. Is it large enough to accommodate my wife and children? And you *must* do something to protect Washington! The Air Force may not be able to shoot down either the Command-Post, or the missile aimed at Jacobson, before they go off. If that happens over a populated area –"

"Now as to Matt and Clairie," diffidently mentioned Karéin-Mayréij, "As they are now among the New People, I will certainly arrange for their safety – as much as this can be done, with – it seems – every schemer in your government, tossing these 'atom-smashing bombs' around like so many, ahh, 'basket-balls'. But why would I risk my life for *you*, sir? My responsibility is to safeguard my family and friends – then to find some way to rescue Min-ee, then to warn and succor Sam Jacobson and his compatriots... in that order. You tried repeatedly to *murder* my family and me; I have settled that score with you; the balance is in alignment. I owe you *nothing*, further! Deal with these horrific weapons, as best you can... for whatever that it is worth, I wish you all success in the coming battle, sir. May the power of my ancestors, be with you."

"I want Clairie and Matt to stay with *us*, Clark!" demanded the First Lady. "I can't *abide* with the idea of her taking them off somewhere, to pervert them, with this 'alien' poison of hers!"

"If you so desire I will take you and your husband along with these two princelings, and I say this as one woman to another," countered the Storied Watcher, "I attest that the powers bestowed upon Matt and Clairie are, as yet, far too weak to withstand one of these 'atom-smashing bombs', if it detonates nearby. Not only will *you* die... but your *children*, too! What kind of 'mother', pleads for such a doom?"

"You're no 'woman'," spat the First Lady. "The right word for *you* is –"

"*Okay*, Kathy," gamely interrupted the President, "I think she understands what you think of her, but we're not accomplishing anything here. Karéin... it demeans me to beg, but if you want me to, then I'll get on my *knees* and say this : you've *got* to help us deal with these threats! I'm grateful that you're so considerate of Matt and Clairie – but do the lives of *millions* of other innocent people – including many children among them – mean *nothing* to you?"

"They... of *course* they do!" stammered the alien-girl, obviously taken off-guard. "Least among all thinking beings on this planet, do I want such a cruel fate upon your subjects; and by now undoubtedly you know that the threats that I made, some time back, to bring ruin to your country – those were idle and empty ones, of which I am ashamed to have uttered. But I had nothing *at all* to do with how these latest, accursed weapons came to *beset* you! Why does it fall to *me*, to fix this?"

"Because you're the only one who *can* fix it," responded the President.

"Because you were *meant* to, all along!" added Kaysten. "Starting with that nasty little bite you landed on me, right in this office. All part of the *plan*... the same one you kicked off, yourself, up there in Canada... can't you *see*, kiddo?"

"But the plan – the quest – that was only supposed to prove that *you* all were –" a defensive Karéin-Mayréij tried to argue. "Your quests never were meant to deal with these 'bombs' – why should I –"

"Because you're our *angel!*" cried Abruzzio. "You're Earth's Guardian Angel – we've all known that, since you *told* us, while on Sam's spaceship. Like with the comet, this task falls to *you*; but *this* time, *not* to you, alone... you have *us* – your disciples, your friends, your followers – to *help* you, Karéin! We'll back you *up! Believe* in yourself!"

An overcome, nonplussed, desperate look appeared on the face of the Storied Watcher.

She addressed Billings and the boy.

"Bob... Tommy... what... what should I *do?*" she asked. "My allegiance is foremost, to you – equally to Elissha and Sayuri. If I perish, these others are themselves at great risk; they will likely suffer a slow and cruel death by cold and starvation... you *know* why! What can I *do?*"

"Good *point!*" smirked the ex-salesman. "'Gotta look after your own first', as they say. Guess our pal the 'President' should have thought all this through a little better, starting with having the kid and me being guinea-pigs for the Agency. Can we get *going*, now?"

"So... you *see*, sir," the alien-girl tried to explain, "I have *commitments*... loyalties... responsibilities. I cannot –"

Some of them saw the kaleidoscope-effect come to Abruzzio's eyes; but it was the *music* that began to play from anywhere and everywhere, and her low, humming singing, that demanded attention.

Though mixed with the ex-scientist's usual, exciting tune, the melody also contained the notes of a different song; and none around (not even the Storied Watcher), understood how Abruzzio had managed the feat.

Somewhere there's a drifter
Trying to find her way
Somewhere someone's waiting
To hear somebody say
I, believe in you...

Tears came to the eyes of a miserable-looking Karéin-Mayréij, while her jaw quivered.

She hung her head, as the music abated.

"From when first I came to Bob's home in Too-Sawn, I just wanted a quiet, plain life here," she softly remarked. "To be a mother and mate... to live happily among you, taking joy from simple things... from watching my beloved grow up, day by day. I thought that dealing with the comet – that must *surely* be enough!"

"You *will* have that – I *swear*, on all that's holy!" implored Abruzzio. "But, Karéin, God Himself now calls you to a quest that you can't refuse! I doubted you before... no more! Take me *with* you, Storied Watcher – and whatever happens, I'll be there *beside* you, all the way through!"

Two heretofore-absent figures appeared in the doorway leading to the outside gardens. They were Hector Ramirez and Melissa Claremont.

"We've been listening for the past ten minutes, Karéin," said the Tex-Mex scientist, "It was pretty hard staying at our posts when we heard the sounds of a fight down here, but we managed... then there didn't seem to be a good time to break into the conversation and introduce ourselves. Your war-children – led by *Vîrya Ahn'jë* – are helping Saquina stand guard over the *Express*. We're with you... whatever you want us to do. That goes for Mrs. White, too."

"Oh *God*, Hector!" breathed an overjoyed Abruzzio, "Are you *ever* a sight for sore eyes!"

"You too," answered Ramirez, with a broad smile. "*Told* you I'd hunt you down!"

Despite the fact that she was still evidently maintaining a communications-link, Abruzzio (accompanied by her dog), managed to rush over to embrace her fellow ex-scientist.

"Nice to meet you two," offered the President. "If you don't mind my asking... what do you – uhh – *do*? Alien-power-wise, that is."

"We allowed to *tell* him?" asked Ramirez, in the Storied Watcher's direction..

"I would tell him the truth... though perhaps not the *whole* truth," phlegmatically suggested the alien-girl, while wiping her eyes.

"Ah jus' fly 'round up there," laconically offered Melissa, with a shrug. "Oh – an' ah blows shi... uh, *stuff*, out of the sky, too. But only if it *'dis* me."

"Well, Mr. President," explained Ramirez, "You can call me 'Mr. Hurricane', I suppose. Only Cat 2 or 3 right now... but Cat 5's just a matter of *time*. Get the idea?"

"*Interesting*," offered the U.S. leader. "I've gotten to know Ms. Abruzzio reasonably well, lately... and I've learned not to under-estimate these 'powers' of hers. If yours are similar..."

"Equivalent... but different," obliquely noted Abruzzio.

"Great to see you, Hector!" added Kaysten. "You too, Melissa."

Ramirez nodded, while the teenager acknowledged with a "Yo."

"Brother... sister... do you understand what we will be *up* against?" riposted the Storied Watcher, in the direction of the newcomers. "*Two* of these damnable 'atom-smashing' bombs! One such, nearly *killed* us, up on yonder island. The risk is *immense!*"

Silence fell on the group.

The Storied Watcher again addressed her mate.

"*Bob...*" she started.

Many pairs of eyes stared balefully at the former flooring-tile salesman.

"You *know* how much I care about the government's problems... but... uhh..."

He thought long and hard, swallowed and then offered,

"Well, Sari... you once told me you weren't sure if you were an 'angel'... maybe now's your chance to find out. What are those voices in your head telling you, honey?"

Those in the room held their breath, as the anguished alien-girl's survival-instincts plainly battled her beliefs of duty and loyalty.

She bent her head, with shuttered eyelids; but at length, the now-familiar – but still *never*-familiar – visage of godly, dignified, surreal power came to Karéin-Mayréij.

Her face seemed illuminated from below while her eyes started to glow.

The flames of *Amaiish* burned brightly within her body.

"May the God of this planet – in whose benevolence, both Devon and now Sylvia do attest – may He again fortify this 'angel'," she vowed. "I do not know why – and it is against my wisdom and my judgment... but yes – I *will* fly into battle, to protect my kin – and also those who slumber, unknowing of this peril!"

Abruzzio was weeping, as she and Sullivan crossed themselves.

"*Yeah!* You *go*, girl!" enthusiastically cheered Kaysten.

"My arts say that we must tarry here briefly... but we dare not more than that," the back-in-charge alien-girl commanded. "Hector, Melissa – use this time to assist Matt and Clairie; call on Saquina if you need help – you can use the mind-push skill to carry the two young ones to our ship. Let Bob, Tommy and all else who wish to, go with you, and prepare to depart. Moira – as a trusted friend of my sister Sylvia – if you will have her, I bestow the grace of my mighty ancestors upon you on this day, and I beg your assistance in ushering our friends aboard the sky-ship. Attend to their needs as you can, my sister. Welcome to our company... and may the light of the Holy *Fire* strengthen and guide you!"

An awed Sullivan managed to say, "Oh... for *sure!*"

With a wry smile and an embrace, Abruzzio whispered to her school-friend, "Here we *go*, Moira... and, 'congratulations, new sister'!"

The Storied Watcher turned to address the two GrayWar pseudo-soldiers, in the next room.

"And to *you*, new-found ones... you have accompanied my sister Sylvia, albeit for a short while... and thus the choice is yours as to what you will do, and as to with whom you will go. I will only say, 'if you travel with me and my kin, much will be expected – Warriors of the Light do not, ahh, 'get long week-ends'. And that drug that now imposes such indolence, no more shall it affect you. If you elect to join me, you will be welcome. You have a very short time in which to decide – may that choice be well-considered."

Those with "Mars Ears" heard the one say to the other, "How the *fuck* she knows that? What the fuck do we do *now*?"

"Mr. President," requested the Storied Watcher, "Do you have a map around here? And may I have your assent for what we shall soon do?"

"*Now* you're talking!" eagerly replied the ex-salesman.

Billings exited the door, followed in quick succession by the boy, who had recovered from his recent ordeal with amazing speed.

The President answered, "I'm always reluctant to approve plans that I don't understand – but considering the complete lack of an alternative... 'yes' – as long as you'll protect my people."

"So do I hope and pray, sir," pledged Karéin-Mayréij, "Though this fate rests on an edge yet more acute than that of *Væran Fàiagàryuu;* and *his*, is the sharpest on this planet. I give you fair notice – should we succeed and survive, you and your kingdom will shortly be in *great* debt to myself and the New People. I will shortly demand *concessions*, when this is over with. I came to your planet intending not to rule – still not do I so desire – but that is a different thing from 'standing idly by, while kings vex the meek.' Your ways must *change!* Is this clear?"

Abruzzio's mind reached out to that of her school-friend.

Good girl, Storied Watcher, she sent.

Grab 'em and twist... serves him right!

A perplexed, wide-eyed Sullivan blurted out, "Sylvia... did you *say* something?"

The former JPL scientist just smiled in her friend's direction.

Glumly, the U.S. leader replied, "I won't be doing any more bluffing, Karéin... we both know that I have no other options. Save D.C. and I'll agree to *anything* – provided that it's reasonable, and that it doesn't change our basic system of government. Fair enough?"

"Verily then... we have a 'deal'," said the Storied Watcher. "And I will hold you *to* it!"

"Yeah – we got a map," offered Kaysten. "But it's just one of those old-school roll-down types, back here, near where you, uhh, *bit* me. Just a sec..."

The President tried to pay attention to this conversation, but he was simultaneously directing his Marine guards in efforts to vector the Air Force against Chu's aircraft.

He reached for a remote-control device and a large map of the entire continental United States descended from the ceiling above the rear parts of the Oval Office, on the opposite side of the two couches from the Resolute Desk.

"I got a marker-pen somewhere... there it is," added the former Chief of Staff, briefly fumbling for something within his jacket-pocket, then retrieving a black permanent-tip marker. Here..."

"Jer-ee... where is Min-ee's airplane, now?" asked Karéin-Mayréij.

"Minnie?" he called out. "You got a fix on where you're now at?"

"Just a second," replied the remote voice.

She issued a few local commands, listened to a faint response, and then said, "Looks like we're just to the west of I-81, between Martinsburg, Maryland, and Winchester, Virginia... about 30,000 feet and slowly descending... I can't guarantee anything about if the flight-plan will go on like this, since Crowford's calling the shots up here. By the way – Sam's plane has been going in and out of track, because he's flying through the mountains, but the last fix we've got on him is... let me see... it was about twenty kilometers north-west of Harrisonburg, Virginia. Ha! *There's* something funny – if he stays on track, he's due to intercept this aircraft, right over D.C.."

"Mark those places on the map," demanded the Storied Watcher. "Min-ee – please monitor these com-pu-ters, and tell us immediately if anything changes."

"Of *course*, Karéin," complied the former team-leader.

Kaysten used the marker, placing an "X" symbol in the appropriate places.

The Storied Watcher briefly closed her eyes and murmured something, as if she were concentrating. In about one second, the outside door re-opened, though there did not appear to be any visible entity responsible for this action.

"*Vîrya Ahn'jë*," intoned the alien-girl to no obvious addressee, "Can thee read this electro-signal – that is, the one that sister Sylvia now reinforces?"

After a short pause, she continued, "Excellent! I bid thee so to do, and never to lose it, until this all is done; we shall thus stay in contact, as much as we can. But beware these signals being used to track us... warn me if thou detect that."

The weirding-armor – her infernal essence immediately apparent to all around – appeared to plain view.

Vîrya Ahn'jë floated, self-levitating about a foot and a half above the Oval Office carpet, just to one side of her mother.

"What in God's name is *that* –" demanded the First Lady.

"Remember how you met *Vîrya I'ëà'b'*, back at your house, Ma'am? The *shield*, I mean." answered Kaysten. "Well… this is her, uhh, 'sister'. Hi, kiddo! Great to see you – uhh, sorry, 'thou'… or was it, 'thee' – again!"

The armor – evidently, overlooking slights related to pronoun-use – chirped happily.

"It's on *fire!*" protested a nonplussed and fearful Presidential wife. "Get it *out* of here!"

"There, *there*, dear child," intervened Karéin-Mayréij, "The lady means not to demean thee – she is just unaccustomed to thy ways. Please forgive her! Now, Min-ee – how fast do all these aircraft and weapons, transit the skies?"

"I'm going at about 550 kilometers per hour... Jacobson's airspeed is about 250," replied Chu's remote voice. "Also note, my Air Force helpers here, are saying that the missile on the bomber – once launched – it can fly at about 800 kilometers per hour."

"Oh-kay," mused the Storied Watcher. "That means... they shall be at their closest, approximately *here*..."

She seemed lost in thought for a few seconds.

"This quest of courage and guile will test the limits of our abilities… and of our craft in deploying them," remarked the alien-girl. "If any fail or falter… then *all* may perish."

"Karéin?" nervously voiced Abruzzio. "You aren't thinking what I *think* you're thinking... *are* you?"

The light of a goddess, again shone from the face of Karéin-Mayréij, as she addressed the others, arrayed all around her.

"I crushed a *comet*, you know," she said.

"Now..." she declared, "It is *your* turn."

Cass Mountain Drop-Off

The V-37, with as many post-humans as could reliably fly or levitate on their own, holding above it, had staggered uncertainly into the air at maximum load; indeed, for a few agonizing seconds, Jacobson – who had insisted on temporarily relieving the trucker at the controls – almost aborted the take-off, fearing that the transport's straining turbofans would fail. But the apprehension proved unnecessary, and soon they were on their way.

The timing was fortunate, as in the next ten seconds after lift-off, White's frozen barriers failed altogether, and a crowd rushed in to the part of the parking-lot that had previously accommodated the V-37. It would have been both unsafe and irresponsible to have tried to power up the engines with so many people milling around.

The transport cruised at the lowest of low altitudes for a few minutes, dodging hill-tops and following the contour of the land; then it arrived (apparently, as near as the group could tell, without being tracked by the Air Force) at the hide-out suggested by the mountain-man.

This, luckily, was uninhabited, although it bore signs of recent occupation.

"Jus' tell them boys that Dorsie sent y'all," the hillbilly advised, on seeing this. "Got some solar hooked up to the batteries on th' lower level, should run y'all fine for two or three day, an' there's a diesel generator down there too, but lay off of it 'less y'all absolutely got to... it makes lots of noise an' that ain't a good thing. An' don' use none of that 'alien' shit, 'less y'all want Ezra 'n Cooter to shoot first 'n ask questions later. Don't touch their guns or their brew neither... they take that kind of thing *personal*."

The counsel was kept in mind in case of future encounters, but Jacobson's attention – and that of White, Boyd and also Wolf – was preoccupied with Tanaka, who, though she had not worsened, seemed not to have improved very much either. She lay half-conscious on her stretcher, with all four of her male companions doting on her, until it was not wise to tarry any further.

"I wonder if we're doing the right thing," quietly remarked Jacobson, as they (with Boyd carefully maintaining a station several paces back, due to persistent, unnerving growls and other negative feedback from Tanaka's living-armor) carried the more-than-a-woman down the V-37's back-ramp, into the crisp night air, thence into a well-hidden shack, with a much larger and even better-hidden basement-complex, that Dorsie had directed them to.

They proceeded into what must have been the brewing-room, which was big enough to accommodate all of those who would stay behind.

"Cherie deserves a crack at the President, as much as any of us do, you know," he continued. "She'll probably be *pissed* when she wakes up here and finds out that we've flown off east without her... can't say I'd blame her."

"Neither would I," agreed an equally soft-toned Boyd, "But we *got* to do this... we all know the reasons why. I just hope the Professor understands."

"Well," grunted Wolf, "Don't be surprised if she wakes up and decides to drop in to the White House, right after all of us. She's damn *fast* when she gets goin' up there... as some of us can personally attest."

"Yeah," ruefully confirmed Boyd. "You got *that* right."

Jacobson called the group to attention.

"Alright, everybody," he announced. "You know the plan... and you know that we'll be back, as soon as we've completed our mission. Any last comments or questions?"

"'Last comments'... now don't I just *love* the way you put that, Jacobson," grumbled Boatman.

"We'll be okay," countered Hendricks. "But I wish Miss Angel-Face had let us turn off this damn 'anti-poison' thing that's on us until *forever*, what with all this fine moonshine lying around down here."

"That's *'nother* thing that Cooter 'n Ezra might take *personal*, if'n y'all dip into it, without them sayin' y'all can, ahead of time," warned the mountain-man.

"See?" opined Donny. "She got us all on the straight and narrow – might as well be in a damn temperance-meetin' – for our own good. But man... I could still use a good Jack Daniels and a smoke..."

Wolf flicked his thumb as if it were a cigarette-lighter, producing a nice long flame.

"Now all you need is a pack of Luckys, pardner," he quipped.

"I'll look around," shrugged the trucker. "Hope them 'billies who's Dorsie's kin, ain't as possessive of that, as that 'shine of theirs."

Jacobson's teenaged daughter raced to his side.

"Daddy... I want to come along!" she demanded.

"You *know* why I can't allow that, Jen," he deflected.

"I'm 18... I'm an *adult* now, you know!" she pressed. "And I want to *tell* the President what I think of the *bullshit* that the government did to Mom, myself, and our whole family... Ammy too... not to mention the Wades and the Youngs!"

He took her off to one side, out of easy human hearing-distance, and embraced her, whispering in her ear, "Sweetheart... you know that if we weren't flying into a potential war-zone, my decision would be different. But – and don't let Mom know I told you this – there *is* a chance that some or all of us, won't be coming back from this mission. If – God forbid – something like that *does* come to pass, you'll be the eldest of the family other than for Mom... and I want you to be there for Jeannie and Riley. If I'm no longer here, I want you to call for the Storied Watcher in the way that Mrs. Boyd explained to you... and tell Karéin that we tried to set things right, as best we knew how. Do what she requests of you, and if she offers you the *Fire* – accept it, say the pledge and carry on the good fight, in my place. Will you do that for me?"

With a shocked, but equally, serious look on her face, Jennifer Jacobson replied, "I will, Daddy... I *promise!*"

Tears came to her eyes as she embraced her father, then let go.

There were a few other "goodbyes", lasting perhaps ten minutes or so, and then the former Mars Mission commander announced, "Well... time to go, I guess."

Silence accompanied him and the rest of those leaving for the Capitol.

They boarded the V-37 through the back ramp. Jacobson and Boyd took the first turn at the pilots' stations, gradually guiding the transport into the cold night air, while the bounty-hunter engaged his alien-powers and flew above the aircraft.

As the top of Cass Mountain receded into the dark distance, Boyd turned to address his former boss.

"You know, Commander," he said, "Wendy's only ten years old... but I had the same talk with her."

Jacobson – momentarily lost in thought, with rueful acknowledgment on his face – stared forward through the windshield, in the direction of Washington, D.C..

The V-37 – its control-responsiveness much-improved, due its lightened weight – still cruised on a north-east course, just above the mountain-tops of West Virginia.

Boyd, who had taken over the controls, asked Jacobson, "Any sign of the Air Force yet?"

"Negative from the sensors... such as they are," replied the former Mars mission commander. "So far, the RWR has alerted properly, when we get painted by those FC radars... but I'm sure that there's *something* they can fire at us, that we're blind to. Hopefully Wolf will warn us if we're about to get bounced."

"Yeah... well, I don't trust that guy," muttered Boyd. "He'll probably head off to burn down every town on the way between here and D.C., just for the fun of it. Plus, his IR-sig will light up the Air Force's thermal-seekers like no tomorrow. Frankly I got no idea why Karéin gave him those alien-powers of his. What she sees in him... I'll never know."

He paused for a second or two, then asked, "Okay... cleared another set of hills... still pretty dark down there, I guess at least *some* folks are obeying the curfew... where are we, Commander?"

Jacobson took a second or two to survey the old-school moving-map display (the GPS-2 feed, and all other network links, had been disabled long ago), comparing the display to a hand-held paper map procured from a recently-visited gas-station, and then announced, "Hmm... better progress than I thought... just crossed Route 220... one more ridge and then we'll be pretty much out of the highest part of the hills, so let's drop the altitude if you can safely do so. We should see I-81 to the east and Harrisonburg south and east. Keep your eyes peeled. Remember that we won't have terrain-contour to mask our radar-returns, when we get down there."

"Affirmative," confirmed Boyd, as he carefully maneuvered the transport's flight-path upward, so as to clear the Blue Ridge mountain-tops. "She's sure handling easier, now... but damn, does this ever feel *clumsy*, after flying on my own..."

"Wish I knew," grumbled Jacobson. "I'm leaping way up there these days... but somehow I always seem to come back down."

"Yeah, well, Captain," interjected White, "Y'all figure it out, eventually. I ain't quite got my own English down on it... but I'm well on my way, I'd say. I've been studyin' Mr. Hot-Shot up there... how he uses them fire-jets to maneuver with. Almost got the same thang goin', but with my ice. When he gets tired, I'll take my turn, topside, with Misha... play 'round with it a bit more, you know?"

"Offer gladly accepted," said the former Mars commander, with a bemused half-smile.

They flew on for a couple more minutes. Boyd observed, "Clearing top of Blue Ridge now... hey... you see *that?* I think that's D.C.!"

And indeed, it was true. Far off in the distance – just a bit closer than the dark, even expanse of the Atlantic behind – was the sprawling, well-lit Washington metropolitan area.

Smaller spots of light, each illustrating a town or small city, dotted the countryside between the elongated mountain-ridge behind the V-37 and their objective.

"You figured out what you're going to say to the bastard, first?" inquired the former Mars mission pilot.

"It'll probably start like, 'you threaten my family, one more time, mother-fucker' –" started Jacobson; but then, his stare re-directed to the aircraft's systems status display, a small, green-text on black-background, old-school computer-screen.

"What do you make of *that?*" he asked.

"Of *what*... oh, right... *wait* a minute," stammered Boyd. "Devon – have a look at *this!* What the *hell*...?"

"Ain't that thang s'posed to be reportin', like, bypass-ratio on the turbofans, or something?" queried White. "What the fuck's it doin', displayin' a message like, 'You're flyin' into danger, turn right zero two five, ascend and maintain thirty thousand, three zero zero knots'?"

"That'll take us *way* south of D.C. – out over the Atlantic!" exclaimed Boyd. "Over my dead body!"

"Yeah... and we're depressurized, remember," added Jacobson. "Unless Karéin's alien-powers can protect us from it... we'd be dealing with hypoxia."

"Prolly some fuckin' trick by the President... since he knows his damn ass is grass, when we show up for a friendly little visit –" opined White.

But then the display showed a different message.

Looker to Diamondback, Sunburn, Barbecue, Grozny, Thunderchild and Snowcone, it started.

Missile with a nuke warhead, on your tail!

Could be fired at any second!

I'm on President's Command-Post plane.

Under 100 km. north of you.

Don't come to D.C.!

"*Fuck!*" swore Boyd. "That's *got* to be... *Minnie?* Or did the government get to her and tortured her for our call-signs... or maybe just intercepted them some other way?"

"I don't *know*," muttered Jacobson. "But knowing her, and her abilities, I doubt that's the case. Is there any way we can reply... ask for clarification? How the hell is it being *sent*, in the first place? I thought we're flying EMCON?"

"We *are!*" replied a frustrated Boyd, "I turned off all the bidirectional systems, and I physically disconnected the ones that couldn't be disabled. This has *got* to be some kind of targeted, unidirectional broadcast. The DF-gear isn't enabled, so I can't tell where it's coming from... unless that 'north' message was accurate. And if it was faked... *my* guess is, the government just wants us to head out over the Atlantic so they can grease us easy, and avoid a lot of casualties on the ground. I say, 'ignore it'."

"Brent," requested Jacobson, "See if you can get a fix on the originating-point. With the RF-tracker, that is."

"But re-enabling that might let them get a target-lock on us!" warned Boyd. "They could home in on the transponder and signal-booster."

"Seems to me that they got *that* down straight already," offered White. "If they can send them messages right into our systems... y'all know?"

"I don't think this is a great idea," complained the former Mars mission pilot, "But Devon's probably right... they want to fire a missile up our asses, they might already be able to do so. Okay, enabling the DF-tracker... we just gotta wait for another message..."

It was not long in coming.

Looker here... don't see your course changing, it advised.
Your display-buffer may fail if I send too much more.
You'll have to land and power-down, to reset it.
Fuckers murdered Otis and Will!
I'm holding FBI director and Vice-President, hostage.
Crowford (religious nut) has taken over cockpit.
He smuggled a H-bomb on-board this plane!
He can set it off any time!
Please turn away, if you want to live!
My plane will crash into White House.
But we have a plan.
President had a visit from –

The LCD-screen went blank, and then showed an error-message.

A stunned silence enveloped the company of more-than-human adventurers.

"She's *got* to be fuckin' *kidding!*" eventually inveighed White. "A fuckin' *bomb* on board Air Force One, or Two, or whatever? What the *fuck?*"

"Well," mordantly observed Jacobson, "I think we can agree that these messages are probably authentic."

"She doesn't know that Hendricks and Boatman survived the fall," mentioned Boyd. "If this is all made up by the government... they're being more creative than I'd ever give them credit for."

"You get a fix?" anxiously demanded Jacobson.

"Checking..." replied Boyd, while the other two held their breath.

"Yeah... accuracy's not that great – it's not meant for precision-targeting, after all – but I think... *there* it is," announced the former Mars mission pilot. "Twelve degrees off due north, distance approximately 77 kilometers."

"Assuming that we maintain current speed... what's our ETA to close proximity with them... say, five to ten clicks?" asked the Mars-Gang leader.

"I'd guess about 16 minutes or thereabouts," mentioned White. "But we should be able to see 'em – at least with our Mars eyes – much sooner'n that. Maybe right now, that we know where to look."

"I can probably cut that time down to about ten, by forcing up our speed," noted Boyd, "Although that might burn out the engines, to say nothing of the effect on the airframe – she's taken quite a beating up to this point. But so we get there... what comes *next?*"

"I don't know," muttered Jacobson. "A lot of this doesn't add up. I mean... why is Minnie staying on that aircraft? We've all seen *her* alien-powers; she's more than capable of blasting her way out of it and then, I suppose, parachuting to safety. And why would Crowford – who the hell's *he –*"

"Wasn't he the new President's Spiritual Adviser... or something?" speculated Boyd. "He used to be one of those televangelists, I think."

"I believe in God – but I ain't never had no time for the shit they're always talkin'," grumbled White. "More interested in linin' their own pockets, than doin' anything that the Lord would approve of."

"If this is true, there's now little point in us continuing to D.C.," remarked Jacobson. "The President would *certainly* have been evacuated from the White House, the moment that the government got wind of all this... whether or not it turns out to be true. We have no idea where he'd be going –"

"Andrews? Mount Weather?" interjected Boyd.

"Those'd be *obvious* targets, for anyone – including us – who was trying to kill the President," argued Jacobson. "We could go on a wild-goose chase to either one, or to dozens of other potential hiding-places... and still come up empty. And we now have a *different* consideration – namely, 'millions of lives in downtown D.C.'. If that really *is* Minnie sending us these messages – and if what she's saying is accurate – we have a disaster of *unprecedented* proportions, flying to the north of us. We've *got* to stop it!"

"And just how y'all proposin' we do *that,* Captain?" countered White. "Nobody here got enough goin' in the telekinesis department, to pull a rig *that* size – it's, like, a jumbo 747 as I recall – away from where it's goin'... not even Angel-Girl herself might be able to do that. And to even *try*, we'd have to get so fuckin' close that we'd have no chance at all, if the damn thing went off. Same might happen if we just tried to shoot down the Command-Post and have it crashin' and blowin' up over some unlucky small town. Fuckin' situation's beyond our abilities, if y'all ask me."

"*Unless,*" portentously suggested Jacobson, "We – or *some* of us – accept the outcome that might happen, by trying to stop the Command-Post, short of the city."

"You're talking a *suicide-mission*, Commander!" argued Boyd. "I'd like to get my name on a few schools as much as you would... but we both have families who are depending on us to return. Why does it fall to *us* to do this – where the *fuck*'s the *Air Force?* Why don't they have every fighter in the continental U.S., in the air, with a lock-on against this flying bomb?"

"Well... we shot down quite a few of those fighters, getting this far," phlegmatically offered the former Mars mission leader. "Whatever's left might be already in the air, or maybe vectored against us – we should ask Wolf and Misha if they've detected any, to the north or the east – but remember... Minnie said that the Vice-President and the FBI director are on the plane, along with her. The government might be reluctant to fire against the Command-Post, until the last possible moment. There are *lots* of possible explanations. Are we willing to take a chance on a million or more innocent people in the Capitol Region, being killed, just because we don't know all the facts?"

None of the three could speak on this, for a few seconds.

Then Jacobson proposed,

"There may be another way, you know."

"Yeah?" asked White.

"The Air Force," offered the former Mars mission leader, "Has a lock on this *aircraft*... not on *us*. We've got a programmable auto-pilot... we could descend low enough to drop us off, then rig her to execute a course, flying at max speed, to collide with the Command-Post... *assuming*, of course, that that plane continues on its own current flight-plan. We could knock her down from a safe distance. If they fire that nuke-tipped missile against our plane, so much the better. It would just hit the Command-Post... which is a lost cause anyway."

"What about our families, back on the mountain?" challenged Boyd. "They'll be *stranded...*"

"And what about Minnie?" exclaimed White. "She'll be –"

"I *know*," unhappily interrupted Jacobson. "I don't like the idea either... but Minnie has already warned us away and we have to assume that she understands the consequences. Are you willing to take the chance of being right next to a thermonuclear blast, if her messages are authentic?"

"That'd be a 'no'," admitted White.

"Given the proximity-factor, which is diminishing as we speak, we're *very* short of time," noted Boyd. "We don't have a homing-system on this plane, so if this is going to work, we'd have to do it by a pre-planned course... let me see..."

He worked feverishly to enter data into the V-37's on-board computers.

"It's do-able, only if we throttle up to max... and here's a trick... I can re-route the fuel-dump circuits to spray into the exhaust-shrouds," said the former Mars mission pilot.

"Yo... *brilliant*, 'bro!" congratulated White. "Instant afterburner!"

"Guesstimating the thrust, I figure it'll get us another fifty miles per hour – of course it'll wreck the engines after a few minutes... not that that matters," noted Boyd, "But the timing's *critical*. If we don't get it lit up and going in the next five minutes, we simply won't be able to intersect the Command-Post's flight-path, far enough away from D.C., for it to make any difference. It'd still blow over the western suburbs – we're talking hundreds of *thousands* dead!"

"Where we gonna bail?" asked White. "And where the hell we go after that?"

Jacobson and Boyd hunched over the moving-map display.

"How about this little town here, on State Road 688... what's its name... yeah, 'Orlean'... that's it," stated the former Mars mission pilot. "We can drop to about 1500 feet – you can survive a drop from that altitude, can't you?"

"*Sure* I can – could probably do it from a few thousand," confirmed Jacobson.

With a wry grin, he added, "Do you know how *insane* it sounds... hearing myself saying that?"

"Only a bit more crazy than me saying, 'I'll start flying all by myself, then try to lock on to you and carry you onward to wherever', Commander," mentioned Boyd. "And as to what happens next, or where we go... I honestly got no idea. 'Try not to be right under the bomb, when and if it goes off', sounds good to me. Anybody got a better plan?"

"Y'all fuckin' not just whistlin' 'Dixie' there, my man," ruefully agreed White. "And listen – I'll try to back y'all up, with the 'tractor-beam' stuff," volunteered White, "'Long as y'all understand... Commander, y'all bein' kept from goin' under, by somebody who's barely swimmin' himself."

"No promises... no problem," acknowledged Jacobson. "Brent – can you get the new course programmed in?"

"Already on it," confirmed the former Mars mission pilot, as he again worked to quickly enter data into the autopilot.

"And then," requested Jacobson, "Somebody will need to go topside and warn Misha and Wolf, of the change in flight-plans."

Bird In Flight

The underground room had benefited by an impromptu make-over; there was now a plain wooden table precisely in its middle, accompanied by a similarly-austere wooden chair. There was a transparent cup of clear, distilled water on the table.

Despite dry lips, nobody in the vicinity had yet taken a drink.

In the chair, sat the Agency director, his usually-unflappable demeanor perhaps showing a hint of frustration, today.

He activated the flat-screen display on the far wall. The Agency logo appeared.

"This is Top Dog," announced the director, toward the screen.

"ID-value is Molehill 461, Blackdragon 95, Trapezoid 8K. Do you copy?"

"Copy, all signatures confirmed," came back the audio-only remote response. "ID value here for HQ Gopher is Airfoil 21D92, Sample 01, Multitude 2A24. Do you confirm, sir?"

"Confirmed," said the director. "I've received the latest briefs, and I have the necessary equipment with me. But we need a last check. What is the situation? Any updates?"

"It's been *extremely* difficult to maintain contact with our assets on the Command-Post, sir," explained the remote Agency subordinate. "Remember that we're trying to jam the communications between this 'Chu' person and the White House, as well as doing the same for the military channels and whatever that the former Spiritual Adviser is using... and our asset's transmissions have to ride on a sub-carrier to one of those channels, so –"

"*Enough* with the excuses!" gruffly countermanded the director. "Find a way! That's an *order!*"

"Acknowledged, sir," committed the remote voice. "Do you want the summary, now?"

"Yes," the Agency leader demanded.

"So here it is," said the subordinate. "Last track on the Jacobson plane had it *en route* to the District, north-east over northern West Virginia, almost at the Virginia state line. We have the Command-Post on a direct, declining-altitude path to D.C., to arrive there in less than an hour. If our calculations are correct, the two aircraft will converge over the Capitol, very close to each other, but the Command-Post will crash into downtown Washington. Unfortunately our attempts to over-ride the NCP's controls have all failed; Mr. Crowford has done a very good job of shutting off all the over-ride circuits, and he seems to be completely in charge of the aircraft's flight-plan –"

"Do we have any idea what he *wants?*" inquired the director. "That conversation that the Palace detected, the one that he had with this 'Chu' woman in the communications-shack – *surely* NSA's been able to replay it by now!"

"Sir... I can only tell you what the Palace has told me," apologized the voice, "But they only know that the two of them – Chu and Crowford I mean – had a long conversation over a closed internal circuit, on the plane. We don't know what was said and the Palace warned me that unless it went into the flight data recorders, we may *never* know. We've had our best situational analysts on this and nothing adds up... our people can't figure out why the Spiritual Adviser would have *shot* his way into the cockpit, when he could just have issued orders on his authority to take over the plane."

"*Unless,* of course," muttered the director, "Chu and Crowford are in this, *together!* I was *personally* in meetings in which he argued for her being allowed to stay on the aircraft, against the recommendations of several other Executive Branch staff. So *she* takes over all air-to-ground communications, and *he* commandeers the cockpit – one terrorist in charge of each of the Command-Post's most critical systems. And then they crash the airplane into the Capitol Buildings or maybe the Supreme Court – bail out at the last minute and get picked up by Jacobson's gang of traitors, who 'just happen' to be in the vicinity at that precise time! Don't forget that he has a VTOL plane that could land anywhere in D.C. that Crowford and Chu parachute down to... and whatever they don't destroy, Jacobson and his crew can clean up, while they're in town – didn't our so-called analysts consider *that* one? Fits the known facts so far, *perfectly*, I'd say!"

"Can't argue with you *there*, sir," offered the remote voice. "The only reason why the team couldn't settle on that scenario, was the lack of a written set of demands... I mean, it's not like non-Muslim terrorists to hijack a plane and then *not* say what concessions they want out of the government. But all the other pieces *do* fit, sir. We know that Chu had many direct interactions with Jacobson and defended his actions whenever she could. The conspiracy probably needed a senior-level plant in the Executive Branch and Crowford would be a perfect fit for *that* role. They pretended to argue with each other to throw us off and give the scheme the cover that it needed. No, sir... I'm afraid you're likely right about the whole thing."

"Yeah, well, it is getting really annoying having to always be the one who figures these things out, hours or days before our so-called 'analysts' do," complained the director. "In any event... we're almost out of *time*. What about the channels to the White House? We saw the broadcast... is the former President still there?"

"We've picked up orders to get helicopters in to the White House, sir," explained the remote subordinate. "It looks like there's an evacuation going on, but the ETA is very close to when the Command-Post will be over D.C, if our calculations are right. As to the data-feeds from the facility, NSA is trying to recover that data, too. It's apparently only weakly-encrypted, but breaking the keys is still going to take them some time. On top of that, the last few minutes of transmissions are being reverse-jammed in some way that we don't understand. We're *working* on it, sir."

"Keep trying... but as of now, I have all the information I need, to make a final decision," growled the Agency leader. "And I want these next words to be recorded, for historical purposes. We have a conspiracy involving the highest levels of the Executive Branch – probably being masterminded by the former President, who undoubtedly plans to act as a figurehead leader, with Jacobson and possibly the alien itself, pulling the strings from behind the curtain – that has taken control of the Airborne Command-Post. I mean... Clark invited both the alien and Jacobson to the *White House!* How obvious does it have to *be?*"

"No argument there, sir," mentioned the under-study. "Our analysts confirm that those broadcasts to the media were *filled* with coded messages. *Perfectly* fits the scenario."

"And," expostulated the director, "Unfortunately, the lawfully-appointed President and FBI Director are either now dead, or *will* be killed when their aircraft impacts in D.C.. The outcome will be the replacement of our entire government by alien rule, aided and abetted by Crawford's treason... I wonder what positions that Chu, Jacobson and the alien have promised him and the former President, in exchange for their collective treachery."

He paused for a second and then continued, "Under these circumstances, and pursuant to Contingency Plan Memorandum CA-199, I have no alternative other than to eliminate the conspiracy using any means possible, and while less, uhh, 'maximal' methodologies would obviously be preferable... this is likely our only chance to catch *all* these terrorists in the same place, at the same time. We need to intercept them over Washington, D.C., when the Command-Post and the Jacobson aircraft will both be within... what did the instructions say, again... yes, *there* it is... within about five miles of each other."

"Accordingly, therefore," stated the Agency director, in his controlled monotone, "Under my authority, I am authorizing re-targeting of the special tools, at my disposal. I am now,"

He placed an aluminum-encased suitcase on the desk and opened it.

Within, was a data-entry keyboard, with a small computer-display just above it. There was also a black-colored push-button, protected by a fold-down shield.

"Enabling the weapon, yield set to maximum... loiter-capability selected, for optimal trajectory to intercept-point and air-burst altitude," he droned on, while typing commands using the keyboard. "Cruise set at 70,000 feet, which should provide optimal look-down target-discrimination. Incidentally – please make sure to thank the Agency staff who sent the instruction-manual... it was very complete and helpful."

"Sir," carefully asked the remote voice, "I assume you *understand* what will happen? That weapon is *very* powerful. There are nearly a *million* people living within the expected blast-radius!"

"Those consequences have been assessed, and the risk is explicitly accepted," smoothly declared the director. "I sincerely regret the expected collateral damage... but we have to assume that the legitimate President and others on the Command-Post are already either dead, or shortly will be, *regardless* of what we do. The 'alternative' to us taking decisive action at this time – namely, 'the loss of our entire way of life, and its replacement by an alien-directed tyranny' – would be *immeasurably* worse! When this is over with, I'll direct the Agency to guide the country back to Constitutional rule, with a firm hand, preventing any more disasters like the one that we're now dealing with, *long* before they get started. Any remaining half-humans that the alien has infected with her sinister magic... they'll be hunted down, one by one, and rendered permanently ineffective. In my view... this is the *only* way."

"Understood, sir," acknowledged the subordinate. "If I may, sir... you'll go down in *history*, for this one."

"Indeed... as will we both," confirmed the Agency director. "I only wish that I had *two* such weapons at my disposal, so I could use the other one against Jacobson as a safety-option. But presumably he'll be close enough to the Command-Post to... well."

Then – without any more to say – he flipped the protective-cover to its "open" position, stared at the black button for a second or two, and... pushed it.

A status light shone bright, within the suitcase's interior panels.

"The bird," he announced, "Is now in flight."

The Captain And His Ship

The two teenagers – still semi-comatose, although random words had been occasionally heard coming from the girl – had been moved to the air-ship, as had been most of Karéin-Mayréij's family and companions (including the two shell-shocked GrayWar guys, who mumbled something about "we better get a fuckin' big book deal outta this" as they stepped aboard the *Mailànkh Express*).

As to the Storied Watcher's adoptive son, the operation had taken some cajoling on her part, along with a patient explanation of "Tommy dear, it would be rude of us to burn our names into this carpet, as a 'going-away present'"; the boy had argued vociferously, pointing to the top of the Washington Monument in the White House lawn, as an example of alien-girl hypocrisy.

She had to promise him the opportunity to deface the obelisk at a later time, in exchange for cooperation in the near-term.

It was noted that – despite alien-powers being used to hide the goings-on, as much as possible, some of what was happening, had evidently been overseen by the crowds and media-teams, who were gathered at the periphery of the White House grounds.

"Mr. President," proposed Kaysten, just after they had exited the Oval Office and proceeded to the outside grassed area, "Shouldn't we, uhh, *warn* these folks?"

"We'll just cause panic," deflected the U.S. leader.

"Is this 'panic'," commented the Storied Watcher, "Worse than being unprotected, underneath an 'atom-smashing bomb', when it detonates? This is but the first example – undoubtedly of many yet to come – of how your ways must *change*, sir! You must rule by the assent of the peasantry, in their interests – not by sly deceit, division and cruelty. How you do this is up to you... but I expect it to happen!"

"How could we possibly communicate... wait, *I* know," offered the President. "Jerry – could you –"

"*On* it, sir!" enthusiastically committed Kaysten.

"You've got a minute… preferably less," ordered the President.

The former Chief of Staff nodded, and in the blink of an eye, he had scorched a trail across the White House lawn, re-appearing outside one of the main gates by Pennsylvania Avenue. To the amazement of the crowds, he effortlessly hopped ten or more feet high, up to a concrete pillar with a small flat area on top. From there, Kaysten began to address the crowds, and immediately, those in the White House heard a moan of fear and apprehension coming from their direction. This was followed by a great commotion as people began running away from the White House grounds, in every which direction.

"How much more time do we have?" shouted the President, toward the communications-room and the several Secret Service staff who were inside it. "Any sign of the helicopters?"

"Command-Post's course hasn't changed, sir," called back a faint voice. "They're due overhead in about 21 minutes. The 'copters seem to be about two minutes behind."

"Damn!" cursed the U.S. leader.

"You and your mate *must* come with us, sir!" demanded the Storied Watcher, "In our *Mailànkh Express*. You will find her, ahh, 'creature-comforts' to be basic, but adequate. *Come* now! Every wasted second may be one that we cannot afford!"

Kaysten returned, as quickly as he had departed, and was ordered into the sky-ship by his alien mentor.

"I'll wait for you in here, Mr. President," he declared, before disappearing into the *Express*.

"Clark… *surely* you can't expect me to get into that accursed thing!" protested the First Lady. "It's *evil* – just like *her!*"

The President stopped and shot an irritated stare at his wife.

"What would you have me *do*, Kathy?" he replied. "You just heard yourself – the evac 'copters aren't going to be here, in time. We don't have time to argue about this. Get aboard!"

Karéin-Mayréij stepped back by about two feet, calling the names of her war-children.

"*Ahn'jë! Fàiagàryuu! I'ëà'b'! Ksé'l'ch'! Ss'éth'ch'!*" she cried; and instantly, her countenance – already imposing – waxed greatly, as she was clad in her full retinue of weirding-arms and -armor.

With glowing eyes, barely-disguised fangs and the energy of *Amaiish* – combined the infernal flames of *Vìrya Ahn'jë* – suffusing her body, the alien-girl came and knelt before the terrified, recoiling First Lady.

"Madam," she intoned, "Though I would prefer to call you 'friend'… that part of it is up to you, and perhaps never will it come to be. But your husband speaks the truth – if you stay here, and if we should fail in our quest, in even the slightest manner – you *surely* will die! Please come with us and be with your children, to guide and love them as they awake, newly-empowered. I swear on the blood of my noble ancestors, that we shall not further interfere with your family. The blessing of the *Khùl-Algrenàthi'i* thus is with-held from yourself; you need not fear 'becoming an alien'. Kathy... please, *please* come with us!"

"I don't believe we're on a first-name basis!" spat back the First Lady. "I'm staying right *here*, in the White House, where Clark and I *belong!* If God wants me to come home to Him – then what will be... will be. But I'm not getting trapped in that devil-machine that you've parked outside!"

The Storied Watcher sent a desperate glance at the President.

"Sir – if this scheme is to work, we must go, *now!*" she exclaimed. "Impress upon her, do whatever you will – but in thirty seconds, we are airborne, come what may! I will *not* use my powers on your mate; she must come of her own free will."

The President dashed over to embrace his wife.

"Kathy..." he started; but all she did was to close her eyes and hide her head under his chin.

With a sad – but 'at-peace' look on his face – he turned to address the Storied Watcher.

"She's *right*, you know," quietly remarked the U.S. leader. "*This* is where she – and I – belong; 'the Captain goes down with his ship'... I need to be here, to re-assure the people. I don't expect you to understand, but... I need to be at her side, even if – *especially* if – it's the end."

"No, sir," answered the alien-girl, "I understand... *perfectly*. Madam – is there *no* way that you will change your mind?"

"None," said the First Lady, never opening her eyes.

"Then... I take back my proscription," offered Karéin-Mayréij. "May the grace of my ancestors, protect you from this impending evil. Now... it is time that I leave."

"Whatever happens, Karéin," pleaded the President, "Keep Matt and Clairie safe. I *beg* this of you."

"Sir," pledged the Storied Watcher, "Long and great, shall be their days; and these shall be but started – never ended – on this night. Take care of yourself. And... you know what?"

"No... what?" he weakly responded.

"I have met many rulers weaker and less worthy, than yourself," she said, with a kindly smile. "I would tell you their stories, if you would listen, and thereby take lessons of state-craft. May you live past tonight... and may we again meet, in better circumstances!"

He just nodded.

The alien-girl floated away, with her powers becoming more and more manifest, with every second. She stopped just ahead of and above the bow of the *Mailànkh Express*.

The air-ship's entrance-hatch closed, accompanied a second or two later, by the faint sounds of frantic shouts, apparently coming from Kaysten, demanding "Let me out – or I'll fucking *wreck* this thing!"

Again the craft's doorway opened and out dashed the former Chief of Staff, to an interrogatory glare on the part of the Storied Watcher.

"Jerr-ee," she implored, "Where *go* you?"

"To be with the President," he responded. "To be where I *belong*. Don't try to stop me!"

The alien-girl had a distraught look on her face.

As she wiped a tear, she said, "I will not. Of all those of the Holy *Fire – still* the bravest and most loyal are you, my beloved brother. May the Gods protect you!"

She sent a stern glance at *Vîrya I'ëà'b'*, who – with obvious reluctance, however one might have so discerned from a living-shield – rejoined the arm of Karéin-Mayréij.

"This peril is too much for thee, dear child," whispered the Storied Watcher. "Even thy mighty skills, cannot protect dear Jerr-ee from it! Better to pray that he live through this day."

Kaysten was at the President's side in less than half a second.

"God bless you, son," was what the others heard, out of the U.S. leader.

Looking downward, the Storied Watcher called out to Abruzzio, Melissa Claremont, and Ramirez, who were positioned on the White House lawn, close to the starboard-, port- and stern-points of the air-ship, respectively; and she called to her son, who was riding on top of the *Express*.

"Every one of you, knows his or her appointed duty," she counseled, "And all know the consequences of mis-timing, or of failure. Are you ready?"

"We *are!*" came back the unanimous response.

"Then… bring your powers to full-flower, and fly with me into sacred *battle*, noble children of the *Fire!*" commanded Karéin-Mayréij, in a Stentorian voice that echoed everywhere.

Four exciting – yea – *thrilling*, war-songs – supplemented and strengthened, by a fifth, indescribably more powerful one – were now heard for many blocks in every direction, as the *Mailànkh Express* began to lift off. It was accompanied by the three more-than-humans, each of whom used his or her unique alien-powers (Ramirez' kicked up a debris-storm, as his hurricane began to roar) to fly in formation.

Tommy, meanwhile, was fully-energized, although he remained standing on the *Express'* upper hull as it rose up.

Faster and faster, it receded into the dark night sky, heading north by northwest.

In a few seconds, the air-ship had disappeared altogether.

The President looked at his wife and then pointed to the Oval Office.

"We should get in there and turn back the 'copters," he said.

Two Now For You, Ms. Chu

Chu had tried several of the mental-meditation tricks taught to her by the Storied Watcher, back at the Canadian forest camp; but nothing had worked, and the former FBI team-leader still paced nervously back and forth, within the Command-Post's communications-center.

"Any change in our course?" she demanded of the Air Force technician, who was sitting in a swivel-chair in front of a computer control-panel.

"None, Ma'am," he replied. "We're now down to 24,000 feet and still due to impact with the White House. ETA's about 25 minutes."

"Christ..." muttered the more-than-a-woman. "I can't let this go on... I *can't!*"

Warnock spoke up, his beady little eyes squinting maliciously.

"You *heard* him," he observed. "I don't care *what* you told Clark, about blasting him to smithereens... you go up there and try anything, and it'll be the death of *all* of us!"

"That's preferable to killing a million people on the ground in Washington, you know," ominously commented Chu. "Even if it involves my own death."

"What if he's just lying?" challenged the former Vice-President. "Harold is full of shit, with all that 'religious' nonsense that he's always gassing on about... it's probably all a bluff –"

"It's *not*," contradicted Chu. "You also heard Karéin, and how she confirmed the accuracy of my visions. This ability is every bit as valid as is my death-gaze. The only question-mark in *my* mind, is whether he can really detonate it remotely, and if so, if there's a delay between when he pushes the button, and when it goes off... in other words, 'if I might have enough time to get far enough away from this plane, to survive the explosion' –"

The normally-courteous Air Force staffer interjected, "Ma'am – don't you think that's a little *unfair?* I mean... there are *hundreds* of people on this plane, including me, who've done nothing at all bad to you and who have tried to help you as best we can. Are you going to let us all get vaporized?"

"No – I'm *not*," countered the team-leader, "It would be *Crawford*, who'd be doing that. Before this became an issue, I stated that I'd try to avoid loss of life on this plane, to the extent that I could. But I can't fight a nuke – I don't think that even the Storied Watcher herself, could. Don't lay this one at *my* doorstep! For what it's worth... I'm sorry... I truly *am*, son. Unlike some in this room," – she sent a cold glance in the direction of the Vice-President and Warnock – "You don't deserve the fate that's likely to engulf you. But then neither did my friends Otis and Will... you know?"

"I just don't want to d – oh, **shit!**" he exclaimed.

"What is it?" called Chu, as she rushed over to the control-panel, to look down upon it over the man's shoulder.

"Look at the bomber – over here – the small bright red symbol moving away from it –" stammered the Air Force guy.

"Omigod," gasped Chu, "Is that… what I *think* it is?"

"Yeah… it's on its way," he confirmed. "Calculating trajectory and impact-point… it's, uhh, climbing rapidly, not a surprise, probably proportional navigation… so the expected target is… it is… *fuck…*"

"Yes?" she prodded.

"It's… uhh… aimed at *us*, Ma'am!" stated the ashen-faced staffer.

The President was preparing an emergency address to the nation (due to the absence of Kaysten and many of his regular staffers, the preparations were going slowly), when the call came in to the White House communications-room.

Agent Kortish, who had temporarily taken over liaison duties, shouted out, "Sir – high-priority message from the woman in the plane!"

"Put her on," requested the U.S. leader.

"White House – White House – Defense Department – if anyone's listening – please pick up, *immediately!*" came the former team-leader's desperate-sounding voice.

"This is the President," he answered. "The First Lady's here with me, along with my bodyguards from the Service and the Marines. The Storied Watcher and her friends – including, thank the Lord, Clairie and Matt – left about a minute ago. What's your status?"

"Mr. President – what in God's name are you *doing*, still there, sir?" riposted a perplexed Chu. "*Surely* you know what's going to happen, if –"

"Of *course* I know, Minnie!" he softly offered. "So do Kathy and all the others who have chosen to stay at their posts. I told the same to Karéin, and she understood. Our fate is in God's hand's now, frankly. We're at peace… whatever may come."

"Well, sir… I have more 'fun news' for you," warned the remote voice. "They've fired the missile – the *other* one, with the nuclear warhead on it, that I warned you and DeWitt about, a few minutes ago – but the damn thing's aimed at *me*, here on the Command-Post plane!"

"I… I… can't *believe* this!" he stuttered. "You mean they didn't fire it at Jacobson, after all? How long do you have?"

"That's right – I have no idea what's going on here, but maybe somebody on the ground down there has learned of Crowford's plans… systems here are saying that it's due to hit shortly before we arrive over the White House," said Chu. "It's fast enough to hit us much before that, but it seems to be on a trajectory that's deliberately set to delay until we get to Washington. So even if we figure out some way to deal with the nuke that's already on-board –"

"I don't know what to *say*," offered the horrified President. "This seals the fate of millions of people… including mine…"

"Incidentally," added Chu, "I've tried to advise Jacobson of this – but, as you know – I have no way to tell if he's actually received the message."

The First Lady sat down on one of the Oval Office couches and started reading prayers from a handy Bible.

"Sir – you *have* to get the Air Force to shoot down this plane – the one that I'm on!" demanded the team-leader. "As soon as possible… it's the only *way!* If the nuke that I'm sitting on top of is going to blow, then at least let's have it go off over somewhere relatively unpopulated. And can the Air Force shoot down the other missile? Can they *do* that?"

"I've been trying to get a stable link to DoD for several minutes now," interrupted Kortish, "I asked for a status-check on the fighters out of Dover and Langley, but the interference on the channel is ramping up again, after the alien and Ms. Abruzzio departed. I think I can –"

There was a short pause.

"Yes, Curt?" pressed the President.

"It's… *damn it,* anyway!" called back the frustrated Secret Service agent. "Sorry for the language, Mr. President… but the link's gone dead… that analog noise has knocked it out."

"There has to be *some* way to communicate outside of this office!" complained the U.S. leader. "The fate of the *country* may depend on it!"

"We can try the media, sir," offered Kortish. "Perhaps someone will be monitoring the news-channels. We have many other ones dedicated to the government, but the chances of the people who you want to communicate with, happening to listen to a particular one, are pretty low. That's about the best I can come up with, I'm afraid."

"The media… everyone in the whole damn country, or the *world,* in fact… alright," glumly responded the President. "I have no idea how I'm going to explain my way out of this, if in fact I'm alive to say anything by tomorrow morning, but…"

"Yes, sir?" asked the Secret Service leader.

"Curt," ordered the President, "Get the TV-feeds going."

Awake And On Her Way

"Don't *rag* on me, Dorsie!" warned Hendricks, as he rummaged around in the bar-fridge in the underground Cass Mountain moonshine-factory. "I don't give a flying *fuck* what your 'kinfolk' are going to say about finding a beer or two missing, when they get back here."

"Even if you won't get a buzz from drinkin' it… or from drinkin' twenty or more of 'em?" chided Boatman. "Don't you just *love* her, now?"

"Even if," confirmed the third agent. "I can't get shit-faced any more – well… 'life's a bitch'. The taste still reminds me of fun times – tailgate-parties, Super Bowl parties… you know?"

"Guess I cain't argue too much 'gainst that," retreated the mountain-man, who had been vociferously protesting Hendricks' repeated trips to the beer-fridge. "Ah cain't imagine not tastin' beer fer the rest of my life... but y'all gonna have to answer to Ezra 'n Cooter, yourself, if'n they find out."

"Risk accepted," said the third agent. "I'll tell them that –"

A young woman's voice (it turned out to be "Jeannie", the younger Jacobson daughter) called in from the next room in the underground facility.

"Mr. Hendricks – Mr. Boatman – come here right *now!*" it demanded.

With little further ado – although the third agent did not abandon his can of Budweiser, in so doing – the two hurried out one door, out into a short corridor and back in through another. They were followed by the teenager.

Inside, was a groggy Cherie Tanaka. She was still on her stretcher, although her fore-body was now being propped up by outstretched arms behind her midriff.

Her sentient breast-plate was wrapped around her torso; its semi-translucent presence seemed less anxious and defensive than had earlier been the case.

Tanaka's physical wounds seemed almost completely healed, though there were still some obvious scars and tears in her garments.

"*Cherie!*" exclaimed Hendricks. "Great to see you back! You *okay?*"

For a second, the former Mars mission Science Officer seemed dazed; but then she responded, "Better... not 100 per cent."

She took another opportunity to shake the cobwebs out of her head, and then inquired, "Will... Otis... thanks for looking after me while I was out. I'm assuming it *was* you?"

"Yeah... more or less," confirmed the third agent.

"Well... 'thanks again'," she said. "Let me give you two a bit of advice," – she mentioned, while wincing as she pivoted on the cot and positioned her feet unsteadily on the floor – "And *that* would be... 'don't get hit by Brent's laser-light-show'."

"I hope you all don't take this the wrong way, Cherie," spoke Boatman, "But... if you don't mind my askin'... what did it *feel* like? Gettin' *hit*, I mean."

Tanaka now stood upright, and her vitality and energy seemed to be visibly returning with each passing second.

"That's an... *interesting* question," she reflectively responded. "As you know, when we were up at the camp by Jasper, Karéin made us scale our primary alien-power-attacks *way* down, when someone else from our group might have ended up in the line of fire – now I know why. How can I explain it to you? There really aren't any words..."

"Try to tell us," pressed Hendricks.

There was a dim glow in his eyes for a second, which he quickly hid.

"I had my force-screen up almost all the way – I was worried about being hit by Air Force missiles, that's happened before and it *hurts*, I can assure you, like being hit by a giant's baseball-bat, and you're the softball," explained Tanaka. "I saw something below me that I thought might be a stealth-missile, and it was hurtling right for the V-37… I fired by reflex, but my aim was off. I saw him dodge and execute a turn, just above the forest-top, that would be impossible for any missile that I'm aware of… I slowed down, hoping to get close enough to find out what the hell I was fighting, and then… '*kapow*'! His attack blanketed everywhere I could fly – there was simply no *way* to evade it!"

She shook her head, as if re-living a bad memory, and continued, "I felt my force-shield stopping – I don't know, maybe 60 or 70 per cent of it – and I guess *Vîrya Sài'ymë* helped to protect me too, but I think Brent's power must have some kind of 'piercing' effect – part of it went right *through* my shield. Whatever was left over, was like putting your face right next to an exploding incandescent light-bulb. It's supposed to be a 'photon' attack… right? But it felt like I was being peppered by molten shrapnel! I honestly don't know how I didn't end up totally blind… I drifted downward, unable to navigate… *Vîrya Sài'ymë* was really the only thing that kept me airborne. Then you guys found me, thank God. That's about it."

"*Jaysus!*" inveighed the black ex-agent, shaking his head. "Remind me not to get that boy mad at me. For what it's worth… he felt *terrible* about it… told us so, several times. I guess you two's just lucky that both of you survived that little 'misunderstandin'."

"Yeah," agreed Tanaka. "Speaking of Brent – not to mention Sam and the rest of the crew – where *are* they? Why aren't they here with us? And by the way… where *is*, 'here'? This looks like a basement or something, and I had expected to be in the transport –"

Donny had now approached. He was accompanied by numerous other members of the combined Jacobson, Boyd, Wade and Young families (as well as other hangers-on). He said,

"They fucked off for points east, not least of which would be the White House. We got dropped off on top of a mountain, where Dorsie's kin brew moonshine… pretty off the beaten track, figure it'll be a while 'till the Man pays us a visit up here. Good to see you back in the land of the livin', Cherie. Y'all want a brewskie? We got lots 'round here, it seems."

"They… *what?*" stammered a perplexed and immediately-upset Tanaka. "Pass on the beer for now. You mean the V-37's taken off *without* me? With who on board?"

"Devon, Misha, Brent, Wolf and Sam went on the plane," explained Hendricks. "They figured that you weren't in any shape to fight – at the time, it sure didn't look to *me*, like you were – and they didn't know how long it would take you to come around. Like, 'would it take minutes, hours or days' kind of thing. That little breastplate you got on wasn't making it any easier – zappin' folks who it – uhh, sorry, 'she' – doesn't trust if they get too near you; she's taken a real dislike to Mr. Boyd, among other things. So they left Otis, Donny and yours truly to guard their families and Dorsie's – excuse me, his *cousin's* – moonshine, until you were 'with it' enough to participate."

"Which now you are, I'd assume," added Boatman. "I believe the idea was that you all would be the only one among us who could really fight off a large-scale attack by the military... so you were s'posed to hang around here until they get back. *If* that's alright by you."

"No... it's *not* 'alright'," complained the former Mars mission science officer. "I can't *believe* they'd *do* this!"

"But Ms. Tanaka," demanded Boyd's ten-year-old, "If you don't protect us... the Army could blow us all up! Commander Jacobson and Daddy *warned* us about that! Oh... and he asked me to tell you, how really sorry he was, about hitting you with his, uhh, 'death-ray'. He *promises* not to do it *ever* again!"

The Professor walked over and gave Wendy Boyd a quick, friendly embrace.

"That makes *two* of us, who don't want anything like that to happen again, honey," said Tanaka. "And for the record, it was *me* who fired first, at your Dad... so I'm really not in a great position to rake him over the coals about it. How long has it been since they left?"

"About fifteen to twenty minutes," offered Yvonne Jacobson. "I asked him to wait around, Cherie... but when Sam gets his mind up to do something like this, there's no talking him out of it. I'm sure you know."

"Yes," quietly responded the former science officer, while avoiding the wife's glance, "I *know*."

Tanaka turned to address the crowd-at-large.

"Do we have any idea about what's actually going *on*... in the outside world, I mean?" she asked.

"Not really," said the trucker, with a shrug. "Ain't nothin' but moonshine-brewin'-gear and some food down here in the basement, where they put you, and the rest of us... we got no way of even hearin' a news-report –"

"Well... Ezra 'n Cooter *do* got one of them old-style TVs up there in the shack – topside I mean," contradicted Dorsie. "Pretty much th' same rig as we got back at our own 'shine still. They told me it's hooked to one of them cheap-ass antennas, kind y'all kin buy in th' dollar store... they got it so's they could watch West Virginny State High School Division football-games, from some station 'round here –"

"Football?" interjected an elated Hendricks.

"We had better go up there and turn it on," proposed Tanaka. "Worst happens is it doesn't work – or Will's game got pre-empted by an infomercial."

She headed for the door, followed by many others.

The above-ground, plywood-walled shack was even more primitive than the larger basement-area underground; it consisted of one decent-sized room with the stairs to the lower levels right in the middle, two small windows, a kitchenette with a propane-gas portable stove and a bar-fridge, along with a few chairs on either side of a half-sized couch, the latter decorated by numerous cigarette-burn-marks. The walls were mostly covered by unpainted plywood and did not seem to be insulated. However, there were a couple of space-heaters at different ends of the room.

A small ULED, 2D television (its screen no more than about seventeen inches in width), covered with dust and probably twenty or more years old, was on a coffee table in front of the couch. The unit was connected by a thin wire to a square UHF antenna affixed to one of the walls, near to a window.

Overall, the place was surprisingly uncluttered, but Dorsie explained that this was only because "Ezra 'n Cooter don' come up here too much... they's spendin' most of their time brewin' shine down below."

Thick layers of dust, which had to be hand-swept off of most horizontal surfaces, confirmed the accuracy of this observation.

"You know how to get this going?" asked Tanaka, of the mountain-man. She had sat down on the couch, in front of the TV.

"More or less," he said, while going over to the unit and fiddling with its remote-control box. "If'n it's the same as mine... jus' wait a sec..."

The television came on, though its screen was filled with static.

"Pretty funny to hear *you* sayin' that, Cherie," needled Boatman. "I mean... weren't you Number One Scientist on board that Mars ship? I wouldn't have thought that tunin' a TV would be too hard for you."

"I just got *up*," she deflected, "And most of the instrumentation on the *Eagle* and *Infinity*, that I used, I developed the operating instructions for, myself. Dorsie... do we have any channels that we know, *do* work?"

"Well... 'search' function's there, on th' box," he stated. "Give it a try."

Tanaka nodded and played around with the remote-control for a few seconds, examining it closely.

"Oh, wait – *there* it is," she mentioned. "Somebody set it for ATSC version 5, but on VHF – everybody *knows* that won't work! Here... I'll change to legacy ATSC 3.0 and force it to UHF jumbo-band... let's see what we get, now..."

"You *had* to ask her, man," quipped Donny.

"Only 'jumbo' I know of, is a big bag of chips at the tailgate-party," added Hendricks.

"Shush!" admonished the former Mars mission science officer. "I think I've got... wait... now *there's* a break – looks like a news-broadcast –"

Multiple pairs of intensely-interested eyes now focused on the TV-screen, with many of those there, clustered either on the couch with Tanaka or standing behind it, looking over her shoulder.

The scene on the television included a male reporter (a clean-cut Caucasian guy in his mid-thirties, with dark hair and a conservative business-suit) in the foreground, and the White House a long distance off – probably at least a quarter-mile – in the background.

A small crowd was in the vicinity, but it could not advance closer to the Presidential residence because of a series of movable barriers that had apparently been erected across the street. The police presence seemed oddly sparse, considering what else was going on. One of the onlookers had a sign saying, in big red letters, "REPENT : THE END IS NIGH".

"Fred... are we on... are we *on?*" asked the reporter, momentarily casting a glance to one side, off the camera.

"Okay," he indicated.

Now looking directly at the screen, the reporter stated, "This is Bill Marco-Haig of WHSV-TV Disney News Harrisonburg, reporting to you tonight on the developing crisis in and around the White House, here in Washington."

"Shit... them boys must have turned on the jets *real* good, to git there an' shit all over th' President, *that* fast," observed Dorsie.

"Hmm," remarked Tanaka, while the reporter was interviewing one of the on-scene passers-by, "You say they've been gone for about twenty minutes? Well, knowing how fast that Brent and Wolf can fly – and both of them are somewhat slower than I am – I *guess* that's possible... but only just, and only if they abandoned the V-37, since it could never hit anything like their maximum speed... and why would they do *that*?"

"Yeah... and they sure wouldn't have a lot of time to introduce themselves to the President," noted Boatman. "Unless that's what's going on now –"

"Just a sec," cautioned Tanaka. "He's talking again."

"So," announced the reporter, "Here's what we know, at the present time. The President's spokesman – Chief of Staff Jerry Kaysten, who demonstrated some very unusual abilities in so doing, just a few minutes ago – gave crowds who had gathered outside the White House grounds, a warning that the Capitol Region was under imminent threat of nuclear attack –"

"Oh my sweet *Lord!*" gasped Boatman. The expression was echoed throughout the cabin, by many others.

"And that everyone should immediately go home, take shelter, and wait for the President's next address to the nation, which is expected momentarily," said the man on TV. "In the words of the Chief of Staff, 'the government is doing everything that it can to protect Washington, but at this time, you all need to get to your basements, turn on your TVs and say a prayer' – understandably, this has caused widespread panic, and there are reports of looting in some downtown stores."

"Jerry's back at the *White House?*" mentioned Hendricks. "*Lot* of shit going on here, that we don't know about –"

"What's that, Fred?" said the reporter, again peering to one side. "Oh... okay. Ladies and gentlemen... we now have the President of the United States, coming straight from the White House; let's hear what he has to say."

The screen flickered, and then the street-scene was replaced by one coming from the Oval Office, with the familiar, fatherly face and figure of the President, looking straight at the camera.

Unusually – though his suit and tie were the similar to what had been used in other broadcasts – they bore subtle marks of recent damage; and the President's skin-texture wasn't dulled and flattened by make-up. It even appeared as if he might have been sweating a little, recently.

"This is the old dude... the *first* one, I mean," commented Donny.

"My fellow Americans," stated the President, in a deeply-serious tone of voice, "I address you tonight at a time of the most grave national emergency; and because the time that we have is so short, I'll be as brief as possible."

"A few minutes ago," stated the U.S. leader, "I received credible information that a nuclear weapon might be detonated by terrorists in, or near to, the Washington, D.C. Capitol Region. As this is an ongoing military and intelligence operation, I'm afraid I can't provide you with a detailed explanation on the nature of the threat, or of the measures that your government is now undertaking to stop it... except to say the following."

"What's he *doing* in the White House... if someone is going to drop a *bomb* on Washington?" asked Jennifer Jacobson.

"My *God* – if *Sam's* there, too –" wailed a horrified Yvonne Jacobson.

"And Brent –" exclaimed an equally-distraught Laura Boyd.

The President stared forcefully at the camera and declared, "First of all, if the terrorist ring-leader is listening, the *only* thing that you will accomplish by doing this, is your own death – and the utter discrediting of the cause that you claim to advance. You *must* surrender, *immediately!* Despite your treason and betrayal, in the interests of saving innocent human life, if you comply, I give my personal assurance that you'll be given a fair trial... or, alternately, safe passage to a third-party country of your choice."

"But *if*," the President vowed, "You persist in this appalling scheme... you *will* be stopped! You should know that the government of the United States has," – he sent an especially steely look at the camera – "Recourse to the most powerful resources on this *planet!* We will not *hesitate* to deploy these effectively against you, to protect the American people! You have been *warned*... govern yourself accordingly!"

"He sounds like he's talking to a single person," remarked Laura Boyd. "How does that make *sense?*"

"And with regard to the resources to which I have just referred," obscurely mentioned the President, "Because the time's so short, I must now speak directly *to* them. To our Armed Forces and to those of you who are involved – you know who you are – 'two – *not* just one, as we had believed – are on the way, and one is aimed at the plane; it will arrive, just before the plane does... you *must* stop both'! I'm sorry that I can't be more specific... but that's all I can say, at this time."

"Now, to my fellow Americans in the D.C. area – I must warn you that despite the measures that your government is undertaking to negate this threat, there's unfortunately the possibility that," – he reflexively cleared his throat – "One or more nuclear weapons *will* detonate, near to or over Washington, within the next twenty minutes to an hour. If this happens, we can expect nearly total destruction within one to three miles from the center of the explosion, and you could be seriously injured if you are as far as twenty miles away. So it's *imperative* that everyone in the D.C. area should get to shelter, *immediately!* Stay in your basements, away from doors and windows. Do *not* leave your sheltering-places until you hear that the emergency is over with; afterwards law-enforcement and public-safety services will be there to assist you. Radioactive fallout can be extremely dangerous up to three weeks from when it's first deposited– so stay indoors."

He concluded by saying, "I want you all to know that Kathy and I will be staying here at the White House, trusting in Almighty God and in whatever fate He has for us. If that means our lives will end tonight, then we'll accept that; but your government – and our way of life – *will* continue on, saddened by unbowed by this tragic situation. If – as we pray – the Lord, our brave Armed Forces and our other resources, deliver us from this peril, I'll personally advise you of that – but only when we're certain that the danger is actually over with. God bless all of you; and God bless the United States of America."

The scene was replaced by a blue-screen, superimposed upon which was the Presidential seal.

Several members of the Boyd and Jacobson families were openly crying, while most of the rest were white-faced with shock at the ominous news.

"This can't be *happening!*" cried Laura Boyd. "Brent's flying right into a *death-trap!*"

"Yeah... and unless they've already showed up there, I bet neither he, nor Sam, nor any of the others even *know* about this shit," noted Hendricks. "I mean... we had the plane's radios turned off for most of the flight here – so the Air Force couldn't use 'em as a beacon to fire a missile at us with – and that's probably how they're still doing it. So they won't even have *heard* Mr. Doom-and-Gloom's speech –"

"Mrs. Boyd, I sure do understand why you all's concerned," interjected Boatman, "But we gotta think this *through*. What you s'pose he means by, 'most powerful resources on the planet'? And what about '*two* are aimed at the plane'? Does he mean the plane that the Commander and those other folks, are headin' to D.C., in? That is... the V-37?"

Uncertain stares were returned to the black ex-agent.

"I wouldn't put it past the government to try to smoke the 'Mars Gang' with the biggest bomb they've got," remarked the third agent, "But... why only *now?* They could've used it against him all the way back from Texas, after all... not to mention after he picked us all up, back in Fayetteville."

"Maybe they just didn't have it ready yet," said the younger of the two Jacobson daughters.

"Well maybe the Air Force figured that Mr. Space Man's on his way to D.C., and decided to pull the trigger before he got too close," opined the trucker.

Tanaka had a far-off look in her eyes as she responded, "Somehow... I don't think so. Not even the asshole government that we're used to dealing with, would set off a nuclear weapon over the Capitol, just to get either Sam, or us. Remember – we were *invited* to the White House... yes, I *know* it might have been a trap, but that would mean that the President – the 'old' one, the 'legitimate' one, I mean – would be committing suicide, in so doing. No... there's something *more* going on here..."

She stood up, with her eyes starting to glow, and the tendrils of *Amaiish* lighting her up, from inside.

"And I mean to find *out!*" vowed Tanaka, in a voice that impressed even the other *Fire*-users. "If Sam and the others are flying into a trap, I may not be able to stop it – but maybe I *can* warn them!"

"Wait a minute, Cherie – *wait* a minute!" implored Hendricks. "I don't blame you for wanting to try... but you're out of time here. If you leave right now you might have only 15 minutes, and you don't even know where the fucking thing *is* – it could blow up right *next* to you!"

"It's well over a hundred miles from here to D.C.," added Boatman. "You think you can make it there, in a quarter of an hour? You're flyin' in the dark, after all."

"No," countered the former Mars mission science officer, "Although *Vîrya Sài'ymë* can help me navigate. But if I don't try, I'll never *forgive* myself!"

"What if the Army comes and kills us all, Ms. Tanaka?" whined Wendy Boyd. "Dad said you'd *protect* us!"

"Uncles Will and Otis can cover for me in that department," parried Tanaka.

As their voices rose to protest, she went over to Hendricks.

"Brother," she calmly directed, "Lay your hands on me... on my arms."

Many in the vicinity – but not Boatman – were puzzled by what she was trying to do.

The third agent complied, looking her straight in the face.

"Your arts grow... I can *smell* it," she purred. "Now use the special one that *Sensei* gifted you with – and may you be worthy of what I now give you, of my own free will. May you never use her for ill... only for good."

Hendricks just nodded, never taking his eyes off Tanaka.

Her arms were held straight out, thumbs pointing upward, palms facing each other, about a foot and a half apart.

"*Learn* from me!" she commanded.

The third agent's eyes began to dimly glow, matching Tanaka's greater brilliance. Small charges of lightening began to jump back and forth between her hands, almost like a science-fair static-electricity exhibit.

"Do you *feel* it?" she asked.

"Yes... yes!" he confirmed.

"You're a fast learner – and I think we're done," she stated.

Again, Hendricks nodded. He broke his hold on Tanaka's arms.

Then, he stepped back by a couple of paces, and held his palms facing each other, mimicking the gesture that she had just done.

The third agent closed his eyes, concentrated, and then – to a chorus of "oohs" and "aahs" from the onlookers – a facsimile, considerably weaker and dimmer but impressive none the less – of Tanaka's lightening-discharge, bounded back and forth between his hands.

"Okay... so I can make it... the electricity, that is," remarked Hendricks. "Damn weird feeling – it *should* hurt like hell... but it doesn't. But... uhh... how do you *aim* it?"

"You point in the right direction and let fly," she advised, with a wry smile. "It's not a precise science... it'll hit somewhere near where you aimed it. Getting it right on center... *that*, takes time and practice. Same as it does, for figuring out how to fire more discharges with less energy, as opposed to fewer, more powerful ones. Its range depends on how much *Amaiish* you put into each bolt. Fewer shots go further and hit harder when they land home. You got that?"

"*Right*," uncertainly agreed the third agent. "Well, folks... I guess I'm better off defending you all, than I was a few minutes ago. For whatever *that's* worth."

"I have complete confidence in you, Will," responded Tanaka. "*They* should, too. Anyway – with all that's going on in D.C., it's not likely that you'll run into any trouble; but if you *do*... you *know* what to do."

"No way we can talk you out of this?" unhappily commented Boatman.

"You'll be okay," she parried. "As for me – who knows? But time's a-wasting. It's time for me to *fly!*"

With that, Tanaka moved toward the cabin's door to the outside. It opened without any apparent human intervention, revealing the cold darkness outside.

Her eyes were glowing, as her war-song began to reverberate all around.

She walked to the doorway and stopped momentarily. Then she turned around to send them a final glance.

"Goodbye, Ms. Tanaka," spoke one of the Jacobson offspring. "Thank you *so* much for saving us, back there in Texas!"

She silently nodded with a half-smile on her face.

"Hey... 'Thunderchild'," added Donny. "Give 'em *hell!*"

Tanaka's smile broadened, and the others saw her do an odd half-curtsy, as they had observed from another, in times before. Then she turned to face the dark outside.

"*Vîrya Sài'ymë*," she cried, while her exciting, inspiring war-song, began to roar, "*Gird* thyself... for we fly now, to *war! Full **power!***"

Then she rocketed upward, out of sight, to the east, with her song receding into the distance.

"Damn," grunted Donny, "Wish *I* could do that! Guess I'm just an also-ran 'round here, though."

"You're *my* 'super-hero'," gushed Sammie, instantly draped over his arm.

"Don't choke on that bubble-gum," whispered the one Jacobson teenager to the other, while subtly gesturing at the working-girl.

Hendricks shot the trucker a wry glance.

"Didn't just do a number on those lightening-bolts of hers, you know," he declared. "Or to put it another way – gimme an hour, a day, a week… and 'off we go, into the wild blue yonder'."

To The Deadly Heavens Above

Upward through the cold, dark, partly-cloudy Eastern Seaboard air, lifted the *Mailànkh Express*, its ovoid, one-third-translucent, weirding form and exterior belying its pedestrian origins.

The war-songs – always almost at their zenith, at the start of such an adventure, though in fact most powerful at the most critical moment – had subsided somewhat, although their exciting, energizing admixture could still be heard and felt, by all in the area.

To the right of the air-ship – about ten feet distant from it – was Sylvia Abruzzio, her eyes and body encased in a close-fitting, scintillating kaleidoscope of ever-changing colors; to its left was glowing-eyed Melissa Claremont, about the same distance off, enveloped in a much less-easily-visible force-field; and to the rear was Hector Ramirez, with a *Fire*-screen similar to the black teenager's one, exulting in his newly-found powers of flight. (He had secretly quavered at the thought of failing, upon hearing the Storied Watcher's command to take to the skies – but the worry lasted only a few seconds, after which something deep within, from he knew not where, guided him as if the challenge was old hat.)

Ramirez' body was not only protected by an "ordinary" force-field; he was also surrounded by a roaring, rushing, howling gale, its atmospheric modules propelled into a secondary protective bubble. Part of this had been redirected so as to provide propulsive thrust for the *Express*, driving the craft forward at a speed in the low hundreds of miles per hour.

Leading the *Mailànkh Express* on with the air-ship firmly in tow by her telekinetic grasp, about twenty feet in front of its prow, was mighty Karéin-Mayréij herself. She was adorned in full battle-gear, with the flickering blue-orange flames of *Vìrya Ahn'jë* bent slightly back by rearward-inertia, yet still forming a fearsome protective-barrier all around her body.

At first she had reflexively and anxiously checked to validate that her son – secured by both an improvised, chain-link seat-belt (connected to cleats welded to the top of the vessel), as well as by hand-holds – was still positioned on top of the air-ship; but after a couple of cheery waves from Tommy – protected by his own force-field, with eyes also dimly-glowing in the darkness – she concluded that by his own volition would he succeed or fail.

As a warrior-goddess, that thought was accepted with equanimity.

As a mother, Karéin-Mayréij was – inwardly – terrified; though, she did her best to hide her apprehension.

The glow of the Storied Watcher's energized eyes was hidden by her sunglasses-cum-bionetic-goggles, their outward appearance showing a dimly-roiling, TV-interference pattern.

Had any the ability to so inspect, what the spectacles displayed to the alien-girl was an intricately-detailed visual, auditory and psychic depiction of the outside tactical-situation, akin to an alien HUD-display with far more complete and sophisticated sensory-inputs than any human fighter-pilot (including, somehow, the ability to detect threats coming from behind), could ever hope to have at his disposal.

The torrent of situational-awareness information coming continuously at her – including chatter from each of her "war-children", all of whose individual sensory-abilities were now running full-bore – would have instantly overwhelmed any normal human mind. Updates came in from every direction.

There was even some dubious-sounding message, coming from somewhere ahead, saying something like "the harlot is on this airplane, she dies..." Unfortunately – despite a sense of foreboding – the Storied Watcher had not the time to ponder the import of the message; and there were too many other warnings coming in simultaneously.

Yet – despite all this, and notwithstanding all her other, equally- or more-formidable arts – Karéin-Mayréij was beset by a combination of fear and doubt as she hurtled through the air, upward and to the north-west.

Children... this 'speech' that ye detect the President having given, after we took to the skies? What is this about "'one is aimed at the plane'"?

What means he, by that?

We must ponder this – but too many other threats, to deal with...

As to the present quest... I withstood the cruel energies of this world's star, and each of these 'atom-smashing bombs'... that is scarcely a fraction of the power of a star, bathing one in refulgent energy, each second.

But... I was a different – far greater, more noble – Storied Watcher, then.

I was the old... 'me'.

The one who I tried to explain to dear Bob, back at his now-wrecked home, in Too-Sawn.

She who shrugs off, such things as we now confront, with nary a concern... how shall I return to her?

To... me?

But now, I am someone... different. Someone all too... 'human'.

Weak, in so many ways... but I like being 'human'... except...

That 'atom-smashing bomb' over the northern sea, that almost killed me – and what is worse, it almost ended Tommy's life... Cherie's... as well.

O my ancestors... what risk we, for this so-called "President"?

What was I thinking?

Scarce days ago, did I threaten war against him... and justly so!

But dear you Mother him word your gave, came a little voice.

Yes... that I did, grimly resolved Karéin-Mayréij.

The solemn vow of the Khùl-Algrenàthi'i – *that shall* not *be retracted... nor shall it be shirked!*

Now she turned her attentions to the sky ahead, activating the fullest sensory-abilities of *Vîrya Ahn'jë* to scan forward, looking for signs of danger – and of her intended target.

Little ones, she counseled, *be ye all most-alert.*

Much may occur, seemingly all upon a single moment. Many war-birds and other "air-o-planes" are in these heavens, and we know not if friend or foe they may be – hold now –

That big air-plane, much akin to the "Laser Battle-Station" that earlier I forced my way aboard, flying on a slight downward path towards the city, perhaps fifty of these "kil-o-meters" ahead... it is likely be Min-ee's one, but... foreboding stars...

Children – the special sight, to see the particle-shine – as potent as ye can so deliver!

Her gaze was set upon the lumbering aircraft ahead of her.

Curses... I see nothing, within or about this air-plane... perhaps it is not the right one?

Or, the particle-shine might be shielded by heavy elements... I have read that this is sometimes done...

From the south and west, a war-song – its owner and melody still indistinct, out of range – could barely be detected.

It seemed to be nearing, though it was still far-off.

But now the Storied Watcher, guided by both intellect and instinct, turned her gaze involuntarily upwards.

Wait – what in the accursed name of – what is that?

Far up yonder, almost at the zenith, where the air meets the void – flying fast, but slowing down every few seconds, as if it means not to strike at once, but rather at a planned time... most unlike the war-arrows we have fought before...

A faint glimmer of the shine is there, but I cannot precisely track – such as this should be easy to detect, in this cold darkness – of course – that damnable "stealth"-echo that the President's death-weapons often use... come on, come on, little ones, try, try harder, push the vision-arts to their limits...

Wait – yes, now the hellish thing reveals itself – larger and differently-shaped than mundane air-arrows – akin to that which we made to detonate over the northern seas... and its course arcs to intersect with the path of that air-plane!

Could this be the "second one" of which the President spoke... but who fired – ah, no time for that now!

This throws our plan into disarray! I must –

What in... more *war-songs? But not from our sky-ship? From the south-direction, and below... who?*

Now the Storied Watcher sent a thought in the direction of the *Mailànkh Express.*

A missile – probably an atom-smashing bomb within – falling from far above... and it is aimed for Min-ee's airplane!

This peril falls to me and the little ones... we must stop it, or Min-ee and many others below, will be killed!

Brothers – sisters – blessed Bob, beloved Tommy – you are now on your own, remember the plan, do the best that you can, as my war-children and I must deal with this evil new thing –

The rest was pre-empted by a chorus of alarms from her war-children.

Us at coming behind from – dear Mother – arrows-war, shine-particle ray-dar!

Barely turning her head, she looked over her right shoulder and immediately understood the truth of the warning.

A formation of fighter-planes far off to the south and west, beyond visual range in fact – at least seven of them, maybe more, judging from the number of projectiles – had fired a volley of air-to-air missiles, apparently at Karéin-Mayréij herself, at the air-ship in her tow.

Oddly, however, some of the rockets seemed to be following a peculiarly-low-altitude track, while another group of them were traveling much higher than would have made sense for an attack on the air-ship behind the Storied Watcher.

I thought that this damnable 'President' had forsworn attacks on us, she angrily mused,

But perhaps they obey him not...

Ah heard that! came Melissa's mental communication.

Hector, Sylvia – y'all take over – ah'll deal with the ones below us!

Angel Lady – y'all gots to handle that shit comin' from up high!

The *Mailànkh Express* listed momentarily to port, as the teenager released both her physical and psychic grasps on the vessel and, with her *Fire* and war-song blazing, rocketed downward and to the rear.

A second later, it regained its stability, but began to slowly lose altitude.

The alien-girl felt Tommy's war-powers becoming fully-energized.

Son, she sent, *you cannot yet fly fast enough –*

I know, Mom, he returned.

I'll stay here and knock down anything that gets too close... okay?

My only son! she answered, wiping a tear.

The Storied Watcher – her attention being pulled in multiple directions simultaneously – re-empowered the fast-thinking skill.

Arts of War – reveal ye the battlefield, to me!

And the understanding of it came to her mind, as it had so many times before, in battles uncounted, eons past.

Gods of my home-world! she grimly inveighed.

After smashing a comet... now... this!

Venerable One – if thy weirding arts still prevail on this world of reason and techno – deploy them now – with as much force as thou can muster!

Pouring *Amaiish* into her force-screen and her propulsive-skills, Karéin-Mayréij executed a brutal, super-G-force turn, blazing an incandescent trail towards the upper stratosphere.

My son... my daughters... my mate... I love you all so much! she sent.

Fire In Any Direction But "Down"

Perhaps more than anyone in the Storied Watcher's extended entourage – with the notable exception of Billings – and despite years of Air Force and NASA air combat and space-travel training, Sam Jacobson *hated* doing this.

How the hell did I end up as the only one who just jumps and can't fly? he peevishly mused.

Maybe she's getting back at me, for slapping her pretty little face?

He tried not to look downward; but despite the darkness of the cold night skies, his damn extra-accurate Mars senses kept inconveniently advising him of the relative distance from where he was, to the fields and trees of central Virginia.

I know I'll just bounce back – probably by several thousand feet – if he drops me from this altitude, thought Jacobson.

But still... he silently prayed that Boyd wouldn't do so.

I'll just bounce.

From 1500 feet.

Yeah... right.

Sure I will!

There she goes, came the former Mars mission pilot's mental broadcast, directing his erstwhile boss's direction upward and to the north.

Luckily, his grasp – both physical and psychic – seemed quite firm and steady.

Sorry to see the old crate sent to her demise, added Boyd.

Like the Eagle *and* Infinity... *she served us well.*

Hoping her last mission's more successful than theirs was.

Jacobson caught a glance of the V-37's tail-empennage and jet-engine exhaust-nozzles (the latter glowing brightly, from Boyd's rigged-up *ersatz* afterburners), as the transport rapidly departed on its pre-programmed suicide-path. He then cast his eyes and Mars sensory-abilities around in all directions.

Red-eyed Wolf – enshrouded and hard to make out, in his meteor-like blaze of flame – was cruising slightly above and to the left of Boyd.

Devon White's proud face showed on the opposite side; the first man to set foot on Mars was propelled by a jet of ice-crystals only scarcely less formidable than the bounty-hunter's fire.

Equally-impressive was the Russian, who – though Jacobson could somehow sense his mental lock-on to Boyd, who did not seem to be resisting – was tagging along behind the former Mars pilot, evidently partly under Misha's own invisible arts of aerial propulsion. The Russian's two war-child daggers, for their part, were flying perpetual, protective lazy-eight patterns around his body, in a manner similar to what had been seen with the alien-girl's own ones, several times before.

Okay, sent Jacobson, *We've seen her off... and 'good luck' to her.*

Time to put down, I guess...

We never thought through where that is, came Boyd's reply.

Where we go, after releasing the V-37, I mean.

Well... I'd suggest that downtown D.C. ain't a good idea, offered White's broadcast.

Two fuckin' nukes headin' that way... two more than I want to deal with... y'understand?

Yeah, agreed Boyd, *But something in me thinks, it'd be kind of crass just to land at the next town and watch the whole damn thing going down over coffee and donuts... I mean, there's* got *to be –*

His mental communications stopped abruptly, as Boyd – along with both of his former Mars mission companions – took note of frantic arm-gestures on the part of the flaming bounty-hunter.

They picked up a note of severe alarm from Wolf's direction, and saw him yelling something, but whatever he was trying to say was being blocked by his protective force-field. Suddenly – with his war-song quickly roaring – he abruptly reversed course and rocketed to the south-west, climbing in altitude as he flew.

What the f – ! came White's broadcast. *Why the hell's he doin' that?*

Now a message came from what had to be the Russian. It was garbled, as if someone who could barely speak English was "mind-talking".

Fire-spirit... missiles... attack! warned Misha.

Why can't we see them, then – oh, right, Wolf's symbiote – better senses, maybe, sent Jacobson.

Ask him if he knows where – started Boyd.

Then he ruefully acknowledged,

Yeah – shit – I forgot... those two haven't got the "mind-talking" thing completely down yet.

We'd have to drop our force-shields to yell back and forth... and at this speed, with the air-noise, we'd hardly hear anything, anyway...

Another glance at the Russian revealed that – somehow – though he was flying forward along with White, Boyd and the suspended Jacobson, Misha was actually facing backwards. He seemed to be tracking the receding Wolf.

A single huge "boom", followed by multiple smaller explosions, echoed off in the distance, to the south-west. Oddly, the noises seemed to be coming from a point considerably above where the bounty-hunter was hurtling toward.

Though he dared not do so for more than a second or two at each instance, Boyd himself cast his eyes backwards to try to see what was happening.

Hmm... got to be easier to see in Um'nàhr'é...

Mars eyes, do your stuff...

He forced the infra-red-sight to become predominant (though, as always, the human-friendly part of the electromagnetic spectrum was still visible as background-imagery), and scanned as far to each side and up and down as he had time to do.

What the hell*!* Boyd mentally called to his two Mars mission associates.

Devon – you see that?

What y'all talkin' about – oh, okay, Mars eyes – damn... yeah! came back White's reply.

But who –

I'm tracking Wolf – with that IR-sig of his, hard to miss, observed Boyd.

Twenty or more low-intensity heat-plumes coming at him – those gotta be AAMs – bugger had better watch his ass, if they got IR-seekers they'll lock on for sure – but what's that above and far back?

As if to emphasize the point, there were booming-sounds and bright flashes, coming from the bounty-hunter's direction.

One nearer – just above our altitude, flying away from us – the other far off, much higher, approaching; I think they're on a converging track –

Both look to me like they's Angel Lady's kin... judgin' from... shit, I don't know from what, man – this is all voodoo magic anyways, offered White.

But them two certainly don't look like no missiles.

One's comin' from back where we were – Hendricks learn to fly for real, maybe?

Too far away for me to recognize who it is, sent Boyd.

But then who's the other one? And where'd he or she come from?

Hold on – looks like it's slowing down, or maybe reversing course...

Y'all got me, bro, complained White.

Too much shit goin' on up here, and I'm sure y'all know why we got to get a positive ID before we start shootin'...

Yeah, ruefully acknowledged the former Mars mission pilot.

That's for sure –

Hold on – second bunch of missiles, inbound from south-west – but they're tracking above of Wolf and us... what the hell are they shooting *at?*

I don't think it's us, came Jacobson's thought-pattern. *Different target.*

I'm scanning forward – damn, what's that, ahead, above us and to the north-west?

Boyd now cast his own gaze and sensory-ability to the north.

Don't see anything – wait – if I focus – hell, yeah!

Gotta be ten miles away at the very least... keeps going in and out of track, but when I get a glimpse, from this angle it sure looks like the... *no, that's* impossible!

Well then what else could *it* be? argued the former Mars mission commander.

And it looks like it's on a course to intercept Minnie's ACP.

See the two signatures that look a lot like the ones aft of us? returned Boyd. *They're outside – one to the aft, one on the flank... hold on, there goes the one from the side, moving away from the object, heading fast towards the ACP – other one's still astern of the object – oh, and now there's a smaller signature on the object's dorsal surfaces... none of this makes* sense... whoa – *Commander, look up* there!

They both directed their senses upward and beheld a bright infra-red signature, rocketing at an oblique angle, already almost past the upper limits of the troposphere.

That looks a lot like – but she said that she wouldn't intervene – didn't she? mentally gasped Jacobson.

Then what the hell's she *doing* here? asked White, who had also temporarily reversed the direction of his sensory-scan.

It might not be her, countered Boyd.

What if it's some new Air Force missile – or wait... didn't she say that she could suppress her IR-sig?

At this range, impossible to tell –

Way *too fast to be a missile by Uncle Sam,* countered White.

Guys, demanded Jacobson, *Situation's changed!*

We need a new plan!

'Scuse my French, sir, broadcasted White, *But what the fuck would that 'new plan' have us doin' in the next five minutes?*

We should – started Jacobson; but his proposal was aborted by another warning-cry from the Russian.

Missiles! was the one word (of several) that the others were able to understand.

Again, White changed his facing, and his dismayed message came through loud and clear.

They're either trackin' us... or they're locked on to the V-37, he warned.

I figure we got about twenty to thirty seconds before they're close enough for prox fuses – if they hit the 'plane, I guess that's a wash, but if they hit us... well, that ain't too fuckin' great... understand what I'm sayin'?

I can try to – White was going to add; but his planned commitment was pre-empted by the Russian, who now abruptly left the airborne-gaggle.

Misha – his war-song roaring, his eyes and body lit up by careening charges of *Amaiish,* with his two daggers surrounding him in protective-pattern – darted aftward, flying on a course similar to the one that the bounty-hunter had recently taken.

Jaysus, commented Boyd, *That guy learned how to fly and maneuver, real fast... didn't he?*

He sure has improved since that episode down at the airfield, noted Jacobson.

President may have had a point, when he bitched at us about "why did you let non-Americans get the Fire".

Well, offered White, *Given what the man did with Her Angelic Highness, back there in Tucson, it was only a matter of time... don't y'all know? Not a whole hell of a lot we could do about that, I mean.*

I'm facin' backwards – I'll try to knock down any that get past him – if, that is, they ain't immune to bein' chilled a bit –

You'll get the IR-seekers no problem, remarked Boyd.

I'll try to zap any that get past you.

Captain – I'm going to climb – we need to get an altitude-advantage here – I'll head for the unknown object ahead and above of us... understood?

Yeah... okay, came back Jacobson's unhappy broadcast.

But I feel like a fifth wheel here.

What if it is the Express?

And what if we have another "friendly fire" incident, with whomever's guarding it?

There were multiple explosions from the area where the Russian had flown; gratifyingly, his own signature still showed as "active and healthy", as near as the others could tell.

Let's play our war-songs at full-volume, as we approach, suggested Boyd.

Hopefully that – and if they see my energy-discharges, maybe Devon's too – they'll hold their fire.

Hopefully...

Uh-oh, interrupted White, *Here come them mothers!*

Sno-Cone!

His *Fire*-melody reverberated as he fired a spreading barrage of ice-jets at the oncoming missiles, accompanied a half-second later by a zeppelin-sized, floating barrier of unbelievably-cold air; so frigid in fact was it, that the others' wary Mars eyes could see oxygen and hydrogen deliquescing from within. These two defensive-measures neutered all but two of the air-to-air missiles, which hurtled ever nearer.

Three-two-one-Shine! broadcasted Boyd.

The other two reflexively shut their eyes, a split-second before the former Mars mission pilot's own attack lit up the heavens for miles in every direction. His photon-beams struck dead-on, resulting in double explosions at uncomfortably close range.

Luckily – although all three of White, Boyd and Jacobson felt shrapnel-impacts – their protective-arts, now energized almost to full-capability, easily stopped these.

You guys still functional? inquired Jacobson.

Yeah, answered Boyd.

Took some hits... but nothing got through... I think. How about you?

Somehow the Mars mission commander's mind-talking conveyed pride, as he replied,

The mosquitoes around here aren't anything to worry about.

White, for his part, offered, *Good one there Commander... by the way, my ice bounced 'em off like they was spitballs... but what makes me think that them nukes ain't gonna be so easy?*

And that's where we're going, grimly resolved Boyd.

If it is the Express... we've got to warn them about where they're headed – the V-37 will impact with Minnie's plane, in only a few minutes – they need to turn around, ASAP!

Yvonne... mused Jacobson... forgive me... but it had to be done...

My sentiments exactly, commented Boyd.

"Regards to next-of-kin", you know.

War-songs on "high", guys... up we go!

Find The Key Of Solomon

For the past short eternity, the former Spiritual Adviser had amused himself by repetitively moving the safety on his customized, pearl-handled .45, back and forth to and from the "on" position. But the novelty of this exercise was waning, and he was fighting the effects of fatigue.

Keep it together, soldier of Jesus, he resolved.

The Lord won't excuse slackin' off... 'specially when we're so close.

He looked out the flight-deck windscreen.

The lights of D.C.'s built-up area – sometimes obscured by clouds moving in and out of the flight-path – beckoned like a huge, Earthbound star-cluster, tantalizingly near, slightly south of east. Beyond this lay the dark reaches of the North Atlantic.

Still pretty high up and runnin' out of time... where is that accursed witch, anyways?

"Wake up!" he demanded of the co-pilot.

The poor guy had passed out, possibly from shock but more likely from exhaustion and blood-loss. Luckily, he was right-handed and it had been his now-bandaged left arm that had taken the bullet; while still lucid, he had obeyed Crowford's orders and had programmed their current course into the auto-pilot.

The Presidential Detail Air Force crewman had protested mightily, given that the requested flight-path terminated at zero altitude, precisely at 1600 Pennsylvania Avenue. But a loaded semi-automatic pistol pointed at the side of his head, had been all the convincing that was needed.

That, and the crumpled, dead body of his friend the senior pilot, lying in a corner, covered by a blood-splattered flight-jacket.

"Whaa... whaa... oh," mumbled the crippled man.

"I need some information out of you," demanded the Spiritual Adviser.

"Whaa... what you want?" gasped the co-pilot.

"Tell me how – *wait* a minute –" started Crowford; but then he stopped, staring back into the flight-deck as if pondering something important.

"What..." asked the co-pilot.

"Hush up!" came back the directive.

There was a slight pause, and then the Spiritual Adviser asked, "You *hear* that?"

"Hear... *what*..." replied the dazed, slowly-recovering co-pilot. Unlike the Spiritual Adviser, he did not detect the distant, rhythmic sound of a war-song, its up-and-down melody telling of burgeoning *Fire*-powers. The song was similar to what Crowford remembered of Chu's one, but it was different in an entrancing, stirring way.

The co-pilot was, however, conscious enough to notice that one of the aft starboard-sector threat-proximity warning-lights had been tripped. He was disinclined to report this to his captor and assailant.

"Sounded like that damnable 'music' – oh, *no*, she don't!" growled Crowford.

The Spiritual Adviser unlatched the safety on his gun, took a step into the vacated pilot's seat, made sure that he had the trigger on the EMP-bomb easily within reach, turned to one side and engaged the intercom-channel back to the ACP's communications-shack.

Unlike Crowford – who was concentrating on some perceived threat and facing mostly backward into the plane – the co-pilot was facing forward into the windscreen.

Before his eyes, the scene outside shimmered, as if a huge plate of translucent, crazy-house distortion-glass had suddenly been dropped in front of the aircraft.

The effect lasted only a second or two, and then the Washington metropolitan area reappeared; however, he could only see its northern half, as the rest of it was now out of the line of sight, apparently to the right. It also seemed as if the lights of D.C. had receded slightly into the distance, horizontally – though they looked as if they were closer, vertically.

In his weakened state, the co-pilot couldn't tell if he was hallucinating, or if something really *strange* had just happened outside the aircraft.

"Listen..." he tried to mention; but he was cut off by Crowford.

"You stop right *there!*" bellowed the Spiritual Adviser into a nearby microphone, "Or I'll fry the controls and we go down right here and now!"

After only a second or so, Minnie Chu's voice sounded on the speakers.

"Crowford?" she inquired. "That *you*? What are you *talking* about, sir?"

"Don't *lie* to me, girlie!" he angrily retorted. "I *heard* that, uhh, what you call it again, 'battle-music' – and if you take one more step towards the cockpit –"

"It's called a 'war-song'," corrected Chu. "But I *still* don't get what you're talking about. I'm still back here in the communications-room; I haven't made any moves against you... I *swear!* Anyway – as long as we're talking – I have some very important news that you need to hear! There's *another* –"

Again, he cut her off.

"I *know* what I heard!" he barked. "And if it ain't yourself – then I know *who* it's **got** to *be!* She's come to rescue you, dearie... but she's in for a *surprise!*"

He flipped a switch, and now his voice could be heard over all the speakers in the airplane.

"The key to truth, is the Key of Solomon," he calmly – but loudly and firmly – pronounced. "It's time to find that key! And as for *you*, harlot witch... if you want me... come and *get* me!"

"What the hell are *those* riddles supposed to mean?" demanded Chu. "Sir, you need to know –"

Secretly, she began to ask the special insight, the same question, as Crowford turned off his microphone and ended the dialog over the speakers.

In another part of the ACP, a cold chill of fear – mixed with traces of excitement and hope – washed over the man calling himself "Sergeant First Class Simon Grassleigh".

Yet still, did he race for the entrance to the aircraft's cargo-hold, after being very sure that he had a certain small, digital device, at the ready.

A sweating, agitated Crowford grabbed the co-pilot by the shoulders and gave the man a rough shake, to rouse him from his apparent stupor.

"Wake up... wake up! No *daydreamin'!*" barked the former Spiritual Adviser.

"Whaa... okay," wearily acknowledged the co-pilot.

"You *look* out there lately, Mister?" shouted a visibly upset Crowford. "We're off-*course!* We're headin' too far north, our nose is low, and we must have been slowin' down, because the city's still way off! What you *do?*"

"The... the... yeah," spoke the co-pilot. "I can see. You were busy... and also..."

"'Also'... *what?*" challenged the severe man.

"Well..." the Presidential Detail Air Force crewman tried to explain, "The INS and auto-pilot co-ordinates look nominal... and airspeed hasn't changed as far as I can see from the instruments. That means we're still on course, sir."

"You're talkin' *shit*, my friend!" growled Crowford. "Look outside – anybody who can see, and that includes both of us, can't miss the fact that we're now headin' north-east, between D.C. and Baltimore... and we're on *way* too steep an incline! So you'd better –"

"But the auto-pilot and Sat-Nav –" the co-pilot tried to argue.

The next thing he knew, there was a pistol pointed right at the side of his head.

"You want me to be flyin' this rig *myself*... after I dump what's left of your body out of that-there chair?" hissed the former Spiritual Adviser. "I got multi-engine experience... I can *do* that. You got three seconds to put us back on a course to hit the White House – and to speed up so we do that on the schedule that I told you of, when, uhh, I had to take control up here. *Got* it?"

"No... *no!*" quailed the desperate man. "I'll do it... I'll *do* it!"

"That's *better*," unctuously replied Crowford. "Now get *on* with it!"

"I'll have to disengage the auto-pilot and fly the aircraft under my own control," said the co-pilot, as he flipped switches on the control-console and adjusted various dials and instrument-settings. "I need to turn off the linkage-systems that we're not using, like the artificial horizon and the correct airspeed regulator, so they don't try to over-ride my manual inputs. Judging from what's out there, beyond the windscreen I mean... uhh... I'm estimating... okay... increasing airspeed, nose up seven degrees, banking twenty degrees starboard... *now...*"

The ACP went into a gentle turn to the right, and – to Crowford's satisfaction – the bright lights of downtown Washington, D.C., were again directly in front of the big plane. He had to hold on to the pilot's-chair to steady himself, and was gratified to feel how the aircraft's vertical orientation had been corrected and was now not in the steep, premature descent that had surely been the case previously.

There was a subtle flicker that momentarily caused an odd optical effect on the scenery outside, but the Spiritual Adviser put this down to the clouds that the ACP occasionally flew through, on its way down to Pennsylvania Avenue.

"Now that we're back on course," requested Crowford of the co-pilot, "I need you to set up a radio-broadcast, on as many channels as possible. Just a repeating, short message. Can you do that?"

"I... I think so, sir," the co-pilot responded. "We do have a multi-channel S.O.S. beacon... I can type the message into the console and it will go out as both digital text and synthesized voice on every standard civilian and military frequency. It has a limit of 160 characters, however. What do you want the advisory to say?"

"Type the following," demanded the former Spiritual Adviser. "To Karéin-Mayréij : Your harlot, Minnie Chu, is on this airplane. She dies in ten minutes unless you appear here. No more chances. The Lord's will be *done!*"

"Uhh... okay," answered the co-pilot. "But *surely* you know, sir... if she hears this, the alien will –"

Crowford jammed the business-end of his .45 into the back of the other man's head.

"More typin'... less *talkin'!*" he growled.

Turn The Key Of Solomon

Chu – her eyes still exhibiting a dull glow – bent forward over the electronics-control console and turned to address the Air Force guy sitting in front of the instruments.

"Anything more?" she demanded.

"He's cut the connection," advised the man. "Flight-deck's isolated from anything we can do. S.O.P. for dealing with terrorist incidents, of course."

"Of *course*," ruefully echoed the former FBI team-leader. "Damn 'terrorists'. You still have a track on the nuke?"

"Yeah," the Air Force guy answered. "Peculiar... it's going *very* slow considering what it's capable of – almost loiter-speed, in fact. Could have hit us in the next minute or two, if whoever fired it, had wanted it to... but it's still on the original, high-to-medium-altitude intercept-course that I showed you. It's nearing its terminal dive initiation-point, according to the path-prediction gear."

"How long have we got?" nervously asked Chu.

"Assuming it doesn't speed up or change course," he stated, in a flat and even tone, "I'd say twelve to fourteen minutes... *max*. Probably less."

"*Shit!*" gulped the more-than-a-woman.

"Make sure that what I'm about to say," she ordered, "Doesn't get broadcast to anywhere outside this room."

"Yes ma'am," the Air Force guy obliged. "Outside circuits are off."

She turned to address the others in the ACP communications-center.

"Listen," Chu announced, "We're out of time – and I'm now going to have to make some very tough decisions. I'll allow no arguing."

She paused for a second, lowering her eyes, and then again spoke up.

"Remaining on this aircraft is a guaranteed death-sentence," she said. "I'm going to blow Harold Crowford to Kingdom Come; then, I'll change our flight-path away from populated areas, if I can; then, I'll shoot out one of the front-end access-doors and jump for it. Anyone who wants to come with me – with the exception of *you*, Mr. Vice-President, and *you*, Warnock – are welcome to do so. You can also just run, when I knock out the door. If you know where on the aircraft to grab a parachute from, I'd suggest you do that."

"What if Crowford sets off the bomb before we can get away from the plane?" asked one of the Air Force staffers (a different one from the one with whom Chu had been conversing).

"Then we die," evenly responded the former FBI team-leader.

"What if that other missile hits us while this is all going on?" asked another.

"Then we *die*," repeated Chu.

She turned to regard Warnock and the *faux*-President.

"I *should* set both of you afire, so you die slowly, in pain and terror... like must have happened to the two best agents that the Bureau has ever known – that is, Will Hendricks and Otis Boatman," she spat. "But unlike you, I'm not into cold-blooded murder – so stay in this room until I'm out of sight, and I'll leave you in God's hands. Surprised? Well... when She gets through with you... you'll be *begging* for my Evil Eye. May you rot in a Hell so richly-deserved!"

Wisely, the two said nothing.

"I'll kill anyone who tries to help them in any way," Chu warned to the others.

She pre-empted any more questions by energizing her *Fire*, wheeling in place and unleashing her *Gaze*, aiming it carefully at its lowest power-level, against the locking-mechanism of the doorway leading to the corridor outside the communications-room.

The door swung open with a light touch of her telekinetic powers. She waited for a few seconds, and though Chu had expected an immediate battle with Secret Service agents and Marine-guards, in fact – much too her surprise – there was nobody right outside.

She advanced and cautiously stepped into the corridor, looking for booby-traps, but none seemed to be around. She noted a jury-rigged patch-job on the aircraft-window where her attack had earlier struck, with alarm.

Goddamn, mused the former team-leader,

Almost depressurized the whole plane, right there... and one more bullet or shot from my Gaze...

Chu looked forward and backward. Two camouflage-uniformed figures, far away down the corridor toward the aft of the ACP, darted out of sight. There did not appear to be anyone within visual-range toward the bow, but there were many twists and turns, any of which could have been hiding her opponents.

With her personal force-field at almost maximum-power, she stepped forward, heading towards the bow in determined fashion. A quick glance behind her revealed that most of those inside the communications-room – with the notable exception of the Air Force guy who had been at the instrument-console – had dashed in the opposite direction, toward the stern of the aircraft. There was no sign of either the Vice-President or the imposter-FBI-director.

"Thanks for the vote of confidence... I *think*," offered Chu to the man, under her voice, while she continued cautiously walking forward. "By the way... what's your name?"

"Flight Communications Technician First Class Stephen Mooney, ma'am," he answered, keeping pace behind her.

He had to crouch a bit, because he was significantly taller.

"Remember... I let you use my phone, a couple of times?"

"Oh... yeah," acknowledged the more-than-a-woman. "Well, son... you can call me 'Minnie', if you want. Welcome to the wonderful world of the Storied

Watcher – for however long you and I have to live within it. Keep your head down. They can't shoot through me – at least I don't *believe* that they can – but if they miss me and hit *you*... get the picture?"

With a grim expression on his face, the technician nodded affirmation that he had understood.

"Figured if I'm dead already... I should find out what the F it's all about first... *ma'am*," he sourly remarked. "Two nukes about to blow over my head – so *ask* me if I give a *shit* about guns."

The two (plus Chu's hidden weirding-child) advanced as cautiously as could be managed, given the need to proceed quickly. They had gone perhaps a third of the way toward the flight-deck, when two Secret Service agents jumped out from hiding-places behind rows of airplane-seats to Chu's left. The one in front crouched in classic LEA-style and began firing a pistol, while the one behind stood upright and raised a shotgun.

But by now, the former FBI team-leader was becoming more confident in, and comfortable with, her alien-powers. Her humming, stirring, exciting war-song came automatically from everywhere and nowhere, and Chu put the tactics that had been taught by the alien-girl, to deadly use.

With her arms instantly-outstretched in front, she rotated her palms so that the finger-tips of each arm and hand – at first vertically-oriented – pointed to the right and left respectively. This gesture invoked one of Karéin-Mayréij's "martial-arts-by-*Fire*" tricks, propelling a pulverizing, invisible wall of telekinetic energy at her two assailants.

Her attack deflected all the incoming shots and shredded the tops and sides of several rows of airplane-seats between Chu and her human targets, who were in turn themselves struck, a half-second later. Bits of debris went flying hither and yon, as the wave of force rocketed forward and eventually dissipated, some ten to twenty feet down the corridor.

"Jesus H. –" gasped Mooney, upon seeing the wave of destruction.

The crouching opponent was knocked rolling backward, being thrown like the proverbial rag-doll against the lower supporting struts of some of the aircraft-seats; badly-bruised and hurt, he coughed out blood from his mouth while more dripped from his ears and nostrils.

The guy with the shotgun, who was somewhat bigger and heavier, was none the less knocked back on his heels and thence to a prone position. Though he suffered much the same damage as the first gunman, he managed to get a round off. It must have been a slug rather than buckshot, because – as the shotgun had been knocked wildly off-target – the round had hit the roof of the aircraft-cabin, punching a hole in the hull about the size of a quarter.

Morosely, she thought,

If only I had been sure I didn't have to use the Gaze, *and that I'd still have survived the fight, a few hours ago!*

Several people who were just doing their duty, might still be alive.

What did Karéin tell me?

Yeah... "you cannot be sentimental in war, Min-ee"... wasn't that it?
I'll have to save the crying and the guilt, for later...

While the two Service agents – both clearly *hors de combat* – gasped, bled and struggled for breath, a hissing-sound could easily be heard.

Her war-song abated.

"*Shit!*" exclaimed Chu. "I think the pressure-hull's been perforated! How long before –"

"Depends on a lot of things – like if the hole gets any bigger," observed Mooney. "Might happen if the fuselage's put under stress from rapid maneuvers and so on. If it stays that size... maybe twenty minutes, before the O2 in the main deck of the plane gets depleted – that'd be my guess."

"Swell!" muttered the former team-leader. "Well... that's longer than we have with the nukes – so we had better get this over with, ASAP. Let's *go!*"

A second later, she stopped abruptly.

"You notice that?" she asked of the Air Force guy.

"Yeah," he remarked. "Banking slightly to starboard... I think we're climbing, or at least leveling-out. I'd know for sure if it wasn't so damn dark out there, and I could look out a window to find the horizon."

"Oh-kay, then," said Chu, with a far-off look in her eyes. "That's what I figured, too."

She pressed on forward, using her enhanced senses to detect the slightest signs of more assailants. None were encountered until the team-leader and her new-found partner had reached the bow, just short of the staircases leading to the front-section upper-decks of the aircraft.

There, in what had at one time been the headquarters of the Presidential Security Guard, they found what must have been most of the remaining Marine and Secret Service guards. These numbered no more than five or six visible soldiers, along with another four or five who Chu somehow knew were secreted in the vicinity. The detachment all seemed badly-fatigued and they were not nearly as alert as would normally have been the case.

The guards were protecting the staircases and their assent – or elimination – would obviously be necessary to get to the flight deck and Crowford. However, the ACP's exit-doors (one to port, the other to starboard) were now within sprinting-distance, although also within easy shooting-range of the Marines and Secret Service agents.

Guns were being raised while Chu shouted, "Hold your *fire!* We've got to talk... there's very little time!"

"Hide behind something," she whispered to the Air Force guy. "This could get ugly, pretty fast."

Mooney quickly dashed behind a row of seats, itself behind a bulkhead.

"This is Major Todd Brown," came a gruff, military voice. "And I'm still authorized to use lethal force against yourself. You've been *warned!*"

"They'll try to flank you and hit you from behind," warned Mooney.

"Major – hold off on the 'war' business for a few minutes, and keep your men at their stations... *please!*" argued Chu. "Come back here and talk to me... I give you my word, you'll not be harmed!"

Amazingly, Brown complied, walking deliberately sternward. He brandished a large side-arm.

The Marine commander stopped at a point about eight feet away from Chu. Coldly, he announced,

"Not sure what you could possibly have to say, that I need to hear... but I guess I've got plenty of time to listen. Are you aware that the President's Spiritual Adviser – Harold Crowford – has *shot* his way into the flight-deck, killed the pilot and commandeered the aircraft? My men have him isolated, but he's threatening to crash the plane if we make a move against him. We've cut his access to the ship's video-monitors but we can't keep him off the intercom, unfortunately. And by the way... how the hell can you *see* anything, with those eyes glowing like that?"

"You're *so* wrong about that, Major!" quickly retorted the former team-leader. "I can see just *fine* – much better than a human can, if you want to know – and no, there *isn't* a lot of time... we're almost out of it, in fact. I'll get right to the point : yes, I know all *about* Mr. Crowford, and there's a nuclear-tipped missile flying right at us as I speak, and it's going to blow us all to *bits* in the next five to ten minutes, and there's 'SFA' that any of us – including Yours Truly – can do to *stop* it!"

'Whaa... *what?*" said the stunned Marine commander.

"Oh... it gets better than *that!*" added Chu. "Crowford's got *another* nuke onboard this plane somewhere – and he's got us on a course that will have us crash right into the White House. I mean to *kill* him and re-direct the ACP so it gets nuked somewhere that millions of civilians won't die as well. I *might* just pull that off if you and your men don't stand in my way... but if you *do*, he'll hear the commotion for sure and set his bomb off, immediately. He's made me aware that he can and *will* do that. Is anything I've explained, *unclear*, sir?"

An ashen expression appeared on the man's face.

"This... this... makes no sense... it can't be *true!*" gasped Brown. "There's no *way* – the aircraft is *secure*... except for how he smuggled a gun... no, sorry, lady, I don't believe you –"

"Stephen," spoke Chu, "Is anything that I've just said, untrue or inaccurate?"

The communications-technician showed his face.

"Major Brown, sir," he offered, "I've been on this rig for almost my entire time in the Armed Forces, and I can personally attest... what she's saying is one hundred per cent true. I sure wish it *wasn't*... but it *is*. I was there on the threat-display and I plotted the missile-trajectory; it's bearing down on us right now. Fact is – you, me, her, *all* of us – we're *fucked*, sir! Let her do what she wants, so when we meet God – which I figure is in about five minutes from now – we've done something good, on the way out. Know what I mean?"

There's always *hope, son,* the more-than-a-woman sent to him, realizing that his mind wouldn't get the message... although a second later, there was a bewildered look on Mooney's face.

"I... I don't... I'll have to ask the Service," argued Brown. "They have the final say –"

"No *time!*" countered Chu. "Yes or no! You either say 'yes' and order both the Marines and the Service to stand down... or you say 'no' and I let you walk back to your position... and I make no guarantees about what happens then. You have three seconds to decide."

Shit, she considered.

I could try to bewitch him... but his mind's already very suspicious, he'd resist... no time to fiddle around with that skill...

"One," counted Chu.

"I need more *time!*" protested the Marine commander.

"Two," repeated the team-leader.

"Then... 'no'," said Brown. "You gave me your word... so no hostilities... right?"

"I don't *have* to," mumbled a deflated Chu. "You'll be dead in a few minutes, either way. Maybe that's a better thing, anyway. When it happens... it'll be over with so quickly, you won't feel a *thing*. I hope that's comforting."

"I'll be *going*, now," said Brown.

He began to step backward, with his gun clearly at the ready.

An even more worried look showed on Chu's face. Her brow furrowed, as if she was pondering something.

"What's up?" asked the Air Force guy. "Other than us fixing to die, that is."

"Gunshots... yelling... somewhere behind us, on the plane... maybe a floor lower, it sounds like it's coming from the storage-bays – those are on the lower-levels, aren't they?" she observed.

"Yeah," he confirmed. "But I don't hear anything..."

"'Mars ears'," she said. "I can hear and see a lot of stuff that you can't. I'm still hearing the sounds of a battle... damn... I hope they don't breach the hull, 'cause if they *do*..."

She grimaced.

"So what we do *now?*" whispered Mooney to Chu. "You gonna zap Brown's guys? Go *easy* on 'em, please – they don't know what you're capable of, you know."

"I could easily do that, of course," she quietly replied, while crouching near his hiding-place. "But either way... I've *failed!* If I start a fire-fight with those guys – given how heavily-armed they are and considering that some of them are hidden – I can't *possibly* finish it before Crowford throws the switch; and either they or I might miss and blow the hull wide-open, crashing us immediately and triggering his wonderful bomb, *that* way. I'll just die with their blood needlessly on my own hands. If there *is* a God... I'd prefer not to have that added to my ledger. No... we're down to 'Plan B', I'm afraid."

"What... uhh... is *that?*" nervously asked the communications-technician.

"Stephen," Chu stated, trying to hide the fear in her own voice, "I won't mislead you... our chances aren't good – but I have the power of an *angel* within me... and she taught me *never* to give up. We're going to get *off* this rig – and we'll do our best to get far enough away to survive, when either or both of these damnable nukes go off."

"There... uhh... aren't any parachutes around here," he noted. "I think they're back in the tail-section or something... and by the time we hunted them down and got 'em on us –"

Chu let out a weak chuckle, shook her head, hung it down for a second, then lifted it again, with her alien-powered eyes glowing even more brightly than before.

"No argument about *that*," she explained. "Not part of the plan. See that outside-access-door, up ahead of us, starboard-side?"

"Yeah," said Mooney.

"I'm going to shoot out its lock and force it open... and you're going to jump through it, to the great skies beyond," she proposed. "I'll follow you, reel you in with my telekinesis, and as we exit the area I'll power up my force-field and we'll fly as fast as I can manage, to a safe distance... I *hope*. Take a deep breath before you jump, curl up into a tight ball at first but then spread your arms and legs out to slow your fall and make you a bigger target – and when you feel my telekinetic grasp, clear your mind and try not to resist, because doing that makes it much harder for me to lock on. Starting at this altitude, I should have plenty of time to locate you... at least two minutes to ground-level. Okay?"

She bent her head down and touched the amulet on its chain.

"You *got* that, Warden?" Chu said out loud. "Mommy will need all the help that she can get. Try to protect Stephen here too, as much as you can."

A chirping-sound was heard even by human ears.

"Who you *talking* to?" the perplexed Air Force guy inquired.

"My, uhh, 'war-child'," she answered. "Kind of like the Storied Watcher's intelligent sword, shield, daggers and armor... except, he's, uhh, a locket. He's called 'Warden' – and yes, he *is* very much, 'alive'. Long story – fill you in later."

An incredulous Mooney shook his head.

"Shoot... jump... blow up the plane... you *nuts?*" he exclaimed, more loudly than was called-for. "That's a 400-knot slipstream out there, it's pitch-dark, and it's minus 15 degrees to boot! If I hit the wing, or the tail, or the tailwings, or get sucked into the engines – and then when we hit the ground –"

"Is that better or worse than being right on the plane, when it gets struck by an H-bomb?" she parried.

"It's still suicide... just *slower* suicide!" he complained. "If what Crowford says is true... we'll be *way* too close to the plane when he sets his bomb off! This can't possibly *work!*"

"When you got on this plane, Stephen," Chu patiently remarked, "Would you have believed that I could have done what you saw me do, back in the communications-room? It's time to believe the unbelievable! I ask you to believe in me... and in yourself. I *like* you, son... and if we live through this, I have someone who I want you to meet."

"But... but," he stammered.

Chu stood up, feigned a smile, and began to walk slowly forward, so as to be within a long-jump's distance to the ACP's access-door.

"Try to stay behind me... unless you want to fly with a whole lot of bullet-holes," she advised, to the sweating, utterly-unnerved Air Force guy.

The two of them advanced at a brisk pace, with Mooney crouching behind Chu, so as not to provide any more target-surface than was absolutely necessary. They reached a spot about ten feet away from the Marine-guards and Secret Service-agents, and an equal distance from the starboard outside access-door.

The more-than-a-woman removed both of her slip-on shoes, compressed them as best she could, and stored them in the pockets of her dress-suit. She was now walking without the benefit of the low heels in the footgear, which made her look even shorter compared to Mooney.

She raised her left arm, with her palm upward in a peace-gesture.

"*Please* don't *shoot!*" she demanded. "Before I do what I'll do next – and it won't be an attack, unless you fire first – I have three things to say."

"Yeah?" asked one of the dispirited, disheveled Service agents.

There was a look of sad resignation on his face, and this man was far from unique.

Evidently, Brown had already delivered the bad news to his subordinates.

"First," Chu stated, "I'm *terribly* sorry for having had to defend myself and thus cause the death of some of your fellow-agents. I only did it to save my own life, but for what it's worth... I feel *awful* about what happened back there. Second... by now you know that staying on-board this aircraft is a death-sentence. When I do what I'm about to do, you're free to follow me. Be warned – I probably can't save all of you... maybe not *any* of you. If you just want to stay here, at least you'll die instantly and, I hope... painlessly. I can't promise the same, if you go with me."

She paused for a second or two, and a different man – a Marine-guard – asked, "This is all bullshit anyway – we're all *fucked* regardless... but what was the third thing, lady?"

Her war-song began to surge.

"The *third* thing," she declared, with her body and eyes lighting up and the music of power flowing from every syllable she spoke, "Is a way *out!* Hold *on* to something – or get ready to *jump!*"

Chu turned and fired her death-gaze – being careful to use near to the least amount of *Amaiish* that she could muster – at the door's locking-mechanism. It sparked and charred, but the egress-hatch remained firmly closed, despite her use of moderate-power telekinesis against it.

A small, red-colored light, positioned in the corridor-ceiling above the door, began to pulsate on and off.

A klaxon sounded somewhere further forward.

Several of the guards brought their weapons to the ready, but – thankfully – none of them aimed or fired.

Now, Crowford's voice boomed over the intercom. It was obviously being broadcast all over the aircraft.

"So... you're finally *here!* You're *late*, Satanic *bitch!*" he bellowed. "But regardless... it's time for everyone on this 'plane to turn to Jesus – and it's time to *turn the Key of Solomon!*"

"What the *fuck's* he gassin' on about?" cursed another one of the Marine guards.

"Fucker's been batshit-crazy from the start," grunted a Secret Service agent. "As anybody who's spent five minutes in his company, will attest –"

Mother Honored, came Warden's psychic voice,

Wrong very something is!

Feet below place particle-glow backwards brightly is coming from!

Well... "something is wrong"... no kidding, she ruefully sent back.

What do you mean, *exactly?*

Particle-shine rapidly increasing is! persisted her fantastical alter-ego.

Us behind from down and!

God in Heaven! gulped Chu.

He's triggered the fucking thing!

Silently wondering why she wasn't already dead, the more-than-a-woman shrieked out loud,

"That was a coded message to set off the bomb! **We only have** *seconds* **left!**"

With her war-song surging, Chu hit the door-handle with a powerful discharge of her deadly *Gaze*, blasting its mechanism apart and also causing the flight-deck to begin rapid decompression, via a fist-size hole blown outward. She locked her mind-push forces on what was left of the portal, shattering it and sending its component-pieces tumbling into the blackness outside.

Immediately, hurricane-force winds beset all in the vicinity, as explosive decompression began to affect the aircraft.

The ACP shuddered and went into a more pronounced starboard bank, throwing several of the anguished, terrified soldiers and Secret Service agents off their feet.

The former team-leader yelled,

"Stephen! Jump! Now!"

The communications-technician made a cross-sign over his chest as he sprinted forward, muttering a string of obscenities mixed with what must have been a prayer.

At the last possible point, as his feet reached the threshold, he closed his eyes, held his nose tightly shut with one hand and executed an impressive flying-leap into the cold void beyond.

A war-song – clearly not Chu's own, but luxurious and stirring in its theme of power, none the less – reverberated from the outside darkness.

"May God save you all!" she shouted, above the howling winds.

Calling on the power of an angel, she levitated above the aircraft's corridor-floor.

Then Minnie Chu rocketed out the wrecked egress-hatch, hoping against hope that she could learn how to fly.

– Here ends –

Against Time